THEODORE DREISER was born in Terre Haute, Indiana, in 1871. He received his early education in the public schools and later attended Indiana University. He began his writing career as a newspaperman, working in Chicago, St. Louis, and Pittsburgh. In 1907 he was appointed editor-in-chief of the Butterick Publications in New York City. Meanwhile his first novel, *Sister Carrie* (1900), had been published by a publisher who thought it objectionable and made little effort to promote its sale; however, some review copies were distributed and the book managed to attract the attention of many prominent writers. With the publication of *The Financier* (1912), a novel based on the life of Charles T. Yerkes, Dreiser was able to give up newspaper work and devote himself to writing. *The Titan* appeared in 1914. *The "Genius"* (1915), a novel of the egocentric artistic personality, was banned, but a year later a petition protesting this was signed by almost five hundred American writers. *An American Tragedy* (1925), based on an actual criminal case history, brought the author widespread recognition and popularity. It was successfully dramatized by Patrick Kearney. In 1944 Dreiser was awarded the Merit Medal for Fiction by the American Academy of Arts and Letters. Although he published little during the later years of his life, *The Bulwark* (1946) and *The Stoic* (1947) appeared posthumously, both showing his later interest in religious philosophy. He died at his home in southern California in 1945.

OTHER WORKS BY THEODORE DREISER

Sister Carrie, 1900 Novel (Signet CT86)
Jennie Gerhart, 1911 Novel
A Traveler at Forty, 1913 Autobiography
The "Genius," 1915 Novel
A Hoosier Holiday, 1916 Autobiography
Plays of the Natural and Supernatural, 1916
Free and Other Stories, 1918
Twelve Men, 1919 Biographical Sketches
A Book About Myself (Newspaper Days),
   1922 Autobiography
Moods, 1922 Poems
The Color of a Great City, 1923 Essays
An American Tragedy, 1925 Novel
   (Signet CQ235)
Dreiser Looks at Russia, 1928 Travel
Dawn, 1931 Autobiography
Tragic America, 1932 Study
The Bulwark, 1946 Novel
The Stoic, 1947 Novel

The TITAN

THEODORE DREISER

With an Afterword by
John Berryman

A SIGNET **C** CLASSIC

PUBLISHED BY THE NEW AMERICAN LIBRARY,
NEW YORK AND TORONTO

CONTENTS

I.	The New City	9
II.	A Reconnoiter	13
III.	A Chicago Evening	20
IV.	Peter Laughlin & Co.	26
V.	Concerning a Wife and Family	31
VI.	The New Queen of the Home	35
VII.	Chicago Gas	42
VIII.	Now This Is Fighting	49
IX.	In Search of Victory	55
X.	A Test	66
XI.	The Fruits of Daring	73
XII.	A New Retainer	80
XIII.	The Die Is Cast	90
XIV.	Undercurrents	101
XV.	A New Affection	113
XVI.	A Fateful Interlude	119
XVII.	An Overture to Conflict	128
XVIII.	The Clash	132
XIX.	"Hell Hath No Fury—"	143
XX.	"Man and Superman"	149
XXI.	A Matter of Tunnels	154
XXII.	Street-railways at Last	164
XXIII.	The Power of the Press	171
XXIV.	The Coming of Stephanie Platow	184
XXV.	Airs from the Orient	192

XXVI.	Love and War	197
XXVII.	A Financier Bewitched	206
XXVIII.	The Exposure of Stephanie	213
XXIX.	A Family Quarrel	221
XXX.	Obstacles	230
XXXI.	Untoward Disclosures	237
XXXII.	A Supper Party	244
XXXIII.	Mr. Lynde to the Rescue	253
XXXIV.	Enter Hosmer Hand	260
XXXV.	A Political Agreement	268
XXXVI.	An Election Draws Near	276
XXXVII.	Aileen's Revenge	281
XXXVIII.	An Hour of Defeat	291
XXXIX.	The New Administration	302
XL.	A Trip to Louisville	311
XLI.	The Daughter of Mrs. Fleming	319
XLII.	F. A. Cowperwood, Guardian	324
XLIII.	The Planet Mars	330
XLIV.	A Franchise Obtained	340
XLV.	Changing Horizons	346
XLVI.	Depths and Heights	354
XLVII.	American Match	362
XLVIII.	Panic	372
XLIX.	Mount Olympus	383
L.	A New York Mansion	395
LI.	The Revival of Hattie Starr	401
LII.	Behind the Arras	412
LIII.	A Declaration of Love	418
LIV.	Wanted—Fifty-year Franchises	426
LV.	Cowperwood and the Governor	437
LVI.	The Ordeal of Berenice	445
LVII.	Aileen's Last Card	453
LVIII.	A Marauder upon the Commonwealth	464
LIX.	Capital and Public Rights	470
LX.	The Net	477
LXI.	The Cataclysm	482
LXII.	The Recompense	497
	Afterword	503

The TITAN

CHAPTER I

The New City

When Frank Algernon Cowperwood emerged from the Eastern District Penitentiary in Philadelphia he realized that the old life he had lived in that city since boyhood was ended. His youth was gone, and with it had been lost the great business prospects of his earlier manhood. He must begin again.

It would be useless to repeat how a second panic following upon a tremendous failure—that of Jay Cooke & Co.—had placed a second fortune in his hands. This restored wealth softened him in some degree. Fate seemed to have his personal welfare in charge. He was sick of the stock exchange, anyhow, as a means of livelihood, and now decided that he would leave it once and for all. He would get in something else—street-railways, land deals, some of the boundless opportunities of the Far West. Philadelphia was no longer pleasing to him. Though now free and rich, he was still a scandal to the pretenders, and the financial and social world was not prepared to accept him. He must go his way alone, unaided, or only secretly so, while his quondam friends watched his career from afar. So, thinking of this, he took the train one day, his charming mistress, now only twenty-six, coming to the station to see him off. He looked at her quite tenderly, for she was the quintessence of a certain type of feminine beauty.

"Bye-bye, dearie." He smiled as the train bell signaled the approaching departure. "You and I will get out of this shortly. Don't grieve. I'll be back in two or three weeks, or I'll send for you. I'd take you now, only I don't know how that country is out there. We'll fix on some place, and then you watch me settle this fortune question. We'll not live under a cloud always. I'll get a divorce, and we'll marry, and things will come right with a bang. Money will do that."

He looked at her with his large, cool, penetrating eyes, and she clasped his cheeks between her hands.

"Oh, Frank," she exclaimed, "I'll miss you so! You're all I have."

"In two weeks." He smiled as the train began to move. "I'll wire or be back. Be good, sweet."

She followed him with adoring eyes—a fool of love, a spoiled child, a family pet, amorous, eager, affectionate, the type so strong a man would naturally like—she tossed her pretty red-gold head and waved him a kiss. Then she walked away with rich, sinuous, healthy strides—the type that men turn to look after.

"That's her—that's that Butler girl," observed one railroad clerk to another. "Gee! a man wouldn't want anything better than that, would he?"

It was the spontaneous tribute that passion and envy invariably pay to health and beauty. On that pivot swings the world.

Never in all his life until this trip had Cowperwood been farther west than Pittsburgh. His amazing commercial adventures, brilliant as they were, had been almost exclusively confined to the dull, staid world of Philadelphia, with its sweet refinement in sections, its pretensions to American social supremacy, its cool arrogation of traditional leadership in commercial life, its history, conservative wealth, unctuous respectability, and all the taste and avocations which these imply. He had, as he recalled, almost mastered that pretty world and made its sacred precincts his own when the crash came. Practically he had been admitted. Now he was an Ishmael, an ex-convict, albeit a millionaire. But wait! The race is to the swift, he said to himself over and over. Yes, and the battle is to the strong. He would test whether the world would trample him underfoot or no.

Chicago, when it finally dawned on him, came with a rush on the second morning. He had spent two nights in the gaudy Pullman then provided—a car intended to make up for some of the inconveniences of its arrangements by an over-elaboration of plush and tortured glass—when the first lone outposts of the prairie metropolis began to appear. The side-tracks along the roadbed over which he was speeding became more and more numerous, the telegraph poles more and more hung with arms and strung smoky-thick with wires. In the far distance, cityward, was, here and there, a lone workingman's cottage, the home of some adventurous soul who had planted his bare hut thus far out in order to reap the small but certain advantage which the growth of the city would bring.

The land was flat—as flat as a table—with a waning growth of brown grass left over from the previous year, and stirring faintly in the morning breeze. Underneath were signs of the new green—the New Year's flag of its disposition. For some reason a crystalline atmosphere enfolded the distant, hazy outlines of the city, holding the latter like a fly in amber and giving it an artistic subtlety which touched him. Already a devotee of art, ambitious for connoisseurship, who had had his joy, training, and sorrow out of the collection he had made and lost in Philadelphia, he appreciated almost every suggestion of a delightful picture in nature.

The tracks, side by side, were becoming more and more numerous. Freight cars were assembled here by thousands from all parts of the country—yellow, red, blue, green, white. (Chicago, he recalled, already had thirty railroads terminating here, as though it were the end of the world.) The little, low one- and two-story houses, quite new as to wood, were frequently unpainted and already smoky—in places grimy. At grade crossings, where ambling streetcars and wagons and muddy-wheeled buggies waited, he noted how flat the streets were, how unpaved, how sidewalks went up and down rhythmically—here a flight of steps, a veritable platform before a house, there a long stretch of boards laid flat on the mud of the prairie itself. What a city! Presently a branch of the filthy, arrogant, self-sufficient little Chicago River came into view, with its mass of sputtering tugs, its black, oily water, its tall red, brown, and green grain elevators, its immense black coal pockets and yellowish-brown lumberyards.

Here was life; he saw it at a flash. Here was a seething city in the making. There was something dynamic in the very air which appealed to his fancy. How different, for some reason, from Philadelphia! That was a stirring city, too. He had thought it wonderful at one time, quite a world; but this thing, while obviously infinitely worse, was better. It was more youthful, more hopeful. In a flare of morning sunlight pouring between two coal pockets, and because the train had stopped to let a bridge swing and half a dozen great grain and lumber boats go by—a half-dozen in either direction—he saw a group of Irish stevedores idling on the bank of a lumberyard whose wall skirted the water. Healthy men they were, in blue or red shirt-sleeves, stout straps about their waists, short pipes in their mouths, fine, hardy, nutty-brown specimens of humanity. Why were they so appealing? he asked himself. This raw, dirty town seemed naturally to compose itself into stirring artistic pictures. Why, it fairly sang! The world was young here. Life was doing something new. Perhaps he had better not go on to the Northwest at all; he would decide that question later.

In the meantime he had letters of introduction to distinguished Chicagoans, and these he would present. He wanted to talk to some bankers and grain and commission men. The stock exchange of Chicago interested him, for the intricacies of that business he knew backward and forward, and some great grain transactions had been made here.

The train finally rolled past the shabby backs of houses into a long, shabbily covered series of platforms—sheds having only roofs—and amidst a clatter of trucks hauling trunks, and engines belching steam, and passengers hurrying to and fro, he made his way out into Canal Street and hailed a waiting cab—one of a long line of vehicles that bespoke a metropolitan spirit. He had fixed on the Grand Pacific as the most important hotel—the one with the most social significance—and thither he asked to be driven. On the way he studied these streets as in the matter of art he would have studied a picture. The little yellow, blue, green, white, and brown streetcars which he saw trundling here and there, the tired, bony horses, jingling bells at their throats, touched him. They were flimsy affairs, these cars, merely highly varnished kindling wood with bits of polished brass and glass stuck about them, but he realized what fortunes they portended if the city grew. Streetcars, he knew, were his natural vocation. Even more than stockbrokerage, even more than banking, even more than stock organization, he loved the thought of streetcars and the vast manipulative life it suggested.

CHAPTER II

A Reconnoiter

The city of Chicago, with whose development the personality of Frank Algernon Cowperwood was soon to be definitely linked! To whom may the laurels as laureate of this Florence of the West yet fall? This singing flame of a city, this all-America, this poet in chaps and buckskin, this rude, raw Titan, this Burns of a city! By its shimmering lake it lay, a king of shreds and patches, a maundering yokel with an epic in its mouth, a tramp, a hobo among cities, with the grip of Caesar in its mind, the dramatic force of Euripides in its soul. A very bard of a city, this, singing of high deeds and high hopes, its heavy brogans buried deep in the mire of circumstance. Take Athens, oh, Greece! Italy, do you keep Rome! This was the Babylon, the Troy, the Nineveh of a younger day. Here came the gaping West and the hopeful East to see. Here hungry men, raw from the shops and fields, idylls and romances in their minds, builded them an empire, crying glory in the mud.

From New York, Vermont, New Hampshire, Maine, had come a strange company, earnest, patient, determined, unschooled in even the primer of refinement, hungry for something the significance of which, when they had it, they could not even guess, anxious to be called great, determined so to be without ever knowing how. Here came the dreamy gentleman of the South, robbed of his patrimony; the hopeful student of Yale and Harvard and Princeton; the enfranchised miner of California and the Rockies, his bags of gold and silver in his hands. Here was already the bewildered foreigner, an alien speech confounding him—the Hun, the Pole, the Swede, the German, the Russian—seeking his homely colonies, fearing his neighbor of another race.

Here were the Negro, the prostitute, the blackleg, the gam-

bler, the romantic adventurer par excellence. A city with but
a handful of native-born; a city packed to the doors with
all the riffraff of a thousand towns. Flaring were the lights
of the bagnio; tinkling the banjos, zithers, mandolins of the
so-called gin mill; all the dreams and the brutality of the
day seemed gathered to rejoice (and rejoice they did) in this
newfound wonder of a metropolitan life in the West.

The first prominent Chicagoan whom Cowperwood sought
out was the president of the Lake City National Bank, the
largest financial organization in the city, with deposits of
over fourteen million dollars. It was located in Dearborn
Street, at Munroe, but a block or two from his hotel.

"Find out who that man is," ordered Mr. Judah Addison,
the president of the bank, on seeing him enter the president's
private waiting room.

Mr. Addison's office was so arranged with glass windows
that he could, by craning his neck, see all who entered his
reception room before they saw him, and he had been struck
by Cowperwood's face and force. Long familiarity with the
banking world and with great affairs generally had given a
rich finish to the ease and force which the latter naturally
possessed. He looked strangely replete for a man of thirty-
six—suave, steady, incisive, with eyes as fine as those of a
Newfoundland or a Collie and as innocent and winsome.
They were wonderful eyes, soft and springlike at times,
glowing with a rich human understanding, which on the
instant could harden and flash lightning. Deceptive eyes, un-
readable, but alluring alike to men and to women in all
walks and conditions of life.

The secretary addressed came back with Cowperwood's
letter of introduction, and immediately Cowperwood followed.

Mr. Addison instinctively arose—a thing he did not always
do. "I'm pleased to meet you, Mr. Cowperwood," he said
politely. "I saw you come in just now. You see how I keep
my windows here, so as to spy out the country. Sit down.
You wouldn't like an apple, would you?" He opened a left-
hand drawer, producing several polished red winesaps, one of
which he held out. "I always eat one about this time in the
morning."

"Thank you, no," replied Cowperwood pleasantly, estimating as he did so his host's temperament and mental

caliber. "I never eat between meals, but I appreciate your kindness. I am just passing through Chicago, and I thought I would present this letter now rather than later. I thought you might tell me a little about the city from an investment point of view."

As Cowperwood talked, Addison, a short, heavy, rubicund man with grayish-brown sideburns extending to his earlobes and hard, bright, twinkling gray eyes—a proud, happy, self-sufficient man—munched his apple and contemplated Cowperwood. As is so often the case in life, he frequently liked or disliked people on sight, and he prided himself on his judgment of men. Almost foolishly, for one so conservative, he was taken with Cowperwood—a man immensely his superior—not because of the Drexel letter, which spoke of the latter's "undoubted financial genius" and the advantage it would be to Chicago to have him settle there, but because of the swimming wonder of his eyes. Cowperwood's personality, maintaining an unbroken outward reserve, breathed a tremendous humanness which touched his fellow banker. Both men were in their way walking enigmas, the Philadelphian far the subtler of the two. Addison was ostensibly a church member, a model citizen; he represented a point of view to which Cowperwood would never have stooped. Both men were ruthless after their fashion, avid of a physical life; but Addison was the weaker in that he was still afraid—very much afraid—of what life might do to him. The man before him had no sense of fear. Addison contributed judiciously to charity, subscribed outwardly to a dull social routine, pretended to love his wife, of whom he was weary, and took his human pleasure secretly. The man before him subscribed to nothing, refused to talk to intimates whom he controlled spiritually, and did as he pleased.

"Why, I'll tell you, Mr. Cowperwood," Addison replied. "We people out here in Chicago think so well of ourselves that sometimes we're afraid to say all we think for fear of appearing a little extravagant. We're like the youngest son in the family that knows he can lick all the others, but doesn't want to do it—not just yet. We're not as handsome as we might be—did you ever see a growing boy that was?—but we're absolutely sure that we're going to be. Our pants and shoes and coat and hat get too small for us every six months, and so we don't look very fashionable, but there are big, strong, hard muscles and bones underneath, Mr. Cowperwood, as you'll discover when you get to looking around. Then you won't mind the clothes so much."

Mr. Addison's round, frank eyes narrowed and hardened for a moment. A kind of metallic hardness came into his voice. Cowperwood could see that he was honestly enamored of his adopted city. Chicago was his most beloved mistress. A moment later the flesh about his eyes crinkled, his mouth softened, and he smiled. "I'll be glad to tell you anything I can," he went on. "There are a lot of interesting things to tell."

Cowperwood beamed back on him encouragingly. He inquired after the condition of one industry and another, one trade or profession and another. This was somewhat different from the atmosphere which prevailed in Philadelphia—more breezy and generous. The tendency to expatiate and make sure of local advantages was western. He liked it, however, as one aspect of life, whether he chose to share in it or not. It was favorable to his own future. He had a prison record to live down; a wife and two children to get rid of—in the legal sense, at least (he had no desire to rid himself of financial obligation toward them). It would take some such loose, enthusiastic western attitude to forgive in him the strength and freedom with which he ignored and refused to accept for himself current convention. *I satisfy myself*, was his private law, but so to do he must assuage and control the prejudices of other men. He felt that this banker, while not putty in his hands, was inclined to a strong and useful friendship.

"My impressions of the city are entirely favorable, Mr. Addison," he said after a time, though he inwardly admitted to himself that this was not entirely true; he was not sure whether he could bring himself ultimately to live in so excavated and scaffolded a world as this or not. "I only saw a portion of it coming in on the train. I like the snap of things. I believe Chicago has a future."

"You came over the Fort Wayne, I presume," replied Addison loftily. "You saw the worst section. You must let me show you some of the best parts. By the way, where are you staying?"

"At the Grand Pacific."

"How long will you be here?"

"Not more than a day or two."

"Let me see," and Mr. Addison drew out his watch. "I

suppose you wouldn't mind meeting a few of our leading men—and we have a little luncheon room over at the Union League Club where we drop in now and then. If you'd care to do so, I'd like to have you come along with me at one. We're sure to find a few of them—some of our lawyers, businessmen, and judges."

"That will be fine," said the Philadelphian simply. "You're more than generous. There are one or two other people I want to meet in between, and"—he arose and looked at his own watch—"I'll find the Union Club. Where is the office of Arneel & Co.?"

At the mention of the great beef packer, who was one of the bank's heaviest depositors, Addison stirred slightly with approval. This young man, at least eight years his junior, looked to him like a future grand seigneur of finance.

At the Union Club, at this noontime luncheon, after talking with the portly, conservative, aggressive Arneel and the shrewd director of the stock exchange, Cowperwood met a varied company of men, ranging in age from thirty-five to sixty-five, gathered about the board in a private dining room of heavily carved black walnut, with pictures of elder citizens of Chicago on the walls and an attempt at artistry in stained glass in the windows. There were short and long men, lean and stout, dark and blond men, with eyes and jaws which varied from those of the tiger, lynx, and bear to those of the fox, the tolerant mastiff, and the surly bulldog. There were no weaklings in this selected company.

Mr. Arneel and Mr. Addison, Cowperwood approved of highly as shrewd, concentrated men. Another who interested him was Anson Merrill, a small, polite, recherché soul, suggesting mansions and footmen and remote luxury generally, who was pointed out by Addison as the famous drygoods prince of that name, quite the leading merchant, in the retail and wholesale sense, in Chicago.

Still another was a Mr. Rambaud, pioneer railroad man, to whom Addison, smiling jocosely, observed: "Mr. Cowperwood is in from Philadelphia, Mr. Rambaud, trying to find out whether he wants to lose any money out here. Can't you sell him some of that bad land you have up in the Northwest?"

Rambaud—a spare, pale, black-bearded man of much force and exactness, dressed, as Cowperwood observed, in much better taste than some of the others—looked at Cowperwood shrewdly but in a gentlemanly, retiring way, with a gracious, enigmatic smile. He caught a glance in return which he could not possibly forget. The eyes of Cowperwood said more than any words ever could. Instead of jesting faintly, Mr. Rambaud decided to explain some things about the Northwest. Perhaps this Philadelphian might be interested.

To a man who has gone through a great life struggle in one metropolis and tested all the phases of human duplicity, decency, sympathy, and chicanery in the controlling group of men that one invariably finds in every American city at last, the temperament and significance of another group in another city is not so much, and yet it is. Long since, Cowperwood had parted company with the idea that humanity at any angle or under any circumstances, climatic or otherwise, is in any way different. To him the most noteworthy characteristic of the human race was that it was strangely chemic, being anything or nothing, as the hour and the condition afforded. In his leisure moments—those free from practical calculation, which were not many—he often speculated as to what life really was. If he had not been a great financier and, above all, a marvelous organizer he might have become a highly individualistic philosopher—a calling which, if he had thought anything about it at all at this time, would have seemed rather trivial. His business as he saw it was with the material facts of life, or, rather, with those third- and fourth-degree theorems and syllogisms which control material things and so represent wealth. He was here to deal with the great general needs of the Middle West—to seize upon, if he might, certain wellsprings of wealth and power, and rise to recognized authority. In his morning talks he had learned of the extent and character of the stockyards' enterprises, of the great railroad and ship interests, of the tremendous rising importance of real estate, grain speculation, the hotel business, the hardware business. He had learned of universal manufacturing companies—one that made cars, another elevators, another binders, another windmills, another engines. Apparently, any new industry seemed to do well in Chicago. In his talk with the one director of the Board of Trade to whom he had a letter he had learned that few, if any, local stocks were dealt in on 'change. Wheat, corn, and grains of all kinds were principally speculated in. The big stocks of the East were gambled in by way of leased wires on the New York Stock Exchange—not otherwise.

As he looked at these men, all pleasantly civil, all general in their remarks, each safely keeping his vast plans under his vest, Cowperwood wondered how he would fare in this community. There were such difficult things ahead of him to do. No one of these men, all of whom were in their commercial-social way agreeable, knew that he had only recently been in the penitentiary. How much difference would that make in their attitude? No one of them knew that, although he was married and had two children, he was planning to divorce his wife and marry the girl who had appropriated to herself the role which his wife had once played.

"Are you seriously contemplating looking into the Northwest?" asked Mr. Rambaud interestedly, toward the close of the luncheon.

"That is my present plan after I finish here. I thought I'd take a short run up there."

"Let me put you in touch with an interesting party that is going as far as Fargo and Duluth. There is a private car leaving Thursday, most of them citizens of Chicago, but some Easterners. I would be glad to have you join us. I am going as far as Minneapolis."

Cowperwood thanked him and accepted. A long conversation followed about the Northwest, its timber, wheat, land sales, cattle, and possible manufacturing plants. What Fargo, Minneapolis, and Duluth were to be civically and financially were the chief topics of conversation. Naturally Mr. Rambaud, having under his direction vast railroad lines which penetrated this region, was confident of the future of it. Cowperwood gathered it all, almost by instinct. Gas, street-railways, land speculations, banks, wherever located, were his chief thoughts.

Finally he left the club to keep his other appointments, but something of his personality remained behind him. Mr. Addison and Mr. Rambaud, among others, were sincerely convinced that he was one of the most interesting men they had met in years. And he scarcely had said anything at all— just listened.

CHAPTER III

A Chicago Evening

After his first visit to the bank over which Addison presided, and an informal dinner at the latter's home, Cowperwood had decided that he did not care to sail under any false colors so far as Addison was concerned. He was too influential and well connected. Besides, Cowperwood liked him too much. Seeing that the man's leaning toward him was strong, in reality a fascination, he made an early morning call a day or two after he had returned from Fargo, whither he had gone at Mr. Rambaud's suggestion, on his way back to Philadelphia, determined to volunteer a smooth presentation of his earlier misfortunes, and trust to Addison's interest to make him view the matter in a kindly light. He told him the whole story of how he had been convicted of technical embezzlement in Philadelphia and had served out his term in the Eastern Penitentiary. He also mentioned his divorce and his intention of marrying again.

Addison, who was the weaker man of the two and yet forceful in his own way, admired this courageous stand on Cowperwood's part. It was a braver thing than he himself could or would have achieved. It appealed to his sense of the dramatic. Here was a man who apparently had been dragged down to the very bottom of things, his face forced in the mire, and now he was coming up again strong, hopeful, urgent. The banker knew many highly respected men in Chicago whose early careers, as he was well aware, would not bear too close an inspection, but nothing was thought of that. Some of them were in society, some not, but all of them were powerful. Why should not Cowperwood be allowed to begin all over? He looked at him steadily, at his eyes, at his stocky body, at his smooth, handsome, moustached face. Then he held out his hand.

20

"Mr. Cowperwood," he said finally, trying to shape his words appropriately, "I needn't say that I am pleased with this interesting confession. It appeals to me. I'm glad you have made it to me. You needn't say any more at any time. I decided the day I saw you walking into that vestibule that you were an exceptional man; now I know it. You needn't apologize to me. I haven't lived in this world fifty years and more without having my eyeteeth cut. You're welcome to the courtesies of this bank and of my house as long as you care to avail yourself of them. We'll cut our cloth as circumstances dictate in the future. I'd like to see you come to Chicago, solely because I like you personally. If you decide to settle here I'm sure I can be of service to you and you to me. Don't think anything more about it; I shan't ever say anything one way or another. You have your own battle to fight, and I wish you luck. You'll get all the aid from me I can honestly give you. Just forget that you told me, and when you get your matrimonial affairs straightened out bring your wife out to see us."

With these things completed Cowperwood took the train back to Philadelphia.

"Aileen," he said when these two met again—she had come to the train to meet him—"I think the West is the answer for us. I went up to Fargo and looked around up there, but I don't believe we want to go that far. There's nothing but prairie grass and Indians out in that country. How'd you like to live in a board shanty, Aileen," he asked banteringly, "with nothing but fried rattlesnakes and prairie dogs for breakfast? Do you think you could stand that?"

"Yes," she replied gaily, hugging his arm, for they had entered a closed carriage; "I could stand it if you could. I'd go anywhere with you, Frank. I'd get me a nice Indian dress with leather and beads all over it and a feather hat like they wear, and—"

"There you go! Certainly! Pretty clothes first of all in a miner's shack. That's the way."

"You wouldn't love me long if I didn't put pretty clothes first," she replied spiritedly. "Oh, I'm so glad to get you back!"

"The trouble is," he went on, "that that country up there isn't as promising as Chicago. I think we're destined to live in Chicago. I made an investment in Fargo, and we'll have to go up there from time to time, but we'll eventually locate in Chicago. I don't want to go out there alone again. It isn't pleasant for me." He squeezed her hand. "If we can't arrange this thing at once I'll just have to introduce you as my wife for the present."

"You haven't heard anything more from Mr. Steger?" she put in. She was thinking of Steger's efforts to get Mrs. Cowperwood to grant him a divorce.

"Not a word."

"Isn't it too bad?" she sighed.

"Well, don't grieve. Things might be worse."

He was thinking of his days in the penitentiary, and so was she. After commenting on the character of Chicago he decided with her that so soon as conditions permitted they would remove themselves to the western city.

It would be pointless to do more than roughly sketch the period of three years during which the various changes which saw the complete elimination of Cowperwood from Philadelphia and his introduction into Chicago took place. For a time there were merely journeys to and fro, at first more especially to Chicago, then to Fargo, where his transported secretary, Walter Whelpley, was managing under his direction the construction of Fargo business blocks, a short street-car line, and a fairground. This interesting venture bore the title of the Fargo Construction and Transportation Company, of which Frank A. Cowperwood was president. His Philadelphia lawyer, Mr. Harper Steger, was for the time being general master of contracts.

For another short period he might have been found living at the Tremont in Chicago, avoiding for the time being, because of Aileen's company, anything more than a nodding contact with the important men he had first met, while he looked quietly into the matter of a Chicago brokerage arrangement—a partnership with some established broker who, without too much personal ambition, would bring him a knowledge of Chicago Stock Exchange affairs, personages, and Chicago ventures. On one occasion he took Aileen with him to Fargo, where with a haughty, bored insouciance she surveyed the state of the growing city.

"Oh, Frank!" she exclaimed, when she saw the plain wooden, four-story hotel, the long, unpleasing business street, with its motley collection of frame and brick stores, the gaping stretches of houses, facing in most directions unpaved streets. Aileen in her tailored spick-and-spanness, her self-conscious vigor, vanity, and tendency to overornament, was a strange contrast to the rugged self-effacement and indifference to personal charm which characterized most of the men and women in this new metropolis. "You didn't seriously think of coming out here to live, did you?"

She was wondering where her chance for social exchange would come in—her opportunity to shine. Suppose her Frank were to be very rich; suppose he did make very much money—much more than he had ever had even in the past— what good would it do her here? In Philadelphia, before his failure, before she had been suspected of the secret liaison with him, he had been beginning (at least) to entertain in a very pretentious way. If she had been his wife then she might have stepped smartly into Philadelphia society. Out here, good gracious! She turned up her pretty nose in disgust. "What an awful place!" was her one comment at this most stirring of western boom towns.

When it came to Chicago, however, and its swirling, increasing life, Aileen was much interested. Between attending to many financial matters Cowperwood saw to it that she was not left alone. He asked her to shop in the local stores and tell him about them; and this she did, driving around in an open carriage, attractively arrayed, a great brown hat emphasizing her pink and white complexion and red-gold hair. On different afternoons of their stay he took her to drive over the principal streets. When Aileen was permitted for the first time to see the spacious beauty and richness of Prairie Avenue, the North Shore Drive, Michigan Avenue, and the new mansions on Ashland Boulevard, set in their grassy spaces, the spirit, aspirations, hope, tang of the future Chicago began to work in her blood as it had in Cowperwood's. All of these rich homes were so very new. The great people of Chicago were all newly rich like themselves. She forgot that as yet she was not Cowperwood's wife; she felt herself truly to be so. The streets, set in most instances with a pleasing creamish-brown flagging, lined with young, newly planted trees, the lawns sown to smooth green grass, the windows of the houses trimmed with bright awnings and hung with intricate lace, blowing in a June breeze, the roadways a gray, gritty macadam—all these things touched her fancy. On one drive they skirted the lake on the North Shore, and Aileen, contemplating the chalky, bluish-green waters, the distant sails, the gulls, and then the new bright homes, reflected that in all certitude she would someday be the mistress of one of these splendid mansions. How haughtily she would carry herself; how she would dress! They would have a splendid house, much finer, no doubt, than Frank's old one in Philadelphia, with a great ballroom and dining room where she could give dances and dinners, and where Frank and she would receive as the peers of these Chicago rich people.

"Do you suppose we will ever have a house as fine as one of these, Frank?" she asked him longingly.

"I'll tell you what my plan is," he said. "If you like this Michigan Avenue section we'll buy a piece of property out here now and hold it. Just as soon as I make the right connections here and see what I am going to do we'll build a house—something really nice—don't worry. I want to get this divorce matter settled, and then we'll begin. Meanwhile, if we have to come here, we'd better live rather quietly. Don't you think so?"

It was now between five and six, that richest portion of a summer day. It had been very warm but was now cooling, the shade of the western building line shadowing the roadway, a moted, winelike air filling the street. As far as the eye could see were carriages, the one great social diversion of Chicago, because there was otherwise so little opportunity for many to show that they had means. The social forces were not as yet clear or harmonious. Jingling harness of nickel, silver, and even plated gold were the sign manual of social hope, if not of achievement. Here sped homeward from the city—from office and manufactory—along this one exceptional southern highway, the Via Appia of the South Side, all the urgent aspirants to notable fortunes. Men of wealth who had met only casually in trade here nodded to each other. Smart daughters, society-bred sons, handsome wives, came downtown in traps, victorias, carriages, and vehicles of the latest design to drive home their trade-weary fathers or brothers, relatives or friends. The air was gay with a social hope, a promise of youth and affection, and that fine flush of material life that recreates itself in delight. Lithe, handsome, well-bred animals, singly and in jingling pairs, paced each other down the long, wide, grass-lined street, its fine homes agleam with a rich, complaisant materiality.

"Oh!" exclaimed Aileen all at once, seeing the vigorous,

forceful men, the handsome matrons, and young women and boys, the nodding and the bowing, feeling a touch of the romance and wonder of it all. "I should like to live in Chicago. I believe it's nicer than Philadelphia."

Cowperwood, who had fallen so low there, despite his immense capacity, set his teeth in two even rows. His handsome moustache seemed at this moment to have an especially defiant curl. The pair he was driving was physically perfect, lean and nervous, with spoiled, petted faces. He could not endure poor horseflesh. He drove as only a horse-lover can, his body bolt upright, his own energy and temperament animating his animals. Aileen sat beside him, very proud, consciously erect.

"Isn't she beautiful?" some of the women observed as they passed, going north. "What a stunning young woman!" thought or said the men.

"Did you see her?" asked a young brother of his sister.

"Never mind, Aileen," commented Cowperwood, with that iron determination that brooks no defeat. "We will be a part of this. Don't fret. You will have everything you want in Chicago, and more besides."

There was tingling over his fingers, into the reins, into the horses, a mysterious vibrating current that was his chemical product, the off-giving of his spirit battery that made his hired horses prance like children. They chafed and tossed their heads and snorted.

Aileen was fairly bursting with hope and vanity and longing. Oh, to be Mrs. Frank Algernon Cowperwood here in Chicago, to have a splendid mansion, to have her cards of invitation practically commands which might not be ignored!

"Oh, dear!" she sighed to herself mentally. "If only it were all true—now."

It is thus that life at its topmost toss irks and pains. Beyond is ever the unattainable, the lure of the infinite with its infinite ache.

"Oh, life! oh, youth! oh, hope! oh, years!
Oh pain-winged fancy, beating forth with fears."

CHAPTER IV

Peter Laughlin & Co.

The partnership which Cowperwood eventually made with an old-time Board of Trade operator, Peter Laughlin, was eminently to his satisfaction. Laughlin was a tall, gaunt speculator who had spent most of his living days in Chicago, having come there as a boy from western Missouri. He was a typical Chicago Board of Trade operator of the old school, having an Andrew Jacksonish countenance, and a Henry Clay-Davy Crockett-"Long John" Wentworth build of body.

Cowperwood from his youth up had had a curious interest in quaint characters, and he was interesting to them; they took to him. He could, if he chose to take the trouble, fit himself in with the odd psychology of almost any individual. In his early peregrinations in La Salle Street he inquired after clever traders on 'change, and then gave them one small commission after another in order to get acquainted. Thus he stumbled one morning on old Peter Laughlin, wheat and corn trader, who had an office in La Salle Street near Madison, and who did a modest business gambling for himself and others in grain and eastern railway shares. Laughlin was a shrewd, canny American, originally, perhaps, of Scotch extraction, who had all the traditional American blemishes of uncouthness, tobacco-chewing, profanity, and other small vices. Cowperwood could tell from looking at him that he must have a fund of information concerning every current Chicagoan of importance, and this fact alone was certain to be of value. Then the old man was direct, plainspoken, simple-appearing, and wholly unpretentious—qualities which Cowperwood deemed invaluable.

Once or twice in the last three years Laughlin had lost

heavily on private corners that he had attempted to engineer, and the general feeling was that he was now becoming cautious, or, in other words, afraid. "Just the man," Cowperwood thought. So one morning he called upon Laughlin, intending to open a small account with him.

"Henry," he heard the old man say, as he entered Laughlin's fair-sized but rather dusty office, to a young, preternaturally solemn-looking clerk, a fit assistant for Peter Laughlin, "git me them there Pittsburgh and Lake Erie sheers, will you?" Seeing Cowperwood waiting, he added, "What kin I do for ye?"

Cowperwood smiled. "So he calls them 'sheers,' does he?" he thought. "Good! I think I'll like him."

He introduced himself as coming from Philadelphia, and went on to say that he was interested in various Chicago ventures, inclined to invest in any good stock which would rise, and particularly desirous to buy into some corporation —public utility preferred—which would be certain to grow with the expansion of the city.

Old Laughlin, who was now all of sixty years of age, owned a seat on the Board, and was worth in the neighborhood of $200,000, looked at Cowperwood quizzically.

"Well, now, if you'da come along here ten or fifteen years ago you mighta got in on the ground floor of a lot of things," he observed. "There was these here gas companies, now, that them Otway and Apperson boys got in on, and then all these here street railways. Why, I'm the feller that told Eddie Parkinson what a fine thing he could make out of it if he would go and organize that North State Street line. He promised me a bunch of sheers if he ever worked it out, but he never give 'em to me. I didn't expect him to, though," he added wisely, and with a glint. "I'm too old a trader for that. He's out of it now, anyway. That Michaels-Kennelly crowd skinned him. Yep, if you'da been here ten or fifteen years ago you mighta got in on that. 'Tain't no use a-thinkin' about that, though, anymore. Them sheers is sellin' fer clost onto a hundred and sixty."

Cowperwood smiled. "Well, Mr. Laughlin," he observed, "you must have been on 'change a long time here. You seem to know a good deal of what has gone on in the past."

"Yep, ever since 1852," replied the old man. He had a thick growth of upstanding hair looking not unlike a rooster's comb, a long and what threatened eventually to become a

Punch-and-Judy chin, a slightly aquiline nose, high cheek-bones, and hollow, brown-skinned cheeks. His eyes were as clean and sharp as those of a lynx.

"To tell you the truth, Mr. Laughlin," went on Cowperwood, "what I'm really out here in Chicago for is to find a man with whom I can go into partnership in the brokerage business. Now, I'm in the banking and brokerage business myself in the East. I have a firm in Philadelphia and a seat on both the New York and Philadelphia exchanges. I have some affairs in Fargo, also. Any trade agency can tell you about me. You have a Board of Trade seat here, and no doubt you do some New York and Philadelphia exchange business. The new firm, if you would go in with me, could handle it all direct. I'm a rather strong outside man myself. I'm thinking of locating permanently in Chicago. What would you say now to going into business with me? Do you think we could get along in the same office space?"

Cowperwood had a way, when he wanted to be pleasant, of beating the fingers of his two hands together, finger for finger, tip for tip. He also smiled at the same time—or, rather, beamed—his eyes glowing with a warm, magnetic, seemingly affectionate light.

As it happened, old Peter Laughlin had arrived at that psychological moment when he was wishing that some such opportunity as this might appear and be available. He was a lonely man, never having been able to bring himself to trust his peculiar temperament in the hands of any woman. As a matter of fact, he had never understood women at all, his relations being confined to those sad immoralities of the cheapest character which only money—grudgingly given, at that—could buy. He lived in three small rooms in West Harrison Street, near Throup, where he cooked his own meals at times. His one companion was a small spaniel, simple and affectionate, a she-dog, Jennie by name, with whom he slept. Jennie was a docile, loving companion, waiting for him patiently by day in his office until he was ready to go home at night. He talked to this spaniel quite as he would to a human being (even more intimately, perhaps), taking the dog's glances, tail-waggings, and general movements for answer. In the morning when he arose, which was often as early as half past four, or even four—he was a brief sleeper—he would begin by pulling on his trousers (he seldom bathed any more except at a downtown barbershop) and talking to Jennie.

"Git up now, Jinnie," he would say. "It's time to git up. We've got to make our coffee now and git some breakfast. I can see yuh lyin' there, pertendin' to be asleep. Come on, now! You've had sleep enough. You've been sleepin' as long as I have."

Jennie would be watching him out of the corner of one loving eye, her tail tap-tapping on the bed, her free ear going up and down.

When he was fully dressed, his face and hands washed, his old string tie pulled around into a loose and convenient knot, his hair brushed upward, Jennie would get up and jump demonstratively about, as much as to say, "You see how prompt I am."

"That's the way," old Laughlin would comment. "Allers last. Yuh never git up first, do yuh, Jinnie? Allers let yer old man do that, don't you?"

On bitter days, when the car wheels squeaked and one's ears and fingers seemed to be in danger of freezing, old Laughlin, arrayed in a heavy, dusty greatcoat of ancient vintage, and a square hat, would carry Jennie downtown in a greenish-black bag along with some of his beloved "sheers" which he was meditating on. Only then could he take Jennie in the cars. On other days they would walk, for he liked exercise. He would get to his office as early as seven-thirty or eight, though business did not usually begin until after nine, and remain until four-thirty or five, reading the papers or calculating during the hours when there were no customers. Then he would take Jennie and go for a walk or to call on some business acquaintance. His home room, the newspapers, the floor of the exchange, his offices, and the streets were his only resources. He cared nothing for plays, books, pictures, music—and for women only in his one-angled mentally impoverished way. His limitations were so marked that to a lover of character like Cowperwood he was fascinating— but Cowperwood only used character. He never idled over it long artistically.

As Cowperwood suspected, what old Laughlin did not know about Chicago financial conditions, deals, opportunities, and individuals was scarcely worth knowing. Being only a trader by instinct, neither an organizer nor an executive, he had never been able to make any great constructive use of his knowledge. His gains and losses he took with reasonable equanimity, exclaiming over and over when he lost: "Shucks! I hadn't orter have done that," and snapping his fingers. When he won heavily or was winning he munched tobacco with a seraphic smile, and occasionally in the midst of trading would exclaim: "You fellers better come in. It's a-gonta rain some more." He was not easy to trap in any small gambling game, and only lost or won when there was a free, open struggle in the market, or when he was engineering some little scheme of his own.

The matter of this partnership was not arranged at once, although it did not take long. Old Peter Laughlin wanted to think it over, although he had immediately developed a personal fancy for Cowperwood. In a way he was the latter's victim and servant from the start. They met day after day to discuss various details and terms; finally, true to his instincts, old Peter demanded a full half interest.

"Now, you don't want that much, Laughlin," Cowperwood suggested quite blandly. They were sitting in Laughlin's private office between four and five in the afternoon, and Laughlin was chewing tobacco with the sense of having a fine, interesting problem before him. "I have a seat on the New York Stock Exchange," he went on, "and that's worth forty thousand dollars. My seat on the Philadelphia exchange is worth more than yours here. They will naturally figure as the principal assets of the firm. It's to be in your name. I'll be liberal with you, though. Instead of a third, which would be fair, I'll make it forty-nine percent, and we'll call the firm Peter Laughlin & Co. I like you, and I think you can be of a lot of use to me. I know you will make more money through me than you have alone. I could go in with a lot of these silk-stocking fellows around here, but I don't want to. You'd better decide right now, and let's get to work."

Old Laughlin was pleased beyond measure that young Cowperwood should want to go in with him. He had become aware of late that all of the young, smug newcomers on 'change considered him an old fogy. Here was a strong, brave young easterner, twenty years his junior, evidently as shrewd as himself—more so, he feared—who actually proposed a business alliance. Besides, Cowperwood, in his young, healthy, aggressive way, was like a breath of spring.

"I ain't keerin' so much about the name," rejoined Laughlin. "You can fix it thataway if you want to. Givin' you fifty-one percent gives you charge of this here shebang. All right, though; I ain't a-kickin'. I guess I can manage allus to git what's a-comin' to me."

"It's a bargain, then," said Cowperwood. "We'll want new offices, Laughlin, don't you think? This one's a little dark."

"Fix it up any way you like, Mr. Cowperwood. It's all the same to me. I'll be glad to see how yer do it."

In a week the details were completed, and two weeks later the sign of Peter Laughlin & Co., grain and commission merchants, appeared over the door of a handsome suite of rooms on the ground floor of a corner at La Salle and Madison, in the heart of the Chicago financial district.

"Get on to old Laughlin, will you?" one broker observed to another, as they passed the new, pretentious commission house with its splendid plate glass windows, and observed the heavy, ornate bronze sign placed on either side of the door, which was located exactly on the corner. "What's struck him? I thought he was almost all through. Who's the Company?"

"I don't know. Some fellow from the East, I think."

"Well, he's certainly moving up. Look at the plate glass, will you?"

It was thus that Frank Algernon Cowperwood's Chicago financial career was definitely launched.

CHAPTER V

Concerning a Wife and Family

If anyone fancies for a moment that this commercial move on the part of Cowperwood was either hasty or ill-considered he but little appreciates the incisive, apprehensive psychology of the man. His thoughts as to life and control (tempered and hardened by thirteen months of reflection in the Eastern District Penitentiary) had given him a fixed policy. He could, should, and would rule alone. No

man must ever again have the least claim on him save
that of a suppliant. He wanted no more dangerous combinations such as he had had with Stener, the man through
whom he had lost so much in Philadelphia, and others. By
right of financial intellect and courage he was first, and
would so prove it. Men must swing around him as planets
around the sun.

Moreover, since his fall from grace in Philadelphia he had
come to think that never again, perhaps, could he hope to
become socially acceptable in the sense in which the so-
called best society of a city interprets the phrase; and pondering over this at odd moments, he realized that his future
allies in all probability would not be among the rich and
socially important—the clannish, snobbish elements of society—but among the beginners and financially strong men
who had come or were coming up from the bottom, and who
had no social hopes whatsoever. There were many such. If
through luck and effort he became sufficiently powerful
financially he might then hope to dictate to society. Individualistic and even anarchistic in character, and without a
shred of true democracy, yet temperamentally he was in
sympathy with the mass more than he was with the class, and
he understood the mass better. Perhaps this, in a way, will
explain his desire to connect himself with a personality so
naive and strange as Peter Laughlin. He had annexed him as
a surgeon selects a special knife or instrument for an operation, and shrewd as old Laughlin was, he was destined to be
no more than a tool in Cowperwood's strong hands, a mere
hustling messenger, content to take orders from this swiftest
of moving brains. For the present Cowperwood was satisfied
to do business under the firm name of Peter Laughlin & Co.
—as a matter of fact, he preferred it; for he could thus keep
himself sufficiently inconspicuous to avoid undue attention,
and gradually work out one or two coups by which he hoped
to firmly fix himself in the financial culture of Chicago.

As the most essential preliminary to the social as well as
the financial establishment of himself and Aileen in Chicago,
Harper Steger, Cowperwood's lawyer, was doing his best all
this while to ingratiate himself in the confidence of Mrs.
Cowperwood, who had no faith in lawyers any more than
she had in her recalcitrant husband. She was now a tall,
severe, and rather plain woman, but still bearing the marks
of the former passive charm that had once interested Cow-

perwood. Notable crow's-feet had come about the corners of her nose, mouth, and eyes. She had a remote, censorious, subdued, self-righteous, and even injured air.

The catlike Steger, who had all the graceful contemplative air of a prowling tom, was just the person to deal with her. A more suavely cunning and opportunistic soul never was. His motto might well have been, Speak softly and step lightly.

"My dear Mrs. Cowperwood," he argued, seated in her modest West Philadelphia parlor one spring afternoon, "I need not tell you what a remarkable man your husband is, nor how useless it is to combat him. Admitting all his faults —and we can agree, if you please, that they are many"— Mrs. Cowperwood stirred with irritation—"still it is not worthwhile to attempt to hold him to a strict account. You know"—and Mr. Steger opened his thin, artistic hands in a deprecatory way—"what sort of a man Mr. Cowperwood is, and whether he can be coerced or not. He is not an ordinary man, Mrs. Cowperwood. No man could have gone through what he has and be where he is today, and be an average man. If you take my advice you will let him go his way. Grant him a divorce. He is willing, even anxious, to make a definite provision for you and your children. He will, I am sure, look liberally after their future. But he is becoming very irritable over your unwillingness to give him a legal separation, and unless you do I am very much afraid that the whole matter will be thrown into the courts. If before it comes to that I could effect an arrangement agreeable to you, I would be much pleased. As you know, I have been greatly grieved by the whole course of your recent affairs. I am intensely sorry that things are as they are."

Mr. Steger lifted his eyes in a very pained, deprecatory way. He regretted deeply the shifty currents of this troubled world.

Mrs. Cowperwood for perhaps the fifteenth or twentieth time heard him to the end in patience. Cowperwood would not return. Steger was as much her friend as any other lawyer would be. Besides, he was socially agreeable to her. Despite his Machiavellian profession, she half believed him. He went over, tactfully, a score of additional points. Finally on the twenty-first visit, and with seemingly great distress, he told her that her husband had decided to break with her financially, to pay no more bills, and do nothing until his responsibility had been fixed by the courts, and that he,

Steger, was about to retire from the case. Mrs. Cowperwood felt that she must yield; she named her ultimatum. If he would fix $200,000 on her and the children (this was Cowperwood's own suggestion) and later on do something commercially for their only son, Frank, junior, she would let him go. She disliked to do it. She knew that it meant the triumph of Aileen Butler, such as it was. But, after all, that wretched creature had been properly disgraced in Philadelphia. It was not likely she could ever raise her head socially anywhere any more. She agreed to file a plea which Steger would draw up for her, and by that oily gentleman's machinations it was finally wormed through the local court in the most secret manner imaginable. The merest item in three of the Philadelphia papers some six weeks later reported that a divorce had been granted. When Mrs. Cowperwood read it she wondered greatly that so little attention had been attracted by it. She had feared a much more extended comment. She little knew the catlike prowlings, legal and journalistic, of her husband's interesting counsel. When Cowperwood read it on one of his visits to Chicago he heaved a sigh of relief. At last it was really true. Now he could make Aileen his wife. He telegraphed her an enigmatic message of congratulation. When Aileen read it she thrilled from head to foot. Now, shortly, she would become the legal bride of Frank Algernon Cowperwood, the newly enfranchised Chicago financier, and then—

"Oh," she said in her Philadelphia home, when she read it, "isn't that splendid! Now I'll be Mrs. Cowperwood. Oh, dear!"

Mrs. Frank Algernon Cowperwood number one, thinking over her husband's liaison, failure, imprisonment, pyrotechnic operations at the time of the Jay Cooke failure, and his present financial ascendancy, wondered at the mystery of life. There must be a God. The Bible said so. Her husband, evil though he was, could not be utterly bad, for he had made ample provision for her, and the children liked him. Certainly, at the time of the criminal prosecution he was no worse than some others who had gone free. Yet he had been convicted, and she was sorry for that and had always been. He was an able and ruthless man. She hardly knew what to think. The one person she really did blame was the wretched, vain, empty-headed, ungodly Aileen Butler, who had been his seductress and was probably now to be his wife.

God would punish her, no doubt. He must. So she went to church on Sundays and tried to believe, come what might, that all was for the best.

CHAPTER VI

The New Queen of the Home

The day Cowperwood and Aileen were married—it was in an obscure village called Dalston, near Pittsburgh, in western Pennsylvania, where they had stopped off to manage this matter—he had said to her: "I want to tell you, dear, that you and I are really beginning life all over. Now it depends on how well we play this game as to how well we succeed. If you will listen to me we won't try to do anything much socially in Chicago for the present. Of course we'll have to meet a few people. That can't be avoided. Mr. and Mrs. Addison are anxious to meet you, and I've delayed too long in that matter as it is. But what I mean is that I don't believe it's advisable to push this social exchange too far. People are sure to begin to make inquiries if we do. My plan is to wait a little while and then build a really fine house so that we won't need to rebuild. We're going to go to Europe next spring, if things go right, and we may get some ideas over there. I'm going to put in a good big gallery," he concluded. "While we're traveling we might as well see what we can find in the way of pictures and so on."

Aileen was thrilling with anticipation. "Oh, Frank," she said to him quite ecstatically, "you're so wonderful! You do everything you want, don't you?"

"Not quite," he said deprecatingly; "but it isn't for not wanting to. Chance has a little to say about some of these things, Aileen."

She stood in front of him as she often did, her plump, ringed hands on his shoulders, and looked into those steady, lucid pools—his eyes. Another man, less leonine, and with all his shifting thoughts, might have had to contend with the handicap of a shifty gaze; he fronted the queries and suspicions of the world with a seeming candor that was as disarming as that of a child. The truth was he believed in himself, and himself only, and thence sprang his courage to think as he pleased. Aileen wondered, but could get no answer.

"Oh, you big tiger!" she said. "You great big lion! Boo!"

He pinched her cheek and smiled. "Poor Aileen!" he thought. She little knew the unsolvable mystery that he was even to himself—to himself most of all.

Immediately after their marriage Cowperwood and Aileen journeyed to Chicago direct, and took the best rooms that the Tremont provided, for the time being. A little later they heard of a comparatively small furnished house at Twenty-third and Michigan Avenue, which, with horses and carriages thrown in, was to be had for a season or two on lease. They contracted for it at once, installing a butler, servants, and the general service of a well-appointed home. Here, because he thought it was only courteous, and not because he thought it was essential or wise at this time to attempt a social on-slaught, he invited the Addisons and one or two others whom he felt sure would come—Alexander Rambaud, president of the Chicago & Northwestern, and his wife, and Taylor Lord, an architect whom he had recently called into consultation and whom he found socially acceptable. Lord, like the Addisons, was in society, but only as a minor figure.

Trust Cowperwood to do the thing as it should be done. The place they had leased was a charming little graystone house, with a neat flight of granite, balustraded steps leading up to its wide-arched door, and a judicious use of stained glass to give its interior an artistically subdued atmosphere. Fortunately, it was furnished in good taste. Cowperwood turned over the matter of the dinner to a caterer and decorator. Aileen had nothing to do but dress, and wait, and look her best.

"I needn't tell you," he said in the morning, on leaving, "that I want you to look nice tonight, pet. I want the Addisons and Mr. Rambaud to like you."

A hint was more than sufficient for Aileen, though really it was not needed. On arriving in Chicago she had sought and discovered a French maid. Although she had brought plenty of dresses from Philadelphia, she had been having additional winter costumes prepared by the best and most expensive mistress of the art in Chicago—Theresa Donovan. Only the day before she had welcomed home a golden-yellow silk under heavy green lace, which, with her reddish-gold hair and her white arms and neck, seemed to constitute an unusual harmony. Her boudoir on the night of the dinner presented a veritable riot of silks, satins, laces, lingerie, hair ornaments, perfumes, jewels—anything and everything which might contribute to the feminine art of being beautiful. Once in the throes of a toilet composition, Aileen invariably became restless and energetic, almost fidgety, and her maid, Fadette, was compelled to move quickly. Fresh from her bath, a smooth ivory Venus, she worked quickly through silken lingerie, stockings and shoes, to her hair. Fadette had an idea to suggest for the hair. Would Madame let her try a new swirl she had seen? Madame would—yes. So there were movings of her mass of rich, glinting tresses this way and that. Somehow it would not do. A braided effect was then tried, and instantly discarded; finally a double looping, without braids, low over the forehead, caught back with two dark green bands crossing like an X above the center of her forehead and fastened with a diamond sunburst, served admirably. In her filmy, lacy boudoir costume of pink silk Aileen stood up and surveyed herself in the full-length mirror.

"Yes," she said, turning her head this way and that.

Then came the dress from Donovan's, rustling and crisping. She slipped into it wonderingly, critically, while Fadette worked at the back, the arms, about her knees, doing one little essential thing after another.

"Oh, Madame!" she exclaimed. "Oh, *charmant!* Ze hair, it go weeth it perfect. It ees so full, so beyutiful here"—she pointed to the hips, where the lace formed a clinging basque. "Oh, tees varee, varee nize."

Aileen glowed, but with scarcely a smile. She was concerned. It wasn't so much her toilet, which must be everything that it should be—but this Mr. Addison, who was so rich and in society, and Mr. Rambaud, who was very powerful, Frank said, must like her. It was the necessity to put her best foot forward now that was really troubling her. She must interest men mentally, perhaps, as well as physically, and with social graces, and that was not so easy. For all her money and comfort in Philadelphia she had never been in society in its best aspects, had never done social entertaining of any real importance. Frank was the most important man who had ever crossed her path. No doubt Mr. Rambaud had a severe, old-fashioned wife. How would she talk to her? And Mrs. Addison! She would know and see everything. Aileen almost talked out loud to herself in a consoling way as she dressed, so strenuous were her thoughts; but she went on, adding the last touches to her physical graces.

When she finally went downstairs to see how the dining and reception rooms looked, and Fadette began putting away the welter of discarded garments, she was a radiant vision —a splendid greenish-gold figure, with gorgeous hair, smooth, soft, shapely ivory arms, a splendid neck and bust, and a swelling form. She felt beautiful, and yet she was a little nervous—truly. Frank himself would be critical. She went about looking into the dining room, which by the cater- er's art had been transformed into a kind of jewel box glow- ing with flowers, silver, gold, tinted glass, and the snowy whiteness of linen. It reminded her of an opal flashing all its soft fires. She went into the general reception room, where was a grand piano finished in pink and gold, upon which, with due thought to her one accomplishment—her playing— she had arranged the songs and instrumental pieces she did best. Aileen was really not a brilliant musician. For the first time in her life she felt matronly—as if now she were not a girl any more, but a woman grown, with some serious re- sponsibilities, and yet she was not really suited to the role. As a matter of fact, her thoughts were always fixed on the artistic, social, and dramatic aspects of life, with unfortu- nately a kind of nebulosity of conception which permitted no condensation into anything definite or concrete. She could only be wildly and feverishly interested. Just then the door clicked to Frank's key—it was nearing six—and in he came, smiling, confident, a perfect atmosphere of assurance.

"Well!" he observed, surveying her in the soft glow of the reception room lighted by wall candles judiciously ar- ranged. "Who's the vision floating around here? I'm almost afraid to touch you. Much powder on those arms?"

He drew her into his arms, and she put up her mouth with a sense of relief. Obviously, he must think that she looked charming.

"I am chalky, I guess. You'll just have to stand it, though. You're going to dress, anyhow."

She put her smooth, plump arms about his neck, and he felt pleased. This was the kind of woman to have—a beauty. Her neck was resplendent with a string of turquoise, her fingers too heavily jeweled, but still beautiful. She was faintly redolent of hyacinth or lavender. Her hair appealed to him, and, above all, the rich yellow silk of her dress, flashing fulgurously through the closely netted green.

"Charming, girlie. You've outdone yourself. I haven't seen this dress before. Where did you get it?"

"Here in Chicago."

He lifted her warm fingers, surveying her train, and turned her about.

"You don't need any advice. You ought to start a school."

"Am I all right?" she queried smartly, but with a sense of self-distrust for the moment, and all because of him.

"You're perfect. Couldn't be nicer. Splendid!"

She took heart.

"I wish your friends would think so. You'd better hurry."

He went upstairs, and she followed, looking first into the dining room again. At least that was right. Surely Frank was a master.

At seven the plop of the feet of carriage horses was heard, and a moment later Louis, the butler, was opening the door. Aileen went down, a little nervous, a little frigid, trying to think of many pleasant things, and wondering whether she would really succeed in being entertaining. Cowperwood accompanied her, a very different person insofar as mood and self-poise were concerned. To himself his own future was always secure, and that of Aileen's if he wished to make it so. The arduous, upward-ascending rungs of the social ladder that were troubling her had no such significance to him.

The dinner, as such simple things go, was a success from what might be called a managerial and pictorial point of view. Cowperwood, because of his varied tastes and interests, could discuss railroading with Mr. Rambaud in a very definite and illuminating way; could talk architecture with Mr. Lord as a student, for instance, of rare promise would talk with a master; and with a woman like Mrs. Addison or Mrs. Rambaud he could suggest or follow appropriate leads. Aileen, unfortunately, was not so much at home, for her natural state and mood were remote not so much from a serious as from an accurate conception of life. So many things, except in a very nebulous and suggestive way, were sealed books to Aileen—merely faint, distant tinklings. She knew nothing of literature except certain authors who to the truly cultured might seem banal. As for art, it was merely a jingle of names gathered from Cowperwood's private comments. Her one redeeming feature was that she was truly beautiful herself—a radiant, vibrating *objet d'art*. A man like Rambaud, remote, conservative, constructive, saw the place of a woman like Aileen in the life of a man like Cowperwood on the instant. She was such a woman as he would have prized himself in a certain capacity.

Sex interest in all strong men usually endures unto the end, governed sometimes by a stoic resignation. The experiment of such attraction can, as they well know, be made over and over, but to what end? For many it becomes too troublesome. Yet the presence of so glittering a spectacle as Aileen on this night touched Mr. Rambaud with an ancient ambition. He looked at her almost sadly. Once he was much younger. But, alas, he had never attracted the flaming interest of any such woman. As he studied her now he wished that he might have enjoyed such good fortune.

In contrast with Aileen's orchid glow and tinted richness Mrs. Rambaud's simple gray silk, the collar of which came almost to her ears, was disturbing—almost reproving—but Mrs. Rambaud's ladylike courtesy and generosity made everything all right. She came out of intellectual New England —the Emerson-Thoreau-Channing Phillips school of philosophy—and was broadly tolerant. As a matter of fact, she liked Aileen and all the Orient richness she represented. "Such a sweet little house this is," she said smiling. "We've noticed it often. We're not so far removed from you but what we might be called neighbors."

Aileen's eyes spoke appreciation. Although she could not fully grasp Mrs. Rambaud, she understood her in a way, and liked her. She was probably something like her own mother would have been if the latter had been highly educated. While they were moving into the reception room Taylor Lord was announced. Cowperwood took his hand and brought him forward to the others.

"Mrs. Cowperwood," said Lord admiringly—a tall, rugged, thoughtful person—"let me be one of many to welcome you to Chicago. After Philadelphia you will find some things to desire at first, but we all come to like it eventually."

"Oh, I'm sure I shall," smiled Aileen.

"I lived in Philadelphia years ago, but only for a little while," added Lord. "I left there to come here."

The observation gave Aileen the least pause, but she passed it over lightly. This sort of accidental reference she must learn to expect; there might be much worse bridges to cross.

"I find Chicago all right," she replied briskly. "There's nothing the matter with it. It has more snap than Philadelphia ever had."

"I'm glad to hear you say that. I like it so much. Perhaps it's because I find such interesting things to do here."

He was admiring the splendor of her arms and hair. What need had a beautiful woman to be intellectual, anyhow, he was saying to himself, sensing that Aileen might be deficient in ultimate refinement.

Once more an announcement from the butler, and now Mr. and Mrs. Addison entered. Addison was not at all concerned over coming here—liked the idea of it; his own position and that of his wife in Chicago were secure. "How are you, Cowperwood?" he beamed, laying one hand on the latter's shoulder. "This is fine of you to have us in tonight. Mrs. Cowperwood, I've been telling your husband for nearly a year now that he should bring you out here. Did he tell you?" (Addison had not as yet confided to his wife the true history of Cowperwood and Aileen.)

"Yes, indeed," replied Aileen gaily, feeling that Addison was charmed by her beauty. "I've been wanting to come, too. It's his fault that I wasn't here sooner."

Addison, looking circumspectly at Aileen, said to himself that she was certainly a stunning-looking woman. So she was the cause of the first wife's suit. No wonder. What a splendid creature! He contrasted her with Mrs. Addison, and to his wife's disadvantage. She had never been as striking, as standupish as Aileen, though possibly she might have more sense. Jove! if he could find a woman like Aileen today. Life would take on a new luster. And yet he had women—very carefully, very subterraneously. But he had them.

"It's such a pleasure to meet you," Mrs. Addison, a corpulent, bejeweled lady, was saying to Aileen. "My husband and yours have become the best of friends, apparently. We must see more of each other."

She babbled on in a puffy social way, and Aileen felt as though she were getting along swiftly. The butler brought in a great tray of appetizers and cordials, and put them softly on a remote table. Dinner was served, and the talk flowed on; they discussed the growth of the city, a new church that Lord was building ten blocks farther out; Rambaud told about some humorous land swindles. It was quite gay. Meanwhile Aileen did her best to become interested in Mrs. Rambaud and Mrs. Addison. She liked the latter somewhat better, solely because it was a little easier to talk to her. Mrs. Rambaud Aileen knew to be the wiser and more charitable woman, but she frightened her a little; presently she had to fall back on Mr. Lord's help. He came to her rescue gallantly, talking of everything that came into his mind. All the men outside of Cowperwood were thinking how splendid Aileen was physically, how white were her arms, how rounded her neck and shoulders, how rich her hair.

CHAPTER VII

Chicago Gas

Old Peter Laughlin, rejuvenated by Cowperwood's electric ideas, was making money for the house. He brought many bits of interesting gossip from the floor, and such shrewd guesses as to what certain groups and individuals were up to that Cowperwood was able to make some very brilliant deductions.

"By gosh! Frank, I think I know exactly what them fellers are trying to do," Laughlin would frequently remark of a morning, after he had lain in his lonely Harrison Street bed meditating the major portion of the night. "That there stockyards gang" (and by gang he meant most of the great manipulators, like Arneel, Hand, Schryhart and others) "are after corn again. We want to git long o' that now, or I miss my guess. What do you think, huh?"

Cowperwood, schooled by now in many western subtleties which he had not previously known, and daily becoming wiser, would as a rule give an instantaneous decision.

"You're right. Risk a hundred thousand bushels. I think New York Central is going to drop a point or two in a few days. We'd better go short a point."

Laughlin could never figure out quite how it was that Cowperwood always seemed to know and was ready to act quite as quickly in local matters as he was himself. He understood his wisdom concerning eastern shares and things dealt in on the eastern exchange, but these Chicago matters?

"Whut makes you think that?" he asked Cowperwood one day, quite curiously.

"Why, Peter," Cowperwood replied quite simply, "Anton Videra" (one of the directors of the Wheat and Corn Bank) "was in here yesterday while you were on 'change, and he was telling me." He described a situation which Videra had outlined.

Laughlin knew Videra as a strong, wealthy Pole who had come up in the last few years. It was strange how Cowperwood naturally got in with these wealthy men and won their confidence so quickly. Videra would never have become so confidential with him.

"Huh!" he exclaimed. "Well, if he says it it's more'n likely so."

So Laughlin bought, and Peter Laughlin & Co. won.

But this grain and commission business, while it was yielding a profit which would average about twenty thousand a year to each partner, was nothing more to Cowperwood than a source of information.

He wanted to get in on something that was sure to bring very great returns within a reasonable time and that would not leave him in any such desperate situation as he was at the time of the Chicago fire—spread out very thin, as he put it. He had interested in his ventures a small group of Chicago men who were watching him—Judah Addison, Alexander Rambaud, Millard Bailey, Anton Videra—men who, although not supreme figures by any means, had free capital. He knew that he could go to them with any truly sound proposition. The one thing that most attracted his attention was the Chicago gas situation, because there was a chance to step in almost unheralded in an as yet unoccupied territory; with franchises once secured—the reader can quite imagine how—he could present himself, like a Hamilcar Barca in the heart of Spain or a Hannibal at the gates of Rome, with a demand for surrender and a division of spoils.

There were at this time three gas companies operating in the three different divisions of the city—the three sections, or sides, as they were called—South, West, and North, and of these the Chicago Gas, Light, and Coke Company, organized in 1848 to do business on the South Side, was the most flourishing and important. The People's Gas, Light, and Coke Company, doing business on the West Side, was a few years younger than the South Chicago company, and had been allowed to spring into existence through the foolish self-confidence of the organizer and directors of the South Side company, who had fancied that neither the West Side nor the North Side was going to develop very rapidly for a number of years to come, and had counted on the city council's allowing them to extend their mains at any time to these other portions of the city. A third company, the North Chicago Gas Illuminating Company, had been organized almost simultaneously with the West Side company by the same process through which the other companies had been brought into life—their avowed intention, like that of the West Side company, being to confine their activities to the sections from which the organizers presumably came.

Cowperwood's first project was to buy out and combine the three old city companies. With this in view he looked up the holders in all three corporations—their financial and social status. It was his idea that by offering them three for one, or even four for one, for every dollar represented by the market value of their stock, he might buy in and capitalize the three companies as one. Then, by issuing sufficient stock to cover all his obligations, he would reap a rich harvest and at the same time leave himself in charge. He approached Judah Addison first as the most available man to help float a scheme of this kind. He did not want him as a partner so much as he wanted him as an investor.

"Well, I'll tell you how I feel about this," said Addison finally. "You've hit on a great idea here. It's a wonder it hasn't occurred to someone else before. And you'll want to keep rather quiet about it, or someone else will rush in and do it. We have a lot of venturesome men out here. But I like you, and I'm with you. Now, it wouldn't be advisable for me to go in on this personally—not openly, anyhow—but I'll promise to see that you get some of the money you want. I like your idea of a central holding company, or pool, with you in charge as trustee, and I'm perfectly willing that you should manage it, for I think you can do it. Anyhow, that leaves me out, apparently, except as an investor. But you will have to get two or three others to help carry this guarantee with me. Have you anyone in mind?"

"Oh yes," replied Cowperwood. "Certainly. I merely came to you first." He mentioned Rambaud, Videra, Bailey, and others.

"They're all right," said Addison, "if you can get them. But I'm not sure, even then, that you can induce these other fellows to sell out. They're not investors in the ordinary sense. They're people who look on this gas business as their private business. They started it. They like it. They built the gas tanks and laid the mains. It won't be easy."

Cowperwood found, as Addison predicted, that it was not such an easy matter to induce the various stockholders and directors in the old companies to come in on any such scheme of reorganization. A closer, more unresponsive set of men he was satisfied he had never met. His offer to buy outright at three or four for one they refused absolutely. The stock in each case was selling from 170 to 210, and intrinsically was worth more every year, as the city was growing larger and its need of gas greater. At the same time they were suspicious —one and all—of any combination scheme by an outsider. Who was he? Whom did he represent? He could make it clear that he had ample capital, but not who his backers were. The old officers and directors fancied that it was a scheme on the part of some of the officers and directors of one of the other companies to get control and oust them. Why should they sell? Why be tempted by greater profits from their stock when they were doing very well as it was? Because of his newness to Chicago and his lack of connection as yet with large affairs Cowperwood was eventually compelled to turn to another scheme—that of organizing new companies in the suburbs as an entering wedge of attack upon the city proper. Suburbs such as Lake View and Hyde Park, having town or village councils of their own, were permitted to grant franchises to water, gas, and street railway companies duly incorporated under the laws of the state.

Cowperwood calculated that if he could form separate and seemingly distinct companies for each of the villages and towns, and one general company for the city later, he would be in a position to dictate terms to the older organizations. It was simply a question of obtaining his charters and franchises before his rivals had awakened to the situation.

The one difficulty was that he knew absolutely nothing of the business of gas—its practical manufacture and distribution—and had never been particularly interested in it. Street railroading, his favorite form of municipal profit seeking, and one upon which he had acquired an almost endless fund of specialized information, offered no present practical opportunity for him here in Chicago. He meditated on the situation, did some reading on the manufacture of gas, and then suddenly, as was his luck, found an implement ready to his hand.

It appeared that in the course of the life and growth of the South Side company there had once been a smaller organization founded by a man by the name of Sippens—Henry De Soto Sippens—who had entered and actually secured, by some hocus-pocus, a franchise to manufacture and sell gas in the downtown districts, but who had been annoyed by all sorts of legal processes until he had finally been driven out or persuaded to get out. He was now in the real estate business in Lake View. Old Peter Laughlin knew him.

"He's a smart little cuss," Laughlin told Cowperwood. "I thort onct he'd make a go of it, but they ketched him where his hair was short, and he had to let go. There was an explosion in his tank over here near the river onct, an' I think he thort them fellers blew him up. Anyhow, he got out. I ain't seen ner heard sight of him fer years."

Cowperwood sent old Peter to look up Mr. Sippens and find out what he was really doing, and whether he would be interested to get back in the gas business. Enter, then, a few days later into the office of Peter Laughlin & Co. Henry De Soto Sippens. He was a very little man, about fifty years of age; he wore a high, four-cornered stiff felt hat, with a short brown business coat (which in summer became seersucker) and square-toed shoes; he looked for all the world like a country drug- or bookstore owner, with perhaps the air of a country doctor or lawyer superadded. His cuffs protruded too far from his coat sleeves, his necktie bulged too far out of his vest, and his high hat was set a little too far back on his forehead; otherwise he was acceptable, pleasant, and interesting. He had short sideburns—reddish brown—which stuck out quite defiantly, and his eyebrows were heavy.

"Mr. Sippens," said Cowperwood blandly, "you were once in the gas manufacturing and distributing business here in Chicago, weren't you?"

"I think I know as much about the manufacture of gas as anyone," replied Sippens almost contentiously. "I worked at it for a number of years."

"Well, now, Mr. Sippens, I was thinking that it might be interesting to start a little gas company in one of these outlying villages that are growing so fast and see if we couldn't make some money out of it. I'm not a practical gas man myself, but I thought I might interest someone who was." He looked at Sippens in a friendly, estimating way. "I have heard of you as someone who has had considerable experience in this field here in Chicago. If I should get up a company of this kind, with considerable backing, do you think you might be willing to take the management of it?"

"Oh, I know all about this gas field," Mr. Sippens was about to say. "It can't be done." But he changed his mind before opening his lips. "If I were paid enough," he said cautiously. "I suppose you know what you have to contend with?"

"Oh yes," Cowperwood replied, smiling. "What would you consider 'paid enough' to mean?"

"Oh, if I were given six thousand a year and a sufficient interest in the company—say, a half, or something like that —I might consider it," replied Sippens, determined, as he thought, to frighten Cowperwood off by his exorbitant demands. He was making almost six thousand dollars a year out of his present business.

"You wouldn't think that four thousand in several companies—say up to fifteen thousand dollars—and an interest of about a tenth in each would be better?"

Mr. Sippens meditated carefully on this. Plainly, the man before him was no trifling beginner. He looked at Cowperwood shrewdly and saw at once, without any additional explanation of any kind, that the latter was preparing a big fight of some sort. Ten years before Sippens had sensed the immense possibilities of the gas business. He had tried to get in on it, but had been sued, waylaid, enjoined, financially blockaded, and finally blown up. He had always resented the treatment he had received, and he had bitterly regretted his inability to retaliate. He had thought his days of financial effort were over, but here was a man who was subtly suggesting a stirring fight, and who was calling him, like a hunter with horn, to the chase.

"Well, Mr. Cowperwood," he replied, with less defiance and more camaraderie, "if you could show me that you have a legitimate proposition in hand, I am a practical gas man. I know all about mains, franchise contracts, and gas machinery. I organized and installed the plant at Dayton, Ohio, and Rochester, New York. I would have been rich if I had got here a little earlier." The echo of regret was in his voice.

"Well, now, here's your chance, Mr. Sippens," urged Cowperwood subtly. "Between you and me there's going to be a big new gas company in the field. We'll make these old fellows step up and see us quickly. Doesn't that interest you? There'll be plenty of money. It isn't that that's wanting— it's an organizer, a fighter, a practical gas man to build the plant, lay the mains, and so on." Cowperwood rose suddenly, straight and determined—a trick with him when he wanted to really impress anyone. He seemed to radiate force, conquest, victory. "Do you want to come in?"

"Yes, I do, Mr. Cowperwood!" exclaimed Sippens, jumping to his feet, putting on his hat, and shoving it far back on his head. He looked like a chest-swollen bantam rooster.

Cowperwood took his extended hand.

"Get your real estate affairs in order. I'll want you to get me a franchise in Lake View shortly and build me a plant. I'll give you all the help you need. I'll arrange everything to your satisfaction within a week or so. We will want a good lawyer or two."

Sippens smiled ecstatically as he left the office. Oh, the wonder of this, and after ten years! Now he would show those crooks. Now he had a real fighter behind him—a man like himself. Now, by George, the fur would begin to fly! Who was this man, anyhow? What a wonder! He would look him up. He knew that from now on he would do almost anything Cowperwood wanted him to do.

CHAPTER VIII

Now This Is Fighting

When Cowperwood, after failing in his overtures to the three city gas companies, confided to Addison his plan of organizing rival companies in the suburbs, the banker glared at him appreciatively. "You're a smart one!" he finally exclaimed. "You'll do! I back you to win!" He went on to advise Cowperwood that he would need the assistance of some of the strong men on the various village councils. "They're all as crooked as eels' teeth," he went on. "But there are one or two that are more crooked than others and safer—bellwethers. Have you got your lawyer?"

"I haven't picked one yet, but I will. I'm looking around for the right man now."

"Well, of course, I needn't tell you how important that is. There is one man, old General Van Sickle, who has had considerable training in these matters. He's fairly reliable."

The entrance of General Judson P. Van Sickle threw at the very outset a suggestive light on the whole situation. The old soldier, over fifty, had been a general of division during the Civil War, and had got his real start in life by filing false titles to property in southern Illinois, and then bringing suits to substantiate his fraudulent claims before friendly associates. He was now a prosperous go-between, requiring heavy retainers, and yet not overprosperous. There was only one kind of business that came to the general—this kind; and one instinctively compared him to that decoy sheep at the stockyards that had been trained to go forth into nervous, frightened flocks of its fellow sheep, balking at being driven into the slaughtering pens, and lead them peacefully into the shambles, knowing enough always to make his own way quietly to the rear during the onward progress and thus escape. A dusty old lawyer, this, with heaven knows

49

what welter of altered wills, broken promises, suborned juries, influenced judges, bribed councilmen and legislators, double-intentioned agreements and contracts, and a whole world of shifty legal calculations and false pretenses floating around in his brain. Among the politicians, judges, and lawyers generally, by reason of past useful services, he was supposed to have some powerful connections. He liked to be called into any case largely because it meant something to do and kept him from being bored. When compelled to keep an appointment in winter, he would slip on an old great-coat of gray twill that he had worn until it was shabby; then, taking down a soft felt hat, twisted and pulled out of shape by use, he would pull it low over his dull gray eyes and amble forth. In summer his clothes looked as crinkled as though he had slept in them for weeks. He smoked. In cast of countenance he was not wholly unlike General Grant, with a short gray beard and moustache which always seemed more or less unkempt, and hair that hung down over his forehead in a gray mass. The poor general! He was neither very happy nor very unhappy—a doubting Thomas without faith or hope in humanity and without any particular affection for anybody.

"I'll tell you how it is with these small councils, Mr. Cowperwood," observed Van Sickle sagely, after the preliminaries of the first interview had been dispensed with. "They're worse than the city council almost, and that's about as bad as it can be. You can't do anything without money where these little fellows are concerned. I don't like to be too hard on men, but these fellows—" He shook his head.

"I understand," commented Cowperwood. "They're not very pleasing, even after you make all allowances."

"Most of them," went on the general, "won't stay put when you think you have them. They sell out. They're just as apt as not to run to this North Side Gas Company and tell them all about the whole thing before you get well under way. Then you have to pay them more money, rival bills will be introduced, and all that." The old general pulled a long face. "Still, there are one or two of them that are all right," he added, "if you can once get them interested—Mr. Duniway and Mr. Gerecht."

"I'm not so much concerned with how it has to be done, General," suggested Cowperwood amiably, "but I want to be sure that it will be done quickly and quietly. I don't want to be bothered with details. Can it be done without too much publicity, and about what do you think it is going to cost?"

"Well, that's pretty hard to say until I look into the matter," said the general thoughtfully. "It might cost only four and it might cost all of forty thousand dollars—even more. I can't tell. I'd like to take a little time and look into it." The old gentleman was wondering how much Cowperwood was prepared to spend.

"Well, we won't bother about that now. I'm willing to be as liberal as necessary. I've sent for Mr. Sippens, the president of the Lake View Gas and Fuel Company, and he'll be here in a little while. You will want to work with him as closely as you can."

The energetic Sippens came after a few moments, and he and Van Sickle, after being instructed to be mutually helpful and to keep Cowperwood's name out of all matters relating to this work, departed together. They were an odd pair—the dusty old general, phlegmatic, disillusioned, useful, but not inclined to feel so; and the smart, chipper Sippens, determined to wreak a kind of poetic vengeance on his old-time enemy, the South Side Gas Company, via this seemingly remote North Side conspiracy. In ten minutes they were hand in glove, the general describing to Sippens the penurious and unscrupulous brand of Councilman Duniway's politics and the friendly but expensive character of Jacob Gerecht. Such is life.

In the organization of the Hyde Park company Cowperwood, because he never cared to put all his eggs in one basket, decided to secure a second lawyer and a second dummy president, although he proposed to keep De Soto Sippens as general practical adviser for all three or four companies. He was thinking this matter over when there appeared on the scene a very much younger man than the old general, one Kent Barrows McKibben, the only son of ex-Judge Marshall Scammon McKibben of the State Supreme Court. Kent McKibben was thirty-three years old, tall, athletic, and, after a fashion, handsome. He was not at all vague intellectually—that is, in the matter of the conduct of his business—but dandified and at times remote. He had an office in one of the best blocks in Dearborn Street, which he reached in a reserved, speculative mood every morning at nine, unless something important called him downtown earlier. It so happened that he had drawn up the deeds and agreements for the real estate company that sold Cowperwood his lots at Thirty-seventh Street and Michigan Avenue, and when they were ready he journeyed to the latter's office to ask if there were any additional details which Cowperwood might want to have taken into consideration. When he was ushered in, Cowperwood turned to him his keen, analytical eyes and saw at once a personality he liked. McKibben was just remote and artistic enough to suit him. He liked his clothes, his agnostic unreadableness, his social air. McKibben, on his part, caught the significance of the superior financial atmosphere at once. He noted Cowperwood's light brown suit picked out with strands of red, his maroon tie, and small cameo cuff links. His desk, glass-covered, looked clean and official. The woodwork of the rooms was all cherry, hand-rubbed and oiled, the pictures interesting steel engravings of American life, appropriately framed. The typewriter—at that time just introduced—was in evidence, and the stock ticker—also new—was ticking volubly the prices current. The secretary who waited on Cowperwood was a young Polish girl named Antoinette Nowak, reserved, seemingly astute, dark, and very attractive.

"What sort of business is it you handle, Mr. McKibben?" asked Cowperwood quite casually in the course of the conversation. And after listening to McKibben's explanation he added idly: "You might come and see me some time next week. It is just possible that I may have something in your line."

In another man McKibben would have resented this remote suggestion of future aid. Now, instead, he was intensely pleased. The man before him gripped his imagination. His remote intellectuality relaxed. When he came again and Cowperwood indicated the nature of the work he might wish to have done, McKibben rose to the bait like a fish to a fly.

"I wish you would let me undertake that, Mr. Cowperwood," he said quite eagerly. "It's something I've never done, but I'm satisfied I can do it. I live out in Hyde Park and know most of the councilmen. I can bring considerable influence to bear for you."

Cowperwood smiled pleasantly.

So a second company, officered by dummies of McKibben's selection, was organized. De Soto Sippens, without old General Van Sickle's knowledge, was taken in as practical adviser. An application for a franchise was drawn up, and Kent Barrows McKibben began silent, polite work on the South Side, coming into the confidence, by degrees, of the various councilmen.

There was still a third lawyer, Burton Stimson, the youngest but assuredly not the least able of the three, a pale, dark-haired Romeoish youth with burning eyes, whom Cowperwood had encountered doing some little work for Laughlin, and who was engaged to work on the West Side with old Laughlin as ostensible organizer and the sprightly De Soto Sippens as practical adviser. Stimson was no mooning Romeo, however, but an eager, incisive soul, born very poor, eager to advance himself. Cowperwood detected that pliability of intellect which, while it might spell disaster to some, spelled success for him. He wanted the intellectual servants. He was willing to pay them handsomely, to keep them busy, to treat them with almost princely courtesy, but he must have the utmost loyalty. Stimson, while maintaining his calm and reserve, could have kissed the archiepiscopal hand. Such is the subtlety of contact.

Behold then at once on the North Side, the South Side, the West Side—dark goings on to and fro and walkings up and down in the earth. In Lake View old General Van Sickle and De Soto Sippens, conferring with shrewd Councilman Duniway, druggist, and with Jacob Gerecht, ward boss and wholesale butcher, both of whom were agreeable but exacting, holding pleasant back room and drugstore confabs with almost tabulated details of rewards and benefits. In Hyde Park Mr. Kent Barrows McKibben, smug and well dressed, a Chesterfield among lawyers, and with him one J. J. Bergdoll, a noble hireling, long-haired and dusty, ostensibly president of the Hyde Park Gas and Fuel Company, conferring with Councilman Alfred B. Davis, manufacturer of willow and rattan ware, and Mr. Patrick Gilgan, saloonkeeper, arranging a prospective distribution of shares, offering certain cash considerations, lots, favors, and the like. Observe also in the village of Douglas and West Park on the West Side, just over the city line, the angular, humorous Peter Laughlin and Burton Stimson arranging a similar deal or deals.

The enemy, the city gas companies, being divided into three factions, were in no way prepared for what was now

coming. When the news finally leaked out that applications
for franchises had been made to the several corporate
village bodies each old company suspected the other of invasion, treachery, robbery. Pettifogging lawyers were sent,
one by each company, to the village council in each particular territory involved, but no one of the companies had
as yet the slightest idea who was back of it all or of the
general plan of operations. Before any one of them could
reasonably protest, before it could decide that it was willing
to pay a very great deal to have the suburb adjacent to its
particular territory left free, before it could organize a legal
fight, councilmanic ordinances were introduced giving the
applying company what it sought; and after a single reading
in each case and one open hearing, as the law compelled,
they were almost unanimously passed. There were loud cries
of dismay from minor suburban papers which had almost
been forgotten in the arrangement of rewards. The large
city newspapers cared little at first, seeing these were outlying districts; they merely made the comment that the villages were beginning well, following in the steps of the city
council in its distinguished career of crime.

Cowperwood smiled as he saw in the morning papers
the announcement of the passage of each ordinance granting him a franchise. He listened with comfort thereafter on
many a day to accounts by Laughlin, Sippens, McKibben, and
Van Sickle of overtures made to buy them out, or to take
over their franchises. He worked on plans with Sippens looking to the actual introduction of gas plants. There were
bond issues now to float, stock to be marketed, contracts for
supplies to be awarded, actual reservoirs and tanks to be
built, and pipes to be laid. A pumped-up public opposition
had to be smoothed over. In all this De Soto Sippens proved
a trump. With Van Sickle, McKibben, and Stimson as his
advisers in different sections of the city he would present
tabloid propositions to Cowperwood, to which the latter had
merely to bow his head in assent or say no. Then De Soto
would buy, build, and excavate. Cowperwood was so pleased
that he was determined to keep De Soto with him permanently. De Soto was pleased to think that he was being
given a chance to pay up old scores and to do large things;
he was really grateful.

"We're not through with those sharpers," he declared to
Cowperwood triumphantly one day. "They'll fight us with

suits. They may join hands later. They blew up my gas plant.
They may blow up ours."

"Let them blow," said Cowperwood. "We can blow, too,
and sue also. I like lawsuits. We'll tie them up so that they'll
beg for quarter." His eyes twinkled cheerfully.

CHAPTER IX

In Search of Victory

In the meantime the social affairs of Aileen had
been prospering in a small way, for while it was plain that
they were not to be taken up at once—that was not to be expected—it was also plain that they were not to be ignored
entirely. One thing that helped in providing a nice harmonious working atmosphere was the obvious warm affection of Cowperwood for his wife. While many might consider Aileen a little brash or crude, still in the hands of so
strong and capable a man as Cowperwood she might prove
available. So thought Mrs. Addison, for instance, and Mrs.
Rambaud. McKibben and Lord felt the same way. If Cowperwood loved her, as he seemed to do, he would probably
put her through successfully. And he really did love her,
after his fashion. He could never forget how splendid she
had been to him in those old days, when, knowing full well
the circumstances of his home, his wife, his children, the
probable opposition of her own family, she had thrown over
convention and sought his love. How freely she had given of
hers! No petty, squeamish bickering and dickering here. He
had been "her Frank" from the start, and he still felt keenly
that longing in her to be with him, to be his, which had produced those first wonderful, almost terrible days. She might
quarrel, fret, fuss, argue, suspect, and accuse him of flirtation with other women; but slight variations from the norm
in his case did not trouble her—at least she argued that they
wouldn't. She had never had any evidence. She was ready to

forgive him anything, she said, and she was, too, if only he
would love her.

"You devil," she used to say to him playfully. "I know
you. I can see you looking around. That's a nice stenographer you have in the office. I suppose it's her."

"Don't be silly, Aileen," he would reply. "Don't be coarse.
You know I wouldn't take up with a stenographer. An office
isn't the place for that sort of thing."

"Oh, isn't it? Don't silly me. I know you. Any old place
is good enough for you."

He laughed, and so did she. She could not help it. She
loved him so. There was no particular bitterness in her as-
saults. She loved him, and very often he would take her in
his arms, kiss her tenderly, and coo: "Are you my fine big
baby? Are you my redheaded doll? Do you really love me
so much? Kiss me, then." Frankly, pagan passion in these
two ran high. So long as they were not alienated by ex-
traneous things he could never hope for more delicious human contact. There was no reaction either, to speak of, no
gloomy disgust. She was physically acceptable to him. He
could always talk to her in a genial, teasing way, even tender, for she did not offend his intellectuality with prudish or
conventional notions. Loving and foolish as she was in some
ways, she would stand blunt reproof or correction. She
could suggest in a nebulous, blundering way things that
would be good for them to do. Most of all at present their
thoughts centered upon Chicago society, the new house,
which by now had been contracted for, and what it would
do to facilitate their introduction and standing. Never did a
woman's life look more rosy, Aileen thought. It was almost
too good to be true. Her Frank was so handsome, so loving,
so generous. There was not a small idea about him. What
if he did stray from her at times? He remained faithful to
her spiritually, and she knew as yet of no single instance in
which he had failed her. She little knew, as much as she
knew, how blandly he could lie and protest in these matters. But he was fond of her just the same, and he really had
not strayed to any extent.

By now also, Cowperwood had invested about $100,000
in his gas company speculations, and he was jubilant over
his prospects; the franchises were good for twenty years.
By that time he would be nearly sixty, and he would probably have bought, combined with, or sold out to the older

companies at a great profit. The future of Chicago was all
in his favor. He decided to invest as much as $30,000 in pic-
tures, if he could find the right ones, and to have Aileen's
portrait painted while she was still so beautiful. This matter of art was again beginning to interest him immensely.
Addison had four or five good pictures—a Rousseau, a
Greuze, a Wouverman, and one Lawrence—picked up heaven
knows where. A hotel man by the name of Collard, a dry-
goods and real estate merchant, was said to have a very
striking collection. Addison had told him of one Davis
Trask, a hardware prince, who was now collecting. There
were many homes he knew where art was beginning to be
assembled. He must begin, too.

Cowperwood, once the franchises had been secured, had
installed Sippens in his own office, giving him charge for
the time being. Small rented offices and clerks were maintained in the region where practical plant building was going
on. All sorts of suits to enjoin, annul, and restrain had been
begun by the various old companies, but McKibben, Stimson,
and old General Van Sickle were fighting these with Trojan
vigor and complacency. It was a pleasant scene. Still no one
knew very much of Cowperwood's entrance into Chicago as
yet. He was a very minor figure. His name had not even
appeared in connection with this work. Other men were
being celebrated daily, a little to his envy. When would he
begin to shine? Soon, now, surely. So off they went in June,
comfortable, rich, gay, in the best of health and spirits, intent upon enjoying to the full their first holiday abroad.

It was a wonderful trip. Addison was good enough to
telegraph flowers to New York for Mrs. Cowperwood, to be
delivered on shipboard. McKibben sent books of travel.
Cowperwood, uncertain whether anybody would send flowers, ordered them himself—two amazing baskets, which with
Addison's made three—and these, with attached cards,
awaited them in the lobby of the main deck. Several at the
captain's table took pains to seek out the Cowperwoods.
They were invited to join several card parties and to attend
informal concerts. It was a rough passage, however, and
Aileen was sick. It was hard to make herself look just nice
enough, and so she kept to her room. She was very haughty,
distant to all but a few, and to these careful of her conversation. She felt herself coming to be a very important person.

Before leaving she had almost exhausted the resources of the Donovan establishment in Chicago. Lingerie, boudoir costumes, walking costumes, riding costumes, evening costumes she possessed in plenty. She had a jewel bag hidden away about her person containing all of thirty thousand dollars' worth of jewels. Her shoes, stockings, hats, and accessories in general were innumerable. Because of all this Cowperwood was rather proud of her. She had such a capacity for life. His first wife had been pale and rather anemic, while Aileen was fairly bursting with sheer physical vitality. She hummed and jested and primped and posed. There are some souls that just are, without previous revision or introspection. The earth with all its long past was a mere suggestion to Aileen, dimly visualized if at all. She may have heard that there were once dinosaurs and flying reptiles, but if so it made no deep impression on her. Somebody had said, or was saying, that we were descended from monkeys, which was quite absurd, though it might be true enough. On the sea the thrashing hills of green water suggested a kind of immensity and terror, but not the immensity of the poet's heart. The ship was safe, the captain at table in brass buttons and blue uniform eager to be nice to her—told her so. Her faith, really, was in the captain. And there with her, always, was Cowperwood, looking at this whole moving spectacle of life with a suspicious, not apprehensive, but wary eye, and saying nothing about it.

In London letters given them by Addison brought several invitations to the opera, to dinner, to Goodwood for a weekend, and so on. Carriages, tallyhoes, cabs for riding were invoked. A weekend invitation to a houseboat on the Thames was secured. Their English hosts, looking on all this as a financial adventure, good financial wisdom, were courteous and civil, nothing more. Aileen was intensely curious. She noted servants, manners, forms. Immediately she began to think that America was not good enough, perhaps; it wanted so many things.

"Now, Aileen, you and I have to live in Chicago for years and years," commented Cowperwood. "Don't get wild. These people don't care for Americans, can't you see that? They wouldn't accept us if we were over here—not yet anyhow. We're merely passing strangers, being courteously entertained." Cowperwood saw it all.

Aileen was being spoiled in a way, but there was no help.

She dressed and dressed. The Englishmen used to look at her—in Hyde Park, where she rode and drove; at Claridges', where they stayed; in Bond Street, where she shopped. The Englishwomen, the majority of them remote, ultraconservative, simple in their tastes, lifted their eyes. Cowperwood sensed the situation, but said nothing. He loved Aileen, and she was satisfactory to him, at least for the present, anyhow, beautiful. If he could adjust her station in Chicago, that would be sufficient for a beginning. After three weeks of very active life, during which Aileen patronized the ancient and honorable glories of England, they went on to Paris.

Here she was quickened to a childlike enthusiasm. "You know," she said to Cowperwood quite solemnly the second morning, "the English don't know how to dress. I thought they did, but the smartest of them copy the French. Take those men we saw last night in the Café d'Anglais. There wasn't an Englishman I saw that compared with them."

"My dear, your tastes are exotic," replied Cowperwood, who was watching her with pleased interest while he adjusted his tie. "The French smart crowd are almost too smart, dandified. I think some of those young fellows had on corsets."

"What of it?" replied Aileen. "I like it. If you're going to be smart, why not be very smart?"

"I know that's your theory, my dear," he said, "but it can be overdone. There is such a thing as going too far. You have to compromise even if you don't look as well as you might. You can't be too very conspicuously different from your neighbors, even in the right direction."

"You know," she said, stopping and looking at him, "I believe you're going to get very conservative someday—like my brothers."

She came over and touched his tie and smoothed his hair.

"Well, one of us ought to be, for the good of the family," he commented, half smiling.

"I'm not so sure, though, that it will be you, either."

"It's a charming day. See how nice those white marble statues look. Shall we go to the Cluny or Versailles or Fontainbleau? Tonight we ought to see Bernhardt at the Française."

Aileen was so gay. It was so splendid to be traveling with her true husband at last.

It was on this trip that Cowperwood's taste for art and life and his determination to possess them revived to the fullest. He made the acquaintance in London, Paris, and Brussels of the important art dealers. His conceptions of great masters and the older schools of art shaped themselves. By one of the dealers in London, who at once recognized in him a possible future patron, he was invited with Aileen to view certain private collections, and here and there was an artist, such as Lord Leighton, Dante Gabriel Rossetti, or Whistler, to whom he was introduced casually, an interested stranger. These men only saw a strong, polite, remote, conservative man. He realized the emotional, egotistic, and artistic soul. He felt on the instant that there could be little in common between such men and himself insofar as personal contact was concerned, yet there was mutual ground on which they could meet. He could not be a slavish admirer of anything, only a princely patron. So he walked and saw, wondering how soon his dreams of grandeur were to be realized.

In London he bought a portrait by Raeburn; in Paris a plowing scene by Millet, a small Jan Steen, a battle piece by Meissonier, and a romantic courtyard scene by Isabey. Thus began the revival of his former interest in art; the nucleus of that future collection which was to mean so much to him in later years.

On their return, the building of the new Chicago mansion created the next interesting diversion in the lives of Aileen and Cowperwood. Because of some châteaus they saw in France, that form, or rather a modification of it as suggested by Taylor Lord, was adopted. Mr. Lord figured that it would take all of a year, perhaps a year and a half, to deliver it in perfect order, but time was of no great importance in this connection. In the meanwhile they could strengthen their social connections and prepare for that interesting day when they should be of the Chicago elite.

There were, at this time, several elements in Chicago—those who, having grown suddenly rich from dull poverty, could not so easily forget the village church and the village social standards; those who, having inherited wealth, or migrated from the East where wealth was old, understood more of the *savoir faire* of the game; and those who, being newly born into wealth and seeing the drift toward a smarter

American life, were beginning to wish they might shine in it—these last the very young people. The latter were just beginning to dream of dances at Kinsley's, a stated kermis, and summer diversions of the European kind, but they had not arrived as yet. The first class, although by far the dullest and most bovine, was still the most powerful because they were the richest, money as yet providing the highest standard. The functions which these people provided were stupid to the verge of distraction; really they were only the weekday receptions and Sunday afternoon calls of Squeedunk and Hohokus raised to the nth power. The purpose of the whole matter was to see and be seen. Novelty in either thought or action was decidedly eschewed. It was, as a matter of fact, customariness of thought and action and the quintessence of convention that were desired. The idea of introducing a "play actress," for instance, as was done occasionally in the East or in London—never; even a singer or an artist was eyed askance. One could easily go too far! But if a European prince should have strayed to Chicago (which he never did) or if an eastern social magnate chanced to stay over a train or two, then the topmost circle of local wealth was prepared to strain itself to the breaking point.

Cowperwood had sensed all this on his arrival, but he fancied that if he became rich and powerful enough he and Aileen, with their fine house to help them, might well be the leaven which would lighten the whole lump. Unfortunately, Aileen was too obviously on the qui vive for those opportunities which might lead to social recognition and equality, if not supremacy. Like the savage, unorganized for protection and at the mercy of the horrific caprice of nature, she was almost tremulous at times with thoughts of possible failure. Almost at once she had recognized herself as unsuited temperamentally for association with certain types of society women. The wife of Anson Merrill, the great dry-goods prince, whom she saw in one of the downtown stores one day, impressed her as much too cold and remote. Mrs. Merrill was a woman of superior mood and education who found herself, in her own estimation, hard put to it for suitable companionship in Chicago. She was eastern-bred —Boston—and familiar in an offhand way with the superior world of London, which she had visited several times. Chicago at its best was to her a sordid commercial mess. She preferred New York or Washington, but she had to live here.

Thus she patronized nearly all of those with whom she condescended to associate, using an upward tilt of the head, a
tired droop of the eyelids, and a fine upward arching of the
brows to indicate how trite it all was.

It was a Mrs. Henry Huddlestone who had pointed out
Mrs. Merrill to Aileen. Mrs. Huddlestone was the wife of
a soap manufacturer living very close to the Cowperwoods'
temporary home, and she and her husband were on the outer
fringe of society. She had heard that the Cowperwoods were
people of wealth, that they were friendly with the Addisons,
and that they were going to build a $200,000 mansion. (The
value of houses always grows in the telling.) That was
enough. She had called, being three doors away, to leave her
card; and Aileen, willing to curry favor here and there, had
responded. Mrs. Huddlestone was a little woman, not very
attractive in appearance, clever in a social way, and eminently practical.

"Speaking of Mrs. Merrill," commented Mrs. Huddlestone
on this particular day, "there she is—near the dress-goods
counter. She always carries that lorgnette in just that way."

Aileen turned and examined critically a tall, dark, slender
woman of the high world of the West, very remote, disdainful, superior.

"You don't know her?" questioned Aileen curiously, surveying her at leisure.

"No," replied Mrs. Huddlestone defensively. "They live on
the North Side, and the different sets don't mingle so much."

As a matter of fact, it was just the glory of the principal
families that they were above this arbitrary division of sides,
and could pick their associates from all three divisions.

"Oh!" observed Aileen nonchalantly. She was secretly irritated to think that Mrs. Huddlestone should find it necessary
to point out Mrs. Merrill to her as a superior person.

"You know, she darkens her eyebrows a little, I think,"
suggested Mrs. Huddlestone, studying her enviously. "Her
husband, they say, isn't the most faithful person in the world.
There's another woman, a Mrs. Gladdens, that lives very
close to them that he's very much interested in."

"Oh!" said Aileen cautiously. After her own Philadelphia
experience she had decided to be on her guard and not
indulge in too much gossip. Arrows of this particular kind
could so readily fly in her direction.

"But her set is really much the smartest," complimented Aileen's companion.

Thereafter it was Aileen's ambition to associate with Mrs. Anson Merrill, to be fully and freely accepted by her. She did not know, although she might have feared, that that ambition was never to be realized.

But there were others who had called at the first Cowperwood home, or with whom the Cowperwoods managed to form an acquaintance. There were the Sunderland Sledds, Mr. Sledd being general traffic manager of one of the southwestern railways entering the city, and a gentleman of taste and culture and some wealth; his wife an ambitious nobody. There were the Walter Rysam Cottons, Cotton being a wholesale coffee broker, but more especially a local social litterateur; his wife a graduate of Vassar. There were the Norrie Simmses, Simms being secretary and treasurer of the Douglas Trust and Savings Company, and a power in another group of financial people, a group entirely distinct from that represented by Addison and Rambaud. Others included the Stanislau Hoecksemas, wealthy furriers; the Duane Kingslands, wholesale flour; the Webster Israelses, packers; the Bradford Candas, jewelers. All these people amounted to something socially. They all had substantial homes and substantial incomes, so that they were worthy of consideration. The difference between Aileen and most of the women involved a difference between naturalism and illusion. But this calls for some explanation.

To really know the state of the feminine mind at this time, one would have to go back to that period in the Middle Ages when the Church flourished and the industrious poet, half schooled in the facts of life, surrounded women with a mystical halo. Since that day the maiden—and the matron as well—has been schooled to believe that she is of a finer clay than man, that she was born to uplift him, and that her favors are priceless. This rose-tinted mist of romance, having nothing to do with personal morality, has brought about, nevertheless, a holier-than-thou attitude of women toward men, and even of women toward women. Now, the Chicago atmosphere in which Aileen found herself was composed in part of this very illusion. The ladies to whom she had been introduced were of this high world of fancy. They conceived themselves to be perfect, even as they were represented in religious art and in fiction. Their husbands must

be models, worthy of their high ideals, and other women must
have no blemish of any kind. Aileen, urgent, elemental, would
have laughed at all this if she could have understood. Not
understanding, she felt diffident and uncertain of herself in
certain presences.

Instance in this connection Mrs. Norrie Simms, who was
a satellite of Mrs. Anson Merrill. To be invited to the Anson
Merrills' for tea, dinner, luncheon, or to be driven downtown by Mrs. Merrill, was paradise to Mrs. Simms. She loved
to recite the bon mots of her idol, to discourse upon her
astonishing degree of culture, to narrate how people refused
on occasion to believe that she was the wife of Anson
Merrill, even though she herself declared it—those old chestnuts of the social world which must have had their origin
in Egypt and Chaldea. Mrs. Simms herself was of a non-
descript type, not a real personage, clever, good-looking, taste-
ful, a social climber. The two Simms children (little girls) had
been taught all the social graces of the day—to pose, smirk,
genuflect, and the like, to the immense delight of their elders.
The nurse in charge was in uniform, the governess was a
much put-upon person. Mrs. Simms had a high manner, eyes
for those above her only, a serene contempt for the commonplace world in which she had to dwell.

During the first dinner at which she entertained the Cowperwoods Mrs. Simms attempted to dig into Aileen's Philadelphia history, asking if she knew the Arthur Leighs, the
Trevor Drakes, Roberta Willing, or the Martyn Walkers. Mrs.
Simms did not know them herself, but she had heard Mrs.
Merrill speak of them, and that was enough of a handle
whereby to swing them. Aileen, quick on the defense, ready
to lie manfully on her own behalf, assured her that she had
known them, as indeed she had—very casually—and before
the rumor which connected her with Cowperwood had
been voiced abroad. This pleased Mrs. Simms.

"I must tell Nellie," she said, referring thus familiarly to
Mrs. Merrill.

Aileen feared that if this sort of thing continued it would
soon be all over town that she had been a mistress before
she had been a wife, that she had been the unmentioned
correspondent in the divorce suit, and that Cowperwood had
been in prison. Only his wealth and her beauty could save
her; and would they?

One night they had been to dinner at the Duane Kingslands', and Mrs. Bradford Canda had asked her, in what seemed a very significant way, whether she had ever met her friend Mrs. Schuyler Evans, of Philadelphia. This frightened Aileen.

"Don't you suppose they must know, some of them, about us?" she asked Cowperwood on the way home.

"I suppose so," he replied thoughtfully. "I'm sure I don't know. I wouldn't worry about that if I were you. If you worry about it you'll suggest it to them. I haven't made any secret of my term in prison in Philadelphia, and I don't intend to. It wasn't a square deal, and they had no right to put me there."

"I know, dear," replied Aileen, "it might not make so much difference if they did know. I don't see why it should. We are not the only ones that have had marriage troubles, I'm sure."

"There's just one thing about this; either they accept us or they don't. If they don't, well and good; we can't help it. We'll go on and finish the house, and give them a chance to be decent. If they won't be, there are other cities. Money will arrange matters in New York—that I know. We can build a real place there, and go in on equal terms if we have money enough—and I will have money enough," he added, after a moment's pondering. "Never fear. I'll make millions here, whether they want me to or not, and after that—well, after that, we'll see what we'll see. Don't worry. I haven't seen many troubles in this world that money wouldn't cure."

His teeth had that even set that they always assumed when he was dangerously in earnest. He took Aileen's hand, however, and pressed it gently.

"Don't worry," he repeated. "Chicago isn't the only city, and we won't be the poorest people in America, either, in ten years. Just keep up your courage. It will all come out right. It's certain to."

Aileen looked out on the lamp-lit length of Michigan Avenue, down which they were rolling past many silent mansions. The tops of all the lamps were white, and gleamed through the shadows, receding to a thin point. It was dark, but fresh and pleasant. Oh, if only Frank's money could buy them position and friendship in this interesting world; if it only would! She did not quite realize how much on her own personality, or the lack of it, this struggle depended.

CHAPTER X

A Test

The opening of the house in Michigan Avenue occurred late in November in the fall of 1878, when Aileen and Cowperwood had been in Chicago about two years. Altogether, between people whom they had met at the races, at various dinners and teas, and at receptions of the Union and Calumet Clubs (to which Cowperwood, through Addison's backing, had been admitted) and those whom McKibben and Lord influenced, they were able to send invitations to about 300, of whom some 250 responded. Up to this time, owing to Cowperwood's quiet manipulation of his affairs, there had been no comment on his past—no particular interest in it. He had money, affable ways, a magnetic personality. The businessmen of the city—those whom he met socially—were inclined to consider him fascinating and very clever. Aileen, being beautiful and graceful for attention, was accepted at more or less her own value, though the kingly high world knew them not.

It is amazing what a showing the socially unplaced can make on occasion where tact and discrimination are used. There was a weekly social paper published in Chicago at this time, a rather able publication as such things go, which Cowperwood, with McKibben's assistance, had pressed into service. Not much can be done under any circumstances where the cause is not essentially strong; but where, as in this case, there are a semblance of respectability, considerable wealth, and great force and magnetism, all things are possible. Kent McKibben knew Horton Biggers, the editor, who was a rather desolate and disillusioned person of forty-five, gray and depressed-looking—a sort of human sponge or barnacle who was only galvanized into seeming interest and cheerfulness by sheer necessity. Those were the days when the society

66

editor was accepted as a member of society—*de facto*—and treated more as a guest than a reporter, though even then the tendency was toward elimination. Working for Cowperwood and liking him, McKibben said to Biggers one evening:

"You know the Cowperwoods, don't you, Biggers?"

"No," replied the latter, who devoted himself barnacle-wise to the more exclusive circles. "Who are they?"

"Why, he's a banker over here in La Salle Street. They're from Philadelphia. Mrs. Cowperwood's a beautiful woman —young and all that. They're building a house out here on Michigan Avenue. You ought to know them. They're going to get in, I think. The Addisons like them. If you were to be nice to them now I think they'd appreciate it later. He's rather liberal, and a good fellow."

Biggers pricked up his ears. This social journalism was thin picking at best, and he had very few ways of turning an honest penny. The would-bes and half-ins who expected nice things said of them had to subscribe, and rather liberally, to his paper. Not long after this brief talk Cowperwood received a subscription blank from the business office of the *Saturday Review*, and immediately sent a check for one hundred dollars to Mr. Horton Biggers direct. Subsequently certain not very significant personages noticed that when the Cowperwoods dined at their boards the function received comment by the *Saturday Review*, not otherwise. It looked as though the Cowperwoods must be favored; but who were they, anyhow?

The danger of publicity, and even moderate social success, is that scandal loves a shining mark. When you begin to stand out the least way in life, as separate from the mass, the cognoscenti wish to know who, what, and why. The enthusiasm of Aileen, combined with the genius of Cowperwood, was for making their opening entertainment a very exceptional affair, which, under the circumstances, and all things considered, was a dangerous thing to do. As yet Chicago was exceedingly slow socially. Its movements were, as has been said, more or less bovine and phlegmatic. To rush in with something utterly brilliant and pyrotechnic was to take notable chances. The more cautious members of Chicago society, even if they did not attend, would hear, and then would come ultimate comment and decision.

The function began with a reception at four which lasted until six-thirty, and this was followed by a dance at nine, with music by a famous stringed orchestra of Chicago, a musical program by artists of considerable importance, and a gorgeous supper from eleven until one in a Chinese fairyland of lights, at small tables filling three of the ground-floor rooms. As an added fillip to the occasion Cowperwood had hung not only the important pictures which he had purchased abroad but a new one—a particularly brilliant Gérôme, then in the heyday of his exotic popularity—a picture of nude odalisques of the harem, idling beside the highly colored stone marquetry of an Oriental bath. It was more or less "loose" art for Chicago, shocking to the uninitiated, though harmless enough to the illuminati; but it gave a touch of color to the art gallery which the latter needed. There was also, newly arrived and newly hung, a portrait of Aileen by a Dutch artist, Jan van Beers, whom they had encountered the previous summer at Brussels. He had painted Aileen in nine sittings, a rather brilliant canvas, high in key, with a summery, out-of-door world behind her—a low stone-curbed pool, the red corner of a Dutch brick palace, a tulip bed, and a blue sky with fleecy clouds. Aileen was seated on the curved arm of a stone bench, green grass at her feet, a pink and white parasol with a lacy edge held idly to one side; her rounded, vigorous figure clad in the latest mode of Paris, a white-and-blue-striped silk walking suit, with a blue-and-white-banded straw hat, wide-brimmed, airy, shading her lusty, animal eyes. The artist had caught her spirit quite accurately, the dash, the assumption, the bravado based on the courage of inexperience, or lack of true subtlety. A refreshing thing in its way, a little showy, as everything that related to her was, and inclined to arouse jealousy in those not so liberally endowed by life, but fine, as a character piece. In the warm glow of the guttered gas jets she looked particularly brilliant here, pampered, idle, jaunty— the well-kept, stall-fed pet of the world. Many stopped to see, and many were the comments, private and otherwise.

This day began with a flurry of uncertainty and worried anticipation on the part of Aileen. At Cowperwood's suggestion she had employed a social secretary, a poor hack of a girl, who had sent out all the letters, tabulated the replies, run errands, and advised on one detail and another. Fadette, her French maid, was in the throes of preparing for two toilets which would have to be made this day, one by two o'clock at least, another between six and eight. Her

"mon dieus" and *"par bleus"* could be heard continuously
as she hunted for some article of dress or polished an ornament, buckle, or pin. The struggle of Aileen to be perfect
was, as usual, severe. Her meditations as to the most becoming gown to wear were trying. Her portrait was on the
east wall in the art gallery, a spur to emulation; she felt as
though all society were about to judge her. Theresa Donovan,
the local dressmaker, had given some advice; but Aileen
decided on a heavy brown velvet constructed by Worth of
Paris—a thing of varying aspects, showing her neck and arms
to a perfection, and composing charmingly with her flesh and
hair. She tried amethyst earrings and changed to topaz; she
stockinged her legs in brown silk, and her feet were shod in
brown slippers with red enamel buttons.

The trouble with Aileen was that she never did these things
with that ease which is a sure sign of the socially efficient.
She never quite so much dominated a situation as she permitted it to dominate her. Only the superior ease and gra-
ciousness of Cowperwood carried her through at times; but
that always did. When he was near she felt quite the great
lady, suited to any realm. When she was alone her courage,
great as it was, often trembled in the balance. Her dangerous
past was never quite out of her mind.

At four Kent McKibben, smug in his afternoon frock,
his quick, receptive eyes approving only partially of all this
show and effort, took his place in the general reception room,
talking to Taylor Lord, who had completed his last observation and was leaving to return later in the evening. If these
two had been closer friends, quite intimate, they would have
discussed the Cowperwoods' social prospects; but as it was,
they confined themselves to dull conventionalities. At this
moment Aileen came downstairs for a moment, radiant. Kent
McKibben thought he had never seen her look more beautiful.
After all, contrasted with some of the stuffy creatures who
moved about in society, shrewd, hard, bony, calculating, trading on their assured position, she was admirable. It was a pity
she did not have more poise; she ought to be a little harder
—not quite so genial. Still, with Cowperwood at her side,
she might go far.

"Really, Mrs. Cowperwood," he said, "it is all most charming. I was just telling Mr. Lord here that I consider the
house a triumph."

From McKibben, who was in society, and with Lord, another "in" standing by, this was like wine to Aileen. She beamed joyously.

Among the first arrivals were Mrs. Webster Israels, Mrs. Bradford Canda, and Mrs. Walter Rysam Cotton, who were to assist in receiving. These ladies did not know that they were taking their future reputations for sagacity and discrimination in their hands; they had been carried away by the show of luxury of Aileen, the growing financial repute of Cowperwood, and the artistic qualities of the new house. Mrs. Webster Israels's mouth was of such a peculiar shape that Aileen was always reminded of a fish; but she was not utterly homely, and today she looked brisk and attractive. Mrs. Bradford Canda, whose old rose-and-silver-gray dress made up in part for an amazing angularity, but who was charming withal, was the soul of interest, for she believed this to be a very significant affair. Mrs. Walter Rysam Cotton, a younger woman than either of the others, had the polish of Vassar life about her, and was "above" many things. Somehow she half suspected the Cowperwoods might not do, but they were making strides, and might possibly surpass all other aspirants. It behooved her to be pleasant.

Life passes from individuality and separateness at times to a sort of Monticelliesque mood of color, where individuality is nothing, the glittering totality all. The new house, with its charming French windows on the ground floor, its heavy bands of stone flowers and deep-sunk florated door, was soon crowded with a moving, colorful flow of people. Many whom Aileen and Cowperwood did not know at all had been invited by McKibben and Lord; they came, and were now introduced. The adjacent side streets and the open space in front of the house were crowded with champing horses and smartly veneered carriages. All with whom the Cowperwoods had been the least intimate came early, and finding the scene colorful and interesting, they remained for some time. The caterer, Kinsley, had supplied a small army of trained servants who were posted like soldiers, and carefully supervised by the Cowperwood butler. The new dining room, rich with a Pompeian scheme of color, was aglow with a wealth of glass and an artistic arrangement of delicacies. The afternoon costumes of the women, ranging through autumnal grays, purples, browns, and greens, blended effectively with the brown-tinted walls of the entry hall, the deep gray and gold of the general living room, the old Roman

red of the dining room, the white and gold of the music
room, and the neutral sepia of the art gallery.

Aileen, backed by the courageous presence of Cowperwood, who, in the dining room, the library, and the art
gallery, was holding a private levee of men, stood up in her
vain beauty, a thing to see—almost to weep over, embody-
ing the vanity of all seeming things, the mockery of having
and yet not having. This parading throng that was more
curious than interested, more jealous than sympathetic, more
critical than kind, was coming almost solely to observe.

"Do you know, Mrs. Cowperwood," Mrs. Simms remarked
lightly, "your house reminds me of an art exhibit today.
I hardly know why."

Aileen, who caught the implied slur, had no clever words
wherewith to reply. She was not gifted in that way, but she
flared with resentment.

"Do you think so?" she replied caustically.

Mrs. Simms, not all dissatisfied with the effect she had
produced, passed on with a gay air, attended by a young
artist who followed amorously in her train.

Aileen saw from this and other things like it how little
she was really in. The exclusive set did not take either her or
Cowperwood seriously as yet. She almost hated the comparatively dull Mrs. Israels, who had been standing beside
her at the time, and who had heard the remark; and yet
Mrs. Israels was much better than nothing. Mrs. Simms had
condescended a mild "How'd do" to the latter.

It was in vain that the Addisons, Sledds, Kingslands,
Hoecksemas, and others made their appearance; Aileen was
not reassured. However, after dinner the younger set, influenced by McKibben, came to dance, and Aileen was at
her best in spite of her doubts. She was gay, bold, attractive.
Kent McKibben, a past master in the mazes and mysteries
of the grand march, had the pleasure of leading her in that
airy, fairy procession, followed by Cowperwood, who gave
his arm to Mrs. Simms. Aileen, in white satin with a touch
of silver here and there, and necklet, bracelet, earrings, and
hair ornament of diamonds, glittered in almost an exotic
way. She was positively radiant. McKibben, almost smitten,
was most attentive.

"This is such a pleasure," he whispered intimately. "You
are very beautiful—a dream!"

"You would find me a very substantial one," returned Aileen.

"Would that I might find," he laughed gaily; and Aileen, gathering the hidden significance, showed her teeth teasingly. Mrs. Simms, engrossed by Cowperwood, could not hear as she would have liked.

After the march Aileen, surrounded by a half-dozen of gay, rudely thoughtless young bloods, escorted them all to see her portrait. The conservative commented on the flow of wine, the intensely nude Gérôme at one end of the gallery, and the sparkling portrait of Aileen at the other, the enthusiasm of some of the young men for her company. Mrs. Rambaud, pleasant and kindly, remarked to her husband that Aileen was "very eager for life," she thought. Mrs. Addison, astonished at the material flare of the Cowperwoods, quite transcending in glitter if not in size and solidity anything she and Addison had ever achieved, remarked to her husband that "he must be making money very fast."

"The man's a born financier, Ella," Addison explained sententiously. "He's a manipulator, and he's sure to make money. Whether they can get into society I don't know. He could if he were alone, that's sure. She's beautiful, but he needs another kind of woman, I'm afraid. She's almost too good-looking."

"That's what I think, too. I like her, but I'm afraid she's not going to play her cards right. It's too bad, too."

Just then Aileen came by, a smiling youth on either side, her own face glowing with a warmth of joy engendered by much flattery. The ballroom, which was composed of the music and drawing rooms thrown into one, was now the objective. It glittered before her with a moving throng; the air was full of the odor of flowers and the sound of music and voices.

"Mrs. Cowperwood," observed Bradford Canda to Horton Biggers, the society editor, "is one of the prettiest women I have seen in a long time. She's almost too pretty."

"How do you think she's taking?" queried the cautious Biggers.

"Charming, but she's hardly cold enough, I'm afraid; hardly clever enough. It takes a more serious type. She's a little too high-spirited. These old women would never want to get near her; she makes them look too old. She'd do better if she were not so young and so pretty."

"That's what I think exactly," said Biggers. As a matter of fact, he did not think so at all; he had no power of drawing any such accurate conclusions. But he believed it now, because Bradford Canda had said it.

CHAPTER XI

The Fruits of Daring

Next morning, over the breakfast cups at the Norrie Simmses' and elsewhere, the import of the Cowperwoods' social efforts was discussed and the problem of their eventual acceptance or nonacceptance carefully weighed.

"The trouble with Mrs. Cowperwood," observed Mrs. Simms, "is that she is too gauche. The whole thing was much too showy. The idea of her portrait at one end of the gallery and that Gérôme at the other! And then this item in the *Press* this morning! Why, you'd really think they were in society." Mrs. Simms was already a little angry at having let herself be used, as she now fancied she had been, by Taylor Lord and Kent McKibben, both friends of hers.

"What did you think of the crowd?" asked Norrie, buttering a roll.

"Why, it wasn't representative at all, of course. We were the most important people they had there, and I'm sorry now that we went. Who are the Israelses and the Hoecksemas, anyhow? That dreadful woman!" (She was referring to Mrs. Hoecksema.) "I never listened to duller remarks in my life."

"I was talking to Haguenin of the *Press* in the afternoon," observed Norrie. "He says that Cowperwood failed in Philadelphia before he came here, and that there were a lot of lawsuits. Did you ever hear that?"

"No. But she says she knows the Drakes and the Walkers there. I've been intending to ask Nellie about that. I have often wondered why he should leave Philadelphia if he was getting along so well. People don't usually do that."

Simms was envious already of the financial showing Cowperwood was making in Chicago. Besides, Cowperwood's manner bespoke supreme intelligence and courage, and that is always resented by all save the suppliants or the triumphant masters of other walks in life. Simms was really interested at last to know something more about Cowperwood, something definite.

Before this social situation had time to adjust itself one way or the other, however, a matter arose which in its way was far more vital, though Aileen might not have thought so. The feeling between the new and old gas companies was becoming strained; the stockholders of the older organization were getting uneasy. They were eager to find out who was back of these new gas companies which were threatening to poach on their exclusive preserves. Finally one of the lawyers who had been employed by the North Chicago Gas Illuminating Company to fight the machinations of De Soto Sippens and old General Van Sickle, finding that the Lake View Council had finally granted the franchise to the new company and that the Appellate Court was about to sustain it, hit upon the idea of charging conspiracy and wholesale bribery of councilmen. Considerable evidence had accumulated that Duniway, Jacob Gerecht, and others on the North Side had been influenced by cash, and to bring legal action would delay final approval of the franchises and give the old company time to think what else to do. This North Side company lawyer, a man by the name of Parsons, had been following up the movements of Sippens and old General Van Sickle, and had finally concluded that they were mere dummies and pawns, and that the real instigator in all this excitement was Cowperwood, or, if not he, then men whom he represented. Parsons visited Cowperwood's office one day in order to see him; getting no satisfaction, he proceeded to look up his record and connections. These various investigations and counterschemings came to a head in a court proceeding filed in the United States Circuit Court late in November, charging Frank Algernon Cowperwood, Henry De Soto Sippens, Judson P. Van Sickle, and others with conspiracy; this again was followed almost immediately by suits begun by the West and South Side companies charging the same thing. In each case Cowperwood's name was mentioned as the secret power behind the new companies, conspiring to force the old companies to buy him out. His Philadelphia history was published, but only in part—a highly modified account he had furnished the newspapers some time before. Though conspiracy and bribery are ugly words, still lawyers' charges prove nothing. But a penitentiary record, for whatever reason served, coupled with previous failure, divorce, and scandal (though the newspapers made only the most guarded reference to all this), served to whet public interest and to fix Cowperwood and his wife in the public eye.

Cowperwood himself was solicited for an interview, but his answer was that he was merely a financial agent for the three new companies, not an investor; and that the charges, insofar as he was concerned, were untrue, mere legal folderol trumped up to make the situation as annoying as possible. He threatened to sue for libel. Nevertheless, although these suits eventually did come to nothing (for he had fixed it so that he could not be traced save as a financial agent in each case), yet the charges had been made, and he was now revealed as a shrewd, manipulative factor, with a record that was certainly spectacular.

"I see," said Anson Merrill to his wife one morning at breakfast, "that this man Cowperwood is beginning to get his name in the papers." He had the *Times* on the table before him, and was looking at a headline which, after the old-fashioned pyramids then in vogue, read: "Conspiracy charged against various Chicago citizens. Frank Algernon Cowperwood, Judson P. Van Sickle, Henry De Soto Sippens, and others named in Circuit Court complaint." It went on to specify other facts. "I supposed he was just a broker."

"I don't know much about them," replied his wife, "except what Bella Simms tells me. What does it say?"

He handed her the paper.

"I have always thought they were merely climbers," continued Mrs. Merrill. "From what I hear she is impossible. I never saw her."

"He begins well for a Philadelphian," smiled Merrill. "I've seen him at the Calumet. He looks like a very shrewd man to me. He's going about his work in a brisk spirit, anyhow."

Similarly Mr. Norman Schryhart, a man who up to this time had taken no thought of Cowperwood, although he had noted his appearance about the halls of the Calumet and Union League Clubs, began to ask seriously who he was. Schryhart, a man of great physical and mental vigor, six feet tall, hale and stolid as an ox, a very different type of man from Anson Merrill, met Addison one day at the Calumet Club shortly after the newspaper talk began. Sinking into a great leather divan beside him, he observed:

"Who is this man Cowperwood whose name is in the papers these days, Addison? You know all these people. Didn't you introduce him to me once?"

"I surely did," replied Addison cheerfully, who, in spite of the attacks on Cowperwood, was rather pleased than otherwise. It was quite plain from the concurrent excitement that attended all this struggle that Cowperwood must be managing things rather adroitly, and, best of all, he was keeping his backers' names from view. "He's a Philadelphian by birth. He came out here several years ago and went into the grain and commission business. He's a banker now. A rather shrewd man, I should say. He has a lot of money."

"Is it true, as the papers say, that he failed for a million in Philadelphia in 1871?"

"Insofar as I know, it is."

"Well, was he in the penitentiary down there?"

"I think so—yes. I believe it was for nothing really criminal, though. There appears to have been some political-financial mix-up, from all I can learn."

"And is he only forty, as the papers say?"

"About that, I should judge. Why?"

"Oh, this scheme of his looks rather pretentious to me—holding up the old gas companies here. Do you suppose he'll manage to do it?"

"I don't know that. All I know is what I have read in the papers," replied Addison cautiously. As a matter of fact, he did not care to talk about this business at all. Cowperwood was busy at this very time, through an agent, attempting to effect a compromise and union of all interests concerned. It was not going very well.

"Humph!" commented Schryhart. He was wondering why men like himself, Merrill, Arneel, and others had not worked into this field long ago or bought out the old companies. He went away interested, and a day or two later—even the next morning—had formulated a scheme. Not unlike Cowperwood, he was a shrewd, hard, cold man. He believed in Chicago implicitly and in all that related to its future. This gas situation, now that Cowperwood had seen the point, was very clear to him. Even yet it might not be impossible for a third party to step in and by intricate manipulation secure the much coveted rewards. Perhaps Cowperwood himself could be taken over—who could tell?

Mr. Schryhart, being a very dominating type of person, did not believe in minor partnerships or investments. If he went into a thing of this kind it was his preference to rule. He decided to invite Cowperwood to visit the Schryhart office and talk matters over. Accordingly, he had his secretary pen a note, which in rather lofty phrases invited Cowperwood to call "on a matter of importance."

Now just at this time, it so chanced, Cowperwood was feeling rather secure as to his place in the Chicago financial world, although he was still smarting from the bitterness of the aspersions recently cast upon him from various quarters. Under such circumstances it was his temperament to evince a rugged contempt for humanity, rich and poor alike. He was well aware that Schryhart, although introduced, had never previously troubled to notice him.

"Mr. Cowperwood begs me to say," wrote Miss Antoinette Nowak at his dictation, "that he finds himself very much pressed for time at present, but he would be glad to see Mr. Schryhart at his office at any time."

This irritated the dominating, self-sufficient Schryhart a little, but nevertheless he was satisfied that a conference could do no harm in this instance—was advisable, in fact. So one Wednesday afternoon he journeyed to the office of Cowperwood, and was most hospitably received.

"How do you do, Mr. Schryhart," observed Cowperwood cordially, extending his hand. "I'm glad to see you again. I believe we met once before several years ago."

"I think so myself," replied Mr. Schryhart, who was broad-shouldered, square-headed, black-eyed, and with a short black moustache gracing a firm upper lip. He had hard, dark, piercing eyes. "I see by the papers, if they can be trusted," he said, coming directly to the point, "that you are interesting yourself in local gas. Is that true?"

"I'm afraid the papers cannot be generally relied on," replied Cowperwood quite blandly. "Would you mind telling me what makes you interested to know whether I am or not?"

"Well, to tell the truth," replied Schryhart, staring at the financier, "I am interested in this local gas situation myself. It offers a rather profitable field for investment, and several members of the old companies have come to me recently

to ask me to help them combine." (This was not true at all.)
"I have been wondering what chance you thought you had
of winning along the lines you are now taking."

Cowperwood smiled. "I hardly care to discuss that," he
said, "unless I know much more of your motives and connections than I do at present. Do I understand that you
have really been appealed to by stockholders of the old
companies to come in and help adjust this matter?"

"Exactly," said Schryhart.

"And you think you can get them to combine? On what
basis?"

"Oh, I should say it would be a simple matter to give
each of them two or three shares of a new company for one
in each of the old. We could then elect one set of officers,
have one set of offices, stop all these suits, and leave everybody happy."

He said this in an easy, patronizing way, as though Cowperwood had not really thought it all out years before. It
amazed the latter no little to see his own scheme patronizingly brought back to him, and that, too, by a very powerful man locally—one who thus far had chosen to overlook
him utterly.

"On what basis," asked Cowperwood cautiously, "would
you expect these new companies to come in?"

"On the same basis as the others, if they are not too
heavily capitalized. I haven't thought out all the details.
Two or three for one, according to investment. Of course,
the prejudices of these old companies have to be considered."

Cowperwood meditated. Should or should he not entertain this offer? Here was a chance to realize quickly by
selling out to the old companies. Only Schryhart, not himself, would be taking the big end in this manipulative deal.
Whereas if he waited—even if Schryhart managed to combine the three old companies into one—he might be able to
force better terms. He was not sure. Finally he asked, "How
much stock of the new company would be left in your
hands—or in the hands of the organizing group—after each
of the old and new companies had been provided for on
this basis?"

"Oh, possibly thirty-five or forty percent of the whole,"
replied Schryhart ingratiatingly. "The laborer is worthy of
his hire."

"Quite so," replied Cowperwood, smiling, "but seeing that

I am the man who has been cutting the pole to knock this persimmon, it seems to me that a pretty good share of that should come to me; don't you think so?"

"Just what do you mean?"

"Just what I have said. I personally have organized the new companies which have made this proposed combination possible. The plan you propose is nothing more than what I have been proposing for some time. The officers and directors of the old companies are angry at me merely because I am supposed to have invaded the fields that belong to them. Now, if on account of that they are willing to operate through you rather than through me, it seems to me that I should have a much larger share in the surplus. My personal interest in these new companies is not very large. I am really more of a fiscal agent than anything else." (This was not true, but Cowperwood preferred to have his guest think so.)

Schryhart smiled. "But, my dear sir," he explained, "you forget that I will be supplying nearly all the capital to do this."

"You forget," retorted Cowperwood, "that I am not a novice. I will guarantee to supply all the capital myself, and give you a good bonus for your services, if you want that. The plants and franchises of the old and new companies are worth something. You must remember that Chicago is growing."

"I know that," replied Schryhart evasively, "but I also know that you have a long, expensive fight ahead of you. As things are now you cannot, of yourself, expect to bring these old companies to terms. They won't work with you, as I understand it. It will require an outsider like myself— someone of influence, or perhaps, I had better say, of old standing in Chicago, someone who knows these people— to bring about this combination. Have you anyone, do you think, who can do it better than I?"

"It is not at all impossible that I will find someone," replied Cowperwood quite easily.

"I hardly think so; certainly not as things are now. The old companies are not disposed to work through you, and they are through me. Don't you think you had better accept my terms and allow me to go ahead and close this matter up?"

"Not at all on that basis," replied Cowperwood quite

simply. "We have invaded the enemies' country too far and done too much. Three for one or four for one—whatever terms are given the stockholders of the old companies—is the best I will do about the new shares, and I must have one-half of whatever is left for myself. At that I will have to divide with others." (This was not true either.)

"No," replied Schryhart evasively and opposingly, shaking his square head. "It can't be done. The risks are too great. I might allow you one-fourth, possibly—I can't tell yet."

"One-half or nothing," said Cowperwood definitely.

Schryhart got up. "That's the best you will do, is it?" he inquired.

"The very best."

"I'm afraid, then," he said, "we can't come to terms. I'm sorry. You may find this a rather long and expensive fight."

"I have fully anticipated that," replied the financier.

CHAPTER XII

A New Retainer

Cowperwood, who had rebuffed Schryhart so courteously but firmly, was to learn that he who takes the sword may well perish by the sword. His own watchful attorney, on guard at the state capitol, where certificates of incorporation were issued in the city and village councils, in the courts and so forth, was not long in learning that a countermovement of significance was under way. Old General Van Sickle was the first to report that something was in the wind in connection with the North Side company. He came in late one afternoon, his dusty greatcoat thrown loosely about his shoulders, his small, soft hat low over his shaggy eyes, and in response to Cowperwood's "Evening, General, what can I do for you?" seated himself portentously.

"I think you'll have to prepare for real rough weather

in the future, Captain," he remarked, addressing the financier with a courtesy title that he had fallen in the habit of using.

"What's the trouble now?" asked Cowperwood.

"No real trouble as yet, but there may be. Someone—I don't know who—is getting these three old companies together in one. There's a certificate of incorporation been applied for at Springfield for the United Gas and Fuel Company of Chicago, and there are some directors' meetings now going on at the Douglas Trust Company. I got this from Duniway, who seems to have friends somewhere that know."

Cowperwood put the ends of his fingers together in his customary way and began to tap them lightly and rhythmically.

"Let me see—the Douglas Trust Company. Mr. Simms is president of that. He isn't shrewd enough to organize a thing of that kind. Who are the incorporators?"

The general produced a list of four names, none of them officers or directors of the old companies.

"Dummies, every one," said Cowperwood succinctly. "I think I know," he said after a few moments' reflection, "who is behind it, General; but don't let that worry you. They can't harm us if they do unite. They're bound to sell out to us or buy us out eventually."

Still, it irritated him to think that Schryhart had succeeded in persuading the old companies to combine on any basis; he had meant to have Addison go shortly, posing as an outside party, and propose this very thing. Schryhart, he was sure, had acted swiftly following their interview. He hurried to Addison's office in the Lake National.

"Have you heard the news?" exclaimed that individual the moment Cowperwood appeared. "They're planning to combine. It's Schryhart. I was afraid of that. Simms of the Douglas Trust is going to act as the fiscal agent. I had the information not ten minutes ago."

"So did I," replied Cowperwood calmly. "We should have acted a little sooner. Still, it isn't our fault exactly. Do you know the terms of agreement?"

"They're going to pool their stock on a basis of three to one, with about thirty percent of the holding company left for Schryhart to sell or keep, as he wants to. He guarantees the interest. We did that for him—drove the game right into his bag."

"Nevertheless," replied Cowperwood, "he still has us to deal with. I propose now that we go into the city council and ask for a blanket franchise. It can be had. If we should get it, it will bring them to their knees. We will really be in a better position than they are with these smaller companies as feeders. We can unite with ourselves."

"That will take considerable money, won't it?"

"Not so much. We may never need to lay a pipe or build a plant. They will offer to sell out, buy, or combine before that. We can fix the terms. Leave it to me. You don't happen to know by any chance this Mr. McKenty who has so much say in local affairs here—John J. McKenty?"

Cowperwood was referring to a man who was at once gambler, rumored owner or controller of a series of houses of prostitution, rumored maker of mayors and aldermen, rumored financial backer of many saloons and contracting companies—in short, the patron saint of the political and social underworld of Chicago, and who was naturally to be reckoned with in matters which related to the city and state legislative program.

"I don't," said Addison, "but I can get you a letter. Why?"

"Don't trouble to ask me that now. Get me as strong an introduction as you can."

"I'll have one for you today some time," replied Addison efficiently. "I'll send it over to you."

Cowperwood went out while Addison speculated as to this newest move. Trust Cowperwood to dig a pit into which the enemy might fall. He marveled sometimes at the man's resourcefulness. He never quarreled with the directness and incisiveness of Cowperwood's action.

The man, McKenty, whom Cowperwood had in mind in this rather disturbing hour, was as interesting and forceful an individual as one would care to meet anywhere, a typical figure of Chicago and the West at the time. He was a pleasant, smiling, bland, affable person, not unlike Cowperwood in magnetism and subtlety, but different by a degree of animal coarseness (not visible on the surface) which Cowperwood would scarcely have understood, and in a kind of temperamental pull drawing to him that vast pathetic life of the underworld in which his soul found its solution. There is a kind of nature, not artistic, not spiritual, in no way emotional, nor yet unduly philosophical, that is nevertheless a sphered content of life; not crystalline, perhaps, and yet not utterly dark—an agate temperament, cloudy and strange. As a three-year-old child McKenty had been brought from Ireland by his emigrant parents during a period of famine. He had been raised on the far South Side in a shanty which stood near a maze of railroad tracks, and as a naked baby he had crawled on its earthen floor. His father had been promoted to a section boss after working for years as a day laborer on the adjoining railroad, and John junior, one of eight other children, had been sent out early to do many things—to be an errand boy in a store, a messenger boy for a telegraph company, an emergency sweep about a saloon, and finally a bartender. This last was his true beginning, for he was discovered by a keen-minded politician and encouraged to run for the state legislature and to study law. Even as a stripling what things had he not learned—robbery, ballot-box stuffing, the sale of votes, the appointive power of leaders, graft, nepotism, vice exploitation—all the things that go to make up (or did) the American world of politics and financial and social strife. There is a strong assumption in the upper walks of life that there is nothing to be learned at the bottom. If you could have looked into the capacious but balanced temperament of John J. McKenty you would have seen a strange wisdom there, and stranger memories—whole worlds of brutalities, tendernesses, errors, immoralities suffered, endured, even rejoiced in—the hardy, eager life of the animal that has nothing but its perceptions, instincts, appetites to guide it. Yet the man had the air and the poise of a gentleman.

Today, at forty-eight, McKenty was an exceedingly important personage. His roomy house on the West Side, at Harrison Street and Ashland Avenue, was visited at sundry times by financiers, businessmen, officeholders, priests, saloonkeepers—in short, the whole range and gamut of active, subtle political life. From McKenty they could obtain that counsel, wisdom, surety, solution which all of them on occasion were anxious to have, and which in one deft way and another—often by no more than gratitude and an acknowledgment of his leadership—they were willing to pay for. To police captains and officers whose places he occasionally saved, when they should justly have been discharged; to mothers whose erring boys or girls he took out of prison and sent home again; to keepers of bawdy houses whom he protected from a too-harsh invasion of the grafting propensities

of the local police; to politicians and saloonkeepers who were
in danger of being destroyed by public upheavals of one
kind and another, he seemed, in hours of stress, when his
smooth, genial, almost artistic face beamed on them, like a
heaven-sent son of light, a kind of western god, all-powerful, all-merciful, perfect. On the other hand, there were
ingrates, uncompromising or pharisaical religionists and reformers, plotting, scheming rivals, who found him deadly to
contend with. There were many henchmen—runners from
an almost imperial throne—to do his bidding. He was simple in dress and taste, married and (apparently) very happy,
a professing though virtually non-practicing Catholic, a suave,
genial, Buddha-like man, powerful and enigmatic.

When Cowperwood and McKenty first met, it was on a
spring evening at the latter's home. The windows of the large
house were pleasantly open, though screened, and the curtains were blowing faintly in a light air. Along with a sense
of the new green life everywhere came a breath of stockyards.

On the presentation of Addison's letter and of another,
secured through Van Sickle from a well-known political
judge, Cowperwood had been invited to call. On his arrival
he was offered a drink, a cigar, introduced to Mrs. McKenty
—who, lacking an organized social life of any kind, was always pleased to meet these celebrities of the upper world, if
only for a moment—and shown eventually into the library.
Mrs. McKenty, as he might have observed if he had had the
eye for it, was plump and fifty, a sort of superannuated
Aileen, but still showing traces of a former hardy beauty,
and concealing pretty well the evidences that she had once
been a prostitute. It so happened that on this particular
evening McKenty was in a most genial frame of mind. There
were no immediate political troubles bothering him just now.
It was early in May. Outside the trees were budding, the sparrows and robins were voicing their several moods. A delicious haze was in the air, and some early mosquitoes were
reconnoitering the screens which protected the windows and
doors. Cowperwood, in spite of his various troubles, was in
a complacent state of mind himself. He liked life—even its
very difficult complications—perhaps its complications best
of all. Nature was beautiful, tender at times, but difficulties,
plans, plots, schemes to unravel and make smooth—these
things were what made existence worthwhile.

"Well, now, Mr. Cowperwood," McKenty began, when they finally entered the cool, pleasant library, "what can I do for you?"

"Well, Mr. McKenty," said Cowperwood, choosing his words and bringing the finest resources of his temperament into play, "it isn't so much, and yet it is. I want a franchise from the Chicago city council, and I want you to help me get it if you will. I know you may say to me why not go to the councilmen direct. I would do that, except that there are certain other elements—individuals—who might come to you. It won't offend you, I know, when I say that I have always understood that you are a sort of clearinghouse for political troubles in Chicago."

Mr. McKenty smiled. "That's flattering," he replied dryly.

"Now, I am rather new myself to Chicago," went on Cowperwood softly. "I have been here only a year or two. I come from Philadelphia. I have been interested as a fiscal agent and an investor in several gas companies that have been organized in Lake View, Hyde Park, and elsewhere outside the city limits, as you may possibly have seen by the papers lately. I am not their owner in the sense that I have provided all or even a good part of the money invested in them. I am not even their manager, except in a very general way. I might better be called their promoter and guardian; but I am that for other people and myself."

Mr. McKenty nodded.

"Now, Mr. McKenty, it was not very long after I started out to get franchises to do business in Lake View and Hyde Park before I found myself confronted by the interests which control the three old city gas companies. They were very much opposed to our entering the field in Cook County anywhere, as you may imagine, although we were not really crowding in on their field. Since then they have fought me with lawsuits, injunctions, and charges of bribery and conspiracy."

"I know," put in Mr. McKenty. "I have heard something of it."

"Quite so," replied Cowperwood. "Because of their opposition I made them an offer to combine these three companies and the three new ones into one, take out a new charter, and give the city a uniform gas service. They would not do that—largely because I was an outsider, I think. Since then another person, Mr. Schryhart"—McKenty nodded—"who has never had anything to do with the gas business here, has stepped in and offered to combine them. His plan is to do exactly what I wanted to do; only his further proposition is, once he has the three old companies united, to invade this new gas field of ours and hold us up, or force us to sell by obtaining rival franchises in these outlying places. There is talk of combining these suburbs with Chicago, as you know, which would allow these three downtown franchises to become mutually operative with our own. This makes it essential for us to do one of several things, as you may see—either to sell out on the best terms we can now, or to continue the fight at a rather heavy expense without making any attempt to strike back, or to get into the city council and ask for a franchise to do business in the downtown section—a general blanket franchise to sell gas in Chicago alongside of the old companies—with the sole intention of protecting ourselves, as one of my officers is fond of saying," added Cowperwood humorously.

McKenty smiled again. "I see," he said. "Isn't that a rather large order, though, Mr. Cowperwood, seeking a new franchise? Do you suppose the general public would agree that the city needs an extra gas company? It's true the old companies haven't been any too generous. My own gas isn't of the best." He smiled vaguely, prepared to listen further.

"Now, Mr. McKenty, I know that you are a practical man," went on Cowperwood, ignoring this interruption, "and so am I. I am not coming to you with any vague story concerning my troubles and expecting you to be interested as a matter of sympathy. I realize that to go into the city council of Chicago with a legitimate proposition is one thing. To get it passed and approved by the city authorities is another. I need advice and assistance, and I am not begging it. If I could get a general franchise, such as I have described, it would be worth a very great deal of money to me. It would help me to close up and realize on these new companies which are entirely sound and needed. It would help me to prevent the old companies from eating me up. As a matter of fact, I must have such a franchise to protect my interests and give me a running fighting chance. Now, I know that none of us are in politics or finance for our health. If I could get such a franchise it would be worth from one-fourth to one-half of all I personally would make out of it, providing my plan of combining

these new companies with the old ones should go through
—say, from three to four hundred thousand dollars." (Here
again Cowperwood was not quite frank, but safe.) "It is
needless to say to you that I can command ample capital.
This franchise would do that. Briefly, I want to know if
you won't give me your political support in this matter and
join in with me on the basis that I propose? I will make it
perfectly clear to you beforehand who my associates are. I
will put all the data and details on the table before you
so that you can see for yourself how things are. If you should
find at any time that I have misrepresented anything you
are at full liberty, of course, to withdraw. As I said before,"
he concluded, "I am not a beggar. I am not coming here to
conceal any facts or to hide anything which might deceive
you as to the worth of all this to us. I want you to know the
facts. I want you to give me your aid on such terms as you
think are fair and equitable. Really the only trouble with
me in this situation is that I am not a silk stocking. If I
were this gas war would have been adjusted long ago.
These gentlemen who are so willing to reorganize through
Mr. Schryhart are largely opposed to me because I am—comparatively—a stranger in Chicago and not in their set. If I
were"—he moved his hand slightly—"I don't suppose I
would be here this evening asking for your favor, although
that does not say that I am not glad to be here, or that I
would not be glad to work with you in any way that I might.
Circumstances simply have not thrown me across your path
before."

As he talked his eye fixed McKenty steadily, almost innocently; and the latter, following him clearly, felt all the
while that he was listening to a strange, able, dark, and very
forceful man. There was no beating about the bush here,
no squeamishness of spirit, and yet there was subtlety—
the kind McKenty liked. While he was amused by Cowperwood's casual reference to the silk stockings who were keeping him out, it appealed to him. He caught the point of view
as well as the intention of it. Cowperwood represented a new
and rather pleasing type of financier to him. Evidently, he
was traveling in able company if one could believe the men
who had introduced him so warmly. McKenty, as Cowperwood was well aware, had personally no interest in the old
companies and also—though this he did not say—no particular sympathy with them. They were just remote finan-

cial corporations to him, paying political tribute on demand, expecting political favors in return. Every few weeks now they were in council, asking for one gas-main franchise after another (special privileges in certain streets), asking for better (more profitable) light contracts, asking for dock privileges in the river, a lower tax rate, and so forth and so on. McKenty did not pay much attention to these things personally. He had a subordinate in council, a very powerful henchman by the name of Patrick Dowling, a meaty, vigorous Irishman and a true watchdog of graft for the machine, who worked with the mayor, the city treasurer, the city tax-receiver—in fact, all the officers of the current administration—and saw that such minor matters were properly equalized. Mr. McKenty had only met two or three of the officers of the South Side Gas Company, and that quite casually. He did not like them very well. The truth was that the old companies were officered by men who considered politicians of the McKenty and Dowling stripe as very evil men; if they paid them and did other such wicked things it was because they were forced to do so.

"Well," McKenty replied, fingering his thin gold watch chain in a thoughtful manner, "that's an interesting scheme you have. Of course the old companies wouldn't like your asking for a rival franchise, but once you had it they couldn't object very well, could they?" He smiled. Mr. McKenty spoke with no suggestion of a brogue. "From one point of view it might be looked upon as bad business, but not entirely. They would be sure to make a great cry, though they haven't been any too kind to the public themselves. But if you offered to combine with them I see no objection. It's certain to be as good for them in the long run as it is for you. This merely permits you to make a better bargain."

"Exactly," said Cowperwood.

"And you have the means, you tell me, to lay mains in every part of the city, and fight with them for business if they won't give in?"

"I have the means," said Cowperwood, "or if I haven't I can get them."

Mr. McKenty looked at Mr. Cowperwood very solemnly. There was a kind of mutual sympathy, understanding, and admiration between the two men, but it was still heavily veiled by self-interest. To Mr. McKenty Cowperwood was in-

teresting because he was one of the few businessmen he
had met who were not ponderous, pharisaical, even hypo-
critical when they were dealing with him.

"Well, I'll tell you what I'll do, Mr. Cowperwood," he said
finally. "I'll take it all under consideration. Let me think it
over until Monday, anyhow. There is more of an excuse
now for the introduction of a general gas ordinance than
there would be a little later—I can see that. Why don't you
draw up your proposed franchise and let me see it? Then we
might find out what some of the other gentlemen of the city
council think."

Cowperwood almost smiled at the word "gentlemen."

"I have already done that," he said. "Here it is."

McKenty took it, surprised and yet pleased at this evidence
of business proficiency. He liked a strong manipulator of this
kind—the more since he was not one himself, and most of
those that he did know were thin-blooded and squeamish.

"Let me take this," he said. "I'll see you next Monday
again if you wish. Come Monday."

Cowperwood got up. "I thought I'd come and talk to you
direct, Mr. McKenty," he said, "and now I'm glad that I did.
You will find, if you will take the trouble to look into this
matter, that it is just as I represent it. There is a very
great deal of money here in one way and another, though
it will take some little time to work it out."

Mr. McKenty saw the point. "Yes," he said sweetly, "to
be sure."

They looked into each other's eyes as they shook hands.

"I'm not sure but you haven't hit upon a very good idea
here," concluded McKenty sympathetically. "A very good idea,
indeed. Come and see me again next Monday, or about that
time, and I'll let you know what I think. Come any time
you have anything else you want of me. I'll always be
glad to see you. It's a fine night, isn't it?" he added, looking
out as they neared the door. "A nice moon, that!" he
added. A sickle moon was in the sky. "Good night."

CHAPTER XIII

The Die Is Cast

The significance of this visit was not long in manifesting itself. At the top, in large affairs, life goes off into almost inexplicable tangles of personalities. Mr. McKenty, now that the matter had been called to his attention, was interested to learn about this gas situation from all sides—whether it might not be more profitable to deal with the Schryhart end of the argument, and so on. But his eventual conclusion was that Cowperwood's plan, as he had outlined it, was the most feasible for political purposes, largely because the Schryhart faction, not being in a position where they needed to ask the city council for anything at present, were so obtuse as to forget to make overtures of any kind to the buccaneering forces at the City Hall.

When Cowperwood next came to McKenty's house the latter was in a receptive frame of mind. "Well," he said after a few genial preliminary remarks, "I've been learning what's going on. Your proposition is fair enough. Organize your company, and arrange your plan conditionally. Then introduce your ordinance, and we'll see what can be done." They went into a long, intimate discussion as to how the forthcoming stock should be divided, how it was to be held in escrow by a favorite bank of Mr. McKenty's until the terms of the agreement under the eventual affiliation with the old companies or the new union company should be fulfilled, and details of that sort. It was rather a complicated arrangement, not as satisfactory to Cowperwood as it might have been, but satisfactory in that it permitted him to win. It required the undivided services of General Van Sickle, Henry De Soto Sippens, Kent Barrows McKibben, and Alderman Dowling for some little time. But finally all was in readiness for the coup.

On a certain Monday night, therefore, following the Thursday on which, according to the rules of the city council, an ordinance of this character would have to be introduced, the plan, after being publicly broached but this very little while, was quickly considered by the city council and passed. There had been really no time for public discussion. This was just the thing, of course, that Cowperwood and McKenty were trying to avoid. On the day following the particular Thursday on which the ordinance had been broached in council as certain to be brought up for passage, Schryhart, through his lawyers and the officers of the old individual gas companies, had run to the newspapers and denounced the whole thing as plain robbery; but what were they to do? There was so little time for agitation. True the newspapers, obedient to this larger financial influence, began to talk of "fair play to the old companies," and the uselessness of two large rival companies in the field when one would serve as well. Still, the public, instructed or urged by the McKenty agents to the contrary, were not prepared to believe it. They had not been so well treated by the old companies as to make any outcry on their behalf.

Standing outside the city council door, on the Monday evening when the bill was finally passed, Mr. Samuel Blackman, president of the South Side Gas Company, a little wispy man with shoe-brush whiskers, declared emphatically:

"This is a scoundrelly piece of business. If the mayor signs that he should be impeached. There is not a vote in there tonight that has not been purchased—not one. This is a fine element of brigandage to introduce into Chicago; why, people who have worked years and years to build up a business are not safe!"

"It's true, every word of it," complained Mr. Jordan Jules, president of the North Side company, a short, stout man with a head like an egg lying lengthwise, a mere fringe of hair, and hard blue eyes. He was with Mr. Hudson Baker, tall and ambling, who was president of the West Chicago company. All of these had come to protest. "It's that scoundrel from Philadelphia. He's the cause of all our troubles. It's high time the respectable business element of Chicago realized just what sort of a man they have to deal with in him. He ought to be driven out of here. Look at his Philadelphia record. They sent him to the penitentiary down there, and they ought to do it here."

Mr. Baker, very recently the guest of Schryhart, and his henchman, too, was also properly chagrined. "The man is a charlatan," he protested to Blackman. "He doesn't play fair. It is plain that he doesn't belong in respectable society."

Nevertheless, and in spite of this, the ordinance was passed. It was a bitter lesson for Mr. Norman Schryhart, Mr. Norrie Simms, and all those who had unfortunately become involved. A committee composed of all three of the old companies visited the mayor; but the latter, a tool of McKenty, giving his future into the hands of the enemy, signed it just the same. Cowperwood had his franchise, and groan as they might, it was now necessary, in the language of a later day, "to step up and see the captain." Only Schryhart felt personally that his score with Cowperwood was not settled. He would meet him on some other ground later. The next time he would try to fight fire with fire. But for the present, shrewd man that he was, he was prepared to compromise.

Thereafter, dissembling his chagrin as best he could, he kept on the lookout for Cowperwood at both of the clubs of which he was a member; but Cowperwood had avoided them during this period of excitement, and Mahomet would have to go to the mountain. So one drowsy June afternoon Mr. Schryhart called at Cowperwood's office. He had on a bright new steel-gray suit and a straw hat. From his pocket, according to the fashion of the time, protruded a neat, blue-bordered silk handkerchief, and his feet were immaculate in new, shining Oxford ties.

"I'm sailing for Europe in a few days, Mr. Cowperwood," he remarked genially, "and I thought I'd drop round to see if you and I could reach some agreement in regard to this gas situation. The officers of the old companies naturally feel that they do not care to have a rival in the field, and I'm sure that you are not interested in carrying on a useless rate war that won't leave anybody any profit. I recall that you were willing to compromise on a half-and-half basis with me before, and I was wondering whether you were still of that mind."

"Sit down, sit down, Mr. Schryhart," remarked Cowperwood cheerfully, waving the newcomer to a chair. "I'm pleased to see you again. No, I'm no more anxious for a rate war than you are. As a matter of fact, I hope to avoid it; but as you see, things have changed somewhat since I saw you. The gentlemen who have organized and invested their money in this new city gas company are perfectly willing— rather anxious, in fact—to go on and establish a legitimate business. They feel all the confidence in the world that they can do this, and I agree with them. A compromise might be effected between the old and the new companies, but not on the basis on which I was willing to settle some time ago. A new company has been organized since then, stock issued, and a great deal of money expended." (This was not true.) "That stock will have to figure in any new agreement. I think a general union of all the companies is desirable, but it will have to be on a basis of one, two, three, or four shares —whatever is decided—at par for all stock involved."

Mr. Schryhart pulled a long face. "Don't you think that's rather steep?" he said solemnly.

"Not at all, not at all!" replied Cowperwood. "You know these new expenditures were not undertaken voluntarily." (The irony of this did not escape Mr. Schryhart, but he said nothing.)

"I admit all that, but don't you think, since your shares are worth practically nothing at present, that you ought to be satisfied if they were accepted at par?"

"I can't see why," replied Cowperwood. "Our future prospects are splendid. There must be an even adjustment here or nothing. What I want to know is how much treasury stock you would expect to have in the safe for the promotion of this new organization after all the old stockholders have been satisfied?"

"Well, as I thought before, from thirty to forty percent of the total issue," replied Schryhart, still hopeful of a profitable adjustment. "I should think it could be worked on that basis."

"And who gets that?"

"Why, the organizer," said Schryhart evasively. "Yourself, perhaps, and myself."

"And how would you divide it? Half and half, as before?"

"I should think that would be fair."

"It isn't enough," returned Cowperwood incisively. "Since I talked to you last I have been compelled to shoulder obligations and make agreements which I did not anticipate then. The best I can do now is to accept three-fourths."

Schryhart straightened up determinedly and offensively. This was outrageous, he thought, impossible! The effrontery of it!

"It can never be done, Mr. Cowperwood," he replied forcefully. "You are trying to unload too much worthless stock on the company as it is. The old companies' stock is selling right now, as you know, for from one-fifty to two-ten. Your stock is worth nothing. If you are to be given two or three for one for that, and three-fourths of the remainder in the treasury, I for one want nothing to do with the deal. You would be in control of the company, and it will be water-logged, at that. Talk about getting something for nothing! The best I would suggest to the stockholders of the old companies would be half and half. And I may say to you frankly, although you may not believe it, that the old companies will not join in with you in any scheme that gives you control. They are too much incensed. Feeling is running too high. It will mean a long, expensive fight, and they will never compromise. Now, if you have anything really reasonable to offer I would be glad to hear it. Otherwise I am afraid these negotiations are not going to come to anything."

"Share and share alike, and three-fourths of the remainder," repeated Cowperwood grimly. "I do not want to control. If they want to raise the money and buy me out on that basis I am willing to sell. I want a decent return for investments I have made, and I am going to have it. I cannot speak for the others behind me, but as long as they deal through me that is what they will expect."

Mr. Schryhart went angrily away. He was exceedingly wroth. This proposition as Cowperwood now outlined it was buccaneering at its best. He proposed for himself to withdraw from the old companies if necessary, to close out his holdings and let the old companies deal with Cowperwood as best they could. So long as he had anything to do with it, Cowperwood should never gain control of the gas situation. Better to take him at his suggestion, raise the money and buy him out, even at an exorbitant figure. Then the old gas companies could go along and do business in their old-fashioned way without being disturbed. This buccaneer! This upstart! What a shrewd, quick, forceful move he had made! It irritated Mr. Schryhart greatly.

The end of all this was a compromise in which Cowperwood accepted one-half of the surplus stock of the new general issue, and two for one of every share of stock for which his new companies had been organized, at the same time selling out to the old companies—clearing out completely. It was a most profitable deal, and he was enabled to provide handsomely not only for Mr. McKenty and Addison, but for all the others connected with him. It was a splendid coup, as McKenty and Addison assured him. Having now done so much, he began to turn his eyes elsewhere for other fields to conquer.

But this victory in one direction brought with it corresponding reverses in another: the social future of Cowperwood and Aileen was now in great jeopardy. Schryhart, who was a force socially, having met with defeat at the hands of Cowperwood, was now bitterly opposed to him. Norrie Simms naturally sided with his old associates. But the worst blow came through Mrs. Anson Merrill. Shortly after the housewarming, and when the gas argument and the conspiracy charges were rising to their heights, she had been to New York and had there chanced to encounter an old acquaintance of hers, Mrs. Martyn Walker of Philadelphia, one of the circle which Cowperwood once upon a time had been vainly ambitious to enter. Mrs. Merrill, aware of the interest the Cowperwoods had aroused in Mrs. Simms and others, welcomed the opportunity to find out something definite.

"By the way, did you ever chance to hear of a Frank Algernon Cowperwood or his wife in Philadelphia?" she inquired of Mrs. Walker.

"Why, my dear Nellie," replied her friend, nonplussed that a woman so smart as Mrs. Merrill should even refer to them, "have those people established themselves in Chicago? His career in Philadelphia was, to say the least, spectacular. He was connected with a city treasurer there who stole five hundred thousand dollars, and they both went to the penitentiary. That wasn't the worst of it! He became intimate with some young girl—a Miss Butler, the sister of Owen Butler, by the way, who is now such a power down there, and—" She merely lifted her eyes. "While he was in the penitentiary her father died and the family broke up. I even heard it rumored that the old gentleman killed himself." (She was referring to Aileen's father, Edward Malia Butler.) "When he came out of the penitentiary Cowperwood disappeared, and I did hear someone say that he had gone West, and divorced his wife and married again. His first wife is still living in Philadelphia somewhere with his two children."

Mrs. Merrill was properly astonished, but she did not show it. "Quite an interesting story, isn't it?" she commented distantly, thinking how easy it would be to adjust the Cowperwood situation, and how pleased she was that she had never shown any interest in them. "Did you ever see her—his new wife?"

"I think so, but I forget where. I believe she used to ride and drive a great deal in Philadelphia."

"Did she have red hair?"

"Oh yes. She was a very striking blonde."

"I fancy it must be the same person. They have been in the papers recently in Chicago. I wanted to be sure."

Mrs. Merrill was meditating some fine comments to be made in the future.

"I suppose now they're trying to get into Chicago society?" Mrs. Walker smiled condescendingly and contemptuously—as much at Chicago society as at the Cowperwoods.

"It's possible that they might attempt something like that in the East and succeed—I'm sure I don't know," replied Mrs. Merrill caustically, resenting the slur, "but attempting and achieving are quite different things in Chicago."

The answer was sufficient. It ended the discussion. When next Mrs. Simms was rash enough to mention the Cowperwoods, or, rather, the peculiar publicity in connection with him, her future viewpoint was definitely fixed for her.

"If you take my advice," commented Mrs. Merrill finally, "the less you have to do with these friends of yours the better. I know all about them. You might have seen that from the first. They can never be accepted."

Mrs. Merrill did not trouble to explain why, but Mrs. Simms through her husband soon learned the whole truth, and she was righteously indignant and even terrified. Who was to blame for this sort of thing, anyhow? she thought. Who had introduced them? The Addisons, of course. But the Addisons were socially unassailable, if not all-powerful, and so the best had to be made of that. But the Cowperwoods could be dropped from the lists of herself and her friends instantly, and that was now done. A sudden slump in their social significance began to manifest itself, though not so swiftly but what for the time being it was slightly deceptive.

The first evidence of change which Aileen observed was when the customary cards and invitations for receptions and the like, which had come to them quite freely of late, began to decline sharply in number, and when the guests to her own Wednesday afternoons, which rather prematurely she had ventured to establish, became a mere negligible handful. At first she could not understand this, not being willing to believe that following so soon upon her apparent triumph as a hostess in her own home there could be so marked a decline in her local importance. Of a possible seventy-five or fifty who might have called or left cards, within three weeks after the housewarming only twenty responded. A week later it had declined to ten, and within five weeks, all told, there was scarcely a caller. It is true that a very few of the unimportant—those who had looked to her for influence and the self-protecting Taylor Lord and Kent McKibben, who were commercially obligated to Cowperwood—were still faithful, but they were really worse than nothing. Aileen was beside herself with disappointment, opposition, chagrin, shame. There are many natures, rhinoceros-hided and iron-souled, who can endure almost any rebuff in the hope of eventual victory, who are almost too thick-skinned to suffer, but hers was not one of these. Already, in spite of her original daring in regard to the opinion of society and the rights of the former Mrs. Cowperwood, she was sensitive on the score of her future and what her past might mean to her. Really her original actions could be attributed to her youthful passion and the powerful sex magnetism of Cowperwood. Under more fortunate circumstances she would have married safely enough and without the scandal which followed. As it was now, her social future here needed to end satisfactorily in order to justify herself to herself, and, she thought, to him.

"You may put the sandwiches in the icebox," she said to Louis, the butler, after one of the earliest of the "at home" failures, referring to the undue supply of pink-and-blue-ribboned tidbits which, uneaten, honored some fine Sèvres with their presence. "Send the flowers to the hospital. The servants may drink the claret cup and lemonade. Keep some of the cakes fresh for dinner."

The butler nodded his head. "Yes, Madame," he said. Then, by way of pouring oil on what appeared to him to be a troubled situation he added: "Eet's a rough day. I suppose zat has somepsing to do weeth it."

Aileen was aflame in a moment. She was about to exclaim: "Mind your business!" but changed her mind. "Yes, I presume so," was her answer as she ascended to her room. If a single poor "at home" was to be commented on by servants, things were coming to a pretty pass. She waited until the next week to see whether this was the weather or a real change in public sentiment. It was worse than the one before. The singers she had engaged had to be dismissed without performing the service for which they had come.

Kent McKibben and Taylor Lord, very well aware of the rumors now flying about, called, but in a remote and troubled spirit. Aileen saw that, too. An affair of this kind, with only these two and Mrs. Webster Israels and Mrs. Henry Huddlestone calling, was a sad indication of something wrong. She had to plead illness and excuse herself. The third week, fearing a worse defeat than before, Aileen pretended to be ill. She would see how many cards were left. There were just three. That was the end. She realized that her "at homes" were a notable failure.

At the same time Cowperwood was not to be spared his share in the distrust and social opposition which were now rampant.

His first inkling of the true state of affairs came in connection with a dinner, which, on the strength of an old invitation, they unfortunately attended at a time when Aileen was still uncertain. It had been originally arranged by the Sunderland Sledds, who were not so much socially, and who at the time it occurred were as yet unaware of the ugly gossip going about, or at least of society's new attitude toward the Cowperwoods. At this time it was understood by nearly all —the Simmses, Candas, Cottons, and Kingslands—that a great mistake had been made, and that the Cowperwoods were by no means admissible.

To this particular dinner a number of people whom the latter knew had been invited. Uniformly all, when they learned or recalled that the Cowperwoods were expected, sent eleventh-hour regrets—"So sorry." Outside the Sledds there was only one other couple—the Stanislau Hoecksemas, for whom the Cowperwoods did not particularly care. It was a dull evening. Aileen complained of a headache, and they went home.

Very shortly afterward, at a reception given by their neighbors, the Haatstaedts, to which they had long since been invited, there was an evident shyness in regard to them, quite new in its aspect, although the hosts themselves were still friendly enough. Previous to this, when strangers of prominence had been present at an affair of this kind they were glad to be brought over to the Cowperwoods, who were always conspicuous because of Aileen's beauty. On this day, for no reason obvious to Aileen or Cowperwood (although both suspected), introductions were almost uniformly refused. There were a number who knew them, and who talked casually, but the general tendency on the part of all was to steer clear of them. Cowperwood sensed the difficulty at once. "I think we'd better leave early," he remarked to Aileen after a little while. "This isn't very interesting."

They returned to their own home, and Cowperwood to avoid discussion went downtown. He did not care to say what he thought of this as yet.

It was previous to a reception given by the Union League that the first real blow was struck at him personally, and that in a roundabout way. Addison, talking to him at the Lake National Bank one morning had said quite confidentially, and out of a clear sky:

"I want to tell you something, Cowperwood. You know by now something about Chicago society. You also know where I stand in regard to some things you told me about your past when I first met you. Well, there's a lot of talk going around about you now in regard to all that, and these two clubs to which you and I belong are filled with a lot of two-faced, double-breasted hypocrites who've been stirred up by this talk of conspiracy in the papers. There are four or five stockholders of the old companies who are members, and they are trying to drive you out. They've looked up that story you told me, and they're talking about filing charges with the house committees at both places. Now, nothing can come of it in either case—they've been talking to me; but when this next reception comes along you'll know what to do. They'll have to extend you an invitation; but they won't mean it." (Cowperwood understood.) "This whole thing is certain to blow over, in my judgment; it will if I have anything to do with it; but for the present—"

He stared at Cowperwood in a friendly way.

The latter smiled. "I expected something like this, Judah, to tell you the truth," he said easily. "I've expected it all along. You needn't worry about me. I know all about this. I've seen which way the wind is blowing, and I know how to trim my sails."

Addison reached out and took his hand. "But don't resign, whatever you do," he said cautiously. "That would be a confession of weakness, and they don't expect you to. I wouldn't want you to. Stand your ground. This whole thing will blow over. They're jealous, I think."

"I never intended to," replied Cowperwood. "There's no legitimate charge against me. I know it will all blow over if

I'm given time enough." Nevertheless, he was chagrined to think that he should be subjected to such a conversation as this with anyone.

Similarly in other ways society—so called—was quite able to enforce its mandates and conclusions.

The one thing that Cowperwood most resented, when he learned of it much later, was a snub directly given to Aileen at the door of the Norrie Simmses'; she called there only to be told that Mrs. Simms was not at home, although the carriages of others were in the street. A few days afterward Aileen, much to his regret and astonishment—for he did not then know the cause—actually became ill.

If it had not been for Cowperwood's eventual financial triumph over all opposition—the complete routing of the situation would have been hard indeed. As it was, Aileen suffered bitterly; she felt that the slight was principally directed at her, and would remain in force. In the privacy of their own home they were compelled eventually to admit, the one to the other, that their house of cards, resplendent and forceful-looking as it was, had fallen to the ground. Personal confidences between people so closely united are really the most trying of all. Human souls are constantly trying to find each other, and rarely succeeding.

"You know," he finally said to her once, when he came in rather unexpectedly and found her sick in bed, her eyes wet, and her maid dismissed for the day, "I understand what this is all about. To tell you the truth, Aileen, I rather expected it. We have been going too fast, you and I. We have been pushing this matter too hard. Now, I don't like to see you taking it this way, dear. This battle isn't lost. Why, I thought you had more courage than this. Let me tell you something which you don't seem to remember. Money will solve all this sometime. I'm winning in this fight right now, and I'll win in others. They are coming to me. Why, dearie, you oughtn't to despair. You're too young. I never do. You'll win yet. We can adjust this matter right here in Chicago, and when we do we will pay up a lot of scores at the same time. We're rich, and we're going to be richer. That will settle it. Now put on a good face and look pleased; there are plenty of things to live for in this world besides society. Get up now and dress, and we'll go for a drive and dinner downtown. You have me yet. Isn't that something?"

"Oh yes," sighed Aileen heavily; but she sank back

again. She put her arms about his neck and cried, as much
out of joy over the consolation he offered as over the loss
she had endured. "It was as much for you as for me," she
sighed.

"I know that," he soothed; "but don't worry about it
now. You will come out all right. We both will. Come, get
up." Nevertheless, he was sorry to see her yield so weakly.
It did not please him. He resolved someday to have a grim
adjustment with society on this score. Meanwhile Aileen was
recovering her spirits. She was ashamed of her weakness
when she saw how forcefully he faced it all.

"Oh, Frank," she exclaimed finally, "you're always so wonderful. You're such a darling."

"Never mind," he said cheerfully. "If we don't win this
game here in Chicago, we will somewhere."

He was thinking of the brilliant manner in which he had
adjusted his affairs with the old gas companies and Mr.
Schryhart, and how thoroughly he would handle some other
matters when the time came.

CHAPTER XIV

Undercurrents

It was during the year that followed their social
repudiation, and the next and the next, that Cowperwood
achieved a keen realization of what it would mean to spend
the rest of his days in social isolation, or, at least, confined
in his sources of entertainment to a circle or element which
constantly reminded him of the fact that he was not identified with the best, or, at least, not the most significant, however dull that might be. When he had first attempted to introduce Aileen into society it was his idea that however tame
they might chance to find it to begin with, they themselves,
once admitted, could make it into something very interesting and even brilliant. Since the time the Cowperwoods had
been repudiated, however, they had found it necessary, if
they wished any social diversion at all, to fall back upon

such various minor elements as they could scrape an acquaintance with—passing actors and actresses to whom occasionally they could give a dinner; artists and singers whom they could invite to the house upon gaining an introduction; and, of course, a number of the socially unimportant, such as the Haatstaedts, Hoecksemas, Videras, Baileys, and others still friendly and willing to come in a casual way. Cowperwood found it interesting from time to time to invite a business friend, a lover of pictures, or some young artist to the house to dinner or for the evening, and on these occasions Aileen was always present. The Addisons called or invited them occasionally. But it was a dull game, the more so since their complete defeat was thus all the more plainly indicated.

This defeat, as Cowperwood kept reflecting, was really not his fault at all. He had been getting along well enough personally. If Aileen had only been a somewhat different type of woman! Nevertheless, he was in no way prepared to desert or reproach her. She had clung to him through his stormy prison days. She had encouraged him when he needed encouragement. He would stand by her and see what could be done a little later; but this ostracism was a rather dreary thing to endure. Besides, personally, he appeared to be becoming more and more interesting to men and to women. The men friends he had made he retained —Addison, Bailey, Videra, McKibben, Rambaud, and others. There were women in society, a number of them, who regretted his disappearance if not that of Aileen. Occasionally the experiment would be tried of inviting him without his wife. At first he refused invariably; later he went alone occasionally to a dinner party without her knowledge.

It was during this interregnum that Cowperwood for the first time clearly began to get the idea that there was a marked difference between him and Aileen intellectually and spiritually; and that while he might be in accord with her in many ways—emotionally, physically, idyllically—there were, nevertheless, many things which he could do alone which she could not do—heights to which he could rise where she could not possibly follow. Chicago society might be a negligible quantity, but he was now to contrast her sharply with the best of what the Old World had to offer in the matter of femininity, for following their social expulsion in Chicago and his financial victory, he once more decided to go abroad.

In Rome, at the Japanese and Brazilian embassies (where because of his wealth he gained introduction), and at the newly established Italian court, he encountered at a distance charming social figures of considerable significance—Italian countesses, English ladies of high degree, talented American women of strong artistic and social proclivities. As a rule they were quick to recognize the charm of his manner, the incisiveness and grip of his mind, and to estimate at all its worth the high individuality of his soul; but he could also always see that Aileen was not so acceptable. She was too rich in her entourage, too showy. Her glowing health and beauty were a species of affront to the paler, more sublimated souls of many who were not in themselves unattractive.

"Isn't that the typical American for you," he heard a woman remark at one of those large, very general court receptions to which so many are freely admitted, and to which Aileen had been determined to go. He was standing aside talking to an acquaintance he had made—an English-speaking Greek banker stopping at the Grand Hotel—while Aileen promenaded with the banker's wife. The speaker was an Englishwoman. "So gaudy, so self-conscious, and so naive!"

Cowperwood turned to look. It was Aileen, and the lady speaking was undoubtedly well-bred, thoughtful, good-looking. He had to admit that much that she said was true, but how were you to gauge a woman like Aileen, anyhow? She was not reprehensible in any way—just a full-blooded animal glowing with a love of life. She was attractive to him. It was too bad that people of obviously more conservative tendencies were so opposed to her. Why could they not see what he saw—a kind of childish enthusiasm for luxury and show which sprang, perhaps, from the fact that in her youth she had not enjoyed the social opportunities which she needed and longed for. He felt sorry for her. At the same time he was inclined to feel that perhaps now another type of woman would be better for him socially. If he had a harder type, one with keener artistic perceptions and a penchant for just the right social touch or note, how much better he would do! He came home bringing a Perugino, brilliant examples of Luini, Previtali, and Pinturicchio (this last a portrait of Caesar Borgia), which he picked up in Italy, to say nothing of two red African vases of great size that he found in Cairo, a tall gilt Louis XV standard of carved wood that he discovered in Rome, two ornate candelabra from Venice for his walls, and a pair of Italian torchères from Naples to decorate the corners of his library. It was thus by degrees that his art collection was growing.

At the same time it should be said, in the matter of women and the sex question, his judgment and views had begun to change tremendously. When he had first met Aileen he had many keen intuitions regarding life and sex, and, above all, clear faith that he had a right to do as he pleased. Since he had been out of prison and once more on his upward way there had been many a stray glance cast in his direction; he had so often had it clearly forced upon him that he was fascinating to women. Although he had only so recently acquired Aileen legally, yet she was years old to him as a mistress, and the first engrossing—it had been almost all-engrossing—enthusiasm was over. He loved her not only for her beauty but for her faithful enthusiasm; but the power of others to provoke in him a momentary interest, and passion even, was something which he did not pretend to understand, explain, or moralize about. So *it* was and so *ye* was. He did not want to hurt Aileen's feelings by letting her know that his impulses thus wantonly strayed to others, but so it was.

Not long after he had returned from the European trip he stopped one afternoon in the one exclusive dry-goods store in State Street to purchase a tie. As he was entering a woman crossed the aisle before him from one counter to another—a type of woman which he was coming to admire, but only from a rather distant point of view, seeing them going here and there in the world. She was a dashing type, essentially smart and trig, with a neat figure, dark hair and eyes, an olive skin, small mouth, quaint nose—all in all quite a figure for Chicago at the time. She had, furthermore, a curious look of current wisdom in her eyes, an air of saucy insolence which aroused Cowperwood's sense of mastery, his desire to dominate. To the look of provocation and defiance which she flung him for the fraction of a second he returned a curiously leonine glare which went over her like a dash of cold water. It was not a hard look, however, merely urgent and full of meaning. She was the vagrom-minded wife of a prosperous lawyer who was absorbed in his business and in himself. She pretended indifference for a moment after the first glance, but paused a little way off as if to examine some laces. Cowperwood looked after her to catch a second fleeting, attracted look. He was on his way to several engagements which he did not wish to break, but he took out a notebook, wrote on a slip of paper the name of a hotel, and underneath: "Parlor, second floor, Tuesday, 1 P.M." Passing by where she stood, he put it into her gloved hand, which was hanging by her side. The fingers closed over it automatically. She had noted his action. On the day and hour suggested she was there, although he had given no name. That liaison, while delightful to him, was of no great duration. The lady was interesting, but too fanciful.

Similarly, at the Henry Huddlestones', one of their neighbors at the first Michigan Avenue house they occupied, he encountered one evening at a small dinner party a girl of twenty-three who interested him greatly—for the moment. Her name was not very attractive—Ella F. Hubby, as he eventually learned—but she was not unpleasing. Her principal charm was a laughing, hoydenish countenance and roguish eyes. She was the daughter of a well-to-do commission merchant in South Water Street. That her interest should have been aroused by that of Cowperwood in her was natural enough. She was young, foolish, impressionable, easily struck by the glitter of a reputation, and Mrs. Huddlestone had spoken highly of Cowperwood and his wife and the great things he was doing or was going to do. When Ella saw him, and saw that he was still young looking, with the love of beauty in his eyes and a force of presence which was not at all hard where she was concerned, she was charmed; and when Aileen was not looking her glance kept constantly wandering to his with a laughing signification of friendship and admiration. It was the most natural thing in the world for him to say to her, when they had adjourned to the drawing room, that if she were in the neighborhood of his office someday she might care to look in on him. The look he gave her was one of keen understanding, and brought a look of its own kind, warm and flushing, in return. She came, and there began a rather short liaison. It was interesting but not brilliant. The girl did not have sufficient temperament to bind him beyond a period of rather idle investigation.

There was still, for a little while, another woman whom he had known—a Mrs. Josephine Ledwell, a smart widow, who came primarily to gamble on the Board of Trade but

who began to see at once, on introduction, the charm of a
flirtation with Cowperwood. She was a woman not unlike
Aileen in type, a little older, not so good-looking, and of a
harder, more subtle, commercial type of mind. She rather
interested Cowperwood because she was so trig, self-
sufficient, and careful. She did her best to lure him on to a
liaison with her, which finally resulted, her apartment on
the North Side being the center of this relationship. It lasted
perhaps six weeks. Through it all he was quite satisfied that
he did not like her so very well. Anyone who associated
with him had Aileen's present attractiveness to contend with,
as well as the original charm of his first wife. It was no
easy matter.

It was during this period of social dullness, however,
which somewhat resembled, though it did not exactly parallel,
his first years with his first wife, that Cowperwood finally
met a woman who was destined to leave a marked impression
on his life. He could not soon forget her. Her name was Rita
Sohlberg. She was the wife of Harold Sohlberg, a Danish
violinist who was then living in Chicago, a very young man;
but she was not a Dane, and he was by no means a remarkable violinist, though he had unquestionably the musical
temperament.

You have perhaps seen the would-bes, the nearlys, the
pretenders in every field—interesting people all—devoted
with a kind of mad enthusiasm to the thing they wish to do.
They manifest in some ways all the externals or earmarks
of their professional traditions, and yet are as sounding brass
and tinkling cymbals. You would have had to know Harold
Sohlberg only a little while to appreciate that he belonged to
this order of artists. He had a wild, stormy, November eye,
a wealth of loose brownish-black hair combed upward from
the temples, with one lock straggling Napoleonically down
toward the eyes; cheeks that had almost a babyish tint to
them; lips much too rich, red, and sensuous; a nose that was
fine and large and full, but only faintly aquiline; and eyebrows and moustache that somehow seemed to flare quite
like his errant and foolish soul. He had been sent away
from Denmark (Copenhagen) because he had been a ne'er-
do-well up to twenty-five and because he was constantly
falling in love with women who would not have anything to
do with him. Here in Chicago as a teacher, with his small
pension of forty dollars a month sent him by his mother, he

had gained a few pupils, and by practicing a kind of erratic economy, which kept him well dressed or hungry by turns, he had managed to make an interesting showing and pull himself through. He was only twenty-eight at the time he met Rita Greenough, of Wichita, Kansas, and at the time they met Cowperwood Harold was thirty-four and she twenty-seven.

She had been a student at the Chicago Fine Arts School, and at various student affairs had encountered Harold when he seemed to play divinely, and when life was all romance and art. Given the spring, the sunshine on the lake, white sails of ships, a few walks and talks on pensive afternoons when the city swam in a golden haze, and the thing was done. There was a sudden Saturday afternoon marriage, a runaway day to Milwaukee, a return to the studio now to be fitted out for two, and then kisses, kisses, kisses until love was satisfied or eased.

But life cannot exist on that diet alone, and so by degrees the difficulties had begun to manifest themselves. Fortunately, the latter were not allied with sharp financial want. Rita was not poor. Her father conducted a small but profitable grain elevator at Wichita, and after her sudden marriage, decided to continue her allowance, though this whole idea of art and music in its upper reaches was to him a strange, far-off, uncertain thing. A thin, meticulous, genial person interested in small trade opportunities, and exactly suited to the rather sparse social life of Wichita, he found Harold as curious as a bomb, and preferred to handle him gingerly. Gradually, however, being a very human if simple person, he came to be very proud of it—boasted in Wichita of Rita and her artist husband, invited them home to astound the neighbors during the summertime, and the fall brought his almost farmerlike wife on to see them and to enjoy trips, sight-seeing, studio teas. It was amusing, typically American, naive, almost impossible from many points of view.

Rita Sohlberg was of the semiphlegmatic type, soft, full-blooded, with a body that was going to be fat at forty, but which at present was deliciously alluring. Having soft, silky, light brown hair, the color of light dust, and moist gray-blue eyes, with fair skin and even white teeth, she was flatteringly self-conscious of her charms. She pretended in a gay, childlike way to be unconscious of the thrill she sent through many susceptible males, and yet she knew well enough all the while what she was doing and how she was doing it; it pleased her so to do. She was conscious of the wonder of her smooth, soft arms and neck, the fullness and seductiveness of her body, the grace and perfection of her clothing, or, at least, the individuality and taste which she made them indicate. She could take an old straw-hat form, a ribbon, a feather, or a rose, and with an innate artistry of feeling turn it into a bit of millinery which somehow was just the effective thing for her. She chose naive combinations of white and blues, pinks and white, browns and pale yellows, which somehow suggested her own soul, and topped them with great sashes of silky brown (or even red) ribbon tied about her waist, and large, soft-brimmed, face-haloing hats. She was a graceful dancer, could sing a little, could play feelingly—sometimes brilliantly—and could draw. Her art was a makeshift, however; she was no artist. The most significant things about her were her moods and her thoughts, which were uncertain, casual, anarchic. Rita Sohlberg, from the conventional point of view, was a dangerous person, and yet from her own point of view at this time she was not so at all—just dreamy and sweet.

A part of the peculiarity of her state was that Sohlberg had begun to disappoint Rita—sorely. Truth to tell, he was suffering from that most terrible of all maladies, uncertainty of soul and inability to truly find himself. At times he was not sure whether he was cut out to be a great violinist or a great composer, or merely a great teacher, which last he was never willing really to admit. "I am an arteest," he was fond of saying. "Ho, how I suffer from my temperament!" And again: "These dogs! These cows! These pigs!" This of other people. The quality of his playing was exceedingly erratic, even though at times it attained to a kind of subtlety, tenderness, awareness, and charm which brought him some attention. As a rule, however, it reflected the chaotic state of his own brain. He would play violently, feverishly, with a wild passionateness of gesture which robbed him of all ability to control his own technique.

"Oh, Harold!" Rita used to exclaim at first, ecstatically. Later she was not so sure.

Life and character must really get somewhere to be admirable, and Harold, really and truly, did not seem to be getting anywhere. He taught, stormed, dreamed, wept; but he ate his three meals a day, Rita noticed, and he took an excited interest at times in other women. To be the be-all and end-all of some one man's life was the least that Rita could conceive or concede as the worth of her personality, and so, as the years went on and Harold began to be unfaithful, first in moods, transports, then in deeds, her mood became dangerous. She counted them up—a girl music pupil, then an art student, then the wife of a banker at whose house Harold played socially. There followed strange, sullen moods on the part of Rita, visits home, groveling repentance on the part of Harold, tears, violent, passionate reunions, and then the same thing over again. What would you?

Rita was not jealous of Harold any more; she had lost faith in his ability as a musician. But she was disappointed that her charms were not sufficient to blind him to all others. That was the fly in the ointment. It was an affront to her beauty, and she was still beautiful. She was unctuously full-bodied, not quite so tall as Aileen, not really as large, but rounder and plumper, softer and more seductive. Physically she was not so well set up, so vigorous; but her eyes and mouth and the roving character of her mind held a strange lure. Mentally she was much more aware than Aileen, much more precise in her knowledge of art, music, literature, and current events; and in the field of romance she was much more vague and alluring. She knew many things about flowers, precious stones, insects, birds, characters in fiction, and poetic prose and verse generally.

At the time the Cowperwoods first met the Sohlbergs the latter still had their studio in the New Arts Building, and all was seemingly as serene as a May morning, only Harold was not getting along very well. He was drifting. The meeting was at a tea given by the Haatstaedts, with whom the Cowperwoods were still friendly, and Harold played. Aileen, who was there alone, seeing a chance to brighten her own life a little, invited the Sohlbergs, who seemed rather above the average, to her house to a musical evening. They came.

On this occasion Cowperwood took one look at Sohlberg and placed him exactly. "An erratic, emotional temperament," he thought. "Probably not able to place himself for want of consistency and application." But he liked him after a fashion. Sohlberg was interesting as an artistic type or figure—quite like a character in a Japanese print might be. He greeted him pleasantly.

"And Mrs. Sohlberg, I suppose," he remarked feelingly, catching a quick suggestion of the rhythm and sufficiency and naive taste that went with her. She was in simple white and blue—small blue ribbons threaded above lacy flounces in the skirt. Her arms and throat were deliciously soft and bare. Her eyes were quick, and yet soft and babyish—petted eyes.

"You know," she said to him, with a peculiar rounded formation of the mouth, which was a characteristic of her when she talked—a pretty, pouty mouth, "I thought we would never get heah at all. There was a fire"—she pronounced it fy-yah—"at Twelfth Street" (the Twelfth was Twalfth in her mouth) "and the engines were all about there. Oh, such sparks and smoke! And the flames coming out of the windows! The flames were a very dark red—almost orange and black. They're pretty when they're that way—don't you think so?"

Cowperwood was charmed. "Indeed I do," he said genially, using a kind of superior and yet sympathetic air which he could easily assume on occasion. He felt as though Mrs. Sohlberg might be a charming daughter to him—she was so cuddling and shy—and yet he could see that she was definite and individual. Her arms and face, he told himself, were lovely. Mrs. Sohlberg only saw before her a smart, cold, exact man—capable, very, she presumed—with brilliant, incisive eyes. How different from Harold, she thought, who would never be anything much—not even famous.

"I'm so glad you brought your violin," Aileen was saying to Harold, who was in another corner. "I've been looking forward to your coming to play for us."

"Very nize ov you, I'm sure," Sohlberg replied with his sweety drawl. "Such a nize plaze you have here—all these loafly books, and jade, and glass."

He had an unctuous, yielding way which was charming, Aileen thought. He should have a strong, rich woman to take care of him. He was like a stormy, erratic boy.

After refreshments were served Sohlberg played. Cowperwood was interested by his standing figure—his eyes, his hair—but he was much more interested in Mrs. Sohlberg, to whom his look constantly strayed. He watched her hands on the keys, her fingers, the dimples at her elbows. What an adorable mouth, he thought, and what light, fluffy hair! But more than that, there was a mood that invested it all— a bit of tinted color of the mind that reached him and made him sympathetic and even passionate toward her. She was the kind of woman he would like. She was somewhat like Aileen when she was six years younger (Aileen was now thirty-three, and Mrs. Sohlberg twenty-seven), only Aileen had always been more robust, more vigorous, less nebulous. Mrs. Sohlberg (he finally thought it out for himself) was like the rich, tinted interior of a South Sea oystershell—warm, colorful, delicate. But there was something firm there, too. Nowhere in society had he seen anyone like her. She was rapt, sensuous, beautiful. He kept his eyes on her until finally she became aware that he was gazing at her, and then she looked back at him in an arch, smiling way, fixing her mouth in a potent line. Cowperwood was captivated. Was she vulnerable? was his one thought. Did that faint smile mean anything more than mere social complaisance? Probably not, but could not a temperament so rich and full be awakened to feeling by his own? When she was through playing he took occasion to say: "Wouldn't you like to stroll into the gallery? Are you fond of pictures?" He gave her his arm.

"Now, you know," said Mrs. Sohlberg quaintly—very captivatingly, he thought, because she was so pretty—"at one time I thought I was going to be a great artist. Isn't that funny! I sent my father one of my drawings inscribed 'to whom I owe it all.' You would have to see the drawing to see how funny that is."

She laughed softly.

Cowperwood responded with a refreshed interest in life. Her laugh was as grateful to him as a summer wind. "See," he said gently, as they entered the room aglow with the soft light produced by guttered jets, "here is a Luini bought last winter." It was "The Mystic Marriage of St. Catharine." He paused while she surveyed the rapt expression of the attenuated saint. "And here," he went on, "is my greatest find so far." They were before the crafty countenance of Caesar Borgia painted by Pinturicchio.

"What a strange face!" commented Mrs. Sohlberg naively. "I didn't know anyone had ever painted him. He looks somewhat like an artist himself, doesn't he?" She had never read the involved and quite Satanic history of this man, and only knew the rumor of his crimes and machinations.

"He was, in his way," smiled Cowperwood, who had had an outline of his life, and that of his father, Pope Alexander VI, furnished him at the time of the purchase. Only so recently had his interest in Caesar Borgia begun. Mrs. Sohlberg scarcely gathered the sly humor of it.

"Oh yes, and here is Mrs. Cowperwood," she commented, turning to the painting by Van Beers. "It's high in key, isn't it?" she said loftily, but with an innocent loftiness that appealed to him. He liked spirit and some presumption in a woman. "What brilliant colors! I like the idea of the garden and the clouds."

She stepped back, and Cowperwood, interested only in her, surveyed the line of her back and the profile of her face. Such coordinated perfection of line and color! "Where every motion weaves and sings," he might have commented. Instead he said: "That was in Brussels. The clouds were an afterthought, and that vase on the wall, too."

"It's very good, I think," commented Mrs. Sohlberg, and moved away.

"How do you like this Israels?" he asked. It was the painting called "The Frugal Meal."

"I like it," she said, "and also your Bastien Le-Page," referring to "The Forge." "But I think your old masters are much more interesting. If you get many more you ought to put them together in a room. Don't you think so? I don't care for your Gérôme very much." She had a cute drawl which he considered infinitely alluring.

"Why not?" asked Cowperwood.

"Oh, it's rather artificial; don't you think so? I like the color, but the women's bodies are too perfect, I should say. It's very pretty, though."

He had little faith in the ability of women aside from their value as objects of art; and yet now and then, as in this instance, they revealed a sweet insight which sharpened his own. Aileen, he reflected, would not be capable of making a remark such as this. She was not as beautiful now as this woman—not as alluringly simple, naive, delicious, nor yet as wise. Mrs. Sohlberg, he reflected shrewdly, had a kind of fool for a husband. Would she take an interest in him, Frank Cowperwood? Would a woman like this surrender on any basis outside of divorce and marriage? He wondered. On her part, Mrs. Sohlberg was thinking what a forceful man Cowperwood was, and how close he had stayed by her. She

felt his interest, for she had often seen these symptoms in
other men and knew what they meant. She knew the pull of
her own beauty, and while she heightened it as artfully as
she dared, yet she kept aloof, too, feeling that she had never
met anyone as yet for whom it was worthwhile to be different. But Cowperwood—he needed someone more soulful than
Aileen, she thought.

CHAPTER XV

A New Affection

The growth of a relationship between Cowperwood
and Rita Sohlberg was fostered quite accidentally by Aileen,
who took a foolishly sentimental interest in Harold which yet
was not based on anything of real meaning. She liked him
because he was a superlatively gracious, flattering, emotional
man where women—pretty women—were concerned. She had
some idea she could send him pupils, and, anyhow, it was
nice to call at the Sohlberg studio. Her social life was dull
enough as it was. So she went, and Cowperwood, mindful of
Mrs. Sohlberg, came also. Shrewd to the point of destruction,
he encouraged Aileen in her interest in them. He suggested
that she invite them to dinner, that they give a musical at
which Sohlberg could play and be paid. There were boxes at
the theaters, tickets for concerts sent, invitations to drive
Sundays or other days.

The very chemistry of life seems to play into the hands
of a situation of this kind. Once Cowperwood was thinking
vividly, forcefully, of her, Rita began to think in like manner
of him. Hourly he grew more attractive, a strange, gripping
man. Beset by his mood, she was having the devil's own time
with her conscience. Not that anything had been said as
yet, but he was investing her, gradually beleaguering her, seal-
ing up, apparently, one avenue after another of escape. One
Thursday afternoon, when neither Aileen nor he could attend

the Sohlberg tea, Mrs. Sohlberg received a magnificent bunch of Jacqueminot roses. "For your nooks and corners," said a card. She knew well enough from whom it came and what it was worth. There were all of fifty dollars' worth of roses. It gave her breath of a world of money that she had never known. Daily she saw the name of his banking and brokerage firm advertised in the papers. Once she met him in Merrill's store at noon, and he invited her to lunch; but she felt obliged to decline. Always he looked at her with such straight, vigorous eyes. To think that her beauty had done or was doing this! Her mind, quite beyond herself, ran forward to an hour when perhaps this eager, magnetic man would take charge of her in a way never dreamed of by Harold. But she went on practicing, shopping, calling, reading, brooding over Harold's inefficiency, and stopping oddly sometimes to think—the etherealized grip of Cowperwood upon her. Those strong hands of his—how fine they were—and those large, soft-hard, incisive eyes. The puritanism of Wichita (modified some time since by the art life of Chicago, such as it was) was having a severe struggle with the manipulative subtlety of the ages—represented in this man.

"You know you are very elusive," he said to her one evening at the theater when he sat behind her during the entr'-acte, and Harold and Aileen had gone to walk in the foyer. The hubbub of conversation drowned the sound of anything that might be said. Mrs. Sohlberg was particularly pleasing in a lacy evening gown.

"No," she replied amusedly, flattered by his attention and acutely conscious of his physical nearness. By degrees she had been yielding herself to his mood, thrilling at his every word. "It seems to me I am very stable," she went on. "I'm certainly substantial enough."

She looked at her full, smooth arm lying on her lap.

Cowperwood, who was feeling all the drag of her substantiality, but in addition the wonder of her temperament, which was so much richer than Aileen's, was deeply moved. Those little blood moods that no words ever (or rarely) indicate were coming to him from her—faint zephyrlike emanations of emotions, moods, and fancies in her mind which allured him. She was like Aileen in animality, but better, still sweeter, more delicate, much richer spiritually. Or was he just tired of Aileen for the present? he asked himself at times. No, no, he told himself that could not be. Rita

Sohlberg was by far the most pleasing woman he had ever known.

"Yes, but elusive just the same," he went on, leaning toward her. "You remind me of something that I can find no word for—a bit of color or a perfume or tone—a flash of something. I follow you in my thoughts all the time now. Your knowledge of art interests me. I like your playing—it is like you. You make me think of delightful things that have nothing to do with the ordinary run of my life. Do you understand?"

"It is very nice," she said, "if I do." She took a breath, softly, dramatically. "You make me think vain things, you know." (Her mouth was a delicious O.) "You paint a pretty picture." She was warm, flushed, suffused with a burst of her own temperament.

"You are like that," he went on insistently. "You make me feel like that all the time. You know," he added, leaning over her chair, "I sometimes think you have never lived. There is so much that would complete your perfectness. I should like to send you abroad or take you—anyhow, you should go. You are very wonderful to me. Do you find me at all interesting to you?"

"Yes, but"—she paused—"you know I am afraid of all this and of you." Her mouth had that same delicious formation which had first attracted him. "I don't think we had better talk like this, do you? Harold is very jealous, or would be. What do you suppose Mrs. Cowperwood would think?"

"I know very well, but we needn't stop to consider that now, need we? It will do her no harm to let me talk to you. Life is between individuals, Rita. You and I have very much in common. Don't you see that? You are infinitely the most interesting woman I have ever known. You are bringing me something I have never known. Don't you see that? I want you to tell me something truly. Look at me. You are not happy as you are, are you? Not perfectly happy?"

"No." She smoothed her fan with her fingers.

"Are you happy at all?"

"I thought I was once. I'm not any more, I think."

"It is so plain why," he commented. "You are so much more wonderful than your place gives you scope for. You are an individual, not an acolyte to swing a censer for another. Mr. Sohlberg is very interesting, but you can't be happy that way. It surprises me you haven't seen it."

"Oh," she exclaimed, with a touch of weariness, "but perhaps I have."

He looked at her keenly, and she thrilled. "I don't think we'd better talk so here," she replied. "You'd better be——"

He laid his hand on the back of her chair, almost touching her shoulder.

"Rita," he said, using her given name again, "you wonderful woman!"

"Oh!" she breathed.

Cowperwood did not see Mrs. Sohlberg again for over a week—ten days exactly—when one afternoon Aileen came for him in a new kind of trap, having stopped first to pick up the Sohlbergs. Harold was up in front with her and she had left a place behind for Cowperwood with Rita. She did not in the vaguest way suspect how interested he was—his manner was so deceptive. Aileen imagined that she was the superior woman of the two, the better-looking, the better-dressed, hence the more ensnaring. She could not guess what a lure this woman's temperament had for Cowperwood, who was so brisk, dynamic, seemingly unromantic, but who, just the same, in his nature concealed (under a very forceful exterior) a deep underlying element of romance and fire.

"This is charming," he said, sinking down beside Rita. "What a fine evening! And the nice straw hat with the roses, and the nice linen dress. My, my!" The roses were red; the dress white, with thin green ribbon run through it here and there. She was keenly aware of the reason for his enthusiasm. He was so different from Harold, so healthy and out-of-doorish, so able. Today Harold had been in tantrums over fate, life, his lack of success.

"Oh, I shouldn't complain so much if I were you," she had said to him bitterly. "You might work harder and storm less."

This had produced a scene which she had escaped by going for a walk. Almost at the very moment when she had returned Aileen had appeared. It was a way out. She had cheered up and accepted, dressed. So had Sohlberg. Apparently smiling and happy, they had set out on the drive. Now, as Cowperwood spoke, she glanced about her contentedly. "I'm lovely," she thought, "and he loves me. How wonderful it would be if we dared." But she said aloud: "I'm not so very nice. It's just the day—don't you think so? It's a simple dress. I'm not very happy, though, tonight, either."

"What's the matter?" he asked cheeringly, the rumble of the traffic destroying the carrying power of their voices. He leaned toward her, very anxious to solve any difficulty which might confront her, perfectly willing to ensnare her by kindness. "Isn't there something I can do? We're going now for a long ride to the pavilion in Jackson Park, and then, after dinner, we'll come back by moonlight. Won't that be nice? You must be smiling now and like yourself—happy. You have no reason to be otherwise that I know of. I will do anything for you that you want done—that can be done. You can have anything you want that I can give you. What is it? You know how much I think of you. If you leave your affairs to me you would never have any troubles of any kind."

"Oh, it isn't anything you can do—not now, anyhow. My affairs! Oh yes. What are they? Very simple, all."

She had that delicious atmosphere of remoteness even from herself. He was enchanted.

"But you are not simple to me, Rita," he said softly, "nor are your affairs. They concern me very much. You are so important to me. I have told you that. Don't you see how true it is? You are a strange complexity to me—wonderful. I'm mad over you. Ever since I saw you last I have been thinking, thinking. If you have troubles let me share them. You are so much to me—my only trouble. I can fix your life. Join it with mine. I need you, and you need me."

"Yes," she said, "I know." Then she paused. "It's nothing much," she went on—"just a quarrel."

"What over?"

"Over me, really." The mouth was delicious. "I can't swing the censer always, as you say." That thought of his had stuck. "It's all right now, though. Isn't the day lovely, be-yoot-i-ful!"

Cowperwood looked at her and shook his head. She was such a treasure—so inconsequential. Aileen, busy driving and talking, could not see or hear. She was interested in Sohlberg, and the southward crush of vehicles on Michigan Avenue was distracting her attention. As they drove swiftly past budding trees, kempt lawns, fresh-made flower beds, open windows—the whole seductive world of spring—Cowperwood felt as though life had once more taken a fresh start. His magnetism, if it had been visible, would have enveloped him like a glittering aura. Mrs. Sohlberg felt that this was going to be a wonderful evening.

The dinner was at the park—an open-air chicken à la Maryland affair, with waffles and champagne to help out. Aileen, flattered by Sohlberg's gaiety under her spell, was having a delightful time, jesting, toasting, laughing, walking on the grass. Sohlberg was making love to her in a foolish, inconsequential way, as many men were inclined to do; but she was putting him off gaily with "silly boy" and "hush." She was so sure of herself that she was free to tell Cowperwood afterward how emotional he was and how she had to laugh at him. Cowperwood, quite certain that she was faithful, took it all in good part. Sohlberg was such a dunce and such a happy convenience ready to his hand. "He's not a bad sort," he commented. "I rather like him, though I don't think he's so much of a violinist."

After dinner they drove along the lake shore and out through an open bit of tree-blocked prairie land, the moon shining in a clear sky, filling the fields and topping the lake with a silvery effulgence. Mrs. Sohlberg was being inoculated with the virus Cowperwood, and it was taking deadly effect. The tendency of her own disposition, however lethargic it might seem, once it was stirred emotionally, was to act. She was essentially dynamic and passionate. Cowperwood was beginning to stand out in her mind as the force that he was. It would be wonderful to be loved by such a man. There would be an eager, vivid life between them. It frightened and drew her like a blazing lamp in the dark. To get control of herself she talked of art, people, of Paris, Italy, and he responded in like strain, but all the while he smoothed her hand, and once, under the shadow of some trees, he put his hand to her hair, turned her face, and put his mouth softly to her cheek. She flushed, trembled, turned pale, in the grip of this strange storm, but drew herself together. It was wonderful—heaven. Her old life was obviously going to pieces.

"Listen," he said guardedly. "Will you meet me tomorrow at three just beyond the Rush Street bridge? I will pick you up promptly. You won't have to wait a moment."

She paused, meditating, dreaming, almost hypnotized by his strange world of fancy.

"Will you?" he asked eagerly.

"Wait," she said softly. "Let me think. Can I?"

She paused.

"Yes," she said after a time, drawing in a deep breath. "Yes"—as if she had arranged something in her mind.

"My sweet," he whispered, pressing her arm, while he looked at her profile in the moonlight.

"But I'm doing a great deal," she replied softly, a little breathless and a little pale.

CHAPTER XVI

A Fateful Interlude

Cowperwood was enchanted. He kept the proposed tryst with eagerness and found her all that he had hoped. She was sweeter, more colorful, more elusive than anybody he had ever known. In their charming apartment on the North Side which he at once engaged, and where he sometimes spent mornings, evenings, afternoons, as opportunity afforded, he studied her with the most critical eye and found her almost flawless. She had that boundless value which youth and a certain insouciance of manner contribute. There was, delicious to relate, no melancholy in her nature, but a kind of innate sufficiency which neither looked forward to nor back upon troublesome ills. She loved beautiful things but was not extravagant; and what interested him and commanded his respect was that no urgings of his toward prodigality, however subtly advanced, could affect her. She knew what she wanted, spent carefully, bought tastefully, arrayed herself in ways which appealed to him as the flowers did. His feeling for her became at times so great that he wished, one might almost have said, to destroy it—to appease the urge and allay the pull in himself, but it was useless. The charm of her endured. His transports would leave her refreshed, apparently, prettier, more graceful than ever, it seemed to him, putting back her ruffled hair with her hand, mouthing at herself prettily in the glass, thinking of many remote, delicious things at once.

"Do you remember that picture we saw in the art store the other day, Algernon?" she would drawl, calling him by his second name, which she had adopted for herself as being more suited to his moods when with her and more pleasing to her. Cowperwood had protested, but she held to it. "Do you remember that lovely blue of the old man's coat?" (It was an "Adoration of the Magi.") "Wasn't that be-yoot-i-ful?"

She drawled so sweetly and fixed her mouth in such an odd way that he was impelled to kiss her. "You clover blossom," he would say to her, coming over and taking her by the arms. "You sprig of cherry bloom. You Dresden china dream."

"Now, are you going to muss my hair when I've just managed to fix it?"

The voice was the voice of careless, genial innocence—and the eyes.

"Yes, I am, minx."

"Yes, but you mustn't smother me, you know. Really, you know you almost hurt me with your mouth. Aren't you going to be nice to me?"

"Yes, sweet. But I want to hurt you, too."

"Well, then, if you must."

But for all his transports the lure was still there. She was like a butterfly, he thought, yellow and white or blue and gold, fluttering over a hedge of wild rose.

In these intimacies it was that he came quickly to understand how much she knew of social movements and tendencies, though she was just an individual of the outer fringe. She caught at once a clear understanding of his social point of view, his art ambition, his dreams of something better for himself in every way. She seemed to see clearly that he had not as yet realized himself, that Aileen was not just the woman for him, though she might be one. She talked of her own husband after a time in a tolerant way—his foibles, defects, weaknesses. She was not unsympathetic, he thought, just weary of a state that was not properly balanced either in love, ability, or insight. Cowperwood had suggested that she could take a larger studio for herself and Harold—do away with the petty economies that had hampered her and him—and explain it all on the grounds of a larger generosity on the part of her family. At first she objected; but Cowperwood was tactful and finally brought it about. He again suggested a little while later that she should persuade Harold to go to Europe. There would be the same ostensible reason —additional means from her relatives. Mrs. Sohlberg, thus urged, petted, made over, assured, came finally to accept his liberal rule—to bow to him; she became as contented as a cat. With caution she accepted of his largess, and made the cleverest use of it she could. For something over a year neither Sohlberg nor Aileen was aware of the intimacy which had sprung up. Sohlberg, easily bamboozled, went back to Denmark for a visit, then to study in Germany. Mrs. Sohlberg followed Cowperwood to Europe the following year. At Aix-les-Bains, Biarritz, Paris, even London, Aileen never knew that there was an additional figure in the background. Cowperwood was trained by Rita into a really finer point of view. He came to know better music, books, even the facts. She encouraged him in his idea of a representative collection of the old masters, and begged him to be cautious in his selection of moderns. He felt himself to be delightfully situated indeed.

The difficulty with this situation, as with all such where an individual ventures thus buccaneeringly on the sea of sex, is the possibility of those storms which result from misplaced confidence, and from our built-up system of ethics relating to property in women. To Cowperwood, however, who was a law unto himself, who knew no law except such as might be imposed upon him by his lack of ability to think, this possibility of entanglement, wrath, rage, pain, offered no particular obstacle. It was not at all certain that any such thing would follow. Where the average man might have found one such liaison difficult to manage, Cowperwood, as we have seen, had previously entered on several such affairs almost simultaneously; and now he had ventured on yet another; in the last instance with much greater feeling and enthusiasm. The previous affairs had been emotional makeshifts at best—more or less idle philanderings in which his deeper moods and feelings were not concerned. In the case of Mrs. Sohlberg all this was changed. For the present at least she was really all in all to him. But this temperamental characteristic of his relating to his love of women, his artistic if not emotional subjection to their beauty and the mystery of their personalities led him into still a further affair, and this last was not so fortunate in its outcome.

Antoinette Nowak had come to him fresh from a West Side high school and a Chicago business college, and had been engaged as his private stenographer and secretary. This girl had blossomed forth into something exceptional, as American children of foreign parents are wont to do. You would have scarcely believed that she, with her fine, lithe body, her good taste in dress, her skill in stenography, bookkeeping, and business details, could be the daughter of a struggling Pole, who had first worked in the Southwest Chicago Steel Mills, and who had later kept a fifth-rate cigar, news, and stationery store in the Polish district, the merchandise of playing cards and a back room for idling and casual gaming being the principal reasons for its existence. Antoinette, whose first name had not been Antoinette at all, but Minka (the Antoinette having been borrowed by her from an article in one of the Chicago Sunday papers), was a fine dark, brooding girl, ambitious and hopeful, who ten days after she had accepted her new place was admiring Cowperwood and following his every daring movement with almost excited interest. To be the wife of such a man, she thought—to even command his interest, let alone his affection—must be wonderful. After the dull world she had known—it seemed dull compared to the upper rarefied realms which she was beginning to glimpse through him—and after the average men in the real estate office over the way where she had first worked, Cowperwood, in his good clothes, his remote mood, his easy, commanding manner, touched the most ambitious chords of her being. One day she saw Aileen sweep in from her carriage, wearing warm brown furs, smart polished boots, a street suit of corded brown wool, and a fur toque sharpened and emphasized by a long dark-red feather which shot upward like a dagger or a quill pen. Antoinette hated her. She conceived herself to be better, or as good at least. Why was life divided so unfairly? What sort of a man was Cowperwood, anyhow? One night after she had written out a discreet but truthful history of him which he had dictated to her, and which she had sent to the Chicago newspapers for him soon after the opening of his brokerage office in Chicago, she went home and dreamed of what he had told her, only altered, of course, as in dreams. She thought that

Cowperwood stood beside her in his handsome private office in La Salle Street and asked her:

"Antoinette, what do you think of me?" Antoinette was nonplussed but brave. In her dream she found herself intensely interested in him.

"Oh, I don't know what to think. I'm so sorry," was her answer. Then he laid his hand on hers, on her cheek, and she awoke. She began thinking what a pity, what a shame that such a man should ever have been in prison. He was so handsome. He had been married twice. Perhaps his first wife was very homely or very mean-spirited. She thought of this, and the next day went to work meditatively. Cowperwood, engrossed in his own plans, was not thinking of her at present. He was thinking of the next moves in his interesting gas war. And Aileen, seeing her one day, merely considered her an underling. The woman in business was such a novelty that as yet she was *déclassé*. Aileen really thought nothing of Antoinette at all.

Somewhat over a year after Cowperwood had become intimate with Mrs. Sohlberg his rather practical business relations with Antoinette Nowak took on a more intimate color. What shall we say of this—that he had already wearied of Mrs. Sohlberg? Not in the least. He was desperately fond of her. Or that he despised Aileen, whom he was thus grossly deceiving? Not at all. She was to him at times as attractive as ever—perhaps more so for the reason that her self-imagined rights were being thus roughly infringed upon. He was sorry for her, but inclined to justify himself on the ground that these other relations—with possibly the exception of Mrs. Sohlberg—were not enduring. If it had been possible to marry Mrs. Sohlberg he might have done so, and he did speculate at times as to whether anything would ever induce Aileen to leave him; but this was more or less idle speculation. He rather fancied they would live out their days together, seeing that he was able thus easily to deceive her. But as for a girl like Antoinette Nowak, she figured in that braided symphony of mere sex attraction which somehow makes up that geometric formula of beauty which rules the world. She was charming in a dark way, beautiful, with eyes that burned with an unsatisfied fire; and Cowperwood, although at first only in the least moved by her, became by degrees interested in her, wondering at the amazing, transforming power of the American atmosphere.

"Are your parents English, Antoinette?" he asked her one morning, with that easy familiarity which he assumed to all underlings and minor intellects—an air that could not be resented in him, and which was usually accepted as a compliment.

Antoinette, clean and fresh in a white shirtwaist, a black walking skirt, a ribbon of black velvet about her neck, and her long black hair laid in a heavy braid low over her forehead and held close by a white celluloid comb, looked at him with pleased and grateful eyes. She had been used to such different types of men—the earnest, fiery, excitable, sometimes drunken and swearing men of her childhood, always striking, marching, praying in the Catholic churches; and then the men of the business world, crazy over money, and with no understanding of anything save some few facts about Chicago and its momentary possibilities. In Cowperwood's office, taking his letters and hearing him talk in his quick, genial way with old Laughlin, Sippens, and others, she had learned more of life than she had ever dreamed existed. He was like a vast open window out of which she was looking upon an almost illimitable landscape.

"No, sir," she replied, dropping her slim, firm white hand, holding a black lead pencil restfully on her notebook. She smiled quite innocently because she was pleased.

"I thought not," he said, "and yet you're American enough."

"I don't know how it is," she said quite solemnly. "I have a brother who is quite as American as I am. We don't either of us look like our father or mother."

"What does your brother do?" he asked indifferently.

"He's one of the weighers at Arneel & Company. He expects to be a manager sometime." She smiled.

Cowperwood looked at her speculatively, and after a momentary return glance she dropped her eyes. Slowly, in spite of herself, a telltale flush rose and mantled her brown cheeks. It always did when he looked at her.

"Take this letter to General Van Sickle," he began, on this occasion quite helpfully, and in a few minutes she had recovered. She could not be near Cowperwood for long at a time, however, without being stirred by a feeling which was not of her own willing. He fascinated and suffused her with a dull fire. She sometimes wondered whether a man so remarkable would ever be interested in a girl like her.

The end of this essential interest, of course, was the eventual assumption of Antoinette. One might go through all the dissolving details of days in which she sat taking dictation, receiving instructions, going about her office duties in a state of apparently chill, practical, commercial single-mindedness; but it would be to no purpose. As a matter of fact, without in any way affecting the preciseness and accuracy of her labor, her thoughts were always upon the man in the inner office—the strange master who was then seeing his men, and in between, so it seemed, a whole world of individuals, solemn and commercial, who came, presented their cards, talked at times almost interminably, and went away. It was the rare individual, however, she observed, who had the long conversation with Cowperwood, and that interested her the more. His instructions to her were always of the briefest, and he depended on her native intelligence to supply much that he scarcely more than suggested.

"You understand, do you?" was his customary phrase.

"Yes," she would reply.

She felt as though she were fifty times as significant here as she had ever been in her life before.

The office was clean, hard, bright, like Cowperwood himself. The morning sun, streaming in through an almost solid glass east front shaded by pale green roller curtains, came to have an almost romantic atmosphere for her. Cowperwood's private office, as in Philadelphia, was a solid cherrywood box in which he could shut himself completely—sightproof, soundproof. When the door was closed it was sacrosanct. He made it a rule, sensibly, to keep his door open as much as possible, even when he was dictating, sometimes not. It was in these half-hours of dictation—the door open, as a rule, for he did not care for too much privacy—that he and Miss Nowak came closest. After months and months, and because he had been busy with the other woman mentioned, of whom she knew nothing, she came to enter sometimes with a sense of suffocation, sometimes of maidenly shame. It would never have occurred to her to admit frankly that she wanted Cowperwood to make love to her. It would have frightened her to have thought of herself as yielding easily, and yet there was not a detail of his personality that was not now burned in her brain. His light, thick, always smoothly parted hair, his wide, clear, inscrutable eyes, his carefully manicured hands, so full and firm, his fresh clothing of delicate, intricate patterns—how these fascinated her! He seemed always remote except just at the moment of doing something, when, curiously enough, he seemed intensely intimate and near.

One day, after many exchanges of glances in which her own always fell sharply—in the midst of a letter—he arose and closed the half-open door. She did not think so much of that, as a rule—it had happened before—but now, today, because of a studied glance he had given her, neither tender nor smiling, she felt as though something unusual were about to happen. Her own body was going hot and cold by turns —her neck and hands. She had a fine figure, finer than she realized, with shapely limbs and torso. Her head had some of the sharpness of the old Greek coinage, and her hair was plaited as in ancient cut stone. Cowperwood noted it. He came back, and without taking his seat, bent over her and intimately took her hand.

"Antoinette," he said, lifting her gently.

She looked up, then arose—for he slowly drew her— breathless, the color gone, much of the capable practicality that was hers completely eliminated. She felt limp, inert. She pulled at her hand faintly, and then, lifting her eyes, was fixed by that hard, insatiable gaze of his. Her head swam— her eyes were filled with a telltale confusion.

"Antoinette!"

"Yes," she murmured.

"You love me, don't you?"

She tried to pull herself together, to inject some of her native rigidity of soul into her air—that rigidity which she always imagined would never desert her—but it was gone. There came instead to her a picture of the far Blue Island Avenue neighborhood from which she emanated—its low brown cottages, and then this smart, hard office and this strong man. He came out of such a marvelous world, apparently. A strange foaming seemed to be in her blood. She was deliriously, deliciously numb and happy.

"Antoinette!"

"Oh, I don't know what I think," she gasped. "I— Oh yes, I do, I do."

"I like your name," he said simply. "Antoinette." And then, pulling her to him, he slipped his arm about her waist.

She was frightened, numb, and then suddenly, not so much from shame as shock, tears rushed to her eyes. She turned and put her hand on the desk and hung her head and sobbed.

"Why, Antoinette," he asked gently, bending over her, "are you so much unused to the world? I thought you said you loved me. Do you want me to forget all this and go on as before? I can, of course, if you can, you know."

He knew that she loved him, wanted him.

She heard him plainly enough, shaking.

"Do you?" he said after a time, giving her moments in which to recover.

"Oh, let me cry!" she recovered herself sufficiently to say quite wildly. "I don't know why I'm crying. It's just because I'm nervous, I suppose. Please don't mind me now."

"Antoinette," he repeated, "look at me! Will you stop?"

"Oh no, not now. My eyes are so bad."

"Antoinette! Come, look!" He put his hand under her chin. "See, I'm not so terrible."

"Oh," she said, when her eyes met his again, "I. . . ." And then she folded her arms against his breast while he petted her hand and held her close.

"I'm not so bad, Antoinette. It's you as much as it is me. You do love me, then?"

"Yes, yes—oh yes!"

"And you don't mind?"

"No. It's all so strange." Her face was hidden.

"Kiss me, then."

She put up her lips and slipped her arms about him. He held her close.

He tried teasingly to make her say why she cried, thinking the while of what Aileen or Rita would think if they knew, but she would not at first—admitting later that it was a sense of evil. Curiously, she also thought of Aileen, and how, on occasion, she had seen her sweep in and out. Now she was sharing with her (the dashing Mrs. Cowperwood, so vain and superior) the wonder of his affection. Strange as it may seem, she looked on it now as rather an honor. She had risen in her own estimation—her sense of life and power. Now, more than ever before, she knew something of life because she knew something of love and passion. The future seemed tremulous with promise. She went back to her machine after a while, thinking of this. What would it all come to? she wondered wildly. You could not have told by her eyes that she had been crying. Instead, a rich glow in her

brown cheeks heightened her beauty. No disturbing sense of
Aileen was involved with all this. Antoinette was of the
newer order that was beginning to privately question ethics
and morals. She had a right to her life, lead where it would.
And to what it would bring her? The feel of Cowperwood's
lips was still fresh on hers. What would the future reveal to
her now? What?

CHAPTER XVII

An Overture to Conflict

The result of this understanding was not so important to Cowperwood as it was to Antoinette. In a vagrant
mood he had unlocked a spirit here which was fiery, passionate, but in this case hopelessly worshipful. However much
she might be grieved by him, Antoinette, as he subsequently
learned, would never sin against his personal welfare. Yet
she was unwittingly the means of first opening the flood-
gates of suspicion on Aileen, thereby establishing in the latter's mind the fact of Cowperwood's persistent unfaithful-
ness.

The incidents which led up to this were comparatively
trivial—nothing more, indeed, at first than the sight of Miss
Nowak and Cowperwood talking intimately in his office one
afternoon when the others had gone and the fact that she
appeared to be a little bit disturbed by Aileen's arrival.
Later came the discovery—though of this Aileen could not
be absolutely sure—of Cowperwood and Antoinette in a
closed carriage one stormy November afternoon in State
Street when he was supposed to be out of the city. She was
coming out of Merrill's store at the time, and just happened
to glance at the passing vehicle, which was running near the
curb. Aileen, although uncertain, was greatly shocked. Could
it be possible that he had not left town? She journeyed to
his office on the pretext of taking old Laughlin's dog, Jennie,

AN OVERTURE TO CONFLICT 129

a pretty collar she had found; actually to find out if Antoinette were away at the same time. Could it be possible, she kept asking herself, that Cowperwood had become interested in his own stenographer? The fact that the office assumed that he was out of town and that Antoinette was not there gave her pause. Laughlin quite innocently informed her that he thought Miss Nowak had gone to one of the libraries to make up certain reports. It left her in doubt.

What was Aileen to think? Her moods and aspirations were linked so closely with the love and success of Cowperwood that she could not, in spite of herself, but take fire at the least thought of losing him. He himself wondered sometimes, as he threaded the meshlike paths of sex, what she would do once she discovered his variant conduct. Indeed, there had been little occasional squabbles, not sharp, but suggestive, when he was trifling about with Mrs. Kittridge, Mrs. Ledwell, and others. There were, as may be imagined, from time to time absences, brief and unimportant, which he explained easily, passional indifferences which were not explained so easily, and the like; but since his affections were not really involved in any of those instances, he had managed to smooth the matter over quite nicely.

"Why do you say that?" he would demand, when she suggested, apropos of a trip or a day when she had not been with him, that there might have been another. "You know there hasn't. If I am going in for that sort of thing you'll learn it fast enough. Even if I did, it wouldn't mean that I was unfaithful to you spiritually."

"Oh, wouldn't it?" exclaimed Aileen resentfully, and with some disturbance of spirit. "Well, you can keep your spiritual faithfulness. I'm not going to be content with any sweet thoughts."

Cowperwood laughed even as she laughed, for he knew she was right and he felt sorry for her. At the same time her biting humor pleased him. He knew that she did not really suspect him of actual infidelity; he was obviously so fond of her. But she also knew that he was innately attractive to women, and that there were enough of the philandering type to want to lead him astray and make her life a burden. Also that he might prove a very willing victim.

Sex desire and its fruition being such an integral factor in the marriage and every other sex relation, the average woman is prone to study the periodic manifestations that go with it quite as one dependent on the weather—a sailor, for example—might study the barometer. In this Aileen was no exception. She was so beautiful herself, and had been so much to Cowperwood physically, that she had followed the corresponding evidences of feeling in him with the utmost interest, accepting the recurring ebullitions of his physical emotions as an evidence of her own enduring charm. As time went on, however—and that was long before Mrs. Sohlberg or anyone else had appeared—the original flare of passion had undergone a form of subsidence, though not noticeable enough to be disturbing. Aileen thought and thought, but she did not investigate. Indeed, because of the precariousness of her own situation as a social failure she was afraid to do so.

With the arrival of Mrs. Sohlberg and then of Antoinette Nowak as factors in the potpourri, the situation became more difficult. Humanly fond of Aileen as Cowperwood was, and because of his lapses and her affection, desirous of being kind, yet for the time being he was alienated almost completely from her. He grew remote according as his clandestine affairs were drifting or blazing, without, however, losing his firm grip on his financial affairs, and Aileen noticed it. It worried her. She was so vain that she could scarcely believe that Cowperwood could long be indifferent, and for a while her sentimental interest in Sohlberg's future and unhappiness of soul beclouded her judgment; but she finally began to feel the drift of affairs. The pathos of all this is that it so quickly descends into the realm of the unsatisfactory, the banal, the pseudo intimate. Aileen noticed it at once. She tried protestations. "You don't kiss me the way you did once," and then a little later, "You haven't noticed me hardly for four whole days. What's the matter?"

"Oh, I don't know," replied Cowperwood easily; "I guess I want you as much as ever. I don't see that I am any different." He took her in his arms and petted and caressed her; but Aileen was suspicious, nervous.

The psychology of the human animal, when confronted by these tangles, these ripping tides of the heart, has little to do with so-called reason or logic. It is amazing how in the face of passion and the affections and the changing face of life all plans and theories by which we guide ourselves fall to the ground. Here was Aileen talking bravely at the time she invaded Mrs. Lillian Cowperwood's domain of the necessity of "her Frank" finding a woman suitable to his needs, tastes, abilities, but now that the possibility of another woman equally or possibly better suited to him was looming in the offing—although she had no idea who it might be—she could not reason in the same way. Her ox, God wot, was the one that was being gored. What if he should find someone whom he could want more than he did her? Dear heaven, how terrible that would be! What would she do? she asked herself thoughtfully. She lapsed into the blues one afternoon —almost cried—she could scarcely say why. Another time she thought of all the terrible things she would do, how difficult she would make it for any other woman who invaded her preserves. However, she was not sure. Would she declare war if she discovered another? She knew she would eventually; and yet she knew, too, that if she did, and Cowperwood were set in his passion, thoroughly alienated, it would do no good. It would be terrible, but what could she do to win him back? That was the issue. Once warned, however, by her suspicious questioning, Cowperwood was more mechanically attentive than ever. He did his best to conceal his altered mood—his enthusiasm for Mrs. Sohlberg, his interest in Antoinette Nowak—and this helped somewhat.

But finally there was a detectable change. Aileen noticed it first after they had been back from Europe nearly a year. At this time she was still interested in Sohlberg, but in a harmlessly flirtatious way. She thought he might be interesting physically, but would he be as delightful as Cowperwood? Never! When she felt that Cowperwood himself might be changing she pulled herself up at once, and when Antoinette appeared—the carriage incident—Sohlberg lost his, at best, unstable charm. She began to meditate on what a terrible thing it would be to lose Cowperwood, seeing that she had failed to establish herself socially. Perhaps that had something to do with his defection. No doubt it had. Yet she could not believe, after all his protestations of affection in Philadelphia, after all her devotion to him in those dark days of his degradation and punishment, that he would really turn on her. No, he might stray momentarily, but if she protested enough, made a scene, perhaps, he would not feel so free to injure her—he would remember and be loving and devoted again. After seeing him, or imagining she had seen him, in the carriage, she thought at first that she would question him, but later decided that she would wait and watch more closely. Perhaps he was beginning to run around with other women. There was safety in numbers—that she knew. Her heart, her pride, were hurt, but not broken.

CHAPTER XVIII

The Clash

The peculiar personality of Rita Sohlberg was such that by her very action she ordinarily allayed suspicion, or, rather, distracted it. Although a novice, she had a strange ease, courage, or balance of soul which kept her whole and self-possessed under the most trying of circumstances. She might have been overtaken in the most compromising of positions, but her manner would always have indicated ease, a sense of innocence, nothing unusual, for she had no sense of moral degradation in this matter—no troublesome emotion as to what was to flow from a relationship of this kind, no worry as to her own soul, sin, social opinion, or the like. She was really interested in art and life—a pagan, in fact. Some people are thus hardily equipped. It is the most notable attribute of the hardier type of personalities—not necessarily the most brilliant or successful. You might have said that her soul was naively unconscious of the agony of others in loss. She would have taken any loss to herself with an amazing equableness—some qualms, of course, but not many—because her vanity and sense of charm would have made her look forward to something better or as good.

She had called on Aileen quite regularly in the past, with or without Harold, and had frequently driven with the Cowperwoods or joined them at the theater or elsewhere. She had decided, after becoming intimate with Cowperwood, to study art again, which was a charming blind, for it called for attendance at afternoon or evening classes, which she frequently skipped. Besides, since Harold had more money

he was becoming gayer, more reckless and enthusiastic over
women, and Cowperwood deliberately advised her to en-
courage him in some liaison which, in case exposure should
subsequently come to them, would effectually tie his hands.

"Let him get in some affair," Cowperwood told Rita.
"We'll put detectives on his trail and get evidence. He won't
have a word to say."

"We don't really need to do that," she protested sweetly,
naively. "He's been in enough scrapes as it is. He's given
me some of the letters"—she pronounced it "lettahs"—"written him."

"But we'll need actual witnesses if we ever need anything
at all. Just tell me when he's in love again, and I'll do the
rest."

"You know, I think," she drawled amusingly, "that he is
now. I saw him on the street the other day with one of his
students—rather a pretty girl, too."

Cowperwood was pleased. Under the circumstances he
would almost have been willing—not quite—for Aileen to
succumb to Sohlberg in order to entrap her and make his
situation secure. Yet he really did not wish it in the last
analysis—would have been grieved temporarily if she had
deserted him. However, in the case of Sohlberg, detectives
were employed, the new affair with the flighty pupil was
unearthed and sworn to by witnesses, and this, combined
with the "lettahs" held by Rita, constituted ample material
wherewith to hush up the musician if ever he became unduly obstreperous. So Cowperwood and Rita's state was quite
comfortable.

But Aileen, meditating over Antoinette Nowak, was beside herself with curiosity, doubt, worry. She did not want
to injure Cowperwood in any way after his bitter Philadelphia
experience, and yet when she thought of his deserting her
in this way she fell into a great rage. Her vanity, as much as
her love, was hurt. What could she do to justify or set at
rest her suspicions? Watch him personally? She was too dignified and vain to lurk about street corners or offices or
hotels. Never! Start a quarrel without additional evidence?—
that would be silly. He was too shrewd to give her further
evidence once she spoke. He would merely deny it. She
brooded irritably, recalling after a time, and with an aching
heart, that her father had put detectives on her track once
ten years before, and had actually discovered her relations

with Cowperwood and their rendezvous. Bitter as that memory was—torturing—yet now the same means seemed not too abhorrent to employ under the circumstances. No harm had come to Cowperwood in the former instance, she reasoned to herself—no especial harm—from that discovery (this was not true), and none would come to him now. (This also was not true.) But one must forgive a fiery, passionate soul, wounded to the quick, some errors of judgment. Her thought was that she would first be sure just what it was her beloved was doing, and then decide what course to take. But she knew that she was treading on dangerous ground, and mentally she recoiled from the consequences which might follow. He might leave her if she fought him too bitterly. He might treat her as he had treated his first wife, Lillian.

She studied her liege lord curiously these days, wondering if it were true that he had deserted her already, as he had deserted his first wife thirteen years before, wondering if he could really take up with a girl as common as Antoinette Nowak—wondering, wondering, wondering—half afraid and yet courageous. What could be done with him? If only he still loved her all would be well yet—but oh!

The detective agency to which she finally applied, after weeks of soul-racking suspense, was one of those disturbingly human implements which many are not opposed to using on occasion, when it is the only means of solving a troublous problem of wounded feelings or jeopardized interests. Aileen, being obviously rich, was forthwith shamefully overcharged; but the services agreed upon were well performed. To her amazement, chagrin, and distress, after a few weeks of observation Cowperwood was reported to have affairs not only with Antoinette Nowak, whom she did suspect, but also with Mrs. Sohlberg. And these two affairs at one and the same time. For the moment it left Aileen actually stunned and breathless.

The significance of Rita Sohlberg to her in this hour was greater than that of any woman before or after. Of all living things, women dread women most of all, and of all women the clever and beautiful. Rita Sohlberg had been growing on Aileen as a personage, for she had obviously been prospering during this past year, and her beauty had been amazingly enhanced thereby. Once Aileen had encountered Rita in a light trap on the Avenue, very handsome and very new, and she had commented on it to Cowperwood, whose reply had been: "Her father must be making some money. Sohlberg could never earn it for her."

Aileen sympathized with Harold because of his temperament, but she knew that what Cowperwood said was true.

Another time, at a box party at the theater, she had noted the rich elaborateness of Mrs. Sohlberg's dainty frock, the endless pleatings of pale silk, the startling charm of the needlework, and the ribbons—countless, rosetted, small—that meant hard work on the part of someone.

"How lovely this is," she had commented.

"Yes," Rita had replied airily; "I thought, don't you know, my dressmaker would never get done working on it."

It had cost, all told, $220, and Cowperwood had gladly paid the bill.

Aileen went home at the time thinking of Rita's taste and of how well she had harmonized her materials to her personality. She was truly charming.

Now, however, when it appeared that the same charm that had appealed to her had appealed to Cowperwood, she conceived an angry, animal opposition to it all. Rita Sohlberg! Ha! A lot of satisfaction she'd get knowing, as she would soon, that Cowperwood was sharing his affection for her with Antoinette Nowak—a mere stenographer. And a lot of satisfaction Antoinette would get—the cheap upstart —when she learned, as she would, that Cowperwood loved her so lightly that he would take an apartment for Rita Sohlberg and let a cheap hotel or an assignation-house do for her.

But in spite of this savage exultation her thoughts kept coming back to herself, to her own predicament, to torture and destroy her. Cowperwood, the liar! Cowperwood, the pretender! Cowperwood, the sneak! At one moment she conceived a kind of horror of the man because of all his protestations to her; at the next a rage—bitter, swelling; at the next a pathetic realization of her own altered position. Say what one will, to take the love of a man like Cowperwood away from a woman like Aileen was to leave her high and dry on land, like a fish out of its native element, to take all the wind out of her sails—almost to kill her. Whatever position she had once thought to hold through him was now jeopardized. Whatever joy or glory she had had in being Mrs. Frank Algernon Cowperwood, it was now tarnished. She sat in her room, this same day after

the detectives had given their report, a tired look in her
eyes, the first set lines her pretty mouth had ever known
showing about it, her past and her future whirling painfully and nebulously in her brain. Suddenly she got up,
and seeing Cowperwood's picture on her dresser, his still-
impressive eyes contemplating her, she seized it and threw
it on the floor, stamping on his handsome face with her
pretty foot, and raging at him in her heart. The dog! The
brute! Her brain was full of the thought of Rita's white arms
about him, of his lips to hers. The spectacle of Rita's
fluffy gowns, her enticing costumes, was in her eyes. Rita
should not have him; she should not have anything connected with him, nor, for that matter, Antoinette Nowak,
either—the wretched upstart, the hireling. To think he
should stoop to an office stenographer! Once on that
thought, she decided that he should not be allowed to have
a woman as an assistant any more. He owed it to her to love
her after all she had done for him, the coward, and to let
other women alone. Her brain whirled with strange thoughts.
She was really not sane in her present state. She was so
wrought up by her prospective loss that she could only
think of rash, impossible, destructive things to do. She
dressed swiftly, feverishly, and calling a closed carriage
from the coach house, ordered herself to be driven to the
New Arts Building. She would show this rosy cat of a
woman, this smiling piece of impertinence, this she-devil,
whether she would lure Cowperwood away. She meditated
as she rode. She would not sit back and be robbed as Mrs.
Cowperwood had been by her. Never! He could not treat
her that way. She would die first! She would kill Rita Sohlberg and Antoinette Nowak and Cowperwood and herself
first. She would prefer to die that way rather than lose his
love. Oh yes, a thousand times!

Fortunately, Rita Sohlberg was not at the New Arts
Building, or Sohlberg, either. They had gone to a reception. Nor was she at the apartment on the North Side, where,
under the name of Jacobs, as Aileen had been informed by
the detectives, she and Cowperwood kept occasional tryst.
Aileen hesitated for a moment, feeling it useless to wait;
then she ordered the coachman to drive her to her husband's
office. It was now nearly five o'clock. Antoinette and Cowperwood had both gone, but she did not know it. She
changed her mind, however, before she reached the office

—for it was Rita Sohlberg she wished to reach first—and ordered her coachman to drive back to the Sohlberg studio. But still they had not returned. In a kind of aimless rage she went home, wondering how she should reach Rita Sohlberg first and alone. Then, to her savage delight, the game walked into her bag. The Sohlbergs, returning home at six o'clock from some reception farther out Michigan Avenue, had stopped, at the wish of Harold, merely to pass the time of day with Mrs. Cowperwood. Rita was exquisite in a pale blue and lavender concoction, with silver braid worked in here and there. Her gloves and shoes were pungent bits of romance, her hat a dream of graceful lines. At the sight of her, Aileen, who was still in the hall and had opened the door herself, fairly burned to seize her by the throat and strike her; but she restrained herself sufficiently to say, "Come in." She still had sense enough and self-possession enough to conceal her wrath and to close the door. Beside his wife Harold was standing, offensively smug and inefficient in the fashionable frock coat and silk hat of the time, a restraining influence as yet. He was bowing and smiling.

"Oh." This sound was neither an "oh" nor an "ah," but a kind of Danish inflected "awe," which was usually not unpleasing to hear. "How are you, once more, Meeses Cowperwood? It eez sudge a pleasure to see you again—awe."

"Won't you two just go in the reception room a moment," said Aileen almost hoarsely. "I'll be right in. I want to get something." Then, as an afterthought, she called very sweetly: "Oh, Mrs. Sohlberg, won't you come up to my room for a moment? I have something I want to show you."

Rita responded promptly. She always felt it incumbent upon her to be very nice to Aileen.

"We have only a moment to stay," she replied, archly and sweetly, and coming out in the hall, "but I'll come up."

Aileen stayed to see her go first, then followed upstairs swiftly, surely, entered after Rita, and closed the door. With a courage and rage born of a purely animal despair, she turned and locked it; then she wheeled swiftly, her eyes lit with a savage fire, her cheeks pale, but later aflame, her hands, her fingers, working in a strange, unconscious way.

"So," she said, looking at Rita, and coming toward her quickly and angrily, "you'll steal my husband, will you? You'll live in a secret apartment, will you? You'll come here smiling and lying to me, will you? You beast! You cat! You prostitute! I'll show you now! You towheaded beast! I know you now for what you are! I'll teach you once for all! Take that, and that, and that!"

Suiting action to word, Aileen had descended upon her in a whirlwind, animal fashion, striking, scratching, choking, tearing her visitor's hat from her head, ripping the laces from her neck, beating her in the face, and clutching violently at her hair and throat to choke and mar her beauty if she could. For the moment she was really crazy with rage.

By the suddenness of this onslaught Rita Sohlberg was taken back completely. It all came so swiftly, so terribly, she scarcely realized what was happening before the storm was upon her. There was no time for arguments, pleas, anything. Terrified, shamed, nonplussed, she went down quite limply under this almost lightning attack. When Aileen began to strike her she attempted in vain to defend herself, uttering at the same time piercing screams which could be heard throughout the house. She screamed shrilly, strangely, like a wild dying animal. On the instant all her fine civilized poise had deserted her. From the sweetness and delicacy of the reception atmosphere—the polite cooings, posturings, and mouthings so charming to contemplate, so alluring in her —she had dropped on the instant to that native animal condition that shows itself in fear. Her eyes had a look of hunted horror, her lips and cheeks were pale and drawn. She retreated in a staggering, ungraceful way; she writhed and squirmed, screaming in the strong clutch of the irate and vigorous Aileen.

Cowperwood entered the hall below just before the screams began. He had followed the Sohlbergs almost immediately from his office, and chancing to glance in the reception room, he had observed Sohlberg smiling, radiant, an intangible air of self-ingratiating, social, and artistic sycophancy about him, his long black frock coat buttoned smoothly around his body, his silk hat still in his hands.

"Awe, how do you do, Meezter Cowperwood," he was beginning to say, his curly head shaking in a friendly manner, "I'm soa glad to see you again," when—but who can imitate a scream of terror? We have no words, no symbols even, for those essential sounds of fright and agony. They filled the hall, the library, the reception room, the distant kitchen, even, and basement with a kind of vibrant terror.

Cowperwood, always the man of action as opposed to nervous cogitation, braced up on the instant like taut wire. What, for heaven's sake, could that be? What a terrible cry! Sohlberg the artist, responding like a chameleon to the various emotional complexions of life, began to breathe stertorously, to blanch, to lose control of himself.

"My God!" he exclaimed, throwing up his hands, "that's Rita! She's upstairs in your wife's room! Something must have happened. Oh—" On the instant he was quite beside himself, terrified, shaking, almost useless. Cowperwood, on the contrary, without a moment's hesitation had thrown his coat to the floor, dashed up the stairs, followed by Sohlberg. What could it be? Where was Aileen? As he bounded upward a clear sense of something untoward came over him; it was sickening, terrifying. Scream! Scream! Scream! came the sounds. "Oh, my God! don't kill me! Help! Help!" Scream—this last a long, terrified, ear-piercing wail.

Sohlberg was about to drop from heart failure, he was so frightened. His face was an ashen gray. Cowperwood seized the doorknob vigorously, and finding the door locked, shook, rattled, and banged at it.

"Aileen!" he called sharply. "Aileen! What's the matter in there? Open this door, Aileen!"

"Oh, my God! Oh, help! help! Oh, mercy—o-o-o-o-oh!"

It was the moaning voice of Rita.

"I'll show you, you she-devil!" he heard Aileen calling. "I'll teach you, you beast! You cat, you prostitute! There! there! there!"

"Aileen!" he called hoarsely. "Aileen!" Then, getting no response, and the screams continuing, he turned angrily.

"Stand back!" he exclaimed to Sohlberg, who was moaning helplessly. "Get me a chair, get me a table—anything." The butler ran to obey, but before he could return Cowperwood had found an implement. "Here!" he said, seizing a long, thin, heavily carved and heavily wrought oak chair which stood at the head of the stairs on the landing. He whirled it vigorously over his head. Smash! The sound rose louder than the screams inside.

Smash! The chair creaked and almost broke, but the door did not give.

Smash! The chair broke and the door flew open. He had knocked the lock loose and had leaped in to where Aileen, kneeling over Rita on the floor, was choking and beating her into insensibility. Like an animal he was upon her.

"Aileen," he shouted fiercely, in a hoarse, ugly, guttural voice, "you fool! You idiot—let go! What the devil's the matter with you? What are you trying to do? Have you lost your mind?—you crazy idiot!"

He seized her strong hands and ripped them apart. He fairly dragged her back, half twisting and half throwing her over his knee, loosing her clutching hold. She was so insanely furious that she still struggled and cried, saying: "Let me at her! Let me at her! I'll teach her! Don't you try to hold me, you dog! I'll show you, too, you brute—oh—"

"Pick up that woman," called Cowperwood firmly to Sohlberg and the butler, who had entered. "Get her out of here, quick! My wife has gone crazy. Get her out of here, I tell you! This woman doesn't know what she's doing. Take her out and get a doctor. What sort of a hell's melee is this, anyway?"

"Oh," moaned Rita, who was torn and fainting, almost unconscious from sheer terror.

"I'll kill her!" screamed Aileen. "I'll murder her! I'll murder you, too, you dog! Oh"—she began striking at him—"I'll teach you how to run around with other women, you dog, you brute!"

Cowperwood merely gripped her hands and shook her vigorously, forcefully.

"What the devil has got into you, anyway, you fool!" he said to her bitterly, as they carried Rita out. "What are you trying to do, anyway—murder her? Do you want the police to come in here? Stop your screaming and behave yourself, or I'll shove a handkerchief in your mouth! Stop, I tell you! Stop! Do you hear me? This is enough, you fool!" He clapped his hand over her mouth, pressing it tight and forcing her back against him. He shook her brutally, angrily. He was very strong. "Now will you stop," he insisted, "or do you want me to choke you quiet? I will, if you don't. You're out of your mind. Stop, I tell you! So this is the way you carry on when things don't go to suit you?" She was sobbing, struggling, moaning, half screaming, quite beside herself.

"Oh, you crazy fool!" he said, swinging her round, and with an effort getting out a handkerchief, which he forced over her face and in her mouth. "There," he said, relievedly, "now will you shut up?" Holding her tight in an iron grip, he let her struggle and turn, quite ready to put an end to her breathing if necessary.

Now that he had conquered her, he continued to hold her tightly, stooping beside her on one knee, listening and meditating. Hers was surely a terrible passion. From some points of view he could not blame her. Great was her provocation, great her love. He knew her disposition well enough to have anticipated something of this sort. Yet the wretchedness, shame, scandal of the terrible affair upset his customary equilibrium. To think anyone should give away to such a storm as this! To think that Aileen should do it! To think that Rita should have been so mistreated! It was not at all unlikely that she was seriously injured, marred for life— possibly even killed. The horror of that! The ensuing storm of public rage! A trial! His whole career gone up in one terrific explosion of woe, anger, death! Great God!

He called the butler to him by a nod of his head when the latter, who had gone out with Rita, hurried back.

"How is she?" he asked desperately. "Seriously hurt?"

"No, sir; I think not. I believe she's just fainted. She'll be all right in a little while, sir. Can I be of any service, sir?"

Ordinarily Cowperwood would have smiled at such a scene. Now he was cold sober.

"Not now," he replied with a sigh of relief, still holding Aileen firmly. "Go out and close the door. Call a doctor. Wait in the hall. When he comes, call me."

Aileen, conscious of things being done for Rita, of sympathy being extended to her, tried to get up, to scream again; but she couldn't; her lord and master held her in an ugly hold. When the door was closed he said again: "Now, Aileen, will you hush? Will you let me get up and talk to you, or must we stay here all night? Do you want me to drop you forever after tonight? I understand all about this, but I am in control now, and I am going to stay so. You will come to your senses and be reasonable, or I will leave you tomorrow as sure as I am here." His voice rang convincingly. "Now, shall we talk sensibly, or will you go on making a fool of yourself—disgracing me, disgracing the house, making yourself and myself the laughingstock of

the servants, the neighborhood, the city? This is a fine
showing you've made today. Good God! A fine showing,
indeed! A brawl in this house, a fight! I thought you had
better sense—more self-respect—really I did. You have
seriously jeopardized my chances here in Chicago. You have
seriously injured and possibly killed a woman. You could
even be hanged for that. Do you hear me?"

"Oh, let them hang me," groaned Aileen. "I want to die."

He took away his hand from her mouth, loosened his
grip upon her arms, and let her get to her feet. She was
still torrential, impetuous, ready to upbraid him, but once
standing she was confronted by him, cold, commanding, fixing her with a fishy eye. He wore a look now she had never
seen on his face before—a hard, wintry, dynamic flare,
which no one but his commercial enemies, and only those occasionally, had seen.

"Now stop!" he exclaimed. "Not one more word! Not one!
Do you hear me?"

She wavered, quailed, gave way. All the fury of her
tempestuous soul fell, as the sea falls under a lapse of wind.
She had had it in heart, on her lips, to cry again, "You
dog! you brute!" and a hundred other terrible, useless things,
but somehow, under the pressure of his gaze, the hardness
of his heart, the words on her lips died away. She
looked at him uncertainly for a moment; then, turning, she
threw herself on the bed nearby, clutched her cheeks and
rocking back and forth in an agony of woe, she began to sob:

"Oh, my God! my God! My heart! My life! I want to
die! I want to die!"

Standing there watching her, there suddenly came to
Cowperwood a keen sense of her soul hurt, her heart hurt,
and he was moved.

"Aileen," he said after a moment or two, coming over
and touching her quite gently, "Aileen! Don't cry so. I
haven't left you yet. Your life isn't utterly ruined. Don't
cry. This is bad business, but perhaps it is not without
remedy. Come now, pull yourself together, Aileen!"

For answer she merely rocked and moaned, uncontrolled
and uncontrollable.

Being anxious about conditions elsewhere, he turned and
stepped out into the hall. He must make some show for the
benefit of the doctor and the servants; he must look after

Rita, and offer some sort of passing explanation to Sohlberg.

"Here," he called to a passing servant, "shut that door and watch it. If Mrs. Cowperwood comes out call me instantly."

CHAPTER XIX

"Hell Hath No Fury—"

Rita was not dead by any means—only seriously bruised, scratched, and choked. Her scalp was cut in one place. Aileen had repeatedly beaten her head on the floor, and this might have resulted seriously if Cowperwood had not entered as quickly as he had. Sohlberg, for the moment—for some little time, in fact—was under the impression that Aileen had truly lost her mind, had suddenly gone crazy, and that those shameless charges he had heard her making were the emanations of a disordered brain. Nevertheless, the things she had said haunted him. He was in a bad state himself—almost a subject for the doctor. His lips were bluish, his cheeks blanched. Rita had been carried into an adjoining bedroom and laid upon a bed; cold water, ointments, a bottle of arnica had been procured; and when Cowperwood appeared she was conscious and somewhat better. But she was still very weak and smarting from her wounds, both mental and physical. When the doctor arrived he had been told that a lady, a guest, had fallen downstairs; when Cowperwood came in the physician was dressing her wounds.

As soon as he had gone Cowperwood said to the maid in attendance, "Go get me some hot water." As the latter disappeared he bent over and kissed Rita's bruised lips, putting his finger to his own in warning sign.

"Rita," he asked, softly, "are you fully conscious?"

She nodded weakly.

"Listen, then," he said, bending over and speaking slowly. "Listen carefully. Pay strict attention to what I'm saying.

You must understand every word, and do as I tell you. You are not seriously injured. You will be all right. This will blow over. I have sent for another doctor to call on you at your studio. Your husband has gone for some fresh clothes. He will come back in a little while. My carriage will take you home when you are a little stronger. You mustn't worry. Everything will be all right, but you must deny everything, do you hear? Everything! Insofar as you know, Mrs. Cowperwood is insane. I will talk to your husband tomorrow. I will send you a trained nurse. Meantime, you must be careful of what you say and how you say it. Be perfectly calm. Don't worry. You are perfectly safe here, and you will be there. Mrs. Cowperwood will not trouble you anymore. I will see to that. I am so sorry; but I love you. I am near you all the while. You must not let this make any difference. You will not see her anymore."

Still he knew that it would make a difference.

Reassured as to Rita's condition, he went back to Aileen's room to plead with her again—to soothe her if he could. He found her up and dressing, a new thought and determination in her mind. Since she had thrown herself on the bed sobbing and groaning, her mood had gradually changed; she began to reason that if she could not dominate him, could not make him properly sorry, she had better leave. It was evident, she thought, that he did not love her anymore, seeing that his anxiety to protect Rita had been so great, his brutality in restraining her so marked; and yet she did not want to believe that this was so. He had been so wonderful to her in times past. She had not given up all hope of winning a victory over him and these other women—she loved him too much—but only a separation would do it. That might bring him to his senses. She would get up, dress, and go downtown to a hotel. He should not see her anymore unless he followed her. She was satisfied that she had broken up the liaison with Rita Sohlberg, anyway for the present, and as for Antoinette Nowak, she would attend to her later. Her brain and her heart ached. She was so full of woe and rage, alternating, that she could not cry any more now. She stood before her mirror, trying with trembling fingers to do over her toilet and adjust a street costume. Cowperwood was disturbed, nonplussed, at this unexpected sight.

"Aileen," he said finally, coming up behind her, "can't

you and I talk this thing over peacefully now? You don't
want to do anything that you'll be sorry for. I don't want
you to. I'm sorry. You don't really believe that I've ceased
to love you, do you? I haven't, you know. This thing isn't
as bad as it looks. I should think you would have a little
more sympathy with me after all we have been through together. You haven't any real evidence of wrongdoing on
which to base any such outburst as this."

"Oh, haven't I?" she exclaimed, turning from the mirror,
where, sorrowfully and bitterly, she was smoothing her red-
gold hair. Her cheeks were flushed, her eyes red. Just now
she seemed as remarkable to him as she had seemed that
first day, years ago, when in a red cape he had seen her, a
girl of sixteen, running up the steps of her father's house in
Philadelphia. She was so wonderful then. It mellowed his
mood toward her.

"That's all you know about it, you liar!" she declared.
"It's little you know what I know. I haven't had detectives
on your trail for weeks for nothing. You sneak! You'd like
to smooth around now and find out what I know. Well, I
know enough, let me tell you that. You won't fool me any
longer with your Rita Sohlbergs and your Antoinette Nowaks
and your apartments and your houses of assignation. I know
what you are, you brute! And after all your protestations of
love for me! Ugh!"

She turned fiercely to her task while Cowperwood stared
at her, touched by her passion, moved by her force. It was
fine to see what a dramatic animal she was—really worthy
of him in many ways.

"Aileen," he said softly, hoping still to ingratiate himself
by degrees, "please don't be so bitter toward me. Haven't
you any understanding of how life works—any sympathy
with it? I thought you were more generous, more tender.
I'm not so bad."

He eyed her thoughtfully, tenderly, hoping to move her
through her love for him.

"Sympathy! Sympathy!" She turned on him, blazing. "A
lot you know about sympathy! I suppose I didn't give you
any sympathy when you were in the penitentiary in Philadelphia, did I? A lot of good it did me—didn't it? Sympathy! Bah! To have you come out here to Chicago and
take up with a lot of prostitutes—cheap stenographers and
wives of musicians! You have given me a lot of sympathy,

haven't you?—with that woman lying in the next room to prove it!"

She smoothed her lithe waist and shook her shoulders, preparatory to putting on a hat and adjusting her wrap. She proposed to go just as she was, and send Fadette back for all her belongings.

"Aileen," he pleaded, determined to have his way, "I think you're very foolish. Really I do. There is no occasion for all this—none in the world. Here you are talking at the top of your voice, scandalizing the whole neighborhood, fighting, leaving the house. It's abominable. I don't want you to do it. You love me yet, don't you? You know you do. I know you don't mean all you say. You can't. You really don't believe that I have ceased to love you, do you, Aileen?"

"Love!" fired Aileen. "A lot you know about love! A lot you have ever loved anybody, you brute! I know how you love. I thought you loved me once. Humph! I see how you loved me—just as you've loved fifty other women, as you love that snippy little Rita Sohlberg in the next room—the cat!—the dirty little beast!—the way you love Antoinette Nowak—a cheap stenographer! Bah! You don't know what the word means." And yet her voice trailed off into a kind of sob and her eyes filled with tears, hot, angry, aching. Cowperwood saw them and came over, hoping in some way to take advantage of them. He was truly sorry now—anxious to make her feel tender toward him once more.

"Aileen," he pleaded, "please don't be so bitter. You shouldn't be so hard on me. I'm not so bad. Aren't you going to be reasonable?" He put out a smoothing hand, but she jumped away.

"Don't you touch me, you brute!" she exclaimed angrily. "Don't you lay a hand on me. I don't want you to come near me. I'll not live with you. I'll not stay in the same house with you and your mistresses. Go and live with your dear, darling Rita on the North Side if you want to. I don't care. I suppose you've been in the next room comforting her—the beast! I wish I had killed her—Oh, God!" She tore at her throat in a violent rage, trying to adjust a button.

Cowperwood was literally astonished. Never had he seen such an outburst as this. He had not believed Aileen to be capable of it. He could not help admiring her. Nevertheless, he resented the brutality of her assault on Rita and on his own promiscuous tendency, and this feeling vented itself in one last unfortunate remark.

"I wouldn't be so hard on mistresses if I were you, Aileen," he ventured pleadingly. "I should have thought your own experience would have—"

He paused, for he saw on the instant that he was making a grave mistake. This reference to her past as a mistress was crucial. On the instant she straightened up, and her eyes filled with a great pain. "So that's the way you talk to me, is it?" she asked. "I knew it! I knew it! I knew it would come!"

She turned to a tall chest of drawers as high as her breasts, laden with silverware, jewel boxes, brushes and combs, and putting her arms down, she laid her head upon them and began to cry. This was the last straw. He was throwing up her lawless girlhood love to her as an offense.

"Oh!" she sobbed, and shook in a hopeless, wretched paroxysm.

Cowperwood came over quickly. He was distressed, pained. "I didn't mean that, Aileen," he explained. "I didn't mean it in that way—not at all. You rather drew that out of me; but I didn't mean it as a reproach. You were my mistress, but good Lord, I never loved you any the less for that—rather more. You know I did. I want you to believe that; it's true. These other matters haven't been so important to me—they really haven't—"

He looked at her helplessly as she moved away to avoid him; he was distressed, nonplussed, immensely sorry. As he walked to the center of the room again she suddenly suffered a great revulsion of feeling, but only in the direction of more wrath. This was too much.

"So this is the way you talk to me," she exclaimed, "after all I have done for you! You say that to me after I waited for you and cried over you when you were in prison for nearly two years? Your mistress! That's my reward, is it? Oh!"

Suddenly she observed her jewel case, and resenting all the gifts he had given her in Philadelphia, in Paris, in Rome, here in Chicago, she suddenly threw open the lid, and grabbing the contents by handfuls, began to toss them toward him—to actually throw them in his face. Out they came, handfuls of gauds that he had given her in real affection: a jade necklace and bracelet of pale apple-green set in spun gold, with clasps of white ivory; a necklace of pearls, assorted as to size and matched in color, that shone with a tinted, pearly flame in the evening light; a handful of rings and brooches, diamonds, rubies, opals, amethysts; a dog collar of emeralds, and a diamond hair ornament. She flung them at him excitedly, strewing the floor, striking him on the neck, the face, the hands. "Take that! and that! and that! There they are! I don't want anything more of yours. I don't want anything more to do with you. I don't want anything that belongs to you. Thank God, I have money enough of my own to live on! I hate you—I despise you—I never want to see you anymore. Oh—" And trying to think of something more, but failing, she dashed swiftly down the hall and down the stairs, while he stood for just one moment overwhelmed. Then he hurried after.

"Aileen!" he called. "Aileen, come back here! Don't go, Aileen!" But she only hurried faster; she opened and closed the door and actually ran out in the dark, her eyes wet, her heart bursting. So this was the end of that youthful dream that had begun so beautifully. She was no better than the others—just one of his mistresses. To have her past thrown up to her as a defense for the others! To be told that she was no better than they! This was the last straw. She choked and sobbed as she walked, vowing never to return, never to see him anymore. But as she did so Cowperwood came running after, determined for once, as lawless as he was, that this should not be the end of it all. She had loved him, he reflected. She had laid every gift of passion and affection on the altar of her love. It wasn't fair, really. She must be made to stay. He caught up at last, reaching her under the dark of the November trees.

"Aileen," he said, laying hold of her and putting his arms around her waist. "Aileen, dearest, this is plain madness. It is insanity. You're not in your right mind. Don't go! Don't leave me! I love you! Don't you know I do? Can't you really see that? Don't run away like this, and don't cry. I do love you, and you know it. I always shall. Come back now. Kiss me. I'll do better. Really I will. Give me another chance. Wait and see. Come now—won't you? That's my girl, my Aileen. Do come. Please!"

She pulled on, but he held her, smoothing her arms, her neck, her face.

"Aileen!" he entreated.

She tugged so that he was finally compelled to work her about into his arms; then, sobbing, she stood there agonized but happy once more, in a way.

"But I don't want to," she protested. "You don't love me anymore. Let me go."

But he kept hold of her, urging, and finally she said, her head upon his shoulder as of old, "Don't make me come back tonight. I don't want to. I can't. Let me go downtown. I'll come back later, maybe."

"Then I'll go with you," he said endearingly. "It isn't right. There are a lot of things I should be doing to stop this scandal, but I'll go."

And together they sought a streetcar.

CHAPTER XX

"Man and Superman"

It is a sad commentary on all save the most chemic unions—those dark red flowers of romance that bloom most often only for a tragic end—that they cannot endure the storms of disaster that are wont to overtake them. A woman like Rita Sohlberg, with a seemingly urgent feeling for Cowperwood, was yet not so charmed by him but that this shock to her pride was a marked sedative. The crushing weight of such an exposure as this, the Homeric laughter inherent, if not indicated in the faulty planning, the failure to take into account beforehand all the possibilities which might lead to such a disaster, were too much for her to endure. She was stung almost to desperation, maddened, at the thought of the gay, idle way in which she had walked into Mrs. Cowperwood's clutches and been made into a spectacle and a laughingstock by her. What a brute she was— what a demon! Her own physical weakness under the circumstances was no grief to her—rather a salve to her superior disposition; but just the same she had been badly beaten, her beauty turned into a ragamuffin show, and that was enough. This evening, in the Lake Shore Sanitarium, where she had been taken, she had but one thought—to get away when it should all be over and rest her wearied brain. She did not want to see Sohlberg anymore; she did not want to see Cowperwood anymore. Already Harold, suspicious and determined to get at the truth, was beginning to question her as to the strangeness of Aileen's attack—her probable reason. When Cowperwood was announced, Sohlberg's manner modified somewhat, for whatever his suspicions were, he was not prepared to quarrel with this singular man as yet.

"I am so sorry about this unfortunate business," said Cowperwood, coming in with brisk assurance. "I never knew my wife to become so strangely unbalanced before. It was most fortunate that I arrived when I did. I certainly owe you both every amend that can be made. I sincerely hope, Mrs. Sohlberg, that you are not seriously injured. If there is anything I can possibly do—anything either of you can suggest"—he looked around solicitously at Sohlberg—"I shall only be too glad to do it. How would it do for you to take Mrs. Sohlberg away for a little while for a rest? I shall so gladly pay all expenses in connection with her recovery."

Sohlberg, brooding and heavy, remained unresponsive, smoldering; Rita, cheered by Cowperwood's presence, but not wholly relieved by any means, was questioning and disturbed. She was afraid there was to be a terrific scene between them. She declared she was better and would be all right—that she did not need to go away, but that she preferred to be alone.

"It's very strange," said Sohlberg sullenly, after a little while. "I daunt onderstand it! I daunt onderstand it at all. Why should she do soach a thing? Why should she say soach things? Here we have been the best of friends opp to now. Then suddenly she attacks my wife and sais all these strange things."

"But I have assured you, my dear Mr. Sohlberg, that my wife was not in her right mind. She has been subject to spells of this kind in the past, though never to anything so violent as this tonight. Already she has recovered her normal state, and she does not remember. But, perhaps, if we are going to discuss things now we had better go out in the hall. Your wife will need all the rest she can get."

Once outside, Cowperwood continued with brilliant assurance: "Now, my dear Sohlberg, what is it I can say? What is it you wish me to do? My wife has made a lot of groundless charges, to say nothing of injuring your wife most seriously and shamefully. I cannot tell you, as I have said, how sorry I am. I assure you Mrs. Cowperwood is suffering from a gross illusion. There is absolutely nothing to do, nothing to say, so far as I can see, but to let the whole matter drop. Don't you agree with me?"

Harold was twisting mentally in the coils of a trying situation. His own position, as he knew, was not formidable. Rita had reproached him over and over for infidelity. He began to swell and bluster at once.

"That is all very well for you to say, Mr. Cowperwood," he commented defiantly, "but how about me? Where do I come in? I daunt know what to theenk yet. It ees very strange. Supposing what your wife sais was true? Supposing my wife has been going around weeth *someone?* That ees what I want to find out. Eef she has! Eef eet is what I theenk it ees I shall—I shall—I daunt know what I shall do. I am a very violent man."

Cowperwood almost smiled, concerned as he was over avoiding publicity; he had no fear of Sohlberg physically.

"See here," he exclaimed suddenly, looking sharply at the musician and deciding to take the bull by the horns, "you are in quite as delicate a situation as I am, if you only stop to think. This affair, if it gets out, will involve not only me and Mrs. Cowperwood, but yourself and your wife, and if I am not mistaken, I think your own affairs are not in any too good shape. You cannot blacken your wife without blackening yourself—that is inevitable. None of us is exactly perfect. For myself I shall be compelled to prove insanity, and I can do this easily. If there is anything in your past which is not precisely what it should be, it could not long be kept a secret. If you are willing to let the matter drop I will make handsome provision for you both; if, instead, you choose to make trouble, to force this matter into the daylight, I shall leave no stone unturned to protect myself, to put as good a face on this matter as I can."

"What!" exclaimed Sohlberg. "You threaten me? You try to frighten me after your wife charges that you have been running around weeth my wife? You talk about my past! I like that. Haw! We shall see about dis! What is it you knaw about me?"

"Well, Mr. Sohlberg," rejoined Cowperwood calmly, "I know, for instance, that for a long while your wife has not loved you, that you have been living on her as any pensioner might, that you have been running around with as many as six or seven women in as many years or less. For months I have been acting as your wife's financial adviser, and in that time, with the aid of detectives, I have learned of Anna Stelmak, Jessie Laska, Bertha Reese, Georgia Du Coin—do I need to say anymore? As a matter of fact, I have a number of your letters in my possession."

"Saw that ees it!" exclaimed Sohlberg, while Cowperwood eyed him fixedly. "You have been running around weeth my wife? Eet ees true, then. A fine situation! And you come here now weeth these threats, these lies to booldoze me. Haw! We weel see about them. We weel see what I can do. Wait teel I can consult a lawyer first. Then we weel see!"

Cowperwood surveyed him coldly, angrily. "What an ass!" he thought.

"See here," he said, urging Sohlberg, for privacy's sake, to come down into the lower hall, and then into the street before the sanitarium, where two gas lamps were fluttering fitfully in the dark and wind, "I see very plainly that you are bent on making trouble. It is not enough that I have assured you that there is nothing in this—that I have given you my word. You insist on going further. Very well, then. Supposing for argument's sake that Mrs. Cowperwood was not insane; that every word she said was true; that I had been misconducting myself with your wife? What of it? What will you do?"

He looked at Sohlberg smoothly, ironically, while the latter flared up.

"Haw!" he shouted melodramatically. "Why, I would keel you, that's what I would do. I would keel her. I weel make a terrible scene. Just let me knaw that this is so, and then see!"

"Exactly," replied Cowperwood grimly. "I thought so. I believe you. For that reason I have come prepared to serve you in just the way you wish." He reached in his coat and took out two small revolvers, which he had taken from a drawer at home for this very purpose. They gleamed in the dark. "Do you see these?" he continued. "I am going to save you the trouble of further investigation, Mr. Sohlberg. Every word that Mrs. Cowperwood said tonight—and I am saying this with a full understanding of what this means to you and to me—is true. She is no more insane than I am. Your wife has been living in an apartment with me on the North Side for months, though you cannot prove that. She does not love you, but me. Now if you want to kill me here is a gun." He extended his hand. "Take your choice. If I am to die you might as well die with me."

He said it so coolly, so firmly, that Sohlberg, who was an innate coward, and who had no more desire to die than any other healthy animal, paled. The look of cold steel was too much. The hand that pressed them on him was hard and firm. He took hold of one, but his fingers trembled. The steely, metallic voice in his ear was undermining the little courage that he had. Cowperwood by now had taken on the proportions of a dangerous man—the lineaments of a demon. He turned away, mortally terrified.

"My God!" he exclaimed, shaking like a leaf. "You want to keel me, do you? I weel not have anything to do with you! I weel not talk to you! I weel see my lawyer. I weel talk to my wife first."

"Oh no you won't," replied Cowperwood, intercepting him as he turned to go and seizing him firmly by the arm. "I am not going to have you do anything of the sort. I am not going to kill you if you are not going to kill me; but I am going to make you listen to reason for once. Now, here is what else I have to say, and then I am through. I am not unfriendly to you. I want to do you a good turn, little as I care for you. To begin with, there is nothing in those charges my wife made, not a thing. I merely said what I did just now to see if you were in earnest. You do not love your wife anymore. She doesn't love you. You are no good to her. Now, I have a very friendly proposition to make to you. If you want to leave Chicago and stay away three years or more, I will see that you are paid five thousand dollars every year on January first—on the nail—five thousand dollars! Do you hear? Or you can stay here in Chicago and hold your tongue and I will make it three thousand—monthly or yearly, just as you please. But—and this is what I want you to remember—if you don't get out of town or hold your tongue, if you make one single rash move against me, I will kill you, and I will kill you on sight. Now, I want you to go away from here and behave yourself. Leave your wife alone. Come and see me in a day or two—the money is ready for you any time."

He paused while Sohlberg stared—his eyes round and glassy. This was the most astonishing experience of his life. This man was either devil or prince, or both. "Good God!" he thought. "He will do that, too. He will really kill me." Then the astounding alternative—five thousand dollars a year—came to his mind. Well, why not? His silence gave consent.

"If I were you I wouldn't go upstairs again tonight," continued Cowperwood sternly. "Don't disturb her. She needs rest. Go on downtown and come and see me tomorrow—or if you want to go back I will go with you. I want to say to Mrs. Sohlberg what I have said to you. But remember what I've told you."

"Nau, thank you," replied Sohlberg feebly. "I will go downtown. Good night." And he hurried away.

"I'm sorry," said Cowperwood to himself defensively. "It is too bad, but it was the only way."

CHAPTER XXI

A Matter of Tunnels

The question of Sohlberg adjusted thus simply, if brutally, Cowperwood turned his attention to Mrs. Sohlberg. But there was nothing much to be done. He explained that he had now completely subdued Aileen and Sohlberg, that the latter would make no more trouble, that he was going to pension him, that Aileen would remain permanently quiescent. He expressed the greatest solicitude for her, but Rita was now sickened of this tangle. She had loved him, as she thought, but through the rage of Aileen she saw him in a different light, and she wanted to get away. His money, plentiful as it was, did not mean as much to her as it might have meant to some women; it simply spelled luxuries, without which she could exist if she must. His charm for her had, perhaps, consisted mostly in the atmosphere of flawless security which seemed to surround him—a glittering bubble of romance. That, by one fell attack, was now burst. He was seen to be quite as other men, subject to the same storms, the same danger of shipwreck. Only he was a better sailor than most. She recuperated gradually; left for home; left for Europe; details too long to be narrated. Sohlberg, after much meditating and fuming, finally accepted the offer of Cowperwood and returned to Denmark. Aileen, after a few days of quarreling in which he agreed to dispense with Antoinette Nowak, returned home.

Cowperwood was in no wise pleased by this rough denouement. Aileen had not raised her own attractions in his estimation, and yet, strange to relate, he was not unsympathetic with her. He had no desire to desert her as yet, though for some time he had been growing in the feeling that Rita would have been a much better type of wife for him. But what he could not have, he could not have. He turned his attention with renewed force to his business; but it was with many a backward glance at those radiant hours when, with Rita in his presence or enfolded by his arms, he had seen life from a new and poetic angle. She was so charming, so naive—but what could he do?

For several years thereafter Cowperwood was busy following the Chicago street-railway situation with increasing interest. He knew it was useless to brood over Rita Sohlberg—she would not return—and yet he could not help it; but he could work hard, and that was something. His natural aptitude and affection for street-railway work had long since been demonstrated, and it was now making him restless. One might have said of him quite truly that the tinkle of car bells and the plop of plodding horses' feet was in his blood. He surveyed these extending lines, with their jingling cars, as he went about the city, with an almost hungry eye. Chicago was growing fast, and these little horsecars on certain streets were crowded night and morning—fairly bulging with people at the rush hours. If he could only secure an octopus-grip on one or all of them; if he could combine and control them all! What a fortune! That, if nothing else, might salve him for some of his woes—a tremendous fortune—nothing less. He forever busied himself with various aspects of the scene quite as a poet might have concerned himself with rocks and rills. To own these street-railways! To own these street-railways! So rang the song of his mind.

Like the gas situation, the Chicago street-railway situation was divided into three parts—three companies representing and corresponding with the three different sides or divisions of the city. The Chicago City Railway Company, occupying the South Side and extending as far south as Thirty-ninth Street, had been organized in 1859, and represented in itself a mine of wealth. Already it controlled some seventy miles of track, and was annually being added to on Indiana Avenue, on Wabash Avenue, on State Street, and on Archer Avenue. It owned over 150 cars of the old-fashioned, straw-strewn, no-stove type, and over 1,000 horses; it employed 170 conductors, 160 drivers, a hundred stablemen, and black-smiths, harness-makers, and repairers in interesting numbers. Its snowplows were busy on the street in winter, its sprinkling cars in summer. Cowperwood calculated its shares, bonds, rolling stock, and other physical properties as totaling in the vicinity of over 2 million dollars. The trouble with this company was that its outstanding stock was principally controlled by Norman Schryhart, who was now decidedly inimical to Cowperwood or anything he might wish to do, and by Anson Merrill, who had never manifested any signs of friendship. He did not see how he was to get control of this property. Its shares were selling around $250.

The North Chicago City Railway was a corporation which had been organized at the same time as the South Side company, but by a different group of men. Its management was old, indifferent, and incompetent, its equipment about the same. The Chicago West Division Railway had originally been owned by the Chicago City or South Side Railway, but was now a separate corporation. It was not yet so profitable as the other divisions of the city, but all sections of the city were growing. The horse bell was heard everywhere tinkling gaily.

Standing on the outside of this scene, contemplating its promise, Cowperwood, much more than anyone else connected financially with the future of these railways at this time, was impressed with their enormous possibilities—their enormous future if Chicago continued to grow, and was concerned with the various factors which might further or impede their progress.

Not long before he had discovered that one of the chief handicaps to street-railway development, on the North and West Sides, lay in the congestion of traffic at the bridges spanning the Chicago River. Between the street ends that abutted on it and connected the two sides of the city ran this amazing stream—dirty, odorous, picturesque, compact—of a heavy, delightful, constantly crowding and moving boat traffic, which kept the various bridges momentarily turning and tied up the street traffic on either side of the river until it seemed at times as though the tangle of teams and boats would never anymore be straightened out. It was lovely, human, natural, Dickensesque—a fit subject for a Daumier, a Turner, or a Whistler. The idlest of bridge-tenders judged for himself when the boats and when the teams should be made to wait, and how long, while in addition to the regular pedestrians a group of idlers stood at gaze fascinated by the crowd of masts, the crush of wagons, and the picturesque tugs in the foreground below. Cowperwood, as he sat in his light runabout, annoyed by a delay, or dashed swiftly forward to get over before a bridge turned, had long since noted that the streetcar service in the North and West Sides was badly hampered. The unbroken South Side, unthreaded by a river, had no such problem, and was growing rapidly.

Because of this he was naturally interested to observe one day, in the course of his peregrinations, that there existed in two places under the Chicago River—in the first place at La Salle Street, running north and south, and in the second at Washington Street, running east and west—two now soggy and rat-infested tunnels which were never used by anybody—dark, dank, dripping affairs only vaguely lighted with oil lamps, and oozing with water. Upon investigation he learned that they had been built years before to accommodate this same tide of wagon traffic which now congested at the bridges, and which even then had been rapidly rising. Being forced to pay a toll in time to which a slight toll in cash, exacted for the privilege of using a tunnel, had seemed to the investors and public infinitely to be preferred, this traffic had been offered this opportunity of avoiding the delay. However, like many another handsome commercial scheme on paper or bubbling in the human brain, the plan did not work exactly. These tunnels might have proved profitable if they had been properly built with long, low percent grades, wide roadways, and a sufficiency of light and air; but, as a matter of fact, they had not been judiciously adapted to public convenience. Norman Schryhart's father had been an investor in these tunnels, and Anson Merrill. When they had proved unprofitable, after a long period of pointless manipulation—cost, one million dollars—they had been sold to the city for exactly that sum each, it being poetically deemed that a growing city could better afford to lose so disturbing an amount than any of its humble, ambitious, and respectable citizens. That was a little affair by which members of council had profited years before; but that also is another story.

After discovering these tunnels Cowperwood walked through them several times—for though they were now boarded up, there was still an uninterrupted footpath—and wondered why they could not be utilized. It seemed to him that if the streetcar traffic were heavy enough, profitable enough, and these tunnels, for a reasonable sum, could be made into a lower grade, one of the problems which now hampered the growth of the North and West Sides would be obviated. But how? He did not own the tunnels. He did not own the street-railways. The cost of leasing and rebuilding the tunnels would be enormous. Helpers and horses and extra drivers on any grade, however slight, would have to be used, and that meant an extra expense. With streetcar horses as the only means of traction, and with the long, expensive grades, he was not so sure that this venture would be a profitable one.

However, in the fall of 1880, or a little earlier (when he was still very much entangled with the preliminary sex affairs that led eventually to Rita Sohlberg), he became aware of a new system of traction relating to streetcars, which together with the arrival of the arc light, the telephone, and other inventions, seemed destined to change the character of city life entirely.

Recently in San Francisco, where the presence of hills made the movement of crowded street-railway cars exceedingly difficult, a new type of traction had been introduced —that of the cable, which was nothing more than a traveling rope of wire running over guttered wheels in a conduit, and driven by immense engines conveniently located in adjacent stations, or powerhouses. The cars carried a readily manip-

ulated grip lever, or steel hand, which reached down
through a slot into a conduit and gripped the moving cable.
This invention solved the problem of hauling heavily laden
streetcars up and down steep grades. About the same time
he also heard, in a roundabout way, that the Chicago City
Railway, of which Schryhart and Merrill were the principal
owners, was about to introduce this mode of traction on its
lines—to cable State Street, and attach the cars of other lines
running farther out into unprofitable districts as trailers.
At once the solution of the North and West Side problems
flashed upon him—cables.

Outside of the bridge crush and the tunnels above mentioned, there was one other special condition which had
been for some time past attracting Cowperwood's attention.
This was the waning energy of the North Chicago City Railway Company—the lack of foresight on the part of its directors which prevented them from perceiving the proper solution of their difficulties. The road was in a rather unsatisfactory state financially—really open to a coup of some sort.
In the beginning it had been considered unprofitable, so
thinly populated was the territory it served, and so short the
distance from the business heart. Later, however, as the territory filled up, it did better; only then the long waits at
the bridges occurred. The management, feeling that the lines
were likely to be poorly patronized, had put down poor little lightweight rails, and run slimpsy cars which were as
cold as ice in winter and as hot as stove ovens in summer.
No attempt had been made to extend the downtown terminus
of the several lines into the business center—they stopped
just over the river which bordered it at the north. (On the
South Side Mr. Schryhart had done much better for his
patrons. He had already installed a loop for his cable
about Merrill's store.) As on the West Side, straw was strewn
in the bottom of all the cars in winter to keep the feet of the
passengers warm, and but few open cars were used in summer. The directors were averse to introducing them because
of the expense. So they had gone on and on, adding lines
only where they were sure they would make a good profit
from the start, putting down the same style of cheap rail
that had been used in the beginning, and employing the same
antique type of car, which rattled and trembled as it ran
until the patrons were enraged to the point of anarchy.
Only recently, because of various suits and complaints in-

augurated, the company had been greatly annoyed, but they scarcely knew what to do, how to meet the onslaught. Though there was here and there a man of sense—such as Terrence Mulgannon, the general superintendent; Edwin Kaffrath, a director; William Johnson, the constructing engineer of the company—yet such other men as Onias C. Skinner, the president, and Walter Parker, the vice-president, were reactionaries of an elderly character, conservative, meditative, stingy, and worst of all, fearful or without courage for great adventure. It is a sad commentary that age almost invariably takes away the incentive to new achievement and makes "Let well enough alone" the most appealing motto.

Mindful of this, Cowperwood, with a now splendid scheme in his mind, one day invited John J. McKenty over to his house to dinner on a social pretext. When the latter, accompanied by his wife, had arrived, and Aileen had smiled on them both sweetly, and was doing her best to be nice to Mrs. McKenty, Cowperwood remarked:

"McKenty, do you know anything about these two tunnels that the city owns under the river at Washington and La Salle streets?"

"I know that the city took them over when it didn't need them, and that they're no good for anything. That was before my time, though," explained McKenty cautiously. "I think the city paid a million for them. Why?"

"Oh, nothing much," replied Cowperwood, evading the matter for the present. "I was wondering whether they were in such condition that they couldn't be used for anything. I see occasional references in the papers to their uselessness."

"They're in pretty bad shape, I'm afraid," replied McKenty. "I haven't been through either of them in years and years. The idea was originally to let the wagons go through them and break up the crowding at the bridges. But it didn't work. They made the grade too steep and the tolls too high, and so the drivers preferred to wait for the bridges. They were pretty hard on horses. I can testify to that myself. I've driven a wagonload through them more than once. The city should never have taken them over at all by rights. It was a deal. I don't know who all was in it. Carmody was mayor then, and Aldrich was in charge of public works."

He relapsed into silence, and Cowperwood allowed the matter of the tunnels to rest until after dinner when they

had adjourned to the library. There he placed a friendly
hand on McKenty's arm, an act of familiarity which the
politician rather liked.

"You felt pretty well satisfied with the way that gas business came out last year, didn't you?" he inquired.

"I did," replied McKenty warmly. "Never more so. I told
you that at the time." The Irishman liked Cowperwood, and
was grateful for the swift manner in which he had been
made richer by the sum of several hundred thousand dollars.

"Well, now, McKenty," continued Cowperwood abruptly
and with a seeming lack of connection, "has it ever occurred to you that things are shaping up for a big change in
the street-railway situation here? I can see it coming. There's
going to be a new motor power introduced on the South
Side within a year or two. You've heard of it?"

"I read something of it," replied McKenty, surprised and a
little questioning. He took a cigar and prepared to listen.
Cowperwood, never smoking, drew up a chair.

"Well, I'll tell you what that means," he explained. "It
means that eventually every mile of street-railway track in
this city—to say nothing of all the additional miles that will
be built before this change takes place—will have to be done
over on an entirely new basis. I mean this cable-conduit system. These old companies that are hobbling along now with
any old equipment will have to make the change. They'll have
to spend millions and millions before they can bring their
equipment up-to-date. If you've paid any attention to the
matter you must have seen what a condition these North and
West Side lines are in."

"It's pretty bad; I know that," commented McKenty.

"Just so," replied Cowperwood emphatically. "Well, now,
if I know anything about these old managements from studying them, they're going to have a hard time bringing themselves to do this. Two to three million are two to three million, and it isn't going to be an easy matter for them to
raise the money—not as easy, perhaps, as it would be for
some of the rest of us, supposing we wanted to go into the
street-railway business."

"Yes, supposing," replied McKenty jovially. "But how are
you to get in it? There's no stock for sale that I know of."

"Just the same," said Cowperwood, "we can if we want
to, and I'll show you how. But at present there's just one
thing in particular I'd like you to do for me. I want to know

if there is any way that we can get control of either of those two old tunnels that I was talking to you about a little while ago. I'd like both if I might. Do you suppose that is possible?"

"Why, yes," replied McKenty, wondering; "but what have they got to do with it? They're not worth anything. Some of the boys were talking about filling them in some time ago—blowing them up. The police think crooks hide in them."

"Just the same, don't let anyone touch them—don't lease them or anything," replied Cowperwood forcefully. "I'll tell you frankly what I want to do. I want to get control, just as soon as possible, of all the street-railway lines I can on the North and West Sides—new or old franchises. Then you'll see where the tunnels come in."

He paused to see whether McKenty caught the point of all he meant, but the latter failed.

"You don't want much, do you?" he said cheerfully. "But I don't see how you can use the tunnels. However, that's no reason why I shouldn't take care of them for you, if you think that's important."

"It's this way," said Cowperwood thoughtfully. "I'll make you a preferred partner in all the ventures that I control if you do as I suggest. The street-railways, as they stand now, will have to be taken up lock, stock, and barrel and thrown into the scrap heap within eight or nine years at the latest. You see what the South Side company is beginning to do now. When it comes to the West and North Side companies they won't find it so easy. They aren't earning as much as the South Side, and besides they have those bridges to cross. That means a severe inconvenience to a cable line. In the first place, the bridges will have to be rebuilt to stand the extra weight and strain. Now the question arises at once— at whose expense? The city's?"

"That depends on who's asking for it," replied Mr. McKenty amiably.

"Quite so," assented Cowperwood. "In the next place, this river traffic is becoming impossible from the point of view of a decent streetcar service. There are waits now of from eight to fifteen minutes while these tows and vessels get through. Chicago has five hundred thousand population to-day. How much will it have in 1890? In 1900? How will it be when it has eight hundred thousand or a million?"

"You're quite right," interpolated McKenty. "It will be pretty bad."

"Exactly. But what is worse, the cable lines will carry trailers, or single cars, from feeder lines. There won't be single cars waiting at these draws—there will be trains, crowded trains. It won't be advisable to delay a cable train from eight to fifteen minutes while boats are making their way through a draw. The public won't stand for that very long, will it, do you think?"

"Not without making a row, probably," replied McKenty.

"Well, that means what, then?" asked Cowperwood. "Is the traffic going to get any lighter? Is the river going to dry up?"

Mr. McKenty stared. Suddenly his face lighted. "Oh, I see," he said shrewdly. "It's those tunnels you're thinking about. Are they in any shape to be used?"

"They can be made over cheaper than new ones can be built."

"True for you," replied McKenty, "and if they're in any sort of repair they'd be just what you'd want." He was emphatic, almost triumphant. "They belong to the city. They cost pretty near a million apiece, those things."

"I know it," said Cowperwood. "Now, do you see what I'm driving at?"

"Do I see!" smiled McKenty. "That's a real idea you have, Cowperwood. I take off my hat to you. Say what you want."

"Well, then, in the first place," replied Cowperwood genially, "it is agreed that the city won't part with those two tunnels under any circumstances until we can see what can be done about this other matter?"

"It will not."

"In the next place, it is understood, is it, that you won't make it any easier than you can possibly help for the North and West Side companies to get ordinances extending their lines, or anything else, from now on? I shall want to introduce some franchises for feeders and outlying lines myself."

"Bring in your ordinances," replied McKenty, "and I'll do whatever you say. I've worked with you before. I know that you keep your word."

"Thanks," said Cowperwood warmly. "I know the value of keeping it. In the meanwhile I'll go ahead and see what can be done about the other matter. I don't know just how many men I will need to let in on this, or just what form the organization will take. But you may depend upon it that your interests will be properly taken care of, and that whatever is done will be done with your full knowledge and consent."

"All very good," answered McKenty, thinking of the new field of activity before them. A combination between himself and Cowperwood in a matter like this must prove very beneficial to both. And he was satisfied, because of their previous relations, that his own interests would not be neglected.

"Shall we go and see if we can find the ladies?" asked Cowperwood jauntily, laying hold of the politician's arm.

"To be sure," assented McKenty gaily. "It's a fine house you have here—beautiful. And your wife is as pretty a woman as I ever saw, if you'll pardon the familiarity."

"I have always thought she was rather attractive myself," replied Cowperwood innocently.

CHAPTER XXII

Street-railways at Last

Among the directors of the North Chicago City company there was one man, Edwin L. Kaffrath, who was young and of a forward-looking temperament. His father, a former heavy stockholder of this company, had recently died and left all his holdings and practically his directorship to his only son. Young Kaffrath was by no means a practical street-railway man, though he fancied he could do very well at it if given a chance. He was the holder of nearly eight hundred of the five thousand shares of stock; but the rest of it was so divided that he could only exercise a minor influence. Nevertheless, from the day of his entrance into the company—which was months before Cowperwood began seriously to think over the situation—he had been strong for improvements—extensions, more franchises, better cars, better horses, stoves in the cars in winter, and the like, all of which suggestions sounded to his fellow directors like mere manifestations of the reckless impetuosity of youth, and were almost uniformly opposed.

"What's the matter with them cars?" asked Albert Thorsen, one of the elder directors, at one of the meetings at which Kaffrath was present and offering his usual protest. "I don't see anything the matter with 'em. I ride in 'em."

Thorsen was a heavy, dusty, tobacco-bestrewn individual of sixty-six, who was a little dull but genial. He was in the paint business, and always wore a very light steel-gray suit much crinkled in the seat and arms.

"Perhaps that's what's the matter with them, Albert," chirped up Solon Kaempfaert, one of his cronies on the board.

The sally drew a laugh.

"Oh, I don't know. I see the rest of you on board often enough."

"Why, I tell you what's the matter with them," replied Kaffrath. "They're dirty, and they're flimsy, and the windows rattle so you can't hear yourself think. The track is no good, and the filthy straw we keep in them in winter is enough to make a person sick. We don't keep the track in good repair. I don't wonder people complain. I'd complain myself."

"Oh, I don't think things are as bad as all that," put in Onias C. Skinner, the president, who had a face which with its very short side-whiskers was as bland as a Chinese god. He was sixty-eight years of age. "They're not the best cars in the world, but they're good cars. They need painting and varnishing pretty badly, some of them, but outside of that there's many a good year's wear in them yet. I'd be very glad if we could put in new rolling stock, but the item of expense will be considerable. It's these extensions that we have to keep building and the long hauls for five cents which eat up the profits." The so-called long hauls were only two or three miles at the outside, but they seemed long to Mr. Skinner.

"Well, look at the South Side," persisted Kaffrath. "I don't know what you people are thinking of. Here's a cable system introduced in Philadelphia. There's another in San Francisco. Someone has invented a car, as I understand it, that's going to run by electricity, and here we are running cars—barns, I call them—with straw in them. Good Lord, I should think it was about time that some of us took a tumble to ourselves!"

"Oh, I don't know," commented Mr. Skinner. "It seems to me we have done pretty well by the North Side. We have done a good deal."

Directors Solon Kaempfaert, Albert Thorsen, Isaac White, Anthony Ewer, Arnold C. Benjamin, and Otto Matjes, being solemn gentlemen all, merely sat and stared.

The vigorous Kaffrath was not to be so easily repressed, however. He repeated his complaints on other occasions. The fact that there was also considerable complaint in the newspapers from time to time in regard to this same North Side service pleased him in a way. Perhaps this would be the proverbial fire under the terrapin which would cause it to move along.

By this time, owing to Cowperwood's understanding with McKenty, all possibility of the North Side company's securing additional franchises for unoccupied streets, or even the use of the La Salle Street tunnel, had ended. Kaffrath did not know this. Neither did the directors or officers of the company, but it was true. In addition, McKenty, through the aldermen, who were at his beck and call on the North Side, was beginning to stir up additional murmurs and complaints in order to discredit the present management. There was a great to-do in council over a motion on the part of somebody to compel the North Side company to throw out its old cars and lay better and heavier tracks. Curiously, this did not apply so much to the West and South Sides, which were in the same condition. The rank and file of the city, ignorant of the tricks which were constantly being employed in politics to effect one end or another, were greatly cheered by this so-called public uprising. They little knew the pawns they were in the game, or how little sincerity constituted the primal impulse.

Quite by accident, apparently, one day, Addison, thinking of the different men in the North Side company who might be of service to Cowperwood, and having finally picked young Kaffrath as the ideal agent, introduced himself to the latter at the Union League.

"That's a pretty heavy load of expense that's staring

you North and West Side street-railway people in the face,"
he took occasion to observe.

"How's that?" asked Kaffrath curiously, anxious to hear
anything which concerned the development of the business.

"Well, unless I'm greatly mistaken, you, all of you, are
going to be put to the expense of doing over your lines completely in a very little while—so I hear—introducing this
new motor or cable system that they are getting on the South
Side." Addison wanted to convey the impression that the city
council or public sentiment or something was going to force
the North Chicago company to indulge in this great and expensive series of improvements.

Kaffrath pricked up his ears. What was the city council
going to do? He wanted to know all about it. They discussed
the whole situation—the nature of the cable conduits, the
cost of the powerhouses, the need of new rails, and the
necessity of heavier bridges, or some other means of getting
over or under the river. Addison took very good care to point
out that the Chicago City or South Side Railway was in a
much more fortunate position than either of the other two
by reason of its freedom from the river-crossing problem.
Then he again commiserated the North Side company on its
rather difficult position. "Your company will have a very
great deal to do, I fancy," he reiterated.

Kaffrath was duly impressed and appropriately depressed,
for his eight hundred shares would be depressed in value by
the necessity of heavy expenditures for tunnels and other
improvements. Nevertheless, there was some consolation in
the thought that such betterment, as Addison now described,
would in the long run make the lines more profitable. But
in the meantime there might be rough sailing. The old directors ought to act soon now, he thought. With the South Side
company being done over, they would have to follow suit.
But would they? How could he get them to see that even
though it were necessary to mortgage the lines for years to
come, it would pay in the long run? He was sick of old, conservative, cautious methods.

After the lapse of a few weeks Addison, still acting for
Cowperwood, had a second and private conference with
Kaffrath. He said, after exacting a promise of secrecy for
the present, that since their previous conversation he had become aware of new developments. In the interval he had been
visited by several men of long connection with street-railways

in other localities. They had been visiting various cities, looking for a convenient outlet for their capital, and had finally picked on Chicago. They had looked over the various lines here, and had decided that the North Chicago City railway was as good a field as any. He then elaborated with exceeding care the idea which Cowperwood had outlined to him. Kaffrath, dubious at first, was finally won over. He had too long chafed under the dusty, poky attitude of the old regime. He did not know who these new men were, but this scheme was in line with his own ideas. It would require, as Addison pointed out, the expenditure of several millions of dollars, and he did not see how the money could be raised without outside assistance, unless the lines were heavily mortgaged. If these new men were willing to pay a high rate for 51 percent of this stock for ninety-nine years and would guarantee a satisfactory rate of interest on all the stock as it stood, besides inaugurating a forward policy, why not let them? It would be just as good as mortgaging the soul out of the old property, and the management was of no value, anyhow. Kaffrath could not see how fortunes were to be made for these new investors out of subsidiary construction and equipment companies, in which Cowperwood would be interested, how by issuing watered stock on the old and new lines the latter need scarcely lay down a dollar once he had the necessary opening capital (the "talking capital," as he was fond of calling it) guaranteed. Cowperwood and Addison had by now agreed, if this went through, to organize the Chicago Trust Company with millions back of it to manipulate all their deals. Kaffrath only saw a better return on his stock, possibly a chance to get in on the ground plan, as a new phrase expressed it, of the new company.

"That's what I've been telling these fellows for the past three years," he finally exclaimed to Addison, flattered by the latter's personal attention and awed by his great influence; "but they never have been willing to listen to me. The way this North Side system has been managed is a crime. Why, a child could do better than we have done. They've saved on track and rolling stock, and lost on population. People are what we want up there, and there is only one way that I know of to get them, and that is to give them decent car service. I'll tell you frankly we've never done it."

Not long after this Cowperwood had a short talk with Kaffrath, in which he promised the latter not only six hundred dollars a share for all the stock he possessed or would part with on lease, but a bonus of new company stock for his influence. Kaffrath returned to the North Side jubilant for himself and for his company. He decided after due thought that a roundabout way would best serve Cowperwood's ends, a line of subtle suggestion from some seemingly disinterested party. Consequently he caused William Johnson, the directing engineer, to approach Albert Thorsen, one of the most vulnerable of the directors, declaring he had heard privately that Isaac White, Arnold C. Benjamin, and Otto Matjes, three other directors and the heaviest owners, had been offered a very remarkable price for their stock, and that they were going to sell, leaving the others out in the cold.

Thorsen was beside himself with grief. "When did you hear that?" he asked.

Johnson told him, but for the time being kept the source of his information secret. Thorsen at once hurried to his friend, Solon Kaempfaert, who in turn went to Kaffrath for information.

"I have heard something to that effect," was Kaffrath's only comment, "but really I do not know."

Thereupon Thorsen and Kaempfaert imagined that Kaffrath was in the conspiracy to sell out and leave them with no particularly valuable pickings. It was very sad.

Meanwhile, Cowperwood, on the advice of Kaffrath, was approaching Isaac White, Arnold C. Benjamin, and Otto Matjes direct—talking with them as if they were the only three he desired to deal with. A little later Thorsen and Kaempfaert were visited in the same spirit, and agreed in secret fear to sell out, or rather lease at the very advantageous terms Cowperwood offered, providing he could get the others to do likewise. This gave the latter a strong backing of sentiment on the board. Finally Isaac White stated at one of the meetings that he had been approached with an interesting proposition, which he then and there outlined. He was not sure what to think, he said, but the board might like to consider it. At once Thorsen and Kaempfaert were convinced that all Johnson had suggested was true. It was decided to have Cowperwood come and explain to the full board just what his plan was, and this he did in a long, bland, smiling talk. It was made plain that the road would have to be put in shape in the near future, and that this proposed plan relieved all of them of work, worry, and care.

Moreover, they were guaranteed more interest at once than they had expected to earn in the next twenty or thirty years. Thereupon it was agreed that Cowperwood and his plan should be given a trial. Seeing that if he did not succeed in paying the proposed interest promptly the property once more became theirs, so they thought, and that he assumed all obligations—taxes, water rents, old claims, a few pensions —it appeared in the light of a rather idyllic scheme.

"Well, boys, I think this is a pretty good day's work myself," observed Anthony Ewer, laying a friendly hand on the shoulder of Mr. Albert Thorsen. "I'm sure we can all unite in wishing Mr. Cowperwood luck with his adventure." Mr. Ewer's seven hundred and fifteen shares, worth seventy-one thousand, five hundred dollars, having risen to a valuation of four hundred and twenty-nine thousand dollars, he was naturally jubilant.

"You're right," replied Thorsen, who was parting with four hundred and eighty shares out of a total of seven hundred and ninety, and seeing them all bounce in value from two hundred dollars to six hundred dollars. "He's an interesting man. I hope he succeeds."

Cowperwood, waking the next morning in Aileen's room —he had been out late the night before with McKenty, Addison, Videra, and others—turned, and patting her neck where she was dozing, said: "Well, pet, yesterday afternoon I wound up that North Chicago Street Railway deal. I'm president of the new North Side company just as soon as I get my board of directors organized. We're going to be of some real consequence in this village, after all, in a year or two."

He was hoping that this fact, among other things, would end in mollifying Aileen toward him. She had been so gloomy, remote, weary these many days—ever since the terrific assault on Rita.

"Yes?" she replied, with a halfhearted smile, rubbing her waking eyes. She was clad in a foamy nightgown of white and pink. "That's nice, isn't it?"

Cowperwood brought himself up on one elbow and looked at her, smoothing her round, bare arms, which he always admired. The luminous richness of her hair had never lost its charm completely.

"That means that I can do the same thing, with the

Chicago West Division company in a year or so," he went on. "But there's going to be a lot of talk about this, I'm afraid, and I don't want that just now. It will work out all right. I can see Schryhart and Merrill and some of these other people taking notice pretty soon. They've missed out on two of the biggest things Chicago ever had—gas and railways."

"Oh yes, Frank, I'm glad for you," commented Aileen rather drearily, who, in spite of her sorrow over his defection, was still glad that he was going on and forward. "You'll always do all right."

"I wish you wouldn't feel so badly, Aileen," he said, with a kind of affectional protest. "Aren't you going to try and be happy with me? This is as much for you as for me. You will be able to pay up old scores even better than I will."

He smiled winningly.

"Yes," she replied, reproachfully but tenderly at that, a little sorrowfully, "a lot of good money does me. It was your love I wanted."

"But you have that," he insisted. "I've told you that over and over. I never ceased to care for you really. You know I didn't."

"Yes, I know," she replied, even as he gathered her close in his arms. "I know how you care." But that did not prevent her from responding to him warmly, for back of all her fuming protest was heartache, the wish to have his love intact, to restore that pristine affection which she had once assumed would endure forever.

CHAPTER XXIII
The Power of the Press

The morning papers, in spite of the efforts of Cowperwood and his friends to keep this transfer secret, shortly thereafter were full of rumors of a change in "North Chicago." Frank Algernon Cowperwood, hitherto unmentioned in connection with Chicago street-railways, was pointed to as the probable successor to Onias C. Skinner, and Edwin L. Kaffrath, one of the old directors, as future vice-president. The men back of the deal were referred to as "in all likelihood eastern capitalists." Cowperwood, as he sat in Aileen's room examining the various morning papers, saw that before the day was over he would be sought out for an expression of opinion and further details. He proposed to ask the newspaper men to wait a few days until he could talk to the publishers of the papers themselves—win their confidence—and then announce a general policy; it would be something that would please the city, and the residents of the North Side in particular. At the same time he did not care to promise anything which he could not easily and profitably perform. He wanted fame and reputation, but he wanted money even more; he intended to get both.

To one who had been working thus long in the minor realms of finance, as Cowperwood considered that he had so far been doing, this sudden upward step into the more conspicuous regions of high finance and control was an all-inspiring thing. So long had he been stirring about in a lesser region, paving the way by hours and hours of private thought and conference and scheming, that now when he actually had achieved his end he could scarcely believe for the time being that it was true. Chicago was such a splendid city. It was growing so fast. Its opportunities were so wonderful. These men who had thus foolishly parted with an indefinite lease of their holdings had not really considered what they were doing. This matter of Chicago street-railways, once he had them well in hand, could be made to yield such splendid profits! He could incorporate and overcapitalize. Many subsidiary lines, which McKenty would secure for him for a song, would be worth millions in the future, and they should be his entirely; he would not be indebted to the directors of the old North Chicago company for any interest on those. By degrees, year by year, as the city grew, the lines which were still controlled by this old company, but were practically his, would become a mere item, a central core, in the so very much larger system of new lines which he would build up about it. Then the West Side, and even the South Side sections—but why dream? He might readily become the sole master of street-railway traffic in Chicago! He might readily become the most princely financial figure in the city—and one of the few great financial magnates of the nation.

In any public enterprise of any kind, as he knew, where the suffrages of the people or the privileges in their possessions are desired, the newspapers must always be considered. As Cowperwood even now was casting hungry eyes in the direction of the two tunnels—one to be held in view of an eventual assumption of the Chicago West Division company, the other to be given to the North Chicago Street Railway, which he had now organized, it was necessary to make friends with the various publishers. How to go about it?

Recently, because of the influx of a heavy native- and foreign-born population (thousands and thousands of men of all sorts and conditions looking for the work which the growth of the city seemed to promise), and because of the dissemination of stirring ideas through radical individuals of foreign groups concerning anarchism, socialism, communism, and the like, the civic idea in Chicago had become most acute. This very May, in which Cowperwood had been going about attempting to adjust matters in his favor, there had been a tremendous national flare-up, when in a great public place on the West Side known as the Haymarket, at one of a number of labor meetings, dubbed anarchistic because of the principles of some of the speakers, a bomb had been hurled by some excited fanatic, which had exploded, and maimed or killed a number of policemen, injuring slightly several others. This had brought to the fore, once and for all, as by a flash of lightning, the whole problem of mass against class, and had given it such an airing as in view of the cheerful, optimistic, almost inconsequential American mind had not previously been possible. It changed, quite as an eruption might, the whole face of the commercial landscape. Man thought thereafter somewhat more accurately of national and civic things. What was anarchism? What socialism? What rights had the rank and file, anyhow, in economic and governmental development? Such were interesting questions, and following the bomb—which acted as a great stone cast in the water—these ripple rings of thought were still widening and emanating until they took in such supposedly remote and impregnable quarters as editorial offices, banks and financial institutions generally, and the haunts of political dignitaries and their jobs.

In the face of this, however, Cowperwood was not disturbed. He did not believe in either the strength of the masses or their ultimate rights, though he sympathized with the condition of individuals, and did believe that men like himself were sent into the world to better perfect its mechanism and habitable order. Often now, in these pre-liminary days, he looked at the large companies of men with their horses gathered in and about the several carbarns of the company, and wondered at their state. So many of them were so dull. They were rather like animals, patient, inartistic, hopeless. He thought of their shabby homes, their long hours, their poor pay, and then concluded that if anything at all could be done for them it would be pay them decent living wages, which he proposed to do—nothing more. They could not be expected to understand his dreams or his visions, or to share in the magnificence and social dominance which he craved. He finally decided that it would be as well for him to personally visit the various newspaper publishers and talk the situation over with them. Addison, when consulted as to this project, was somewhat dubious. He had small faith in the newspapers. He had seen them play petty politics, follow up enmities and personal grudges, and even sell out, in certain cases, for pathetically small rewards.

"I tell you how it is, Frank," remarked Addison on one occasion. "You will have to do all this business on cotton heels, practically. You know that old gas crowd are still down on you, in spite of the fact that you are one of their largest stockholders. Schryhart isn't at all friendly, and he practically owns the *Chronicle*. Ricketts will just about say what he wants him to say. Hyssop, of the *Mail* and the *Transcript*, is an independent man, but he's a Presbyterian and a cold, self-righteous moralist. Braxton's paper, the *Globe*, practically belongs to Merrill, but Braxton's a nice fellow, at that. Old General MacDonald, of the *Inquirer*, is old General MacDonald. It's all according to how he feels when he gets up in the morning. If he should chance to like your looks he might support you forever and forever until you crossed his conscience in some way. He's a fine old walrus. I like him. Neither Schryhart nor Merrill nor anyone else can get anything out of him unless he wants to give it. He may not live so many years, however, and I don't trust that son of his. Haguenin, of the *Press*, is all right, and friendly to you, as I understand. Other things being equal, I think he'd naturally support you in anything he thought was fair and reasonable. Well, there you have them. Get them all on your side if you can. Don't ask for the La Salle Street tunnel right away. Let it come as an afterthought—a great public need. The main thing will be to avoid having the other companies stirring up a real fight against you. Depend on it, Schryhart will be thinking pretty hard about this whole business from now on. As for Merrill—well, if you can show him where he can get something out of it for his store, I guess he'll be for you."

It is one of the splendid yet sinister fascinations of life that there is no tracing to their ultimate sources all the winds of influence that play upon a given bark—all the breaths of chance that fill or desert our bellied or our sagging sails. We plan and plan, but who by taking thought can add a cubit to his stature? Who can overcome or even assist the Providence that shapes our ends, rough hew them as we may. Cowperwood was now entering upon a great public career, and the various editors and public personalities of the city were watching him with interest. Augustus M. Haguenin, a free agent with his organ, the *Press,* and yet not free, either, because he was harnessed to the necessity of making his paper pay, was most interested. Lacking the commanding magnetism of a man like MacDonald, he was nevertheless an honest man, well-intentioned, thoughtful, careful. Haguenin, ever since the outcome of Cowperwood's gas transaction, had been intensely interested in the latter's career. It seemed to him that Cowperwood was probably destined to become a significant figure. Raw, glittering force, however, compounded of the cruel Machiavellianism of nature, if it be but Machiavellian, seems to exercise a profound attraction for the conventionally rooted. Your cautious citizen of average means, looking out through the eye of his dull world of seeming fact, is often the first to forgive or condone the grim butcheries of theory by which the strong rise. Haguenin, observing Cowperwood, conceived of him as a man perhaps as much sinned against as sinning, a man who would be faithful to friends, one who could be relied upon in hours of great stress. As it happened, the Haguenins were neighbors of the Cowperwoods, and since those days when the latter had attempted unsuccessfully to enter Chicago society this family had been as acceptable as any of those who had remained friendly.

And so, when Cowperwood arrived one day at the office of the *Press* in a blowing snowstorm—it was just before the Christmas holidays—Haguenin was glad to see him. "It's certainly real winter weather we're having now, isn't it?" he observed cheerfully. "How goes the North Chicago Street Railway business?" For months he, with the other publishers, had been aware that the whole North Side was to be made over by fine cable tracks, powerhouses, and handsome cars; and there already was talk that some better arrangement was to be made to bring the passengers into the downtown section.

"Mr. Haguenin," said Cowperwood smilingly—he was arrayed in a heavy fur coat, with a collar of beaver and driving gauntlets of dogskin—"we have reached the place in this street-railway problem on the North Side where we are going to require the assistance of the newspapers, or at least their friendly support. At present our principal difficulty is that all our lines, when they come downtown, stop at Lake Street —just this side of the bridges. That means a long walk for everybody to all the streets south of it, and as you probably know, there has been considerable complaint. Besides that, this river traffic is becoming more and more what I may say it has been for years—an intolerable nuisance. We have all suffered from it. No effort has ever been made to regulate it, and because it is so heavy I doubt whether it ever can be systematized in any satisfactory way. The best thing in the long run would be to tunnel under the river; but that is such an expensive proposition that as things are now we are in no position to undertake it. The traffic on the North Side does not warrant it. It really does not warrant the reconstruction of the three bridges which we now use at State, Dearborn, and Clark; yet if we introduce the cable system, which we now propose, these bridges will have to be done over. It seems to me, seeing that this is an enterprise in which the public is as much interested almost as we are, that it would only be fair if the city should help pay for this reconstruction work. All the land adjacent to these lines, and the property served by them, will be greatly enhanced in value. The city's taxing power will rise tremendously. I have talked to several financiers here in Chicago, and they agree with me; but as is usual in all such cases, I find that some of the politicians are against me. Since I have taken charge of the North Chicago company the attitude of one or two papers has not been any too friendly." (In the *Chronicle*, controlled by Schryhart, there had already been a number of references to the probability that now, since Cowperwood and his friends were in charge, the skyrocketing tactics of the old

Lake View, Hyde Park, and other gas organizations would be repeated. Braxton's *Globe,* owned by Merrill, being semineutral, had merely suggested that it hoped that no such methods would be repeated here.) "Perhaps you may know," Cowperwood continued, "that we have a very sweeping program of improvement in mind, if we can obtain proper public consideration and assistance."

At this point he reached down in one of his pockets and drew forth astutely drafted maps and blueprints, especially prepared for this occasion. They showed main cable lines on North Clark, La Salle, and Wells streets. These lines coming downtown converged at Illinois and La Salle streets on the North Side—and though Cowperwood made no reference to it at the moment, they were indicated on the map in red as running over or under the river at La Salle Street, where there was no bridge, and emerging therefrom, following a loop along La Salle to Munroe, to Dearborn, to Randolph, and thence into the tunnel again. Cowperwood allowed Haguenin to gather the very interesting traffic significance of it all before he proceeded.

"On the map, Mr. Haguenin, I have indicated a plan which, if we can gain the consent of the city, will obviate any quarrel as to the great expense of reconstructing the bridges, and will make use of a piece of property which is absolutely without value to the city at present, but which can be made into something of vast convenience to the public. I am referring, as you see"—he laid an indicative finger on the map in Mr. Haguenin's hands—"to the old La Salle Street tunnel, which is now boarded up and absolutely of no use to anyone. It was built apparently under a misapprehension as to the grade the average loaded wagon could negotiate. When it was found to be unprofitable it was sold to the city and locked up. If you have ever been through it you know what condition it is in. My engineers tell me the walls are leaking, and that there is great danger of a cave-in unless it is very speedily repaired. I am also told that it will require about four hundred thousand dollars to put it in suitable condition for use. My theory is that if the North Chicago Street Railway is willing to go to this expense for the sake of solving this bridge crush problem, and giving the residents of the North Side a sensible and uninterrupted service into the business heart, the city ought to be willing to make us a present of this tunnel for the time being, or at least a long lease at a purely nominal rental."

Cowperwood paused to see what Haguenin would say. The latter was looking at the map gravely, wondering whether it was fair for Cowperwood to make this demand, wondering whether the city should grant it to him without compensation, wondering whether the bridge traffic problem was as serious as he pointed out, wondering, indeed, whether this whole move was not a clever ruse to obtain something for nothing.

"And what is this?" he asked, laying a finger on the aforementioned loop.

"That," replied Cowperwood, "is the only method we have been able to figure out of serving the downtown business section and the North Side, and of solving this bridge problem. If we obtain the tunnel, as I hope we shall, all the cars of these North Side lines will emerge here"—he pointed to La Salle and Randolph—"and swing around—that is, they will if the city council gives us the right of way. I think, of course, there can be no reasonable objection to that. There is no reason why the citizens of the North Side shouldn't have as comfortable an access to the business heart as those of the West or South Side."

"None in the world," Mr. Haguenin was compelled to admit. "Are you satisfied, however, that the council and the city should sanction the gift of a loop of this kind without some form of compensation?"

"I see no reason why they shouldn't," replied Cowperwood in a somewhat injured tone. "There has never been any question of compensation where other improvements have been suggested for the city in the past. The South Side company has been allowed to turn in a loop around State and Wabash. The Chicago West Division Railway has a loop in Adams and Washington streets."

"Quite so," said Mr. Haguenin vaguely. "That is true. But this tunnel, now—do you think that should fall in the same category of public beneficences?"

At the same time he could not help thinking, as he looked at the proposed loop indicated on the map, that the new cable line, with its string of trailers, would give downtown Chicago a truly metropolitan air and would provide a splendid outlet for the North Side. The streets in question were magnificent commercial thoroughfares, crowded even at this date with structures five, six, seven, and even eight stories high, and brimming with heavy streams of eager life —young, fresh, optimistic. Because of the narrow area into which the commercial life of the city tended to congest itself, this property and these streets were immensely valuable —among the most valuable in the whole city. Also he observed that if this loop did come here, its cars, on their return trip along Dearborn Street, would pass by his very door—the office of the *Press*—thereby enhancing the value of that property of which he was the owner.

"I certainly do, Mr. Haguenin," returned Cowperwood emphatically, in answer to his query. "Personally, I should think Chicago would be glad to pay a bonus to get its street-railway service straightened out, especially where a corporation comes forward with a liberal, conservative program such as this. It means millions in growth of property values on the North Side. It means millions to the business heart to have this loop system laid down just as I suggest."

He put his finger firmly on the map which he had brought, and Haguenin agreed with him that the plan was undoubtedly a sound business proposition. "Personally, I should be the last to complain," he added, "for the line passes my door. At the same time this tunnel, as I understand it, cost in the neighborhood of eight hundred thousand or a million dollars. It is a delicate problem. I should like to know what the other editors think of it, and how the city council itself would feel toward it."

Cowperwood nodded. "Certainly, certainly," he said. "With pleasure. I would not come here at all if I did not feel that I had a perfectly legitimate proposition—one that the press of the city should unite in supporting. Where a corporation such as ours is facing large expenditures, which have to be financed by outside capital, it is only natural that we should wish to allay useless, groundless opposition in advance. I hope we may command your support."

"I hope you may," smiled Mr. Haguenin. They parted the best of friends.

The other publishers, guardians of the city's privileges, were not quite so genial as Haguenin in their approval of Cowperwood's proposition. The use of a tunnel and several of the most important downtown streets might readily be essential to the development of Cowperwood's North Side schemes, but the gift of them was a different matter. Already, as a matter of fact, the various publishers and editors had been consulted by Schryhart, Merrill, and others with a view to discovering how they felt as to this new venture, and whether Cowperwood would be cheerfully indorsed or not. Schryhart, smarting from the wounds he had received in the gas war, viewed this new activity on Cowperwood's part with a suspicious and envious eye. To him much more than to the others it spelled a new and dangerous foe in the street-railway field, although all the leading citizens of Chicago were interested.

"I suppose now," he said one evening to the Honorable Walter Melville Hyssop, editor and publisher of the *Transcript* and the *Evening Mail,* whom he met at the Union League, "that this fellow Cowperwood will attempt some disturbing coup in connection with street-railway affairs. He is just the sort. I think, from an editorial point of view, his political connections will bear watching." Already there were rumors abroad that McKenty might have something to do with the new company.

Hyssop, a medium-sized, ornate, conservative person, was not so sure. "We shall find out soon enough, no doubt, what propositions Mr. Cowperwood has in hand," he remarked. "He is very energetic and capable, as I understand it."

Hyssop and Schryhart, as well as the latter and Merrill, had been social friends for years and years.

After his call on Mr. Haguenin, Cowperwood's naturally selective and self-protective judgment led him next to the office of the *Inquirer,* old General MacDonald's paper, where he found that because of rheumatism and the severe, inclement weather of Chicago, the old general had sailed only a few days before for Italy. His son, an aggressive, mercantile type of youth of thirty-two, and a managing editor by the name of Du Bois were acting in his stead. In the son, Truman Leslie MacDonald, an intense, calm, and penetrating young man, Cowperwood encountered someone who, like himself, saw life only from the point of view of sharp, self-centered, personal advantage. What was he, Truman Leslie MacDonald, to derive from any given situation, and how was he to make the *Inquirer* an even greater property than it had been under his father before him? He did not propose to be overwhelmed by the old general's rather flowery reputation. At the same time he meant to become imposingly rich. An active member of a young and very smart set which had been growing up on the North Side, he rode, drove, was instrumental in organizing a new and exclusive country club, and despised the rank and file as unsuited to the fine atmosphere to which he aspired. Mr. Clifford Du Bois, the managing editor, was a cool reprobate of forty, masquerading as a gentleman, and using the *Inquirer* in subtle ways for furthering his personal ends, and that under the old general's very nose. He was osseous, sandy-haired, blue-eyed, with a keen, formidable nose and a solid chin. Clifford Du Bois was always careful never to let his left hand know what his right hand did.

It was this sapient pair that received Cowperwood in the old general's absence, first in Mr. Du Bois's room and then in that of Mr. MacDonald. The latter had already heard much of Cowperwood's doings. Men who had been connected with the old gas war—Jordan Jules, for instance, president of the old North Chicago Gas Company, and Hudson Baker, president of the old West Chicago Gas Company—had denounced him long before as a buccaneer who had pirated them out of very comfortable sinecures. Here he was now invading the North Chicago street-railway field and coming with startling schemes for the reorganization of the downtown business heart. Why shouldn't the city have something in return; or, better yet, those who helped to formulate the public opinion, so influential in the success of Cowperwood's plans? Truman Leslie MacDonald, as has been said, didn't see life from his father's point of view at all. He had in mind a sharp bargain, which he could drive with Cowperwood during the old gentleman's absence. The general need never know.

"I understand your point of view, Mr. Cowperwood," he commented loftily, "but where does the city come in? I see very clearly how important this is to the people of the North Side, and even to the merchants and real estate owners in the downtown section; but that simply means that it is ten times as important to you. Undoubtedly, it will help the city, but the city is growing, anyhow, and that will help you. I've said all along that these public franchises were worth more than they used to be worth. Nobody seems to see it very clearly as yet, but it's true just the same. That tunnel is worth more now than the day it was built. Even if the city can't use it, somebody can."

He was meaning to indicate a rival car line.

Cowperwood bristled internally.

"That's all very well," he said, preserving his surface composure, "but why make fish of one and flesh of another? The South Side company has a loop for which it never paid a dollar. So has the Chicago West Division Railway. The North Side company is planning more extensive improvements than were ever undertaken by any single company before. I hardly think it is fair to raise the question of compensation and a franchise tax at this time, and in connection with this one company only."

"Um—well, that may be true of the other companies. The South Side company had those streets long ago. They merely connected them up. But this tunnel, now—that's a different matter, isn't it? The city bought and paid for that, didn't it?"

"Quite true—to help out men who saw that they couldn't make another dollar out of it," said Cowperwood acidly. "But it's of no use to the city. It will cave in pretty soon if it isn't repaired. Why, the consent of property owners alone, along the line of this loop, is going to aggregate a considerable sum. It seems to me instead of hampering a great work of this kind the public ought to do everything in its power to assist it. It means giving a new metropolitan flavor to this downtown section. It is time Chicago was getting out of its swaddling clothes."

Mr. MacDonald, the younger, shook his head. He saw clearly enough the significance of the points made, but he was jealous of Cowperwood and of his success. This loop franchise and tunnel gift meant millions for someone. Why shouldn't there be something in it for him? He called in Mr. Du Bois and went over the proposition with him. Quite without effort the latter sensed the drift of the situation.

"It's an excellent proposition," he said. "I don't see but that the city should have something, though. Public sentiment is rather against gifts to corporations just at present."

Cowperwood caught the drift of what was in young MacDonald's mind.

"Well, what would you suggest as a fair rate of compensation to the city?" he asked cautiously, wondering whether this aggressive youth would go so far as to commit himself in any way.

"Oh, well, as to that," MacDonald replied with a deprecatory wave of his hand, "I couldn't say. It ought to bear a reasonable relationship to the value of the utility as it now stands. I should want to think that over. I shouldn't want to see the city demand anything unreasonable. Certainly, though, there is a privilege here that is worth something."

Cowperwood flared inwardly. His greatest weakness, if he had one, was that he could but ill brook opposition of any kind. This young upstart, with his thin, cool face and sharp, hard eyes! He would have liked to tell him and his paper to go to the devil. He went away, hoping that he could influence the *Inquirer* in some other way upon the old general's return.

As he was sitting next morning in his office in North Clark Street he was aroused by the still novel-sounding bell of the telephone—one of the earliest in use—on the wall back of him. After a parley with his secretary, he was informed that a gentleman connected with the *Inquirer* wished to speak with him.

"This is the *Inquirer*," said a voice which Cowperwood, his ear to the receiver, thought he recognized as that of young Truman MacDonald, the general's son. "You wanted to know," continued the voice, "what would be considered adequate compensation so far as that tunnel matter is concerned. Can you hear me?"

"Yes," replied Cowperwood.

"Well, I should not care to influence your judgment one way or the other; but if my opinion were asked I should say about fifty thousand dollars' worth of North Chicago Street Railway stock would be satisfactory."

The voice was young, clear, steely.

"To whom would you suggest that it might be paid?" Cowperwood asked softly, quite genially.

"That, also, I would suggest, might be left to your very sound judgment."

The voice ceased. The receiver was hung up.

"Well, I'll be damned!" Cowperwood said, looking at the floor reflectively. A smile spread over his face. "I'm not going to be held up like that. I don't need to be. It isn't worth it. Not at present, anyhow." His teeth set.

He was underestimating Mr. Truman Leslie MacDonald, principally because he did not like him. He thought his father might return and oust him. It was one of the most vital mistakes he ever made in his life.

CHAPTER XXIV

The Coming of Stephanie Platow

During this period of what might have been called financial and commercial progress, the affairs of Aileen and Cowperwood had been to a certain extent smoothed over. Each summer now, partly to take Aileen's mind off herself and partly to satisfy his own desire to see the world and collect objects of art, in which he was becoming more and more interested, it was Cowperwood's custom to make with his wife a short trip abroad or to foreign American lands, visiting in these two years Russia, Scandinavia, Argentina, Chile, and Mexico. Their plan was to leave in May or June with the outward rush of traffic, and return in September or early October. His idea was to soothe Aileen as much as possible, to fill her mind with pleasing anticipations as to her eventual social triumph somewhere—in New York or London, if not Chicago—to make her feel that in spite of his physical desertion he was still spiritually loyal.

By now also Cowperwood was so shrewd that he had the ability to simulate an affection and practice a gallantry which he did not feel, or, rather, that was not backed by real passion. He was the soul of attention; he would buy her flowers, jewels, knickknacks, and ornaments; he would see that her comfort was looked after to the last detail; and yet, at the very same moment, perhaps, he would be looking cautiously about to see what life might offer in the way of illicit entertainment. Aileen knew this, although she could not prove it to be true. At the same time she had an affection and an admiration for the man which gripped her in spite of herself.

You have, perhaps, pictured to yourself the mood of some general who has perhaps suffered a great defeat; the employee who after years of faithful service finds himself discharged. What shall life say to the loving when their love is no longer of any value, when all that has been placed upon the altar of affection has been found to be a vain sacrifice? Philosophy? Give that to dolls to play with. Religion? Seek first the metaphysical-minded. Aileen was no longer the lithe, forceful, dynamic girl of 1865, when Cowperwood first met her. She was still beautiful, it is true, a fair, full-blown, matronly creature not more than thirty-five, looking perhaps thirty, feeling, alas, that she was a girl and still as attractive as ever. It is a grim thing to a woman, however fortunately placed, to realize that age is creeping on, and that love, that singing will-o'-the-wisp, is fading into the ultimate dark. Aileen, within the hour of her greatest triumph, had seen love die. It was useless to tell herself, as she did sometimes, that it might come back, revive. Her ultimately realistic temperament told her this could never be. Though she had routed Rita Sohlberg, she was fully aware that Cowperwood's original constancy was gone. She was no longer happy. Love was dead. That sweet illusion, with its pearly pink for heart and borders, that laughing cherub that lures with Cupid's mouth and misty eye, that young tendril of the vine of life that whispers of eternal springtime, that calls and calls where aching, wearied feet by legion follow, was no longer in existence.

In vain the tears, the storms, the self-tortures; in vain the looks in the mirror, the studied examination of plump, sweet features still fresh and inviting. One day, at the sight of tired circles under her eyes, she ripped from her neck a lovely ruche that she was adjusting, and throwing herself on her bed, cried as though her heart would break. Why primp? Why ornament? Her Frank did not love her. What to her now was a handsome residence in Michigan Avenue, the refinements of a French boudoir, or clothing that ran the gamut of the dressmaker's art, hats that were like orchids blooming in serried rows? In vain, in vain! Like the raven that perched above the lintel of the door, sad memory was here, grave in her widow weeds, crying, "Nevermore." Aileen knew that the sweet illusion which had bound Cowperwood to her for a time had gone and would never come again. He was here. His step was in the room mornings and evenings; at night for long, prosaic, uninterrupted periods she could hear him breathing by her side, his hand on her body. There were other nights when he was not there—when he was "out of the city"—and she resigned herself to accept his excuses at their face value. Why quarrel? she asked herself. What could she do? She was waiting, waiting, but for what?

And Cowperwood, noting the strange, unalterable changes which time works in us all, the inward lap of the marks of age, the fluted recession of that splendor and radiance which is youth, sighed at times, perhaps, but turned his face to that dawn which is forever breaking where youth is. Not for him that poetic loyalty which substitutes for the perfection of young love its memories, or takes for the glitter of passion and desire that once was the happy thoughts of companionship—the crystal memories that like early dews congealed remain beaded recollections to comfort or torture for the end of former joys. On the contrary, after the vanishing of Rita Sohlberg, with all that she meant in the way of a delicate insouciance which Aileen had never known, his temperament ached, for he must have something like that. Truth to say, he must always have youth, the illusion of beauty, vanity in womanhood, the novelty of a new, untested temperament, quite as he must have pictures, old porcelain, music, a mansion, illuminated missals, power, the applause of the great, unthinking world.

As has been said, this promiscuous attitude on Cowperwood's part was the natural flowering out of a temperament that was chronically promiscuous, intellectually uncertain, and philosophically anarchistic. From one point of view it might have been said of him that he was seeking the realization of an ideal, yet to one's amazement our very ideals change at times and leave us floundering in the dark. What is an ideal, anyhow? A wraith, a mist, a perfume in the wind, a dream of fair water. The soul yearning of a girl like Antoinette Nowak was a little too strained for him. It was too ardent, too clinging, and he had gradually extricated himself, not without difficulty, from that particular entanglement. Since then he had been intimate with other women for brief periods, but to no great satisfaction— Dorothy Ormsby, Jessie Belle Hinsdale, Toma Lewis, Hilda

Jewell; but they shall be names merely. One was an actress, one a stenographer, one the daughter of one of his stock patrons, one a church worker, a solicitor for charity coming to him to seek help for an orphans' home. It was a pathetic mess at times, but so are all defiant variations from the accustomed drift of things. In the hardy language of Napoleon, one cannot make an omelette without cracking a number of eggs.

The coming of Stephanie Platow, Russian Jewess on one side of her family, southwestern American on the other, was an event in Cowperwood's life. She was tall, graceful, brilliant, young, with much of the optimism of Rita Sohlberg, and yet endowed with a strange fatalism which, once he knew her better, touched and moved him. He met her on shipboard on the way to Göteborg. Her father, Isadore Platow, was a wealthy furrier of Chicago. He was a large, meaty, oily type of man—a kind of ambling, gelatinous formula of the male, with the usual sound commercial instincts of the Jew, but with an errant philosophy which led him to believe first one thing and then another so long as neither interfered definitely with his business. He was an admirer of Henry George and of so altruistic a program as that of Robert Owen, and, also, in his way, a social snob. And yet he had married Susetta Osborn, a Texas girl who was once his bookkeeper. Mrs. Platow was lithe, amiable, subtle, with an eye always to the main social chance—in other words, a climber. She was shrewd enough to realize that a knowledge of books and art and current events was essential, and so she went in for these things.

It is curious how the temperaments of parents blend and revivify in their children. As Stephanie grew up she had repeated in her very differing body some of her father's and mother's characteristics—an interesting variability of soul. She was tall, dark, sallow, lithe, with a strange moodiness of heart and a recessive, fulgurous gleam in her chestnut-brown, almost brownish-black eyes. She had a full, sensuous Cupid's mouth, a dreamy and even languishing expression, a graceful neck, and a heavy, dark, and yet pleasingly modeled face. From both her father and mother she had inherited a penchant for art, literature, philosophy, and music. Already at eighteen she was dreaming of painting, singing, writing poetry, writing books, acting—anything and everything. Serene in her own judgment of what was worthwhile, she was like to lay stress on any silly mood or fad, thinking it exquisite—the last word. Finally, she was a rank voluptuary, dreaming dreams of passionate union with first one and then another type of artist, poet, musician—the whole gamut of the artistic and emotional world.

Cowperwood first saw her on board the *Centurion* one June morning, as the ship lay at dock in New York. He and Aileen were en route for Norway, she and her father and mother for Denmark and Switzerland. She was hanging over the starboard rail looking at a flock of wide-winged gulls, which were besieging the port of the cook's galley. She was musing soulfully—conscious (fully) that she was musing soulfully. He paid very little attention to her, except to note that she was tall, rhythmic, and that a dark gray plaid dress, and an immense veil of gray silk wound about her shoulders and waist and over one arm, after the manner of a Hindu shawl, appeared to become her much. Her face seemed very sallow, and her eyes ringed as if indicating dyspepsia. Her black hair under a chic hat did not escape his critical eye. Later she and her father appeared at the captain's table, to which the Cowperwoods had also been invited.

Cowperwood and Aileen did not know how to take this girl, though she interested them both. They little suspected the chameleon character of her soul. She was an artist, and as formless and unstable as water. It was a mere passing gloom that possessed her. Cowperwood liked the semi-Jewish cast of her face, a certain fullness of the neck, her dark, sleepy eyes. But she was much too young and nebulous, he thought, and he let her pass. On this trip, which endured for ten days, he saw much of her, in different moods, walking with a young Jew in whom she seemed greatly interested, playing at shuffleboard, reading solemnly in a corner out of the reach of the wind or spray, and usually looking naive, preternaturally innocent, remote, dreamy. At other times she seemed possessed of a wild animation, her eyes alight, her expression vigorous, an intense glow in her soul. Once he saw her bent over a small wood block, cutting a bookplate with a thin steel graving tool.

Because of Stephanie's youth and seeming unimportance, her lack of what might be called compelling, rosy charm, Aileen had become reasonably friendly with the girl. Far subtler, even at her years, than Aileen, Stephanie gathered a very good impression of the former, of her mental girth, and how to take her. She made friends with her, made a bookplate for her, made a sketch of her. She confided to Aileen that in her own mind she was destined for the stage, if her parents would permit; and Aileen invited her to see her husband's pictures on their return. She little knew how much of a part Stephanie would play in Cowperwood's life.

The Cowperwoods, having been put down at Göteborg, saw no more of the Platows until late October. Then Aileen, being lonely, called to see Stephanie, and occasionally thereafter Stephanie came over to the South Side to see the Cowperwoods. She liked to roam about their house, to dream meditatively in some nook of the rich interior, with a book for company. She liked Cowperwood's pictures, his jades, his missals, his ancient radiant glass. From talking with Aileen she realized that the latter had no real love for these things, that her expressions of interest and pleasure were pure make-believe, based on their value as possessions. For Stephanie herself certain of the illuminated books and bits of glass had a heavy, sensuous appeal, which only the truly artistic can understand. They unlocked dark dream moods and pageants for her. She responded to them, lingered over them, experienced strange moods from them as from the orchestrated richness of music.

And in doing so she thought of Cowperwood often. Did he really like these things, or was he just buying them to be buying them? She had heard much of the pseudo artistic —the people who made a show of art. She recalled Cowperwood as he walked the deck of the *Centurion*. She remembered his large, comprehensive, embracing blue-gray eyes that seemed to blaze with intelligence. He seemed to her quite obviously a more forceful and significant man than her father, and yet she could not have said why. He always seemed so trigly dressed, so well put together. There was a friendly warmth about all that he said or did, though he said or did little. She felt that his eyes were mocking, that back in his soul there was some kind of humor over something which she did not understand quite.

After Stephanie had been back in Chicago six months, during which time she saw very little of Cowperwood, who was busy with his street-railway program, she was swept into the net of another interest, which carried her away from

him and Aileen for the time being. On the West Side, among
a circle of her mother's friends, had been organized an
amateur dramatic league, with no less object than to ele-
vate the stage. That world-old problem never fails to interest the new and the inexperienced. It all began in the
home of one of the new rich of the West Side—the Timber-
lakes. They, in their large house on Ashland Avenue, had a
stage, and Georgia Timberlake, a romantic-minded girl of
twenty with flaxen hair, imagined she could act. Mrs. Timberlake, a fat, indulgent mother, rather agreed with her. The
whole idea, after a few discursive performances of Milton's
masque *Comus, Pyramus and Thisbe,* and an improved
Harlequin and Columbine, written by one of the members,
was transferred to the realm of the studios, then quartered
in the New Arts Building. An artist by the name of Lane
Cross, a portrait painter, who was much less of an artist
than he was a stage director, and not much of either, but
who made his living by hornswoggling society into the belief
that he could paint, was induced to take charge of these
stage performances.

By degrees the "Garrick Players," as they chose to call
themselves, developed no little skill and craftsmanship in
presenting one form and another of classic and semiclassic
play. *Romeo and Juliet,* with few properties of any kind,
The Learned Ladies of Molière, Sheridan's *The Rivals,* and
the *Electra* of Sophocles were all given. Considerable ability of one kind and another was developed, the group including two actresses of subsequent repute on the American stage, one of whom was Stephanie Platow. There were
some ten girls and women among the active members, and
almost as many men—a variety of characters much too extended to discuss here. There was a dramatic critic by the
name of Gardner Knowles, a young man, very smug and
handsome, who was connected with the Chicago *Press.* Whipping his neatly trousered legs with his bright little cane, he
used to appear at the rooms of the players at the Tuesday,
Thursday, and Saturday teas which they inaugurated, and
discuss the merits of the venture. Thus the Garrick Players
were gradually introduced into the newspapers. Lane Cross,
the smooth-faced, pasty-souled artist who had charge, was
a rake at heart, a subtle seducer of women, who, however,
escaped detection by a smooth, conventional bearing. He was
interested in such girls as Georgia Timberlake, Irma Ottley,

a rosy, aggressive maiden who essayed comic roles, and Stephanie Platow. These, with another girl, Ethel Tuckerman, very emotional and romantic, who could dance charmingly and sing, made up a group of friends which became very close. Presently intimacies sprang up; only in this realm, instead of ending in marriage, they merely resulted in sex liberty. Thus Ethel Tuckerman became the mistress of Lane Cross; an illicit attachment grew up between Irma Ottley and a young society idler by the name of Bliss Bridge; and Gardner Knowles, ardently admiring Stephanie Platow, literally seized upon her one afternoon in her own home, when he went ostensibly to interview her, and overpersuaded her. She was only reasonably fond of him, not in love; but being generous, nebulous, passionate, emotional, inexperienced, voiceless, and vainly curious, without any sense of the meums and tuums that govern society in such matters, she allowed this rather brutal thing to happen. She was not a coward—was too nebulous and yet forceful to be such. Her parents never knew. And once so launched, another world—that of sex satisfaction—began to dawn on her.

Were these young people evil? Let the social philosopher answer. One thing is certain: They did not establish homes and raise children. On the contrary, they led a gay, butterfly existence for nearly two years; then came a rift in the lute. Quarrels developed over parts, respective degrees of ability, and leadership. Ethel Tuckerman fell out with Lane Cross because she discovered him making love to Irma Ottley. Irma and Bliss Bridge released each other, the latter transferring his affections to Georgia Timberlake. Stephanie Platow, by far the most individual of them all, developed a strange inconsequence as to her deeds. It was when she was drawing near the age of twenty that the affair with Gardner Knowles began. After a time Lane Cross, with his somewhat earnest attempt at artistic interpretation and his superiority in the matter of years—he was forty, and young Knowles only twenty-four—seemed more interesting to Stephanie, and he was quick to respond. There followed an idle, passionate union with this man, which seemed important, but was not so at all. And then it was that Stephanie began dimly to perceive that it was on and on that the blessings lie, that somewhere there might be some man much more remarkable than either of these; but this was only a dream. She thought of Cowperwood at times; but he seemed to her to be too wrapped up in grim, tremendous things, far apart from this romantic world of amateur dramatics in which she was involved.

CHAPTER XXV

Airs from the Orient

Cowperwood gained his first real impression of Stephanie at the Garrick Players, where he went with Aileen once to witness a performance of *Electra*. He liked Stephanie particularly in this part, and thought her beautiful. One evening not long afterward he noticed her in his own home looking at his jades, particularly a row of bracelets and earrings. He liked the rhythmic outline of her body, which reminded him of a letter S in motion. Quite suddenly it came over him that she was a remarkable girl—very—destined, perhaps, to some significant future. At the same time Stephanie was thinking of him.

"Do you find them interesting?" he asked, stopping beside her.

"I think they're wonderful. Those dark greens, and that pale, fatty white! I can see how beautiful they would be in a Chinese setting. I have always wished we could find a Chinese or Japanese play to produce sometime."

"Yes, with your black hair those earrings would look well," said Cowperwood.

He had never deigned to comment on a feature of hers before. She turned her dark, brown-black eyes on him—velvety eyes with a kind of black glow in them—and now he noticed how truly fine they were, and how nice were her hands—brown almost as a Malay's.

He said nothing more; but the next day an unlabeled box was delivered to Stephanie at her home, containing a pair of jade earrings, a bracelet, and a brooch with Chinese characters intagliated. Stephanie was beside herself with delight. She gathered them up in her hands and kissed them, fastening the earrings in her ears and adjusting the bracelet and ring. Despite her experience with her friends and relatives, her stage associates, and her paramours, she was still a little unschooled in the world. Her heart was essentially poetic and innocent. No one had ever given her much of anything—not even her parents. Her allowance thus far in life had been a pitiful six dollars a week, outside of clothing. As she surveyed these pretty things in the privacy of her room she wondered oddly whether Cowperwood was going to like her. Would such a strong, hard businessman be interested in her? She had heard her father say he was becoming very rich. Was she a great actress, as some said she was, and would strong, able types of men like Cowperwood take to her—eventually? She had heard of Rachel, of Nell Gwynne, of the divine Sarah and her loves. She took the precious gifts and locked them in a black iron box which was sacred to her trinkets and her secrets.

The mere acceptance of these things in silence was sufficient indication to Cowperwood that she was of a friendly turn of mind. He waited patiently until one day a letter came to his office—not his house—addressed, "Frank Algernon Cowperwood, Personal." It was written in a small, neat, careful hand, almost printed.

I don't know how to thank you for your wonderful present. I didn't mean you should give them to me, and I know you sent them. I shall keep them with pleasure and wear them with delight. It was so nice of you to do this.

STEPHANIE PLATOW

Cowperwood studied the handwriting, the paper, the phraseology. For a girl of only a little over twenty this was wise and reserved and tactful. She might have written to him at his residence. He gave her the benefit of a week's time, and then found her in his own home one Sunday afternoon. Aileen had gone calling, and Stephanie was pretending to await her return.

"It's nice to see you there in that window," he said. "You fit your background perfectly."

"Do I?" The black-brown eyes burned soulfully. The paneling back of her was of dark oak, burnished by the rays of an afternoon winter sun.

Stephanie Platow had dressed for this opportunity. Her full, rich, short black hair was caught by a childish band of blood-red ribbon, holding it low over her temples and ears. Her lithe body, so harmonious in its graven roundness, was clad in an apple-green bodice and a black skirt with gussets of red about the hem; her smooth arms, from the elbow down, were bare. On one wrist was the jade bracelet he had given her. Her stockings were apple-green silk, and despite the chill of the day, her feet were shod in enticingly low slippers with brass buckles.

Cowperwood retired to the hall to hang up his overcoat, and came back smiling.

"Isn't Mrs. Cowperwood about?"

"The butler says she's out calling, but I thought I'd wait a little while, anyhow. She may come back."

She turned up a dark, smiling face to him, with languishing, inscrutable eyes, and he recognized the artist at last, full and clear.

"I see you like my bracelet, don't you?"

"It's beautiful," she replied, looking down and surveying it dreamily. "I don't always wear it. I carry it in my muff. I've just put it on for a little while. I carry them all with me always. I love them so. I like to feel them."

She opened a small chamois bag beside her—lying with her handkerchief and a sketchbook which she always carried —and took out the earrings and brooch.

Cowperwood glowed with a strange feeling of approval and enthusiasm at this manifestation of real interest. He liked jade himself very much, but more than that the feeling that prompted this expression in another. Roughly speaking, it might have been said of him that youth and hope in women—particularly youth when combined with beauty and ambition in a girl—touched him. He responded keenly to her impulse to do or be something in this world, whatever it might be, and he looked on the smart, egoistic vanity of so many with a kindly, tolerant, almost parental eye. Poor little organisms growing on the tree of life—they would burn out and fade soon enough. He did not know the ballad of the roses of yesterday, but if he had it would have appealed to him. He did not care to rifle them, willy-nilly; but should their temperaments or tastes incline them in his direction, they would not suffer vastly in their lives because of him. The fact was, the man was essentially generous where women were concerned.

"How nice of you!" he commented, smiling. "I like that." And then, seeing a notebook and pencil beside her, he asked, "What are you doing?"

"Just sketching."

"Let me see?"

"It's nothing much," she replied deprecatingly. "I don't draw very well."

"Gifted girl!" he replied, picking it up. "Paints, draws, carves on wood, plays, sings, acts."

"All rather badly," she sighed, turning her head languidly and looking away. In her sketchbook she had put all of her best drawings; there were sketches of nude women, dancers, torsos, bits of running figures, sad, heavy, sensuous heads and necks of sleeping girls—chins up, eyelids down—studies of her brothers and sister, and of her father and mother.

"Delightful!" exclaimed Cowperwood, keenly alive to a new treasure. Good heavens, where had been his eyes all this while? Here was a jewel lying at his doorstep—innocent, untarnished—a real jewel. These drawings suggested a fire of perception, smoldering and somber, which thrilled him.

"These are beautiful to me, Stephanie," he said simply, a strange, uncertain feeling of real affection creeping over him. The man's greatest love was for art. It was hypnotic to him. "Did you ever study art?" he asked.

"No."

"And you never studied acting?"

"No."

She shook her head in a slow, sad, enticing way. The black hair concealing her ears moved him strangely.

"I know the art of your stage work is real, and you have a natural art which I just seem to see. What has been the matter with me, anyhow?"

"Oh no," she sighed. "It seems to me that I merely play at everything. I could cry sometimes when I think how I go on."

"At twenty?"

"That is old enough." She smiled archly.

"Stephanie," he asked cautiously, "how old are you, exactly?"

"I will be twenty-one in April," she answered.

"Have your parents been very strict with you?"

She shook her head dreamily. "No; what makes you ask? They haven't paid very much attention to me. They've always liked Lucille and Gilbert and Ormond best." Her voice had a plaintive, neglecting ring. It was the voice she used in her best scenes on the stage.

"Don't they realize that you are very talented?"

"I think perhaps my mother feels that I may have some ability. My father doesn't, I'm sure. Why?"

She lifted those languorous, plaintive eyes.

"Why, Stephanie, if you want to know, I think you're wonderful. I thought so the other night when you were looking at those jades. It all came over me. You are an artist, truly, and I have been so busy I have scarcely seen it. Tell me one thing."

"Yes."

She drew in a soft breath, filling her chest and expanding her bosom, while she looked at him from under her black hair. Her hands were crossed idly in her lap. Then she looked demurely down.

"Look, Stephanie! Look up! I want to ask you something. You have known something of me for over a year. Do you like me?"

"I think you're very wonderful," she murmured.

"Is that all?"

"Isn't that much?" She smiled, shooting a dull, black-opal look in his direction.

"You wore my bracelet today. Were you very glad to get it?"

"Oh yes," she sighed with aspirated breath, pretending a kind of suffocation.

"How beautiful you really are!" he said, rising and looking down at her.

She shook her head.

"No."

"Yes!"

"No."

"Come, Stephanie! Stand by me and look at me. You are so tall and slender and graceful. You are like something out of Asia."

She sighed, turning in a sinuous way, as he slipped his arm about her.

"I don't think we should, should we?" she asked naively after a moment, pulling away from him.

"Stephanie!"

"I think I'd better go now, please."

CHAPTER XXVI

Love and War

It was during the earlier phases of his connection with Chicago street-railways that Cowperwood, ardently interesting himself in Stephanie Platow, developed as serious a sex affair as any that had yet held him. At once, after a few secret interviews with her, he adopted his favorite ruse in such matters and established bachelor quarters in the downtown section as a convenient meeting ground. Several conversations with Stephanie were not quite as illuminating as they might have been, for wonderful as she was—a kind of artistic godsend in this dull western atmosphere—she was also enigmatic and elusive, very. He learned speedily, in talking with her on several days when they met for lunch, of her dramatic ambitions, and of the seeming spiritual and artistic support she required from someone who would have faith in her and inspire her by his or her confidence. He learned all about the Garrick Players, her home intimacies and friends, the growing quarrels in the dramatic organization. He asked her, as they sat in a favorite and inconspicuous resort of his finding, during one of those moments when blood and not intellect was ruling between them, whether she had ever—

"Once," she naively admitted.

It was a great shock to Cowperwood. He had fancied her refreshingly innocent. But she explained it was all so accidental, so unintentional on her part, very. She described it all so gravely, soulfully, pathetically, with such a brooding, contemplative, backward searching of the mind, that he was astonished and in a way touched. What a pity! It was Gardner Knowles who had done this, she admitted. But he was not very much to blame, either. It just happened. She had tried to protest, but— Wasn't she angry? Yes, but then she was sorry to do anything to hurt Gardner Knowles. He was such a charming boy, and he had such a lovely mother and sister, and the like.

Cowperwood was astonished. He had reached that point in life where the absence of primal innocence in a woman was not very significant; but in Stephanie, seeing that she was so utterly charming, it was almost too bad. He thought what fools the Platows must be to tolerate this art atmosphere for Stephanie without keeping a sharp watch over it. Nevertheless, he was inclined to believe from observation thus far that Stephanie might be hard to watch. She was ingrainedly irresponsible, apparently—so artistically nebulous, so non-self-protective. To go on and be friends with this scamp! And yet she protested that never after that had there been the least thing between them. Cowperwood could scarcely believe it. She must be lying, and yet he liked her so. The very romantic, inconsequential way in which she narrated all this staggered, amused, and even fascinated him.

"But Stephanie," he argued curiously, "there must have been some aftermath to all this. What happened? What did you do?"

"Nothing." She shook her head.

He had to smile.

"But oh, don't let's talk about it!" she pleaded. "I don't want to. It hurts me. There was nothing more."

She sighed, and Cowperwood meditated. The evil was now done, and the best that he could do, if he cared for her at all —and he did—was to overlook it. He surveyed her oddly, wonderingly. What a charming soul she was, anyhow! How naive—how brooding! She had art—lots of it. Did he want to give her up?

As he might have known, it was dangerous to trifle with a type of this kind, particularly once awakened to the significance of promiscuity, and unless mastered by some absorbing passion. Stephanie had had too much flattery and affection heaped upon her in the past two years to be easily absorbed. Nevertheless, for the time being, anyhow, she was fascinated by the significance of Cowperwood. It was wonderful to have so fine, so powerful a man care for her. She

conceived of him as a very great artist in his realm rather
than as a businessman, and he grasped this fact after a very
little while and appreciated it. To his delight, she was even
more beautiful physically than he had anticipated—a smoldering, passionate girl who met him with a fire which, though
somber, quite rivaled his own. She was different, too, in her
languorous acceptance of all that he bestowed from anyone
he had ever known. She was as tactful as Rita Sohlberg—
more so—but so preternaturally silent at times.

"Stephanie," he would exclaim, "do talk. What are you
thinking of? You dream like an African native."

She merely sat and smiled in a dark way or sketched or
modeled him. She was constantly penciling something, until
moved by the fever of her blood, when she would sit and
look at him or brood silently, eyes down. Then, when he
would reach for her with seeking hands, she would sigh, "Oh
yes, oh yes!"

Those were delightful days with Stephanie.

In the matter of young MacDonald's request for fifty thousand dollars in securities, as well as the attitude of the other
editors—Hyssop, Braxton, Ricketts, and so on—who had
proved subtly critical, Cowperwood conferred with Addison
and McKenty.

"A likely lad, that," commented McKenty, succinctly,
when he heard it. "He'll do better than his father in one
way, anyhow. He'll probably make more money."

McKenty had seen old General MacDonald just once in
his life, and liked him.

"I should like to know what the general would think of
that if he knew," commented Addison, who admired the old
editor greatly. "I'm afraid he wouldn't sleep very well."

"There is just one thing," observed Cowperwood thoughtfully. "This young man will certainly come into control of the
Inquirer sometime. He looks to me like someone who
would not readily forget an injury." He smiled sardonically.
So did McKenty and Addison.

"Be that as it may," suggested the latter, "he isn't editor
yet." McKenty, who never revealed his true views to anyone
but Cowperwood, waited until he had the latter alone to observe:

"What can they do? Your request is a reasonable one.
Why shouldn't the city give you the tunnel? It's no good to

anyone as it is. And the loop is no more than the other roads have now. I'm thinking it's the Chicago City Railway and that silk-stocking crowd in State Street or that gas crowd that's talking against you. I've heard them before. Give them what they want, and it's a fine moral cause. Give it to anyone else, and there's something wrong with it. It's little attention I pay to them. We have the council. Let it pass the ordinances. It can't be proved that they don't do it willingly. The mayor is a sensible man. He'll sign them. Let young MacDonald talk if he wants to. If he says too much you can talk to his father. As for Hyssop, he's an old grandmother anyhow. I've never known him to be for a public improvement yet that was really good for Chicago unless Schryhart or Merrill or Arneel or someone else of that crowd wanted it. I know them of old. My advice is to go ahead and never mind them. To hell with them! Things will be sweet enough, once you are as powerful as they are. They'll get nothing in the future without paying for it. It's little enough they've ever done to further anything that I wanted."

Cowperwood, however, remained cool and thoughtful. Should he pay young MacDonald? he asked himself. Addison knew of no influence that he could bring to bear. Finally, after much thought, he decided to proceed as he had planned. Consequently, the reporters around the City Hall and the council chamber, who were in touch with Alderman Thomas Dowling, McKenty's leader on the floor of council, and those who called occasionally—quite regularly, in fact—at the offices of the North Chicago Street Railway Company, Cowperwood's comfortable new offices in the North Side, were now given to understand that two ordinances—one granting the free use of the La Salle Street tunnel for an unlimited period (practically a gift of it), and another granting a right of way in La Salle, Munroe, Dearborn, and Randolph streets for the proposed loop—would be introduced in council very shortly. Cowperwood granted a very flowery interview, in which he explained quite enthusiastically all that the North Chicago company was doing and proposed to do, and made clear what a splendid development it would assure to the North Side and to the business center.

At once Schryhart, Merrill, and some individuals connected with the Chicago West Division Company began to complain in the newspaper offices and at the clubs to Ricketts, Braxton, young MacDonald, and the other editors. Envy of the pyrotechnic progress of the man was as much a factor in this as anything else. It did not make the slightest difference, as Cowperwood had sarcastically pointed out, that every other corporation of any significance in Chicago had asked and received without money and without price. Somehow his career in connection with Chicago gas, his venturesome if unsuccessful effort to enter Chicago society, his self-acknowledged Philadelphia record, rendered the sensitive cohorts of the ultraconservative exceedingly fearful. In Schryhart's *Chronicle* appeared a news column which was headed, "Plain Grab of City Tunnel Proposed." It was a very truculent statement, and irritated Cowperwood greatly. The *Press* (Mr. Haguenin's paper), on the other hand, was most cordial to the idea of the loop, while appearing to be a little uncertain as to whether the tunnel should be granted without compensation or not. Editor Hyssop felt called upon to insist that something more than merely nominal compensation should be made for the tunnel, and that "riders" should be inserted in the loop ordinance making it incumbent upon the North Chicago company to keep those thoroughfares in full repair and well lighted. The *Inquirer,* under Mr. MacDonald, junior, and Mr. Du Bois, was in rumbling opposition. No free tunnels, it cried; no free ordinances for privileges in the downtown heart. It had nothing to say about Cowperwood personally. The *Globe,* Mr. Braxton's paper, was certain that no free rights to the tunnel should be given, and that a much better route for the loop could be found—one larger and more serviceable to the public, one that might be made to include State Street or Wabash Avenue, or both, where Mr. Merrill's store was located. So it went, and one could see quite clearly to what extent the interests of the public figured in the majority of these particular viewpoints.

Cowperwood, individual, reliant, utterly indifferent to opposition of any kind, was somewhat angered by the manner in which his overtures had been received, but still felt that the best way out of his troubles was to follow McKenty's advice and get power first. Once he had his cable conduit down, his new cars running, the tunnel rebuilt, brilliantly lighted, and the bridge crush disposed of, the public would see what a vast change for the better had been made and would support him. Finally all things were in readiness and the ordinance jammed through. McKenty, being a little dubious of the outcome, had a rocking-chair brought into the council chamber itself during the hours when the ordinances were up for consideration. In this he sat, presumably as a curious spectator, actually as a master dictating the course of liquidation in hand. Neither Cowperwood nor anyone else knew of McKenty's action until too late to interfere with it. Addison and Videra, when they read about it as sneeringly set forth in the news columns of the papers, lifted and then wrinkled their eyebrows.

"That looks like pretty rough work to me," commented Addison. "I thought McKenty had more tact. That's his early Irish training."

Alexander Rambaud, who was an admirer and follower of Cowperwood's, wondered whether the papers were lying, whether it really could be true that Cowperwood had a serious political compact with McKenty which would allow him to walk roughshod over public opinion. Rambaud considered Cowperwood's proposition so sane and reasonable that he could not understand why there should be serious opposition, or why Cowperwood and McKenty should have to resort to such methods.

However, the streets requisite for the loop were granted. The tunnel was leased for 999 years at the nominal sum of five thousand dollars per year. It was understood that the old bridges over State, Dearborn, and Clark streets should be put in repair or removed; but there was a joker inserted elsewhere which nullified this. Instantly there were stormy outbursts in the *Chronicle, Inquirer,* and *Globe;* but Cowperwood, when he read them, merely smiled. "Let them grumble," he said to himself. "I put a very reasonable proposition before them. Why should they complain? I'm doing more now than the Chicago City Railway. It's jealousy, that's all. If Schryhart or Merrill had asked for it, there would have been no complaint."

McKenty called at the offices of the Chicago Trust Company to congratulate Cowperwood. "The boys did as I thought they would," he said. "I had to be there, though, for I heard someone say that about ten of them intended to ditch us at the last moment."

"Good work, good work!" replied Cowperwood cheerfully. "This row will all blow over. It would be the same whenever we asked. The air will clear up. We'll give them such a fine service that they'll forget all about this, and be glad they gave us the tunnel."

Just the same, the morning after the enabling ordinances had passed, there was much derogatory comment in influential quarters. Mr. Norman Schryhart, who, through his publisher, had been fulminating defensively against Cowperwood, stared solemnly at Mr. Ricketts when they met.

"Well," said the magnate, who imagined he foresaw a threatened attack on his Chicago City Railway preserves, "I see our friend Mr. Cowperwood has managed to get his own way with the council. I am morally certain he uses money to get what he is after as freely as a fireman uses water. He's as slippery as an eel. I should be glad if we could establish that there is a community of interest between him and these politicians around City Hall, or between him and Mr. McKenty. I believe he has set out to dominate this city politically as well as financially, and he'll need constant watching. If public opinion can be aroused against him he may be dislodged in the course of time. Chicago may get too uncomfortable for him. I know Mr. McKenty personally, but he is not the kind of man I care to do business with."

Mr. Schryhart's method of negotiating at City Hall was through certain reputable but somewhat slow-going lawyers who were in the employ of the South Side company. They had never been able to reach Mr. McKenty at all. Ricketts echoed a hearty approval. "You're very right," he said with owlish smugness, adjusting a waistcoat button that had come loose, and smoothing his cuffs. "He's a prince of politicians. We'll have to look sharp if we ever trap him." Mr. Ricketts would have been glad to sell out to Mr. Cowperwood if he had not been so heavily obligated to Mr. Schryhart. He had no especial affection for Cowperwood, but he recognized in him a coming man.

Young MacDonald, talking to Clifford Du Bois in the office of the *Inquirer,* and reflecting how little his private telephone message had availed him, was in a waspish, ironic frame of mind.

"Well," he said, "it seems our friend Cowperwood hasn't taken our advice. He may make his mark, but the *Inquirer* isn't through with him by a long shot. He'll be wanting other things from the city in the future."

Clifford Du Bois regarded his acid young superior with a curious eye. He knew nothing of MacDonald's private telephone message to Cowperwood; but he knew how he himself would have dealt with the crafty financier had he been in MacDonald's position.

"Yes, Cowperwood is shrewd," was his comment. "Pritchard, our political man, says the ways of the City Hall are greased straight up to the mayor and McKenty, and that Cowperwood can have anything he wants at any time. Tom Dowling eats out of his hand, and you know what that means. Old General Van Sickle is working for him in some way. Did you ever see that old buzzard flying around if there wasn't something dead in the woods?"

"He's a slick one," remarked MacDonald. "But as for Cowperwood, he can't get away with this sort of thing very long. He's going too fast. He wants too much."

Mr. Du Bois smiled quite secretly. It amused him to see how Cowperwood had brushed MacDonald and his objections aside—dispensed for the time being with the services of the *Inquirer*. Du Bois confidently believed that if the old general had been at home he would have supported the financier.

Within eight months after seizing the La Salle Street tunnel and gobbling four of the principal downtown streets for his loop, Cowperwood turned his eyes toward the completion of the second part of the program—that of taking over the Washington Street tunnel and the Chicago West Division company, which was still drifting along under its old horse-car regime. It was the story of the North Side company all over again. Stockholders of a certain type—the average—are extremely nervous, sensitive, fearsome. They are like that peculiar bivalve, the clam, which at the slightest sense of untoward pressure withdraws into its shell and ceases all activity. The city tax department began by instituting proceedings against the West Division company, compelling them to disgorge various unpaid streetcar taxes which had hitherto been conveniently neglected. The city highway department was constantly jumping on them for neglect of street repairs. The city water department, by some hocus-pocus, made it its business to discover that they had been stealing water. On the other hand were the smiling representatives of Cowperwood, Kaffrath, Addison, Videra, and others, approaching one director or stockholder after another with glistening accounts of what a splendid day would set in for the Chicago West Division company if only it would lease 51 percent of its holdings—51 percent of 1250 shares, par value two hundred dollars—for the fascinating sum of six hundred dollars per share, and 30 percent interest on all stock not assumed.

Who could resist? Starve and beat a dog on the one hand; wheedle, pet, and hold meat in front of it on the other, and it can soon be brought to perform. Cowperwood knew this. His emissaries for good and evil were tireless. In the end—and it was not long in coming—the directors and chief stockholders of the Chicago West Division company succumbed; and then, lo! the sudden leasing by the Chicago West Division company of all its property to the North Chicago Street Railway Company, lessee in turn of the Chicago City Passenger Railway, a line which Cowperwood had organized to take over the Washington Street tunnel. How had he accomplished it? The question was on the tip of every financial tongue. Who were the men or the organization providing the enormous sums necessary to pay six hundred dollars per share for 650 shares of the 1250 belonging to the old West Division company, and 30 percent per year on all the remainder? Where was the money coming from to cable all these lines? It was simple enough if they had only thought.

Before the newspapers or the public could suitably protest, crowds of men were at work day and night in the business heart of the city, their flaring torches and resounding hammers making a fitful bedlamic world of that region; they were laying the first great cable loop and repairing the La Salle Street tunnel. It was the same on the North and West Sides, where concrete conduits were being laid, new grip and trailer cars built, new carbarns erected, and large, shining powerhouses put up. The city, so long used to the old bridge delays, the straw-strewn, stoveless horsecars on their jumping rails, was agog to see how fine this new service would be. The La Salle Street tunnel was soon aglow with white plaster and electric lights. The long streets and avenues of the North Side were threaded with concrete-lined conduits and heavy street rails. The powerhouses were completed and the system was started, even while the contracts for the changes on the West Side were being let.

Schryhart and his associates were amazed at this swiftness of action, this dizzy phantasmagoria of financial operations. It looked very much to the conservative traction interests of Chicago as if this young giant out of the East had it in mind to eat up the whole city. The Chicago Trust Company, which he, Addison, McKenty, and others had organized to manipulate the principal phases of the local bond issues, and of which he was rumored to be in control, was in a flourishing condition. Apparently he could now write his check for millions, and yet he was not beholden, so far as the older and more conservative multimillionaires of Chicago were concerned, to any one of them. The worst of it was that this Cowperwood—an upstart, a jailbird, a stranger whom they had done their best to suppress financially and ostracize socially, had now become an attractive, even a sparkling figure in the eyes of the Chicago public. His views and opinions on almost any topic were freely quoted; the newspapers, even the most antagonistic, did not dare to neglect him. Their owners were now fully alive to the fact that a new financial rival had appeared who was worthy of their steel.

CHAPTER XXVII

A Financier Bewitched

It was interesting to note how, able though he was, and bound up with this vast street-railway enterprise which was beginning to affect several thousand men, his mind could find intense relief and satisfaction in the presence and actions of Stephanie Platow. It is not too much to say that in her, perhaps, he found revivified the spirit and personality of Rita Sohlberg. Rita, however, had not contemplated disloyalty—it had never occurred to her to be faithless to Cowperwood so long as he was fond of her anymore than for a long time it had been possible for her, even after all his philanderings, to be faithless to Sohlberg. Stephanie, on the other hand, had the strange feeling that affection was not necessarily identified with physical loyalty, and that she could be fond of Cowperwood and still deceive him—a fact which was based on her lack as yet of a true enthusiasm for him. She loved him and she didn't. Her attitude was not necessarily

identified with her heavy, lizardish animality, though that
had something to do with it; but rather with a vague, kindly
generosity which permitted her to feel that it was hard to
break with Gardner Knowles and Lane Cross after they had
been so nice to her. Gardner Knowles had sung her praises
here, there, and everywhere, and was attempting to spread
her fame among the legitimate theatrical enterprises which
came to the city, in order that she might be taken up and
made into a significant figure. Lane Cross was wildly fond
of her in an inadequate way which made it hard to break
with him, and yet certain that she would eventually. There
was still another man—a young playwright and poet by the
name of Forbes Gurney—tall, fair, passionate—who had
newly arrived on the scene and was courting her, or, rather,
being courted by her at odd moments, for her time was
her own. In her artistically errant way she had refused to
go to school like her sister, and was idling about, developing,
as she phrased it, her artistic possibilities.

Cowperwood, as was natural, heard much of her stage
life. At first he took all this palaver with a grain of salt, the
babbling of an ardent nature interested in the flighty romance
of the studio world. By degrees, however, he became curious
as to the freedom of her actions, the ease with which she
drifted from place to place—Lane Cross's studio; Bliss
Bridge's bachelor rooms, where he appeared always to be
receiving his theatrical friends of the Garrick Players; Mr.
Gardner Knowles's home on the near North Side, where he
was frequently entertaining a party after the theater. It
seemed to Cowperwood, to say the least, that Stephanie was
leading a rather free and inconsequential existence, and yet
it reflected her exactly—the color of her soul. But he began
to doubt and wonder.

"Where were you, Stephanie, yesterday?" he would ask
when they met for lunch, or in the evenings early, or when
she called at his new offices on the North Side, as she sometimes did to walk or drive with him.

"Oh, yesterday morning I was at Lane Cross's studio trying
on some of his Indian shawls and veils. He has such a lot of
those things—some of the loveliest oranges and blues. You
just ought to see me in them. I wish you might."

"Alone?"

"For a while. I thought Ethel Tuckerman and Bliss Bridge
would be there, but they didn't come until later. Lane Cross

is such a dear. He's sort of silly at times, but I like him. His portraits are so bizarre."

She went off into a description of his pretentious but insignificant art.

Cowperwood marveled, not at Lane Cross's art nor his shawls, but at this world in which Stephanie moved. He could not quite make her out. He had never been able to make her explain satisfactorily that first single relationship with Gardner Knowles, which she declared had ended so abruptly. Since then he had doubted, as was his nature; but this girl was so sweet, childish, irreconcilable with herself, like a wandering breath of air, or a pale-colored flower, that he scarcely knew what to think. The artistically inclined are not prone to quarrel with an enticing sheaf of flowers. She was heavenly to him, coming in, as she did at times when he was alone, with bland eyes, and yielding herself in a kind of summery ecstasy. She had always something artistic to tell of storms, winds, dust, clouds, smoke forms, the outline of buildings, the lake, the stage. She would cuddle in his arms and quote long sections from *Romeo and Juliet, Paolo and Francesca, The Ring and the Book,* Keats's *Eve of St. Agnes.* He hated to quarrel with her, because she was like a wild rose or some art form in nature. Her sketchbook was always full of new things. Her muff, or the light silk shawl she wore in summer, sometimes concealed a modeled figure of some kind which she would produce with a look like that of a doubting child, and if he wanted it, if he liked it, he could have it. Cowperwood meditated deeply. He scarcely knew what to think.

The constant atmosphere of suspicion and doubt in which he was compelled to remain came by degrees to distress and anger him. While she was with him she was clinging enough, but when she was away she was ardently cheerful and happy. Unlike the station he had occupied in so many previous affairs, he found himself, after the first little while, asking her whether she loved him instead of submitting to the same question from her.

He thought that with his means, his position, his future possibilities, he had the power to bind almost any woman once drawn to his personality; but Stephanie was too young and too poetic to be greatly impaired by wealth and fame, and she was not yet sufficiently gripped by the lure of him. She loved him in her strange way; but she was interested also by the latest arrival, Forbes Gurney. This tall, melancholy youth, with brown eyes and pale brown hair, was very poor. He hailed from southern Minnesota, and what between a penchant for journalism, verse-writing, and some dramatic work, was somewhat undecided as to his future. His present occupation was that of an installment collector for a furniture company, which set him free, as a rule, at three o'clock in the afternoon. He was trying, in a mooning way, to identify himself with the Chicago newspaper world, and was a discovery of Gardner Knowles.

Stephanie had seen him about the rooms of the Garrick Players. She had looked at his longish face with its aureole of soft, crinkly hair, his fine wide mouth, deep-set eyes, and good nose, and had been touched by an atmosphere of wistfulness, or, let us say, life-hunger. Gardner Knowles brought a poem of his once, which he had borrowed from him, and read it to the company, Stephanie, Ethel Tuckerman, Lane Cross, and Irma Ottley assembled.

"Listen to this," Knowles had suddenly exclaimed, taking it out of his pocket.

It concerned a garden of the moon with the fragrance of pale blossoms, a mystic pool, some ancient figures of joy, a quavered Lucidian tune.

> With eerie flute and rhythmic thrum
> Of muted strings and beaten drum.

Stephanie Platow had sat silent, caught by a quality that was akin to her own. She asked to see it, and read it in silence.

"I think it's charming," she said.

Thereafter she hovered in the vicinity of Forbes Gurney. Why, she could scarcely say. It was not coquetry. She just drew near, talked to him of stage work and her plays and her ambitions. She sketched him as she had Cowperwood and others, and one day Cowperwood found three studies of Forbes Gurney in her notebook, idyllically done, a note of romantic feeling about them.

"Who is this?" he asked.

"Oh, he's a young poet who comes up to the Players— Forbes Gurney. He's so charming; he's so pale and dreamy."

Cowperwood contemplated the sketches curiously. His eyes clouded.

"Another one of Stephanie's adherents," he commented teasingly. "It's a long procession I've joined. Gardner Knowles, Lane Cross, Bliss Bridge, Forbes Gurney."

Stephanie merely pouted moodily.

"How you talk! Bliss Bridge, Gardner Knowles! I admit I like them all, but that's all I do. They're just sweet and dear. You'd like Lane Cross yourself; he's such a foolish old Polly. As for Forbes Gurney, he just drifts up there once in a while as one of the crowd. I scarcely know him."

"Exactly," said Cowperwood dolefully; "but you sketch him."

For some reason Cowperwood did not believe this. Back in his brain he did not believe Stephanie at all, he did not trust her. Yet he was intensely fond of her—the more so, perhaps, because of this.

"Tell me truly, Stephanie," he said to her one day, urgently and yet very diplomatically. "I don't care at all, so far as your past is concerned. You and I are close enough to reach a perfect understanding. But you didn't tell me the whole truth about you and Knowles, did you? Tell me truly now. I shan't mind. I can understand well enough how it could have happened. It doesn't make the least bit of difference to me, really."

Stephanie was off her guard for once, in no truly fencing mood. She was troubled at times about her various relations, anxious to put herself straight with Cowperwood or with anyone whom she truly liked. Compared to Cowperwood and his affairs, Cross and Knowles were trivial, and yet Knowles was interesting to her. Compared to Cowperwood, Forbes Gurney was a stripling beggar, and yet Gurney had what Cowperwood did not have—a sad, poetic lure. He awakened her sympathies. He was such a lonely boy. Cowperwood was so strong, brilliant, magnetic.

Perhaps it was with some idea of clearing up her moral status generally that she finally said: "Well, I didn't tell you the exact truth about it, either. I was a little ashamed to."

At the close of her confession, which involved only Knowles, and was incomplete at that, Cowperwood burned with a kind of angry resentment. Why trifle with a lying prostitute? That she was an inconsequential free lover at twenty-one was quite plain. And yet there was something so strangely large about the girl, so magnetic, and she was so beautiful after her kind, that he could not think of giving her up. She reminded him of himself.

"Well, Stephanie," he said, trampling underfoot an impulse to insult or rebuke and dismiss her, "you are strange. Why didn't you tell me this before? I have asked and asked. Do you really mean to say that you care for me at all?"

"How can you ask that?" she demanded reproachfully, feeling that she had been rather foolish in confessing. Perhaps she would lose him now, and she did not want to do that. Because his eyes blazed with a jealous hardness she burst into tears. "Oh, I wish I had never told you! There is nothing to tell, anyhow. I never wanted to."

Cowperwood was nonplussed. He knew human nature pretty well, and woman nature; his common sense told him that this girl was not to be trusted, and yet he was drawn to her. Perhaps she was not lying, and these tears were real.

"And you positively assure me that this was all—that there wasn't anyone else before, and no one since?"

Stephanie dried her eyes. They were in his private rooms in Randolph Street, the bachelor rooms he had fitted for himself as a changing place for various affairs.

"I don't believe you care for me at all," she observed dolefully, reproachfully. "I don't believe you understand me. I don't think you believe me. When I tell you how things are you don't understand. I don't lie. I can't. If you are so doubting now, perhaps you had better not see me anymore. I want to be frank with you, but if you won't let me—"

She paused heavily, gloomily, very sorrowfully, and Cowperwood surveyed her with a kind of yearning. What an unreasoning pull she had for him! He did not believe her, and yet he could not let her go.

"Oh, I don't know what to think," he commented morosely. "I certainly don't want to quarrel with you, Stephanie, for telling me the truth. Please don't deceive me. You are a remarkable girl. I can do so much for you if you will let me. You ought to see that."

"But I'm not deceiving you," she repeated wearily. "I should think you could see."

"I believe you," he went on, trying to deceive himself against his better judgment. "But you lead such a free, unconventional life."

"Ah," thought Stephanie, "perhaps I talk too much."

"I am very fond of you. You appeal to me so much. I love you, really. Don't deceive me. Don't run with all these silly simpletons. They are really not worthy of you. I shall be able to get a divorce one of these days, and then I would be glad to marry you."

"But I'm not running with them in the sense that you think. They're not anything to me beyond mere entertainment. Oh, I like them, of course. Lane Cross is a dear in his way, and so is Gardner Knowles. They have all been nice to me."

Cowperwood's gorge rose at her calling Lane Cross dear. It incensed him, and yet he held his peace.

"Do give me your word that there will never be anything between you and any of these men so long as you are friendly with me?" he almost pleaded—a strange role for him. "I don't care to share you with anyone else. I won't. I don't mind what you have done in the past, but I don't want you to be unfaithful in the future."

"What a question! Of course I won't. But if you don't believe me—oh, dear—"

Stephanie sighed painfully, and Cowperwood's face clouded with angry though well-concealed suspicion and jealousy.

"Well, I'll tell you, Stephanie, I believe you now. I'm going to take your word. But if you do deceive me, and I should find it out, I will quit you the same day. I do not care to share you with anyone else. What I can't understand, if you care for me, is how you can take so much interest in all these affairs? It certainly isn't devotion to your art that's impelling you, is it?"

"Oh, are you going to go on quarreling with me?" asked Stephanie naively. "Won't you believe me when I say that I love you? Perhaps—" But here her histrionic ability came to her aid, and she sobbed violently.

Cowperwood took her in his arms. "Never mind," he soothed. "I do believe you. I do think you care for me. Only I wish you weren't such a butterfly temperament, Stephanie."

So this particular lesion for the time being was healed.

CHAPTER XXVIII

The Exposure of Stephanie

At the same time the thought of readjusting her relations so that they would avoid disloyalty to Cowperwood was never further from Stephanie's mind. Let no one quarrel with Stephanie Platow. She was an unstable chemical compound, artistic to her fingertips, not understood or properly guarded by her family. Her interest in Cowperwood, his force and ability, was intense. So was her interest in Forbes Gurney—the atmosphere of poetry that enveloped him. She studied him curiously on the various occasions when they met, and finding him bashful and recessive, set out to lure him. She felt that he was lonely and depressed and poor, and her womanly capacity for sympathy naturally bade her be tender.

Her end was easily achieved. One night when they were all out in Bliss Bridge's singlesticker—a fast-sailing saucer—Stephanie and Forbes Gurney sat forward of the mast looking at the silver moon track which was directly ahead. The rest were in the cockpit cutting up—laughing and singing. It was very plain to all that Stephanie was becoming interested in Forbes Gurney; and since he was charming and she willful, nothing was done to interfere with them, except to throw an occasional jest their way. Gurney, new to love and romance, scarcely knew how to take his good fortune, how to begin. He told Stephanie of his home life in the wheat fields of the Northwest, how his family had moved from Ohio when he was three, and how difficult were the labors he had always undergone. He had stopped in his plowing many a day to stand under a tree and write a poem—such as it was—or to watch the birds or to wish he could go to college or to Chicago. She looked at him with dreamy eyes, her dark skin turned a copper bronze in the moonlight, her black hair irradiated with a strange, luminous grayish blue. Forbes Gurney, alive to beauty in all its forms, ventured finally to touch her hand—she of Knowles, Cross, and Cowperwood—and she thrilled from head to toe. This boy was so sweet. His curly brown hair gave him a kind of Greek innocence and aspect. She did not move but waited, hoping he would do more.

"I wish I might talk to you as I feel," he finally said hoarsely, a catch in his throat.

She laid one hand on his.

"You dear!" she said.

He realized now that he might. A great ecstasy fell upon him. He smoothed her hand, then slipped his arm about her waist, then ventured to kiss the dark cheek turned dreamily from him. Artfully her head sank to his shoulder, and he murmured wild nothings—how divine she was, how artistic, how wonderful! With her view of things it could only end one way. She maneuvered him into calling on her at her home, into studying her books and plays on the top floor sitting room, into hearing her sing. Once fully in his arms, the rest was easy by suggestion. He learned she was no longer innocent, and then—

In the meantime Cowperwood mingled his speculations concerning large powerhouses, immense reciprocating engines, the problem of a wage scale for his new two thousand employees, some of whom were threatening to strike, the problem of securing, bonding, and equipping the La Salle Street tunnel and a downtown loop in La Salle, Munroe, Dearborn, and Randolph Streets, with mental inquiries and pictures as to what possibly Stephanie Platow might be doing. He could only make appointments with her from time to time. He did not fail to note that after he began to make use of information she let drop as to her whereabouts from day to day and her free companionship, he heard less of Gardner Knowles, Lane Cross, and Forbes Gurney, and more of Georgia Timberlake and Ethel Tuckerman. Why this sudden reticence? On one occasion she did say of Forbes Gurney "that he was having such a hard time, and that his clothes weren't as nice as they should be, poor dear!" Stephanie herself, owing to gifts made to her by Cowperwood, was resplendent these days. She took just enough to complete her wardrobe according to her taste.

"Why not send him to me?" Cowperwood asked. "I

might find something to do for him." He would have been
perfectly willing to put him in some position where he could
keep track of his time. However, Mr. Gurney never sought
him for a position, and Stephanie ceased to speak of his
poverty. A gift of two hundred dollars, which Cowperwood
made her in June, was followed by an accidental meeting
with her and Gurney in Washington Street. Mr. Gurney, pale
and pleasant, was very well dressed indeed. He wore a pin
which Cowperwood knew had once belonged to Stephanie.
She was in no way confused. Finally Stephanie let it out
that Lane Cross, who had gone to New Hampshire for the
summer, had left his studio in her charge. Cowperwood decided to have this studio watched.

There was in Cowperwood's employ at this time a young
newspaperman, an ambitious spark aged twenty-six, by the
name of Francis Kennedy. He had written a very intelligent
article for the Sunday *Inquirer*, describing Cowperwood and
his plans, and pointing out what a remarkable man he was.
This pleased Cowperwood. When Kennedy called one day,
announcing smartly that he was anxious to get out of rep-
ortorial work, and inquiring whether he couldn't find something to do in the street-railway world, Cowperwood saw in
him a possibly useful tool.

"I'll try you out as secretary for a while," he said pleasantly. "There are a few special things I want done. If you
succeed in those, I may find something else for you later."

Kennedy had been working for him only a little while when
he said to him one day: "Francis, did you ever hear of a
young man by the name of Forbes Gurney in the newspaper
world?"

They were in Cowperwood's private office.

"No, sir," replied Francis, briskly.

"You have heard of an organization called the Garrick
Players, haven't you?"

"Yes, sir."

"Well, Francis, do you suppose you could undertake a
little piece of detective work for me, and handle it intelligently and quietly?"

"I think so," said Francis, who was the pink of perfection
this morning in a brown suit, garnet tie, and sard sleeve
links. His shoes were immaculately polished, and his young,
healthy face glistened.

"I'll tell you what I want you to do. There is a young

actress, or amateur actress, by the name of Stephanie Platow, who frequents the studio of an artist named Cross in the New Arts Building. She may even occupy it in his absence—I don't know. I want you to find out for me what the relations of Mr. Gurney and this woman are. I have certain business reasons for wanting to know."

Young Kennedy was all attention.

"You couldn't tell me where I could find out anything about this Mr. Gurney to begin with, could you?" he asked.

"I think he is a friend of a critic here by the name of Gardner Knowles. You might ask him. I need not say that you must never mention me."

"Oh, I understand that thoroughly, Mr. Cowperwood."

Young Kennedy departed, meditating. How was he to do this? With true journalistic skill he first sought other newspapermen, from whom he learned—a bit from one and a scrap from another—of the character of the Garrick Players, and of the women who belonged to it. He pretended to be writing a one-act play, which he hoped to have produced.

He then visited Lane Cross's studio, posing as a newspaper interviewer. Mr. Cross was out of town, so the elevator man said. His studio was closed.

Mr. Kennedy meditated on this fact for a moment.

"Does anyone use his studio during the summer months?" he asked.

"I believe there is a young woman who comes here—yes."

"You don't happen to know who it is?"

"Yes, I do. Her name is Platow. What do you want to know for?"

"Looky here," exclaimed Kennedy, surveying the rather shabby attendant with a cordial and persuasive eye, "do you want to make some money—five or ten dollars, and without any trouble to you?"

The elevator man, whose wages were exactly eight dollars a week, pricked up his ears.

"I want to know who comes here with this Miss Platow, when they come—all about it. I'll make it fifteen dollars if I find out what I want, and I'll give you five right now."

The elevator factotum had just sixty-five cents in his pocket at the time. He looked at Kennedy with some uncertainty and much desire.

"Well, what can I do?" he repeated. "I'm not here after six. The janitor runs this elevator from six to twelve."

"There isn't a room vacant anywhere near this one, is there?" Kennedy asked speculatively.

The factotum thought. "Yes, there is. One just across the hall."

"What time does she come here as a rule?"

"I don't know anything about nights. In the day she sometimes comes mornings, sometimes in the afternoon."

"Anybody with her?"

"Sometimes a man, sometimes a girl or two. I haven't really paid much attention to her, to tell you the truth."

Kennedy walked away whistling.

From this day on Mr. Kennedy became a watcher over this very unconventional atmosphere. He was in and out, principally observing the comings and goings of Mr. Gurney. He found what he naturally suspected, that Mr. Gurney and Stephanie spent hours here at peculiar times—after a company of friends had jollified, for instance, and all had left, including Gurney, when the latter would quietly return, with Stephanie sometimes, if she had left with the others, alone if she had remained behind. The visits were of varying duration, and Kennedy, to be absolutely accurate, kept days, dates, the duration of the hours, which he left noted in a sealed envelope for Cowperwood in the morning. Cowperwood was enraged, but so great was his interest in Stephanie that he was not prepared to act. He wanted to see to what extent her duplicity would go.

The novelty of this atmosphere and its effect on him was astonishing. Although his mind was vigorously employed during the day, nevertheless his thoughts kept returning constantly. Where was she? What was she doing? The bland way in which she could lie reminded him of himself. To think that she should prefer anyone else to him, especially at this time when he was shining as a great constructive factor in the city, was too much. It smacked of age, his ultimate displacement by youth. It cut and hurt.

One morning, after a peculiarly exasperating night of thought concerning her, he said to young Kennedy: "I have a suggestion for you. I wish you would get this elevator man you are working with down there to get you a duplicate key to this studio, and see if there is a bolt on the inside. Let me know when you do. Bring me the key. The next time she

is there of an evening with Mr. Gurney step out and telephone
me."

The climax came one night several weeks after this dis-
couraging investigation began. There was a heavy yellow
moon in the sky, and a warm, sweet summer wind was
blowing. Stephanie had called on Cowperwood at his office
about four to say that instead of staying downtown with
him, as they had casually planned, she was going to her home
on the West Side to attend a garden party of some kind at
Georgia Timberlake's. Cowperwood looked at her with—for
him—a morbid eye. He was all cheer, geniality, pleasant
badinage; but he was thinking all the while what a shameless enigma she was, how well she played her part, what a
fool she must take him to be. He gave her youth, her passion, her attractiveness, her natural promiscuity of soul due
credit; but he could not forgive her for not loving him
perfectly, as had so many others. She had on a summery
black and white frock and a fetching brown Leghorn hat,
which, with a rich red poppy ornamenting a flare over her
left ear and a peculiar ruching of white and black silk about
the crown, made her seem strangely young, debonair, a study
in Hebraic and American origins.

"Going to have a nice time, are you?" he asked genially,
politely, eyeing her in his enigmatic and inscrutable way.
"Going to shine among that charming company you keep?
I suppose all the standbys will be there—Bliss Bridge, Mr.
Knowles, Mr. Cross—dancing attendance on you?"

He failed to mention Mr. Gurney.

Stephanie nodded cheerfully. She seemed in an innocent
outing mood.

Cowperwood smiled, thinking how one of these days—
very shortly, perhaps—he was certain to take a signal revenge. He would catch her in a lie, in a compromising position somewhere—in this studio, perhaps—and dismiss her
with contempt. In an elder day, if they had lived in Tur-
key, he would have had her strangled, sewn in a sack, and
thrown into the Bosporus. As it was, he could only dismiss
her. He smiled and smiled, smoothing her hand. "Have a good
time," he called as she left. Later, at his own home—it was
nearly midnight—Mr. Kennedy called him up.

"Mr. Cowperwood?"

"Yes."

"You know the studio in the New Arts Building?"

"Yes."

"It is occupied now."

Cowperwood called a servant to bring him his runabout. He had had a downtown locksmith make a round key stem with a bored clutch at the end of it—a hollow which would fit over the end of such a key as he had to the studio and turn it easily from the outside. He felt in his pocket for it, jumped into his runabout, and hurried away. When he reached the New Arts Building he found Kennedy in the hall and dismissed him. "Thanks," he observed brusquely. "I will take care of this."

He hurried up the stairs, avoiding the elevator, to the vacant room opposite, and thence reconnoitered the studio door. It was as Kennedy had reported. Stephanie was there, and with Gurney. The pale poet had been brought there to furnish her an evening of delight. Because of the stillness of the building at this hour he could hear their muffled voices speaking alternately, and once Stephanie singing the refrain of a song. He was angry and yet grateful that she had, in her genial way, taken the trouble to call and assure him that she was going to a summer lawn party and dance. He smiled grimly, sarcastically, as he thought of her surprise. Softly he extracted the clutch key and inserted it, covering the end of the key on the inside and turning it. It gave solidly without sound. He next tried the knob and turned it, feeling the door spring slightly as he did so. Then inaudibly, because of a gurgled laugh with which he was throughly familiar, he opened it and stepped in.

At his rough, firm cough they sprang up—Gurney to a hiding position behind a curtain, Stephanie to one of concealment behind draperies on the couch. She could not speak, and could scarcely believe that her eyes did not deceive her. Gurney, masculine and defiant, but by no means well composed, demanded: "Who are you? What do you want here?" Cowperwood replied very simply and smilingly: "Not very much. Perhaps Miss Platow there will tell you." He nodded in her direction.

Stephanie, fixed by his cold, examining eye, shrank nervously, ignoring Gurney entirely. The latter perceived on the instant that he had a previous liaison to deal with—an angry and outraged lover—and he was not prepared to act either wisely or well.

"Mr. Gurney," said Cowperwood complacently, after star-

ing at Stephanie grimly and scorching her with his scorn, "I
have no concern with you, and do not propose to do anything to disturb you or Miss Platow after a very few moments. I am not here without reason. This young woman has
been steadily deceiving me. She has lied to me frequently,
and pretended an innocence which I did not believe. Tonight
she told me she was to be at a lawn party on the West Side.
She has been my mistress for months. I have given her
money, jewelry, whatever she wanted. Those jade earrings, by
the way, are one of my gifts." He nodded cheerfully in
Stephanie's direction. "I have come here simply to prove to
her that she cannot lie to me anymore. Heretofore, every
time I have accused her of things like this she has cried
and lied. I do not know how much you know of her, or how
fond you are of her. I merely wish her, not you, to know"
—and he turned and stared at Stephanie—"that the day of
her lying to me is over."

During this very peculiar harangue Stephanie, who, nervous, fearful, fixed, and yet beautiful, remained curled up in
the corner of the suggestive Oriental divan, had been gazing
at Cowperwood in a way which plainly attested, trifle as
she might with others, that she was nevertheless fond of
him—intensely so. His strong, solid figure, confronting her
so ruthlessly, gripped her imagination, of which she had a
world. She had managed to conceal her body in part, but her
brown arms and shoulders, her bosom, trim knees, and feet
were exposed in part. Her black hair and naive face were
now heavy, distressed, sad. She was frightened, really, for
Cowperwood at bottom had always overawed her—a strange,
terrible, fascinating man. Now she sat and looked, seeking
still to lure him by the pathetic cast of her face and soul,
while Cowperwood, scornful of her, and almost openly contemptuous of her lover and his possible opposition, merely
stood smiling before them. It came over her very swiftly
now just what it was she was losing—a grim, wonderful
man. Beside him Gurney, the pale poet, was rather thin—a
mere breath of romance. She wanted to say something, to
make a plea; but it was so plain Cowperwood would have
none of it, and, besides, here was Gurney. Her throat
clogged, her eyes filled, even here, and a mystical bog-fire
state of emotion succeeded the primary one of opposition.
Cowperwood knew the look well. It gave him the only sense
of triumph he had.

"Stephanie," he remarked, "I have just one word to say to you now. We will not meet anymore, of course. You are a good actress. Stick to your profession. You may shine in it if you do not merge it too completely with your loves. As for being a free lover, it isn't incompatible with what you are, perhaps, but it isn't socially advisable for you. Good night."

He turned and walked quickly out.

"Oh, Frank," called Stephanie, in a strange, magnetized, despairing way, even in the face of her astonished lover. Gurney stared with his mouth open.

Cowperwood paid no heed. Out he went through the dark hall and down the stairs. For once the lure of a beautiful, enigmatic, immoral, and promiscuous woman—poison flower though she was—was haunting him.

"D— her!" he exclaimed. "D— the little beast, anyhow! The————! The ————!" He used terms so hard, so vile, so sad, all because he knew for once what it was to love and lose—to want ardently in his way and not to have—now or ever after. He was determined that his path and that of Stephanie Platow should never be allowed to cross again.

CHAPTER XXIX

A Family Quarrel

It chanced that shortly before this liaison was broken off, some troubling information was quite innocently conveyed to Aileen by Stephanie Platow's own mother. One day Mrs. Platow, in calling on Mrs. Cowperwood, commented on the fact that Stephanie was gradually improving in her art, that the Garrick Players had experienced a great deal of trouble, and that Stephanie was shortly to appear in a new role—something Chinese.

"That was such a charming set of jade you gave her," she volunteered genially. "I only saw it the other day for

the first time. She never told me about it before. She prizes
it so very highly that I feel as though I ought to thank
you myself."

Aileen opened her eyes. "Jade!" she observed curiously.
"Why, I don't remember." Recalling Cowperwood's proclivities on the instant, she was suspicious, distraught. Her face
showed her perplexity.

"Why, yes," replied Mrs. Platow, Aileen's show of surprise troubling her. "The earrings and necklet, you know.
She said you gave them to her."

"To be sure," answered Aileen, catching herself as by a
hair. "I do recall it now. But it was Frank who really gave
them. I hope she likes them."

She smiled sweetly.

"She thinks they're beautiful, and they do become her,"
continued Mrs. Platow pleasantly, understanding it all, as
she fancied. The truth was that Stephanie, having forgotten,
had left her make-up box open one day at home, and her
mother, rummaging in her room for something, had discovered them and genially confronted her with them, for
she knew the value of jade. Nonplussed for the moment,
Stephanie had lost her mental, though not her outward,
composure and referred them back casually to an evening
at the Cowperwood home when Aileen had been present
and the gauds had been genially forced upon her.

Unfortunately for Aileen, the matter was not to be allowed to rest just so, for going one afternoon to a reception
given by Rhees Grier, a young sculptor of social proclivities,
who had been introduced to her by Taylor Lord, she was
given a taste of what it means to be a neglected wife from a
public point of view. As she entered on this occasion she
happened to overhear two women talking in a corner behind
a screen erected to conceal wraps. "Oh, here comes Mrs.
Cowperwood," said one. "She's the street-railway magnate's
wife. Last winter and spring he was running with that Platow
girl—of the Garrick Players, you know."

The other nodded, studying Aileen's splendiferous green
velvet gown with envy.

"I wonder if she's faithful to him?" she queried, while
Aileen strained to hear. "She looks daring enough."

Aileen strained to catch a glimpse of her observers later,
when they were not looking, and her face showed her mingled
resentment and feeling; but it did no good. The wretched

gossipers had wounded her in the keenest way. She was hurt, angry, nonplussed. To think that Cowperwood by his variability should expose her to such gossip as this!

One day not so long after her conversation with Mrs. Platow, Aileen happened to be standing outside the door of her own boudoir, the landing of which commanded the lower hall, and there overheard two of her servants discussing the Cowperwood menage in particular and Chicago life in general. One was a tall, angular girl of perhaps twenty-seven or -eight, a chambermaid, the other a short, stout woman of forty who held the position of assistant housekeeper. They were pretending to dust, though gossip conducted in a whisper was the matter for which they were foregathered. The tall girl had recently been employed in the family of Aymar Cochrane, the former president of the Chicago West Division Railway, and now a director of the new West Chicago Street Railway Company.

"And I was that surprised," Aileen heard this girl saying, "to think I should be coming here. I cud scarcely believe me ears when they told me. Why, Miss Florence was runnin' out to meet him two and three times in the week. The wonder to me was that her mother never guessed."

"Och," replied the other, "he's the very divil and all when it comes to the wimmin." (Aileen did not see the upward lift of the hand that accompanied this.) "There was a little girl that used to come here. Her father lives up the street here. Haguenin is his name. He owns that morning paper, the *Press*, and has a fine house up the street here a little way. Well, I haven't seen her very often of late, but more than once I saw him kissing her in this very room. Sure his wife knows all about it. Depend on it. She had an awful fight with some woman here onct, so I hear, some woman that he was runnin' with and bringin' here to the house. I hear it's somethin' terrible the way she beat her up —screamin' and carryin' on. Oh, they're the divil, these men, when it comes to the wimmin."

A slight rustling sound from somewhere sent the two gossipers on their several ways, but Aileen had heard enough to understand. What was she to do? How was she to learn more of these new women, of whom she had never heard at all? She at once suspected Florence Cochrane, for she knew that this servant had worked in the Cochrane family. And then Cecily Haguenin, the daughter of the editor with whom they were on the friendliest terms! Cowperwood kissing her! Was there no end to his liaisons—his infidelity?

She returned, fretting and grieving, to her room, where she meditated and meditated, wondering whether she should leave him, wondering whether she should reproach him openly, wondering whether she should employ more detectives. What good would it do? She had employed detectives once. Had it prevented the Stephanie Platow incident? Not at all. Would it prevent other liaisons in the future? Very likely not. Obviously her home life with Cowperwood was coming to a complete and disastrous end. Things could not go on in this way. She had done wrong, possibly, in taking him away from Mrs. Cowperwood number one, though she could scarcely believe that, for Mrs. Lillian Cowperwood was so unsuited to him—but this repayment! If she had been at all superstitious or religious, and had known her Bible, which she didn't, she might have quoted to herself that very fatalistic statement of the New Testament, "With what measure ye mete, it shall be measured to you again."

The truth was that Cowperwood's continued propensity to rove at liberty among the fair sex could not in the long run fail of some results of an unsatisfactory character. Coincident with the disappearance of Stephanie Platow, he launched upon a variety of episodes—the charming daughter of so worthy a man as Editor Haguenin, his sincerest and most sympathetic journalistic supporter; and the daughter of Aymar Cochrane falling victims, among others, to what many would have called his wiles. As a matter of fact, in most cases he was as much sinned against as sinning, since the provocation was as much offered as given.

The manner in which he came to get in with Cecily Haguenin was simple enough. Being an old friend of the family, and a frequent visitor at her father's house, he found this particular daughter of desire an easy victim. She was a vigorous blonde creature of twenty at this time, very full and plump, with large violet eyes, and with considerable alertness of mind—a sort of doll girl with whom Cowperwood found it pleasant to amuse himself. A playful, gamboling relationship had existed between them when she was a mere child attending school, and had continued through her college years whenever she happened to be at home on a vacation. In these very latest days when Cowperwood on occasion sat in the Haguenin library consulting with the journalist-publisher concerning certain moves which he wished to have put right before the public, he saw considerably more of Cecily. One night, when her father had gone out to look up the previous action of the city council in connection with some matter of franchises, a series of more or less sympathetic and understanding glances suddenly culminated in Cecily's playfully waving a new novel, which she happened to have in her hand, in Cowperwood's face; and he, in reply, laid hold caressingly of her arms.

"You can't stop me so easily," she observed banteringly.

"Oh yes, I can," he replied.

A slight struggle ensued, in which he, with her semiwillful connivance, managed to maneuver her into his arms, her head backward against his shoulder.

"Well," she said, looking up at him with a seminervous, semiprovocative glance, "now what? You'll just have to let me go."

"Not very soon, though."

"Oh yes, you will. My father will be here in a moment."

"Well, not until then, anyhow. You're getting to be the sweetest girl."

She did not resist, but remained gazing half nervously, half dreamily at him, whereupon he smoothed her cheek, and then kissed her. Her father's returning step put an end to this; but from this point on ascent or decent to a perfect understanding was easily made.

In the matter of Florence Cochrane, the daughter of Aymar Cochrane, the president of the Chicago West Division company—a second affair of the period—the approach was only slightly different, the result the same. This girl, to furnish only a brief impression, was a blonde of a different type from Cecily—delicate, picturesque, dreamy. She was mildly intellectual at this time, engaged in reading Marlowe and Jonson; and Cowperwood, busy in the matter of the West Chicago Street Railway, and conferring with her father, was conceived by her as a great personage of the Elizabethan order. In a tentative way she was in revolt against an apple-pie order of existence which was being forced upon her. Cowperwood recognized the mood, trifled with her spiritedly, looked into her eyes, and found the response he wanted. Neither old Aymar Cochrane nor his impeccably respectable wife ever discovered.

Subsequently Aileen, reflecting upon these latest developments, was from one point of view actually pleased or eased. There is always safety in numbers, and she felt that if Cowperwood were going to go on like this it would not be possible for him in the long run to take a definite interest in anyone; and so, all things considered, and other things being equal, he would probably just as leave remain married to her as not.

But what a comment, she could not help reflecting, on her own charms! What an end to an ideal union that had seemed destined to last all their days! She, Aileen Butler, who in her youth had deemed herself the peer of any girl in charm, force, beauty, to be shoved aside thus early in her life—she was only forty—by the younger generation. And such silly snips as they were—Stephanie Platow! and Cecily Haguenin! and Florence Cochrane, in all likelihood another pasty-faced beginner! And here she was—vigorous, resplendent, smooth of face and body, her forehead, chin, neck, eyes without a wrinkle, her hair a rich golden-reddish glow, her step springing, her weight no more than 150 pounds for her very normal height, with all the advantages of a complete toilet cabinet, jewels, clothing, taste, and skill in material selection—being elbowed out by these upstarts. It was almost unbelievable. It was so unfair. Life was so cruel, Cowperwood so temperamentally unbalanced. Dear God! to think that this should be true! Why should he not love her? She studied her beauty in the mirror from time to time, and raged and raged. Why was her body not sufficient for him? Why should he deem anyone more beautiful? Why should he not be true to his reiterated protestations that he cared for her? Other men were true to other women. Her father had been faithful to her mother. At the thought of her own father and his opinion of her conduct she winced, but it did not change her point of view as to her present rights. See her hair! See her eyes! See her smooth, resplendent arms! Why should Cowperwood not love her? Why, indeed?

One night shortly afterward, she was sitting in her boudoir reading, waiting for him to come home, when the telephone bell sounded, and he informed her that he was compelled to remain at the office late. Afterward he said he might be obliged to run on to Pittsburgh for thirty-six hours or thereabouts; but he would surely be back on the third day, counting the present as one. Aileen was chagrined. Her voice showed it. They had been scheduled to go to dinner with the Hoecksemas, and afterward to the theater. Cowperwood suggested that she should go alone, but Aileen declined rather sharply; she hung up the receiver without even the pretense of a good-bye. And then at ten o'clock he telephoned again, saying that he had changed his mind, and that if she were interested to go anywhere—a later supper, or the like—she should dress, otherwise he would come home expecting to remain.

Aileen immediately concluded that some scheme he had had to amuse himself had fallen through. Having spoiled her evening, he was coming home to make as much hay as possible out of this bit of sunshine. This infuriated her. The whole business of uncertainty in the matter of his affections was telling on her nerves. A storm was in order, and it had come. He came bustling in a little later, slipped his arms around her as she came forward, and kissed her on the mouth. He smoothed her arms in a make-believe and yet tender way, and patted her shoulders. Seeing her frown, he inquired, "What's troubling Babykins?"

"Oh, nothing more than usual," replied Aileen irritably. "Let's not talk about that. Have you had your dinner?"

"Yes, we had it brought in." He was referring to McKenty, Addison, and himself, and the statement was true. Being in an honest position for once, he felt called upon to justify himself a little. "It couldn't be avoided tonight. I'm sorry that this business takes up so much of my time, but I'll get out of it someday soon. Things are bound to ease up."

Aileen withdrew from his embrace and went to her dressing table. A glance showed her that her hair was slightly awry, and she smoothed it into place. She looked at her chin, and then went back to her book—rather sulkily, he thought.

"Now, Aileen, what's the trouble?" he inquired. "Aren't you glad to have me up here? I know you have had a pretty rough road of it of late, but aren't you willing to let bygones be bygones and trust to the future a little?"

"The future! The future! Don't talk to me about the future. It's little enough it holds in store for me," she replied.

Cowperwood saw that she was verging on an emotional storm, but he trusted to his powers of persuasion, and her basic affection for him, to soothe and quell her.

"I wish you wouldn't act this way, pet," he went on. "You know I have always cared for you. You know I always shall. I'll admit that there are a lot of little things which interfere with my being at home as much as I would like at present; but that doesn't alter the fact that my feeling is the same. I should think you could see that."

"Feeling! Feeling!" taunted Aileen suddenly. "Yes, I know how much feeling you have. You have feeling enough to give other women sets of jade and jewels, and to run around with every silly little snip you meet. You needn't come home here at ten o'clock, when you can't go anywhere else, and talk about feeling for me. I know how much feeling you have. Pshaw!"

She flung herself irritably back in her chair and opened her book. Cowperwood gazed at her solemnly, for this thrust in regard to Stephanie was a revelation. This woman business could grow peculiarly exasperating at times.

"What do you mean, anyhow?" he observed cautiously and with much seeming candor. "I haven't given any jade or jewels to anyone, nor have I been running around with any 'little snips,' as you call them. I don't know what you are talking about, Aileen."

"Oh, Frank," commented Aileen wearily and incredulously, "you lie so! Why do you stand there and lie? I'm so tired of it; I'm so sick of it all. How should the servants know of so many things to talk of here if they weren't true? I didn't invite Mrs. Platow to come and ask me why you had given her daughter a set of jade. I know why you lie; you want to hush me up and keep quiet. You're afraid I'll go to Mr. Haguenin or Mr. Cochrane or Mr. Platow, or to all three. Well, you can rest your soul on that score. I won't. I'm sick of you and your lies. Stephanie Platow—the thin stick! Cecily Haguenin—the little piece of gum! And Florence Cochrane—she looks like a dead fish!" (Aileen had a genius for characterization at times.) "If it just weren't for the way I acted toward my family in Philadelphia, and the talk it would create, and the injury it would do you financially, I'd act tomorrow. I'd leave you—that's what I'd do. And to think that I should ever have believed that you really loved me, or could care for any woman permanently. Bosh! But I don't care. Go on! Only I'll tell you one thing. You needn't think I'm going to go on enduring all this as I have in the past. I'm not. You're not going to deceive me always. I'm not going to stand it. I'm not so old yet. There are plenty of men who will be glad to pay me attention if you won't. I told you once that I wouldn't be faithful to you if you weren't to me, and I won't be. I'll show you. I'll go with other men. I will! I will! I swear it."

"Aileen," he asked softly, pleadingly, realizing the futility of additional lies under such circumstances, "won't you forgive me this time? Bear with me for the present. I scarcely understand myself at times. I am not like other men. You and I have run together a long time now. Why not wait awhile? Give me a chance! See if I do not change. I may."

"Oh yes, wait! Change. You may change. Haven't I waited? Haven't I walked the floor night after night when you haven't been here? Bear with you—yes, yes! Who's to bear with me when my heart is breaking? Oh, God!" she suddenly added, with passionate vigor, "I'm miserable! I'm miserable! My heart aches! It aches!"

She clutched her breast and swung from the room, moving with that vigorous stride that had once appealed to him so, and still did. Alas, alas! it touched him now, but only as a part of a very shifty and cruel world. He hurried out of the room after her, and (as at the time of the Rita Sohlberg incident) slipped his arm about her waist; but she pulled away irritably. "No, no!" she exclaimed. "Let me alone. I'm tired of that."

"You're really not fair to me, Aileen," with a great show of feeling and sincerity. "You're letting one affair that came between us blind your whole point of view. I give you my word I haven't been unfaithful to you with Stephanie Platow or any other woman. I may have flirted with them a little, but that is really nothing. Why not be sensible? I'm not as black as you paint me. I'm moving in big matters that are as much for your concern and future as for mine. Be sensible, be liberal."

There was much argument—the usual charges and counter-charges—but finally, because of her weariness of heart, his petting, the unsolvability of it all, she permitted him for the time being to persuade her that there were still some crumbs of affection left. She was soul-sick, heartsick. Even he, as he attempted to soothe her, realized clearly that to establish the reality of his love in her belief he would have to make some much greater effort to entertain and comfort her, and that this, in his present mood, and with his leaning toward promiscuity, was practically impossible. For the time being a peace might be patched up, but in view of what she expected of him—her passion and selfish individuality—it could not be. He would have to go on, and she would have to leave him, if need be; but he could not cease or go back. He was too passionate, too radiant, too individual and complex to belong to any one single individual alone.

CHAPTER XXX

Obstacles

The impediments that can arise to baffle a great and swelling career are strange and various. In some instances all the cross waves of life must be cut by the strong swimmer. With other personalities there is a chance, or force, that happily allies itself with them; or they quite unconsciously ally themselves with it, and find that there is a tide that bears them on. Divine will? Not necessarily. There is no understanding of it. Guardian spirits? There are many who so believe, to their utter undoing. (Witness Macbeth.) An unconscious drift in the direction of right, virtue, duty? These are banners of mortal manufacture. Nothing is proved; all is permitted.

Not long after Cowperwood's accession to control on the West Side, for instance, a contest took place between his corporation and a citizen by the name of Redmond Purdy —real estate investor, property trader, and moneylender— which set Chicago by the ears. The La Salle and Washington Street tunnels were now in active service, but because of the great north and south area of the West Side, necessitating the cabling of Van Buren Street and Blue Island Avenue, there was need of a third tunnel somewhere south of Washington Street, preferably at Van Buren Street, because the business heart was thus more directly reached. Cowperwood was willing and anxious to build this tunnel, though he was puzzled how to secure from the city a right of way under Van Buren Street, where a bridge loaded with heavy traffic now swung. There were all sorts of complications. In the first place, the consent of the War Department at Washington had to be secured in order to tunnel under the river at all. Secondly, the excavation, if directly under the bridge, might prove an intolerable nuisance, necessitating the closing or removal of the bridge. Owing to the critical, not to say hostile, attitude of the newspapers, which since the La Salle and Washington tunnel grants were following his every move with a searchlight, Cowperwood decided not to petition the city for privileges in this case, but instead to buy the property rights of sufficient land just north of the bridge, where the digging of the tunnel could proceed without interference.

The piece of land most suitable for this purpose, a lot 150 by 150, lying a little way from the riverbank and occupied by a seven-story loft building, was owned by the previously mentioned Redmond Purdy, a long, thin, angular, dirty person, who wore celluloid collars and cuffs and spoke with a nasal intonation.

Cowperwood had the customary overtures made by seemingly disinterested parties endeavoring to secure the land at a fair price. But Purdy, who was as stingy as a miser and as incisive as a rattrap, had caught wind of the proposed tunnel scheme. He was all alive for a fine profit. "No, no, no," he declared over and over, when approached by the representatives of Mr. Sylvester Toomey, Cowperwood's ubiquitous land agent. "I don't want to sell. Go away."

Mr. Sylvester Toomey was finally at his wits' end, and complained to Cowperwood, who at once sent for those noble beacons of dark and stormy waters, General Van Sickle and the Honorable Kent Barrows McKibben. The general was now becoming a little dolty, and Cowperwood was thinking of pensioning him; but McKibben was in his prime—smug, handsome, deadly, smooth. After talking it over with Mr. Toomey they returned to Cowperwood's office with a promising scheme. The Honorable Nahum Dickensheets, one of the judges of the state court of appeals, and a man long since attached, by methods which need not here be described, to Cowperwood's star, had been persuaded to bring his extensive technical knowledge to bear on the emergency. At his suggestion the work of digging the tunnel was at once begun

—first at the east or Franklin Street end; then, after eight months' digging, at the west or Canal Street end. A shaft was actually sunk some thirty feet back of Mr. Purdy's building—between it and the river—while that gentleman watched with a quizzical gleam in his eye that defiant procedure. He was sure that when it came to the necessity of annexing his property the North and West Chicago Street Railways would be obliged to pay through the nose.

"Well, I'll be cussed," he frequently observed to himself, for he could not see how his exaction of a pound of flesh was to be evaded, and yet he felt strangely restless at times. Finally, when it became absolutely necessary for Cowperwood to secure without further delay this coveted strip, he sent for its occupant, who called in pleasant anticipation of a profitable conversation; this should be worth a small fortune to him.

"Mr. Purdy," observed Cowperwood glibly, "you have a piece of land on the other side of the river that I need. Why don't you sell it to me? Can't we fix this up now in some amicable way?"

He smiled while Purdy cast shrewd, wolfish glances about the place, wondering how much he could really hope to exact. The building, with all its interior equipment, land, and all, was worth in the neighborhood of $200,000.

"Why should I sell? The building is a good building. It's as useful to me as it would be to you. I'm making money out of it."

"Quite true," replied Cowperwood, "but I am willing to pay you a fair price for it. A public utility is involved. This tunnel will be a good thing for the West Side and any other land you may own over there. With what I will pay you you can buy more land in that neighborhood or elsewhere, and make a good thing out of it. We need to put this tunnel just where it is, or I wouldn't trouble to argue with you."

"That's just it," replied Purdy fixedly. "You've gone ahead and dug your tunnel without consulting me, and now you expect me to get out of the way. Well, I don't see that I'm called on to get out of there just to please you."

"But I'll pay you a fair price."

"How much will you pay me?"

"How much do you want?"

Mr. Purdy scratched a foxlike ear. "One million dollars."

"One million dollars!" exclaimed Cowperwood. "Don't you think that's a little steep, Mr. Purdy?"

"No," replied Purdy sagely. "It's not any more than it's worth."

Cowperwood sighed.

"I'm sorry," he replied meditatively, "but this is really too much. Wouldn't you take three hundred thousand dollars in cash now and consider this thing closed?"

"One million," replied Purdy, looking sternly at the ceiling.

"Very well, Mr. Purdy," replied Cowperwood. "I'm very sorry. It's plain to me that we can't do business as I had hoped. I'm willing to pay you a reasonable sum; but what you ask is far too much—preposterous! Don't you think you'd better reconsider? We might move the tunnel even yet."

"One million dollars," said Purdy.

"It can't be done, Mr. Purdy. It isn't worth it. Why won't you be fair? Call it three hundred and twenty-five thousand dollars cash, and my check tonight."

"I wouldn't take five or six hundred thousand dollars if you were to offer it to me, Mr. Cowperwood, tonight or any other time. I know my rights."

"Very well, then," replied Cowperwood, "that's all I can say. If you won't sell, you won't sell. Perhaps you'll change your mind later."

Mr. Purdy went out, and Cowperwood called in his lawyers and his engineers. One Saturday afternoon, a week or two later, when the building in question had been vacated for the day, a company of three hundred laborers, with wagons, picks, shovels, and dynamite sticks, arrived. By sundown of the next day (which, being Sunday, was a legal holiday, with no courts open or sitting to issue injunctions) this comely structure, the private property of Mr. Redmond Purdy, was completely razed and a large excavation substituted in its stead. The gentleman of the celluloid cuffs and collars, when informed about nine o'clock of this same Sunday morning that his building had been almost completely removed, was naturally greatly perturbed. A portion of the wall was still standing when he arrived, hot and excited, and the police were appealed to. But, strange to say, this was of little avail, for they were shown a writ of injunction issued by the court of highest jurisdiction, presided over by the Honorable Nahum Dickensheets, which restrained all and sundry from interfering. (Subsequently, on demand of another court, this remarkable document was discovered to have disappeared; the contention was that it had never really existed or been produced at all.)

The demolition and digging proceeded. Then began a scurrying of lawyers to the door of one friendly judge after another. There were apoplectic cheeks, blazing eyes, and gasps for breath while the enormity of the offense was being noised abroad. Law is law, however. Procedure is procedure, and no writ of injunction was either issuable or returnable on a legal holiday, when no courts were sitting. Nevertheless, by three o'clock in the afternoon an obliging magistrate was found who consented to issue an injunction staying this terrible crime. By this time, however, the building was gone, the excavation complete. It remained merely for the West Chicago Street Railway Company to secure an injunction vacating the first injunction, praying that its rights, privileges, liberties, etc., be not interfered with, and so creating a contest which naturally threw the matter into the state court of appeals, where it could safely lie. For several years there were numberless injunctions, writs of errors, doubts, motions to reconsider, threats to carry the matter from the state to the federal courts on a matter of constitutional privilege, and the like. The affair was finally settled out of court, for Mr. Purdy by this time was a more sensible man. In the meantime, however, the newspapers had been given full details of the transaction, and a story of words against Cowperwood ensued.

But more disturbing than the Redmond Purdy incident was the rivalry of a new Chicago street-railway company. It appeared first as an idea in the brain of one James Furnivale Woolsen, a determined young westerner from California, and developed by degrees into consents and petitions from fully two-thirds of the residents of various streets in the extreme southwest section of the city where it was proposed the new line should be located. This same James Furnivale Woolsen, being an ambitious person, was not to be so easily put down. Besides the consents and petitions, which Cowperwood could not easily get away from him, he had a new form of traction then being tried out in several minor cities—a form of electric propulsion by means of an overhead wire and a traveling pole, which was said to be very

economical, and to give a service better than cables and
cheaper even than horses.

Cowperwood had heard all about this new electric system
some time before, and had been studying it for several years
with the greatest interest, since it promised to revolutionize
the whole business of street-railroading. However, having
but so recently completed his excellent cable system, he did
not see that it was advisable to throw it away. The trolley
was as yet too much of a novelty; certainly it was not advisable to have it introduced into Chicago until he was ready
to introduce it himself—first on his outlying feeder lines, he
thought, then perhaps generally.

But before he could take suitable action against Woolsen,
that engaging young upstart, who was possessed of a high-
power imagination and a gift of gab, had allied himself with
such interested investors as Truman Leslie MacDonald, who
saw here a heaven-sent opportunity of mulcting Cowperwood,
and Jordan Jules, once the president of the North Chicago
Gas Company, who had lost money through Cowperwood in
the gas war. Two better instruments for goading a man whom
they considered an enemy could not well be imagined—Truman Leslie with his dark, waspish, mistrustful, jealous eyes
and his slim, vital body; and Jordan Jules, short, rotund,
sandy, a sickly crop of thin oily light hair growing down
over his coat collar, his forehead and crown glisteningly
bald, his eyes a seeking, searching, revengeful blue. They in
turn brought in Samuel Blackman, once president of the
South Side gas company; Sunderland Sledd, of local railroad management and stock investment fame; and Norrie
Simms, president of the Douglas Trust Company, who, however, was little more than a fiscal agent. The general feeling
was that Cowperwood's defensive tactics—which consisted in
having the city council refuse to act—could be easily met.

"Well, I think we can soon fix that," exclaimed young Mac-
Donald one morning at a meeting. "We ought to be able to
smoke them out. A little publicity will do it."

He appealed to his father, the editor of the *Inquirer*,
but the latter refused to act for the time being, seeing that
his son was interested. MacDonald, enraged at the do-noth-
ing attitude of the council, invaded that body and demanded
of Alderman Dowling, still leader, why this matter of the
Chicago general ordinances was still lying unconsidered. Mr.
Dowling, a large, mushy, placid man with blue eyes, an iron

frame, and a beefy smile, vouchsafed the information that, although he was chairman of the committee on streets and alleys, he knew nothing about it. "I haven't been payin' much attention to things lately," he replied.

Mr. MacDonald went to see the remaining members of this same committee. They were noncommittal. They would have to look into the matter. Somebody claimed that there was a flaw in the petitions.

Evidently there was crooked work here somewhere. Cowperwood was to blame, no doubt. MacDonald conferred with Blackman and Jordan Jules, and it was determined that the council should be harried into doing its duty. This was a legitimate enterprise. A new and better system of traction was being kept out of the city. Schryhart, since he was offered an interest, and since there was considerable chance of his being able to dominate the new enterprise, agreed that the ordinances ought to be acted upon. In consequence there was a renewed hubbub in the newspapers.

It was pointed out through Schryhart's *Chronicle*, through Hyssop's and Merrill's papers, and through the *Inquirer* that such a situation was intolerable. If the dominant party, at the behest of so sinister an influence as Cowperwood, was to tie up all outside traction legislation, there could be but one thing left—an appeal to the voters of the city to turn the rascals out. No party could survive such a record of political trickery and financial jugglery. McKenty, Dowling, Cowperwood, and others were characterized as unreasonable obstructionists and debasing influences. But Cowperwood merely smiled. These were the caterwaulings of the enemy. Later, when young MacDonald threatened to bring legal action to compel the council to do its duty, Cowperwood and his associates were not so cheerful. A mandamus proceeding, however futile, would give the newspapers great opportunity for chatter; moreover, a city election was drawing near. However, McKenty and Cowperwood were by no means helpless. They had offices, jobs, funds, a well-organized party system, the saloons, the dives, and those dark chambers where at late hours ballot boxes are incontinently stuffed.

Did Cowperwood share personally in all this? Not at all. Or McKenty? No. In good tweed and fine linen they frequently conferred in the offices of the Chicago Trust Company, the president's office of the North Chicago Street Railway system, and Mr. Cowperwood's library. No dark scenes were ever enacted there. But just the same, when the time came, the Schryhart-Simms-MacDonald editorial combination did not win. Mr. McKenty's party had the votes. A number of the most flagrantly debauched aldermen, it is true, were defeated; but what is an alderman here and there? The newly elected ones, even in the face of pre-election promises and vows, could be easily suborned or convinced. So the anti-Cowperwood element was just where it was before; but the feeling against him was much stronger, and considerable sentiment generated in the public at large that there was something wrong with the Cowperwood method of street-railway control.

CHAPTER XXXI

Untoward Disclosures

Coincident with these public disturbances and of subsequent bearing upon them was the discovery by Editor Haguenin of Cowperwood's relationship with Cecily. It came about not through Aileen, who was no longer willing to fight Cowperwood in this matter, but through Haguenin's lady society editor, who, hearing rumors in the social world, springing from heaven knows where, and being beholden to Haguenin for many favors, had carried the matter to him in a very direct way. Haguenin, a man of insufficient worldliness in spite of his journalistic profession, scarcely believed it. Cowperwood was so suave, so commercial. He had heard many things concerning him—his past—but Cowperwood's present state in Chicago was such, it seemed to him, as to preclude petty affairs of this kind. Still, the name of his daughter being involved, he took the matter up with Cecily, who, under pressure, confessed. She made the usual plea that she was of age, and that she wished to live her own life —logic which she had gathered largely from Cowperwood's attitude. Haguenin did nothing about it at first, think-

ing to send Cecily off to an aunt in Nebraska; but, finding
her intractable, and fearing some counteradvice or reprisal
on the part of Cowperwood, who, by the way, had indorsed
paper to the extent of $100,000 for him, he decided to dis-
cuss matters first. It meant a cessation of relations and some
inconvenient financial readjustments; but it had to be. He
was just on the point of calling on Cowperwood when the
latter, unaware as yet of the latest development in regard to
Cecily, and having some variation of his council program to
discuss with Haguenin, asked him over the phone to lunch.
Haguenin was much surprised, but in a way relieved. "I am
busy," he said very heavily, "but cannot you come to the
office some time today? There is something I would like to
see you about."

Cowperwood, imagining that there was some editorial or
local political development on foot which might be of interest
to him, made an appointment for shortly after four. He drove
to the publisher's office in the Press Building, and was
greeted by a grave and almost despondent man.

"Mr. Cowperwood," began Haguenin when the financier
entered, smart and trig, his usual air of genial sufficiency
written all over him, "I have known you now for something
like fourteen years, and during this time I have shown you
nothing but courtesy and good will. It is true that quite recently you have done me various financial favors, but that
was more due, I thought, to the sincere friendship you
bore me than to anything else. Quite accidentally I have
learned of the relationship that exists between you and my
daughter. I have recently spoken to her, and she admitted all
that I need to know. Common decency, it seems to me, might
have suggested to you that you leave my child out of the list
of women you have degraded. Since it has not, I merely
wish to say to you"—and Mr. Haguenin's face was very tense
and white—"that the relationship between you and me is
ended. The one hundred thousand dollars you have indorsed
for me will be arranged for otherwise as soon as possible,
and I hope you will return to me the stock of this paper that
you hold as collateral. Another type of man, Mr. Cowperwood, might attempt to make you suffer in another way. I
presume that you have no children of your own, or that if
you have you lack the parental instinct; otherwise you could
not have injured me in this fashion. I believe that you will

live to see that this policy does not pay in Chicago or anywhere else."

Haguenin turned slowly on his heel toward his desk. Cowperwood, who had listened very patiently and very fixedly, without a tremor of an eyelash, merely said:

"There seems to be no common intellectual ground, Mr. Haguenin, upon which you and I can meet in this matter. You cannot understand my point of view. I could not possibly adopt yours. However, as you wish it, the stock will be returned to you upon receipt of my indorsements. I cannot say more than that."

He turned and walked unconcernedly out, thinking that it was too bad to lose the support of so respectable a man, but also that he could do without it. It was silly the way parents insisted on their daughters being something that they did not wish to be.

Haguenin stood by his desk after Cowperwood had gone, wondering where he should get $100,000 quickly, and also what he should do to make his daughter see the error of her ways. It was an astonishing blow he had received, he thought, in the house of a friend. It occurred to him that Walter Melville Hyssop, who was succeeding mightily with his two papers, might come to his rescue, and that later he could repay him when the *Press* was more prosperous. He went out to his house in a quandary concerning life and chance; while Cowperwood went to the Chicago Trust Company to confer with Videra, and later out to his own home to consider how he should equalize this loss. The state and fate of Cecily Haguenin were not of so much importance as many other things on his mind at this time.

Far more serious were his cogitations with regard to a liaison he had recently ventured to establish with Mrs. Hosmer Hand, wife of an eminent investor and financier. Hand was a solid, phlegmatic, heavy-thinking person who had some years before lost his first wife, to whom he had been eminently faithful. After that, for a period of years he had been a lonely speculator, attending to his vast affairs; but finally, because of his enormous wealth, his rather presentable appearance and social rank, he had been entrapped by much social attention on the part of a Mrs. Jessie Drew Barrett into marrying her daughter Caroline, a dashing skip of a girl who was clever, incisive, calculating, and intensely gay. Since she was socially ambitious, and without much heart, the thought of Hand's millions, and how advantageous would be her situation in case he should die, had enabled her to overlook quite easily his heavy, unyouthful appearance and to see him in the light of a lover. There was criticism, of course. Hand was considered a victim, and Caroline and her mother designing minxes and cats; but since the wealthy financier was truly ensnared it behooved friends and future satellites to be courteous, and so they were. The wedding was very well attended. Mrs. Hand began to give house parties, teas, musicales, and receptions on a lavish scale.

Cowperwood never met either her or her husband until he was well launched on his streetcar program. Needing $250,000 in a hurry, and finding the Chicago Trust Company, the Lake City Bank, and other institutions heavily loaded with his securities, he turned in a moment of inspirational thought to Hand. Cowperwood was always a great borrower. His paper was out in large quantities. He introduced himself frequently to powerful men in this way, taking long or short loans at high or low rates of interest, as the case might be, and sometimes finding someone whom he could work with or use. In the case of Hand, though the latter was ostensibly of the enemies' camp—the Schryhart-Union Gas-Douglas Trust Company crowd—nevertheless Cowperwood had no hesitation in going to him. He wished to overcome or forestall any unfavorable impression. Though Hand, a solemn man of shrewd but honest nature, had heard a number of unfavorable rumors, he was inclined to be fair and think the best. Perhaps Cowperwood was merely the victim of envious rivals.

When the latter first called on him at his office in the Rookery Building, he was most cordial. "Come in, Mr. Cowperwood," he said. "I have heard a great deal about you from one person and another—mostly from the newspapers. What can I do for you?"

Cowperwood exhibited $500,000 worth of West Chicago Street Railway stock. "I want to know if I can get two hundred and fifty thousand dollars on those by tomorrow morning."

Hand, a placid man, looked at the securities peacefully. "What's the matter with your own bank?" He was referring to the Chicago Trust Company. "Can't it take care of them for you?"

"Loaded up with other things just now," smiled Cowperwood ingratiatingly.

"Well, if I can believe all the papers say, you're going to wreck these roads or Chicago or yourself; but I don't live by the papers. How long would you want it for?"

"Six months, perhaps. A year, if you choose."

Hand turned over the securities, eyeing their gold seals. "Five hundred thousand dollars' worth of six percent West Chicago preferred," he commented. "Are you earning six percent?"

"We're earning eight right now. You'll live to see the day when these shares will sell at two hundred dollars and pay twelve percent at that."

"And you've quadrupled the issue of the old company? Well, Chicago's growing. Leave them here until tomorrow or bring them back. Send over or call me, and I'll tell you."

They talked for a little while on street-railway and corporation matters. Hand wanted to know something concerning West Chicago land—a region adjoining Ravenswood. Cowperwood gave him his best advice.

The next day he phoned, and the stocks, so Hand informed him, were available. He would send a check over. So thus a tentative friendship began, and it lasted until the relationship between Cowperwood and Mrs. Hand was consummated and discovered.

In Caroline Barrett, as she occasionally preferred to sign herself, Cowperwood encountered a woman who was as restless and fickle as himself, but not so shrewd. Socially ambitious, she was anything but socially conventional, and she did not care for Hand. Once married, she had planned to repay herself in part by a very gay existence. The affair between her and Cowperwood had begun at a dinner at the magnificent residence of Hand on the North Shore Drive overlooking the lake. Cowperwood had gone to talk over with her husband various Chicago matters. Mrs. Hand was excited by his risqué reputation. A little woman in stature, with intensely white teeth, red lips which she did not hesitate to rouge on occasion, brown hair, and small brown eyes which had a gay, searching, defiant twinkle in them, she did her best to be interesting, clever, witty, and she was.

"I know Frank Cowperwood by reputation, anyhow," she exclaimed, holding out a small white, jeweled hand, the nails of which at their juncture with the flesh were tinged with henna, and the palms of which were slightly rouged. Her eyes blazed, and her teeth gleamed. "One can scarcely read of anything else in the Chicago papers."

Cowperwood returned his most winning beam. "I'm delighted to meet you, Mrs. Hand. I had read of you, too. But I hope you don't believe all the papers say about me."

"And if I did it wouldn't hurt you in my estimation. To do is to be talked about in these days."

Cowperwood, because of his desire to employ the services of Hand, was at his best. He kept the conversation within conventional lines; but all the while he was exchanging secret, unobserved smiles with Mrs. Hand, whom he realized at once had married Hand for his money, and was bent, under a somewhat jealous espionage, to have a good time anyhow. There is a kind of eagerness that goes with those who are watched and wish to escape that gives them a gay, electric awareness and sparkle in the presence of an opportunity for release. Mrs. Hand had this. Cowperwood, a past master in this matter of femininity, studied her hands, her hair, her eyes, her smile. After some contemplation he decided, other things being equal, that Mrs. Hand would do, and that he could be interested if she were very much interested in him. Her telling eyes and smiles, the heightened color of her cheeks, indicated after a time that she was.

Meeting him on the street one day not long after they had first met, she told him that she was going for a visit to friends at Oconomowoc, in Wisconsin.

"I don't suppose you ever get up that far north in summer, do you?" she asked with an air, and smiled.

"I never have," he replied; "but there's no telling what I might do if I were bantered. I suppose you ride and canoe?"

"Oh yes; and play tennis and golf, too."

"But where would a mere idler like me stay?"

"Oh, there are several good hotels. There's never any trouble about that. I suppose you ride yourself?"

"After a fashion," replied Cowperwood, who was an expert.

Witness then the casual encounter on horseback, early one Sunday morning in the painted hills of Wisconsin, of Frank Algernon Cowperwood and Caroline Hand. A jaunty, racing canter, side by side; idle talk concerning people, scenery, conveniences; his usual direct suggestions and love-making, and then, subsequently—

The day of reckoning, if such it might be called, came later.

Caroline Hand was, perhaps, unduly reckless. She admired Cowperwood greatly without really loving him. He found her interesting principally because she was young, debonair, sufficient—a new type. They met in Chicago after a time instead of in Wisconsin, then in Detroit (where she had friends), then in Rockford, where a sister had gone to live. It was easy for him with his time and means. Finally, Duane Kingsland, wholesale flour merchant, religious, moral, conventional, who knew Cowperwood and his repute, encountered Mrs. Hand and Cowperwood first near Oconomowoc one summer's day, and later in Randolph Street, near Cowperwood's bachelor rooms. Being the man that he was, and knowing old Hand well, he thought it was his duty to ask the latter if his wife knew Cowperwood intimately. There was an explosion in the Hand home. Mrs. Hand, when confronted by her husband, denied, of course, that there was anything wrong between her and Cowperwood. Her elderly husband, from a certain telltale excitement and resentment in her manner, did not believe this. He thought once of confronting Cowperwood; but being heavy and practical, he finally decided to sever all business relationships with him and fight him in other ways. Mrs. Hand was watched very closely, and a suborned maid discovered an old note she had written to Cowperwood. An attempt to persuade her to leave for Europe—as old Butler had once attempted to send Aileen years before—raised a storm of protest, but she went. Hand, from being neutral if not friendly, became quite the most dangerous and forceful of all Cowperwood's Chicago enemies. He was a powerful man. His wrath was boundless. He looked upon Cowperwood now as a dark and dangerous man—one of whom Chicago would be well rid.

CHAPTER XXXII

A Supper Party

Since the days in which Aileen had been left more or less lonely by Cowperwood, however, no two individuals had been more faithful in their attentions than Taylor Lord and Kent McKibben. Both were fond of her in a general way, finding her interesting physically and temperamentally; but being beholden to the magnate for many favors, they were exceedingly circumspect in their attitude toward her, particularly during those early years in which they knew that Cowperwood was intensely devoted to her. Later they were not so careful.

It was during this latter period that Aileen came gradually, through the agency of these two men, to share in a form of mid-world life that was not utterly dull. In every large city there is a kind of social half world, where artists and the more adventurous of the socially unconventional and restless meet for an exchange of things which cannot be counted mere social form and civility. It is the age-old world of Bohemia. Hither resort those "accidentals" of fancy that make the stage, the drawing room, and all the schools of artistic endeavor interesting or peculiar. In a number of studios in Chicago such as those of Lane Cross and Rhees Grier, such little circles were to be found. Rhees Grier, for instance, a purely parlor artist, with all the airs, conventions, and social adaptability of the tribe, had quite a following. Here and to several other places by turns Taylor Lord and Kent McKibben conducted Aileen, both asking and obtaining permission to be civil to her when Cowperwood was away.

Among the friends of these two at this time was a certain Polk Lynde, an interesting society figure, whose father owned an immense reaper works, and whose time was

244

spent in idling, racing, gambling, socializing—anything, in short, that it came into his head to do. He was tall, dark, athletic, straight, muscular, with a small dark moustache, dark, black-brown eyes, kinky black hair, and a fine, almost military carriage—which he clothed always to the best advantage. A clever philanderer, it was quite his pride that he did not boast of his conquests. One look at him, however, by the initiated, and the story was told. Aileen first saw him on a visit to the studio of Rhees Grier. Being introduced to him very casually on this occasion, she was, nevertheless, clearly conscious that she was encountering a fascinating man, and that he was fixing her with a warm, avid eye. For the moment she recoiled from him as being a little too brazen in his stare, and yet she admired the general appearance of him. He was of that smart world that she admired so much, and from which now apparently she was hopelessly debarred. That trig, bold air of his realized for her at last the type of man, outside of Cowperwood, whom she would prefer within limits to admire her. If she were going to be bad, as she would have phrased it to herself, she would be bad with a man such as he. He would be winsome and coaxing, but at the same time strong, direct, deliciously brutal, like her Frank. He had, too, what Cowperwood could not have, a certain social air or swagger which came with idleness, much loafing, a sense of social superiority and security—a devil-may-care insouciance which recks little of other people's wills or whims.

When she next saw him, which was several weeks later at an affair of the Courtney Tabors, friends of Lord's, he exclaimed:

"Oh yes. By George! You're the Mrs. Cowperwood I met several weeks ago at Rhees Grier's studio. I've not forgotten you. I've seen you in my eye all over Chicago. Taylor Lord introduced me to you. Say, but you're a beautiful woman!"

He leaned ingratiatingly, whimsically, admiringly near.

Aileen realized that for so early in the afternoon, and considering the crowds, he was curiously enthusiastic. The truth was that because of some rounds he had made elsewhere he was verging toward too much liquor. His eye was alight, his color coppery, his air swagger, devil-may-care, bacchanal. This made her a little cautious; but she rather liked his brown, hard face, handsome mouth, and crisp

Jovian curls. His compliment was not utterly improper; but she nevertheless attempted coyly to avoid him.

"Come, Polk, here's an old friend of yours over here—Sadie Boutwell—she wants to meet you again," someone observed, catching him by the arm.

"No, you don't," he exclaimed, genially and yet at the same time a little resentfully—the kind of disjointed resentment a man who has had the least bit too much is apt to feel on being interrupted. "I'm not going to walk all over Chicago thinking of a woman I've seen somewhere only to be carried away the first time I do meet her. I'm going to talk to her first."

Aileen laughed. "It's charming of you, but we can meet again, perhaps. Besides, there's someone here"—Lord was tactfully directing her attention to another woman. Rhees Grier and McKibben, who were present also, came to her assistance. In the hubbub that ensued Aileen was temporarily extricated and Lynde tactfully steered out of her way. But they had met again, and it was not to be the last time. Subsequent to this second meeting, Lynde thought the matter over quite calmly, and decided that he must make a definite effort to become more intimate with Aileen. Though she was not as young as some others, she suited his present mood exactly. She was rich physically—voluptuous and sentient. She was not of his world precisely, but what of it? She was the wife of an eminent financier, who had been in society once, and she herself had a dramatic record. He was sure of that. He could win her if he wanted to. It would be easy, knowing her as he did, and knowing what he did about her.

So not long after, Lynde ventured to invite her, with Lord, McKibben, Mr. and Mrs. Rhees Grier, and a young girl friend of Mrs. Grier who was rather attractive, a Miss Chrystobel Lanman, to a theater and supper party. The program was to hear a reigning farce at Hooley's, then to sup at the Richelieu, and finally to visit a certain exclusive gambling parlor which then flourished on the South Side—the resort of actors, society gamblers, and the like—where roulette, trente-et-quarante, baccarat, and the honest game of poker, to say nothing of various other games of chance, could be played amid exceedingly recherché surroundings.

The party was gay, especially after the adjournment to the Richelieu, where special dishes of chicken, lobster, and a bucket of champagne were served. Later at the Alcott Club, as the gambling resort was known, Aileen, according to Lynde, was to be taught to play baccarat, poker, and any other game that she wished. "You follow my advice, Mrs. Cowperwood," he observed cheerfully at dinner—being host, he had put her between himself and McKibben—"and I'll show you how to get your money back, anyhow. That's more than some others can do," he added spiritedly, recalling by a look a recent occasion when he and McKibben, being out with friends, the latter had advised liberally and had seen his advice go wrong.

"Have you been gambling, Kent?" asked Aileen archly, turning to her longtime social mentor and friend.

"No, I can honestly say I haven't," replied McKibben with a bland smile. "I may have thought I was gambling, but I admit I don't know how. Now, Polk, here, wins all the time, don't you, Polk? Just follow him."

A wry smile spread over Lynde's face at this, for it was on record in certain circles that he had lost as much as ten and even fifteen thousand in an evening. He also had a record of winning twenty-five thousand once at baccarat at an all-night and all-day sitting, and then losing it.

Lynde all through the evening had been casting hard, meaning glances into Aileen's eyes. She could not avoid this, and she did not feel that she wanted to. He was so charming. He was talking to her half the time at the theater, without apparently addressing or even seeing her. Aileen knew well enough what was in his mind. At times, quite as in those days when she had first met Cowperwood, she felt an unwilled titillation in her blood. Her eyes brightened. It was just possible that she could come to love a man like this, although it would be hard. It would serve Cowperwood right for neglecting her. Yet even now the shadow of Cowperwood was over her, but also the desire for love and a full sex life.

In the gambling rooms was gathered an interested and fairly smart throng—actors, actresses, clubmen, one or two very emancipated women of the high local social world, and a number of more or less gentlemanly young gamblers. Both Lord and McKibben began suggesting column numbers for first plays to their protégés, while Lynde leaned caressingly over Aileen's powdered shoulders. "Let me put this on quatre premier for you," he suggested, throwing down a twenty-dollar gold piece.

"Oh, but let it be my money," complained Aileen. "I want to play with my money. I won't feel that it's mine if I don't."

"Very well, but you can't just now. You can't play with bills." She was extracting a crisp roll from her purse. "I'll have to exchange them later for you for gold. You can pay me then. He's going to call now, anyhow. There you are. He's done it. Wait a moment. You may win." And he paused to study the little ball as it circled round and round above the receiving pockets.

"Let me see. How much do I get if I win quatre premier?" She was trying to recall her experiences abroad.

"Ten for one," replied Lynde; "but you didn't get it. Let's try it once more for luck. It comes up every so often —once in ten or twelve. I've made it often on a first play. How long has it been since the last quatre premier?" he asked of a neighbor whom he recognized.

"Seven, I think, Polk. Six or seven. How's tricks?"

"Oh, so-so." He turned again to Aileen. "It ought to come up now soon. I always make it a rule to double my plays each time. It gets you back all you've lost, some time or other." He put down two twenties.

"Goodness," she exclaimed, "that will be two hundred! I had forgotten that."

Just then the call came for all placements to cease, and Aileen directed her attention to the ball. It circled and circled in its dizzy way and then suddenly dropped.

"Lost again," commented Lynde. "Well, now we'll make it eighty," and he threw down four twenties. "Just for luck we'll put something on thirty-six, and thirteen, and nine." With an easy air he laid one hundred dollars in gold on each number.

Aileen liked his manner. This was like Frank. Lynde had the cool spirit of a plunger. His father, recognizing his temperament, had set over a large fixed sum to be paid to him annually. She recognized, as in Cowperwood, the spirit of adventure, only working out in another way. Lynde was perhaps destined to come to some startlingly reckless end, but what of it? He was a gentleman. His position in life was secure. That had always been Aileen's sad, secret thought. Hers had not been and might never be now.

"Oh, I'm getting foozled already," she exclaimed, gaily reverting to a girlhood habit of clapping her hands. "How much will I win if I win?" The gesture attracted attention even as the ball fell.

"By George, you have it!" exclaimed Lynde, who was watching the croupier. "Eight hundred, two hundred, two hundred"—he was counting to himself—"but we lose thirteen. Very good, that makes us nearly one thousand ahead, counting out what we put down. Rather nice for a beginning, don't you think? Now, if you'll take my advice you'll not play quatre premier anymore for a while. Suppose you double a thirteen—you lost on that—and play Bates's formula. I'll show you what that is."

Already, because he was known to be a plunger, Lynde was gathering a few spectators behind him, and Aileen, fascinated, and not knowing these mysteries of chance, was content to watch him. At one stage of the playing Lynde leaned over, and seeing her smile, whispered:

"What adorable hair and eyes you have! You glow like a great rose. You have a radiance that is wonderful."

"Oh, Mr. Lynde! How you talk! Does gambling always affect you this way?"

"No, you do. Always, apparently!" And he stared hard into her upturned eyes. Still playing ostensibly for Aileen's benefit, he now doubled the cash deposit on his system, laying down a thousand in gold. Aileen urged him to play for himself and let her watch. "I'll just put a little money on these odd numbers here and there, and you play any system you want. How will that do?"

"No, not at all," he replied feelingly. "You're my luck. I play with you. You keep the gold for me. I'll make you a fine present if I win. The losses are mine."

"Just as you like. I don't know really enough about it to play. But I surely get the nice present if you win?"

"You do, win or lose," he murmured. "And now you put the money on the numbers I call. Twenty on seven. Eighty on thirteen. Eighty on thirty. Twenty on nine. Fifty on twenty-four." He was following a system of his own, and in obedience Aileen's white, plump arm reached here and there while the spectators paused, realizing that heavier playing was being done by this pair than by anyone else. Lynde was plunging for effect. He lost $1,050 at one clip.

"Oh, all that good money!" exclaimed Aileen mock-pathetically, as the croupier raked it in.

"Never mind, we'll get it back," exclaimed Lynde, throwing two $1,000 bills to the cashier. "Give me gold for those."

The man gave him a double handful, which he put down between Aileen's white arms.

"One hundred on two. One hundred on four. One hundred on six. One hundred on eight."

The pieces were five-dollar gold pieces, and Aileen quickly built up the little yellow stacks and shoved them in place. Again the other players stopped and began to watch the odd pair. Aileen's red-gold head and pink cheeks and swimming eyes, her body swathed in silks and rich laces; and Lynde, erect, his shirt bosom snowy white, his face dark, almost coppery, his eyes and hair black—they were indeed a strikingly assorted pair.

"What's this? What's this?" asked Grier, coming up. "Who's plunging? You, Mrs. Cowperwood?"

"Not plunging," replied Lynde indifferently. "We're merely working out a formula—Mrs. Cowperwood and I. We're doing it together."

Aileen smiled. She was in her element at last. She was beginning to shine. She was attracting attention.

"One hundred on twelve. One hundred on eighteen. One hundred on twenty-six."

"Good heavens, what are you up to, Lynde?" exclaimed Lord, leaving Mrs. Rhees Grier and coming over. She followed. Strangers also were gathering. The business of the place was at its topmost toss—it being two o'clock in the morning—and the rooms were full.

"How interesting!" observed Miss Lanman at the other end of the table, pausing in her playing and staring. McKibben, who was beside her, also paused. "They're plunging. Do look at all the money! Goodness, isn't she daring-looking—and he?" Aileen's shining arm was moving deftly, showily about.

"Look at the bills he's breaking!" Lynde was taking out a thick layer of fresh yellow bills which he was exchanging for gold. "They make a striking pair, don't they?"

The board was now practically covered with Lynde's gold in quaint little stacks. He had followed a system called Mazarin, which should give him five for one, and possibly break the bank. Quite a crowd swarmed about the table, their faces glowing in the artificial light. The exclamation "Plunging!" "Plunging!" was to be heard whispered here and there. Lynde was delightfully cool and straight. His lithe body was quite erect, his eyes reflective, his teeth set over an unlighted cigarette. Aileen was excited as a child, delighted to be once more the center of comment. Lord looked at her with sympathetic eyes. He liked her. Well, let her be amused. It was good for her now; but Lynde was a fool to make a show of himself and risk so much money.

"Table closed!" called the croupier, and instantly the little ball began to spin. All eyes followed it. Round and round it went—Aileen as keen an observer as any. Her face was flushed, her eyes bright.

"If we lose this," said Lynde, "we will make one more bet double, and then if we don't win that we'll quit." He was already out nearly three thousand dollars.

"Oh yes, indeed! Only I think we ought to quit now. Here goes two thousand if we don't win. Don't you think that's quite enough? I haven't brought you much luck, have I?"

"You are luck," he whispered. "All the luck I want. One more. Stand by me for one more try, will you? If we win I'll quit."

The little ball clicked even as she nodded, and the croupier, paying out on a few small stacks here and there, raked all the rest solemnly into the receiving orifice, while murmurs of sympathetic dissatisfaction went up here and there.

"How much did they have on the board?" asked Miss Lanman of McKibben, in surprise. "It must have been a great deal, wasn't it?"

"Oh, two thousand dollars, perhaps. That isn't so high here, though. People do plunge for as much as eight or ten thousand. It all depends." McKibben was in a belittling, depreciating mood.

"Oh yes, but not often, surely."

"For the love of heavens, Polk!" exclaimed Rhees Grier, coming up and plucking at his sleeve; "if you want to give your money away give it to me. I can gather it in just as well as that croupier, and I'll go get a truck and haul it home, where it will do some good. It's perfectly terrible the way you are carrying on."

Lynde took his loss with equanimity. "Now to double it," he observed, "and get all our losses back, or go downstairs and have a rarebit and some champagne. What form of a present would please you best?—but never mind. I know a souvenir for this occasion."

He smiled and bought more gold. Aileen stacked it up showily if a little repentantly. She did not quite approve of this—his plunging—and yet she did; she could not help sympathizing with the plunging spirit. In a few moments it was on the board—the same combination, the same stacks, only doubled—four thousand all told. The croupier called, the ball rolled and fell. Barring three hundred dollars returned, the bank took it all.

"Well, now for a rarebit," exclaimed Lynde easily, turning to Lord, who stood behind him smiling. "You haven't a match, have you? We've had a run of bad luck, that's sure."

Lynde was secretly the least bit disgruntled, for if he had won he had intended to take a portion of the winnings and put it in a necklace or some other gewgaw for Aileen. Now he must pay for it. Yet there was some satisfaction in having made an impression as a calm and indifferent, though heavy, loser. He gave Aileen his arm.

"Well, my lady," he observed, "we didn't win; but we had a little fun out of it, I hope? That combination, if it had come out, would have set us up handsomely. Better luck next time, eh?"

He smiled genially.

"Yes, but I was to have been your luck, and I wasn't," replied Aileen.

"You are all the luck I want, if you're willing to be. Come to the Richelieu tomorrow with me for lunch—will you?"

"Let me see," replied Aileen, who, observing his ready and somewhat iron fervor, was doubtful. "I can't do that," she said finally, "I have another engagement."

"How about Tuesday, then?"

Aileen, realizing of a sudden that she was making much of a situation that ought to be handled with a light hand, answered readily: "Very well—Tuesday! Only call me up before. I may have to change my mind or the time." And she smiled good-naturedly.

After this Lynde had no opportunity to talk to Aileen privately; but in saying good night he ventured to press her arm suggestively. She suffered a peculiar nervous thrill from this, but decided curiously that she had brought it upon herself by her eagerness for life and revenge, and must make up her mind. Did she or did she not wish to go on with this?

This was the question uppermost, and she felt that she must decide. However, as in most such cases, circumstances were to help decide for her, and, unquestionably, a portion of this truth was in her mind as she was shown gallantly to her door by Taylor Lord.

CHAPTER XXXIII

Mr. Lynde to the Rescue

The interested appearance of a man like Polk Lynde at this stage of Aileen's affairs was a bit of fortuitous or gratuitous humor on the part of fate, which is involved with that subconscious chemistry of things of which as yet we know nothing. Here was Aileen brooding over her fate, meditating over her wrongs, as it were; and here was Polk Lynde, an interesting, forceful Lothario of the city, who was perhaps as well suited to her moods and her tastes at this time as any male outside of Cowperwood could be.

In many respects Lynde was a charming man. He was comparatively young—not more than Aileen's own age—schooled, if not educated, at one of the best American colleges, of excellent taste in the matter of clothes, friends, and the details of living with which he chose to surround himself, but at heart a rake. He loved, and had from his youth up, to gamble. He was in one phase of the word a hard and yet by no means a self-destructive drinker, for he had an iron constitution and could consume spirituous waters with the minimum of ill effect. He had what Gibbon was wont to call "the most amiable of our vices," a passion for women, and he cared no more for the cool, patient, almost penitent methods by which his father had built up the immense reaper business, of which he was supposedly the heir, than he cared for the mysteries or sacred rights of the Chaldees. He realized that the business itself was a splendid thing. He liked on occasion to think of it with all its extent of ground space, plain red-brick buildings, tall stacks and yelling whistles; but he liked in no way to have anything to do with the rather commonplace routine of its manipulation.

The principal difficulty with Aileen under these circumstances, of course, was her intense vanity and self-consciousness. Never was there a vainer or more sex-troubled woman. Why, she asked herself, should she sit here in loneliness day after day, brooding about Cowperwood, eating her heart out, while he was flitting about gathering the sweets of life elsewhere? Why should she not offer her continued charms as a solace and a delight to other men who would appreciate them? Would not such a policy have all the essentials of justice in it? Yet even now, so precious had Cowperwood been to her hitherto, and so wonderful, that she was scarcely able to think of serious disloyalty. He was so charming when he was nice—so splendid. When Lynde sought to hold her to the proposed luncheon engagement she at first declined. And there, under slightly differing conditions, the matter might easily have stood. But it so happened that just at this time Aileen was being almost daily harassed by additional evidence and reminders of Cowperwood's infidelity.

For instance, going one day to call on the Haguenins—for she was perfectly willing to keep up the pretense of amity in so long as they had not found out the truth—she was informed that Mrs. Haguenin was "not at home." Shortly thereafter the *Press*, which had always been favorable to Cowperwood, and which Aileen regularly read because of its friendly comment, suddenly veered and began to attack him. There were solemn suggestions at first that his policy and intentions might not be in accord with the best interests of the city. A little later Haguenin printed editorials which referred to Cowperwood as "the wrecker," "the Philadelphia adventurer," "a conscienceless promoter," and the like. Aileen guessed instantly what the trouble was, but she was too disturbed as to her own position to make any comment. She could not resolve the threats and menaces of Cowperwood's envious world any more than she could see her way through her own grim difficulties.

One day, in scanning the columns of that faithful chronicle of Chicago social doings, the Chicago *Saturday Review*, she came across an item which served as a final blow.

For some time in high social circles, [the paragraph ran]

speculation has been rife as to the amours and liaisons of a certain individual of great wealth and pseudo social prominence, who once made a serious attempt to enter Chicago society. It is not necessary to name the man, for all who are acquainted with recent events in Chicago will know who is meant. The latest rumor to affect his already nefarious reputation relates to two women—one the daughter, and the other the wife, of men of repute and standing in the community. In these latest instances it is more than likely that he has arrayed influences of the greatest importance socially and financially against himself, for the husband in the one case and the father in the other are men of weight and authority. The suggestion has more than once been made that Chicago should and eventually would not tolerate his buccaneering methods in finance and social matters; but thus far no definite action has been taken to cast him out. The crowning wonder of all is that the wife, who was brought here from the East, and who—so rumor has it—made a rather scandalous sacrifice of her own reputation and another woman's heart and home in order to obtain the privilege of living with him, should continue so to do.

Aileen understood perfectly what was meant. "The father" of the so-called "one" was probably Haguenin or Cochrane, more than likely Haguenin. "The husband of the other"— but who was the husband of the other? She had not heard of any scandal with the wife of anybody. It could not be the case of Rita Sohlberg and her husband—that was too far back. It must be some new affair of which she had not the least inkling, and so she sat and reflected. Now, she told herself, if she received another invitation from Lynde she would accept it.

It was only a few days later that Aileen and Lynde met in the gold room of the Richelieu. Strange to relate, for one determined to be indifferent she had spent much time in making a fetching toilet. It being February and chill with glittering snow on the ground, she had chosen a dark green broadcloth gown, quite new, with lapis lazuli buttons that worked a Y pattern across her bosom, a seal turban with an emerald plume which complemented a sealskin jacket with immense wrought-silver buttons, and bronze shoes. To perfect it all,

Aileen had fastened lapis lazuli earrings of a small flower form in her ears, and wore a plain, heavy gold bracelet. Lynde came up with a look of keen approval written on his handsome brown face.

"Will you let me tell you how nice you look?" he said, sinking into the chair opposite. "You show beautiful taste in choosing the right colors. Your earrings go so well with your hair."

Although Aileen feared because of his desperateness, she was caught by his sleek force—that air of iron strength under a parlor mask. His long brown, artistic hands, hard and muscular, indicated an idle force that might be used in many ways. They harmonized with his teeth and chin.

"So you came, didn't you?" he went on, looking at her steadily, while she fronted his gaze boldly for a moment, only to look evasively down.

He still studied her carefully, looking at her chin and mouth and piquant nose. In her colorful cheeks and strong arms and shoulders, indicated by her well-tailored suit, he recognized the human vigor he most craved in a woman. By way of diversion he ordered an old-fashioned whiskey cocktail, urging her to join him. Finding her obdurate, he drew from his pocket a little box.

"We agreed when we played the other night on a memento, didn't we?" he said. "A sort of souvenir? Guess?"

Aileen looked at it a little nonplussed, recognizing the contents of the box to be jewelry. "Oh, you shouldn't have done that," she protested. "The understanding was that we were to win. You lost, and that ended the bargain. I should have shared the losses. I haven't forgiven you for that yet, you know."

"How ungallant that would make me!" he said smilingly, as he trifled with the long, thin, lacquered case. "You wouldn't want to make me ungallant, would you? Be a good fellow—a good sport, as they say. Guess, and it's yours."

Aileen pursed her lips at this ardent entreaty.

"Oh, I don't mind guessing," she commented superiorly, "though I shan't take it. It might be a pin, it might be a set of earrings, it might be a bracelet—"

He made no comment, but opened it, revealing a necklace of gold wrought into the form of a grapevine of the most curious workmanship, with a cluster of leaves artistically carved and arranged as a breastpiece, the center of them formed by a black opal, which shone with an enticing luster. Lynde knew well enough that Aileen was familiar with many jewels, and that only one of ornate construction and value would appeal to her sense of what was becoming to her. He watched her face closely while she studied the details of the necklace.

"Isn't it exquisite!" she commented. "What a lovely opal— what an odd design." She went over the separate leaves. "You shouldn't be so foolish. I couldn't take it. I have too many things as it is, and besides—" She was thinking of what she would say if Cowperwood chanced to ask her where she got it. He was so intuitive.

"And besides?" he queried.

"Nothing," she replied, "except that I mustn't take it, really."

"Won't you take it as a souvenir even if—our agreement, you know."

"Even if what?" she queried.

"Even if nothing else comes of it. A memento, then— truly—you know."

He laid hold of her fingers with his cool, vigorous ones.

A year before, even six months, Aileen would have released her hand smilingly. Now she hesitated. Why should she be so squeamish with other men when Cowperwood was so unkind to her?

"Tell me something," Lynde asked, noting the doubt and holding her fingers gently but firmly, "do you care for me at all?"

"I like you, yes. I can't say that it is anything more than that."

She flushed, though, in spite of herself.

He merely gazed at her with his hard, burning eyes. The materiality that accompanies romance in so many temperaments awakened in her, and quite put Cowperwood out of her mind for the moment. It was an astonishing and revolutionary experience for her. She quite burned in reply, and Lynde smiled sweetly, encouragingly.

"Why won't you be friends with me, my sweetheart? I know you're not happy—I can see that. Neither am I. I have a wreckless, wretched disposition that gets me into all sorts of hell. I need someone to care for me. Why won't you? You're just my sort. I feel it. Do you love him so much"—he was referring to Cowperwood—"that you can't love anyone else?"

"Oh, him!" retorted Aileen irritably, almost disloyally. "He doesn't care for me anymore. He wouldn't mind. It isn't him."

"Well, then, what is it? Why won't you? Am I not interesting enough? Don't you like me? Don't you feel that I'm really suited to you?" His hand sought hers softly.

Aileen accepted the caress.

"Oh, it isn't that," she replied feelingly, running back in her mind over her long career with Cowperwood, his former love, his keen protestations. She had expected to make so much out of her life with him, and here she was sitting in a public restaurant flirting with and extracting sympathy from a comparative stranger. It cut her to the quick for the moment and sealed her lips. Hot, unbidden tears welled to her eyes.

Lynde saw them. He was really very sorry for her, though her beauty made him wish to take advantage of her distress. "Why should you cry, dearest?" he asked softly, looking at her flushed cheeks and colorful eyes. "You have beauty; you are young; you're lovely. He's not the only man in the world. Why should you be faithful when he isn't faithful to you? This Hand affair is all over town. When you meet someone that really would care for you, why shouldn't you? If he doesn't want you, there are others."

At the mention of the Hand affair Aileen straightened up. "The Hand affair?" she asked curiously. "What is that?"

"Don't you know?" he replied, a little surprised. "I thought you did, or I certainly wouldn't have mentioned it."

"Oh, I know *about* what it is," replied Aileen, wisely and with a touch of sardonic humor. "There have been so many of the same kind. I suppose it must be the case the Chicago *Review* was referring to—the wife of the prominent financier. Has he been trifling with Mrs. Hand?"

"Something like that," replied Lynde. "I'm sorry that I spoke, though—really I am. I didn't mean to be carrying tales."

"Soldiers in a common fight, eh?" taunted Aileen gaily.

"Oh, not that, exactly. Please don't be mean. I'm not so bad. It's just a principle with me. We all have our little foibles."

"Yes, I know," replied Aileen; but her mind was running

on Mrs. Hand. So she was the latest. "Well, I admire his taste, anyway, in this case," she said archly. "There have been so many, though. She is just one more."

Lynde smiled. He himself admired Cowperwood's taste. Then he dropped the subject.

"But let's forget that," he said. "Please don't worry about him anymore. You can't change that. Pull yourself together." He squeezed her fingers. "Will you?" he asked, lifting his eyebrows in inquiry.

"Will I what?" replied Aileen meditatively.

"Oh, you know. The necklace for one thing. Me, too." His eyes coaxed and laughed and pleaded.

Aileen smiled. "You're a bad boy," she said evasively. This revelation in regard to Mrs. Hand had made her singularly retaliatory in spirit. "Let me think. Don't ask me to take the necklace today. I couldn't. I couldn't wear it, anyhow. Let me see you another time." She moved her plump hand in an uncertain way, and he smoothed her wrist.

"I wonder if you wouldn't like to go around to the studio of a friend of mine here in the tower?" he asked quite nonchalantly. "He has such a charming collection of landscapes. You're interested in pictures, I know. Your husband has some of the finest."

Instantly Aileen understood what was meant—quite by instinct. The alleged studio must be private bachelor quarters.

"Not this afternoon," she replied, quite wrought up and disturbed. "Not today. Another time. And I must be going now. But I will see you."

"And this?" he asked, picking up the necklace.

"You keep it until I do come," she replied. "I may take it then."

She relaxed a little, pleased that she was getting safely away; but her mood was anything but antagonistic, and her spirits were as shredded as wind-whipped clouds. It was time she wanted—a little time—that was all.

CHAPTER XXXIV

Enter Hosmer Hand

It is needless to say that the solemn rage of Hand,
to say nothing of the pathetic anger of Haguenin, coupled
with the wrath of Redmond Purdy, who related to all his sad
story, and of young MacDonald and his associates of the
Chicago General Company, constituted an atmosphere highly
charged with possibilities and potent for dramatic results.
The most serious element in this at present was Hosmer
Hand, who, being exceedingly wealthy and a director in a
number of the principal mercantile and financial institutions
of the city, was in a position to do Cowperwood some real
financial harm. Hand had been extremely fond of his young
wife. Being a man of but few experiences with women, it
astonished and enraged him that a man like Cowperwood
should dare to venture on his preserves in this reckless way,
should take his dignity so lightly. He burned now with a hot,
slow fire of revenge.

Those who know anything concerning the financial world
and its great adventures know how precious is that reputation for probity, solidarity, and conservatism on which so
many of the successful enterprises of the world are based.
If men are not absolutely honest themselves they at least
wish for and have faith in the honesty of others. No set of
men know more about each other, garner more carefully all
the straws of rumor which may affect the financial and social
well being of an individual one way or another, keep a
tighter mouth concerning their own affairs and a sharper eye
on that of their neighbors. Cowperwood's credit had hitherto
been good because it was known that he had a "soft thing"
in the Chicago street-railway field, that he paid his interest
charges promptly, that he had organized the group of men
who now, under him, controlled the Chicago Trust Company

and the North and West Chicago Street Railways, and that the Lake City Bank, of which Addison was still president, considered his collateral sound. Nevertheless, even previous to this time there had been a protesting element in the shape of Schryhart, Simms, and others of considerable import in the Douglas Trust, who had lost no chance to say to one and all that Cowperwood was an interloper, and that his course was marked by political and social trickery and chicanery, if not by financial dishonesty. As a matter of fact, Schryhart, who had once been a director of the Lake City National along with Hand, Arneel, and others, had resigned and withdrawn all his deposits some time before because he found, as he declared, that Addison was favoring Cowperwood and the Chicago Trust Company with loans when there was no need of so doing—when it was not essentially advantageous for the bank so to do. Both Arneel and Hand, having at this time no personal quarrel with Cowperwood on any score, had considered this protest as biased. Addison had maintained that the loans were neither unduly large nor out of proportion to the general loans of the bank. The collateral offered was excellent. "I don't want to quarrel with Schryhart," Addison had protested at the time; "but I am afraid his charge is unfair. He is trying to vent a private grudge through the Lake National. That is not the way nor this the place to do it."

Both Hand and Arneel, sober men both, agreed with this —admiring Addison—and so the case stood. Schryhart, however, frequently intimated to them both that Cowperwood was merely building up the Chicago Trust Company at the expense of the Lake City National, in order to make the former strong enough to do without any aid, at which time Addison would resign and the Lake City would be allowed to shift for itself. Hand had never acted on this suggestion, but he had thought.

It was not until the incidents relating to Cowperwood and Mrs. Hand had come to light that things financial and otherwise began to darken up. Hand, being greatly hurt in his pride, contemplated only severe reprisal. Meeting Schryhart at a directors' meeting one day not long after his difficulty had come upon him, he remarked:

"I thought a few years ago, Norman, when you talked to me about this man Cowperwood, that you were merely jealous—a dissatisfied business rival. Recently a few things have come to my notice which cause me to think differently. It is very plain to me now that the man is thoroughly bad—from the crown of his head to the soles of his feet. It's a pity the city has to endure him."

"So you're just beginning to find that out, are you, Hosmer?" answered Schryhart. "Well, I'll not say I told you so. Perhaps you'll agree with me now that the responsible people of Chicago ought to do something about it."

Hand, a very heavy, taciturn man, merely looked at him. "I'll be ready enough to do," he said, "when I see how and what's to be done."

A little later Schryhart, meeting Duane Kingsland, learned the true source of Hand's feeling against Cowperwood, and was not slow in transferring this tidbit to Merrill, Simms, and others. Merrill, who, though Cowperwood had refused to extend his La Salle tunnel loop about State Street and his store, had hitherto always liked him after a fashion—remotely admired his courage and daring—was now appropriately shocked.

"Why, Anson," observed Schryhart, "the man is no good. He has the heart of a hyena and the friendliness of a scorpion. You heard how he treated Hand, didn't you?"

"No," replied Merrill, "I didn't."

"Well, it's this way, so I hear." And Schryhart leaned over and confidentially communicated considerable information into Mr. Merrill's left ear.

The latter raised his eyebrows. "Indeed!" he said.

"And the way he came to meet her," added Schryhart contemptuously, "was this. He went to Hand originally to borrow two hundred and fifty thousand dollars on West Chicago Street Railway. Angry? The word is no name for it."

"You don't say so," commented Merrill dryly, though privately interested and fascinated, for Mrs. Hand had always seemed very attractive to him. "I don't wonder."

He recalled that his own wife had recently insisted on inviting Cowperwood once.

Similarly Hand, meeting Arneel not so long afterward, confided to him that Cowperwood was trying to repudiate a sacred agreement. Arneel was grieved and surprised. It was enough for him to know that Hand had been seriously injured. Between the two of them they now decided to indicate to Addison, as president of the Lake City Bank, that all relations with Cowperwood and the Chicago Trust Company must cease. The result of this was, not long after, that Addison, very suave and gracious, agreed to give Cowperwood due warning that all his loans would have to be taken care of, and then resigned—to become, seven months later, president of the Chicago Trust Company. This desertion created a great stir at the time, astonishing the very men who had suspected that it might come to pass. The papers were full of it.

"Well, let him go," observed Arneel to Hand sourly, on the day that Addison notified the board of directors of the Lake City of his contemplated resignation. "If he wants to sever his connection with a bank like this to go with a man like that, it's his own lookout. He may live to regret it."

It so happened that by now another election was pending in Chicago, and Hand, along with Schryhart and Arneel—who joined their forces because of friendship for Hand—decided to try to fight Cowperwood through this means.

Hosmer Hand, feeling that he had the burden of a great duty upon him, was not slow in acting. He was always, when aroused, a determined and able fighter. Needing an able lieutenant in the impending political conflict, he finally bethought himself of a man who had recently come to figure somewhat conspicuously in Chicago politics—one Patrick Gilgan, the same Patrick Gilgan of Cowperwood's old Hyde Park gas war days. Mr. Gilgan was now a comparatively well-to-do man. Owing to a genial capacity for mixing with people, a close mouth, and absolutely no understanding of, and consequently no conscience in, matters of large public import (insofar as they related to the so-called rights of the mass), he was a fit individual to succeed politically. His saloon was the finest in all Wentworth Avenue. It fairly glittered with the newly introduced incandescent lamps reflected in a perfect world of beveled and faceted mirrors. His ward, or district, was full of low, rain-beaten cottages crowded together along half-mile streets; but Patrick Gilgan was now a state senator, slated for Congress at the next congressional election, and a possible successor of the Honorable John J. McKenty as dictator of the city, if only the Republican party should come into power. (Hyde Park, before it had been annexed to the city, had always been Republican, and since then, although the larger city was normally

Democratic, Gilgan could not conveniently change.) Hearing from the political discussion which preceded the election that Gilgan was by far the most powerful politician on the South Side, Hand sent for him. Personally, Hand had far less sympathy with the polite moralistic efforts of men like Haguenin, Hyssop, and others, who were content to preach morality and strive to win by the efforts of the unco good, than he had with the cold political logic of a man like Cowperwood himself. If Cowperwood could work through McKenty to such a powerful end, he, Hand, could find someone else who could be made as powerful as McKenty.

"Mr. Gilgan," said Hand, when the Irishman came in, medium tall, beefy, with shrewd, twinkling gray eyes and hairy hands, "you don't know me—"

"I know *of you* well enough," smiled the Irishman, with a soft brogue. "You don't need an introduction to talk to me."

"Very good," replied Hand, extending his hand. "I know of you, too. Then we can talk. It's the political situation here in Chicago I'd like to discuss with you. I'm not a politician myself, but I take some interest in what's going on. I want to know what you think will be the probable outcome of the present situation here in the city."

Gilgan, having no reason for laying his private political convictions bare to anyone whose motive he did not know, merely replied: "Oh, I think the Republicans may have a pretty good show. They have all but one or two of the papers with them, I see. I don't know much outside of what I read and hear people talk."

Mr. Hand knew that Gilgan was sparring, and was glad to find his man canny and calculating.

"I haven't asked you to come here just to be talking over politics in general, as you may imagine, Mr. Gilgan. I want to put a particular problem before you. Do you happen to know either Mr. McKenty or Mr. Cowperwood?"

"I never met either of them to talk to," replied Gilgan. "I know Mr. McKenty by sight, and I've seen Mr. Cowperwood once." He said no more.

"Well," said Mr. Hand, "suppose a group of influential men here in Chicago were to get together and guarantee sufficient funds for a city-wide campaign; now, if you had the complete support of the newspapers and the Republican organization in the bargain, could you organize the opposition here so that the Democratic party could be beaten this fall?

I'm not talking about the mayor merely and the principal city officers, but the council, too—the aldermen. I want to fix things so that the McKenty-Cowperwood crowd couldn't get an alderman or a city official to sell out, once they are elected. I want the Democratic party beaten so thoroughly that there won't be any question in anybody's mind as to the fact that it has been done. There will be plenty of money forthcoming if you can prove to me, or, rather, to the group of men I am thinking of, that the thing can be done."

Mr. Gilgan blinked his eyes solemnly. He rubbed his knees, put his thumbs in the armholes of his vest, took out a cigar, lit it, and gazed poetically at the ceiling. He was thinking very, very hard. Mr. Cowperwood and Mr. McKenty, as he knew, were very powerful men. He had always managed to down the McKenty opposition in his ward, and several others adjacent to it, and in the Eighteenth Senatorial District, which he represented. But to be called upon to defeat him in Chicago, that was different. Still, the thought of a large amount of cash to be distributed through him, and the chance of wresting the city leadership from McKenty, by the aid of the so-called moral forces of the city, was very inspiring. Mr. Gilgan was a good politician. He loved to scheme and plot and make deals—as much for the fun of it as anything else. Just now he drew a solemn face, which, however, concealed a very light heart.

"I have heard," went on Hand, "that you have built up a strong organization in your ward and district."

"I've managed to hold me own," suggested Gilgan, archly. "But this winning all over Chicago," he went on after a moment, "now, that's a pretty large order. There are thirty-one wards in Chicago this election, and all but eight of them are nominally Democratic. I know most of the men that are in them now, and some of them are pretty shrewd men, too. This man Dowling in council is nobody's fool, let me tell you that. Then there's Duvanicki and Ungerich and Tiernan and Kerrigan—all good men." He mentioned four of the most powerful and crooked aldermen in the city. "You see, Mr. Hand, the way things are now the Democrats have the offices, and the small jobs to give out. That gives them plenty of political workers to begin with. Then they have the privilege of collecting money from those in office to help elect themselves. That's another great privilege." He smiled. "Then this man Cowperwood employs all of ten thousand men at present, and any ward boss that's favorable to him can send a man out of work to him and he'll find a place for him. That's a gre-a-eat help in building up a party following. Then there's the money a man like Cowperwood and others can contribute at election time. Say what you will, Mr. Hand, but it's the two-, and five-, and ten-dollar bills paid out at the last moment over the saloon bars and the polling places that do the work. Give me enough money"—and at this noble thought Mr. Gilgan straightened up and slapped one fist lightly in the other, adjusting the same time his half-burned cigar so that it should not burn his hand—"and I can carry every ward in Chicago, bar none. If I have enough money," he repeated, emphasizing the last two words. He put his cigar back in his mouth, blinked his eyes defiantly, and leaned back in his chair.

"Very good," commented Hand simply; "but how much money?"

"Ah, that's another question," replied Gilgan, straightening up once more. "Some wards require more than others. Counting out the eight that are normally Republican as safe, you would have to carry eighteen others to have a majority in council. I don't see how anything under ten to fifteen thousand dollars to a ward would be safe to go on. I should say three hundred thousand dollars would be safer, and that wouldn't be any too much by any means."

Mr. Gilgan restored his cigar and puffed heavily the while he leaned back and lifted his eyes once more.

"And how would that money be distributed exactly?" inquired Mr. Hand.

"Oh, well, it's never wise to look into such matters too closely," commented Mr. Gilgan comfortably. "There's such a thing as cutting your cloth too close in politics. There are ward captains, leaders, block captains, workers. They all have to have money to do with——to work up sentiment——and you can't be too inquiring as to just how they do it. It's spent in saloons, and buying coal for mother, and getting Johnnie a new suit here and there. Then there are torchlight processions and clubrooms and jobs to look after. Sure, there's plenty of places for it. Some men may have to be brought into these wards to live——kept in boardinghouses for a week or ten days." He waved a hand deprecatingly.

Mr. Hand, who had never busied himself with the minutiae

of politics, opened his eyes slightly. This colonizing idea was a little liberal, he thought.

"Who distributes this money!" he asked finally.

"Nominally, the Republican County Committee, if it's in charge; actually, the man or men who are leading the fight. In the case of the Democratic party it's John J. McKenty, and don't you forget it. In my district it's me, and no one else."

Mr. Hand, slow, solid, almost obtuse at times, meditated under lowering brows. He had always been associated with a more or less silk-stocking crew who were unused to the rough usage of back room saloon politics, yet everyone suspected vaguely, of course, at times that ballot boxes were stuffed and ward lodging houses colonized. Everyone (at least everyone of any worldly intelligence) knew that political capital was collected from office seekers, officeholders, beneficiaries of all sorts and conditions under the reigning city administration. Mr. Hand had himself contributed to the Republican party for favors received or about to be. As a man who had been compelled to handle large affairs in a large way he was not inclined to quarrel with this. Three hundred thousand dollars was a large sum, and he was not inclined to subscribe it alone, but fancied that at his recommendation and with his advice it could be raised. Was Gilgan the man to fight Cowperwood? He looked him over and decided—other things being equal—that he was. And forthwith the bargain was struck. Gilgan, as a Republican central committeeman—chairman, possibly—was to visit every ward, connect up with every available Republican force, pick strong, suitable anti-Cowperwood candidates, and try to elect them, while he, Hand, organized the money element and collected the necessary cash. Gilgan was to be given money personally. He was to have the undivided if secret support of all the high Republican elements in the city. His business was to win at almost any cost. And as a reward he was to have the Republican support for Congress, or, failing that, the practical Republican leadership in city and county.

"Anyhow," said Hand, after Mr. Gilgan finally took his departure, "things won't be so easy for Mr. Cowperwood in the future as they were in the past. And when it comes to getting his franchises renewed, if I'm alive, we'll see whether he will or not."

The heavy financier actually growled a low growl as he spoke out loud to himself. He felt a boundless rancor toward the man who had, as he supposed, alienated the affections of his smart young wife.

CHAPTER XXXV

A Political Agreement

In the first and second wards of Chicago at this time—wards including the business heart, South Clark Street, the waterfront, the river levee, and the like—were two men, Michael (alias Smiling Mike) Tiernan and Patrick (alias Emerald Pat) Kerrigan, who, for picturesqueness of character and sordidness of atmosphere, could not be equaled elsewhere in the city, if in the nation at large. Smiling Mike Tiernan, proud possessor of four of the largest and filthiest saloons of this area, was a man of large and genial mold—perhaps six feet one inch in height, broad-shouldered in proportion, with a bovine head, bullet-shaped from one angle, and big, healthy, hairy hands and large feet. He had done many things, from digging in a ditch to occupying a seat in the city council from this his beloved ward, which he sold out regularly for one purpose and another; but his chief present joy consisted in sitting behind a solid mahogany railing at a rosewood desk in the back portion of his largest Clark Street hostelry—The Silver Moon. Here he counted up the returns from his various properties—saloons, gambling resorts, and houses of prostitution—which he manipulated with the connivance or blinking courtesy of the present administration, and listened to the pleas and demands of his henchmen and tenants.

The character of Mr. Kerrigan, Mr. Tiernan's only rival in this rather difficult and sordid region, was somewhat different. He was a small man, quite dapper, with a lean, hollow, and somewhat haggard face, but by no means sickly body, a large, strident moustache, a wealth of coal-black hair parted slickly on one side, and a shrewd, genial brown-black eye—constituting altogether a rather pleasing and ornate figure whom it was not at all unsatisfactory to meet. His ears were large and stood out bat-wise from his head; and his eyes gleamed with a smart, evasive light. He was cleverer financially than Tiernan, richer, and no more than thirty-five, whereas Mr. Tiernan was forty-five years of age. Like Mr. Tiernan in the first ward, Mr. Kerrigan was a power in the second, and controlled a most useful and dangerous floating vote. His saloons harbored the largest floating element that was to be found in the city—longshoremen, railroad hands, stevedores, tramps, thugs, thieves, pimps, rounders, detectives and the like. He was very vain, considered himself handsome, a killer with the ladies. Married, and with two children and a sedate young wife, he still had his mistress, who changed from year to year, and his intermediate girls. His clothes were altogether noteworthy, but it was his pride to eschew jewelry, except for one enormous emerald, value fourteen thousand dollars, which he wore in his necktie on occasions, and the wonder of which, pervading all Dearborn Street and the city council, had won him the soubriquet of Emerald Pat. At first he rejoiced heartily in this title, as he did in a gold and diamond medal awarded him by a Chicago brewery for selling the largest number of barrels of beer of any saloon in Chicago. More recently, the newspapers having begun to pay humorous attention to both him and Mr. Tiernan because of their prosperity and individuality, he resented it.

The relation of these two men to the present political situation was peculiar, and as it turned out, was to constitute the weak spot in the Cowperwood-McKenty campaign. Tiernan and Kerrigan, to begin with, being neighbors and friends, worked together in politics and business, on occasions pooling their issues and doing each other favors. The enterprises in which they were engaged being low and shabby, they needed counsel and consolation. Infinitely beneath a man like McKenty in understanding and a politic grasp of life, they were, nevertheless, as they prospered, somewhat jealous of him and his high estate. They saw, with speculative and somewhat jealous eyes, how after his union with Cowperwood he grew, and how he managed to work his will in many ways—by extracting tolls from the police department, and heavy annual campaign contributions from manufacturers favored by the city gas and water departments. McKenty—a born manipulator in this respect—knew where political funds were to be had in an hour of emergency, and he did not hesitate to demand them. Tiernan and Kerrigan had always been fairly treated by him as politics go; but they had never as yet been included in his inner council of plotters. When he was downtown on one errand or another, he stopped in at their places to shake hands with them, to inquire after business, to ask if there was any favor he could do them; but never did he stoop to ask a favor of them or personally to promise any form of reward. That was the business of Dowling and others through whom he worked.

Naturally men of strong, restive, animal disposition, finding no complete outlet for all their growing capacity, Tiernan and Kerrigan were both curious to see in what way they could add to their honors and emoluments. Their wards, more than any in the city, were increasing in what might be called a vote-piling capacity, the honest, legitimate vote not being so large, but the opportunities afforded for colonizing, repeating, and ballot box stuffing being immense. In a doubtful mayoralty campaign the first and second wards alone, coupled with a portion of the third adjoining them, would register sufficient illegitimate votes (after voting hours, if necessary) to completely change the complexion of the city as to the general officers nominated. Large amounts of money were sent to Tiernan and Kerrigan around election time by the Democratic County Committee to be disposed of as they saw fit. They merely sent in a rough estimate of how much they would need, and always received a little more than they asked for. They never made nor were asked to make accounting afterward. Tiernan would receive as high as fifteen and eighteen, Kerrigan sometimes as much as twenty to twenty-five thousand dollars, his being the pivotal ward under such circumstances.

McKenty had recently begun to recognize that these two men would soon have to be given fuller consideration, for they were becoming more or less influential. But how? Their personalities, let alone the reputation of their wards and the methods they employed, were not such as to command public confidence. In the meantime, owing to the tremendous growth of the city, the growth of their own private business, and the amount of ballot box stuffing, repeating, and the like which was required of them, they were growing more and more restless. Why should not they be slated for higher offices? they now frequently asked themselves. Tiernan would have been delighted to have been nominated for sheriff or city treasurer. He considered himself eminently qualified. Kerrigan at the last city convention had privately urged on Dowling the wisdom of nominating him for the position of commissioner of highways and sewers, which office he was anxious to obtain because of its reported commercial perquisites; but this year, of all times, owing to the need of nominating an unblemished ticket to defeat the sharp Republican opposition, such a nomination was not possible. It would have drawn the fire of all the respectable elements in the city. As a result both Tiernan and Kerrigan, thinking over their services, past and future, felt very much disgruntled. They were really not large enough mentally to understand how dangerous—outside of certain fields of activity—they were to the party.

After his confidence with Hand, Gilgan, going about the city with the promise of ready cash on his lips, was able to arouse considerable enthusiasm for the Republican cause. In the wards and sections where the so-called better element prevailed it seemed probable, because of the heavy moral teaching of the newspapers, that the respectable vote would array itself almost solidly this time against Cowperwood. In the poorer wards it would not be so easy. True, it was possible, by a sufficient outlay in cash, to find certain hardy buccaneers who could be induced to knife their own brothers, but the result was not certain. Having heard through one person and another of the disgruntled mood of both Kerrigan and Tiernan, and recognizing himself, even if he was a Republican, to be a man much more of their own stripe than either McKenty or Dowling, Gilgan decided to visit that lusty pair and see what could be done by way of alienating them from the present center of power.

After due reflection he first sought out Emerald Pat Kerrigan, whom he knew personally but with whom he was by no means intimate politically, at his Emporium Bar in Dearborn Street. This particular saloon, a feature of political Chicago at this time, was a large affair containing among other marvelous saloon fixtures a circular bar of cherrywood twelve feet in diameter, which glowed like a small mountain with the customary plain and colored glasses, bottles, labels, and mirrors. The floor was a composition of small, shaded red and green marbles; the ceiling a daub of pinky, fleshy nudes floating among diaphanous clouds; the walls were alternate panels of cerise and brown set in rosewood. Mr. Kerrigan, when other duties were not pressing, was usually to be found standing chatting with several friends and surveying the wonders of his bar trade, which was very large. On the day of Mr. Gilgan's call he was resplendent in a dark brown suit with a fine red stripe in it, cordovan leather shoes, a wine-colored tie ornamented with the emerald of so much renown, and a straw hat of flaring proportions and novel weave. About his waist, in lieu of a waistcoat, was fastened one of the eccentricities of the day, a manufactured silk sash. He formed an interesting contrast with Mr. Gilgan, who now came up very moist, pink, and warm, in a fine, light tweed of creamy, showy texture, straw hat, and yellow shoes.

"How are you, Kerrigan?" he observed genially, there being no political enmity between them. "How's the first, and how's trade? I see you haven't lost the emerald yet?"

"No. No danger of that. Oh, trade's all right. And so's the first. How's Mr. Gilgan?" Kerrigan extended his hand cordially.

"I have a word to say to you. Have you any time to spare?"

For answer Mr. Kerrigan led the way into the back room. Already he had heard rumors of a strong Republican opposition at the coming election.

Mr. Gilgan sat down. "It's about things this fall I've come to see you, of course," he began smilingly. "You and I are supposed to be on opposite sides of the fence, and we are as a rule, but I am wondering whether we need be this time or not?"

Mr. Kerrigan, shrewd though seemingly simple, fixed him with an amiable eye. "What's your scheme?" he said. "I'm always open to a good idea."

"Well, it's just this," began Mr. Gilgan, feeling his way. "You have a fine big ward here that you carry in your vest pocket, and so has Tiernan, as we all know; and we all know, too, that if it wasn't for what you and him can do there wouldn't always be a Democratic mayor elected. Now, I have an idea, from looking into the thing, that neither you nor Tiernan have got as much out of it so far as you might have."

Mr. Kerrigan was too cautious to comment as to that, though Mr. Gilgan paused for a moment.

"Now, I have a plan, as I say, and you can take it or leave it, just as you want, and no hard feelings one way or the other. I think the Republicans are going to win this fall—McKenty or no McKenty—first, second, and third wards with us or not, as they choose. The doings of the big fellow"—he was referring to McKenty—"with the other fellow in North Clark Street"—Mr. Gilgan preferred to be a little enigmatic at times—"are very much in the wind just now. You see how the papers stand. I happen to know where there's any quantity of money coming into the game from big financial quarters who have no use for this railroad man. It's a solid La Salle and Dearborn Street lineup, so far as I can see. Why, I don't know. But so it is. Maybe you know better than I do. Anyhow, that's the way it stands now. Add to that the fact that there are eight naturally Republican wards as it is, and ten more where there is always a fighting chance, and you begin to see what I'm driving at. Count out these last ten, though, and bet only on the eight that are sure to stand. That leaves twenty-three wards that we Republicans always conceded to you people; but if we manage to carry thirteen of them along with the eight I'm talking about, we'll have a majority in council, and"—flick! he snapped his fingers—"out you go—you, McKenty, Cowperwood, and all the rest. No more franchises, no more street-paving contracts, no more gas deals. Nothing—for two years, anyhow, and maybe longer. If we win we'll take the jobs and the fat deals." He paused and surveyed Kerrigan cheerfully but defiantly.

"Now, I've just been all over the city," he continued, "in every ward and precinct, so I know something of what I am talking about. I have the men and the cash to put up a fight all along the line this time. This fall we win—me and the big fellows over there in La Salle Street, and all the Republicans or Democrats or Prohibitionists, or whoever else comes in with us—do you get me? We're going to put up the biggest political fight Chicago has ever seen. I'm not naming any names just yet, but when the time comes you'll see. Now, what I want to ask of you is this, and I'll not mince me words nor beat around the bush. Will you and

Tiernan come in with me and Edstrom to take over the city
and run it during the next two years? If you will, we can
win hands down. It will be a case of share and share alike
on everything—police, gas, water, highways, street-railways,
everything—or we'll divide beforehand and put it down in
black and white. I know that you and Tiernan work together, or I wouldn't talk about this. Edstrom has the
Swedes where he wants them, and he'll poll twenty thousand
of them this fall. There's Ungerich with his Germans; one
of us might make a deal with him afterward, give him most
any office he wants. If we win this time we can hold the
city for six or eight years anyhow, most likely, and after
that—well, there's no use lookin' too far in the future—
Anyhow, we'd have a majority of the council and carry the
mayor along with it."

"If—" commented Mr. Kerrigan dryly.

"If," replied Mr. Gilgan sententiously. "You're very right.
There's a big 'if' in there, I'll admit. But if these two wards
—yours and Tiernan's—could by any chance be carried
for the Republicans they'd be equal to any four or five of
the others."

"Very true," replied Mr. Kerrigan, "if they could be carried for the Republicans. But they can't be. What do you
want me to do, anyhow? Lose me seat in council and be run
out of the Democratic party? What's your game? You don't
take me for a plain damn fool, do you?"

"Sorry the man that ever took Emerald Pat for that,"
answered Gilgan, with honeyed compliment. "I never would.
But no one is askin' ye to lose your seat in council and be
run out of the Democratic party. What's to hinder you from
electin' yourself and droppin' the rest of the ticket?" He had
almost said "knifing."

Mr. Kerrigan smiled. In spite of all his previous dissatisfaction with the Chicago situation he had not thought of Mr.
Gilgan's talk as leading to this. It was an interesting idea.
He had knifed people before—here and there a particular
candidate whom it was desirable to undo. If the Democratic
party was in any danger of losing this fall, and if Gilgan
was honest in his desire to divide and control, it might not
be such a bad thing. Neither Cowperwood, McKenty, nor
Dowling had ever favored him in any particular way. If they
lost through him, and he could still keep himself in power,
they would have to make terms with him. There was no

chance of their running him out. Why shouldn't he knife the ticket? It was worth thinking over, to say the least.

"That's all very fine," he observed dryly, after his meditations had run their course; "but how do I know that you wouldn't turn around and welch on the agreement afterward?" (Mr. Gilgan stirred irritably at the suggestion.) "Dave Morrissey came to me four years ago to help him out, and a lot of satisfaction I got afterward." Kerrigan was referring to a man whom he had helped make county clerk, and who had turned on him when he asked for return favors and his support for the office of commissioner of highways. Morrissey had become a prominent politician.

"That's very easy to say," replied Gilgan irritably, "but it's not true of me. Ask any man in my district. Ask the men who know me. I'll put my part of the bargain in black and white if you'll put yours. If I don't make good, show me up afterward. I'll take you to the people that are backing me. I'll show you the money. I've got the goods this time. What do you stand to lose, anyhow? They can't run you out for cutting the ticket. They can't prove it. We'll bring police in here to make it look like a fair vote. I'll put up as much money as they will to carry this district, and more."

Mr. Kerrigan suddenly saw a grand coup here. He could "draw down" from the Democrats, as he would have expressed it, twenty to twenty-five thousand dollars to do the dirty work here. Gilgan would furnish him as much and more —the situation being so critical. Perhaps fifteen or eighteen thousand would be necessary to poll the number of votes required either way. At the last hour, before stuffing the boxes, he would learn how the city was going. If it looked favorable for the Republicans it would be easy to complete the victory and complain that his lieutenants had been suborned. If it looked certain for the Democrats he could throw Gilgan and pocket his funds. In either case he would be "in" twenty-five to thirty thousand dollars, and he would still be councilman.

"All very fine," replied Mr. Kerrigan, pretending a dullness which he did not feel; "but it's damned ticklish business at best. I don't know that I want anything to do with it even if we could win. It's true the City Hall crowd have never played into my hands very much; but this is a Democratic district, and I'm a Democrat. If it ever got out that I had thrown the party it would be pretty near all day with me."

"I'm a man of my word," declared Mr. Gilgan emphatically, getting up. "I never threw a man or a bet in my life. Look at me record in the eighteenth. Did you ever hear anyone say that I had?"

"No, I never did," returned Kerrigan mildly. "But it's a pretty large thing you're proposing, Mr. Gilgan. I wouldn't want to say what I thought about it offhand. This ward is supposed to be Democratic. It couldn't be swung over into the Republican column without a good bit of fuss being made about it. You'd better see Mr. Tiernan first and hear what he has to say. Afterward I might be willing to talk about it further. Not now, though—not now."

Mr. Gilgan went away quite jauntily and cheerfully. He was not at all downcast.

CHAPTER XXXVI

An Election Draws Near

Subsequently Mr. Kerrigan called on Mr. Tiernan casually. Mr. Tiernan returned the call. A little later Messrs. Tiernan, Kerrigan, and Gilgan, in a parlor room in a small hotel in Milwaukee (in order not to be seen together), conferred. Finally Messrs. Tiernan, Edstrom, Kerrigan, and Gilgan met and mapped out a program of division far too intricate to be indicated here. Needless to say, it involved the division of chief clerks, pro rata, of police graft, of gambling and bawdy house perquisites, of returns from gas, street-railway, and other organizations. It was sealed with many solemn promises. If it could be made effective this quadrumvirate was to endure for years. Judges, small magistrates, officers large and small, the shrievalty, the water office, the tax office, all were to come within its purview. It was a fine handsome political dream, and as such worthy of every courtesy and consideration; but it was only a political dream in its ultimate aspects, and as such impressed the participants themselves at times.

The campaign was now in full blast. The summer and fall (September and October) went by to the tune of Democratic and Republican marching club bands, to the sound of lusty political voices orating in parks, at street corners, in wooden "wigwams," halls, tents, and parlors—wherever a meager handful of listeners could be drummed up and made by any device to keep still. The newspapers honked and bellowed, as is the way with those profit-appointed advocates and guardians of "right" and "justice." Cowperwood and McKenty were denounced from nearly every street corner in Chicago. Wagons and signboards on wheels were hauled about, labeled "Break the partnership between the street-railway corporations and the city council." "Do you want more streets stolen?" "Do you want Cowperwood to own Chicago?" Cowperwood himself, coming downtown of a morning or driving home of an evening, saw these things. He saw the huge signs, listened to speeches denouncing him, and smiled. By now he was quite aware as to whence this powerful uprising had sprung. Hand was back of it, he knew—for so McKenty and Addison had quickly discovered—and with Hand were Schryhart, Arneel, Merrill, the Douglas Trust Company, the various editors, young Truman Leslie MacDonald, the old gas crowd, the Chicago General Company—all. He even suspected that certain aldermen might possibly be suborned to desert him, though all professed loyalty. McKenty, Addison, Videra, and he were planning the details of their defenses as carefully and effectively as possible. Cowperwood was fully alive to the fact that if he lost this election—the first to be vigorously contested—it might involve a serious chain of events; but he did not propose to be unduly disturbed, since he could always fight in the courts by money, and by preferment in the council, and with the mayor and the city attorney. "There is more than one way to kill a cat," was one of his pet expressions, and it expressed his logic and courage exactly. Yet he did not wish to lose.

One of the amusing features of the campaign was that the McKenty orators had been instructed to shout as loudly for reforms as the Republicans, only instead of assailing Cowperwood and McKenty they were to point out that Schryhart's Chicago City Railway was far more rapacious, and that this was a scheme to give it a blanket franchise of all streets not yet covered by either the Cowperwood or the Schryhart-Hand-Arneel lines. It was a pretty argument. The Democrats could point with pride to a uniformly liberal interpretation of some trying Sunday laws, whereby under Republican and reform administrations it had been occasionally difficult for the honest workingman to get his glass or pail of beer on Sunday. On the other hand, it was possible for the Republican orators to show how "the low dives and gin mills" were everywhere being operated in favor of McKenty, and that under the highly respectable administration of the Republican candidate for mayor this partnership between the city government and vice and crime would be nullified.

"If I am elected," declared the Honorable Chaffee Thayer Sluss, the Republican candidate, "neither Frank Cowperwood nor John McKenty will dare to show his face in the City Hall unless he comes with clean hands and an honest purpose."

"Hoorar!" yelled the crowd.

"I know that ass," commented Addison, when he read this in the *Transcript*. "He used to be a clerk in the Douglas Trust Company. He's made a little money recently in the paper business. He's a mere tool for the Arneel-Schryhart interests. He hasn't the courage of a two-inch fishworm."

When McKenty read it, he simply observed: "There are other ways of going to City Hall than by going yourself." He was depending upon a councilmanic majority at least.

However, in the midst of this uproar the goings to and fro of Gilgan, Edstrom, Kerrigan, and Tiernan were not fully grasped. A more urbanely shifty pair than these latter were never seen. While fraternizing secretly with both Gilgan and Edstrom, laying out their political program most neatly, they were at the same time conferring with Dowling, Duvanicki, even McKenty himself. Seeing that the outcome was, for some reason—he could scarcely see why—looking very uncertain, McKenty one day asked the two of them to come to see him. On getting the letter Mr. Tiernan strolled over to Mr. Kerrigan's place to see whether he also had received a message.

"Sure, sure! I did!" replied Mr. Kerrigan gaily. "Here it is now in me outside coat pocket. 'Dear Mr. Kerrigan,'" he read, "'won't you do me the favor to come over tomorrow evening at seven and dine with me? Mr. Ungerich, Mr. Duvanicki, and several others will very likely drop in afterward. I have asked Mr. Tiernan to come at the same time. Sincerely, John J. McKenty.' That's the way he does it," added Mr. Kerrigan; "just like that."

He kissed the letter mockingly and put it back into his pocket.

"Sure I got one, jist the same way. The very same langwidge, nearly," commented Mr. Tiernan sweetly. "He's beginning to wake up, eh? What! The little old first and second are beginning to look purty big just now eh? What!"

"Tush!" observed Mr. Kerrigan to Mr. Tiernan, with a marked sardonic emphasis, "that combination won't last forever. They've been getting too big for their pants, I'm thinking. Well, it's a long road, eh? It's pretty near time, what?"

"You're right," responded Mr. Tiernan feelingly. "It is a long road. These are the two big wards of the city, and everybody knows it. If we turn on them at the last moment where will they be, eh?"

He put a fat finger alongside of his heavy reddish nose and looked at Mr. Kerrigan out of squinted eyes.

"You're damned right," replied the little politician cheerfully.

They went to the dinner separately, so as not to appear to have conferred before, and greeted each other on arriving as though they had not seen each other for days.

"How's business, Mike?"

"Oh, fair, Pat. How's things with you?"

"So-so."

"Things lookin' all right in your ward for November?"

Mr. Tiernan wrinkled a fat forehead. "Can't tell yet." All this was for the benefit of Mr. McKenty, who did not suspect rank party disloyalty.

Nothing much came of this conference, except that they sat about discussing in a general way wards, pluralities, what Zeigler was likely to do with the twelfth, whether Pinski could make it in the fourteenth, Schlumbohm in the twentieth, and so on. New Republican contestants in old, safe Democratic wards were making things look dubious.

"And how about the first, Kerrigan?" inquired Ungerich, a thin, reflective German-American of shrewd presence. Ungerich was one who had hitherto wormed himself higher in McKenty's favor than either Kerrigan or Tiernan.

"Oh, the first's all right," replied Kerrigan archly. "Of course, you never can tell. This fellow Scully may do something, but I don't think it will be much. If we have the same police protection—"

Ungerich was gratified. He was having a struggle in his own ward, where a rival by the name of Glover appeared to be pouring out money like water. He would require considerably more money than usual to win. It was the same with Duvanicki.

McKenty finally parted with his lieutenants—more feelingly with Kerrigan and Tiernan than he had ever done before. He did not wholly trust these two, and he could not exactly admire them and their methods, which were the roughest of all, but they were useful.

"I'm glad to learn," he said at parting, "that things are looking all right with you, Pat, and you, Mike," nodding to each in turn. "We're going to need the most we can get out of everybody. I depend on you two to make a fine showing —the best of any. The rest of us will not forget it when the plums are being handed around afterward."

"Oh, you can depend on me to do the best I can always," commented Mr. Kerrigan sympathetically. "It's a tough year, but we haven't failed yet."

"And me, Chief! That goes for me," observed Mr. Tiernan raucously. "I guess I can do as well as I have."

"Good for you, Mike!" soothed McKenty, laying a gentle hand on his shoulder. "And you, too, Kerrigan. Yours are the key wards, and we understand that. I've always been sorry that the leaders couldn't agree on you two for something better than councilmen; but next time there won't be any doubt of it, if I have any influence then." He went in and closed the door.

Outside a cool October wind was whipping dead leaves and weed stalks along the pavements. Neither Tiernan nor Kerrigan spoke, though they had come away together, until they were two hundred feet down the avenue toward Van Buren.

"Some talk, that, eh?" commented Mr. Tiernan, eyeing Mr. Kerrigan in the flare of a passing gas lamp.

"Sure. That's the stuff they always hand out when they're up against it. Pretty kind words, eh?"

"And after ten years of about the roughest work that's done, eh? It's about time, what? Say, it's a wonder he didn't think of that last June when the convention was in session."

"Tush! Mikey," smiled Mr. Kerrigan grimly. "You're a bad

little boy. You want your pie too soon. Wait another two or four or six years, like Paddy Kerrigan and the others."

"Yes, I will—not," growled Mr. Tiernan. "Wait'll the sixth."

"No more, will I," replied Mr. Kerrigan. "Say, we know a trick that beats that next-year business to a pulp. What?"

"You're dead right," commented Mr. Tiernan.

And so they went peacefully home.

CHAPTER XXXVII

Aileen's Revenge

The interesting Polk Lynde, rising one morning, decided that his affair with Aileen, sympathetic as it was, must culminate in the one fashion satisfactory to him here and now—this day, if possible, or the next. Since the luncheon some considerable time had elapsed, and although he had tried to seek her out in various ways, Aileen, owing to a certain feeling that she must think and not jeopardize her future, had evaded him. She realized well enough that she was at the turning of the balance, now that opportunity was knocking so loudly at her door, and she was exceedingly coy and distrait. In spite of herself that old grip of Cowperwood was over her—the conviction that he was such a tremendous figure in the world—and this made her strangely disturbed, nebulous, and meditative. Another type of woman, having troubled as much as she had done, would have made short work of it, particularly since the details in regard to Mrs. Hand had been added. Not so Aileen. She could not quite forget the early vows and promises exchanged between them, nor conquer the often-fractured illusions that he might still behave himself.

On the other hand, Polk Lynde, marauder, social adventurer, a buccaneer of the affections, was not so easily to be put aside, delayed, and gainsaid. Not unlike Cowper-

wood, he was a man of real force, and his methods, insofar as women were concerned, were even more daring. Long
trifling with the sex had taught him that they were coy,
uncertain, foolishly inconsistent in their moods, even with
regard to what they most desired. If one contemplated victory, it had frequently to be taken with an iron hand.

From this attitude on his part had sprung his rather dark
fame. Aileen felt it on the day that she took lunch with
him. His solemn dark eyes were treacherously sweet. She
felt as if she might be paving the way for some situation
in which she would find herself helpless before his sudden
mood—and yet she had come.

But Lynde, meditating Aileen's delay, had this day decided that he should get a definite decision, and that it
should be favorable. He called her up at ten in the morning
and chafed her concerning her indecision and changeable
moods. He wanted to know whether she would not come
and see the paintings at his friend's studio—whether she
could not make up her mind to come to a barn dance which
some bachelor friends of his had arranged. When she pleaded
being out of sorts he urged her to pull herself together.
"You're making things very difficult for your admirers," he
suggested sweetly.

Aileen fancied she had postponed the struggle diplomatically for some little time without ending it, when at two
o'clock in the afternoon her doorbell was rung and the
name of Lynde brought up. "He said he was sure you were
in," commented the footman, on whom had been pressed
a dollar, "and would you see him for just a moment? He
would not keep you more than a moment."

Aileen, taken off her guard by this effrontery, uncertain
as to whether there might not be something of some slight
import concerning which he wished to speak to her, quarreling with herself because of her indecision, really fascinated by Lynde as a rival for her affections, and remem-
bering his jesting, coaxing voice of the morning, decided
to go down. She was lonely, and clad in a lavender house
gown with an ermine collar and sleeve cuffs, was reading
a book.

"Show him into the music room," she said to the lackey.
When she entered she was breathing with some slight difficulty, for so Lynde affected her. She knew she had displayed
fear by not going to him before, and previous cowardice

plainly manifested does not add to one's power of resistance.

"Oh!" she exclaimed, with an assumption of bravado which she did not feel. "I didn't expect to see you so soon after your telephone message. You have never been in our house before, have you? Won't you put up your coat and hat and come into the gallery? It's brighter there, and you might be interested in some of the pictures."

Lynde, who was seeking for any pretext whereby he might prolong his stay and overcome her nervous mood, accepted, pretending, however, that he was merely passing and with a moment to spare.

"Thought I'd get just one glimpse of you again. Couldn't resist the temptation to look in. Stunning room, isn't it? Spacious—and there you are! Who did that? Oh, I see— Van Beers. And a jolly fine piece of work it is, too, charming."

He surveyed her and then turned back to the picture where, ten years younger, buoyant, hopeful, carrying her blue-and-white-striped parasol, she sat on a stone bench against the Dutch background of sky and clouds. Charmed by the picture she presented in both cases, he was genially complimentary. Today she was stouter, ruddier—the fiber of her had hardened, as it does with so many as the years come on; but she was still in full bloom—a little late in the summer, but in full bloom.

"Oh yes; and this Rembrandt—I'm surprised! I did not know your husband's collection was so representative. Israels, I see, and Gérôme, and Meissonier! Gad! It is a representative collection, isn't it?"

"Some of the things are excellent," she commented with an air, aping Cowperwood and others, "but a number will be weeded out eventually—that Paul Potter and this Goya— as better examples come into the market."

She had heard Cowperwood say as much, over and over.

Finding that conversation was possible between them in this easy, impersonal way, Aileen become quite natural and interested, pleased and entertained by his discreet and charming presence. Evidently he did not intend to pay much more than a passing social call. On the other hand, Lynde was studying her, wondering what effect his light, distant air was having. As he finished a very casual survey of the gallery he remarked:

"I have always wondered about this house. I knew Lord

did it, of course, and I always heard it was well done. That is the dining room, I suppose?"

Aileen, who had always been inordinately vain of the house in spite of the fact that it had proved of small use socially, was delighted to show him the remainder of the rooms. Lynde, who was used, of course, to houses of all degrees of material splendor—that of his own family being one of the best—pretended an interest he did not feel. He commented as he went on the taste of the decorations and wood carving, the charm of the arrangement that permitted neat brief vistas, and the like.

"Just wait a moment," said Aileen, as they neared the door of her own boudoir. "I've forgotten whether mine is in order. I want you to see that."

She opened it and stepped in.

"Yes, you may come," she called.

He followed. "Oh yes, indeed. Very charming. Very graceful—those little lacy dancing figures—aren't they? A delightful color scheme. It harmonizes with you exactly. It is quite like you."

He paused, looking at the spacious rug, which was of warm blues and creams, and at the gilt ormolu bed. "Well done," he said, and then, suddenly changing his mood and dropping his talk of decoration (Aileen was to his right, and he was between her and the door), he added: "Tell me now why won't you come to the barn dance tonight? It would be charming. You will enjoy it."

Aileen saw the sudden change in his mood. She recognized that by showing him the rooms she had led herself into an easily made disturbing position. His dark, engaging eyes told their own story.

"Oh, I don't feel in the mood to. I haven't for a number of things for some time. I—"

She began to move unconcernedly about him toward the door, but he detained her with his hand. "Don't go just yet," he said. "Let me talk to you. You always evade me in such a nervous way. Don't you like me at all?"

"Oh yes, I like you; but can't we talk just as well down in the music room as here? Can't I tell you why I evade you down there just as well as I can here?" She smiled a winning and now fearless smile.

Lynde showed his even white teeth in two gleaming rows. His eyes filled with a gay maliciousness. "Surely, surely," he replied; "but you're so nice in your own room here. I hate to leave it."

"Just the same," replied Aileen, still gay, but now slightly disturbed also, "I think we might as well. You will find me just as entertaining downstairs."

She moved, but his strength, quite like Cowperwood's, was much too great for her. He was a strong man.

"Really, you know," she said, "you mustn't act this way here. Someone might come in. What cause have I given you to make you think you could do like this with me?"

"What cause?" he asked, bending over her and smoothing her plump arms with his brown hands. "Oh, no definite cause, perhaps. You are a cause in yourself. I told you how sweet I thought you were the night we were at the Alcott. Didn't you understand then? I thought you did."

"Oh, I understood that you liked me, and all that, perhaps. Anyone might do that. But as for anything like—well— taking such liberties with me—I never dreamed of it. But listen. I think I hear someone coming." Aileen, making a sudden vigorous effort to free herself and failing, added: "Please let me go, Mr. Lynde. It isn't very gallant of you, I must say, restraining a woman against her will. If I had given you any real cause— I shall be angry in a moment."

Again the even, smiling teeth and dark, wrinkling, malicious eyes.

"Really! How you go on! You would think I was a perfect stranger. Don't you remember what you said to me at lunch? You didn't keep your promise. You practically gave me to understand that you would come. Why didn't you? Are you afraid of me, or don't you like me, or both? I think you're delicious, splendid, and I want to know."

He shifted his position, putting one arm about her waist, pulling her close to him, looking into her eyes. With the other he held her free arm. Suddenly he covered her mouth with his and then kissed her cheeks. "You care for me, don't you? What did you mean by saying you might come, if you didn't?"

He held her quite firmly, while Aileen struggled. It was a new sensation, this—that of the other man, and this was Polk Lynde, the first individual outside of Cowperwood to whom she had ever felt drawn. But now, here in her own room—and it was within the range of possibilities that Cowperwood might return or the servants enter.

"Oh, but think what you are doing," she protested, not really disturbed as yet as to the outcome of the contest with him, and feeling as though he were merely trying to make her be sweet to him without intending anything more at present —"here in my own room! Really, you're not the man I thought you were at all, if you don't instantly let me go. Mr. Lynde! Mr. Lynde!" (He had bent over and was kissing her.) "Oh, you shouldn't do this! Really! I—I said I might come, but that was far from doing it. And to have you come here and take advantage of me in this way! I think you're horrid. If I ever had any interest in you it is quite dead now, I can assure you. Unless you let me go at once, I give you my word I will never see you anymore. I won't! Really, I won't! I mean it! Oh, please let me go! I'll scream, I tell you! I'll never see you again after this day! Oh—" It was an intense but useless struggle.

Coming home one evening about a week later, Cowperwood found Aileen humming cheerfully, and yet also in a seemingly deep and reflective mood. She was just completing an evening toilet, and looked young and colorful—quite her avid, seeking self of earlier days.

"Well," he asked cheerfully, "how have things gone today?"

Aileen, feeling somehow, as one will on occasions, that if she had done wrong she was justified and that sometime because of this she might even win Cowperwood back, felt somewhat kindlier toward him. "Oh, very well," she replied. "I stopped in at the Hoecksemas' this afternoon for a little while. They're going to Mexico in November. She has the darlingest new basket carriage—if she only looked like anything when she rode in it. Etta is getting ready to enter Bryn Mawr. She is all fussed up about leaving her dog and cat. Then I went down to one of Lane Cross's receptions, and over to Merrill's"—she was referring to the great store— "and home. I saw Taylor Lord and Polk Lynde together in Wabash Avenue."

"Polk Lynde?" commented Cowperwood. "Is he interesting?"

"Yes, he is," replied Aileen. "I never met a man with such perfect manners. He's so fascinating. He's just like a boy, and yet, heaven knows, he seems to have had enough worldly experience."

"So I've heard," commented Cowperwood. "Wasn't he the

one that was mixed up in that Carmen Torriba case here a few years ago?" Cowperwood was referring to the matter of a Spanish dancer traveling in America with whom Lynde had been apparently desperately in love.

"Oh yes," replied Aileen maliciously; "but that oughtn't to make any difference to you. He's charming, anyhow. I like him."

"I didn't say it did, did I? You don't object to my mentioning a mere incident?"

"Oh, I know about the incident," replied Aileen jestingly. "I know you."

"What do you mean by that?" he asked, studying her face.

"Oh, I know you," she replied, sweetly and yet defensively. "You think I'll stay here and be content while you run about with other women—play the sweet and loving wife? Well, I won't. I know why you say this about Lynde. It's to keep me from being interested in him, possibly. Well, I will be if I want to. I told you I would be, and will. You can do what you please about that. You don't want me, so why should you be disturbed as to whether other men are interested in me or not?"

The truth was that Cowperwood was not clearly thinking of any probable relations between Lynde and Aileen any more than he was in connection with her and any other man, and yet in a remote way he was sensing someone. It was this that Aileen felt in him, and that brought forth her seemingly uncalled-for comment. Cowperwood, under the circumstances, attempted to be as suave as possible, having caught the implication clearly.

"Aileen," he cooed, "how you talk! Why do you say that? You know I care for you. I can't prevent anything you want to do, and I'm sure you know I don't want to. It's you that I want to see satisfied. You know that I care."

"Yes, I know how you care," replied Aileen, her mood changing for the moment. "Don't start that old stuff, please. I'm sick of it. I know how you're running around. I know about Mrs. Hand. Even the newspapers make that plain. You've been home just one evening in the last eight days, long enough for me to get more than a glimpse of you. Don't talk to me. Don't try to bill and coo. I've always known. Don't think I don't know who your latest flame is. But don't begin to whine, and don't quarrel with me if I go about and get interested in other men, as I certainly will. It will be all your fault if I do, and you know it. Don't begin and complain. It won't do you any good. I'm not going to sit here and be made a fool of. I've told you that over and over. You don't believe it, but I'm not. I told you that I'd find someone one of these days, and I will. As a matter of fact, I have already."

At this remark Cowperwood surveyed her coolly, critically, and yet not unsympathetically; but she swung out of the room with a defiant air before anything could be said, and went down to the music room, from whence a few moments later there rolled up to him from the hall below the strains of the second Hungarian Rhapsody, feelingly and for once movingly played. Into it Aileen put some of her own wild woe and misery. Cowperwood hated the thought for the moment that someone as smug as Lynde—so good-looking, so suave a society rake—should interest Aileen; but if it must be, it must be. He could have no honest reason for complaint. At the same time a breath of real sorrow for the days that had gone swept over him. He remembered her in Philadelphia in her red cape as a schoolgirl—in his father's house—out horseback-riding, driving. What a splendid, loving girl she had been—such a sweet fool of love. Could she really have decided not to worry about him anymore? Could it be possible that she might find someone else who would be interested in her, and in whom she would take a keen interest? It was an odd thought for him.

He watched her as she came into the dining room later, arrayed in green silk of the shade of copper patina, her hair done in a high coil—and in spite of himself he could not help admiring her. She looked very young in her soul, and yet moody—loving (for someone), eager, and defiant. He reflected for a moment what terrible things passion and love are—how they make fools of us all. "All of us are in the grip of a great creative impulse," he said to himself. He talked of other things for a while—the approaching election, a poster wagon he had seen bearing the question, "Shall Cowperwood own the city?" "Pretty cheap politics, I call that," he commented. And then he told of stopping in a so-called Republican wigwam at State and Sixteenth streets—a great, cheaply erected, unpainted wooden shack with seats, and of hearing himself bitterly denounced by the reigning orator. "I was tempted once to ask that donkey a few questions," he added, "but I decided I wouldn't."

Aileen had to smile. In spite of his faults he was such a wonderful man—to set a city thus by the ears. "Yet, what care I how fair he be, if he be not fair to me."

"Did you meet anyone else besides Lynde you liked?" he finally asked archly, seeking to gather further data without stirring up too much feeling.

Aileen, who had been studying him, feeling sure the subject would come up again, replied: "No, I haven't; but I don't need to. One is enough."

"What do you mean by that?" he asked gently.

"Oh, just what I say. One will do."

"You mean you are in love with Lynde?"

"I mean—oh!" She stopped and surveyed him defiantly. "What difference does it make to you what I mean? Yes, I am. But what do you care? Why do you sit there and question me? It doesn't make any difference to you what I do. You don't want me. Why should you sit there and try to find out, or watch? It hasn't been any consideration for you that has restrained me so far. Suppose I am in love? What difference would it make to you?"

"Oh, I care. You know I care. Why do you say that?"

"Yes, you care," she flared. "I know how you care. Well, I'll just tell you one thing"—rage at his indifference was driving her on—"I am in love with Lynde, and what's more, I'm his mistress. And I'll continue to be. But what do you care? Pshaw!"

Her eyes blazed hotly, her color rose high and strong. She breathed heavily.

At this announcement, made in the heat of spite and rage generated by long indifference, Cowperwood sat up for a moment, and his eyes hardened with quite that implacable glare with which he sometimes confronted an enemy. He felt at once there were many things he could do to make her life miserable and to take revenge on Lynde, but he decided after a moment he would not. It was not weakness, but a sense of superior power that was moving him. Why should he be jealous? Had he not been unkind enough? In a moment his mood changed to one of sorrow for Aileen, for himself, for life, indeed—its tangles of desire and necessity. He could not blame Aileen. Lynde was surely attractive. He had no desire to part with her or to quarrel with him—merely to temporarily cease all intimate relations with her and allow her mood to clear itself up. Perhaps she would want to leave him of her own accord. Perhaps, if he ever found the right woman, this might prove good grounds for leaving her. The right woman—where was she? He had never found her yet.

"Aileen," he said quite softly, "I wish you wouldn't feel so bitterly about this. Why should you? When did you do this? Will you tell me that?"

"No, I'll not tell you that," she replied bitterly. "It's none of your affair, and I'll not tell you. Why should you ask? You don't care."

"But I do care, I tell you," he returned irritably, almost roughly. "When did you? You can tell me that, at least." His eyes had a hard, cold look for the moment, dying away, though, into kindly inquiry.

"Oh, not long ago. About a week," Aileen answered, as though she were compelled.

"How long have you known him?" he asked, curiously.

"Oh, four or five months now. I met him last winter."

"And did you do this deliberately—because you were in love with him, or because you wanted to hurt me?"

He could not believe from past scenes between them that she had ceased to love him.

Aileen stirred irritably. "I like that," she flared. "I did it because I wanted to, and not because of any love for you—I can tell you that. I like your nerve sitting here presuming to question me after the way you have neglected me." She pushed back her plate, and made as if to get up.

"Wait a minute, Aileen," he said simply, putting down his knife and fork and looking across the handsome table where Sèvres, silver, fruit, and dainty dishes were spread, and where under silk-shaded lights they sat opposite each other. "I wish you wouldn't talk that way to me. You know that I am not a petty, fourth-rate fool. You know that whatever you do, I am not going to quarrel with you. I know what the trouble is with you. I know why you are acting this way, and how you will feel afterward if you go on. It isn't anything I will do—" He paused, caught by a wave of feeling.

"Oh, isn't it?" she blazed, trying to overcome the emotion that was rising in herself. The calmness of him stirred up memories of the past. "Well, you keep your sympathy for yourself. I don't need it. I will get along. I wish you wouldn't talk to me."

She shoved her plate away with such force that she upset a glass in which was champagne, the wine making a frayed, yellowish splotch on the white linen; and rising, hurried toward the door. She was choking with anger, pain, shame, regret.

"Aileen! Aileen!" he called, hurrying after her, regardless of the butler, who, hearing the sound of stirring chairs, had entered. These family woes were an old story to him. "It's love you want—not revenge. I know—I can tell. You want to be loved by someone completely. I'm sorry. You mustn't be too hard on me. I shan't be on you." He seized her by the arm and detained her as they entered the next room. By this time Aileen was too ablaze with emotion to talk sensibly or understand what he was doing.

"Let me go!" she exclaimed angrily, hot tears in her eyes. "Let me go! I tell you I don't love you anymore. I tell you I hate you!" She flung herself loose and stood erect before him. "I don't want you to talk to me! I don't want you to speak to me! You're the cause of all my troubles. You're the cause of whatever I do, when I do it, and don't you dare to deny it! You'll see! You'll see! I'll show you what I'll do!"

She twisted and turned, but he held her firmly, until in his strong grasp, as usual, she collapsed and began to cry. "Oh, I cry," she declared, even in her tears, "but it will be just the same. It's too late! too late!"

CHAPTER XXXVIII

An Hour of Defeat

The stoic Cowperwood, listening to the blare and excitement that went with the fall campaign, was much more pained to learn of Aileen's desertion than to know that he had arrayed a whole social element against himself in Chicago. He could not forget the wonder of those first days when Aileen was young, and love and hope had been the substance of her being. The thought ran through all his efforts and cogitations like a distantly orchestrated undertone. In the main, in spite of his activity, he was an introspective man, and art, drama, and the pathos of broken ideals were not beyond him. He harbored in no way any grudge against Aileen—only a kind of sorrow over the inevitable consequences of his own ungovernable disposition, the will to freedom within himself. Change! Change! the inevitable passing of things! Who parts with a perfect thing, even if no more than an unreasoning love, without a touch of self-pity?

But there followed swiftly the sixth of November, with its election, noisy and irrational, and the latter resulted in a resounding defeat. Out of the thirty-two Democratic aldermen nominated only ten were elected, giving the opposition a full two-thirds majority in council, Messrs. Tiernan and Kerrigan, of course, being safely in their places. With them came a Republican mayor and all his Republican associates on the ticket, who were now supposed to carry out the theories of the respectable and the virtuous. Cowperwood knew what it meant and prepared at once to make overtures to the enemy. From McKenty and others he learned by degrees the full story of Tiernan's and Kerrigan's treachery, but he did not store it up bitterly against them. Such was life. They must be looked after more carefully in future, or caught in some trap and utterly undone. According to their own accounts, they had barely managed to scrape through.

"Look at meself! I only won by three hundred votes," archly declared Mr. Kerrigan, on divers and sundry occasions. "By God, I almost lost me own ward!"

Mr. Tiernan was equally emphatic. "The police was no good to me," he declared firmly. "They let the other fellows beat up me men. I only polled six thousand when I should have had nine."

But no one believed them.

While McKenty meditated as to how in two years he should be able to undo this temporary victory, and Cowperwood was deciding that conciliation was the best policy for him, Schryhart, Hand, and Arneel, joining hands with young MacDonald, were wondering how they could make sure that this party victory would cripple Cowperwood and permanently prevent him from returning to power. It was a long, intricate fight that followed, but it involved (before Cowperwood could possibly reach the aldermen) a proposed reintroduction and passage of the much-opposed General Electric franchise, the granting of rights and privileges in outlying districts to various minor companies, and last and worst—a thing which had not previously dawned on Cowperwood as in any way probable—the projection of an ordinance granting to a certain South Side corporation the privilege of erecting and operating an elevated road. This was as severe a blow as any that had yet been dealt Cowperwood, for it introduced a new factor and complication into the Chicago street-railway situation, which had hitherto, for all its troubles, been comparatively simple.

In order to make this plain it should be said that some eighteen or twenty years before in New York there had been devised and erected a series of elevated roads calculated to relieve the congestion of traffic on the lower portion of that long and narrow island, and they had proved an immense success. Cowperwood had been interested in them, along with everything else which pertained to public street traffic, from the very beginning. On his various trips to New York he had made a careful physical inspection of them. He knew all about their incorporation, backers, the expense connected with them, their returns, and so forth. Personally, insofar as New York was concerned, he considered them an ideal solution of traffic on that crowded island. Here in Chicago, where the population was as yet comparatively small—verging now toward a million, and widely scattered over a great area—he did not feel that they would be profitable—certainly not for some years to come. What traffic they gained would be taken from the surface lines, and if he built them he would be merely doubling his expenses to halve his profits. From time to time he had contemplated the possibility of their being built by other men—providing they could secure a franchise, which previous to the late election had not seemed probable—and in this connection he had once said to Addison: "Let them sink their money, and about the time the population is sufficient to support the lines they will have been driven into the hands of receivers. That will simply chase the game into my bag, and I can buy them for a mere song." With this conclusion Addison had agreed. But since this conversation circumstances made the construction of these elevated roads far less problematic.

In the first place, public interest in the idea of elevated roads was increasing. They were a novelty, a factor in the life of New York; and at this time rivalry with the great cosmoplitan heart was very keen in the mind of the average Chicago citizen. Public sentiment in this direction, however naive or unworthy, was nevertheless sufficient to make any elevated road in Chicago popular for the time being. In the second place, it so happened that because of this swelling tide of municipal enthusiasm, this renaissance of the West, Chicago had finally been chosen, at a date shortly preceding the present campaign, as the favored city for an enormous international fair—quite the largest ever given in America. Men such as Hand, Schryhart, Merrill, and Arneel, to say nothing of the various newspaper publishers and editors, had been enthusiastic supporters of the project, and in this Cowperwood had been one with them. No sooner, however, had the award actually been granted than Cowperwood's enemies made it their first concern to utilize the situation against him.

To begin with, the site of the fair, by aid of the new anti-Cowperwood council, was located on the South Side at the terminus of the Schryhart line, thus making the whole city pay tribute to that corporation. Simultaneously the thought suddenly dawned upon the Schryhart faction that it would be an excellent stroke of business if the New York elevated road idea were now introduced into the city—not so much with the purpose of making money immediately, but in order to bring the hated magnate to an understanding that he had a formidable rival which might invade the territory that he now monopolized, curtailing his profits and thus making it advisable for him to close out his holdings and depart. Bland and interesting were the conferences held by Mr. Schryhart with Mr. Hand, and by Mr. Hand with Mr. Arneel, on this subject. Their plan as first outlined was to build an elevated road on the South Side—south of the proposed fairgrounds —and once that was popular—having previously secured franchises which would cover the entire field, West, South, and North—to construct the others at their leisure, and so to bid Mr. Cowperwood a sweet and smiling adieu.

Cowperwood, awaiting the assembling of the new city council one month after election, did not propose to wait in peace and quiet until the enemy should strike at him unprepared. Calling those familiar agents, his corporation attorneys, around him, he was shortly informed of the new elevated road idea, and it gave him a real shock. Obviously Hand and Schryhart were now in deadly earnest. At once he dictated a letter to Mr. Gilgan asking him to call at his office. At the same time he hurriedly adjured his advisers to use due diligence in discovering what influences could be brought to bear on the new mayor, the Honorable Chaffee Thayer Sluss, to cause him to veto the ordinances in case they came before him—to effect in him, indeed, a total change of heart.

The Honorable Chaffee Thayer Sluss, whose attitude in this instance was to prove crucial, was a tall, shapely, somewhat grandiloquent person who took himself and his social and commercial opportunities and doings in the most serious and, as it were, elevated light. You know, perhaps, the type of man or woman who, raised in an atmosphere of comparative comfort and some small social pretension, and being short of those gray convolutions in the human brainpan which permit an individual to see life in all its fortuitousness and uncertainty, proceed because of an absence of necessity and the consequent lack of human experience to take themselves and all that they do in the most reverential and Providence-protected spirit. The Honorable Chaffee Thayer Sluss reasoned that because of the splendid ancestry on which he prided himself, he was an essentially honest man. His father had amassed a small fortune in the wholesale harness business. The wife whom at the age of twenty-eight he had married—a pretty but inconsequential type of woman —was the daughter of a pickle manufacturer, whose wares were in some demand and whose children had been considered good catches in the neighborhood from which the Honorable Chaffee Sluss emanated. There had been a highly conservative wedding feast, and a honeymoon trip to the Garden of the Gods and the Grand Canyon. Then the sleek Chaffee, much in the grace of both families because of his smug determination to rise in the world, had returned to his business, which was that of a paper broker, and had begun with the greatest care to amass a competence on his own account.

The Honorable Chaffee Sluss, be it admitted, had no particular faults, unless those of smugness and a certain overcarefulness as to his own prospects and opportunities can be counted as such. But he had one weakness, which, in view of his young wife's stern and somewhat Puritanic ideas and the religious propensities of his father and father-in-law, was exceedingly disturbing to him. He had an eye for the beauty of women in general, and particularly for plump blonde women with corn-colored hair. Now and then, in spite of the fact that he had an ideal wife and two lovely children, he would cast a meditative and speculative eye after those alluring forms that cross the path of all men, and that seem to beckon slyly by implication if not by actual, open suggestion.

However, it was not until several years after Mr. Sluss had married, and when he might have been considered settled in the ways of righteousness, that he actually essayed to any extent the role of a gay Lothario. An experience or two with the less vigorous and vicious girls of the streets, a tentative love affair with a girl in his office who was not new to the practices she encouraged, and he was fairly launched. He lent himself at first to the great folly of pretending to love truly; but this was taken by one and another intelligent young woman with a grain of salt. The entertainment and preferment he could provide were accepted as sufficient reward. One girl, however, actually seduced, had to be compensated by five thousand dollars—and that after such terrors and heartaches (his wife, her family, and his own looming up horribly in the background) as should have cured him forever of a penchant for stenographers and employees generally. Thereafter for a long time he confined himself strictly to such acquaintances as he could make through agents, brokers, and manufacturers who did business with him, and who occasionally invited him to one form of bacchanalian feast or another.

As time went on he became wiser, if, alas, a little more eager. By association with merchants and some superior politicians whom he chanced to encounter, and because the ward in which he lived happened to be a pivotal one, he began to speak publicly on occasion and to gather dimly the import of that logic which sees life as a pagan wild, and religion and convention as the forms man puts on or off to suit his fancy, mood, and whims during the onward drift of the ages. Not for Chaffee Thayer Sluss to grasp the true meaning of it all. His brain was not big enough. Men led dual lives, it was true; but say what you would, and in the face of his own erring conduct, this was very bad. On Sunday, when he went to church with his wife, he felt that religion was essential and purifying. In his own business he found himself frequently confronted by various little flaws of logic relating to undue profits, misrepresentation, and the like; but say what you would, nevertheless and notwithstanding, God was God, morality was superior, the church was important. It was wrong to yield to one's impulses, as he found it so fascinating to do. One should be better than his neighbor, or pretend to be.

What is to be done with such a ragbag, moralistic ass as this? In spite of all his philanderings, and the resultant qualms due to his fear of being found out, he prospered in business and rose to some eminence in his own community. As he had grown more lax he had become somewhat more genial and tolerant, more generally acceptable. He was a good Republican, a follower in the wake of Norrie Simms and young Truman Leslie MacDonald. His father-in-law was both rich and moderately influential. Having lent himself to some campaign speaking, and to party work in general, he proved quite an adept. Because of all these things—his ability, such as it was, his pliability, and his thoroughly respectable savor—he had been slated as candidate for mayor on the Republican ticket, which had subsequently been elected.

Cowperwood was well aware, from remarks made in the previous campaign, of the derogatory attitude of Mayor Sluss. Already he had discussed it in a conversation with the Honorable Joel Avery (ex-state senator), who was in his employ at the time. Avery had recently been in all sorts of corporation work, and knew the ins and outs of the courts—lawyers, judges, politicians—as he knew his revised statutes. He was a very little man—not more than five feet one inch tall—with a wide forehead, saffron hair and brows, brown, catlike eyes and a mushy underlip that occasionally covered the upper one as he thought. After years and years Mr. Avery had learned to smile, but it was in a strange, exotic way. Mostly he gazed steadily, folded his lower lip over his upper one, and expressed his almost unchangeable conclusions in slow, Addisonian phrases. In the present crisis it was Mr. Avery who had a suggestion to make.

"One thing that I think could be done," he said to Cowperwood one day in a very confidential conference, "would be to have a look into the—the—shall I say the heart affairs —of the Honorable Chaffee Thayer Sluss." Mr. Avery's catlike eyes gleamed sardonically. "Unless I am greatly mistaken, judging the man by his personal presence merely, he is the sort of person who probably has had, or if not might readily be induced to have, some compromising affair with a woman which would require considerable sacrifice on his part to smooth over. We are all human and vulnerable"—up went Mr. Avery's lower lip covering the upper one, and then down again—"and it does not behoove any of us to be too severely ethical and self-righteous. Mr. Sluss is a well-meaning man, but a trifle sentimental, as I take it."

As Mr. Avery paused Cowperwood merely contemplated him, amused no less by his personal appearance than by his suggestion.

"Not a bad idea," he said, "though I don't like to mix heart affairs with politics."

"Yes," said Mr. Avery soulfully, "there may be something in it. I don't know. You never can tell."

The upshot of this was that the task of obtaining an account of Mr. Sluss's habits, tastes, and proclivities was assigned to that now rather dignified legal personage, Mr. Burton Stimson, who in turn assigned it to an assistant, a Mr. Marchbanks. It was an amazing situation in some respects, but those who know anything concerning the intricacies of politics, finance, and corporate control, as they were practiced in those palmy days, would never marvel at the wells of subtlety, sinks of misery, and morasses of disaster which they represented.

From another quarter, the Honorable Patrick Gilgan was not slow in responding to Cowperwood's message. Whatever his political connections and proclivities, he did not care to neglect so powerful a man.

"And what can I be doing for you today, Mr. Cowperwood?" he inquired, when he arrived looking nice and fresh, very spick and span after his victory.

"Listen, Mr. Gilgan," said Cowperwood simply, eyeing the Republican county chairman very fixedly and twiddling his thumbs with fingers interlocked, "are you going to let the city council jam through the General Electric and that South Side L road ordinance without giving me a chance to say a word or do anything about it?"

Mr. Gilgan, so Cowperwood knew, was only one of a new quadrumvirate setting out to rule the city, but he pretended to believe that he was the last word—an all-power and authority—after the fashion of McKenty.

"Me good man," replied Gilgan archly, "you flatter me. I haven't the city council in me vest pocket. I've been county chairman, it's true, and helped to elect some of these men, but I don't own 'em. Why shouldn't they pass the General Electric ordinance? It's an honest ordinance, as far as I know. All the newspapers have been for it. As for this L road ordinance, I haven't anything to do with it. It isn't anything I know much about. Young MacDonald and Mr. Schryhart are looking after that."

As a matter of fact, all that Mr. Gilgan was saying was decidedly true. A henchman of young MacDonald's who was beginning to learn to play politics—an alderman by the name of Klemm—had been scheduled as a kind of field marshal, and it was MacDonald—not Gilgan, Tiernan, Kerrigan, or Edstrom—who was to round up the recalcitrant aldermen, telling them their duty. Gilgan's quadrumvirate had not as yet got their machine in good working order, though they were doing their best to bring this about. "I helped to elect every one of these men, it's true; but that doesn't mean I'm running 'em by any means," concluded Gilgan. "Not yet, anyhow."

At the "not yet" Cowperwood smiled.

"Just the same, Mr. Gilgan," he went on smoothly, "you're the nominal head and front of this whole movement in opposition to me at present, and you're the one I have to look to. You have this present Republican situation almost entirely in your own fingers, and you can do about as you like if you're so minded. If you choose you can persuade the members of the council to take considerable more time than they otherwise would in passing these ordinances—of that I'm sure. I don't know whether you know or not, Mr. Gilgan, though I suppose you do, that this whole fight against me is a strike campaign intended to drive me out of Chicago. Now, you're a man of sense and judgment and considerable experience, and I want to ask you if you think that is fair. I came here some sixteen or seventeen years ago and went into the gas business. It was an open field, the field I undertook to develop—outlying towns on the North, South, and West Sides. Yet the moment I started, the old-line companies began to fight me, though I wasn't invading their territory at all at the time."

"I remember it well enough," replied Gilgan. "I was one of the men that helped you to get your Hyde Park franchise. You'd never have got it if it hadn't been for me. That fellow McKibben," added Gilgan with a grin, "a likely chap, him. He always walked as if he had on rubber shoes. He's with you yet, I suppose?"

"Yes, he's around here somewhere," replied Cowperwood loftily. "But to go back to this other matter, most of the men that are behind this General Electric ordinance and this L road franchise were in the gas business—Blackman, Jules, Baker, Schryhart, and others—and they are angry because I came into their field, and angrier still because they had eventually to buy me out. They're angry because I reorganized these old-fashioned street-railway companies here and put them on their feet. Merrill is angry because I didn't run a loop around his store, and the others are angry because I ever got a loop at all. They're all angry because I managed to step in and do the things that they should have done long before I came here—and that's the whole story in a nutshell. I've had to have the city council with me to be able to do anything at all, and because I managed to make it friendly and keep it so they've turned on me in that section and gone into politics. I know well enough, Mr. Gilgan," concluded Cowperwood, "who has been behind you in this fight. I've known all along where the money has been coming from. You've won, and you've won handsomely, and I for one don't begrudge you your victory in the least; but what I want to know now is, are you going to help them carry this fight on against me in this way, or are you not? Are you going to give me a fighting chance? There's going to be another election in two years. Politics isn't a bed of roses that stays made just because you make it once. These fellows that you have got in with are a crowd of silk stockings. They haven't any sympathy with you or anyone like you. They're willing to be friendly with you now—just long enough to get something out of you and club me to death. But after that how long do you think they will have any use for you—how long?"

"Not very long, maybe," replied Gilgan simply and contemplatively, "but the world is the world, and we have to take it as we find it."

"Quite so," replied Cowperwood, undismayed; "but Chicago is Chicago, and I will be here as long as they will. Fighting me in this fashion—building elevated roads to cut into my profits and giving franchises to rival companies—isn't going to get me out or seriously injure me, either. I'm here to stay, and the political situation as it is today isn't going to remain the same forever and ever. Now, you are an ambitious man; I can see that. You're not in politics for your health—that I know. Tell me exactly what it is you want and whether I can't get it for you as quick if not quicker than these other fellows? What is it I can do for you that will make you see that my side is just as good as theirs and better? I am playing a legitimate game in Chicago. I've been building up an excellent streetcar service. I don't want to be annoyed every fifteen minutes by a rival company coming into the field. Now, what can I do to straighten this out? Isn't there some way that you and I can come together without fighting at every step? Can't you suggest some program we can both follow that will make things easier?"

Cowperwood paused, and Gilgan thought for a long time. It was true, as Cowperwood said, that he was not in politics for his health. The situation, as at present conditioned, was not inherently favorable for the brilliant program he had originally mapped out for himself. Tiernan, Kerrigan, and Edstrom were friendly as yet; but they were already making extravagant demands; and the reformers—those who had been led by the newspapers to believe that Cowperwood was a scoundrel and all his works vile—were demanding that a strictly moral program be adhered to in all the doings of council, and that no jobs, contracts, or deals of any kind be entered into without the full knowledge of the newspapers and of the public. Gilgan, even after the first post-election conference with his colleagues, had begun to feel that he was between the devil and the deep sea, but he was feeling his way, and not inclined to be in too much of a hurry.

"It's rather a flat proposition you're makin' me," he said softly after a time, "askin' me to throw down me friends the moment I've won a victory for 'em. It's not the way I've been used to playin' politics. There may be a lot of truth in what you say. Still, a man can't be jumpin' around like a cat in a bag. He has to be faithful to somebody sometime." Mr. Gilgan paused, considerably nonplussed by his own position.

"Well," replied Cowperwood sympathetically, "think it over. It's difficult business, this business of politics. I'm in it, for one, only because I have to be. If you see any way you can help me, or I can help you, let me know. In the meantime don't take in bad part what I've just said. I'm in the position of a man with his back to the wall. I'm fighting for my life. Naturally, I'm going to fight. But you and I needn't be the worse friends for that. We may become the best of friends yet."

"It's well I know that," said Gilgan, "and it's the best of friends I'd like to be with you. But even if I could take care of the aldermen, which I couldn't alone as yet, there's the mayor. I don't know him at all except to say how-do-ye-do now and then; but he's very much opposed to you, as I understand it. He'll be running around most likely and talking in the papers. A man like that can do a good deal."

"I may be able to arrange for that," replied Cowperwood. "Perhaps Mr. Sluss can be reached. It may be that he isn't as opposed to me as he thinks he is. You never can tell."

CHAPTER XXXIX

The New Administration

Oliver Marchbanks, the youthful fox to whom Stimson had assigned the task of trapping Mr. Sluss in some legally unsanctioned act, had by scurrying about finally pieced together enough of a story to make it exceedingly unpleasant for the Honorable Chaffee in case he were to become the too-willing tool of Cowperwood's enemies. The principal agent in this affair was a certain Claudia Carlstadt—adventuress, detective by disposition, and a sort of smiling prostitute and hireling, who was at the same time a highly presentable and experienced individual. Needless to say, Cowperwood knew nothing of these minor proceedings, though a genial nod from him in the beginning had set in motion the whole machinery of trespass in this respect.

Claudia Carlstadt—the instrument of the Honorable Chaffee Sluss' undoing—was blonde, slender, notably fresh as yet, being only twenty-six, and as ruthless and unconsciously cruel as only the avaricious and unthinking type—unthinking in the larger philosophic meaning of the word—can be. To grasp the reason for her being, one would have had to see the spiritless South Halstead Street world from which she had sprung—one of those neighborhoods of old, cracked, and battered houses where slatterns trudge to and fro with beer cans, and shutters swing on broken hinges. In her youth Claudia had been made to "rush the growler," to sell newspapers at the corner of Halstead and Harrison streets, and to buy cocaine at the nearest drugstore. Her little dresses and underclothing had always been of the poorest and shabbiest material; torn and dirty, her ragged stockings frequently showed the white flesh of her thin little legs, and her shoes were worn and cracked, letting the water and snow seep through in winter. Her companions were wretched little street boys of her own neighborhood, from whom she learned to swear and to understand and indulge in vile practices, though, as is often the case with children, she was not utterly depraved thereby, at that. At eleven, when her mother died, she ran away from the wretched children's home to which she had been committed, and by putting up a piteous tale she was harbored on the West Side by an Irish family whose two daughters were clerks in a large retail store. Through these Claudia became a cashgirl. Thereafter followed an individual career as strange and checkered as anything that had gone before. Sufficient to say that Claudia's native intelligence was considerable. At the age of twenty she had managed—through her connections with the son of a shoe manufacturer and with a rich jeweler—to amass a little cash and an extended wardrobe. It was then that a handsome young western congressman, newly elected, invited her to Washington to take a position in a government bureau. This necessitated a knowledge of stenography and typewriting, which she soon acquired. Later she was introduced by a western senator into that form of secret service which has no connection with legitimate government, but which is profitable. She was used to extract secrets by flattery and cajolery where ordinary bribery would not avail. A matter of tracing the secret financial connections of an Illinois congressman finally brought her back to Chicago, and here young Stimson encountered her. From him she learned of the political and financial conspiracy against Cowperwood, and was in an odd manner fascinated. From her congressmen friends she already knew something of Sluss. Stimson indicated that it would be worth two or three thousand dollars and expenses if the mayor were successfully compromised. Thus Claudia Carlstadt was gently navigated into Mr. Sluss's glowing life.

The matter was not so difficult of accomplishment. Through the Honorable Joel Avery, Marchbanks secured a letter from a political friend of Mr. Sluss in behalf of a young widow— temporarily embarrassed, a competent stenographer, and the like—who wished a place under the new administration. Thus equipped, Claudia presented herself at the mayor's office armed for the fray, as it were, in a fetching black silk of a strangely heavy grain, her throat and fingers ornamented with simple pearls, her yellow hair arranged about her temples in exquisite curls. Mr. Sluss was very busy, but made an appointment. The next time she appeared a yellow-and-red-velvet rose had been added to her corsage. She was a shapely, full-bosomed young woman who had acquired the art of walking, sitting, standing, and bending after the most approved theories of the Washington cocotte. Mr. Sluss was interested at once, but circumspect and careful. He was now mayor of a great city, the cynosure of all eyes. It seemed to him he remembered having already met Mrs. Brandon, as the lady styled herself, and she reminded him where. It had been two years before in the grill of the Richelieu. He immediately recalled details of the interesting occasion.

"Ah, yes, and since then, as I understand it, you married and your husband died. Most unfortunate."

Mr. Sluss had a large, international manner, suited, as he thought, to a man in so exalted a position.

Mrs. Brandon nodded resignedly. Her eyebrows and lashes were carefully darkened so as to sweeten the lines of her face, and a dimple had been made in one cheek by the aid of an orange stick. She was the picture of delicate femininity appealingly distressful, and yet to all appearance commercially competent.

"At the time I met you you were connected with the government service in Washington, I believe."

"Yes, I had a small place in the Treasury Department, but this new administration put me out."

She lifted her eyes and leaned forward, thus bringing

her torso into a ravishing position. She had the air of one who has done many things besides work in the Treasury Department. No least detail, as she observed, was lost on Mr. Sluss. He noted her shoes, which were button patent leather with cloth tops; her gloves, which were glacé black kid with white stitching at the back and fastened by dark garnet buttons; the coral necklace worn on this occasion and her yellow-and-red-velvet rose. Evidently a trig and hopeful widow even if so recently bereaved.

"Let me see," mused Mr. Sluss, "where are you living? Just let me make a note of your address. This is a very nice letter from Mr. Barry. Suppose you give me a few days to think what I can do? This is Tuesday. Come in again on Friday. I'll see if anything suggests itself."

He strolled with her to the official door, and noted that her step was light and springy. At parting she turned a very melting gaze upon him, and at once he decided that if he could he would find her something. She was the most fascinating applicant that had yet appeared.

The end of Chaffee Thayer Sluss was not far distant after this. Mrs. Brandon returned, as requested, her costume enlivened this time by a red silk petticoat, which contrived to show its ingratiating flounces beneath the glistening black broadcloth of her skirt.

"Say, did you get on to that?" observed one of the doormen, a holdover from the previous regime, to another of the same vintage. "Some style to the new administration, hey? We're not so slow, do you think?"

He pulled his coat together and fumbled at his collar to give himself an air of smartness, and gazed gaily at his partner, both of them over sixty, and dusty specimens at that.

The other poked him in the stomach. "Hold your horses there, Bill. Not so fast. We ain't got a real start yet. Give us another six months, and then watch out."

Mr. Sluss was pleased to see Mrs. Brandon. He had spoken to John Bastienelli, the new commissioner of taxes, whose offices were directly over the way in the same hall, and the latter, seeing that he might want favors of the mayor later on, had volubly agreed to take care of the lady.

"I am very glad to be able to give you this letter to Mr. Bastienelli," commented Mr. Sluss as he rang for a stenographer, "not only for the sake of my old friend Mr. Barry, but

for your own as well. Do you know Mr. Barry very well?"
he asked curiously.

"Only slightly," admitted Mrs. Brandon, feeling that Mr.
Sluss would be glad to know she was not very intimate
with those who were recommending her. "I was sent to him
by a Mr. Amerman." (She named an entirely fictitious personage.)

Mr. Sluss was relieved. As he handed her the note she
once more surveyed him with those grateful, persuasive,
appealing eyes. They made him almost dizzy, and set up a
chemical perturbation in his blood which quite dispelled
his good resolutions in regard to the strange woman and his
need of being circumspect.

"You say you are living on the North Side?" he inquired,
smiling weakly, almost foolishly.

"Yes, I have taken such a nice little apartment overlooking Lincoln Park. I didn't know whether I was going
to be able to keep it up, but now that I have this position—
You've been so very kind to me, Mr. Sluss," she concluded,
with the same "I-need-to-be-cared-for" air. "I hope you
won't forget me entirely. If I could be of any personal service
to you at any time—"

Mr. Sluss was rather beside himself at the thought that
this charming baggage of femininity, having come so close
for the minute, was now passing on and might disappear entirely. By a great effort of daring, as they walked toward
the door, he managed to say: "I shall have to look into that
little place of yours sometime and see how you are getting
along. I live up that way myself."

"Oh, do!" she exclaimed warmly. "It would be so kind.
I am practically alone in the world. Perhaps you play cards.
I know how to make a most wonderful punch. I should like
you to see how cozily I am settled."

At this Sluss, now completely in tow of his principal
weakness, capitulated. "I will," he said, "I surely will. And
that sooner than you expect, perhaps. You must let me know
how you are getting along."

He took her hand. She held his quite warmly. "Now I'll
hold you to your promise," she gurgled, in a throaty, coaxing
way. A few days later he encountered her at lunchtime in
his hall, where she had been literally lying in wait for him
in order to repeat her invitation. Then he came.

The holdover employees who worked about the City Hall

in connection with the mayor's office were hereafter instructed to note as witnesses the times of arrival and departure of Mrs. Brandon and Mr. Sluss. A note that he
wrote to Mrs. Brandon was carefully treasured, and sufficient evidence as to their presence at hotels and restaurants
was garnered to make out a damaging case. The whole
affair took about four months; then Mrs. Brandon suddenly
received an offer to return to Washington, and decided to
depart. The letters that followed her were a part of the data
that was finally assembled in Mr. Stimson's office to be used
against Mr. Sluss in case he became too obstreperous in his
opposition to Cowperwood.

In the meantime the organization which Mr. Gilgan had
planned with Mr. Tiernan, Mr. Kerrigan, and Mr. Edstrom
was encountering what might be called rough sledding. It
was discovered that owing to the temperaments of some of
the new aldermen, and to the self-righteous attitude of their
political sponsors, no franchises of any kind were to be
passed unless they had the moral approval of such men as
Hand, Sluss, and the other reformers; above all, no money
of any kind was to be paid to anybody for anything.

"Whaddye think of those damn four-flushers and come-
ons, anyhow?" inquired Mr. Kerrigan of Mr. Tiernan, shortly
subsequent to a conference with Gilgan, from which Tiernan
had been unavoidably absent. "They've got an ordinance
drawn up covering the whole city in an elevated road scheme,
and there ain't anything in it for anybody. Say, whaddye
think they think we are, anyhow? Hey?"

Mr. Tiernan himself, after his own conference with Edstrom,
had been busy getting the lay of the land, as he termed it;
and his investigations led him to believe that a certain
alderman by the name of Klemm, a clever and very respectable German-American from the North Side, was to be the
leader of the Republicans in council, and that he and some
ten or twelve others were determined, because of moral principles alone, that only honest measures should be passed.
It was staggering.

At this news Mr. Kerrigan, who had been calculating on
a number of thousands of dollars for his vote on various
occasions, stared incredulously. "Well, I'll be damned!" he
commented. "They've got a nerve! What?"

"I've been talking to this fellow Klemm of the twentieth,"

said Mr. Tiernan sardonically. "Say, he's a real one! I met him over at the Tremont talkin' to Hvranek. He shakes hands like a dead fish. Whaddye think he had the nerve to say to me. 'This isn't the Mr. Tiernan of the second?' he says.

" 'I'm the same,' says I.

" 'Well, you don't look as savage as I thought you did,' says he. Haw-haw! I felt like sayin', 'If you don't go way I'll give you a slight tap on the wrist.' I'd like just one pass at a stiff like that up a dark alley." (Mr. Tiernan almost groaned in anguish.) "And then he begins to say he doesn't see how there can be any reasonable objection to allowin' various new companies to enter the streetcar field. 'It's sufficiently clear,' he says, 'that the public is against monopolies in any form.' " (Mr. Tiernan was mocking Mr. Klemm's voice and language.) "My eye!" he concluded sententiously. "Wait till he tries to throw that dope into Gumble and Pinski and Schlumbohm—haw, haw, haw!"

Mr. Kerrigan, at the thought of these hearty aldermen, accustomed to all the perquisites of graft and rake-off, leaned back and gave vent to a burst of deep-chested laughter. "I'll tell you what it is, Mike," he said archly, hitching up his tight, very artistic, and almost English trousers, "we're up against a bunch of pikers in this Gilgan crowd, and they've gotta be taught a lesson. He knows it as well as anybody else. None o' that Christian con game goes around where I am. I believe this man Cowperwood's right when he says them fellows are a bunch of soreheads and jealous. If Cowperwood's willing to put down good hard money to keep 'em out of his game, let them do as much to stay in it. This ain't no charity grab bag. We ought to be able to round up enough of these new fellows to make Schryhart and MacDonald come down good and plenty for what they want. From what Gilgan said all along, I thought he was dealing with live ones. They paid to win the election. Now let 'em pay to pull off a swell franchise if they want it, eh?"

"You're damn right," echoed Tiernan. "I'm with you to a T."

It was not long after this conversation that Mr. Truman Leslie MacDonald, acting through Alderman Klemm, proceeded to make a count of noses, and found to his astonishment that he was not as strong as he had thought he was. Political loyalty is such a fickle thing. A number of aldermen with curious names—Horback, Fogarty, McGrane,

Sumulsky—showed signs of being tampered with. He hurried at once to Messrs. Hand, Schryhart, and Arneel with this disconcerting information. They had been congratulating themselves that the recent victory, if it resulted in nothing else, would at least produce a blanket L road franchise, and that this would be sufficient to bring Cowperwood to his knees.

Upon receiving MacDonald's message Hand sent at once for Gilgan. When he inquired as to how soon a vote on the General Electric franchise—which had been introduced by Mr. Klemm—could reasonably be expected, Gilgan declared himself much grieved to admit that in one direction or other considerable opposition seemed to have developed to the measure.

"What's that?" said Hand a little savagely. "Didn't we make a plain bargain in regard to this? You had all the money you asked for, didn't you? You said you could give me twenty-six aldermen who would vote as we agreed. You're not going to go back on your bargain, are you?"

"Bargain! bargain!" retorted Gilgan, irritated because of the spirit of the assault. "I agreed to elect twenty-six Republican aldermen, and that I did. I don't own 'em body and soul. I didn't name 'em in every case. I made deals with the men in the different wards that had the best chance, and that the people wanted. I'm not responsible for any crooked work that's going on behind my back, am I? I'm not responsible for men's not being straight if they're not."

Mr. Gilgan's face was an aggrieved question mark.

"But you had the picking of these men," insisted Mr. Hand aggressively. "Every one of them had your personal indorsement. You made the deals with them. You don't mean to say they're going back on their sacred agreement to fight Cowperwood tooth and nail? There can't be any misunderstanding on their part as to what they were elected to do. The newspapers have been full of the fact that nothing favorable to Cowperwood was to be put through."

"That's all true enough," replied Mr. Gilgan; "but I can't be held responsible for the private honesty of everybody. Sure I selected these men. Sure I did! But I selected them with the help of the rest of the Republicans and some of the Democrats. I had to make the best terms I could—to pick the men that could win. As far as I can find out most of 'em are satisfied not to do anything for Cowperwood. It's passing these ordinances in favor of other people that's stirring up the trouble."

Mr. Hand's broad forehead wrinkled, and his blue eyes surveyed Mr. Gilgan with suspicion. "Who are these men, anyhow?" he inquired. "I'd like to get a list of them."

Mr. Gilgan, safe in his own subtlety, was ready with a toll of the supposed recalcitrants. They must fight their own battles. Mr. Hand wrote down the names, determining meanwhile to bring pressure to bear. He decided also to watch Mr. Gilgan. If there should prove to be a hitch in the program the newspapers should be informed, and commanded to thunder appropriately. Such aldermen as proved unfaithful to the great trust imposed on them should be smoked out, followed back to the wards which had elected them, and exposed to the people who were behind them. Their names should be pilloried in the public press. The customary hints as to Cowperwood's deviltry and trickery should be redoubled.

But in the meantime Messrs. Stimson, Avery, McKibben, Van Sickle, and others were on Cowperwood's behalf acting separately upon various unattached aldermen—those not temperamentally and chronically allied with the reform idea—and making them understand that if they could find it possible to refrain from supporting anti-Cowperwood measures for the next two years, a bonus in the shape of an annual salary of two thousand dollars or a gift in some other form—perhaps a troublesome note indorsed or a mortgage taken care of—would be forthcoming, together with a guarantee that the general public should never know. In no case was such an offer made direct. Friends or neighbors, or suave unidentified strangers, brought mysterious messages. By this method some eleven aldermen—quite apart from the ten regular Democrats who, because of McKenty and his influence, could be counted upon—had been already suborned. Although Schryhart, Hand, and Arneel did not know it, their plans—even as they planned—were being thus undermined, and try as they would, the coveted ordinance for a blanket franchise persistently eluded them. They had to content themselves for the time being with a franchise for a single L road line on the South Side in Schryhart's own territory, and with a franchise to the General Electric covering only one unimportant line, which it would be easy for Cowperwood, if he continued in power, to take over at some later time.

CHAPTER XL

A Trip to Louisville

The most serious difficulty confronting Cowperwood from now on was really not so much political as financial. In building up and financing his Chicago street-railway enterprises he had, in those days when Addison was president of the Lake City National, used that bank as his chief source of supply. Afterward, when Addison had been forced to retire from the Lake City to assume charge of the Chicago Trust Company, Cowperwood had succeeded in having the latter designated as a central reserve and in inducing a number of rural banks to keep their special deposits in its vaults. However, since the war on him and his interests had begun to strengthen through the efforts of Hand and Arneel—men most influential in the control of the other central reserve banks of Chicago, and in close touch with the money barons of New York—there were signs not wanting that some of the country banks depositing with the Chicago Trust Company had been induced to withdraw because of pressure from outside inimical forces, and that more were to follow. It was some time before Cowperwood fully realized to what an extent this financial opposition might be directed against himself. In its very beginning it necessitated speedy hurryings to New York, Philadelphia, Cincinnati, Baltimore, Boston —even London at times—on the chance that there would be loose and ready cash in someone's possession. It was on one of these peregrinations that he encountered a curious personality, which led to various complications in his life, sentimental and otherwise, which he had not hitherto contemplated.

In various sections of the country Cowperwood had met many men of wealth, some grave, some gay, with whom he did business, and among these in Louisville, Kentucky, he encountered a certain Colonel Nathaniel Gillis, very wealthy, a horseman, inventor, roué, from whom he occasionally extracted loans. The colonel was an interesting figure in Kentucky society; and taking a great liking to Cowperwood, he found pleasure, during the brief periods in which they were together, in piloting him about. On one occasion in Louisville he observed: "Tonight, Frank, with your permission, I am going to introduce you to one of the most interesting women I know. She isn't good, but she's entertaining. She has had a troubled history. She is the ex-wife of two of my best friends, both dead, and the ex-mistress of another. I like her because I knew her father and mother, and because she was a clever little girl and still is a nice woman, even if she is getting along. She keeps a sort of house of convenience here in Louisville for a few of her old friends. You haven't anything particular to do tonight, have you? Suppose we go around there?"

Cowperwood, who was always genially sportive when among strong men—a sort of bounding collie—and who liked to humor those who could be of use to him, agreed.

"It sounds interesting to me. Certainly I'll go. Tell me more about her. Is she good-looking?"

"Rather. But better yet, she is connected with a number of women who are." The colonel, who had a small gray goatee and sportive dark eyes, winked the latter solemnly.

Cowperwood arose.

"Take me there," he said.

It was a rainy night. The business on which he was seeing the colonel required another day to complete. There was little or nothing to do. On the way the colonel retailed more of the life history of Nannie Hedden, as he familiarly called her, and explained that, although this was her maiden name, she had subsequently become first Mrs. John Alexander Fleming, then, after a divorce, Mrs. Ira George Carter, and now, alas! was known among the exclusive set of fast livers, to which he belonged, as plain Hattie Starr, the keeper of a more or less secret house of ill repute. Cowperwood did not take so much interest in all this until he saw her, and then only because of two children the colonel told him about, one a girl by her first marriage, Berenice Fleming, who was away in a New York boarding school, the other a boy, Rolfe Carter, who was in a military school for boys somewhere in the West.

"That daughter of hers," observed the Colonel, "is a chip off the old block, unless I miss my guess. I only saw her two or three times a few years ago when I was down East at her mother's summer home; but she struck me as having great charm even for a girl of ten. She's a lady born, if ever there was one. How her mother is to keep her straight, living as she does, is more than I know. How she keeps her in that school is a mystery. There's apt to be a scandal here at any time. I'm very sure the girl doesn't know anything about her mother's business. She never lets her come out here."

"Berenice Fleming," Cowperwood thought to himself. "What a pleasing name, and what a peculiar handicap in life."

"How old is the daughter now?" he inquired.

"Oh, she must be about fifteen—not more than that."

When they reached the house, which was located in a rather somber, treeless street, Cowperwood was surprised to find the interior spacious and tastefully furnished. Presently Mrs. Carter, as she was generally known in society, or Hattie Starr, as she was known to a less satisfying world, appeared. Cowperwood realized at once that he was in the presence of a woman who, whatever her present occupation, was not without marked evidences of refinement. She was exceedingly intelligent, if not highly intellectual, trig, vivacious, anything but commonplace. A certain spirited undulation in her walk, a seeming gay, frank indifference to her position in life, and obvious accustomedness to polite surroundings, took his fancy. Her hair was built up in a loose Frenchy way, after the fashion of the Empire, and her cheeks were slightly mottled with red veins. Her color was too high, and yet it was not utterly unbecoming. She had friendly gray-blue eyes, which went well with her light-brown hair; along with a pink flowered house gown, which became her fulling figure, she wore pearls.

"The widow of two husbands," thought Cowperwood; "the mother of two children!" With the colonel's easy introduction began a light conversation. Mrs. Carter gracefully persisted that she had known of Cowperwood for some time. His strenuous street-railway operations were more or less familiar to her.

"It would be nice," she suggested, "since Mr. Cowperwood is here, if we invited Grace Deming to call."

The latter was a favorite of the colonel's.

"I would be very glad if I could talk to Mrs. Carter," gallantly volunteered Cowperwood—he scarcely knew why. He was curious to learn more of her history. On subsequent occasions, and in more extended conversation with the colonel, it was retailed to him in full.

Nannie Hedden, or Mrs. John Alexander Fleming, or Mrs. Ira George Carter, or Hattie Starr, was by birth a descendant of a long line of Virginia and Kentucky Heddens and Colters, related in a definite or vague way to half the aristocracy of four or five of the surrounding states. Now, although still a woman of brilliant parts, she was the keeper of a select house of assignation in this meager city of perhaps 200,000 population. How had it happened? How could it possibly have come about? She had been in her day a reigning beauty. She had been born to money and had married money. Her first husband, John Alexander Fleming, who had inherited wealth, tastes, privileges, and vices from a long line of slave-holding, tobacco-growing Flemings, was a charming man of the Kentucky-Virginia society type. He had been trained in the law with a view to entering the diplomatic service, but being an idler by nature, had never done so. Instead, horse raising, horse racing, philandering, dancing, hunting, and the like, had taken up his time. When their wedding took place the Kentucky-Virginia society world considered it a great match. There was wealth on both sides. Then came much more of that idle social whirl which had produced the marriage. Even philanderings of a very vital character were not barred, though deception, in some degree at least, would be necessary. As a natural result there followed the appearance in the mountains of North Carolina, during a charming autumn outing, of a gay young spark by the name of Tucker Tanner, and the bestowal on him by the beautiful Nannie Fleming—as she was then called—of her temporary affections. Kind friends were quick to report what Fleming himself did not see, and Fleming, roué that he was, encountering young Mr. Tanner on a high mountain road one evening, said to him, "You get out of this party by night, or I will let daylight through you in the morning." Tucker Tanner, realizing that however senseless and unfair the exaggerated chivalry of the South might be, the end would be bullets just the same, departed. Mrs. Fleming, disturbed but unrepentant, considered herself greatly abused. There was much scandal.

Then came quarrels, drinking on both sides, finally a divorce.
Mr. Tucker Tanner did not appear to claim his damaged love,
but the aforementioned Ira George Carter, a penniless ne'er-
do-well of the same generation and social standing, offered
himself and was accepted. By the first marriage there had
been one child, a girl. By the second there was another
child, a boy. Ira George Carter, before the children were
old enough to impress Mrs. Carter with the importance of
their needs or her own affection for them, had squandered,
in one ridiculous venture after another, the bulk of the property willed to her by her father, Major Wickham Hedden.
Ultimately, after drunkenness and dissipation on the husband's side, and finally his death, came the approach of
poverty. Mrs. Carter was not practical, and still passionate
and inclined to dissipation. However, the aimless, fatuous
going to pieces of Ira George Carter, the looming pathos of
the future of the children, and a growing sense of affection
and responsibility had finally sobered her. The lure of love
and life had not entirely disappeared. But her chance of
sipping at those crystal founts had grown sadly slender. A
woman of thirty-eight and still possessing some beauty, she
was not content to eat the husks provided for the unworthy.
Her gorge rose at the thought of that neglected state into
which the pariahs of society fall on which the inexperienced
so cheerfully comment. Neglected by her own set, shunned
by the respectable, her fortune quite gone, she was nevertheless determined that she would not be a back-street seam-
stress or a pensioner upon the bounty of quondam friends.
By insensible degrees came first unhallowed relationships
through friendship and passing passion, then a curious intermediate state between the high world of fashion and the
half-world of harlotry, until finally, in Louisville, she had
become, not openly but actually, the mistress of a house of
ill repute. Men who knew how these things were done, and
who were consulting their own convenience far more than
her welfare, suggested the advisability of it. Three or four
friends like Colonel Gillis wished rooms—convenient places
in which to loaf, gamble, and bring their women. Hattie
Starr was her name now, and as such she had even become
known in a vague way to the police—but only vaguely—as a
woman whose home was suspiciously gay on occasions.

Cowperwood, with his appetite for the wonders of life,
his appreciation of the dramas which produce either failure

or success, could not help being interested in this spoiled woman who was sailing so vaguely the seas of chance. Colonel Gillis once said that with some strong man to back her, Nannie Fleming could be put back into society. She had a pleasant appeal—she and her two children, of whom she never spoke. After a few visits to her home Cowperwood spent hours talking with Mrs. Carter whenever he was in Louisville. On one occasion, as they were entering her boudoir, she picked up a photograph of her daughter from the dresser and dropped it into a drawer. Cowperwood had never seen this picture before. It was that of a girl of fifteen or sixteen, of whom he obtained but the most fleeting glance. Yet, with that instinct for the essential and vital which invariably possessed him, he gained a keen impression of it. It was of a delicately haggard child with a marvelously agreeable smile, a fine, high-poised head upon a thin neck, and an air of bored superiority. Combined with this was a touch of weariness about the eyelids, which drooped in a lofty way. Cowperwood was fascinated. Because of the daughter he professed an interest in the mother, which he really did not feel.

A little later Cowperwood was moved to definite action by the discovery in a photographer's window in Louisville of a second picture of Berenice—a rather large affair which Mrs. Carter had had enlarged from a print sent her by her daughter some time before. Berenice was standing rather indifferently posed at the corner of a Colonial mantel, a soft straw outing hat held negligently in one hand, one hip sunk lower than the other, a faint, elusive smile playing dimly around her mouth. The smile was really not a smile, but only the wraith of one, and the eyes were wide, disingenuous, mock-simple. The picture, because of its simplicity, appealed to him. He did not know that Mrs. Carter had never sanctioned its display. "A personage," was Cowperwood's comment to himself, and he walked into the photographer's office to see what could be done about its removal and the destruction of the plates. A half-hundred dollars, he found, would arrange it all—plates, prints, everything. Since by this ruse he secured a picture for himself, he promptly had it framed and hung in his Chicago rooms, where sometimes of an afternoon when he was hurrying to change his clothes he stopped to look at it. With each succeeding examination his admiration and curiosity grew. Here was, perhaps he thought, the true society woman, the high-born lady, the realization of that ideal which Mrs. Merrill and many another grande dame had suggested.

It was not so long after this again that, chancing to be in Louisville, he discovered Mrs. Carter in a very troubled social condition. Her affairs had received a severe setback. A certain Major Hagenback, a citizen of considerable prominence, had died in her home under peculiar circumstances. He was a man of wealth, married, and nominally living with his wife in Lexington. As a matter of fact, he spent very little time there, and at the time of his death of heart failure was leading a pleasurable existence with a Miss Trent, an actress, whom he had introduced to Mrs. Carter as his friend. The police, through a talkative deputy coroner, were made aware of all the facts. Pictures of Miss Trent, Mrs. Carter, Major Hagenback, his wife, and many curious details concerning Mrs. Carter's home were about to appear in the papers when Colonel Gillis and others who were powerful socially and politically interfered; the affair was hushed up, but Mrs. Carter was in distress. This was more than she had bargained for. Her quondam friends were frightened away for the nonce. She herself had lost courage. When Cowperwood saw her she had been in the very human act of crying, and her eyes were red.

"Well, well," he commented on seeing her—she was in moody gray in the bargain—"you don't mean to tell me you're worrying about anything, are you?"

"Oh, Mr. Cowperwood," she explained pathetically, "I have had so much trouble since I saw you. You heard of Major Hagenback's death, didn't you?" Cowperwood, who had heard something of the story from Colonel Gillis, nodded. "Well, I have just been notified by the police that I will have to move, and the landlord has given me notice, too. If it just weren't for my two children—"

She dabbed at her eyes pathetically.

Cowperwood meditated interestedly.

"Haven't you any place you can go?" he asked.

"I have a summer place in Pennsylvania," she confessed; "but I can't go there very well in February. Besides, it's my living I'm worring about. I have only this to depend on."

She waved her hand inclusively toward the various rooms.

"Don't you own that place in Pennsylvania?" he inquired.

"Yes, but it isn't worth much, and I couldn't sell it. I've been trying to do that anyhow for some time, because Berenice is getting tired of it."

"And haven't you any money laid away?"

"It's taken all I have to run this place and keep the children in school. I've been trying to give Berenice and Rolfe a chance to do something for themselves."

At the repetition of Berenice's name Cowperwood consulted his own interest or mood in the matter. A little assistance for her would not bother him much. Besides, it would probably eventually bring about a meeting with the daughter.

"Why don't you clear out of this?" he observed finally. "It's no business to be in, anyhow, if you have any regard for your children. They can't survive anything like this. You want to put your daughter back in society, don't you?"

"Oh yes," almost pleaded Mrs. Carter.

"Precisely," commented Cowperwood, who, when he was thinking, almost invariably dropped into a short, cold, curt business manner. Yet he was humanely inclined in this instance.

"Well, then, why not live in your Pennsylvania place for the present, or, if not that, go to New York? You can't stay here. Ship or sell these things." He waved a hand toward the rooms.

"I would only too gladly," replied Mrs. Carter, "if I knew what to do."

"Take my advice and go to New York for the present. You will get rid of your expenses here, and I will help you with the rest—for the present, anyhow. You can get a start again. It is too bad about these children of yours. I will take care of the boy as soon as he is old enough. As for Berenice"—he used her name softly—"if she can stay in school until she is nineteen or twenty the chances are that she will make social connections which will save her nicely. The thing for you to do is to avoid meeting any of this old crowd out here in the future if you can. It might be advisable to take her abroad for a time after she leaves school."

"Yes, if I just could," sighed Mrs. Carter rather lamely.

"Well, do what I suggest now, and we will see," observed Cowperwood. "It would be a pity if your two children were to have their lives ruined by such an accident as this."

Mrs. Carter, realizing that here in the shape of Cowperwood, if he chose to be generous, was the open way out of a lowering dungeon of misery, was inclined to give vent to a bit of grateful emotion, but finding him subtly remote, restrained herself. His manner, while warmly generous at times, was also easily distant, except when he wished it to be otherwise. Just now he was thinking of the high soul of Berenice Fleming and of its possible value to him.

CHAPTER LXI

The Daughter of Mrs. Fleming

Berenice Fleming, at the time Cowperwood first encountered her mother, was an inmate of the Misses Brewster's School for Girls, then on Riverside Drive, New York, and one of the most exclusive establishments of its kind in America. The social prestige and connections of the Heddens, Flemings, and Carters were sufficient to gain her this introduction, though the social fortunes of her mother were already at this time on the downgrade. A tall girl, delicately haggard, as he had imagined her, with reddish-bronze hair of a tinge but distantly allied to that of Aileen's, she was unlike any woman Cowperwood had ever known. Even at seventeen she stood up and out with an inexplicable superiority which brought her the feverish and exotic attention of lesser personalities, whose emotional animality found an outlet in swinging a censer at her shrine.

A strange maiden, decidedly! Even at this age, when she was, as one might suppose, a mere slip of a girl, she was deeply conscious of herself, her sex, her significance, her possible social import. Armed with a fair skin, a few freckles, an almost too-high color at times, strange, deep, night-blue, catlike eyes, a long nose, a rather pleasant mouth, perfect teeth, and a really good chin, she moved always with a feline grace that was careless, superior, sinuous, and yet the acme of harmony and a rhythmic flow of lines. One of her mess hall tricks, when unobserved by her instructors, was to walk with six plates and a water pitcher all gracefully poised on the top of her head after the fashion of the Asiatic and the African, her hips moving, her shoulders, neck, and head still. Girls begged weeks on end to have her repeat this stunt, as they called it. Another was to put her arms behind her and with a rush imitate the Winged Victory, a copy of which graced the library hall.

"You know," one little rosy-cheeked satellite used to urge her on adoringly, "she must have been like you. Her head must have been like yours. You are lovely when you do it."

For answer Berenice's deep, almost black-blue eyes turned on her admirer with solemn, unflattered consideration. She awed always by the something that she did not say.

The school, for all the noble dames who presided over it —solemn, inexperienced, owllike conventionalists who insisted on the last tittle and jot of order and procedure— was a joke to Berenice. She recognized the value of its social import, but even at fifteen and sixteen she was superior to it. She was superior to her superiors and to the specimens of maidenhood—supposed to be perfect socially—who gathered about to hear her talk, to hear her sing, declaim, or imitate. She was deeply, dramatically, urgently conscious of the value of her personality in itself, not as connected with any inherited social standing, but of its innate worth, and of the artistry and wonder of her body. One of her chief delights was to walk alone in her room—sometimes at night, the lamp out, the moon perhaps faintly illuminating her chamber —and to pose and survey her body, and dance in some naive, graceful, airy Greek way a dance that was singularly free from sex consciousness—and yet was it? She was conscious of her body—of every inch of it—under the ivory-white clothes which she frequently wore. Once she wrote in a secret diary which she maintained—another art impulse or an affectation, as you will:

My skin is so wonderful. It tingles so with rich life. I love it and my strong muscles underneath. I love my hands and my hair and my eyes. My hands are long and thin and delicate; my eyes are a dark, deep blue; my hair is a brown, rusty red, thick and sleepy. My long, firm, untired limbs can dance all night. Oh, I love life! I love life!

You would not have called Berenice Fleming sensuous—
though she was—because she was self-controlled. Her eyes
lied to you. They lied to all the world. They looked you
through and through with a calm *savoir faire*, a mocking
defiance, which said with a faint curl of the lips, barely suggested to help them out, "You cannot read me, you cannot
read me." She put her head to one side, smiled, lied (by
implication), assumed that there was nothing. And there was
nothing, as yet. Yet there was something, too—her inmost
convictions, and these she took good care to conceal. The
world—how little it should ever, ever know! How little it
ever could know truly!

The first time Cowperwood encountered this Circe daughter of so unfortunate a mother was on the occasion of a trip
to New York, the second spring following his introduction to
Mrs. Carter in Louisville. Berenice was taking some part in
the closing exercises of the Brewster School, and Mrs. Carter,
with Cowperwood for an escort, decided to go East. Cowperwood having located himself at the Netherlands, and Mrs.
Carter at the much humbler Grenoble, they journeyed together to visit this paragon whose picture he had had hanging
in his rooms in Chicago for months past. When they were
introduced into the somewhat somber reception parlor of the
Brewster School, Berenice came slipping in after a few
moments, a noiseless figure of a girl, tall and slim, and
deliciously sinuous. Cowperwood saw at first glance that she
fulfilled all the promise of her picture, and was delighted.
She had, he thought, a strange, shrewd, intelligent smile,
which, however, was girlish and friendly. Without so much
as a glance in his direction she came forward, extending her
arms and hands in an inimitable histrionic manner, and exclaimed, with a practiced and yet natural inflection: "Mother,
dear! So here you are really! You know, I've been thinking
of you all morning. I wasn't sure whether you would come
today, you change about so. I think I even dreamed of you
last night."

Her skirts, still worn just below the shoe tops, had the
richness of scraping silk then fashionable. She was also
guilty of using a faint perfume of some kind.

Cowperwood could see that Mrs. Carter, despite a certain
nervousness due to the girl's superior individuality and his
presence, was very proud of her. Berenice, he also saw
quickly, was measuring him out of the tail of her eye—a

single sweeping glance which she vouchsafed from beneath her long lashes sufficing; but she gathered quite accurately the totality of Cowperwood's age, force, grace, wealth, and worldly ability. Without hesitation she classed him as a man of power in some field, possibly finance, one of the numerous able men whom her mother seemed to know. She always wondered about her mother. His large gray eyes, that searched her with lightning accuracy, appealed to her as pleasant, able eyes. She knew on the instant, young as she was, that he liked women, and that probably he would think her charming; but as for giving him additional attention it was outside her code. She preferred to be interested in her dear mother exclusively.

"Berenice," observed Mrs. Carter airily, "let me introduce Mr. Cowperwood."

Berenice turned, and for the fraction of a second leveled a frank and yet condescending glance from wells of what Cowperwood considered to be indigo blue.

"Your mother has spoken of you from time to time," he said pleasantly.

She withdrew a cool, thin hand as limp and soft as wax, and turned to her mother again without comment, and yet without the least embarrassment. Cowperwood seemed in no way important to her.

"What would you say, dear," pursued Mrs. Carter, after a brief exchange of commonplaces, "if I were to spend next winter in New York?"

"It would be charming if I could live at home. I'm sick of this silly boarding school."

"Why, Berenice! I thought you liked it."

"I hate it, but only because it's so dull. The girls here are so silly."

Mrs. Carter lifted her eyebrows as much as to say to her escort, "Now what do you think?" Cowperwood stood solemnly by. It was not for him to make a suggestion at present. He could see that for some reason—probably because of her disordered life—Mrs. Carter was playing a game of manners with her daughter; she maintained always a lofty, romantic air. With Berenice it was natural—the expression of a vain, self-conscious, superior disposition.

"A rather charming garden here," he observed, lifting a curtain and looking out into a blooming plot.

"Yes, the flowers are nice," commented Berenice. "Wait;

I'll get some for you. It's against the rules, but they can't do more than send me away, and that's what I want."

"Berenice! Come back here!"

It was Mrs. Carter calling.

The daughter was gone in a fling of graceful lines and flounces.

"Now, what do you make of her?" asked Mrs. Carter, turning to her friend.

"Youth, individuality, energy—a hundred things. I see nothing wrong with her."

"If I could only see to it that she had her opportunities unspoiled."

Already Berenice was returning, a subject for an artist in almost studied lines. Her arms were full of sweet peas and roses which she had ruthlessly gathered.

"You willful girl!" scolded her mother indulgently. "I shall have to go and explain to your superiors. Whatever shall I do with her, Mr. Cowperwood?"

"Load her with daisy chains and transport her to Cytherea," commented Cowperwood, who had once visited this romantic isle, and therefore knew its significance.

Berenice paused. "What a pretty speech that is!" she exclaimed. "I have a notion to give you a special flower for that. I will, too." She presented him with a rose.

For a girl who had slipped in shy and still, Cowperwood commented, her mood had certainly changed. Still, this was the privilege of the born actress, to change. And as he viewed Berenice Fleming now he felt her to be such—a born actress, lissome, subtle, wise, indifferent, superior, taking the world as she found it and expecting it to obey—to sit up like a pet dog and be told to beg. What a charming character! What a pity it should not be allowed to bloom undisturbed in its make-believe garden! What a pity, indeed!

CHAPTER XLII

F. A. Cowperwood, Guardian

It was some time after this first encounter before Cowperwood saw Berenice again, and then only for a few days in that region of the Pocono Mountains where Mrs. Carter had her summer home. It was an idyllic spot on a mountainside some three miles from Stroudsburg, among a peculiar juxtaposition of hills which, from the comfortable recesses of a front veranda, had the appearance, as Mrs. Carter was fond of explaining, of elephants and camels parading in the distance. The humps of the hills—some of them as high as eighteen hundred feet—rose stately and green. Below, quite visible for a mile or more, moved the dusty white road descending to Stroudsburg. Out of her Louisville earnings Mrs. Carter had managed to employ, for the several summer seasons she had been here, a gardener, who kept the sloping front lawn in seasonable flowers. There was a trig two-wheeled trap with a smart horse and harness, and both Rolfe and Berenice were possessed of the latest novelty of the day—low-wheeled bicycles, which had just then superseded the old, high-wheel variety. For Berenice, also, was a music rack full of classic music and song collections, a piano, a shelf of favorite books, painting materials, various athletic implements, and several types of Greek dancing tunics which she had designed herself, including sandals and fillet for her hair. She was an idle, reflective, erotic person, dreaming strange dreams of a near and yet far-off social supremacy, at other times busying herself with such social opportunities as came to her. A more safely calculating and yet willful girl than Berenice Fleming would have been hard to find. By some trick of mental adjustment she had gained a clear prevision of how necessary it was to select the right socially, and to conceal her true motives and feelings; and yet she was by no means a snob, mentally, nor utterly calculating. Certain things in her own and in her mother's life troubled her—quarrels in her early days, from her seventh to her eleventh year, between her mother and her stepfather, Mr. Carter; the latter's drunkenness, verging upon delirium tremens at times; movings from one place to another—all sorts of sordid and depressing happenings. Berenice had been an impressionable child. Some things had gripped her memory mightily—once, for instance, when she had seen her stepfather, in the presence of her governess, kick a table over, and seizing the toppling lamp with demoniac skill, hurl it through a window. She herself had been tossed by him in one of these tantrums, when, in answer to the cries of terror of those about her, he had shouted: "Let her fall! It won't hurt the little devil to break a few bones." This was her keenest memory of her stepfather, and it rather softened her judgment of her mother, made her sympathetic with her when she was inclined to be critical. Of her own father she only knew that he had divorced her mother—why, she could not say. She liked her mother on many counts, though she could not feel that she actually loved her— Mrs. Carter was too fatuous at times, and at other times too restrained. This house at Pocono, or Forest Edge, as Mrs. Carter had named it, was conducted after a peculiar fashion. From June to October only it was open, Mrs. Carter, in the past, having returned to Louisville at that time, while Berenice and Rolfe went back to their respective schools. Rolfe was a cheerful, pleasant-mannered youth, well bred, genial, and courteous, but not very brilliant intellectually. Cowperwood's judgment of him the first time he saw him was that under ordinary circumstances he would make a good confidential clerk, possibly in a bank. Berenice, on the other hand, the child of the first husband, was a creature of an exotic mind and an opalescent heart. After his first contact with her in the reception room of the Brewster School, Cowperwood was deeply conscious of the import of this budding character. He was by now so familiar with types and kinds of women that an exceptional type—quite like an exceptional horse to a judge of horse flesh—stood out in his mind with singular vividness. Quite as in some great racing stable an ambitious horseman might imagine that he detected in some likely filly the signs and lineaments of the future winner of a Derby, so in Berenice Fleming, in the

quiet precincts of the Brewster School, Cowperwood pre-
visioned the central figure of a Newport lawn fete or a
London drawing room. Why? She had the air, the grace, the
lineage, the blood—that was why; and on that score she
appealed to him intensely, quite as no other woman before
had ever done.

It was on the lawn of Forest Edge that Cowperwood now
saw Berenice. The latter had had the gardener set up a tall
pole, to which was attached a tennis ball by a cord, and she
and Rolfe were hard at work on a game of tetherball.
Cowperwood, after a telegram to Mrs. Carter, had been met
at the station in Pocono by her and rapidly driven out to
the house. The green hills pleased him, the upwinding yellow
road, the silver-gray cottage with the brown shingle roof in
the distance. It was three in the afternoon, and bright for a
sinking sun.

"There they are now," observed Mrs. Carter, cheerful
and smiling, as they came out from under a low ledge that
skirted the road a little way from the cottage. Berenice,
executing a tripping, running step to one side, was striking
the tethered ball with her racket. "They are hard at it, as
usual. Two such romps!"

She surveyed them with pleased motherly interest, which
Cowperwood considered did her much credit. He was thinking that it would be too bad if her hopes for her children
should not be realized. Yet possibly they might not be. Life
was very grim. How strange, he thought, was this type of
woman—at once a sympathetic, affectionate mother and a
panderer to the vices of men. How strange that she should
have these children at all.

Berenice had on a white skirt, white tennis shoes, a pale
cream silk waist or blouse, which fitted her very loosely.
Because of exercise her color was high—quite pink—and her
dusty reddish hair was blowy. Though they turned into the
hedge gate and drove to the west entrance, which was at one
side of the house, there was no cessation of the game, not
even a glance from Berenice, so busy was she. He was
merely her mother's friend to her. Cowperwood noted,
with singular vividness of feeling, that the lines of her
movements—the fleeting, momentary positions she assumed
—were full of a wondrous natural charm. He wanted to
say so to Mrs. Carter, but restrained himself.

"It's a brisk game," he commented with a pleased glance. "You play, do you?"

"Oh, I did. I don't much anymore. Sometimes I try a set with Rolfe or Bevy; but they both beat me so badly."

"Bevy? Who is Bevy?"

"Oh, that's short of Berenice. It's what Rolfe called her when he was a baby."

"Bevy! I think that rather nice."

"I always like it, too. Somehow it seems to suit her, and yet I don't know why."

Before dinner Berenice made her appearance, freshened by a bath and clad in a light summer dress that appeared to Cowperwood to be all flounces, and the more graceful in its lines for the problematic absence of a corset. Her face and hands, however—a face thin, long, and sweetly hollow, and hands that were slim and sinewy—gripped and held his fancy. He was reminded in the least degree of Stephanie; but this girl's chin was firmer and more delicately, though more aggressively, rounded. Her eyes, too, were shrewder and less evasive, though subtle enough.

"So I meet you again," he observed with a somewhat aloof air, as she came out on the porch and sank listlessly into a wicker chair. "The last time I met you you were hard at work in New York."

"Breaking the rules. No, I forget; that was my easiest work. Oh, Rolfe," she called over her shoulder indifferently, "I see your pocketknife out on the grass."

Cowperwood, properly suppressed, waited a brief space. "Who won that exciting game?"

"I did, of course. I always win at tetherball."

"Oh, do you?" commented Cowperwood.

"I mean with Brother, of course. He plays so poorly." She turned to the west—the house faced south—and studied the road which came up from Stroudsburg. "I do believe that's Harry Kemp," she added, quite to herself. "If so, he'll have my mail, if there is any."

She got up again and disappeared into the house, coming out a few moments later to saunter down to the gate, which was over a hundred feet away. To Cowperwood she seemed to float, so hale and graceful was she. A smart youth in blue serge coat, white trousers, and white shoes drove by in a high-seated trap.

"Two letters for you," he called in a high, almost falsetto

voice. "I thought you would have eight or nine. Blessed hot, isn't it?" He had a smart though somewhat effeminate manner, and Cowperwood at once wrote him down as an ass. Berenice took the mail with an engaging smile. She sauntered past him reading, without so much as a glance. Presently he heard her voice within.

"Mother, the Haggertys have invited me for the last week in August. I have half a mind to cut Tuxedo and go. I like Bess Haggerty."

"Well, you'll have to decide that, dearest. Are they going to be at Tarrytown or Loon Lake?"

"Loon Lake, of course," come Berenice's voice.

What a world of social doings she was involved in, thought Cowperwood. She had begun well. The Haggertys were rich coal mine operators in Pennsylvania. Harris Haggerty, to whose family she was probably referring, was worth at least six or eight million. The social world they moved in was high.

They drove after dinner to The Saddler, at Saddler's Run, where a dance and "moonlight promenade" was to be given. On the way over, owing to the remoteness of Berenice, Cowperwood for the first time in his life felt himself to be getting old. In spite of the vigor of his mind and body, he realized constantly that he was over fifty-two, while she was only seventeen. Why should this lure of youth continue to possess him? She wore a white concoction of lace and silk which showed a pair of smooth young shoulders and a slender, queenly, inimitably modeled neck. He could tell by the sleek lines of her arms how strong she was.

"It is perhaps too late," he said to himself in comment. "I am getting old."

The freshness of the hills in the pale night was sad.

Saddler's, when they reached there after ten, was crowded with the youth and beauty of the vicinity. Mrs. Carter, who was prepossessing in a ball costume of silver and old rose, expected that Cowperwood would dance with her. And he did, but all the time his eyes were on Berenice, who was caught up by one youth and another of dapper mien during the progress of the evening, and carried rhythmically by in the mazes of the waltz or schottische. There was a new dance in vogue that involved a gay, running step—kicking first one foot and then the other forward, turning and running backward and kicking again, and then swinging with a smart air, back to back, with one's partner. Berenice, in her lithe, rhythmic way, seemed to him the soul of spirited gracious ease—unconscious of everybody and everything save the spirit of the dance itself as a medium of sweet emotion, of some far-off, dreamlike spirit of gaiety. He wondered. He was deeply impressed.

"Berenice," observed Mrs. Carter, when in an intermission she came forward to where Cowperwood and she were sitting in the moonlight discussing New York and Kentucky social life, "haven't you saved one dance for Mr. Cowperwood?"

Cowperwood, with a momentary feeling of resentment, protested that he did not care to dance anymore. Mrs. Carter, he observed to himself, was a fool.

"I believe," said her daughter with a languid air, "that I am full up. I could break one engagement, though, somewhere."

"Not for me, though, please," pleaded Cowperwood. "I don't care to dance anymore, thank you."

He almost hated her at the moment for a chilly cat. And yet he did not.

"Why, Bevy, how you talk! I think you are acting very badly this evening."

"Please, please," pleaded Cowperwood quite sharply. "Not anymore. I don't care to dance anymore."

Bevy looked at him oddly for a moment—a single thoughtful glance.

"But I have a dance, though," she pleaded softly. "I was just teasing. Won't you dance with me?"

"I can't refuse, of course," replied Cowperwood coldly.

"It's the next one," she replied.

They danced, but he scarcely softened to her at first, so angry was he. Somehow, because of all that had gone before, he felt stiff and ungainly. She had managed to break in upon his natural *savoir faire*—this chit of a girl. But as they went on through a second half the spirit of her dancing soul caught him, and he felt more at ease, quite rhythmic. She drew close and swept him into a strange unison with herself.

"You dance beautifully," he said.

"I love it," she replied. She was already of an agreeable height for him.

It was soon over. "I wish you would take me where the ices are," she said to Cowperwood.

He led her, half amused, half disturbed at her attitude toward him.

"You are having a pleasant time teasing me, aren't you?" he asked.

"I am only tired," she replied. "The evening bores me. Really it does. I wish we were all home."

"We can go when you say, no doubt."

As they reached the ices, and she took one from his hand, she surveyed him with those cool, dull blue eyes of hers—eyes that had the flat quality of unglazed Dutch tiles.

"I wish you would forgive me," she said. "I was rude. I couldn't help it. I am all out of sorts with myself."

"I hadn't felt you were rude," he observed, lying grandly, his mood toward her changing entirely.

"Oh yes I was, and I hope you will forgive me. I sincerely wish you would."

"I do with all my heart—the little that there is to forgive."

He waited to take her back, and yielded to a youth who was waiting. He watched her trip away in a dance, and eventually led her mother to the trap. Berenice was not with them on the home drive; someone else was bringing her. Cowperwood wondered when she would come, and where was her room, and whether she was really sorry, and— As he fell asleep Berenice Fleming and her slate-blue eyes were filling his mind completely.

CHAPTER XLIII

The Planet Mars

The banking hostility to Cowperwood, which in its beginning had made necessary his trip to Kentucky and elsewhere, finally reached a climax. It followed an attempt on his part to furnish funds for the building of elevated roads. The hour for this new form of transit convenience had struck. The public demanded it. Cowperwood saw one

elevated road, the South Side Alley Line, being built, and
another, the West Side Metropolitan Line, being proposed,
largely, as he knew, in order to create sentiment for the
idea, and so to make his opposition to a general franchise
difficult. He was well aware that if he did not choose to
build them others would. It mattered little that electricity
had arrived finally as a perfected traction factor, and that
all his lines would soon have to be done over to meet that
condition, or that it was costing him thousands and thousands to stay the threatening aspect of things politically. In
addition he must now plunge into this new realm, gaining
franchises by the roughest and subtlest forms of political
bribery. The most serious aspect of this was not political, but
rather financial. Elevated roads in Chicago, owing to the
sparseness of the population over large areas, were a serious
thing to contemplate. The mere cost of iron, right of way,
rollingstock, and power plants was immense. Being chronically opposed to investing his private funds where stocks
could just as well be unloaded on the public, and the management and control retained by him, Cowperwood, for the
time being, was puzzled as to where he should get credit
for the millions to be laid down in structural steel, engineering fees, labor, and equipment before even a dollar
could be taken out in passenger fares. Owing to the advent
of the world's fair, the South Side L—to which, in order
to have peace and quiet, he had finally conceded a franchise
—was doing reasonably well. Yet it was not making any
such return on the investment as the New York roads. The
new lines which he was preparing would traverse even less
populous sections of the city, and would in all likelihood
yield even a smaller return. Money had to be forthcoming—
something between twelve and fifteen million dollars—and
this on the stocks and bonds of a purely paper corporation
which might not yield paying dividends for years to come.
Addison, finding that the Chicago Trust Company was already heavily loaded, called upon various minor but prosperous local banks to take over the new securities (each in
part, of course). He was astonished and chagrined to find
that one and all uniformly refused.

"I'll tell you how it is, Judah," one bank president confided to him in great secrecy. "We owe Timothy Arneel at
least three hundred thousand dollars that we only have to
pay three percent for. It's a call loan. Besides, the Lake Na-

tional is our main standby when it comes to quick trades, and he's in on that. I understand from one or two friends that he's at outs with Cowperwood, and we can't afford to offend him. I'd like to, but no more for me—not at present, anyhow."

"Why, Simmons," replied Addison, "these fellows are simply cutting off their noses to spite their faces. These stock and bond issues are perfectly good investments, and no one knows it better than you do. All this hue and cry in the newspapers against Cowperwood doesn't amount to anything. He's perfectly solvent. Chicago is growing. His lines are becoming more valuable every year."

"I know that," replied Simmons. "But what about this talk of a rival elevated system? Won't that injure his lines for the time being, anyhow, if it comes into the field?"

"If I know anything about Cowperwood," replied Addison simply, "there isn't going to be any rival elevated road. It's true they got the city council to give them a franchise for one line on the South Side; but that's out of his territory, anyhow, and that other one to the Chicago General Company doesn't amount to anything. It will be years and years before it can be made to pay a dollar, and when the time comes he will probably take it over if he wants it. Another election will be held in two years, and then the city administration may not be so unfavorable. As it is, they haven't been able to hurt him through the council as much as they thought they would."

"Yes; but he lost the election."

"True; but it doesn't follow he's going to lose the next one, or every one."

"Just the same," replied Simmons very secretively, "I understand there's a concerted effort on to drive him out. Schryhart, Hand, Merrill, Arneel—they're the most powerful men we have. I understand Hand says that he'll never get his franchises renewed except on terms that'll make his lines unprofitable. There's going to be an awful smash here one of these days if that's true." Mr. Simmons looked very wise and solemn.

"Never believe it," replied Addison contemptuously. "Hand isn't Chicago, neither is Schryhart, nor Arneel. Cowperwood is a brainy man. He isn't going to be put under so easily. Did you ever hear what was the real bottom cause of all this disturbance?"

"Yes, I've heard," replied Simmons.

"Do you believe it?"

"Oh, I don't know. Yes, I suppose I do. Still, I don't know that that need have anything to do with it. Money envy is enough to make any man fight. This man Hand is very powerful."

Not long after this Cowperwood, strolling into the president's office of the Chicago Trust Company, inquired: "Well, Judah, how about those Northwestern L bonds?"

"It's just as I thought, Frank," replied Addison softly. "We'll have to go outside of Chicago for that money. Hand, Arneel, and the rest of that crowd have decided to combine against us. That's plain. Something has started them off in full cry. I suppose my resignation may have had something to do with it. Anyhow, every one of the banks in which they have any hand has uniformly refused to come in. To make sure that I was right I even called up the little old Third National of Lake View and the Drovers and Traders on Forty-seventh Street. That's Charlie Wallin's bank. When I was over in the Lake National he used to hang around the back door asking for anything I could give him that was sound. Now he says his orders are from his directors not to share in anything we have to offer. It's the same story everywhere—they daren't. I asked Wallin if he knew why the directors were down on the Chicago Trust or on you, and at first he said he didn't. Then he said he'd stop in and lunch with me someday. They're the silliest lot of old ostriches I ever heard of. As if refusing to let us have money on any loan here was going to prevent us from getting it! They can take their little old one-horse banks and play blockhouses with them if they want to. I can go to New York and in thirty-six hours raise twenty million dollars if we need it."

Addison was a little warm. It was a new experience for him. Cowperwood merely curled his moustaches and smiled sardonically.

"Well, never mind," he said. "Will you go down to New York, or shall I?"

It was decided, after some talk, that Addison should go. When he reached New York, he found, to his surprise, that the local opposition to Cowperwood had, for some mysterious reason, begun to take root in the East.

"I'll tell you how it is," observed Joseph Haeckelheimer, to whom Addison applied—a short, smug, pussy person who was the head of Haeckelheimer, Gotloeb & Co., international bankers. "We hear odd things concerning Mr. Cowperwood out in Chicago. Some people say he is sound—some not. He has some very good franchises covering a large portion of the city, but they are only twenty-year franchises, and they will all run out by 1903 at the latest. As I understand it, he has managed to stir up all the local elements—some very powerful ones, too—and he is certain to have a hard time to get his franchises renewed. I don't live in Chicago, of course. I don't know much about it, but our western correspondent tells me this is so. Mr. Cowperwood is a very able man, as I understand it, but if all these influential men are opposed to him they can make him a great deal of trouble. The public is very easily aroused."

"You do a very able man a great injustice, Mr. Haeckelheimer," Addison retorted. "Almost anyone who starts out to do things successfully and intelligently is sure to stir up a great deal of feeling. The particular men you mention seem to feel that they have a sort of proprietor's interest in Chicago. They really think they own it. As a matter of fact, the city made them; they didn't make the city."

Mr. Haeckelheimer lifted his eyebrows. He laid two fine white hands, plump and stubby, over the lower buttons of his protuberant waistcoat. "Public favor is a great factor in all of these enterprises," he almost sighed. "As you know, part of a man's resources lies in his ability to avoid stirring up opposition. It may be that Mr. Cowperwood is strong enough to overcome all that. I don't know. I've never met him. I'm just telling you what I hear."

This offish attitude on the part of Mr. Haeckelheimer was indicative of a new trend. The man was enormously wealthy. The firm of Haeckelheimer, Gotloeb & Co. represented a controlling interest in some of the principal railways and banks in America. Their favor was not to be held in light esteem.

It was plain that these rumors against Cowperwood in New York, unless offset promptly by favorable events in Chicago, might mean—in the large banking quarters, anyhow—the refusal of all subsequent Cowperwood issues. It might even close the doors of minor banks and make private investors nervous.

Addison's report of all this annoyed Cowperwood no little. It made him angry. He saw in it the work of Schryhart,

Hand, and others who were trying their best to discredit him. "Let them talk," he declared crossly. "I have the street-railways. They're not going to rout me out of here. I can sell stocks and bonds to the public direct if need be! There are plenty of private people who are glad to invest in these properties."

At this psychological moment enter, as by the hand of Fate, the planet Mars and the university. This latter, from having been for years a humble Baptist college of the cheapest character, had suddenly, through the beneficence of a great Standard Oil multimillionaire, flared upward into a great university, and was causing a stir throughout the length and breadth of the educational world. It was already a most noteworthy spectacle, one of the sights of the city. Millions were being poured into it; new and beautiful buildings were almost monthly erected. A brilliant, dynamic man had been called from the East as president. There were still many things needed—dormitories, laboratories of one kind and another, a great library; and last but not least, a giant telescope—one that would sweep the heavens with a hitherto unparalleled receptive eye, and wring from it secrets not previously decipherable by the eye and the mind of man.

Cowperwood had always been interested in the heavens and in the giant mathematical and physical methods of interpreting them. It so happened that the warlike planet, with its sinister aspect, was just at this time to be seen hanging in the west, a fiery red; and the easily aroused public mind was being stirred to its shallow depth by reflections and speculations regarding the famous canals of the luminary. The mere thought of the possibility of a larger telescope than any now in existence, which might throw additional light on this evasive mystery, was exciting not only Chicago, but the whole world. Late one afternoon Cowperwood, looking over some open fields which faced his new powerhouse in West Madison Street, observed the planet hanging low and lucent in the evening sky, a warm, radiant bit of orange in a sea of silver. He paused and surveyed it. Was it true that there were canals on it, and people? Life was surely strange.

One day not long after this Alexander Rambaud called him up on the phone and remarked jocosely:

"I say, Cowperwood, I've played a rather shabby trick on you just now. Dr. Hooper, of the university, was in here a few minutes ago asking me to be one of ten to guarantee the cost of a telescope lens that he thinks he needs to run that one-horse school of his out there. I told him I thought you might possibly be interested. His idea is to find someone who will guarantee forty thousand dollars, or eight or ten men who will guarantee four or five thousand each. I thought of you, because I've heard you discuss astronomy from time to time."

"Let him come," replied Cowperwood, who was never willing to be behind others in generosity, particularly where his efforts were likely to be appreciated in significant quarters.

Shortly afterward appeared the doctor himself—short, rotund, rubicund, displaying, behind a pair of clear, thick, gold-rimmed glasses, round, dancing, incisive eyes. Imaginative grip, buoyant, self-delusive self-respect were written all over him. The two men eyed each other—one with that broad-gage examination which sees even universities as futile in the endless shift of things; the other with that faith in the balance for right which makes even great personal forces, such as financial magnates, serve an idealistic end.

"It's not a very long story I have to tell you, Mr. Cowperwood," said the doctor. "Our astronomical work is handicapped just now by the simple fact that we have no lens at all, no telescope worthy of the name. I should like to see the university do original work in this field, and do it in a great way. The only way to do it, in my judgment, is to do it better than anyone else can. Don't you agree with me?" He showed a row of shining white teeth.

Cowperwood smiled urbanely.

"Will a forty-thousand-dollar lens be a better lens than any other lens?" he inquired.

"Made by Appleman Brothers of Dorchester it will," replied the college president. "The whole story is here, Mr. Cowperwood. These men are practical lens-makers. A great lens, in the first place, is a matter of finding a suitable crystal. Large and flawless crystals are not common, as you may possibly know. Such a crystal has recently been found, and is now owned by Mr. Appleman. It takes about four or five years to grind and polish it. Most of the polishing, as you may or may not know, is done by the hand—smoothing it with the thumb and forefinger. The time, judgment, and skill of an optical expert is required. Today, unfortunately,

that is not cheap. The laborer is worthy of his hire, however, I suppose"—he waved a soft, full white hand—"and
forty thousand is little enough. It would be a great honor if
the university could have the largest, most serviceable, and
most perfect lens in the world. It would reflect great credit,
I take it, on the men who would make this possible."

Cowperwood liked the man's artistically educational air;
obviously here was a personage of ability, brains, emotion,
and scientific enthusiasm. It was splendid to him to see any
strong man in earnest, for himself or others.

"And forty thousand will do this?" he asked.

"Yes, sir. Forty thousand will guarantee us the lens, anyhow."

"And how about land, buildings, a telescope frame? Have
you all those things prepared for it?"

"Not as yet, but, since it takes four years at least to grind
the lens, there will be time enough, when the lens is
nearing completion, to look after the accessories. We have
picked our site, however—Lake Geneva—and we would not
refuse either land or accessories if we knew where to get
them."

Again the even, shining teeth, the keen eyes boring
through the glasses.

Cowperwood saw a great opportunity. He asked what
would be the cost of the entire project. Dr. Hooper presumed
that $300,000 would do it all handsomely—lens, telescope,
land, machinery, building—a great monument.

"And how much have you guaranteed on the cost of your
lens?"

"Sixteen thousand dollars, so far."

"To be paid when?"

"In installments—ten thousand a year for four years. Just
enough to keep the lens-maker busy for the present."

Cowperwood reflected. Ten thousand a year for four years
would be a mere salary item, and at the end of that time
he felt sure that he could supply the remainder of the
money quite easily. He would be so much richer; his plans
would be so much more mature. On such a repute (the
ability to give a $300,000 telescope out of hand to be known
as the Cowperwood telescope), he could undoubtedly raise
money in London, New York, and elsewhere for his Chicago enterprise. The whole world would know him in a day.

He paused, his enigmatic eyes revealing nothing of the splendid vision that danced before them. At last! At last!

"How would it do, Mr. Hooper," he said sweetly, "if, instead of ten men giving you four thousand each, as you plan, one man were to give you forty thousand in annual installments of ten thousand each? Could that be arranged as well?"

"My dear Mr. Cowperwood," exclaimed the doctor, glowing, his eyes alight, "do I understand that you personally might wish to give the money for this lens?"

"I might, yes. But I should have to exact one pledge, Mr. Hooper, if I did any such thing."

"And what would that be?"

"The privilege of giving the land and the building—the whole telescope, in fact. I presume no word of this will be given out unless the matter is favorably acted upon?" he added cautiously and diplomatically.

The new president of the university arose and eyed him with a peculiarly approbative and grateful gaze. He was a busy, overworked man. His task was large. Any burden taken from his shoulders in this fashion was a great relief.

"My answer to that, Mr. Cowperwood, if I had the authority, would be to agree now in the name of the university, and thank you. For form's sake, I must submit the matter to the trustees of the university, but I have no doubt as to the outcome. I anticipate nothing but grateful approbation. Let me thank you again."

They shook hands warmly, and the solid collegian bustled forth. Cowperwood sank quietly in his chair. He pressed his fingers together, and for a moment or two permitted himself to dream. Then he called a stenographer and began a bit of dictation. He did not care to think even to himself how universally advantageous all this might yet prove to be.

The result was that in the course of a few weeks the proffer was formally accepted by the trustees of the university, and a report of the matter, with Cowperwood's formal consent, was given out for publication. The fortuitous combination of circumstances already described gave the matter a unique news value. Giant reflectors and refractors had been given and were in use in other parts of the world, but none so large or so important as this. The gift was sufficient to set Cowperwood forth in the light of a public benefactor and patron of science. Not only in Chicago, but in London, Paris, and New York, wherever, indeed, in the great capitals scientific and intellectual men were gathered, this significant gift of an apparently fabulously rich American became the subject of excited discussion. Banking men, among others, took sharp note of the donor, and when Cowperwood's emissaries came around later with a suggestion that the fifty-year franchises about to be voted him for elevated roads should be made a basis of bond and mortgage loans, they were courteously received. A man who could give $300,000 telescopes in the hour of his greatest difficulties must be in a rather satisfactory financial condition. He must have great wealth in reserve. After some preliminaries, during which Cowperwood paid a flying visit to Threadneedle Street in London, and to Wall Street in New York, an arrangement was made with an English-American banking company by which the majority of the bonds for his proposed roads were taken over by them for sale in Europe and elsewhere, and he was given ample means wherewith to proceed. Instantly the stocks of his surface lines bounded in price, and those who had been scheming to bring about Cowperwood's downfall gnashed impotent teeth. Even Haeckelheimer & Co. were interested.

Anson Merrill, who had only a few weeks before given a large field for athletic purposes to the university, pulled a wry face over this sudden eclipse of his glory. Hosmer Hand, who had given a chemical laboratory, and Schryhart, who had presented a dormitory, were depressed to think that a benefaction less costly than theirs should create, because of the distinction of the idea, so much more notable comment. It was merely another example of the brilliant fortune which seemed to pursue the man, the star that set all their plans at defiance.

CHAPTER XLIV

A Franchise Obtained

The money requisite for the construction of elevated roads having been thus pyrotechnically obtained, the acquisition of franchises remained no easy matter. It involved, among other problems, the taming of Chaffee Thayer Sluss, who, quite unconscious of the evidence stored up against him, had begun to fulminate the moment it was suggested in various secret political quarters that a new ordinance was about to be introduced, and that Cowperwood was to be the beneficiary. "Don't you let them do that, Mr. Sluss," observed Mr. Hand, who, for purposes of conference, had courteously but firmly bidden his hireling, the mayor, to lunch. "Don't you let them pass that if you can help it." (As chairman or president of the city council Mr. Sluss held considerable manipulative power over the machinery of procedure.) "Raise such a row that they won't try to pass it over your head. Your political future really depends on it—your standing with the people of Chicago. The newspapers and the respectable financial and social elements will fully support you in this. Otherwise they will wholly desert you. Things have come to a handsome pass when men sworn and elected to perform given services turn on their backers and betray them in this way!"

Mr. Hand was very wroth.

Mr. Sluss, immaculate in black broadcloth and white linen, was very sure that he would fulfill to the letter all of Mr. Hand's suggestions. The proposed ordinance should be denounced by him; its legislative progress heartily opposed in council.

"They shall get no quarter from me!" he declared emphatically. "I know what the scheme is. They know that I know it."

He looked at Mr. Hand quite as one advocate of right-eousness should look at another, and the rich promoter went away satisfied that the reins of government were in safe hands. Immediately afterward Mr. Sluss gave out an inter-view in which he served warning on all aldermen and coun-cilmen that no such ordinance as the one in question would ever be signed by him as mayor.

At half past ten on the same morning on which the in-terview appeared—the hour at which Mr. Sluss usually reached his office—his private telephone bell rang, and an assistant inquired if he would be willing to speak with Mr. Frank A. Cowperwood. Mr. Sluss, somehow anticipating fresh laurels of victory, gratified by the front-page display given his announcement in the morning papers, and swelling internally with civic pride, announced solemnly: "Yes; con-nect me."

"Mr. Sluss," began Cowperwood at the other end, "this is Frank A. Cowperwood."

"Yes. What can I do for you, Mr. Cowperwood?"

"I see by the morning papers that you state that you will have nothing to do with any proposed ordinance which looks to giving me a franchise for any elevated road on the North or West Side?"

"That is quite true," replied Mr. Sluss loftily. "I will not."

"Don't you think it is rather premature, Mr. Sluss, to denounce something which has only a rumored existence?" (Cowperwood, smiling sweetly to himself, was quite like a cat playing with an unsuspicious mouse.) "I should like very much to talk this whole matter over with you personally before you take an irrevocable attitude. It is just possible that after you have heard my side you may not be so com-pletely opposed to me. From time to time I have sent to you several of my personal friends, but apparently you do not care to receive them."

"Quite true," replied Mr. Sluss loftily; "but you must re-member that I am a very busy man, Mr. Cowperwood, and, besides, I do not see how I can serve any of your purposes. You are working for a set of conditions to which I am morally and temperamentally opposed. I am working for another. I do not see that we have any common ground on which to meet. In fact, I do not see how I can be of any service to you whatsoever."

"Just a moment, please, Mr. Mayor," replied Cowperwood, still very sweetly, and fearing that Sluss might choose to hang up the receiver, so superior was his tone. "There may be some common ground of which you do not know. Wouldn't you like to come to lunch at my residence or receive me at yours? Or let me come to your office and talk this matter over. I believe you will find it the part of wisdom as well as of courtesy to do this."

"I cannot possibly lunch with you today," replied Sluss, "and I cannot see you, either. There are a number of things pressing for my attention. I must say also that I cannot hold any back room conferences with you or your emissaries. If you come you must submit to the presence of others."

"Very well, Mr. Sluss," replied Cowperwood cheerfully. "I will not come to your office. But unless you come to mine before five o'clock this afternoon you will face by noon tomorrow a suit for breach of promise, and your letters to Mrs. Brandon will be given to the public. I wish to remind you that an election is coming on, and that Chicago favors a mayor who is privately moral as well as publicly so. Good morning."

Mr. Cowperwood hung up his telephone receiver with a click, and Mr. Sluss sensibly and visibly stiffened and paled. Mrs. Brandon! The charming, lovable, discreet Mrs. Brandon who had so ungenerously left him! Why should she be thinking of suing him for breach of promise, and how did his letters to her come to be in Cowperwood's hands? Good heavens—those mushy letters! His wife! His children! His church and the owlish pastor thereof! Chicago! And its conventional, moral, religious atmosphere! Come to think of it, Mrs. Brandon had scarcely if ever written him a note of any kind. He did not even know her history.

At the thought of Mrs. Sluss—her hard, cold blue eyes —Mr. Sluss arose, tall and distrait, and ran his hand through his hair. He walked to the window, snapping his thumb and middle finger and looking eagerly at the floor. He thought of the telephone switchboard just outside his private office, and wondered whether his secretary, a handsome young Presbyterian girl, had been listening as usual. Oh, this sad world! If the North Side ever learned of this—Hand, the newspapers, young MacDonald—would they protect him? They would not. Would they run him for mayor again? Never! Could the public be induced to vote for him with all the churches fulminating against private immorality, hypocrites, and whited sepulchers? Oh, Lord! Oh, Lord! And he was so very, very much respected and looked up to—that was the worst of it all. This terrible demon Cowperwood had descended on him, and he had thought himself so secure. He had not even been civil to Cowperwood. What if the latter chose to avenge the discourtesy?

Mr. Sluss went back to his chair, but he could not sit in it. He went for his coat, took it down, hung it up again, took it down, announced over the phone that he could not see anyone for several hours, and went out by a private door. Wearily he walked along North Clark Street, looking at the hurly-burly of traffic, looking at the dirty, crowded river, looking at the sky and smoke and gray buildings, and wondering what he should do. The world was so hard at times; it was so cruel. His wife, his family, his political career. He could not conscientiously sign any ordinances for Mr. Cowperwood—that would be immoral, dishonest, a scandal to the city. Mr. Cowperwood was a notorious traitor to the public welfare. At the same time he could not very well refuse, for here was Mrs. Brandon, the charming and unscrupulous creature, playing into the hands of Cowperwood. If he could only meet her, beg of her, plead; but where was she? He had not seen her for months and months. Could he go to Hand and confess all? But Hand was a hard, cold, moral man also. Oh, Lord! Oh, Lord! He wondered and thought, and sighed and pondered—all without avail.

Pity the poor earthling caught in the toils of the moral law. In another country, perhaps, in another day, another age, such a situation would have been capable of a solution, one not utterly destructive to Mr. Sluss, and not entirely favorable to a man like Cowperwood. But here in the United States, here in Chicago, the ethical verities would all, as he knew, be lined up against him. What Lake View would think, what his pastor would think, what Hand and all his moral associates would think—ah, these were the terrible, the incontrovertible consequences of his lapse from virtue.

At four o'clock, after Mr. Sluss had wandered for hours in the snow and cold, belaboring himself for a fool and a knave, and while Cowperwood was sitting at his desk, signing papers, contemplating a glowing fire, and wondering whether the mayor would deem it advisable to put in an appearance, his office door opened and one of his trim stenographers

entered, announcing Mr. Chaffee Thayer Sluss. Enter Mayor
Sluss, sad, heavy, subdued, shrunken, a very different gentleman from the one who had talked so cavalierly over the
wires some five and a half hours before. Gray weather,
severe cold, and much contemplation of seemingly irreconcilable facts had reduced his spirits greatly. He was a little pale
and a little restless. Mental distress has a reducing, congealing
effect, and Mayor Sluss seemed somewhat less than his usual
self in height, weight, and thickness. Cowperwood had seen
him more than once on various political platforms, but he
had never met him. When the troubled mayor entered he
arose courteously and waved him to a chair.

"Sit down, Mr. Sluss," he said genially. "It's a disagree-
able day out, isn't it? I suppose you have come in regard
to the matter we were discussing this morning?"

Nor was this cordiality wholly assumed. One of the primal
instincts of Cowperwood's nature—for all his chicane and
subtlety—was to take no rough advantage of a beaten enemy.
In the hour of victory he was always courteous, bland, gentle,
and even sympathetic; he was so today, and quite honestly,
too.

Mayor Sluss put down the high sugar-loaf hat he wore
and said grandiosely, as was his manner even in the direst
extremity: "Well, you see, I am here, Mr. Cowperwood.
What is it you wish me to do, exactly?"

"Nothing unreasonable, I assure you, Mr. Sluss," replied
Cowperwood. "Your manner to me this morning was a little
brusque, and as I had always wanted to have a sensible private talk with you, I took this way of getting it. I should
like you to dismiss from your mind at once the thought
that I am going to take an unfair advantage of you in any
way. I have no present intention of publishing your cor-
respondence with Mrs. Brandon." (As he said this he took
from his drawer a bundle of letters which Mayor Sluss
recognized at once as the enthusiastic missives which he
had sometime before penned to the fair Claudia. Mr. Sluss
groaned as he beheld this incriminating evidence.) "I am
not trying," continued Cowperwood, "to wreck your career,
or to make you do anything which you do not feel that you
can conscientiously undertake. The letters that I have here,
let me say, have come to me quite by accident. I did not
seek them. But since I do have them, I thought I might as

well mention them as a basis for a possible talk and compromise between us."

Cowperwood did not smile. He merely looked thoughtfully at Sluss; then, by way of testifying to the truthfulness of what he had been saying, thumped the letters up and down, just to show that they were real.

"Yes," said Mr. Sluss heavily, "I see."

He studied the bundle—a small, solid affair—while Cowperwood looked discreetly elsewhere. He contemplated his own shoes, the floor. He rubbed his hands and then his knees.

Cowperwood saw how completely he had collapsed. It was ridiculous, pitiable.

"Come, Mr. Sluss," said Cowperwood amiably, "cheer up. Things are not nearly as desperate as you think. I give you my word right now that nothing which you yourself, on mature thought, could say was unfair will be done. You are the mayor of Chicago. I am a citizen. I merely wish fair play from you. I merely ask you to give me your word of honor that from now on you will take no part in this fight, which is one of pure spite against me. If you cannot conscientiously aid me in what I consider to be a perfectly legitimate demand for additional franchises, you will, at least, not go out of your way to publicly attack me. I will put these letters in my safe, and there they will stay until the next campaign is over, when I will take them out and destroy them. I have no personal feeling against you— none in the world. I do not ask you to sign any ordinance which the council may pass giving me elevated-road rights. What I do wish you to do at this time is to refrain from stirring up public sentiment against me, especially if the council should see fit to pass an ordinance over your veto. Is that satisfactory?"

"But my friends? The public? The Republican party? Don't you see it is expected of me that I should wage some form of campaign against you?" queried Sluss nervously.

"No, I don't," replied Cowperwood succinctly, "and, anyhow, there are ways and ways of waging a public campaign. Go through the motions, if you wish, but don't put too much heart in it. And, anyhow, see some one of my lawyers from time to time when they call on you. Judge Dickensheets is an able and fair man. So is General Van

Sickle. Why not confer with them occasionally?—not publicly, of course, but in some less conspicuous way. You will find both of them most helpful."

Cowperwood smiled encouragingly, quite beneficently, and Chaffee Thayer Sluss, his political hopes gone glimmering, sat and mused for a few moments in a sad and helpless quandary.

"Very well," he said at last, rubbing his hands feverishly. "It is what I might have expected. I should have known. There is no other way, but—" Hardly able to repress the hot tears now burning beneath his eyelids, the Honorable Mr. Sluss picked up his hat and left the room. Needless to add that his preachings against Cowperwood were permanently silenced.

CHAPTER XLV

Changing Horizons

The effect of all this was to arouse in Cowperwood the keenest feelings of superiority he had ever yet enjoyed. Hitherto he had fancied that his enemies might worst him, but at last his path seemed clear. He was now worth, all in all, the round sum of twenty million dollars. His art collection had become the most important in the West—perhaps in the nation, public collections excluded. He began to envision himself as a national figure, possibly even an international one. And yet he was coming to feel that no matter how complete his financial victory might ultimately be, the chances were that he and Aileen would never be socially accepted here in Chicago. He had done too many boisterous things—alienated too many people. He was as determined as ever to retain a firm grip on the Chicago street-railway situation. But he was disturbed for a second time in his life by the thought that, owing to the complexities of his own temperament, he had married unhappily and would find the situation difficult of adjustment. Aileen, whatever might be said of her deficiencies, was by no means as tractable or acquiescent as his first wife. And, besides, he felt that he owed her a better turn. By no means did he actually dislike her as yet; though she was no longer soothing, stimulating, or suggestive to him as she had formerly been. Her woes, because of him, were too many; her attitude toward him too censorious. He was perfectly willing to sympathize with her, to regret his own change of feeling, but what would you? He could not control his own temperament any more than Aileen could control hers.

The worst of this situation was that it was now becoming complicated on Cowperwood's part with the most disturbing thoughts concerning Berenice Fleming. Ever since the days when he had first met her mother he had been coming more and more to feel for the young girl a soul-stirring passion—and that without a single look exchanged or a single word spoken. There is a static something which is beauty, and this may be clothed in the habiliments of a ragged philosopher or in the silks and satins of pampered coquetry. It was a suggestion of this beauty, which is above sex and above age and above wealth, that shone in the blowing hair and night-blue eyes of Berenice Fleming. His visit to the Carter family at Pocono had been a disappointment to him, because of the apparent hopelessness of arousing Berenice's interest, and since that time, and during their casual encounters, she had remained politely indifferent. Nevertheless, he remained true to his persistence in the pursuit of any game he had fixed upon. Mrs. Carter, whose relations with Cowperwood had in the past been not wholly platonic, nevertheless attributed much of his interest in her to her children and their vital chance. Berenice and Rolfe themselves knew nothing concerning the nature of their mother's arrangements with Cowperwood. True to his promise of protectorship and assistance, he had established her in a New York apartment adjacent to her daughter's school, and where he fancied that he himself might spend many happy hours were Berenice but near. Proximity to Berenice! The desire to arouse her interest and command her favor! Cowperwood would scarcely have cared to admit to himself how great a part this played in a thought which had recently been creeping into his mind. It was that of erecting a splendid house in New York.

By degrees this idea of building a New York house had grown upon him. His Chicago mansion was a costly sepulcher in which Aileen sat brooding over the woes which had befallen her. Moreover, aside from the social defeat which it represented, it was becoming merely as a structure, but poorly typical of the splendor and ability of his imagination. This second dwelling, if he ever achieved it, should be resplendent, a monument to himself. In his speculative wanderings abroad he had seen many such great palaces, designed with the utmost care, which had housed the taste and culture of generations of men. His art collection, in which he took an immense pride, had been growing until it was the basis if not the completed substance for a very splendid memorial. Already in it were gathered paintings of all the important schools; to say nothing of collections of jade, illumined missals, porcelains, rugs, draperies, mirror frames, and a beginning at rare originals of sculpture. The beauty of these strange things, the patient laborings of inspired souls of various times and places, moved him, on occasion, to a gentle awe. Of all individuals he respected, indeed revered, the sincere artist. Existence was a mystery, but these souls who set themselves to quiet tasks of beauty had caught something of which he was dimly conscious. Life had touched them with a vision, their hearts and souls were attuned to sweet harmonies of which the common world knew nothing. Sometimes, when he was weary after a strenuous day, he would enter—late in the night—his now silent gallery, and turning on the lights so that the whole sweet room stood revealed, he would seat himself before some treasure, reflecting on the nature, the mood, the time, and the man that had produced it. Sometimes it would be one of Rembrandt's melancholy heads—the sad "Portrait of a Rabbi" —or the sweet introspection of a Rousseau stream. A solemn Dutch housewife, rendered with the bold fidelity and resonant enameled surfaces of a Hals or the cold elegance of an Ingres, commanded his utmost enthusiasm. So he would sit and wonder at the vision and skill of the original dreamer, exclaiming at times: "A marvel! A marvel!"

At the same time, so far as Aileen was concerned, things were obviously shaping up for additional changes. She was in that peculiar state which has befallen many a woman—trying to substitute a lesser ideal for a greater, and finding that the effort is useless or nearly so. In regard to her affair with Lynde, aside from the temporary relief and diversion it had afforded her, she was beginning to feel that she had made a serious mistake. Lynde was delightful, after his fashion. He could amuse her with a different type of experience from any that Cowperwood had to relate. Once they were intimate he had, with an easy, genial air, confessed to all sorts of liaisons in Europe and America. He was utterly pagan—a faun—and at the same time he was truly of the smart world. His open contempt of all but one or two of the people in Chicago whom Aileen had secretly admired and wished to associate with, and his easy references to figures of importance in the East and in Paris and London raised him amazingly in her estimation; it made her feel, sad to relate, that she had by no means lowered herself in succumbing so readily to his forceful charms.

Nevertheless, because he was what he was—genial, complimentary, affectionate, but a playboy, merely, and a soldier of fortune, with no desire to make over her life for her on any new basis—she was now grieving over the futility of this romance, which had got her nowhere, and which, in all probability, had alienated Cowperwood for good. He was still outwardly genial and friendly, but their relationship was now colored by a sense of mistake and uncertainty which existed on both sides, but which, in Aileen's case, amounted to a subtle species of soul torture. Hitherto she had been the aggrieved one, the one whose loyalty had never been in question, and whose persistent affection and faith had been greatly sinned against. Now all this was changed. The manner in which he had sinned against her was plain enough, but the way in which, out of pique, she had forsaken him was in the other balance. Say what one will, the loyalty of woman, whether a condition in nature or an evolved accident of sociology, persists as a dominating thought in at least a section of the race; and women themselves, be it said, are the ones who most loudly and openly subscribe to it. Cowperwood himself was fully aware that Aileen had deserted him, not because she loved him less or Lynde more, but because she was hurt—and deeply so. Aileen knew that he knew this. From one point of view it enraged her and made her defiant; from another it grieved her to think she had uselessly sinned against his faith in her. Now he had ample excuse to do anything he chose.

Her best claim on him—her wounds—she had thrown away
as one throws away a weapon. Her pride would not let her
talk to him about this, and at the same time she could not
endure the easy, tolerant manner with which he took it.
His smiles, his forgiveness, his sometimes pleasant jesting,
were all a horrible offense.

To complete her mental quandary, she was already beginning to quarrel with Lynde over this matter of her un-
breakable regard for Cowperwood. With the sufficiency of
a man of the world Lynde intended that she should succumb
to him completely and forget her wonderful husband. When
with him she was apparently charmed and interested, yielding
herself freely, but this was more out of pique at Cowperwood's neglect than from any genuine passion for Lynde.
In spite of her pretensions of anger, her sneers and criticisms
whenever Cowperwood's name came up, she was, nevertheless, hopelessly fond of him and identified with him spiritually, and it was not long before Lynde began to suspect
this. Such a discovery is a sad one for any master of women
to make. It jolted his pride severely.

"You care for him still, don't you?" he asked, with a
wry smile, upon one occasion. They were sitting at dinner
in a private room at Kinsley's, and Aileen, whose color was
high, and who was becomingly garbed in metallic-green
silk, was looking especially handsome. Lynde had been
proposing that she should make special arrangements to depart with him for a three-months' stay in Europe, but she
would have nothing to do with the project. She did not
dare. Such a move would make Cowperwood feel that she
was alienating herself forever; it would give him an excellent
excuse to leave her.

"Oh, it isn't that," she had declared, in reply to Lynde's
query. "I just don't want to go. I can't. I'm not prepared. It's
nothing but a notion of yours, anyhow. You're tired of
Chicago because it's getting near spring. You go and I'll be
here when you come back, or I may decide to come over
later." She smiled.

Lynde pulled a dark face.

"Hell!" he said. "I know how it is with you. You still stick
to him, even when he treats you like a dog. You pretend
not to love him when as a matter of fact you're mad about
him. I've seen it all along. You don't really care anything
about me. You can't. You're too crazy about him."

"Oh, shut up!" replied Aileen, irritated greatly for the moment by this onslaught. "You talk like a fool. I'm not anything of the sort. I admire him. How could anyone help it?" (At this time, of course, Cowperwood's name was filling the city.) "He's a very wonderful man. He was never brutal to me. He's a full-sized man—I'll say that for him."

By now Aileen had become sufficiently familiar with Lynde to criticize him in her own mind, and even outwardly by innuendo, for being a loafer and idler who had never created in any way the money he was so freely spending. She had little power to psychologize concerning social conditions, but the stalwart constructive persistence of Cowperwood along commercial lines coupled with the current American contempt of leisure reflected somewhat unfavorably upon Lynde, she thought.

Lynde's face clouded still more at this outburst. "You go to the devil," he retorted. "I don't get you at all. Sometimes you talk as though you were fond of me. At other times you're all wrapped up in him. Now you either care for me or you don't. Which is it? If you're so crazy about him that you can't leave home for a month or so you certainly can't care much about me."

Aileen, however, because of her long experience with Cowperwood, was more than a match for Lynde. At the same time she was afraid to let go of him for fear that she should have no one to care for her. She liked him. He was a happy resource in her misery, at least for the moment. Yet the knowledge that Cowperwood looked upon this affair as a heavy blemish on her pristine solidarity cooled her. At the thought of him and of her whole tarnished and troubled career she was very unhappy.

"Hell!" Lynde had repeated irritably, "stay if you want to. I'll not be trying to overpersuade you—depend on that."

They quarreled still further over this matter, and though they eventually made up, both sensed the drift toward an ultimately unsatisfactory conclusion.

It was one morning not long after this that Cowperwood, feeling in a genial mood over his affairs, came into Aileen's room, as he still did on occasions, to finish dressing and pass the time of day.

"Well," he observed gaily, as he stood before the mirror

adjusting his collar and tie, "how are you and Lynde getting along these days—nicely?"

"Oh, you go to the devil!" replied Aileen, flaring up and struggling with her divided feelings, which pained her constantly. "If it hadn't been for you there wouldn't be any chance for your smarty 'how-am-I-getting-alongs.' I am getting along all right—fine—regardless of anything you may think. He's as good a man as you are any day, and better. I like him. At least he's fond of me, and that's more than you are. Why should you care what I do? You don't, so why talk about it? I want you to let me alone."

"Aileen, Aileen, how you carry on! Don't flare up so. I meant nothing by it. I'm sorry as much for myself as for you. I've told you I'm not jealous. You think I'm critical. I'm not anything of the kind. I know how you feel. That's all very good."

"Oh yes, yes," she replied. "Well, you can keep your feelings to yourself. Go to the devil! Go to the devil, I tell you!" Her eyes blazed.

He stood now, fully dressed, in the center of the rug before her, and Aileen looked at him, keen, valiant, handsome—her old Frank. Once again she regretted her nominal faithlessness, and raged at him in her heart for his indifference. "You dog," she was about to add, "you have no heart!" but she changed her mind. Her throat tightened and her eyes filled. She wanted to run to him and say: "Oh, Frank, don't you understand how it all is, how it all came about? Won't you love me again—can't you?" But she restrained herself. It seemed to her that he might understand—that he would, in fact—but that he would never again be faithful, anyhow. And she would so gladly have discarded Lynde and any and all men if he would only have said the word, would only have really and sincerely wished her to do so.

It was one day not long after their morning quarrel in her bedroom that Cowperwood broached the matter of living in New York to Aileen, pointing out that thereby his art collection, which was growing constantly, might be more suitably housed, and that it would give her a second opportunity to enter social life.

"So that you can get rid of me out here," commented Aileen, little knowing of Berenice Fleming.

"Not at all," replied Cowperwood sweetly. "You see how things are. There's no chance of our getting into Chicago society. There's too much financial opposition against me here. If we had a big house in New York, such as I would build, it would be an introduction in itself. After all, these Chicagoans aren't even a snapper on the real society whip. It's the easterners who set the pace, and the New Yorkers most of all. If you want to say the word, I can sell this place and we can live down there, part of the time, anyhow. I could spend as much of my time with you there as I have been doing here—perhaps more."

Because of her soul of vanity Aileen's mind ran forward in spite of herself to the wider opportunities which his words suggested. This house had become a nightmare to her—a place of neglect and bad memories. Here she had fought with Rita Sohlberg; here she had seen society come for a very little while only to disappear; here she had waited this long time for the renewal of Cowperwood's love, which was now obviously never to be restored in its original glamour. As he spoke she looked at him quizzically, almost sadly, in her great doubt. At the same time she could not help reflecting that in New York, where money counted for so much, and with Cowperwood's great and growing wealth and prestige behind her, she might hope to find herself socially at last. "Nothing venture, nothing have" had always been her motto, nailed to her mast, though her equipment for the life she now craved had never been more than the veriest make-believe—painted wood and tinsel. Vain, radiant, hopeful Aileen. Yet how was she to know?

"Very well," she observed finally. "Do as you like. I can live down there as well as I can here, I presume—alone."

Cowperwood knew the nature of her longings. He knew what was running in her mind, and how futile were her dreams. Life had taught him how fortuitous must be the circumstances which could enable a woman of Aileen's handicaps and defects to enter that cold upper world. Yet for all the courage of him, for the very life of him, he could not tell her. He could not forget that once, behind the grim bars in the penitentiary for the Eastern District of Pennsylvania, he had cried on her shoulder. He could not be an ingrate and wound her with his inmost thoughts any more than he could deceive himself. A New York mansion and the dreams of social supremacy which she might there entertain would soothe her ruffled vanity and assuage her disappointed heart; and at the same time he would be nearer

Berenice Fleming. Say what one will of these ferret windings
of the human mind, they are, nevertheless, true and characteristic of the average human being, and Cowperwood was
no exception. He saw it all, he calculated on it—he calculated on the simple humanity of Aileen.

CHAPTER XLVI

Depths and Heights

The complications which had followed his various
sentimental affairs left Cowperwood in a quandary at times
as to whether there could be any peace or satisfaction outside of monogamy, after all. Although Mrs. Hand had gone
to Europe at the crisis of her affairs, she had returned to
seek him out. Cecily Haguenin found many opportunities of
writing him letters and assuring him of her undying affection. Florence Cochrane persisted in seeing or attempting to
see him even after his interest in her began to wane. For another thing Aileen, owing to the complication and general
degeneracy of her affairs, had recently began to drink. Owing
to the failure of her affair with Lynde—for in spite of her
yielding she had never had any real heart interest in it—
and to the cavalier attitude with which Cowperwood took
her disloyalty, she had reached that state of speculative
doldrums where the human animal turns upon itself in bitter
self-analysis; the end with the more sensitive or the less
durable is dissipation or even death. Woe to him who places
his faith in illusion—the only reality—and woe to him who
does not. In one way lies disillusion with its pain, in the
other way regret.

After Lynde's departure for Europe, whither she had refused to follow him, Aileen took up with a secondary personage by the name of Watson Skeet, a sculptor. Unlike most
artists, he was the solitary heir of the president of an immense furniture-manufacturing company in which he refused

to take any interest. He had studied abroad, but had returned to Chicago with a view to propagating art in the West.
A large, blond, soft-fleshed man, he had a kind of archaic
naturalness and simplicity which appealed to Aileen. They
had met at the Rhees Griers'. Feeling herself neglected after
Lynde's departure, and dreading loneliness above all things,
Aileen became intimate with Skeet, but to no intense mental
satisfaction. That driving standard within—that obsessing
ideal which requires that all things be measured by it—was
still dominant. Who has not experienced the chilling memory
of the better thing? How it creeps over the spirit of one's
current dreams! Like the specter at the banquet it stands, its
substanceless eyes viewing with a sad philosophy the make-
shift feast. The what-might-have-been of her life with Cowperwood walked side by side with her wherever she went.
Once occasionally indulging in cigarettes, she now smoked
almost constantly. Once barely sipping at wines, cocktails,
brandy and soda, she now took to the latter, or, rather, to a
new whiskey and soda combination known as highball, with
a kind of vehemence which had little to do with a taste for
the thing itself. True, drinking is, after all, a state of mind,
and not an appetite. She had found on a number of occasions when she had been quarreling with Lynde, or was
mentally depressed that in partaking of these drinks a sort of
warm, speculative indifference seized upon her. She was no
longer so sad. She might cry, but it was in a soft, rainy, relieving way. Her sorrows were as strange, enticing figures in
dreams. They moved about and around her, not as things
actually identical with her, but as ills which she could view
at a distance. Sometimes both she and they (for she saw herself also as in a kind of mirage of inverted vision) seemed
beings of another state, troubled, but not bitterly painful.
The old nepenthe of the bottle had seized upon her. After a
few accidental lapses, in which she found it acted as a solace
or sedative, the highball visioned itself to her as a resource.
Why should she not drink if it relieved her, as it actually
did, of physical and mental pain? There were apparently no
bad aftereffects. The whiskey involved was diluted to an almost watery state. It was her custom now when at home
alone to go to the butler's pantry where the liquors were
stored and prepare a drink for herself, or to order a tray
with a siphon and bottle placed in her room. Cowperwood,

noticing the persistence of its presence there and the fact that she drank heavily at table, commented upon it.

"You're not taking too much of that, are you, Aileen?" he questioned one evening, watching her drink down a tumbler of whiskey and water as she sat contemplating a pattern of needlework with which the table was ornamented.

"Certainly I'm not," she replied irritably, a little flushed and thick of tongue. "Why do you ask?" She herself had been wondering whether in the course of time it might not have a depreciating effect on her complexion. This was the only thing that still concerned her—her beauty.

"Well, I see you have that bottle in your room all the time. I was wondering if you might not be forgetting how much you are using it."

Because she was so sensitive he was trying to be tactful.

"Well," she answered crossly, "what if I am? It wouldn't make any particular difference if I did. I might as well drink as do some other things that are done."

It was a kind of satisfaction to her to bait him in this way. His inquiry, being a proof of continued interest on his part, was of some value. At least he was not entirely indifferent to her.

"I wish you wouldn't talk that way, Aileen," he replied. "I have no objection to your drinking some. I don't suppose it makes any difference to you now whether I object or not. But you are too good-looking, too well set up physically, to begin that. You don't need it, and it's such a short road to hell. Your state isn't so bad. Good heavens! many another woman has been in your position. I'm not going to leave you unless you want to leave me. I've told you that over and over. I'm just sorry people change—we all do. I suppose I've changed some, but that's no reason for your letting yourself go to pieces. I wish you wouldn't be desperate about this business. It may come out better than you think in the long run."

He was merely talking to console her.

"Oh! oh! oh!" Aileen suddenly began to rock and cry in a foolish, drunken way, as though her heart would break, and Cowperwood got up. He was horrified after a fashion.

"Oh, don't come near me!" Aileen suddenly exclaimed, sobering in an equally strange way. "I know why you come. I know how much you care about me or my looks. Don't you worry whether I drink or not. I'll drink if I please, or do anything else if I choose. If it helps me over my difficulties, that's my business, not yours." And in defiance she prepared another glass and drank it.

Cowperwood shook his head, looking at her steadily and sorrowfully. "It's too bad, Aileen," he said. "I don't know what to do about you exactly. You oughtn't to go on this way. Whiskey won't get you anywhere. It will simply ruin your looks and make you miserable in the bargain."

"Oh, to hell with my looks!" she snapped. "A lot of good they've done me." And feeling contentious and sad, she got up and left the table. Cowperwood followed her after a time, only to see her dabbing at her eyes and nose with powder. A half-filled glass of whiskey and water was on the dressing table beside her. It gave him a strange feeling of responsibility and helplessness.

Mingled with his anxiety as to Aileen were thoughts of the alternate rise and fall of his hopes in connection with Berenice. She was such a superior girl, developing so definitely as an individual. To his satisfaction she had, on a few recent occasions when he had seen her, unbent sufficiently to talk to him in a friendly and even intimate way, for she was by no means hoity-toity, but a thinking, reasoning being of the profoundest intellectual, or, rather, the highest artistic tendencies. She was so carefree, living in a high and solitary world, at times apparently enwrapped in thoughts serene, at other times sharing vividly in the current interests of the social world of which she was a part, and which she dignified as much as it dignified her.

One Sunday morning at Pocono, in late June weather, when he had come East to rest for a few days, and all was still and airy on the high ground which the Carter cottage occupied, Berenice came out on the veranda where Cowperwood was sitting, reading a fiscal report of one of his companies and meditating on his affairs. By now they had become somewhat more *simpatico* than formerly, and Berenice had an easy, genial way in his presence. She liked him, rather. With an indescribable smile which wrinkled her nose and eyes, and played about the corners of her mouth, she said:

"Now I am going to catch a bird."

"A what?" asked Cowperwood, looking up and pretending he had not heard, though he had. He was all eyes for any movement of hers. She was dressed in a flouncy morning gown eminently suitable for the world in which she was moving.

"A bird," she replied, with an airy toss of her head. "This is June-time, and the sparrows are teaching their young to fly."

Cowperwood, previously engrossed in financial speculations, was translated, as by the wave of a fairy wand, into another realm, where birds and fledglings and grass and the light winds of heaven were more important than brick and stone and stocks and bonds. He got up and followed her flowing steps across the grass to where, near a clump of alder bushes, she had seen a mother sparrow enticing a fledgling to take wing. From her room upstairs she had been watching this bit of outdoor sociology. It suddenly came to Cowperwood, with great force, how comparatively unimportant in the great drift of life were his own affairs when about him was operative all this splendid will to existence, as sensed by her. He saw her stretch out her hands downward, and run in an airy, graceful way, stooping here and there, while before her fluttered a baby sparrow, until suddenly she dived quickly, and then, turning, her face agleam, cried: "See, I have him! He wants to fight, too! Oh, you little dear!"

She was holding "him," as she chose to characterize it, in the hollow of her hand, the head between her thumb and forefinger, with the forefinger of her free hand petting it the while she laughed and kissed it. It was not so much bird love as the artistry of life and of herself that was moving her. Hearing the parent bird chirping distractedly from a nearby limb, she turned and called: "Don't make such a row! I shan't keep him long."

Cowperwood laughed—trig in the morning sun. "You can scarcely blame her," he commented.

"Oh, she knows well enough I wouldn't hurt him," Berenice replied spiritedly, as though it were literally true.

"Does she, indeed?" inquired Cowperwood. "Why do you say that?"

"Because it's true. Don't you think they know when their children are really in danger?"

"But why should they?" persisted Cowperwood, charmed and interested by the involute character of her logic. She was quite deceptive to him. He could not be sure what she thought.

She merely fixed him a moment with her cool, slate-blue

eyes. "Do you think the senses of the world are only five?"
she asked, in the most charming and nonreproachful way.
"Indeed, they know well enough. She knows." She turned and
waved a graceful hand in the direction of the tree, where
peace now reigned. The chirping had ceased. "She knows I
am not a cat."

Again that enticing, mocking smile that wrinkled her nose,
her eye corners, her mouth. The word "cat" had a sharp,
sweet sound in her mouth. It seemed to be bitten off closely
with force and airy spirit. Cowperwood surveyed her as he
would have surveyed the ablest person he knew. Here was a
woman, he saw, who could and would command the utmost
reaches of his soul in every direction. If he interested her at
all, he would need them all. The eyes of her were at once
so elusive, so direct, so friendly, so cool and keen. "You will
have to be interesting, indeed, to interest me," they seemed
to say; and yet they were by no means averse, apparently,
to a hearty camaraderie. That nose-wrinkling smile said as
much. Here was by no means a Stephanie Platow, nor
yet a Rita Sohlberg. He could not assume her as he had
Ella Hubby, or Florence Cochrane, or Cecily Haguenin.
Here was an iron individuality with a soul for romance and
art and philosophy and life. He could not take her as he had
those others. And yet Berenice was really beginning to think
more than a little about Cowperwood. He must be an extraor-
dinary man; her mother said so, and the newspapers were
always mentioning his name and noting his movements.

A little later, at Southampton, whither she and her mother
had gone, they met again. Together with a young man by the
name of Greanelle, Cowperwood and Berenice had gone into
the sea to bathe. It was a wonderful afternoon. To the east
and south and west spread the sea, a crinkling floor of blue,
and to their left, as they faced it, was a lovely outward-
curving shore of tawny sand. Studying Berenice in blue
silk bathing costume and shoes, Cowperwood had been
stung by the wonder of passing life—how youth comes in,
ever fresh and fresh, and age goes out. Here he was, long,
crowded years of conflict and experience behind him, and
yet this twenty-year-old girl, with her incisive mind and keen
tastes, was apparently as wise in matters of general import as
himself. He could find no flaw in her armor in those matters
which they could discuss. Her knowledge and comments
were so ripe and sane, despite a tendency to pose a little,

which was quite within her rights. Because Greanelle had bored her a little she had shunted him off and was amusing herself talking to Cowperwood, who fascinated her by his compact individuality.

"Do you know," she confided to him on this occasion, "I get so very tired of young men sometimes. They can be so inane. I do declare, they are nothing more than shoes and ties and socks and canes strung together in some unimaginable way. Vaughn Greanelle is for all the world like a perambulating mannequin today. He is just an English suit with a cane attached walking about."

"Well, bless my soul," commented Cowperwood, "what an indictment!"

"It's true," she replied. "He knows nothing at all except polo, and the latest swimming stroke, and where everybody is, and who is going to marry who. Isn't it dull?"

She tossed her head back and breathed as though to exhale the fumes of the dull and the inane from her inmost being.

"Did you tell him that?" inquired Cowperwood curiously.

"Certainly I did."

"I don't wonder he looks so solemn," he said, turning and looking back at Greanelle and Mrs. Carter; they were sitting side by side in sand chairs, the former beating the sand with his toes. "You're a curious girl, Berenice," he went on familiarly. "You are so direct and vital at times."

"Not any more than you are, from all I can hear," she replied, fixing him with those steady eyes. "Anyhow, why should I be bored? He is so dull. He follows me around out here all the time, and I don't want him."

She tossed her head and began to run up the beach to where bathers were fewer and fewer, looking back at Cowperwood as if to say, "Why don't you follow?" He developed a burst of enthusiasm and ran quite briskly, overtaking her near some shallows, where, because of a sandbar offshore, the waters were thin and bright.

"Oh, look!" exclaimed Berenice when he came up. "See, the fish! O-oh!"

She dashed in to where a few feet offshore a small school of minnows as large as sardines were playing, silvery in the sun. She ran as she had for the bird, doing her best to frighten them into a neighboring pocket or pool farther up on the shore. Cowperwood, as gay as a boy of ten, joined in the chase. He raced after them briskly, losing one school, but pocketing another a little farther on and calling to her to come.

"Oh!" exclaimed Berenice at one point. "Here they are now. Come quick! Drive them in here!"

Her hair was blowy, her face a keen pink, her eyes an electric blue by contrast. She was bending low over the water—Cowperwood also—their hands outstretched, the fish, some five in all, nervously dancing before them in their efforts to escape. All at once, having forced them into a corner, they dived; Berenice actually caught one. Cowperwood missed by a fraction, but drove the fish she did catch into her hands.

"Oh," she exclaimed, jumping up, "how wonderful! It's alive. I caught it."

She danced up and down, and Cowperwood, standing before her, was sobered by her charm. He felt an impulse to speak to her of his affection, to tell her how delicious she was to him.

"You," he said, pausing over the word and giving it special emphasis—"you are the only thing here that is wonderful to me."

She looked at him a moment, the live fish in her extended hands, her eyes keying to the situation. For the least fraction of a moment she was uncertain, as he could see, how to take this. Many men had been approximative before. It was common to have compliments paid to her. But this was different. She said nothing, but fixed him with a look which said quite plainly, "You had better not say anything more just now, I think." Then, seeing that he understood, that his manner softened, and that he was troubled, she crinkled her nose gaily and added: "It's like fairyland. I feel as though I had caught it out of another world." Cowperwood understood. The direct approach was not for use in her case; and yet there was something, a camaraderie, a sympathy, which he felt and which she felt. A girl's school, conventions, the need of socially placing herself, her conservative friends and their viewpoint—all were working here. If he were only single now, she told herself, she would be willing to listen to him in a very different spirit, for he was charming. But this way— And he, for his part, concluded that here was one woman whom he would gladly marry if she would have him.

CHAPTER XLVII

American Match

Following Cowperwood's coup in securing cash by means of his seeming gift of $300,000 for a telescope, his enemies rested for a time, but only because of lack of ideas wherewith to destroy him. Public sentiment—created by the newspapers—was still against him. Yet his franchises had still from eight to ten years to run, and meanwhile he might make himself unassailably powerful. For the present he was busy, surrounded by his engineers and managers and legal advisers, constructing his several elevated lines at a whirlwind rate. At the same time, through Videra, Kaffrath, and Addison, he was effecting a scheme of loaning money on call to the local Chicago banks—the very banks which were most opposed to him—so that in a crisis he could retaliate. By manipulating the vast quantity of stocks and bonds of which he was now the master he was making money hand over fist, his one rule being that 6 percent was enough to pay any holder who had merely purchased his stock as an outsider. It was most profitable to himself. When his stocks earned more than that he issued new ones, selling them on 'change and pocketing the difference. Out of the cash drawers of his various companies he took immense sums, temporary loans, as it were, which later he had charged by his humble servitors to "construction," "equipment," or "operation." He was like a canny wolf prowling in a forest of trees of his own creation.

The weak note of this whole project of elevated lines was that for some time it was destined to be unprofitable. Its very competition tended to weaken the value of his surface line companies. His holdings in these as well as in elevated road shares were immense. If anything happened to cause them to fall in price immense numbers of these same stocks

362

held by others would be thrown on the market, thus still further depreciating their value and compelling him to come into the market and buy. With the most painstaking care he began at once to pile up a reserve in government bonds for emergency purposes, which he decided should not be less than eight or nine million dollars, for he feared financial storms as well as financial reprisal, and where so much was at stake he did not propose to be caught napping.

At the time that Cowperwood first entered on elevated road construction there was no evidence that any severe depression in the American money market was imminent. But it was not long before a new difficulty began to appear. It was now the day of the trust in all its watery magnificence. Coal, iron, steel, oil, machinery, and a score of other commercial necessities had already been "trustified," and others, such as leather, shoes, cordage, and the like, were almost hourly being brought under the control of shrewd and ruthless men. Already in Chicago Schryhart, Hand, Arneel, Merrill, and a score of others were seeing their way to amazing profits by underwriting these ventures, which required ready cash, and to which lesser magnates, content with a portion of the leavings of Dives's table, were glad to bring to their attention. On the other hand, in the nation at large there was growing up a feeling that at the top there were a set of giants—Titans—who, without heart or soul, and without any understanding of or sympathy with the condition of the rank and file, were setting forth to enchain and enslave them. The vast mass, writhing in ignorance and poverty, finally turned with pathetic fury to the cure-all of a political leader in the West. This latter prophet, seeing gold becoming scarcer and scarcer and the cash and credits of the land falling into the hands of a few who were manipulating them for their own benefit, had decided that what was needed was a greater volume of currency, so that credits would be easier and money cheaper to come by in the matter of interest. Silver, of which there was a superabundance in the mines, was to be coined at the ratio of sixteen dollars of silver for every one of gold in circulation, and the parity of the two metals maintained by fiat of government. Never again should the few be able to make a weapon of the people's medium of exchange in order to bring about their undoing. There was to be ample money, far beyond the control of central banks and the men in

power over them. It was a splendid dream worthy of a
charitable heart, but because of it a disturbing war for
political control of the government was shortly threatened
and soon began. The money element, sensing the danger of
change involved in the theories of the new political leader,
began to fight him and the element in the Democratic party
which he represented. The rank and file of both parties—
the more or less hungry and thirsty who lie ever at the
bottom on both sides—hailed him as a heaven-sent deliverer,
a new Moses come to lead them out of the wilderness of
poverty and distress. Woe to the political leader who preaches
a new doctrine of deliverance, and who, out of tenderness
of heart, offers a panacea for human ills. His truly shall be
a crown of thorns.

Cowperwood, no less than other men of wealth, was opposed to what he deemed a crackbrained idea—that of maintaining a parity between gold and silver by law. Confiscation was his word for it—the confiscation of the wealth
of the few for the benefit of the many. Most of all was he
opposed to it because he feared that this unrest, which was
obviously growing, foreshadowed a class war in which investors would run to cover and money be locked in
strongboxes. At once he began to shorten sail, to invest only
in the soundest securities, and to convert all his weaker
ones into cash.

To meet current emergencies, however, he was compelled
to borrow heavily here and there, and in doing so he was
quick to note that those banks representing his enemies in
Chicago and elsewhere were willing to accept his various
stocks as collateral, providing he would accept loans subject to call. He did so gladly, at the same time suspecting
Hand, Schryhart, Arneel, and Merrill of some scheme to
wreck him, providing they could get him where the calling
of his loans suddenly and in concert would financially em-
barrass him. "I think I know what that crew are up to,"
he once observed to Addison at this period. "Well, they will
have to rise very early in the morning if they catch me
napping."

The thing that he suspected was really true. Schryhart,
Hand, and Arneel, watching him through their agents and
brokers, had soon discovered—in the very earliest phases
of the silver agitation and before the real storm broke—that
he was borrowing in New York, in London, in certain quar-

ters of Chicago, and elsewhere. "It looks to me," said Schryhart one day to his friend Arneel, "as if our friend has gotten in a little too deep. He has overreached himself. These elevated road schemes of his have eaten up too much capital. There is another election coming on next fall, and he knows we are going to fight tooth and nail. He needs money to electrify his surface lines. If we could trace out exactly where he stands, and where he has borrowed, we might know what to do."

"Unless I am greatly mistaken," replied Arneel, "he is in a tight place or is rapidly getting there. This silver agitation is beginning to weaken stocks and tighten money. I suggest that our banks here loan him all the money he wants on call. When the time comes, if he isn't ready, we can shut him up tighter than a drum. If we can pick up any other loans he's made anywhere else, well and good."

Mr. Arneel said this without a shadow of bitterness or humor. In some tight hour, perhaps, now fast approaching, Mr. Cowperwood would be promised salvation—"saved" on condition that he should leave Chicago forever. There were those who would take over his property in the interest of the city and upright government and administer it accordingly.

Unfortunately, at this very time Messrs. Hand, Schryhart, and Arneel were themselves concerned in a little venture to which the threatened silver agitation could bode nothing but ill. This concerned so simple a thing as matches, a commodity which at this time, along with many others, had been trustified and was yielding a fine profit. "American Match" was a stock which was already listed on every exchange and which was selling steadily around 120.

The geniuses who had first planned a combination of all match concerns and a monopoly of the trade in America were two men, Messrs. Hull and Stackpole—bankers and brokers, primarily. Mr. Phineas Hull was a small, ferretlike, calculating man with a sparse growth of dusty brown hair and an eyelid, the right one, which was partially paralyzed and drooped heavily, giving him a characterful and yet at times a sinister expression.

His partner, Mr. Benoni Stackpole, had been once a stage driver in Arkansas, and later a horse trader. He was a man of great force and calculation—large, oleaginous, politic, and courageous. Without the ultimate brain capacity of such men as Arneel, Hand, and Merrill, he was, nevertheless, resourceful and able. He had started somewhat late in the race for wealth, but now, with all his strength, he was endeavoring to bring to fruition this plan which, with the aid of Hull, he had formulated. Inspired by the thought of great wealth, they had first secured control of the stock of one match company, and had then put themselves in a position to bargain with the owners of others. The patents and processes controlled by one company and another had been combined, and the field had been broadened as much as possible.

But to do all this a great deal of money had been required, much more than was in possession of either Hull or Stackpole. Both of them being western men, they looked first to western capital. Hand, Schryhart, Arneel, and Merrill were in turn appealed to, and great blocks of the new stock were sold to them at inside figures. By the means thus afforded the combination proceeded apace. Patents for exclusive processes were taken over from all sides, and the idea of invading Europe and eventually controlling the market of the world had its inception. At the same time it occurred to each and all of their lordly patrons that it would be a splendid thing if the stock they had purchased at 45, and which was now selling in open market at 120, should go to 300, where, if these monopolistic dreams were true, it properly belonged. A little more of this stock—the destiny of which at this time seemed sure and splendid—would not be amiss. And so there began a quiet campaign on the part of each capitalist to gather enough of it to realize a true fortune on the rise.

A game of this kind is never played with the remainder of the financial community entirely unaware of what is on foot. In the inner circles of brokerage life rumors were soon abroad that a tremendous boom was in store for American Match. Cowperwood heard of it through Addison, always at the center of financial rumor, and the two of them bought heavily, though not so heavily but that they could clear out at any time with at least a slight margin in their favor. During a period of eight months the stock slowly moved upward, finally crossing the 200 mark and reaching 220, at which figure both Addison and Cowperwood sold, realizing nearly a million between them on their investment.

In the meantime the foreshadowed political storm was

brewing. At first a cloud no larger than a man's hand, it matured swiftly in the late months of 1895, and by the spring of 1896 it had become portentous and was ready to burst. With the climacteric nomination of the "Apostle of Free Silver" for President of the United States, which followed in July, a chill settled down over the conservative and financial elements of the country. What Cowperwood had wisely proceeded to do months before, others less farseeing, from Maine to California and from the Gulf to Canada, began to do now. Bank deposits were in part withdrawn; feeble or uncertain securities were thrown upon the market. All at once Schryhart, Arneel, Hand, and Merrill realized that they were in more or less of a trap in regard to their large holdings in American Match. Having gathered vast quantities of this stock, which had been issued in blocks of millions, it was now necessary to sustain the market or sell at a loss. Since money was needed by many holders, and this stock was selling at 220, telegraphic orders began to pour in from all parts of the country to sell on the Chicago Exchange, where the deal was being engineered and where the market obviously existed. All of the instigators of the deal conferred, and decided to sustain the market. Messrs. Hull and Stackpole, being the nominal heads of the trust, were delegated to buy, they in turn calling on the principal investors to take their share, pro rata. Hand, Schryhart, Arneel, and Merrill, weighted with this inpouring flood of stock, which they had to take at 220, hurried to their favorite banks, hypothecating vast quantities at 150 and over, and using the money so obtained to take care of the additional shares which they were compelled to buy.

At last, however, their favorite banks were full to overflowing and at the danger point. They could take no more.

"No, no, no!" Hand declared to Phineas Hull over the phone. "I can't risk another dollar in this venture, and I won't! It's a perfect proposition. I realize all its merits just as well as you do. But enough is enough. I tell you a financial slump is coming. That's the reason all this stock is coming out now. I am willing to protect my interests in this thing up to a certain point. As I told you, I agree not to throw a single share on the market of all that I now have. But more than that I cannot do. The other gentlemen in this agreement will have to protect themselves as best they can.

I have other things to look out for that are just as important to me, and more so, than American Match."

It was the same with Mr. Schryhart, who, stroking a crisp
black moustache, was wondering whether he had not better
throw over what holdings he had and clear out; however, he
feared the rage of Hand and Arneel for breaking the market
and thus bringing on a local panic. It was risky business.
Arneel and Merrill finally agreed to hold firm to what they
had; but, as they told Mr. Hull, nothing could induce them
to "protect" another share, come what might.

In this crisis naturally Messrs. Hull and Stackpole—esti-
mable gentlemen both—were greatly depressed. By no means
so wealthy as their lofty patrons, their private fortunes were
in much greater jeopardy. They were eager to make any
port in so black a storm. Witness, then, the arrival of Benoni
Stackpole at the office of Frank Algernon Cowperwood. He
was at the end of his tether, and Cowperwood was the only
really rich man in the city not yet involved in this speculation. In the beginning he had heard both Hand and Schryhart
say that they did not care to become involved if Cowperwood was in any way, shape, or manner to be included, but
that had been over a year ago, and Schryhart and Hand
were now, as it were, leaving both him and his partner to
their fates. They could have no objection to his dealing
with Cowperwood in this crisis if he could make sure that
the magnate would not sell him out. Mr. Stackpole was six
feet one in his socks and weighed 230 pounds. Clad in a
brown linen suit and straw hat (for it was late July), he
carried a palm-leaf fan as well as his troublesome stocks in
a small yellow leather bag. He was wet with perspiration and
in a gloomy state of mind. Failure was staring him in the
face—giant failure. If American Match fell below two hundred he would have to close his doors as banker and broker,
and in view of what he was carrying, he and Hull would
fail for approximately twenty million dollars. Messrs. Hand,
Schryhart, Arneel, and Merrill would lose in the neighborhood of six or eight millions between them. The local banks
would suffer in proportion, though not nearly so severely,
for, loaning at 150, they would only sacrifice the difference between that and the lowest point to which the stock
might fall.

Cowperwood eyed the newcomer, when he entered, with
an equivocal eye, for he knew well now what was coming.

Only a few days before he had predicted an eventual smash to Addison.

"Mr. Cowperwood," began Stackpole, "in this bag I have fifteen thousand shares of American Match, par value one million five hundred thousand dollars, market value three million three hundred thousand at this moment, and worth every cent of three hundred dollars a share and more. I don't know how closely you have been following the developments of American Match. We own all the patents on labor-saving machines, and what's more, we're just about to close contracts with Italy and France to lease our machines and processes to them for pretty nearly one million dollars a year each. We're dickering with Austria and England, and of course we'll take up other countries later. The American Match Company will yet make matches for the whole world, whether I'm connected with it or not. This silver agitation has caught us right in mid-ocean, and we're having a little trouble weathering the storm. I'm a perfectly frank man when it comes to close business relations of this kind, and I'm going to tell you just how things stand. If we can scull over this rough place that has come up on account of the silver agitation, our stock will go to three hundred before the first of the year. Now, if you want to take it you can have it outright at one hundred and fifty dollars —that is, providing you'll agree not to throw any of it back on the market before next December; or, if you won't promise that" (he paused to see if by any chance he could read Cowperwood's inscrutable face) "I want you to loan me one hundred and fifty dollars a share on these for thirty days at least at ten or fifteen, or whatever rate you care to fix."

Cowperwood interlocked his fingers and twiddled his thumbs as he contemplated this latest evidence of earthly difficulty and uncertainty. Time and chance certainly happened to all men, and here was one opportunity of paying out those who had been nagging him. To take this stock at 150 on loan and peddle it out swiftly and fully at 220 or less would bring American Match crumbling about their ears. When it was selling at 150 or less he could buy it back, pocket his profit, complete his deal with Mr. Stackpole, pocket his interest, and smile like the well-fed cat in the fable. It was as simple as twiddling his thumbs, which he was now doing.

"Who has been backing this stock here in Chicago besides yourself and Mr. Hull?" he asked pleasantly. "I think that I already know, but I should like to be certain, if you have no objection."

"None in the least, none in the least," replied Mr. Stackpole accommodatingly. "Mr. Hand, Mr. Schryhart, Mr. Arneel, and Mr. Merrill."

"That is what I thought," commented Cowperwood easily. "They can't take this up for you? Is that it? Saturated?"

"Saturated," agreed Mr. Stackpole dully. "But there's one thing I'd have to stipulate in accepting a loan on these. Not a share must be thrown on the market, or, at least, not before I have failed to respond to your call. I have understood that there is a little feeling between you and Mr. Hand and the other gentlemen I have mentioned. But, as I say— and I'm talking perfectly frankly now—I'm in a corner, and it's any port in a storm. If you want to help me I'll make the best terms I can, and I won't forget the favor."

He opened the bag and began to take out the securities— long greenish-yellow bundles, tightly gripped in the center by thick elastic bands. They were in bundles of one thousand shares each. Since Stackpole half proffered them to him, Cowperwood took them in one hand and lightly weighed them up and down.

"I'm sorry, Mr. Stackpole," he said sympathetically, after a moment of apparent reflection, "but I cannot possibly help you in this matter. I'm too involved in other things myself, and I do not often indulge in stock speculations of any kind. I have no particular malice toward any one of the gentlemen you mention. I do not trouble to dislike all who dislike me. I might, of course, if I chose, take these stocks and pay them out and throw them on the market tomorrow, but I have no desire to do anything of the sort. I only wish I could help you, and if I thought I could carry them safely for three or four months I would. As it is—" He lifted his eyebrows sympathetically. "Have you tried all the bankers in town?"

"Practically every one."

"And they can't help you?"

"They are carrying all they can stand now."

"Too bad. I'm sorry, very. By the way, do you happen, by any chance, to know Mr. Millard Bailey or Mr. Edwin Kaffrath?"

"No, I don't," replied Stackpole hopefully.

"Well, now, there are two men who are much richer than is generally supposed. They often have very large sums at their disposal. You might look them up on a chance. Then there's my friend Videra. I don't know how he is fixed at present. You can always find him at the Twelfth Ward Bank. He might be inclined to take a good portion of that—I don't know. He's much better off than most people seem to think. I wonder you haven't been directed to some one of these men before." (As a matter of fact, no one of the individuals in question would have been interested to take a dollar of this loan except on Cowperwood's order, but Stackpole had no reason for knowing this. They were not prominently identified with the magnate.)

"Thank you very much. I will," observed Stackpole, restoring his undesired stocks to his bag.

Cowperwood, with an admirable show of courtesy, called a stenographer, and pretended to secure for his guest the home addresses of these gentlemen. He then bade Mr. Stackpole an encouraging farewell. The distrait promoter at once decided to try not only Bailey and Kaffrath, but Videra; but even as he drove toward the office of the first-mentioned, Cowperwood was personally busy reaching him by telephone.

"I say, Bailey," he called, when he had secured the wealthy lumberman on the wire, "Benoni Stackpole, of Hull & Stackpole, was here to see me just now."

"Yes."

"He has with him fifteen thousand shares of American Match—par value one hundred, market value today two-twenty."

"Yes."

"He is trying to hypothecate the lot or any part of it at one-fifty."

"Yes."

"You know what the trouble with American Match is, don't you?"

"No. I only know it's being driven up to where it is now by a bull campaign."

"Well, listen to me. It's going to break. American Match is going to bust."

"Yes."

"But I want you to loan this man five hundred thousand

dollars at one-twenty or less and then recommend that he go to Edwin Kaffrath or Anton Videra for the balance."

"But, Frank, I haven't any five hundred thousand to spare. You say American Match is going to bust."

"I know you haven't, but draw the check on the Chicago Trust, and Addison will honor it. Send the stock to me and forget all about it. I will do the rest. But under no circumstances mention my name, and don't appear too eager. Not more than one-twenty at the outside, do you hear? and less if you can get it. You recognize my voice, do you?"

"Perfectly."

"Drive over afterward if you have time and let me know what happens."

"Very good," commented Mr. Bailey in a businesslike way.

Cowperwood next called for Mr. Kaffrath. Conversing to similar effect with that individual and with Videra, before three-quarters of an hour Cowperwood had arranged completely for Mr. Stackpole's tour. He was to have his total loan at 120 or less. Checks were to be forthcoming at once. Different banks were to be drawn on—banks other than the Chicago Trust Company. Cowperwood would see, in some roundabout way, that these checks were promptly honored, whether the cash was there or not. In each case the hypothecated stocks were to be sent to him. Then, having seen to the perfecting of this little program, and that the banks to be drawn upon in this connection understood perfectly that the checks in question were guaranteed by him or others, he sat down to await the arrival of his henchmen and the turning of the stock into his private safe.

CHAPTER XLVIII

Panic

On August 4, 1896, the city of Chicago, and for that matter the entire financial world, was startled and amazed by the collapse of American Match, one of the strongest of market securities, and the coincident failure of Messrs. Hull and Stackpole, its ostensible promoters, for twenty millions. As early as eleven o'clock of the preceding day the banking and brokerage world of Chicago, trading in this stock, was fully aware that something untoward was on foot in connection with it. Owing to the high price at which the stock was "protected," and the need of money to liquidate, blocks of this stock from all parts of the country were being rushed to the market with the hope of realizing before the ultimate break. About the stock exchange, which frowned like a gray fortress at the foot of La Salle Street, all was excitement—as though a giant anthill had been ruthlessly disturbed. Clerks and messengers hurried to and fro in confused and apparently aimless directions. Brokers whose supply of American Match had been apparently exhausted on the previous day now appeared on 'change bright and early, and at the clang of the gong began to offer the stock in sizable lots of from two hundred to five hundred shares. The agents of Hull & Stackpole were in the market, of course, in the front rank of the scrambling, yelling throng, taking up whatever stock appeared at the price they were hoping to maintain. The two promoters were in touch by phone and wire not only with those various important personages whom they had induced to enter upon this bull campaign, but with their various clerks and agents on 'change. Naturally, under the circumstances both were in a gloomy frame of mind. This game was no longer moving in those large, easy sweeps which characterize the more favorable aspects of high finance. Sad to relate, as in all the troubled flumes of life where vast currents are compressed in narrow, tortuous spaces, these two men were now concerned chiefly with the momentary care of small but nonetheless heartbreaking burdens. Where to find fifty thousand to take care of this or that burden of stock which was momentarily falling upon them? They were as two men called upon, with their limited hands and strength, to seal up the ever-increasing crevices of a dike beyond which raged a mountainous and destructive sea.

At eleven o'clock Mr. Phineas Hull rose from the chair which sat before his solid mahogany desk, and confronted his partner.

"I'll tell you, Ben," he said, "I'm afraid we can't make this. We've hypothecated so much of this stock around town

that we can't possibly tell who's doing what. I know as well
as I'm standing on this floor that someone, I can't say which
one, is selling us out. You don't suppose it could be Cowperwood or any of those people he sent to us, do you?"

Stackpole, worn by his experiences of the past few weeks,
was inclined to be irritable.

"How should I know, Phineas?" he inquired, scowling in
troubled thought. "I don't think so. I didn't notice any signs
that they were interested in stock gambling. Anyhow, we had
to have the money in some form. Any one of the whole
crowd is apt to get frightened now at any moment and throw
the whole thing over. We're in a tight place, that's plain."

For the fortieth time he plucked at a too-tight collar
and pulled up his shirt-sleeves, for it was stifling, and he
was coatless and waistcoatless. Just then Mr. Hull's telephone bell rang—the one connecting with the firm's private office on 'change, and the latter jumped to seize the
receiver.

"Yes?" he inquired irritably.

"Two thousand shares of American offered at two-twenty!
Shall I take them?"

The man who was phoning was in sight of another man
who stood at the railing of the brokers' gallery overlooking
the pit, or central room of the stock exchange, and who
instantly transferred any sign he might receive to the man
on the floor. So Mr. Hull's "yea" or "nay" would be almost
instantly transmuted into a cash transaction on 'change.

"What do you think of that?" asked Hull of Stackpole,
putting his hand over the receiver's mouth, his right eyelid
drooping heavier than ever. "Two thousand more to take up!
Where d'you suppose they are coming from? Tch!"

"Well, the bottom's out, that's all," replied Stackpole heavily and gutturally. "We can't do what we can't do. I say
this, though: support it at two-twenty until three o'clock.
Then we'll figure up where we stand and what we owe. And
meanwhile I'll see what I can do. If the banks won't help us
and Arneel and that crowd want to get from under, we'll
fail, that's all; but not before I've had one more try, by
Jericho! They may not help us, but—"

Actually Mr. Stackpole did not see what was to be done
unless Messrs. Hand, Schryhart, Merrill, and Arneel were
willing to risk much more money, but it grieved and angered
him to think he and Hull should be thus left to sink without

a sigh. He had tried Kaffrath, Videra, and Bailey, but they were adamant. Thus cogitating, Stackpole put on his wide-brimmed straw hat and went out. It was nearly ninety-six in the shade. The granite and asphalt pavements of the down-town district reflected a dry, Turkish bathroom heat. There was no air to speak of. The sky was a burning, milky blue, with the sun gleaming feverishly upon the upper walls of the tall buildings.

Mr. Hand, in his seventh-story suite of offices in the Rookery Building, was suffering from the heat, but much more from mental perturbation. Though not a stingy or penurious man, it was still true that of all earthly things he suffered most from a financial loss. How often had he seen chance or miscalculation sweep apparently strong and valiant men into the limbo of the useless and forgotten! Since the alienation of his wife's affections by Cowperwood, he had scarcely any interest in the world outside his large financial holdings, which included profitable investments in a half-hundred companies. But they must pay, pay, pay heavily in interest—all of them—and the thought that one of them might become a failure or a drain on his resources was enough to give him an almost physical sensation of dis-satisfaction and unrest, a sort of spiritual and mental nausea which would cling to him for days and days or until he had surmounted the difficulty. Mr. Hand had no least corner in his heart for failure.

As a matter of fact, the situation in regard to American Match had reached such proportions as to be almost numb-ing. Aside from the fifteen thousand shares which Messrs. Hull and Stackpole had originally set aside for themselves, Hand, Arneel, Schryhart, and Merrill had purchased five thousand shares each at 40, but had since been compelled to sustain the market to the extent of over five thousand shares more each, at prices ranging from 120 to 220, the largest blocks of shares having been bought at the latter figure. Actually Hand was caught for nearly $1,500,000, and his soul was as gray as a bat's wing. At fifty-seven years of age men who are used only to the most successful financial calculations and the credit that goes with unerring judgment dread to be made a mark by chance or fate. It opens the way for comment on their possibly failing vitality or judg-ment. And so Mr. Hand sat on this hot August afternoon, ensconced in a large carved mahogany chair in the inner recesses of his inner offices, and brooded. Only this morning, in the face of a falling market, he would have sold out openly had he not been deterred by telephone messages from Arneel and Schryhart suggesting the advisability of a pool conference before any action was taken. Come what might on the morrow, he was determined to quit unless he saw some clear way out—to be shut of the whole thing unless the ingenuity of Stackpole and Hull should discover a way of sustaining the market without his aid. While he was meditating on how this was to be done Mr. Stackpole appeared, pale, gloomy, wet with perspiration.

"Well, Mr. Hand," he exclaimed wearily, "I've done all I can. Hull and I have kept the market fairly stable so far. You saw what happened between ten and eleven this morning. The jig's up. We've borrowed our last dollar and hypothecated our last share. My personal fortune has gone into the balance, and so has Hull's. Some one of the outside stockholders, or all of them, are cutting the ground from under us. Fourteen thousand shares since ten o'clock this morning! That tells the story. It can't be done just now— not unless you gentlemen are prepared to go much further than you have yet gone. If we could organize a pool to take care of fifteen thousand more shares—"

Mr. Stackpole paused, for Mr. Hand was holding up a fat pink digit.

"No more of that," he was saying solemnly. "It can't be done. I, for one, won't sink another dollar in this proposition at this time. I'd rather throw what I have on the market and take what I can get. I am sure the others feel the same way."

Mr. Hand, to play safe, had hypothecated nearly all his shares with various banks in order to release his money for other purposes, and he knew he would not dare to throw over all his holdings, just as he knew he would have to make good at the figure at which they had been margined. But it was a fine threat to make.

Mr. Stackpole stared oxlike at Mr. Hand.

"Very well," he said, "I might as well go back, then, and post a notice on our front door. We bought fourteen thousand shares and held the market where it is, but we haven't a dollar to pay for them with. Unless the banks or someone will take them over for us we're gone—we're bankrupt."

Mr. Hand, who knew that if Mr. Stackpole carried out

this decision it meant the loss of his $1,500,000, halted mentally. "Have you been to all the banks?" he asked. "What does Lawrence, of the Prairie National, have to say?"

"It's the same with all of them," replied Stackpole, now quite desperate, "as it is with you. They have all they can carry—every one. It's this damned silver agitation—that's it, and nothing else. There's nothing the matter with this stock. It will right itself in a few months. It's sure to."

"Will it?" commented Mr. Hand sourly. "That depends on what happens next November." (He was referring to the coming national election.)

"Yes, I know," sighed Mr. Stackpole, seeing that it was a condition, and not a theory, that confronted him. Then, suddenly clenching his right hand, he exclaimed, "Damn that upstart!" (He was thinking of the Apostle of Free Silver.) "He's the cause of all this. Well, if there's nothing to be done I might as well be going. There's all those shares we bought today which we ought to be able to hypothecate with somebody. It would be something if we could get even a hundred and twenty on them."

"Very true," replied Hand. "I wish it could be done. I, personally, cannot sink any more money. But why don't you go and see Schryhart and Arneel? I've been talking to them, and they seem to be in a position similar to my own; but if they are willing to confer, I am. I don't see what's to be done, but it may be that all of us together might arrange some way of heading off the slaughter of the stock tomorrow. I don't know. If only we don't have to suffer too great a decline."

Mr. Hand was thinking that Messrs. Hull and Stackpole might be forced to part with all their remaining holdings at fifty cents on the dollar or less. Then if it could possibly be taken and carried by the united banks for them (Schryhart, himself, Arneel) and sold at a profit later, he and his associates might recoup some of their losses. The local banks at the behest of the big quadrumvirate might be coerced into straining their resources still further. But how was this to be done? How, indeed?

It was Schryhart who, in pumping and digging at Stackpole when he finally arrived there, managed to extract from him the truth in regard to his visit to Cowperwood. As a matter of fact, Schryhart himself had been guilty this very

day of having thrown two thousand shares of American
Match on the market, unknown to his confreres. Naturally,
he was eager to learn whether Stackpole or anyone else had
the least suspicion that he was involved. As a consequence
he questioned Stackpole closely, and the latter, being anxious
as to the outcome of his own interests, was not unwilling
to make a clean breast. He had the justification in his own
mind that the quadrumvirate had been ready to desert him,
anyhow.

"Why did you go to him?" exclaimed Schryhart, professing
to be greatly astonished and annoyed, as indeed in one sense
he was. "I thought we had a distinct understanding in the
beginning that under no circumstances was he to be included
in any portion of this. You might as well go to the devil
himself for assistance as go there." At the same time he
was thinking "How fortunate!" Here was not only a loop-
hole for himself in connection with his own subtle side plays,
but also, if the quadrumvirate desired, an excuse for deserting the troublesome fortunes of Hull & Stackpole.

"Well, the truth is," replied Stackpole, somewhat sheepishly
and yet defiantly, "last Thursday I had fifteen thousand shares
on which I had to raise money. Neither you nor any of the
others wanted any more. The banks wouldn't take them. I
called up Rambaud on a chance, and he suggested Cowperwood."

As has been related, Stackpole had really gone to Cowperwood direct, but a lie under the circumstances seemed rather
essential.

"Rambaud!" sneered Schryhart. "Cowperwood's man—he
and all the others. You couldn't have gone to a worse crowd
if you had tried. So that's where this stock is coming from,
beyond a doubt. That fellow or his friends are selling us out.
You might have known he'd do it. He hates us. So you're
through, are you?—not another single trick to turn?"

"Not one," replied Stackpole solemnly.

"Well, that's too bad. You have acted most unwisely in
going to Cowperwood; but we shall have to see what can
be done."

Schryhart's idea, like that of Hand, was to cause Hull &
Stackpole to relinquish all their holdings for nothing to the
banks in order that, under pressure, the latter might carry
the stocks he and the others had hypothecated with them
until such a time as the company might be organized at a

profit. At the same time he was intensely resentful against Cowperwood for having by any fluke of circumstance reaped so large a profit as he must have done. Plainly, the present crisis had something to do with him. Schryhart was quick to call up Hand and Arneel, after Stackpole had gone, suggesting a conference, and together, an hour later, at Arneel's office, they foregathered along with Merrill to discuss this new and very interesting development. As a matter of fact, during the course of the afternoon all of these gentlemen had been growing more and more uneasy. Not that between them they were not eminently capable of taking care of their own losses, but the sympathetic effect of such a failure as this (twenty million dollars), to say nothing of its reaction upon the honor of themselves and the city as a financial center, was a most unsatisfactory if not disastrous thing to contemplate, and now this matter of Cowperwood's having gained handsomely by it all was added to their misery. Both Hand and Arneel growled in opposition when they heard, and Merrill meditated, as he usually did, on the wonder of Cowperwood's subtlety. He could not help liking him.

There is a sort of municipal pride latent in the bosoms of most members of a really thriving community which often comes to the surface under the most trying circumstances. These four men were by no means an exception to this rule. Messrs. Schryhart, Hand, Arneel, and Merrill were concerned as to the good name of Chicago and their united standing in the eyes of eastern financiers. It was a sad blow to them to think that the one great enterprise they had recently engineered—a foil to some of the immense affairs which had recently had their geneses in New York and elsewhere—should have come to so untimely an end. Chicago finance really should not be put to shame in this fashion if it could be avoided. So that when Mr. Schryhart arrived, quite warm and disturbed, and related in detail what he had just learned, his friends listened to him with eager and wary ears.

It was now between five and six o'clock in the afternoon and still blazing outside, though the walls of the buildings on the opposite side of the street were a cool gray, picked out with pools of black shadow. A newsboy's strident voice was heard here and there calling an extra, mingled with the sound of homing feet and streetcars—Cowperwood's streetcars.

"I'll tell you what it is," said Schryhart finally. "It seems to me we have stood just about enough of this man's beggarly interference. I'll admit that neither Hull nor Stackpole had any right to go to him. They laid themselves and us open to just such a trick as has been worked in this case." Mr. Schryhart was righteously incisive, cold, immaculate, waspish. "At the same time," he continued, "any other moneyed man of equal standing with ourselves would have had the courtesy to confer with us and give us, or at least our banks, an opportunity for taking over these securities. He would have come to our aid for Chicago's sake. He had no occasion for throwing these stocks on the market, considering the state of things. He knows very well what the effect of their failure will be. The whole city is involved, but it's little he cares. Mr. Stackpole tells me that he had an express understanding with him, or, rather, with the men who it is plain have been representing him, that not a single share of this stock was to be thrown on the market. As it is, I venture to say not a single share of it is to be found anywhere in any of their safes. I can sympathize to a certain extent with poor Stackpole. His position, of course, was very trying. But there is no excuse—none in the world—for such a stroke of trickery on Cowperwood's part. It's just as we've known all along—the man is nothing but a wrecker. We certainly ought to find some method of ending his career here if possible."

Mr. Schryhart kicked out his well-rounded legs, adjusted his soft-roll collar, and smoothed his short, crisp, wiry, now blackish-gray moustache. His black eyes flashed an undying hate.

At this point Mr. Arneel, with a cogency of reasoning which did not at the moment appear on the surface, inquired: "Do any of you happen to know anything in particular about the state of Mr. Cowperwood's finances at present? Of course we know of the Lake Street L and the Northwestern. I hear he's building a house in New York, and I presume that's drawing on him somewhat. I know he has four hundred thousand dollars in loans from the Chicago Central; but what else has he?"

"Well, there's the two hundred thousand he owes the Prairie National," piped up Schryhart promptly. "From time to time I've heard of several other sums that escape my mind just now."

Mr. Merrill, a diplomatic mouse of a man—gray, Parisian, dandified—was twisting in his large chair, surveying the others with shrewd though somewhat propitiatory eyes. In spite of his old grudge against Cowperwood because of the latter's refusal to favor him in the matter of running street-car lines past his store, he had always been interested in the man as a spectacle. He really disliked the thought of plotting to injure Cowperwood. Just the same, he felt it incumbent to play his part in such a council as this. "My financial agent, Mr. Hill, loaned him several hundred thousand not long ago," he volunteered a little doubtfully. "I presume he has many other outstanding obligations."

Mr. Hand stirred irritably.

"Well, he's owing the Third National and the Lake City as much if not more," he commented. "I know where there are five hundred thousand dollars of his loans that haven't been mentioned here. Colonel Ballinger has two hundred thousand. He must owe Anthony Ewer all of that. He owes the Drovers and Traders all of one hundred and fifty thousand."

On the basis of these suggestions Arneel made a mental calculation, and found that Cowperwood was indebted apparently to the tune of about three million dollars on call, if not more.

"I haven't all the facts," he said at last, slowly and distinctly. "If we could talk with some of the presidents of our banks tonight, we should probably find that there are other items of which we do not know. I do not like to be severe on anyone, but our own situation is serious. Unless something is done tonight Hull & Stackpole will certainly fail in the morning. We are, of course, obligated to the various banks for our loans, and we are in honor bound to do all we can for them. The good name of Chicago and its rank as a banking center is to a certain extent involved. As I have already told Mr. Stackpole and Mr. Hull, I personally have gone as far as I can in this matter. I suppose it is the same with each of you. The only other resources we have under the circumstances are the banks, and they, as I understand it, are pretty much involved with stock on hypothecation. I know, at least, that this is true of the Lake City and the Douglas Trust."

"It's true of nearly all of them," said Hand. Both Schryhart and Merrill nodded assent.

"We are not obligated to Mr. Cowperwood for anything so far as I know," continued Mr. Arneel, after a slight but somewhat portentous pause. "As Mr. Schryhart has suggested here today, he seems to have a tendency to interfere and disturb on every occasion. Apparently he stands obligated to the various banks in the sums we have mentioned. Why shouldn't his loans be called? It would help strengthen the local banks, and possibly permit them to aid in meeting this situation for us. While he might be in a position to retaliate, I doubt it."

Mr. Arneel had no personal opposition to Cowperwood—none, at least, of a deep-seated character. At the same time Hand, Merrill, and Schryhart were his friends. In him, they felt, centered the financial leadership of the city. The rise of Cowperwood, his Napoleonic airs, threatened this. As Mr. Arneel talked he never raised his eyes from the desk where he was sitting. He merely drummed solemnly on the surface with his fingers. The others contemplated him a little tensely, catching quite clearly the drift of his proposal.

"An excellent idea—excellent!" exclaimed Schryhart. "I will join in any program that looks to the elimination of this man. The present situation may be just what is needed to accomplish this. Anyhow, it may help to solve our difficulty. If so, it will certainly be a case of good coming out of evil."

"I see no reason why these loans should not be called," Hand commented. "I'm willing to meet the situation on that basis."

"And I have no particular objection," said Merrill. "I think, however, it would be only fair to give as much notice as possible of any decision we may reach," he added.

"Why not send for the various bankers now," suggested Schryhart, "and find out exactly where he stands, and how much it will take to carry Hull & Stackpole? Then we can inform Mr. Cowperwood of what we propose to do."

To this proposition Mr. Hand nodded an assent, at the same time consulting a large, heavily engraved gold watch of the most ponderous and inartistic design. "I think," he said, "that we have found the solution to this situation at last. I suggest that we get Candish and Kramer, of the stock exchange" (he was referring to the president and secretary, respectively, of that organization), "and Simmons, of the Douglas Trust. We should soon be able to tell what we can do."

The library of Mr. Arneel's home was fixed upon as the most suitable rendezvous. Telephones were forthwith set ringing and messengers and telegrams dispatched in order that the subsidiary financial luminaries and the watchdogs of the various local treasuries might come and, as it were, put their seal on this secret decision, which it was obviously presumed no minor official or luminary would have the temerity to gainsay.

CHAPTER XLIX

Mount Olympus

By eight o'clock, at which hour the conference was set, the principal financial personages of Chicago were truly in a great turmoil. Messrs. Hand, Schryhart, Merrill, and Arneel were personally interested! What would you? As early as seven-thirty there was a pattering of horses' hooves and a jingle of harness, as splendid open carriages were drawn up in front of various exclusive mansions and a bank president, or a director at least, issued forth at the call of one of the big quadrumvirate to journey to the home of Mr. Arneel. Such interesting figures as Samuel Blackman, once president of the old Chicago Gas Company, and now a director of the Prairie National; Hudson Baker, once president of the West Chicago gas company, and now a director of the Chicago Central National; Ormonde Ricketts, publisher of the *Chronicle* and director of the Third National; Norrie Simms, president of the Douglas Trust Company; Walter Rysam Cotton, once an active wholesale coffee broker, but now a director principally of various institutions, were all en route. It was a procession of solemn, superior, thoughtful gentlemen, and all desirous of giving the right appearance and of making the correct impression. For, be it known, of all men none are so proud or vainglorious over the minor trappings of materialism as those who have but newly achieved them. It is so essential, apparently, to fulfill in manner and air, if not in fact, the principle of "presence," which befits the role of conservator of society and leader of wealth. Every one of those named and many more—to the number of thirty—rode thus loftily forth in the hot, dry evening air and were soon at the door of the large and comfortable home of Mr. Timothy Arneel.

That important personage was not as yet present to receive his guests, and neither were Messrs. Schryhart, Hand, nor Merrill. It would not be fitting for such eminent potentates to receive their underlings in person on such an occasion. At the hour appointed these four were still in their respective offices, perfecting separately the details of the plan upon which they had agreed and which, with a show of informality and of momentary inspiration, they would later present. For the time being their guests had to make the best of their absence. Drinks and liquors were served, but these were of small comfort. A rack provided for straw hats was for some reason not used, everyone preferring to retain his own head-gear. Against the background of wood paneling and the chairs covered with summer linen the company presented a galleryesque variety and interest. Messrs. Hull and Stackpole, the corpses or victims over which this serious gathering were about to sit in state, were not actually present within the room, though they were within call in another part of the house, where, if necessary, they could be reached and their advice or explanations heard. This presumably brilliant assemblage of the financial weight and intelligence of the city appeared as solemn as owls under the pressure of a rumored impending financial crisis. Before Arneel's appearance there was a perfect buzz of minor financial gossip, such as:

"You don't say?"

"Is it as serious as that?"

"I knew things were pretty shaky, but I was by no means certain how shaky."

"Fortunately, we are not carrying much of that stock." (This from one of the few really happy bankers.)

"This is a rather serious occasion, isn't it?"

"You don't tell me!"

"Dear, dear!"

Never a word in criticism from any source of either Hand or Schryhart or Arneel or Merrill, though the fact that they were back of the pool was well known. Somehow they were looked upon as benefactors who were calling this conference with a view of saving others from disaster rather than for the purpose of assisting themselves. Such phrases as, "Oh, Mr. Hand! Marvelous man! Marvelous!" or, "Mr. Schryhart—

very able—very able indeed!" or, "You may depend on it
these men are not going to allow anything serious to overtake the affairs of the city at this time," were heard on every
hand. The fact that immense quantities of cash or paper
were involved in behalf of one or another of these four was
secretly admitted by one banker to another. No rumor that
Cowperwood or his friends had been profiting or were in any
way involved had come to anyone present—not as yet.

At eight-thirty exactly Mr. Arneel first ambled in quite in-
formally, Hand, Schryhart, and Merrill appearing separately
very shortly after. Rubbing their hands and mopping their
faces with their handkerchiefs, they looked about them, making an attempt to appear as nonchalant and cheerful as possible under such trying circumstances. There were many old
acquaintances and friends to greet, inquiries to be made as to
the health of wives and children. Mr. Arneel, clad in yellowish linen, with a white silk shirt of lavender stripe, and carrying a palm-leaf fan, seemed quite refreshed; his fine ex-
panse of neck and bosom looked most paternal, and even
Abrahamesque. His round, glistening pate exuded beads of
moisture. Mr. Schryhart, on the contrary, for all the heat,
appeared quite hard and solid, as though he might be carved
out of some dark wood. Mr. Hand, much of Mr. Arneel's
type, but more solid and apparently more vigorous, had
donned for the occasion a blue serge coat with trousers of an
almost gaudy, bright stripe. His ruddy, archaic face was at
once encouraging and serious, as though he were saying,
"My dear children, this is very trying, but we will do the best
we can." Mr. Merrill was as cool and ornate and lazy as it
was possible for a great merchant to be. To one person and
another he extended a cool, soft hand, nodding and smiling
half the time in silence. To Mr. Arneel as the foremost citizen and the one of largest wealth fell the duty (by all agreed
as most appropriate) of assuming the chair—which in this
case was an especially large one at the head of the table.

There was a slight stir as he finally, at the suggestion of
Schryhart, went forward and sat down. The other great men
found seats.

"Well, gentlemen," began Mr. Arneel dryly (he had a low,
husky voice), "I'll be as brief as I can. This is a very unusual
occasion which brings us together. I suppose you all know
how it is with Mr. Hull and Mr. Stackpole. American Match
is likely to come down with a crash in the morning if some-

thing very radical isn't done tonight. It is at the suggestion of a number of men and banks that this meeting is called."

Mr. Arneel had an informal, tête-à-tête way of speaking, as if he were sitting on a chaise longue with one other person.

"The failure," he went on firmly, "if it comes, as I hope it won't, will make a lot of trouble for a number of banks and private individuals which we would like to avoid, I am sure. The principal creditors of American Match are our local banks and some private individuals who have loaned money on the stock. I have a list of them here, along with the amounts for which they are responsible. It is in the neighborhood of ten millions of dollars."

Mr. Arneel, with the unconscious arrogance of wealth and power, did not trouble to explain how he got the list; neither did he show the slightest perturbation. He merely fished down in one pocket in a heavy way and produced it, spreading it out on the table before him. The company wondered whose names and what amounts were down, and whether it was his intention to read it.

"Now," resumed Mr. Arneel seriously, "I want to say here that Mr. Stackpole, Mr. Merrill, Mr. Hand, and myself have been to a certain extent investors in this stock, and up to this afternoon we felt it to be our duty, not so much to ourselves as to the various banks which have accepted this stock as collateral, and to the city at large, to sustain it as much as possible. We believed in Mr. Hull and Mr. Stackpole. We might have gone still further if there had been any hope that a number of others could carry the stock without seriously injuring themselves; but in view of recent developments we know that this can't be done. For some time Mr. Hull and Mr. Stackpole and the various bank officers have had reason to think that someone has been cutting the ground from under them, and now they know it. It is because of this, and because only concerted action on the part of banks and individuals can save the financial credit of the city at this time, that this meeting is called. Stocks are going to continue to be thrown on the market. It is possible that Hull & Stackpole may have to liquidate in some way. One thing is certain: unless a large sum of money is gathered to meet the claim against them in the morning, they will fail. The trouble is due indirectly, of course, to this silver agitation; but it is due a great deal more, we believe, to a piece of local sharp dealing which has just come to light, and which has really been the cause of putting the financial community in the tight place where it stands tonight. I might as well speak plainly as to this matter. It is the work of one man—Mr. Cowperwood. American Match might have pulled through and the city have been spared the danger which now confronts it if Mr. Hull and Mr. Stackpole had not made the mistake of going to this man."

Mr. Arneel paused, and Mr. Norrie Simms, more excitable than most by temperament, chose to exclaim bitterly: "The wrecker!" A stir of interest passed over the others, accompanied by murmurs of disapproval.

"The moment he got the stock in his hands as collateral," continued Mr. Arneel solemnly, "and in the face of an agreement not to throw a share on the market, he has been unloading steadily. That is what has been happening yesterday and today. Over fifteen thousand shares of this stock, which cannot very well be traced to outside sources, have been thrown on the market, and we have every reason to believe that all of it comes from the same place. The result is that American Match, and Mr. Hull and Mr. Stackpole, are on the verge of collapse."

"The scoundrel!" repeated Mr. Norrie Simms bitterly, almost rising to his feet. The Douglas Trust Company was heavily interested in American Match.

"What an outrage!" commented Mr. Lawrence of the Prairie National, which stood to lose at least $300,000 in shrinkage of values on hypothecated stock alone. To this bank that Cowperwood owed at least $300,000 on call.

"Depend on it to find his devil's hoof in it somewhere," observed Jordan Jules, who had never been able to make any satisfactory progress in his fight on Cowperwood in connection with the city council and the development of the Chicago General Company. The Chicago Central, of which he was now a director, was one of the banks from which Cowperwood had judiciously borrowed.

"It's a pity he should be allowed to go on bedeviling the town in this fashion," observed Mr. Sunderland Sledd to his neighbor, Mr. Duane Kingsland, who was a director in a bank controlled by Mr. Hand.

The latter, as well as Schryhart, observed with satisfaction the effect of Mr. Arneel's words on the company.

Mr. Arneel now again fished in his pocket laboriously, and

drew forth a second slip of paper which he spread out before him. "This is a time when frankness must prevail," he went on solemnly, "if anything is to be done, and I am in hopes that we can do something. I have here a memorandum of some of the loans which the local banks have made to Mr. Cowperwood and which are still standing on their books. I want to know if there are any further loans of which any of you happen to know and which you are willing to mention at this time."

He looked solemnly around.

Immediately several loans were mentioned by Mr. Cotton and Mr. Osgood which had not been heard of previously. The company was now very well aware, in a general way, of what was coming.

"Well, gentlemen," continued Mr. Arneel, "I have, previous to this meeting, consulted with a number of our leading men. They agree with me that since so many banks are in need of funds to carry this situation, and since there is no particular obligation on anybody's part to look after the interests of Mr. Cowperwood, it might be just as well if these loans of his, which are outstanding, were called, and the money used to aid the banks and the men who have been behind Mr. Hull and Mr. Stackpole. I have no personal feeling against Mr. Cowperwood—that is, he has never done me any direct injury—but naturally I cannot approve of the course he has seen fit to take in this case. Now, if there isn't money available from some source to enable you gentlemen to turn around, there will be a number of other failures. Runs may be started on a half-dozen banks. Time is the essence of a situation like this, and we haven't any time."

Mr. Arneel paused and looked around. A slight buzz of conversation sprang up, mostly bitter and destructive criticism of Cowperwood.

"It would be only just if he could be made to pay for this," commented Mr. Blackman to Mr. Sledd. "He has been allowed to play fast and loose long enough. It is time some-one called a halt on him."

"Well, it looks to me as though it would be done tonight," Mr. Sledd returned.

Meanwhile, Mr. Schryhart was again rising to his feet. "I think," he was saying, "if there is no objection on any-one's part, Mr. Arneel, as chairman, might call for a formal expression of opinion from the different gentlemen present, which will be on record as the sense of this meeting."

At this point Mr. Kingsland, a tall, whiskered gentleman, arose to inquire exactly how it came that Cowperwood had secured these stocks, and whether those present were absolutely sure that the stock had been coming from him or from his friends. "I would not like to think we were doing any man an injustice," he concluded.

In reply to this Mr. Schryhart called in Mr. Stackpole to corroborate him. Some of the stocks had been positively identified. Stackpole related the full story, which somehow seemed to electrify the company, so intense was the feeling against Cowperwood.

"It is amazing that men should be permitted to do things like this and still hold up their heads in the business world," said one Mr. Vasto, president of the Third National, to his neighbor.

"I should think there would be no difficulty in securing united action in a case of this kind," said Mr. Lawrence, president of the Prairie National, who was very much beholden to Hand for past and present favors.

"Here is a case," put in Schryhart, who was merely waiting for an opportunity to explain further, "in which an unexpected political situation develops an unexpected crisis, and this man uses it for his personal aggrandizement and to the detriment of every other person. The welfare of the city is nothing to him. The stability of the very banks he borrows from is nothing. He is a pariah, and if this opportunity to show him what we think of him and his methods is not used we will be doing less than our duty to the city and to one another."

"Gentlemen," said Mr. Arneel finally, after Cowperwood's different loans had been carefully tabulated, "don't you think it would be wise to send for Mr. Cowperwood and state to him directly the decision we have reached and the reason for it? I presume all of us would agree that he should be notified."

"I think he should be notified," said Mr. Merrill, who saw behind this smooth talk the iron club that was being brandished.

Both Hand and Schryhart looked at each other and Arneel while they politely waited for someone else to make a suggestion. When no one ventured, Hand, who was hoping this would prove a ripping blow to Cowperwood, remarked viciously:

"He might as well be told—if we can reach him. It's sufficient notice, in my judgment. He might as well understand that this is the united action of the leading financial forces of the city."

"Quite so," added Mr. Schryhart. "It is time he understood, I think, what the moneyed men of this community think of him and his crooked ways."

A murmur of approval ran around the room.

"Very well," said Mr. Arneel. "Anson, you know him better than some of the rest of us. Perhaps you had better see if you can get him on the telephone and ask him to call. Tell him that we are here in executive session."

"I think he might take it more seriously if you spoke to him, Timothy," replied Merrill.

Arneel, being always a man of action, arose and left the room, seeking a telephone which was located in a small workroom or office den on the same floor, where he could talk without fear of being overheard.

Sitting in his library on this particular evening, and studying the details of half a dozen art catalogues which had accumulated during the week, Cowperwood was decidedly conscious of the probable collapse of American Match on the morrow. Through his brokers and agents he was well aware that a conference was on at this hour at the house of Arneel. More than once during the day he had seen bankers and brokers who were anxious about possible shrinkage in connection with various hypothecated securities, and tonight his valet had called him to the phone half a dozen times to talk with Addison, with Kaffrath, with a broker by the name of Prosser who had succeeded Laughlin in active control of his private speculations, and also, be it said, with several of the banks whose presidents were at this particular conference. If Cowperwood was hated, mistrusted, or feared by the overlords of these institutions, such was by no means the case with the underlings, some of whom, through being merely civil, were hopeful of securing material benefits from him at some future time. With a feeling of amused satisfaction he was meditating upon how heavily and neatly he had countered on his enemies. Whereas they were speculating as to how to offset their heavy losses on the morrow, he was congratulating himself on corresponding gains. When all his deals should be closed up he would clear within the neighborhood of a million dollars. He did not feel that he had worked Messrs. Hull and Stackpole any great injustice. They were at their wits' end. If he had not seized this opportunity to undercut them Schryhart or Arneel would have done so, anyhow.

Mingled with thoughts of a forthcoming financial triumph were others of Berenice Fleming. There are such things as figments of the brain, even in the heads of colossuses. He thought of Berenice early and late; he even dreamed of her. He laughed at himself at times for thus being taken in the toils of a mere girl—the strands of her ruddy hair—but working in Chicago these days he was always conscious of her, of what she was doing, of where she was going in the East, of how happy he would be if they were only together, happily mated.

It had so happened, unfortunately, that in the course of this summer's stay at Narragansett Berenice, among other diversions, had assumed a certain interest in one Lieutenant Lawrence Braxmar, U.S.N., whom she found loitering there, and who was then connected with the naval station at Portsmouth, New Hampshire. Cowperwood, coming East at this time for a few days' stay in order to catch another glimpse of his ideal, had been keenly disturbed by the sight of Braxmar and by what his presence might signify. Up to this time he had not given much thought to younger men in connection with her. Engrossed in her personality, he could think of nothing as being able to stand long between him and the fulfillment of his dreams. Berenice must be his. That radiant spirit, enwrapped in so fair an outward seeming, must come to see and rejoice in him. Yet she was so young and airy in her mood that he sometimes wondered. How was he to draw near? What say exactly? What do? Berenice was in no way hypnotized by either his wealth or fame. She was accustomed (she little knew to what extent by his courtesy) to a world more resplendent in its social security than his own. Surveying Braxmar keenly upon their first meeting, Cowperwood had liked his face and intelligence, had judged him to be able, but had wondered instantly how he could get rid of him. Viewing Berenice and the lieutenant as they strolled off together along a summery seaside veranda, he had been for once lonely, and had sighed. These uncertain phases of affection could become very trying at times. He wished he were young again, single.

Tonight, therefore, this thought was haunting him like a gloomy undertone, when at half past eleven the telephone rang once more, and he heard a low, even voice which said:

"Mr. Cowperwood? This is Mr. Arneel."

"Yes."

"A number of the principal financial men of the city are gathered here at my house this evening. The question of ways and means of preventing a panic tomorrow is up for discussion. As you probably know, Hull & Stackpole are in trouble. Unless something is done for them tonight they will certainly fail tomorrow for twenty million dollars. It isn't so much their failure that we are considering as it is the effect on stocks in general, and on the banks. As I understand it, a number of your loans are involved. The gentlemen here have suggested that I call you up and ask you to come here, if you will, to help us decide what ought to be done. Something very drastic will have to be decided on before morning."

During this speech Cowperwood's brain had been reciprocating like a well-oiled machine.

"My loans?" he inquired suavely. "What have they to do with the situation? I don't owe Hull & Stackpole anything."

"Very true. But a number of the banks are carrying securities for you. The idea is that a number of these will have to be called—the majority of them—unless some other way can be devised tonight. We thought you might possibly wish to come and talk it over, and that you might be able to suggest some other way out."

"I see," replied Cowperwood caustically. "The idea is to sacrifice me in order to save Hull & Stackpole. Is that it?"

His eyes, quite as though Arneel were before him, emitted malicious sparks.

"Well, not precisely that," replied Arneel conservatively; "but something will have to be done. Don't you think you had better come over?"

"Very good. I'll come," was the cheerful reply. "It isn't anything that can be discussed over the phone anyhow."

He hung up the receiver and called for his runabout. On the way over he thanked the prevision which had caused him, in anticipation of some such attack as this, to set aside in the safety vaults of the Chicago Trust Company several

millions in low-interest-bearing government bonds. Now, if
worst came to worst, these could be drawn on and hypothecated. These men should see at last how powerful he was
and how secure.

As he entered the home of Arneel he was a picturesque and
truly representative figure of his day. In a light summer suit
of cream and gray twill, with a straw hat ornamented by a
blue and white band, and wearing yellow quarter-shoes of
the softest leather, he appeared a very model of trig, well-
groomed self-sufficiency. As he was ushered into the room he
gazed about him in a brave, leonine way.

"A fine night for a conference, gentlemen," he said, walking toward a chair indicated by Mr. Arneel. "I must say I
never saw so many straw hats at a funeral before. I understand that my obsequies are contemplated. What can I do?"

He beamed in a genial, sufficient way, which in anyone
else would have brought a smile to the faces of the company. In him it was an implication of basic power which
secretly enraged and envenomed nearly all those present.
They merely stirred in a nervous and wholly antagonistic
way. A number of those who knew him personally nodded
—Merrill, Lawrence, Simms; but there was no friendly light
in their eyes.

"Well, gentlemen?" he inquired after a moment or two
of ominous silence, observing Hand's averted face and Schryhart's eyes, which were lifted ceilingward.

"Mr. Cowperwood," began Mr. Arneel quietly, in no way
disturbed by Cowperwood's jaunty air, "as I told you over
the phone, this meeting is called to avert, if possible, what
is likely to be a very serious panic in the morning. Hull &
Stackpole are on the verge of failure. The outstanding loans
are considerable—in the neighborhood of seven or eight
million here in Chicago. On the other hand, there are assets
in the shape of American Match stocks and other properties
sufficient to carry them for a while longer if the banks can
only continue their loans. As you know, we are all facing a
falling market, and the banks are short of ready money.
Something has to be done. We have canvassed the situation
here tonight as thoroughly as possible, and the general conclusion is that your loans are among the most available
assets which can be reached quickly. Mr. Schryhart, Mr.
Merrill, Mr. Hand, and myself have done all we can thus
far to avert a calamity, but we find that someone with whom

Hull & Stackpole have been hypothecating stocks has been feeding them out in order to break the market. We shall know how to avoid that in the future" (and he looked hard at Cowperwood), "but the thing at present is immediate cash and your loans are the largest and the most available. Do you think you can find the means to pay them back in the morning?"

Arneel blinked his keen blue eyes solemnly, while the rest, like a pack of genial but hungry wolves, sat and surveyed this apparently whole but now condemned scapegoat and victim. Cowperwood, who was keenly alive to the spirit of the company, looked blandly and fearlessly around. On his knee he held his blue-banded straw hat neatly balanced on one edge. His full moustache curled upward in a jaunty, arrogant way.

"I can meet my loans," he replied easily. "But I would not advise you or any of the gentlemen present to call them." His voice, for all its lightness, had an ominous ring.

"Why not?" inquired Hand grimly and heavily, turning squarely about and facing him. "It doesn't appear that you have extended any particular courtesy to Hull or Stackpole." His face was red and scowling.

"Because," replied Cowperwood, smiling, and ignoring the reference to his trick, "I know why this meeting was called. I know that these gentlemen here, who are not saying a word, are mere cat's-paws and rubber stamps for you and Mr. Schryhart and Mr. Arneel and Mr. Merrill. I know how you four gentlemen have been gambling in this stock, and what your probable losses are, and that it is to save yourselves from further loss that you have decided to make me the scapegoat. I want to tell you here"—and he got up, so that in his full stature he loomed over the room—"you can't do it. You can't make me your cat's-paw to pull your chestnuts out of the fire, and no rubber-stamp conference can make any such attempt successful. If you want to know what to do, I'll tell you—close the Chicago Stock Exchange tomorrow morning and keep it closed. Then let Hull & Stackpole fail, or if not you four put up the money to carry them. If you can't, let your banks do it. If you open the day by calling a single one of my loans before I am ready to pay it, I'll gut every bank from here to the river. You'll have panic, all the panic you want. Good evening, gentlemen."

He drew out his watch, glanced at it, and quickly walked

to the door, putting on his hat as he went. As he bustled jauntily down the wide interior staircase, preceded by a footman to open the door, a murmur of dissatisfaction arose in the room he had just left.

"The wrecker!" reexclaimed Norrie Simms angrily, astounded at this demonstration of defiance.

"The scoundrel!" declared Mr. Blackman. "Where does he get the wealth to talk like that?"

"Gentlemen," said Mr. Arneel, stung to the quick by this amazing effrontery, and yet made cautious by the blazing wrath of Cowperwood, "it is useless to debate this question in anger. Mr. Cowperwood evidently refers to loans which can be controlled in his favor, and of which I for one know nothing. I do not see what can be done until we do know. Perhaps some of you can tell us what they are."

But no one could, and after due calculation advice was borrowed of caution. The loans of Frank Algernon Cowperwood were not called.

CHAPTER L

A New York Mansion

The failure of American Match the next morning was one of those events that stirred the city and the nation and lingered in the minds of men for years. At the last moment it was decided that in lieu of calling Cowperwood's loans Hull & Stackpole had best be sacrificed, the stock exchange closed, and all trading ended. This protected stocks from at least a quotable decline and left the banks free for several days (ten all told) in which to repair their disrupted finances and buttress themselves against the eventual facts. Naturally, the minor speculators throughout the city—those who had expected to make a fortune out of this crash—raged and complained, but, being faced by an adamantine exchange directorate, a subservient press, and the

alliance between the big bankers and the heavy quadrumvirate, there was nothing to be done. The respective bank
presidents talked solemnly of "a mere temporary flurry";
Hand, Schryhart, Merrill, and Arneel went still further into
their pockets to protect their interests; and Cowperwood,
triumphant, was roundly denounced by the smaller fry as a
"buccaneer," a "pirate," a "wolf"—indeed, any opprobrious
term that came into their minds. The larger men faced
squarely the fact that here was an enemy worthy of their
steel. Would he master them? Was he already the dominant
money power in Chicago? Could he thus flaunt their helplessness and his superiority in their eyes and before their underlings and go unwhipped?

"I must give in!" Hosmer Hand had declared to Arneel
and Schryhart, at the close of the Arneel house conference
and as they stood in consultation after the others had departed. "We seem to be beaten tonight, but I, for one, am
not through yet. He has won tonight, but he won't win always. This is a fight to a finish between me and him. The
rest of you can stay in or drop out, just as you wish."

"Hear, hear!" exclaimed Schryhart, laying a fervently sympathetic hand on his shoulder. "Every dollar that I have is at
your service, Hosmer. This fellow can't win eventually. I'm
with you to the end."

Arneel, walking with Merrill and the others to the door,
was silent and dour. He had been cavalierly affronted by
a man who but a few short years before he would have
considered a mere underling. Here was Cowperwood beard-
ing the lion in his den, dictating terms to the principal financial figures of the city, standing up trig and resolute,
smiling in their faces and telling them in so many words
to go to the devil. Mr. Arneel glowered under lowering
brows, but what could he do? "We must see," he said to the
others, "what time will bring. Just now there is nothing much
to do. This crisis has been too sudden. You say you are not
through with him, Hosmer, and neither am I. But we must
wait. We shall have to break him politically in this city,
and I am confident that in the end we can do it." The
others were grateful for his courage even though tomorrow
he and they must part with millions to protect themselves
and the banks. For the first time Merrill concluded that he
would have to fight Cowperwood openly from now on, though
even yet he admired his courage. "But he is too defiant, too

cavalier! A very lion of a man," he said to himself. "A man with the heart of a Numidian lion."

It was true.

From this day on for a little while, and because there was no immediate political contest in sight, there was comparative peace in Chicago, although it more resembled an armed camp operating under the terms of some agreed neutrality than it did anything else. Schryhart, Hand, Arneel, and Merrill were quietly watchful. Cowperwood's chief concern was lest his enemies might succeed in their project of worsting him politically in one or all three of the succeeding elections which were due to occur every two years between now and 1903, at which time his franchises would have to be renewed. As in the past they had made it necessary for him to work against them through bribery and perjury, so in ensuing struggles they might render it more and more difficult for him or his agents to suborn the men elected to office. The subservient and venal councilmen whom he now controlled might be replaced by men who, if no more honest, would be more loyal to the enemy, thus blocking the extension of his franchises. Yet upon a renewal period of at last twenty and preferably fifty years depended the fulfillment of all the colossal things he had begun—his art collection, his new mansion, his growing prestige as a financier, his rehabilitation socially, and the celebration of his triumph by a union, morganatic or otherwise, with someone who would be worthy to share his throne.

It is curious how that first and most potent tendency of the human mind, ambition, becomes finally dominating. Here was Cowperwood at fifty-seven, rich beyond the wildest dream of the average man, celebrated in a local and in some respects in a national way, who was nevertheless feeling that by no means had his true aims been achieved. He was not yet all-powerful as were divers eastern magnates, or even these four or five magnificently moneyed men here in Chicago, who, by plodding thought and labor in many dreary fields such as Cowperwood himself frequently scorned, had reaped tremendous and uncontended profits. How was it, he asked himself, that his path had almost constantly been strewn with stormy opposition and threatened calamity? Was it due to his private immorality? Other men were immoral; the mass, despite religious dogma and folderol theory im-

posed from the top, was generally so. Was it not rather due
to his inability to control without dominating personally—
without standing out fully and clearly in the sight of all
men? Sometimes he thought so. The humdrum conventional
world could not brook his daring, his insouciance, his constant desire to call a spade a spade. His genial sufficiency
was a taunt and a mockery to many. The hard implication of
his eye was dreaded by the weaker as fire is feared by a
burned child. Dissembling enough, he was not sufficiently oily
and make-believe. Well, come what might, he did not need
to be or mean to be so, and there the game must lie; but he
had not by any means attained the height of his ambition.
He was not yet looked upon as a money prince. He could
not rank as yet with the magnates of the East—the serried
Sequoias of Wall Street. Until he could stand with these
men, until he could have a magnificent mansion, acknowl-
edged as such by all, until he could have a world-famous
gallery, Berenice, millions—what did it avail?

The character of Cowperwood's New York house, which
proved one of the central achievements of his latter years,
was one of those flowerings-out of disposition which even-
tuate in the case of men quite as in that of plants. After the
passing of the years neither a modified Gothic (such as his
Philadelphia house had been), nor a conventionalized
Norman-French, after the style of his Michigan Avenue
home, seemed suitable to him. Only the Italian palaces of
medieval or Renaissance origin which he had seen abroad
now appealed to him as examples of what a stately residence should be. He was really seeking something which
should not only reflect his private tastes as to a home, but
should have the more enduring qualities of a palace or even
a museum, which might stand as a monument to his memory. After much searching Cowperwood had found an architect in New York who suited him entirely—one Raymond
Pyne, rake, raconteur, man-about-town—who was still first
and foremost an artist, with an eye for the exceptional and
the perfect. These two spent days and days together meditating on the details of this home museum. An immense
gallery was to occupy the west wing of the house and be
devoted to pictures; a second gallery should occupy the
south wing and be given over to sculpture and large whorls
of art; and these two wings were to swing as an L around
the house proper, the latter standing in the angle between

them. The whole structure was to be of a rich brown-stone, heavily carved. For its interior decoration the richest woods, silks, tapestries, glass, and marbles were canvassed. The main rooms were to surround a great central court with a colonnade of pink-veined alabaster, and in the center there would be an electrically lighted fountain of alabaster and silver. Occupying the east wall a series of hanging baskets of orchids, or of other fresh flowers, were to give a splendid glow of color, a morning-sun effect, to this richly artificial realm. One chamber—a lounge on the second floor—was to be entirely lined with thin-cut transparent marble of a peachblow hue, the lighting coming only through these walls and from without. Here in a perpetual atmosphere of sunrise were to be racks for exotic birds, a trellis of vines, stone benches, a central pool of glistening water, and an echo of music. Pyne assured him that after his death this room would make an excellent chamber in which to exhibit porcelains, jades, ivories, and other small objects of value.

Cowperwood was now actually transferring his possessions to New York, and had persuaded Aileen to accompany him. Fine compound of tact and chicane that he was, he had the effrontery to assure her that they could here create a happier social life. His present plan was to pretend a marital contentment which had no basis solely in order to make this transition period as undisturbed as possible. Subsequently he might get a divorce, or he might make an arrangement whereby his life would be rendered happy outside the social pale.

Of all this Berenice Fleming knew nothing at all. At the same time, the building of this splendid mansion eventually awakened her to an understanding of the spirit of art that occupied the center of Cowperwood's iron personality, and caused her to take a real interest in him. Before this she had looked on him as a kind of western interloper coming East and taking advantage of her mother's good nature to scrape a little social courtesy. Now, however, all that Mrs. Carter had been telling her of his personality and achievements was becoming crystallized into a glittering chain of facts. This house, the papers were fond of repeating, would be a jewel of rare workmanship. Obviously the Cowperwoods were going to try to enter society. "What a pity it is," Mrs. Carter once said to Berenice, "that he couldn't have gotten a divorce from his wife before he began all this. I am so afraid they will never be received. He would be if he only had the right woman; but she——" Mrs. Carter, who had once seen Aileen in Chicago, shook her head doubtfully. "She is not the type," was her comment. "She has neither the air nor the understanding."

"If he is so unhappy with her," observed Berenice thoughtfully, "why doesn't he leave her? She can be happy without him. It is so silly—this cat-and-dog existence. Still, I suppose she values the position he gives her," she added, "since she isn't so interesting herself."

"I suppose," said Mrs. Carter, "that he married her twenty years ago, when he was a very different man from what he is today. She is not exactly coarse, but not clever enough. She cannot do what he would like to see done. I hate to see mismatings of this kind, and yet they are so common. I do hope, Bevy, that when you marry it will be someone with whom you can get along, though I do believe I would rather see you unhappy than poor."

This was delivered as an early breakfast peroration in Central Park South, with the morning sun glittering on one of the nearest park lakes. Bevy, in spring-green and old gold, was studying the social notes in one of the morning papers.

"I think I should prefer to be unhappy with wealth than to be without it," she said idly, without looking up.

Her mother surveyed her admiringly, conscious of her imperious mood. What was to become of her? Would she marry well? Would she marry in time? Thus far no breath of the wretched days in Louisville had affected Berenice. Most of those with whom Mrs. Carter had found herself compelled to deal would be kind enough to keep her secret. But there were others. How near she had been to drifting on the rocks when Cowperwood had appeared!

"After all," observed Berenice thoughtfully, "Mr. Cowperwood isn't a mere money-grabber, is he? So many of these western moneyed men are so dull."

"My dear," exclaimed Mrs. Carter, who by now had become a confirmed satellite of her secret protector, "you don't understand him at all. He is a very astonishing man, I tell you. The world is certain to hear a lot more of Frank Cowperwood before he dies. You can say what you please, but someone has to make the money in the first place. It's little enough that good breeding does for you in poverty.

I know, because I've seen plenty of our friends come down."

In the new house, on a scaffold one day, a famous sculptor and his assistants were at work on a Greek frieze which represented dancing nymphs linked together by looped wreaths. Berenice and her mother happened to be passing. They stopped to look, and Cowperwood joined them. He waved his hand at the figures of the frieze, and said to Berenice, with his old, gay air, "If they had copied you they would have done better."

"How charming of you!" she replied, with her cool, strange blue eyes fixed on him. "They are beautiful." In spite of her earlier prejudices she knew now that he and she had one god in common—Art; and that his mind was fixed on things beautiful as on a shrine.

He merely looked at her.

"This house can be little more than a museum to me," he remarked simply, when her mother was out of hearing; "but I shall build it as perfectly as I can. Perhaps others may enjoy it if I do not."

She looked at him musingly, understandingly, and he smiled. She realized, of course, that he was trying to convey to her that he was lonely.

CHAPTER LI

The Revival of Hattie Starr

Engrossed in the pleasures and entertainments which Cowperwood's money was providing, Berenice had until recently given very little thought to her future. Cowperwood had been most liberal. "She is young," he once said to Mrs. Carter, with an air of disinterested liberality, when they were talking about Berenice and her future. "She is an exquisite. Let her have her day. If she marries well she can pay you back, or me. But give her all she needs now." And he signed checks with the air of a gardener who is growing a wondrous orchid.

The truth was that Mrs. Carter had become so fond of Berenice as an object of beauty, a prospective grande dame, that she would have sold her soul to see her well placed; and as the money to provide the dresses, setting, equipage had to come from somewhere, she had placed her spirit in subjection to Cowperwood and pretended not to see the compromising position in which she was placing all that was near and dear to her.

"Oh, you're so good," she more than once said to him, a mist of gratitude commingled with joy in her eyes. "I would never have believed it of anyone. But Bevy—"

"An aesthete is an aesthete," Cowperwood replied. "They are rare enough. I like to see a spirit as fine as hers move untroubled. She will make her way."

Seeing Lieutenant Braxmar in the foreground of Berenice's affairs, Mrs. Carter was foolish enough to harp on the matter in a friendly, ingratiating way. Braxmar was really interesting after his fashion. He was young, tall, muscular, and handsome, a graceful dancer; but better yet, he represented in his moods lineage, social position, a number of the things which engaged Berenice most. He was intelligent, serious, with a kind of social grace which was gay, courteous, wistful. Berenice met him first at a local dance, where a new step was being practiced—"dancing in the barn," as it was called—and so airily did he tread it with her in his handsome uniform that she was half smitten for the moment.

"You dance delightfully," she said. "Is this a part of your life on the ocean wave?"

"Deep-sea-going dancing," he replied, with a heavenly smile. "All battles are accompanied by balls, don't you know?"

"Oh, what a wretched jest!" she replied. "It's unbelievably bad."

"Not for me. I can make much worse ones."

"Not for me," she replied, "I can't stand them." And they went prancing on. Afterward he came and sat by her; they walked in the moonlight; he told her of naval life, his southern home and connections.

Mrs. Carter, seeing him with Berenice, and having been introduced, observed the next morning, "I like your lieutenant, Bevy. I know some of his relatives well. They come from the Carolinas. He's sure to come into money. The whole family is wealthy. Do you think he might be interested in you?"

"Oh, possibly—yes, I presume so," replied Berenice airily, for she did not take too kindly to this evidence of parental interest. She preferred to see life drift on in some nebulous way at present, and this was bringing matters too close to home. "Still, he has so much machinery on his mind I doubt whether he could take any serious interest in a woman. He is almost more of a battleship than he is a man."

She made a mouth, and Mrs. Carter commented gaily: "You rogue! All the men take an interest in you. You don't think you could care for him, then, at all?"

"Why, Mother, what a question! Why do you ask? Is it so essential that I should?"

"Oh, not that exactly," replied Mrs. Carter sweetly, bracing herself for a word which she felt incumbent upon her; "but think of his position. He comes of such a good family, and he must be heir to a considerable fortune in his own right. Oh, Bevy, I don't want to hurry or spoil your life in any way, but do keep in mind the future. With your tastes and instincts money is so essential, and unless you marry it I don't know where you are to get it. Your father was so thoughtless, and Rolfe's was even worse."

She sighed.

Berenice, for almost the first time in her life, took solemn heed of this thought. She pondered whether she could endure Braxmar as a life partner, follow him around the world, perhaps retransferring her abode to the South; but she could not make up her mind. This suggestion on the part of her mother rather poisoned the cup for her. To tell the truth, in this hour of doubt her thoughts turned vaguely to Cowperwood as one who represented in his avid way more of the things she truly desired. She remembered his wealth, his plaint that his new house could be only a museum, the manner in which he approached her with look and voiceless suggestions. But he was old and married—out of the question, therefore—and Braxmar was young and charming. To think her mother should have been so tactless as to suggest the necessity for consideration in his case! It almost spoiled him for her. And was their financial state, then, as uncertain as her mother indicated?

In this crisis some of her previous social experiences became significant. For instance, only a few weeks previous to her meeting with Braxmar she had been visiting at the country estate of the Corscaden Batjers, at Redding Hills, Long Island, and had been sitting with her hostess in the morning room of Hillcrest, which commanded a lovely though distant view of Long Island Sound.

Mrs. Fredericka Batjer was a chestnut blonde, fair, cool, quiescent—a type out of Dutch art. Clad in a morning gown of gray and silver, her hair piled in a Psyche knot, she had in her lap on this occasion a Java basket filled with some attempt at Norwegian needlework.

"Bevy," she said, "you remember Kilmer Duelma, don't you? Wasn't he at the Haggertys' last summer when you were there?"

Berenice, who was seated at a small Chippendale writing desk penning letters, glanced up, her mind visioning for the moment the youth in question. Kilmer Duelma—tall, stocky, swaggering, his clothes the loose, nonchalant perfection of the season, his walk ambling, studied, lackadaisical, aimless, his color high, his cheeks full, his eyes a little vacuous, his mind acquiescing in a sort of genial, inconsequential way to every query and thought that were put to him. The younger of the two sons of Auguste Duelma, banker, promoter, multimillionaire, he would come into a fortune estimated roughly at between six and eight millions. At the Haggertys' the year before he had hung about her in an aimless fashion.

Mrs. Batjer studied Berenice curiously for a moment, then returned to her needlework. "I've asked him down over this weekend," she suggested.

"Yes?" queried Berenice sweetly. "Are there others?"

"Of course," assented Mrs. Batjer remotely. "Kilmer doesn't interest you, I presume."

Berenice smiled enigmatically.

"You remember Clarissa Faulkner, don't you, Bevy?" pursued Mrs. Batjer. "She married Romulus Garrison."

"Perfectly. Where is she now?"

"They have leased the Château Brieul at Ars for the winter. Romulus is a fool, but Clarissa is so clever. You know, she writes that she is holding a veritable court there this season. Half the smart set of Paris and London are dropping in. It is so charming for her to be able to do those things now. Poor dear! At one time I was quite troubled over her."

Without giving any outward sign Berenice did not fail to gather the full import of the analogy. It was all true. One must begin early to take thought of one's life. She suffered a disturbing sense of duty. Kilmer Duelma arrived at noon Friday with six types of bags, a special valet, and a preposterous enthusiasm for polo and hunting (diseases lately acquired from a hunting set in the Berkshires). A cleverly contrived compliment supposed to have emanated from Miss Fleming and conveyed to him with tact by Mrs. Batjer brought him ambling into Berenice's presence suggesting a Sunday drive to Saddle Rock.

"Haw! haw! You know, I'm delighted to see you again. Haw! haw! It's been an age since I've seen the Haggertys. We missed you after you left. Haw! haw! I did, you know. Since I saw you I have taken up polo—three ponies with me all the time now—haw! haw!—a regular stable nearly."

Bernice strove valiantly to retain a serene interest. Duty was in her mind, the Château Brieul, the winter court of Clarissa Garrison, some first premonitions of the flight of time. Yet the drive was a bore, conversation a burden, the struggle to respond titanic, impossible. When Monday came she fled, leaving three days between that and a weekend at Morristown. Mrs. Batjer—who read straws most capably— sighed. Her own Corscaden was not much beyond his money, but life must be lived, and the ambitious must inherit wealth or gather it wisely. Some impossible scheming silly would soon collect Duelma, and then— She considered Berenice a little difficult.

Berenice could not help piecing together the memory of this incident with her mother's recent appeal in behalf of Lieutenant Braxmar. A great, cloying, disturbing, disintegrating factor in her life was revealed by the dawning discovery that she and her mother were without much money, that aside from her lineage she was in a certain sense an interloper in society. There were never rumors of great wealth in connection with her—no flattering whispers or public notices regarding her station as an heiress. All the smug minor mannequins of the social world were on the qui vive for some cotton-headed doll of a girl with an endless bank account. By nature sybaritic, an intense lover of art, fabrics, of stately functions, of power and success in every

form, she had been dreaming all this while of a great soul
freedom and art freedom under some such circumstances
as the greatest individual wealth of the day, and only that,
could provide. Simultaneously she had vaguely cherished the
idea that if she ever found someone who was truly fond of
her, and whom she could love or even admire intensely—
someone who needed her in a deep, sincere way—she would
give herself freely and gladly. Yet who could it be? She had
been charmed by Braxmar, but her keen, analytic intelligence
required someone harder, more vivid, more ruthless, someone who would appeal to her as an immense force. Yet she
must be conservative, she must play what cards she had to
win.

During his summer visit at Narragansett Cowperwood had
not been long disturbed by the presence of Braxmar, for,
having received special orders, the latter was compelled to
hurry away to Hampton Roads. But the following November,
forsaking temporarily his difficult affairs in Chicago for New
York and the Carter apartment in Central Park South, Cowperwood again encountered the lieutenant, who arrived one
evening brilliantly arrayed in full official regalia in order to
escort Berenice to a ball. A high military cap surmounting his
handsome face, his epaulets gleaming in gold, the lapels of
his cape thrown back to reveal a handsome red silken lining,
his sword clanking by his side, he seemed a veritable singing
flame of youth. Cowperwood, caught in the drift of circumstance—age, unsuitableness, the flaring counterattractions of
romance and vigor—fairly writhed in pain.

Berenice was so beautiful in a storm of diaphanous, clinging garments. He stared at them from an adjacent room,
where he pretended to be reading, and sighed. Alas, how
were his cunning and foresight—even his—to overcome the
drift of life itself? How was he to make himself appealing
to youth? Braxmar had the years, the color, the bearing.
Berenice seemed tonight, as she prepared to leave, to be
fairly seething with youth, hope, gaiety. He arose after a
few moments, and giving business as an excuse, hurried away.
But it was only to sit in his own rooms in a neighboring
hotel and meditate. The logic of the ordinary man under
such circumstances, compounded of the age-old notions of
chivalry, self-sacrifice, duty to higher impulses, and the like,
would have been to step aside in favor of youth, to give
convention its day, and retire in favor of morality and

virtue. Cowperwood saw things in no such moralistic or altruistic light. "I satisfy myself," had ever been his motto, and under that, however much he might sympathize with Berenice in love or with love itself, he was not content to withdraw until he was sure that the end of hope for him had really come. There had been moments between him and Berenice—little approximations toward intimacy—which had led him to believe that by no means was she seriously opposed to him. At the same time this business of the lieutenant, so Mrs. Carter confided to him a little later, was not to be regarded lightly. While Berenice might not care so much, obviously Braxmar did.

"Ever since he has been away he has been storming her with letters," she remarked to Cowperwood one afternoon. "I don't think he is the kind that can be made to take no for an answer."

"A very successful kind," commented Cowperwood dryly.

Mrs. Carter was eager for advice in the matter. Braxmar was a man of parts. She knew his connections. He would inherit at least $600,000 at his father's death, if not more. What about her Louisville record? Supposing that should come out later? Would it not be wise for Berenice to marry, and have the danger over with?

"It is a problem, isn't it?" observed Cowperwood calmly. "Are you sure she's in love?"

"Oh, I wouldn't say that, but such things so easily turn into love. I have never believed that Berenice could be swept off her feet by anyone—she is so thoughtful—but she knows she has her own way to make in the world, and Mr. Braxmar is certainly eligible. I know his cousins, the Clifford Porters, very well."

Cowperwood knitted his brows. He was sick to his soul with this worry over Berenice. He felt that he must have her, even at the cost of inflicting upon her a serious social injury. Better that she should surmount it with him than escape it with another. It so happened, however, that the final grim necessity of acting on any such idea was spared him.

Imagine a dining room in one of the principal hotels of New York, the hour midnight, after an evening at the opera, to which Cowperwood, as host, had invited Berenice, Lieutenant Braxmar, and Mrs. Carter. He was now playing the role of disinterested host and avuncular mentor. His attitude toward Berenice, meditating, as he was, a course which should be destructive to Braxmar, was gentle, courteous, serenely thoughtful. Like a true Mephistopheles he was waiting, surveying Mrs. Carter and Berenice, who were seated in front chairs clad in such exotic draperies as opera-goers affect—Mrs. Carter in pale lemon silk and diamonds; Berenice in purple and old rose, with a jeweled comb in her hair. The lieutenant in his dazzling uniform smiled and talked blandly, complimented the singers, whispered pleasant nothings to Berenice, descanted at odd moments to Cowperwood on naval personages who happened to be present. Coming out of the opera and driving through blowy, windy streets to the Waldorf, they took the table reserved for them, and Cowperwood, after consulting with regard to the dishes and ordering the wine, went back reminiscently to the music, which had been *La Bohème*. The death of Mimi and the grief of Rodolfo, as voiced by the splendid melodies of Puccini, interested him.

"That makeshift studio world may have no connection with the genuine professional artist, but it's very representative of life," he remarked.

"I don't know, I'm sure," said Braxmar seriously. "All I know of Bohemia is what I have read in books—*Trilby*, for instance, and—" He could think of no other, and stopped. "I suppose it is that way in Paris."

He looked at Berenice for confirmation and to win a smile.

Owing to her mobile and sympathetic disposition, she had during the opera been swept from period to period by surges of beauty too gay or pathetic for words, but clearly comprehended of the spirit. Once when she had been lost in dreamy contemplation, her hands folded on her knees, her eyes fixed on the stage, both Braxmar and Cowperwood had studied her parted lips and fine profile with common impulses of emotion and enthusiasm. Realizing after the mood was gone that they had been watching her, Berenice had continued the pose for a moment, then had waked as from a dream with a sigh. This incident now came back to her, as well as her feeling in regard to the opera generally.

"It is very beautiful," she said; "I do not know what to say. People are like that, of course. It is so much better than just dull comfort. Life is really finest when it's tragic, anyhow."

She looked at Cowperwood, who was studying her; then

at Braxmar, who saw himself for the moment on the captain's bridge of a battleship commanding in time of action. To Cowperwood came back many of his principal moments of difficulty. Surely his life had been sufficiently dramatic to satisfy her.

"I don't think I care so much for it," interposed Mrs. Carter. "One gets tired of sad happenings. We have enough drama in real life."

Cowperwood and Braxmar smiled faintly. Berenice looked contemplatively away. The crush of diners, the clink of china and glass, the bustling to and fro of waiters, and the strumming of the orchestra diverted her somewhat, as did the nods and smiles of some entering guests who recognized Braxmar and her, but not Cowperwood.

Suddenly from a neighboring door, opening from the men's café and grill, there appeared the semi-intoxicated figure of an ostensibly swagger society man, his clothing somewhat awry, an opera coat hanging loosely from one shoulder, a crush opera hat dangling in one hand, his eyes a little bloodshot, his underlip protruding slightly and defiantly, and his whole visage proclaiming that devil-may-care, superior, and malicious aspect which the drunken rake does not so much assume as achieve. He looked sullenly, uncertainly about; then, perceiving Cowperwood and his party, made his way thither in the half-determined, half-inconsequential fashion of one not quite sound after his cups. When he was directly opposite Cowperwood's table—the cynosure of a number of eyes—he suddenly paused as if in recognition, and coming over, laid a genial and yet condescending hand on Mrs. Carter's bare shoulder.

"Why, hello, Hattie!" he called leeringly and jeeringly. "What are you doing down here in New York? You haven't given up your business in Louisville, have you, eh, old sport? Say, lemme tell you something. I haven't had a single decent girl since you left—not one. If you open a house down here, let me know, will you?"

He bent over her smirkingly and patronizingly the while he made as if to rummage in his white waistcoat pocket for a card. At the same moment Cowperwood and Braxmar, realizing quite clearly the import of his words, were on their feet. While Mrs. Carter was pulling and struggling back from the stranger, Braxmar's hand (he being the nearest) was on him, and the headwaiter and two assistants had appeared.

"What is the trouble here? What has he done?" they demanded.

Meanwhile the intruder, leering contentiously at them all, was exclaiming in very audible tones: "Take your hands off. Who are you? What the devil have you got to do with this? Don't you think I know what I'm about? She knows me—don't you, Hattie? That's Hattie Starr of Louisville—ask her! She kept one of the swellest —— ever run in Louisville. What do you people want to be so upset about? I know what I'm doing. She knows me."

He not only protested, but contested, and with some vehemence. Cowperwood, Braxmar, and the waiters forming a cordon, he was shoved and hustled out into the lobby and the outer entranceway, and an officer was called.

"This man should be arrested," Cowperwood protested vigorously, when the latter appeared. "He has grossly insulted lady guests of mine. He is drunk and disorderly, and I wish to make that charge. Here is my card. Will you let me know where to come?" He handed it over, while Braxmar, scrutinizing the stranger with military care, added: "I should like to thrash you within an inch of your life. If you weren't drunk I would. If you are a gentleman and have a card I want you to give it to me. I want to talk to you later." He leaned over and presented a cold, hard face to that of Mr. Beales Chadsey of Louisville, Kentucky.

"Tha's all right, Captain," leered Chadsey mockingly. "I got a card. No harm done. Here you are. You c'n see me any time you want—Hotel Buckingham, Fifth Avenue and Fiftieth Street. I got a right to speak to anybody I please, where I please, when I please. See?"

He fumbled and protested while the officer stood by ready to take him in charge. Not finding a card, he added:

"Tha's all right. Write it down. Beales Chadsey, Hotel Buckingham, or Louisville, Kentucky. See me any time you want to. Tha's Hattie Starr. She knows me. I couldn't make a mistake about her—not once in a million. Many's the night I spent in her house."

Braxmar was quite ready to lunge at him had not the officer intervened.

Back in the dining room Berenice and her mother were sitting, the latter quite flustered, pale, distrait, horribly taken aback—by far too much distressed for any convincing measure of deception.

"Why, the very idea!" she was saying. "That dreadful man! How terrible! I never saw him before in my life."

Berenice, disturbed and nonplussed, was thinking of the familiar and lecherous leer with which the stranger had addressed her mother—the horror, the shame of it. Could even a drunken man, if utterly mistaken, be so defiant, so persistent, so willing to explain? What shameful things had she been hearing?

"Come, Mother," she said, gently and with dignity; "never mind, it is all right. We can go home at once. You will feel better when you are out of here."

She called a waiter and asked him to say to the gentlemen that they had gone to the women's dressing room. She pushed an intervening chair out of the way and gave her mother her arm.

"To think I should be so insulted," Mrs. Carter mumbled on, "here in a great hotel, in the presence of Lieutenant Braxmar and Mr. Cowperwood! This is too dreadful. Well, I never."

She half whimpered as she walked; and Berenice, surveying the room with dignity, a lofty superiority in her face, led solemnly forth, a strange, lacerating pain about her heart. What was at the bottom of these shameful statements? Why should this drunken roisterer have selected her mother, of all other women in the dining room, for the object of these outrageous remarks? Why should her mother be stricken, so utterly collapsed, if there were not some truth in what he had said? It was very strange, very sad, very grim, very horrible. What would that gossiping, scandal-loving world of which she knew so much say to a scene like this? For the first time in her life the import and horror of social ostracism flashed upon her.

The following morning, owing to a visit paid to the Jefferson Market Police Court by Lieutenant Braxmar, where he proposed, if satisfaction was not immediately guaranteed to empty cold lead into Mr. Beales Chadsey's stomach, the following letter on Buckingham stationery was written and sent to Mrs. Ira George Carter—36 Central Park South:

DEAR MADAM:

Last evening, owing to a drunken debauch, for which

I have no satisfactory or suitable explanation to make, I was the unfortunate occasion of an outrage upon your feelings and those of your daughter and friends, for which I wish most humbly to apologize. I cannot tell you how sincerely I regret whatever I said or did, which I cannot now clearly recall. My mental attitude when drinking is both contentious and malicious, and while in this mood and state I was the author of statements which I know to be wholly unfounded. In my drunken stupor I mistook you for a certain notorious woman of Louisville—why, I have not the slightest idea. For this wholly shameful and outrageous conduct I sincerely ask your pardon—beg your forgiveness. I do not know what amends I can make, but anything you may wish to suggest I shall gladly do. In the meanwhile I hope you will accept this letter in the spirit in which it is written and as a slight attempt at recompense which I know can never fully be made.

Very sincerely,
BEALES CHADSEY

At the same time Lieutenant Braxmar was fully aware before this letter was written or sent that the charges implied against Mrs. Carter were only too well founded. Beales Chadsey had said drunk what twenty men in all sobriety and even the police at Louisville would corroborate. Chadsey had insisted on making this clear to Braxmar before writing the letter.

CHAPTER LII

Behind the Arras

Berenice, perusing the apology from Beales Chadsey, which her mother—very much fagged and weary—handed her the next morning, thought that it read like the overnight gallantry of someone who was seeking to make amends without changing his point of view. Mrs. Carter was too obviously self-conscious. She protested too much. Berenice knew that she could find out for herself if she chose, but would she choose? The thought sickened her, and yet who was she to judge too severely?

Cowperwood came in bright and early to put as good a face on the matter as he could. He explained how he and Braxmar had gone to the police station to make a charge; how Chadsey, sobered by arrest, had abandoned his bravado and humbly apologized. When viewing the letter handed him by Mrs. Carter he exclaimed:

"Oh yes. He was very glad to promise to write that if we would let him off. Braxmar seemed to think it was necessary that he should. I wanted the judge to impose a fine and let it go at that. He was drunk, and that's all there was to it."

He assumed a very unknowing air when in the presence of Berenice and her mother, but when alone with the latter his manner changed completely.

"Brazen it out," he commanded. "It doesn't amount to anything. Braxmar doesn't believe that this man really knows anything. This letter is enough to convince Berenice. Put a good face on it; more depends on your manner than on anything else. You're much too upset. That won't do at all; you'll tell the whole story that way."

At the same time he privately regarded this incident as a fine windfall of chance—in all likelihood the one thing which would serve to scare the lieutenant away. Outwardly, however, he demanded effrontery, assumption; and Mrs. Carter was somewhat cheered, but when she was alone she cried. Berenice, coming upon her accidentally and finding her eyes wet, exclaimed:

"Oh, Mother, please don't be foolish. How can you act this way? We had better go up in the country and rest a little while if you are so unstrung."

Mrs. Carter protested that it was merely nervous reaction, but to Berenice it seemed that where there was so much smoke there must be some fire.

Her manner in the aftermath toward Braxmar was gracious but remote. He called the next day to say how sorry he was, and to ask her to a new diversion. She was sweet but distant. Insofar as she was concerned it was plain that the Beales Chadsey incident was closed, but she did not accept his invitation.

"Mother and I are planning to go to the country for a few days," she observed genially. "I can't say just when we shall return, but if you are still here we shall meet, no doubt. You must be sure and come to see us." She turned to an east court-window, where the morning sun was gleaming on some flowers in a window box, and began to pinch off a dead leaf here and there.

Braxmar, full of the tradition of American romance, captivated by her vibrant charm, her poise and superiority under the circumstances, her obvious readiness to dismiss him, was overcome, as the human mind frequently is, by a riddle of the spirit, a chemical reaction as mysterious to its victim as to one who is its witness. Stepping forward with a motion that was at once gallant, reverent, eager, unconscious, he exclaimed:

"Berenice! Miss Fleming! Please don't send me away like this. Don't leave me. It isn't anything I have done, is it? I am mad about you. I can't bear to think that anything that has happened could make any difference between you and me. I haven't had the courage to tell you before, but I want to tell you now. I have been in love with you from the very first night I saw you. You are such a wonderful girl! I don't feel that I deserve you, but I love you. I love you with all the honor and force in me. I admire and respect you. Whatever may or may not be true, it is all one and the same to me. Be my wife, will you? Marry me, please! Oh, I'm not fit to be the lacer of your shoes, but I have position and I'll make a name for myself, I hope. Oh, Berenice!" He extended his arms in a dramatic fashion, not outward, but downward, stiff and straight, and declared: "I don't know what I shall do without you. Is there no hope for me at all?"

An artist in all the graces of sex—histrionic, plastic, many-faceted—Berenice debated for the fraction of a minute what she should do and say. She did not love the lieutenant as he loved her by any means, and somehow this discovery concerning her mother shamed her pride, suggesting an obligation to save herself in one form or another which she resented bitterly. She was sorry for his tactless proposal at this time, although she knew well enough the innocence and virtue of the emotion from which it sprang.

"Really, Mr. Braxmar," she replied, turning on him with solemn eyes, "you mustn't ask me to decide that now. I know how you feel. I'm afraid, though, that I may have been a little misleading in my manner. I didn't mean to be. I'm quite sure you'd better forget your interest in me for the present, anyhow. I could only make up my mind in one way if you should insist. I should have to ask you to forget me entirely. I wonder if you can see how I feel—how it hurts me to say this?"

She paused, perfectly poised, yet quite moved really, as charming a figure as one would have wished to see—part Greek, part Oriental—contemplative, calculating.

In that moment, for the first time, Braxmar realized that he was talking to someone whom he could not comprehend really. She was strangely self-contained, enigmatic, more beautiful perhaps because more remote than he had ever seen her before. In a strange flash this young American saw the isles of Greece, Cytherea, the lost Atlantis, Cyprus and its Paphian shrine. His eyes burned with a strange, comprehending luster; his color, at first high, went pale.

"I can't believe you don't care for me at all, Miss Berenice," he went on quite strainedly. "I felt you did care about me. But here," he added all at once, with a real, if summoned, military force, "I won't bother you. You do understand me. You know how I feel. I won't change. Can't we be friends, anyhow?"

He held out his hand, and she took it, feeling now that she was putting an end to what might have been an idyllic romance.

"Of course we can," she said. "I hope I shall see you again soon."

After he was gone she walked into the adjoining room and sat down in a wicker chair, putting her elbows on her knees and resting her chin in her hands. What a denouement to a thing so innocent, so charming! And now he was gone. She would not see him anymore, would not want to see him—not much, anyhow. Life had sad, even ugly facts. Oh yes, yes, and she was beginning to perceive them clearly.

Some two days later, when Berenice had brooded and brooded until she could endure it no longer, she finally went to Mrs. Carter and said: "Mother, why don't you tell me all about this Louisville matter so that I may really know? I can see something is worrying you. Can't you trust me? I am no longer a child by any means, and I am your daughter. It may help me to straighten things out, to know what to do."

Mrs. Carter, who had always played a game of lofty though loving motherhood, was greatly taken aback by this courageous attitude. She flushed and chilled a little; then decided to lie.

"I tell you there was nothing at all," she declared nervously and pettishly. "It is all an awful mistake. I wish that dreadful man could be punished severely for what he said to me. To be outraged and insulted this way before my own child!"

"Mother," questioned Berenice, fixing her with those cool blue eyes, "why don't you tell me all about Louisville? You and I shouldn't have things between us. Maybe I can help you."

All at once Mrs. Carter, realizing that her daughter was no longer a child or a mere social butterfly, but a woman superior, cool, sympathetic, with intuitions much deeper than her own, sank into a heavily flowered wing-chair behind her, and seeking a small pocket-handkerchief with one hand, placed the other over her eyes and began to cry.

"I was so driven, Bevy, I didn't know which way to turn. Colonel Gillis suggested it. I wanted to keep you and Rolfe in school and give you a chance. It isn't true—anything that horrible man said. It wasn't anything like what he suggested. Colonel Gillis and several others wanted me to rent them bachelor quarters, and that's the way it all came about. It wasn't my fault; I couldn't help myself, Bevy."

"And what about Mr. Cowperwood?" inquired Berenice curiously. She had begun of late to think a great deal about Cowperwood. He was so cool, deep, dynamic, in a way resourceful, like herself.

"There's nothing about him," replied Mrs. Carter, looking up defensively. Of all her men friends she best liked Cowperwood. He had never advised her to evil ways or used her house as a convenience to himself alone. "He never did anything but help me out. He advised me to give up my house in Louisville and come East and devote myself to looking after you and Rolfe. He offered to help me until you two should be able to help yourselves, and so I came. Oh, if I had only not been so foolish—so afraid of life! But your father and Mr. Carter just ran through everything."

She heaved a deep, heartfelt sigh.

"Then we really haven't anything at all, have we, Mother —property or anything else?"

Mrs. Carter shook her head, meaning no.

"And the money we have been spending is Mr. Cowperwood's?"

"Yes."

Berenice paused and looked out the window over the wide stretch of park which it commanded. Framed in it like a picture were a small lake, a hill of trees, with a Japanese pagoda effect in the foreground. Over the hill were the yellow towering walls of a great hotel in Central Park West. In the street below could be heard the jingle of streetcars. On a road in the park could be seen a moving line of pleasure vehicles—society taking an airing in the chill November afternoon.

"Poverty, ostracism," she thought. And should she marry rich? Of course, if she could. And whom should she marry? The lieutenant? Never. He was really not masterful enough mentally, and he had witnessed her discomfiture. And who, then? Oh, the long line of sillies, lightweights, rakes, ne'er-do-wells, who, combined with sober, prosperous, conventional, muddleheaded oafs, constituted society. Here and there, at far jumps, was a real man, but would he be interested in her if he knew the whole truth about her?

"Have you broken with Mr. Braxmar?" asked her mother curiously, nervously, hopefully, hopelessly.

"I haven't seen him since," replied Berenice, lying conservatively. "I don't know whether I shall or not. I want to think." She arose. "But don't you mind, Mother. Only I wish we had some other way of living besides being dependent on Mr. Cowperwood."

She walked into her boudoir, and before her mirror began to dress for a dinner to which she had been invited. So it was Cowperwood's money that had been sustaining them all during the last few years; and she had been so liberal with his means—so proud, vain, boastful, superior. And he had only fixed her with those inquiring, examining eyes. Why? But she did not need to ask herself why. She knew now. What a game he had been playing, and what a silly she had been not to see it. Did her mother in any way suspect? She doubted it. This queer, paradoxical, impossible world! The eyes of Cowperwood burned at her as she thought.

CHAPTER LIII

A Declaration of Love

For the first time in her life Berenice now pondered seriously what she could do. She thought of marriage, but decided that instead of sending for Braxmar or taking up some sickening chase of an individual even less satisfactory it might be advisable to announce in a simple social way to her friends that her mother had lost her money, and that she herself was now compelled to take up some form of employment—the teaching of dancing, perhaps, or the practice of it professionally. She suggested this calmly to her mother one day. Mrs. Carter, who had been long a parasite really, without any constructive monetary notions of real import, was terrified. To think that she and Bevy, her wonderful daughter, and by reaction her son, should come to anything so humdrum and prosaic as ordinary struggling life, and after all her dreams. She sighed and cried in secret, writing Cowperwood a cautious explanation and asking him to see her privately in New York when he returned.

"Don't you think we had best go on a little while longer?" she suggested to Berenice. "It just wrings my heart to think that you, with your qualifications, should have to stoop to giving dancing lessons. We had better do almost anything for a while yet. You can make a suitable marriage, and then everything will be all right for you. It doesn't matter about me. I can live. But you—" Mrs. Carter's strained eyes indicated the misery she felt. Berenice was moved by this affection for her, which she knew to be genuine; but what a fool her mother had been, what a weak reed, indeed, she was to lean upon!

Cowperwood, when he conferred with Mrs. Carter, insisted that Berenice was quixotic, nervously awry, to wish to modify her state, to eschew society and invalidate her wondrous

charm by any sort of professional life. By prearrangement
with Mrs. Carter he hurried to Pocono at a time when he
knew that Berenice was there alone. Ever since the Beales
Chadsey incident she had been evading him.

When he arrived, as he did about one in the afternoon of
a crisp January day, there was snow on the ground, and the
surrounding landscape was bathed in a crystalline light that
gave back to the eye endless facets of luster—jewel beams
that cut space with a flash. The automobile had been introduced by now, and he rode in a touring car of eighty horse-
power, that gave back from its dark brown, varnished surface
a lacquered light. In a great fur coat and cap of round
black lamb's wool he arrived at the door.

"Well, Bevy," he exclaimed, pretending not to know of
Mrs. Carter's absence, "how are you? How's your mother?
Is she in?"

Berenice fixed him with her cool, steady-gazing eyes, as
frank and incisive as they were daring, and smiled him an
equivocal welcome. She wore a blue denim painter's apron,
and a palette of many colors glistened under her thumb.
She was painting and thinking—thinking being her special
occupation these days, and her thoughts had been of Braxmar,
Cowperwood, Kilmer Duelma, a half-dozen others, as well
as of the stage, dancing, painting. Her life was in a melting
pot, as it were, before her; again, it was like a disarranged
puzzle, the pieces of which might be fitted together into
some interesting picture if she could but endure.

"Do come in," she said. "It's cold, isn't it? Well, there's
a nice fire here for you. No, Mother isn't here. She went
down to New York. I should think you might have found her
at the apartment. Are you in New York for long?"

She was gay, cheerful, genial, but remote. Cowperwood felt
the protective gap that lay between him and her. It had always been there. He felt that even though she might understand and like him, yet there was something—convention,
ambition, or some deficiency on his part—that was keeping
her from him, keeping her eternally distant. He looked about
the room, at the picture she was attempting (a snowscape,
of a view down a slope), at the view itself which he contemplated from the window, at some dancing sketches she
had recently executed and hung on the wall for the time
being—lovely, short-tunic motives. He looked at her in her
interesting and becoming painter's apron. "Well, Berenice,"

he said, "always the artist first. It is your world. You will never escape it. These things are beautiful." He waved an ungloved hand in the direction of a choric line. "It wasn't your mother I came to see, anyhow. It is you. I had such a curious letter from her. She tells me you want to give up society and take to teaching or something of that sort. I came because I wanted to talk to you about that. Don't you think you are acting rather hastily?"

He spoke now as though there were some reason entirely disassociated from himself that was impelling him to this interest in her.

Berenice, brush in hand, standing by her picture, gave him a look that was cool, curious, defiant, equivocal.

"No, I don't think so," she replied quietly. "You know how things have been, so I may speak quite frankly. I know that Mother's intentions were always of the best." Her mouth moved with the faintest touch of sadness. "Her heart, I am afraid, is better than her head. As for your motives, I am satisfied to believe that they have been of the best also. I know that they have been, in fact—it would be ungenerous of me to suggest anything else." (Cowperwood's fixed eyes, it seemed to her, had moved somewhere in their deepest depths.) "Yet I don't feel we can go on as we have been doing. We have no money of our own. Why shouldn't I do something? What else can I really do?"

She paused, and Cowperwood gazed at her, quite still. In her informal, bunchy painter's apron, and with her blue eyes looking out at him from beneath her loose red hair, it seemed to him she was the most perfect thing he had ever known. Such a keen, fixed, enthroned mind. She was so capable, so splendid, and, like his own, her eyes were unafraid. Her spiritual equipoise was undisturbed.

"Berenice," he said quietly, "let me tell you something. You did me the honor just now to speak of my motives in giving your mother money as of the best. They were—from my own point of view—the best I have ever known. I will not say what I thought they were in the beginning. I know what they were now. I am going to speak quite frankly with you, if you will let me, as long as we are here together. I don't know whether you know this or not, but when I first met your mother I only knew by chance that she had a daughter, and it was of no particular interest to me then. I went to her house as the guest of a financial friend of mine who admired her greatly. From the first I myself admired her, because I found her to be a lady to the manner born—she was interesting. One day I happened to see a photograph of you in her home, and before I could mention it she put it away. Perhaps you recall the one. It is in profile —taken when you were about sixteen."

"Yes, I remember," replied Berenice simply—as quietly as though she were hearing a confession.

"Well, that picture interested me intensely. I inquired about you, and learned all I could. After that I saw another picture of you, enlarged, in a Louisville photographer's window. I bought it. It is in my office now—my private office— in Chicago. You are standing by a mantelpiece."

"I remember," replied Berenice, moved but uncertain.

"Let me tell you a little something about my life, will you? It won't take long. I was born in Philadelphia. My family had always belonged there. I have been in the banking and street-railway business all my life. My first wife was a Presbyterian girl, religious, conventional. She was older than I by six or seven years. I was happy for a while—five or six years. We had two children—both still living. Then I met my present wife. She was younger than myself—at least ten years, and very good-looking. She was in some respects more intelligent than my first wife—at least less conventional, more generous, I thought. I fell in love with her, and when I eventually left Philadelphia I got a divorce and married her. I was greatly in love with her at the time. I thought she was an ideal mate for me, and I still think she has many qualities which make her attractive. But my own ideals in regard to women have all the time been slowly changing. I have come to see, through various experiments, that she is not the ideal woman for me at all. She does not understand me. I don't pretend to understand myself, but it has occurred to me that there might be a woman somewhere who would understand me better than I understand myself, who would see the things that I don't see about myself, and would like me, anyhow. I might as well tell you that I have been a lover of women always. There is just one ideal thing in this world to me, and that is the woman that I would like to have."

"I should think it would make it rather difficult for any one woman to discover just which woman you would like to have?" smiled Berenice whimsically. Cowperwood was un-abashed.

"It would, I presume, unless she should chance to be the very one woman I am talking about," he replied impressively.

"I should think she would have her work cut out for her under any circumstances," added Berenice lightly, but with a touch of sympathy in her voice.

"I am making a confession," replied Cowperwood, seriously and a little heavily. "I am not apologizing for myself. The women I have known would make ideal wives for some men, but not for me. Life has taught me that much. It has changed me."

"And do you think the process has stopped by any means?" she replied quaintly, with that air of superior banter which puzzled, fascinated, defied him.

"No, I will not say that. My ideal has become fixed, though, apparently. I have had it for a number of years now. It spoils other matters for me. There is such a thing as an ideal. We do have a polestar in physics."

As he said this Cowperwood realized that for him he was making a very remarkable confession. He had come here primarily to magnetize her and control her judgment. As a matter of fact, it was almost the other way about. She was almost dominating him. Lithe, slender, resourceful, histrionic, she was standing before him making him explain himself; only he did not see her so much in that light as in the way of a large, kindly, mothering intelligence which could see, feel, and understand. She would know how it was, he felt sure. He could make himself understood if he tried. Whatever he was or had been, she would not take a petty view. She could not. Her answers thus far guaranteed as much.

"Yes," she replied, "we do have a polestar, but you do not seem able to find it. Do you expect to find your ideal in any living woman?"

"I *have* found it," he answered, wondering at the ingenuity and complexity of her mind—and of his own, for that matter—of all mind, indeed. Deep below deep it lay, staggering him at times by its fathomless reaches. "I hope you will take seriously what I am going to say, for it will explain so much. When I began to be interested in your picture I was so be-cause it coincided with the ideal I had in mind—the thing that you think changes swiftly. That was nearly seven years ago. Since then it has never changed. When I saw you at your school on Riverside Drive I was fully convinced. Although I have said nothing, I have remained so. Perhaps you think I had no right to any such feelings. Most people would agree with you. I had them and do have them just the same, and it explains my relation to your mother. When she came to me once in Louisville and told me of her difficulties I was glad to help her for your sake. That has been my reason ever since, although she does not know that. In some respects, Berenice, your mother is a little dull. All this while I have been in love with you—intensely so. As you stand there now you seem to me amazingly beautiful—the ideal I have been telling you about. Don't be disturbed; I shan't press any attentions on you." (Berenice had moved very slightly. She was concerned as much for him as for herself. His power was so wide, his power so great. She could not help taking him seriously when he was so serious.) "I have done whatever I have done in connection with you and your mother because I have been in love with you and because I wanted you to become the splendid thing I thought you ought to become. You have not known it, but you are the cause of my building the house on Fifth Avenue—the principal reason. I wanted to build something worthy of you. A dream? Certainly. Everything we do seems to have something of that quality. Its beauty, if there is any, is due to you. I made it beautiful thinking of you."

He paused, and Berenice gave no sign. Her first impulse had been to object, but her vanity, her love of art, her love of power—all were touched. At the same time she was curious now as to whether he had merely expected to take her as his mistress or to wait until he could honor her as his wife.

"I suppose you are wondering whether I ever expected to marry you or not," he went on, getting the thought out of her mind. "I am no different from many men in that respect, Berenice. I will be frank. I wanted you in any way that I could get you. I was living in the hope all along that you would fall in love with me—as I had with you. I hated Braxmar here, not long ago, when he appeared on the scene, but I could never have thought of interfering. I was quite prepared to give you up. I have envied every man I have ever seen with you—young and old. I have even envied your mother for being so close to you when I could not be. At the same time I have wanted you to have everything that would help you in any way. I did not want to interfere with you in case you found someone whom you could truly love if I knew that you could not love me. There is the whole story outside of anything you may know. But it is not because of this that I came today. Not to tell you this."

He paused, as if expecting her to say something, though she made no comment beyond a questioning "Yes?"

"The thing that I have come to say is that I want you to go on as you were before. Whatever you may think of me or of what I have just told you, I want you to believe that I am sincere and disinterested in what I am telling you now. My dream in connection with you is not quite over. Chance might make me eligible if you should happen to care. But I want you to go on and be happy, regardless of me. I have dreamed, but I daresay it has been a mistake. Hold your head high—you have a right to. Be a lady. Marry anyone you really love. I will see that you have a suitable marriage portion. I love you, Berenice, but I will make it a fatherly affection from now on. When I die I will put you in my will. But go on now in the spirit you were going before. I really can't be happy unless I think you are going to be."

He paused, still looking at her, believing for the time being what he said. If he should die she would find herself in his will. If she were to go on and socialize and seek she might find someone to love, but also she might think of him more kindly before she did so. What would be the cost of her as a ward compared to his satisfaction and delight in having her at least friendly and sympathetic and being in her good graces and confidence?

Berenice, who had always been more or less interested in him, temperamentally biased, indeed, in his direction because of his efficiency, simplicity, directness, and force, was especially touched in this instance by his utter frankness and generosity. She might question his temperamental control over his own sincerity in the future, but she could scarcely question that at present he was sincere. Moreover, his long period of secret love and admiration, the thought of so powerful a man dreaming of her in this fashion, was so flattering. It soothed her troubled vanity and shame in what had gone before. His straightforward confession had a kind of nobility which was electric, moving. She looked at him as he stood there, a little gray about the temples—the most appealing ornament of some men to some women—and for the life of her she could not help being moved by a kind of tenderness, sympathy, mothering affection. Obviously he did need the woman his attitude seemed to show that he needed, some woman of culture, spirit, taste, amorousness; or, at least, he was entitled to dream of her. As he stood before her he seemed a kind of superman, and yet also a bad boy—handsome, powerful, hopeful, not so very much older than herself now, impelled by some blazing internal force which harried him on and on. How much did he really care for her? How much could he? How much could he care for anyone? Yet see all he had done to interest her. What did that mean? To say all this? To do all this? Outside was his car, brown and radiant in the snow. He was the great Frank Algernon Cowperwood of Chicago, and he was pleading with her, a mere chit of a girl, to be kind to him, not to put him out of her life entirely. It touched her intellect, her pride, her fancy.

Aloud she said: "I like you better now. I really believe in you. I never did, quite, before. Not that I think I ought to let you spend your money on me or Mother—I don't. But I admire you. You make me. I understand how it is, I think. I know what your ambitions are. I have always felt that I did, in part. But you mustn't talk to me anymore now. I want to think. I want to think over what you have said. I don't know whether I can bring myself to it or not." (She noticed that his eyes seemed to move somehow in their deepest depths again.) "But we won't talk about it anymore at present."

"But Berenice," he added, with a real plea in his voice, "I wonder if you do understand. I have been so lonely— I am—"

"Yes, I do," she replied, holding out her hand. "We are going to be friends, whatever happens, from now on, because I really like you. You mustn't ask me to decide about the other, though, today. I can't do it. I don't want to. I don't care to."

"Not when I would so gladly give you everything—when I need it so little?"

"Not until I think it out for myself. I don't think so, though. No," she replied with an air. "There, Mr. Guardian Father," she laughed, pushing his hand away.

Cowperwood's heart bounded. He would have given millions to take her close in his arms. As it was he smiled appealingly.

"Don't you want to jump in and come to New York with me? If your mother isn't at the apartment you could stop at the Netherland."

"No, not today. I expect to be in soon. I will let you know, or Mother will."

He bustled out and into the machine after a moment of parley, waving to her over the purpling snow of the evening as his machine tore eastward, planning to make New York by dinnertime. If he could just keep her in this friendly, sympathetic attitude. If he only could!

CHAPTER LIV

Wanted—Fifty-year Franchises

Whatever his momentary satisfaction in her friendly acceptance of his confession, the uncertain attitude of Berenice left Cowperwood about where he was before. By a strange stroke of fate Braxmar, his young rival, had been eliminated, and Berenice had been made to see him, Cowperwood, in his true colors of love and of service for her. Yet plainly she did not accept them at his own valuation. More than ever was he conscious of the fact that he had fallen in tow of an amazing individual, one who saw life from a distinct and peculiar point of view and who was not to be bent to his will. That fact more than anything else—for her grace and beauty merely emblazoned it—caused him to fall into a hopeless infatuation. He said to himself over and over, "Well, I can live without her if I must," but at this stage the mere thought was an actual stab in his vitals. What, after all, were life, wealth, fame, if you couldn't have the woman you wanted—love, that indefinable, unnamable coddling of the spirit which the strongest almost more than the weakest crave? At last he saw clearly, as within a chalicelike nimbus, that the ultimate end of fame, power, vigor was beauty, and that beauty was a compound of the taste, the emotion, the innate culture, passion, and dreams of a woman like Berenice Fleming. That was it: that *was* IT. And beyond were nothing save crumbling age, darkness, silence.

In the meantime, owing to the preliminary activity and tact of his agents and advisers, the Sunday newspapers were vying with one another in describing the wonders of his new house in New York—its cost, the value of its ground, the wealthy citizens with whom the Cowperwoods would now be neighbors. There were double-column pictures of Aileen and Cowperwood, with articles indicating them as prospective entertainers on a grand scale who would unquestionably be received because of their tremendous wealth. As a matter of fact, this was purely newspaper gossip and speculation. While the general columns made news and capital of his wealth, special society columns, which dealt with the ultrafashionable, ignored him entirely. Already the machination of certain Chicago social figures in distributing information as to his past was discernible in the attitude of those clubs, organizations, and even churches, membership in which constitutes a form of social passport to better and higher earthly, if not spiritual, realms. His emissaries were active enough, but soon found that their end was not to be gained in a day. Many were waiting locally, anxious enough to get in, and with social equipment which the Cowperwoods could scarcely boast. After being blackballed by one or two exclusive clubs, seeing his application for a pew at St. Thomas's quietly pigeonholed for the present, and his invitations declined by several multimillionaires whom he met in the course of commercial transactions, he began to feel that his splendid home, aside from its final purpose as an art museum, could be of little value.

At the same time Cowperwood's financial genius was constantly being rewarded by many new phases of materiality, chiefly by an offensive and defensive alliance he was now able to engineer between himself and the house of Haeckelheimer, Gotloeb & Co. Seeing the iron manner in which he had managed to wrest victory out of defeat after the first seriously contested election, these gentlemen had experienced a change of heart and announced that they would now gladly help finance any new enterprise which Cowperwood might undertake. Among many other financiers, they had heard of his triumph in connection with the failure of American Match.

"Dot must be a right cleffer man, dot Cowperwood," Mr. Gotloeb told several of his partners, rubbing his hands and smiling. "I shouldt like to meet him."

And so Cowperwood was maneuvered into the giant banking office, where Mr. Gotloeb extended a genial hand.

"I hear much of Chicawkgo," he explained, in his semi-German, semi-Hebraic dialect, "but almozd more uff you. Are you goink to swallow up all de street-railways unt elefated roats out dere?"

Cowperwood smiled his most ingenuous smile.

"Why? Would you like me to leave a few for you?"

"Not dot exzagly, but I might not mint sharink in some uff dem wit you."

"You can join with me at any time, Mr. Gotloeb, as you must know. The door is always very, very wide open for you."

"I musd look into dot some more. It loogs very promising to me. I am gladt to meet you."

The great external element in Cowperwood's financial success—and one which he himself had foreseen from the very beginning—was the fact that Chicago was developing constantly. What had been when he arrived a soggy, messy plain strewn with shanties, ragged sidewalks, a higgledy-piggledy business heart, was now truly an astounding metropolis, which had passed the million mark in population and which stretched proud and strong over the greater part of Cook County. Where once had been a meager, makeshift financial section, with here and there only a splendid business building or hotel or a public office of some kind, there were now canyonlike streets lined with fifteen- and even eighteen-story office buildings, from the upper stories of which, as from watchtowers, might be surveyed the vast, expanding regions of simple home life below. Farther out were districts of mansions, parks, pleasure resorts, great worlds of train yards and manufacturing areas. In the commercial heart of this world Frank Algernon Cowperwood had truly become a figure of giant significance. How wonderful it is that men grow until, like colossuses, they bestride the world, or, like banyan trees, they drop roots from every branch and are themselves a forest—a forest of intricate commercial life, of which a thousand material aspects are the evidence. His street-railway properties were like a net—the parasite goldthread—linked together as they were, and draining two of the three important sides of the city.

In 1886, when he had first secured a foothold, they had been capitalized at between six and seven millions (every device for issuing a dollar on real property having been exhausted). Today, under his management, they were capitalized at between sixty and seventy millions. The majority of the stock issued and sold was subject to a financial device whereby 20 percent controlled 80 percent, Cowperwood holding that 20 percent and borrowing money on it as hypothecated collateral. In the case of the West Side corporation, a corporate issue of over thirty millions had been made, and these stocks, owing to the tremendous carrying power of the roads and the swelling traffic night and morning of poor sheep who paid their hard-earned nickels, had a market value which gave the road an assured physical value of about three times the sum for which it could have been built. The North Chicago company, which in 1886 had a physical value of little more than a million, could not now be duplicated for less than seven millions, and was capitalized at nearly fifteen millions. The road was valued at over one hundred thousand dollars more per mile than the sum for which it could actually have been replaced. Pity the poor groveling hack at the bottom, who has not the brainpower either to understand or to control that which his very presence and necessities create.

These tremendous holdings, paying from 10 to 12 percent on every hundred-dollar share, were in the control, if not in the actual ownership, of Cowperwood. Millions in loans that did not appear on the books of the companies, he had converted into actual cash, wherewith he had bought houses, lands, equipages, paintings, government bonds of the purest gold value, thereby assuring himself to that extent of a fortune vaulted and locked, absolutely secure. After much toiling and moiling on the part of his overworked legal department he had secured a consolidation, under the title of the Consolidated Traction Company of Illinois, of all outlying lines, each having separate franchises and capitalized separately, yet operated by an amazing hocus-pocus of contracts and agreements in single, harmonious union with all his other properties. The North and West Chicago companies he now proposed to unite into a third company to be called the Union Traction Company. By taking up the 10 and 12 percent issues of the old North and West companies and giving two for one of the new 6 percent one-hundred-dollar-share Union Traction stocks in their stead, he could satisfy the current stockholders, who were apparently made somewhat better off thereby, and still create and leave for himself a handsome margin of nearly eighty million dollars. With a renewal of his franchises for twenty, fifty, or one hundred years, he would have fastened on the city of Chicago the burden of yielding interest on this somewhat fictitious value, and would leave himself personally worth in the neighborhood of one hundred millions.

This matter of extending his franchises was a most difficult and intricate business, however. It involved overcoming or outwitting a recent and very treacherous increase of local sentiment against him. This had been occasioned by various details which related to his elevated roads. To the two lines already built he now added a third property, the Union Loop. This he prepared to connect not only with his own, but with other outside elevated properties, chief among which was Mr. Schryhart's South Side L. He would then farm out to his enemies the privilege of running trains on this new line. However unwillingly, they would be forced to avail themselves of the proffered opportunity, because within the region covered by the new loop was the true congestion—here everyone desired to come either once or twice during the day or night. By this means Cowperwood would secure to his property a paying interest from the start.

This scheme aroused a really unprecedented antagonism in the breasts of Cowperwood's enemies. By the Arneel-Hand-Schryhart contingent it was looked upon as nothing short of diabolical. The newspapers, directed by such men as Haguenin, Hyssop, Ormonde Ricketts, and Truman Leslie MacDonald (whose father was now dead, and whose thoughts as editor of the *Inquirer* were almost solely directed toward driving Cowperwood out of Chicago), began to shout, as a last resort, in the interests of democracy. Seats for everybody (on Cowperwood's lines), no more straps in the rush hours, three-cent fares for workingmen, morning and evening, free transfers from all of Cowperwood's lines north to west and west to north, 20 percent of the gross income of his lines to be paid to the city. The masses should be made cognizant of their individual rights and privileges. Such a course, while decidedly inimical to Cowperwood's interests at the present time, and as such strongly favored by the majority of his opponents, had nevertheless, its disturbing elements to an ultraconservative like Hosmer Hand.

"I don't know about this, Norman," he remarked to Schryhart on one occasion. "I don't know about this. It's one thing to stir up the public, but it's another to make them forget. This is a restless, socialistic country, and Chicago is the very hotbed and center of it. Still, if it will serve to trip him up I suppose it will do for the present. The newspapers can probably smooth it all over later. But I don't know."

Mr. Hand was of that order of mind that sees socialism as a horrible importation of monarchy-ridden Europe. Why couldn't the people be satisfied to allow the strong, intelligent, God-fearing men of the community to arrange things for them? Wasn't that what democracy meant? Certainly it was—he himself was one of the strong. He could not help distrusting all this radical palaver. Still, anything to hurt Cowperwood—anything.

Cowperwood was not slow to realize that public sentiment was now in danger of being thoroughly crystallized against him by newspaper agitation. Although his franchises would not expire—the large majority of them—before January 1, 1903, yet if things went on at this rate it would be doubtful soon whether ever again he would be able to win another election, by methods legitimate or illegitimate. Hungry aldermen and councilmen might be venal and greedy enough to do anything he should ask, provided he was willing to pay enough, but even the thickest-hided, the most voracious and corrupt politician, could scarcely withstand the searching glare of publicity and the infuriated rage of a possibly aroused public opinion. By degrees this last, owing to the untiring efforts of the newspapers, was being whipped into a wild foam. To come into council at this time and ask for a twenty-year extension of franchises not destined to expire for seven years was too much. It could not be done. Even suborned councilmen would be unwilling to undertake it just now. There are some things which even politically are impossible.

To make matters worse, the twenty-year-franchise limit was really not at all sufficient for his present needs. In order to bring about the consolidation of his North and West surface lines, which he was now proposing and on the strength of which he wished to issue at least 200 million dollars' worth of $100 6 percent shares in place of the 70 million

dollars current of 10 and 12 percents, it was necessary for
him to secure a much more respectable term of years than
the brief one now permitted by the state legislature, even
providing that this latter could be obtained.

"Peeble are not ferry much indrested in tees short-time
frangizes," observed Mr. Gotloeb once, when Cowperwood
was talking the matter over with him. He wanted Haeckelheimer & Co. to underwrite the whole issue. "Dey are so in-
sigure. Now if you couldt get, say, a frangize for fifty or
one hunnert years or something like dot your stocks wouldt
go off like hot cakes. I know where I couldt dispose of
fifty million dollars off dem in Chermany alone."

He was most unctuous and pleading.

Cowperwood understood this quite as well as Gotloeb,
if not better. He was not at all satisfied with the thought of
obtaining a beggarly twenty-year extension for his giant
schemes when cities like Philadelphia, Boston, New York,
and Pittsburgh were apparently glad to grant their corporations franchises which would not expire for ninety-nine
years at the earliest, and in most cases were given in perpe-
tuity. This was the kind of franchise favored by the great
moneyed houses of New York and Europe, and which Gotloeb, and even Addison, locally, were demanding.

"It is certainly important that we get these franchises renewed for fifty years," Addison used to say to him, and it
was seriously and disagreeably true.

The various lights of Cowperwood's legal department, constantly on the search for new legislative devices, were
not slow to grasp the import of the situation. It was not long
before the resourceful Mr. Joel Avery appeared with a suggestion.

"Did you notice what the state legislature of New York
is doing in connection with the various local transit problems down there?" asked this honorable gentleman of Cowperwood one morning, ambling in when announced and seat-
ing himself in the great presence. A half-burned cigar was
between his fingers, and a little round felt hat looked peculiarly rakish above his sinister, intellectual, constructive
face and eyes.

"No, I didn't," replied Cowperwood, who had actually
noted and pondered upon the item in question, but who did
not care to say so. "I saw something about it, but I didn't
pay much attention to it. What of it?"

"Well, it plans to authorize a body of four or five men —one branch in New York, one in Buffalo, I presume—to grant all new franchises and extend old ones with the consent of the various local communities involved. They are to fix the rate of compensation to be paid to the state or the city, and the rates of fare. They can regulate transfers, stock issues, and all that sort of thing. I was thinking if at any time we find this business of renewing the franchises too uncertain here we might go into the state legislature and see what can be done about introducing a public-service commission of that kind into this state. We are not the only corporation that would welcome it. Of course, it would be better if there were a general or special demand for it outside of ourselves. It ought not to originate with us."

He stared at Cowperwood heavily, the latter returning a reflective gaze.

"I'll think it over," he said. "There may be something in that."

Henceforth the thought of instituting such a commission never left Cowperwood's mind. It contained the germ of a solution—the possibility of extending his franchises for fifty or even a hundred years.

This plan, as Cowperwood was subsequently to discover, was a thing more or less expressly forbidden by the state constitution of Illinois. The latter provided that no special or exclusive privilege, immunity, or franchise whatsoever should be granted to any corporation, association, or individual. Yet, "What is a little matter like the constitution between friends, anyhow?" someone had already asked. There are fads in legislation, as well as dusty pigeonholes in which phases of older law are tucked away and forgotten. Many earlier ideals of the constitution-makers had long since been conveniently obscured or nullified by decisions, appeals to the federal government, appeals to the state government, communal contracts, and the like—fine cobwebby figments, all, but sufficient, just the same, to render inoperative the original intention. Besides, Cowperwood had but small respect for either the intelligence or the self-protective capacity of such men as constituted the rural voting element of the state. From his lawyers and from others he had heard innumerable droll stories of life in the state legislature, and the state counties and towns—on the bench, at the rural hustings where the state elections were won, in country hotels, on country roads and farms. "One day as I was getting on the train at Petunkey," old General Van Sickle, or Judge Dickensheets, or ex-Judge Avery would begin—and then would follow some amazing narration of rural immorality or dullness, or political or social misconception. Of the total population of the state at this time over half were in the city itself, and these he had managed to keep in control. For the remaining million, divided between twelve small cities and an agricultural population, he had small respect. What did this handful of yokels amount to, anyhow?—dull, frivoling, barn-dancing boors.

The great state of Illinois—a territory as large as England proper and as fertile as Egypt, bordered by a great lake and a vast river, and with a population of over two million freeborn Americans—would scarcely seem a fit subject for corporate manipulation and control. Yet a more trade-ridden commonwealth might not have been found anywhere at this time within the entire length and breadth of the universe. Cowperwood personally, though contemptuous of the bucolic mass when regarded as individuals, had always been impressed by this great community of his election. Here had come Marquette and Joliet, La Salle and Hennepin, dreaming a way to the Pacific. Here Lincoln and Douglas, antagonist and protagonist of slavery argument, had contested; here had arisen "Joe" Smith, propagator of that strange American dogma of the Latter-Day Saints. What a state, Cowperwood sometimes thought; what a figment of the brain, and yet how wonderful! He had crossed it often on his way to St. Louis, to Memphis, to Denver, and had been touched by its very simplicity—the small, new wooden towns, so redolent of American tradition, prejudice, force, and illusion. The white-steepled church, the lawn-faced, tree-shaded village streets, the long stretches of flat, open country where corn grew in serried rows or where in winter the snow bedded lightly—it all reminded him a little of his own father and mother, who had been in many respects suited to such a world as this. Yet nonetheless did he hesitate to press on the measure which was to adjust his own future, to make profitable his issue of 200 million dollars' worth of Union Traction, to secure him a fixed place in the financial oligarchy of America and of the world.

The state legislature at this time was ruled over by a small group of wire-pulling, pettifogging, corporation-controlled individuals who came up from the respective towns, counties, and cities of the state, but who bore the same relation to the communities which they represented and to their superiors and equals in and out of the legislative halls at Springfield that men do to such allies anywhere in any given field. Why do we call them pettifogging and dismiss them? Perhaps they were pettifogging, but certainly no more so than any other shrewd rat or animal that burrows its way onward—and shall we say upward? The deepest controlling principle which animated these individuals was the oldest and first, that of self-preservation. Picture, for example, a common occurrence—that of Senator John H. Southack, conversing with, perhaps, Senator George Mason Wade of Gallatin County, behind a legislative door in one of the senate conference chambers toward the close of a session—Senator Southack, blinking, buttonholing his well-dressed colleague and drawing very near; Senator Wade, curious, confidential, expectant (a genial, solid, experienced, slightly paunchy but well-built Senator Wade—and handsome, too).

"You know, George, I told you there would be something eventually in the Quincy waterfront improvement if it ever worked out. Well, here it is. Ed Truesdale was in town yesterday." (This with a knowing eye, as much as to say, "Mum's the word.") "Here's five hundred; count it."

A quick flashing out of some green and yellow bills from a vest pocket, a light thumbing and counting on the part of Senator Wade. A flare of comprehension, approval, gratitude, admiration, as though to signify, "This is something like." "Thanks, John. I had pretty near forgot all about it. Nice people, eh? If you see Ed again give him my regards. When that Bellville contest comes up let me know."

Mr. Wade, being a good speaker, was frequently in request to stir up the populace to a sense of pro or con in connection with some legislative crisis impending, and it was to some such future opportunity that he now pleasantly referred. O life, O politics, O necessity, O hunger, O burning human appetite and desire on every hand!

Mr. Southack was an unobtrusive, pleasant, quiet man of the type that would usually be patronized as rural and pettifogging by men high in commercial affairs. He was nonetheless well fitted to his task, a capable and diligent beneficiary and agent. He was well dressed, middle-aged—only forty-five—cool, courageous, genial, with eyes that were material but not cold or hard, and a light, springy, energetic step and manner. A holder of some C. W. & I. R.R. shares, a director of one of his local county banks, a silent partner in the Effingham *Herald,* he was a personage in his district, one much revered by local swains. Yet a more game and rascally type was not to be found in all rural legislation.

It was old General Van Sickle who sought out Southack, having remembered him from his earlier legislative days. It was Avery who conducted the negotiations. Primarily, in all state scheming at Springfield, Senator Southack was supposed to represent the C. W. I., one of the great trunk lines traversing the state, and incidentally connecting Chicago with the South, West, and East. This road, having a large local mileage and being anxious to extend its franchises in Chicago and elsewhere, was deep in state politics. By a curious coincidence it was mainly financed by Haeckelheimer, Gotloeb & Co. of New York, though Cowperwood's connection with that concern was not as yet known. Going to Southack, who was the Republican whip in the senate, Avery proposed that he, in conjunction with Judge Dickensheets and one Gilson Bickel, counsel for the C. W. I., should now undertake to secure sufficient support in the state senate and house for a scheme introducing the New York idea of a public-service commission into the governing machinery of the state of Illinois. This measure, be it noted, was to be supplemented by one very interesting and important little proviso to the effect that all franchise-holding corporations should hereby, for a period of fifty years from the date of the enactment of the bill into law, be assured of all their rights, privileges, and immunities—including franchises, of course. This was justified on the ground that any such radical change as that involved in the introduction of a public-service commission might disturb the peace and well-being of corporations with franchises which still had years to run.

Senator Southack saw nothing very wrong with this idea, though he naturally perceived what it was all about and whom it was truly designed to protect.

"Yes," he said succinctly, "I see the lay of that land, but what do I get out of it?"

"Fifty thousand dollars for yourself if it's successful, ten thousand if it isn't—provided you make an honest effort; two thousand dollars apiece for any of the boys who see fit to help you if we win. Is that perfectly satisfactory?"

"Perfectly," replied Senator Southack.

CHAPTER LV

Cowperwood and the Governor

A public-service-commission law might, *ipso facto*, have been quietly passed at this session if the arbitrary franchise-extending proviso had not been introduced, and this on the thin excuse that so novel a change in the working scheme of the state government might bring about hardship to some. This redounded too obviously to the benefit of one particular corporation. The newspapermen—as thick as flies about the halls of the state capitol at Springfield, and essentially watchful and loyal to their papers—were quick to sense the true state of affairs. Never were there such hawks as newspapermen. These wretches (employed by sniveling, mudsnouting newspapers of the opposition) were not only in the councils of politicians, in the pay of rival corporations, in the confidence of the governor, in the secrets of the senators and local representatives, but were here and there in one another's confidence. A piece of news—a rumor, a dream, a fancy—whispered by Senator Smith to Senator Jones, or by Representative Smith to Representative Jones, and confided by him in turn to Charlie White of the *Globe,* or Eddie Burns of the *Democrat,* would in turn be communicated to Robert Hazlitt of the *Press,* or Harry Emonds of the *Transcript.*

All at once a disturbing announcement in one or another of the papers, no one knowing whence it came. Neither Senator Smith nor Senator Jones had told anyone. No word of the confidence reposed in Charlie White or Eddie Burns had ever been breathed. But there you were—the thing was

in the papers; the storm of inquiry, opinion, opposition was
on. No one knew, no one was to blame, but it was on, and
the battle had henceforth to be fought in the open.

Consider also the governor who presided at this time in
the executive chamber at Springfield. He was a strange, tall,
dark, osseous man, who, owing to the brooding, melancholy
character of his own disposition, had a checkered and
somewhat sad career behind him. Born in Sweden, he had
been brought to America as a child, and allowed or compelled to fight his own way upward under all the grinding
aspects of poverty. Owing to an energetic and indomitable
temperament, he had through years of law practice and
public labors of various kinds built up for himself a following among Chicago Swedes which amounted to adoration. He had been city tax-collector, city surveyor, district
attorney, and for six or eight years a state circuit judge. In
all these capacities he had manifested a tendency to do the
right as he saw it and play fair—qualities which en-
deared him to the idealistic. Honest, and with a hopeless,
brooding sympathy for the miseries of the poor, he had as
circuit judge, and also as district attorney, rendered various
decisions which had made him very unpopular with the rich,
and powerful—decisions in damage cases, fraud cases, railroad claim cases where the city or the state was seeking to
oust various powerful railway corporations from possession
of property—yards, water-frontages, and the like, to which
they had no just claim. At the same time the populace, reading the news items of his doings and hearing him speak on
various and sundry occasions, conceived a great fancy
for him. He was primarily softhearted, sweet-minded, fiery,
a brilliant orator, a dynamic presence. In addition he was
woman-hungry—a phase which homely, sex-starved intel-
lectuals the world over will understand, to the shame of a
lying age that because of quixotic dogma belies its greatest
desire, its greatest sorrow, its greatest joy. All these factors
turned an ultraconservative element in the community
against him, and he was considered dangerous. At the same
time he had by careful economy and investment built up a
fair-sized fortune. Recently, however, owing to the craze for
skyscrapers, he had placed much of his holdings in a somewhat poorly constructed and therefore unprofitable office
building. Because of this error financial wreck was threat-

ening him. Even now he was knocking at the doors of large bonding companies for assistance.

This man, in company with the antagonistic financial element and the newspapers, constituted, as regards Cowperwood's public-service-commission scheme, a triumvirate of difficulties not easy to overcome. The newspapers, in due time, catching wind of the true purport of the plan, ran screaming to their readers with the horrible intelligence. In the offices of Schryhart, Arneel, Hand, and Merrill, as well as in other centers of finance, there was considerable puzzling over the situation, and then a shrewd, intelligent deduction was made.

"Do you see what he's up to, Hosmer?" inquired Schryhart of Hand. "He sees that we have him scotched here in Chicago. As things stand now he can't go into the city council and ask for a franchise for more than twenty years under the state law, and he can't do that for three or four years yet, anyhow. His franchises don't expire soon enough. He knows that by the time they do expire we will have public sentiment aroused to such a point that no council, however crooked it may be, will dare to give him what he asks unless he is willing to make a heavy return to the city. If he does that it will end his scheme of selling any two hundred million dollars of Union Traction at six percent. The market won't back him up. He can't pay twenty percent to the city and give universal transfers and pay six percent on two hundred million dollars, and everybody knows it. He has a fine scheme of making a cool hundred million out of this. Well, he can't do it. We must get the newspapers to hammer this legislative scheme of his to death. When he comes into the local council he must pay twenty or thirty percent of the gross receipts of his roads to the city. He must give free transfers from every one of his lines to every other one. Then we have him. I dislike to see socialistic ideas fostered, but it can't be helped. We have to do it. If we ever get him out of here we can hush up the newspapers, and the public will forget about it; at least we can hope so."

In the meantime the governor had heard the whisper of "boodle"—a word of the day expressive of a corrupt legislative fund. Not at all a small-minded man, nor involved in the financial campaign being waged against Cowperwood, nor inclined to be influenced mentally or emotionally by superheated charges against the latter, he nevertheless speculated

deeply. In a vague way he sensed the dreams of Cowperwood. The charge of seducing women so frequently made
against the street-railway magnate, so shocking to the yoked
conventionalists, did not disturb him at all. Back of the onward sweep of the generations he himself sensed the mystic
Aphrodite and her magic. He realized that Cowperwood had
traveled fast—that he was pressing to the utmost a great advantage in the face of great obstacles. At the same time he
knew that the present streetcar service of Chicago was by
no means bad. Would he be proving unfaithful to the trust
imposed on him by the great electorate of Illinois if he
were to advantage Cowperwood's cause? Must he not rather
in the sight of all men smoke out the animating causes here
—greed, overweening ambition, colossal self-interest as opposed to the selflessness of a Christian ideal and of a democratic theory of government?

Life rises to a high plane of the dramatic, and hence of
the artistic, whenever and wherever in the conflict regarding material possession there enters a conception of the
ideal. It was this that lit forever the beacon fires of Troy,
that thundered eternally in the horses' hooves at Arbela and
in the guns at Waterloo. Ideals were here at stake—the dreams
of one man as opposed, perhaps, to the ultimate dreams of a
city or state or nation—the grovelings and wallowings of a
democracy slowly, blindly trying to stagger to its feet. In
this conflict—taking place in an inland cottage-dotted state
where men were clowns and churls, dancing fiddlers at country fairs—were opposed, as the governor saw it, the ideals
of one man and the ideals of men.

Governor Swanson decided after mature deliberation to
veto the bill. Cowperwood, debonair as ever, faithful as
ever to his logic and his conception of individuality, was
determined that no stone should be left unturned that would
permit him to triumph, that would carry him finally to the
gorgeous throne of his own construction. Having first engineered the matter through the legislature by a tortuous process, fired upon at every step by the press, he next sent various
individuals—state legislators, representatives of the C. W. &
I., members of outside corporations, to see the governor,
but Swanson was adamant. He did not see how he could
conscientiously sanction the bill. Finally, one day, as he
was seated in his Chicago business office—a fateful chamber located in the troublesome building which was subse-

quently to wreck his fortune and which was the *raison d'être* of a present period of care and depression—enter the smug, comfortable presence of Judge Nahum Dickensheets, at present senior counsel of the North Chicago Street Railway. He was a very mountain of a man physically—smooth-faced, agreeably clothed, hard and yet ingratiating of eye, a thinker, a reasoner. Swanson knew much of him by reputation and otherwise, although personally they were no more than speaking acquaintances.

"How are you, Governor? I'm glad to see you again. I heard you were back in Chicago. I see by the morning papers that you have that Southack public-service bill up before you. I thought I would come over and have a few words with you about it if you have no objection. I've been trying to get down to Springfield for the last three weeks to have a little chat with you before you reached a conclusion one way or the other. Do you mind if I inquire whether you have decided to veto it?"

The ex-judge, faintly perfumed, clean and agreeable, carried in his hand a large-sized black hand-satchel which he put down beside him on the floor.

"Yes, Judge," replied Swanson, "I've practically decided to veto it. I can see no practical reason for supporting it. As I look at it now, it's specious and special, not particularly called for or necessary at this time."

The governor talked with a slight Swedish accent, intellectual, individual.

A long, placid, philosophic discussion of all the pros and cons of the situation followed. The governor was tired, distrait, but ready to listen in a tolerant way to more argument along a line with which he was already fully familiar. He knew, of course, that Dickensheets was counsel for the North Chicago Street Railway Company.

"I'm very glad to have heard what you have to say, Judge," finally commented the governor. "I don't want you to think I haven't given this matter serious thought—I have. I know most of the things that have been done down at Springfield. Mr. Cowperwood is an able man; I don't charge any more against him than I do against twenty other agencies that are operating down there at this very moment. I know what his difficulties are. I can hardly be accused of sympathizing with his enemies, for they certainly do not sympathize with me. I am not even listening to the newspapers.

This is a matter of faith in democracy—a difference in ideals between myself and many other men. I haven't vetoed the bill yet. I don't say that something may not arise to make me sign it. My present intention, unless I hear something much more favorable in its behalf than I have already heard, is to veto it."

"Governor," said Dickensheets, rising, "let me thank you for your courtesy. I would be the last person in the world to wish to influence you outside the line of your private convictions and your personal sense of fair play. At the same time I have tried to make plain to you how essential it is, how only fair and right, that this local street-railway franchise business should be removed out of the realm of sentiment, emotion, public passion, envy, bunkum, and all the other influences that are at work to frustrate and make difficult the work of Mr. Cowperwood. All envy, I tell you. His enemies are willing to sacrifice every principle of justice and fair play to see him eliminated. That sums it up."

"That may all be true," replied Swanson. "Just the same, there is another principle involved here which you do not seem to see or do not care to consider—the right of the people under the state constitution to a consideration, a revaluation, of their contracts at the time and in the manner agreed upon under the original franchise. What you propose is sumptuary legislation; it makes null and void an agreement between the people and the street-railway companies at a time when the people have a right to expect a full and free consideration of this matter aside from state legislative influence and control. To persuade the state legislature, by influence or by any other means, to step in at this time and interfere is unfair. The propositions involved in those bills should be referred to the people at the next election for approval or not, just as they see fit. That is the way this matter should be arranged. It will not do to come into the legislature and influence or buy votes, and then expect me to write my signature under the whole matter as satisfactory."

Swanson was not heated or antipathetic. He was cool, firm, well-intentioned.

Dickensheets passed his hand over a wide, high temple. He seemed to be meditating something—some hitherto untried statement or course of action.

"Well, Governor," he repeated, "I want to thank you, anyhow. You have been exceedingly kind. By the way, I see you have a large, roomy safe here." He had picked up the bag he was carrying. "I wonder if I might leave this here for a day or two in your care? It contains some papers that I do not wish to carry into the country with me. Would you mind locking it up in your safe and letting me have it when I send for it?"

"With pleasure," replied the governor.

He took it, placed it in lower storage space, and closed and locked the door. The two men parted with a genial handshake. The governor returned to his meditations, the judge hurried to catch a car.

About eleven o'clock the next morning Swanson was still working in his office, worrying greatly over some method whereby he could raise $100,000 to defray interest charges, repairs, and other payments on a structure that was by no means meeting expenses and was hence a drain. At this juncture his office door opened, and his very youthful office boy presented him the card of F. A. Cowperwood. The governor had never seen him before. Cowperwood entered, brisk, fresh, forceful. He was as crisp as a new dollar bill—as clean, sharp, firmly limned.

"Governor Swanson, I believe?"

"Yes, sir."

The two were scrutinizing each other defensively.

"I am Mr. Cowperwood. I come to have a very few words with you. I will take very little of your time. I do not wish to go over any of the arguments that have been gone over before. I am satisfied that you know all about them."

"Yes, I had a talk with Judge Dickensheets yesterday."

"Just so, Governor. Knowing all that you do, permit me to put one more matter before you. I know that you are, comparatively, a poor man—that every dollar you have is at present practically tied in this building. I know of two places where you have applied for a loan of one hundred thousand dollars and have been refused because you haven't sufficient security to offer outside of this building, which is mortgaged up to its limits as it stands. The men, as you must know, who are fighting you are fighting me. I am a scoundrel because I am selfish and ambitious—a materialist. You are not a scoundrel, but a dangerous person because you are an idealist. Whether you veto this bill or not, you will never again be elected Governor of Illinois if the people who are fighting me succeed, as they will succeed, in fighting you."

Swanson's dark eyes burned illuminatively. He nodded his head in assent.

"Governor, I have come here this morning to bribe you, if I can. I do not agree with your ideals; in the last analysis I do not believe that they will work. I am sure I do not believe in most of the things that you believe in. Life is different at bottom, perhaps, from what either you or I may think. Just the same, as compared with other men, I sympathize with you. I will loan you that one hundred thousand dollars and two or three or four hundred thousand dollars more besides if you wish. You need never pay me a dollar—or you can if you wish. Suit yourself. In that black bag which Judge Dickensheets brought here yesterday, and which is in your safe, is three hundred thousand dollars in cash. He did not have the courage to mention it. Sign the bill and let me beat the men who are trying to beat me. I will support you in the future with any amount of money or influence that I can bring to bear in any political contest you may choose to enter, state or national."

Cowperwood's eyes glowed like a large, genial collie's. There was a suggestion of sympathetic appeal in them, rich and deep, and even more than that, a philosophic perception of ineffable things. Swanson arose. "You really don't mean to say that you are trying to bribe me openly, do you?" he inquired. In spite of a conventional impulse to burst forth in moralistic denunciation, solemnly phrased, he was compelled for the moment to see the other man's viewpoint. They were working in different directions, going different ways, to what ultimate end?

"Mr. Cowperwood," continued the governor, his face a physiognomy out of Goya, his eye alight with a kind of understanding sympathy, "I suppose I ought to resent this, but I can't. I see your point of view. I'm sorry, but I can't help you or myself. My political belief, my ideals, compel me to veto this bill; when I forsake these I am done politically with myself. I may not be elected governor again, but that does not matter, either. I could use your money, but I won't. I shall have to bid you good morning."

He moved toward the safe slowly, opened it, took out the bag, and brought it over.

"You must take that with you," he added.

The two men looked at each other a moment curiously, sadly—the one with a burden of financial, political, and moral worry on his spirit, the other with an unconquerable determination not to be worsted even in defeat.

"Governor," concluded Cowperwood, in the most genial, contented, undisturbed voice, "you will live to see another legislature pass and another governor sign some such bill. It will not be done this season, apparently, but it will be done. I am not through, because my case is right and fair. Just the same, after you have vetoed the bill, come and see me, and I will loan you that one hundred thousand if you want it."

Cowperwood went out. Swanson vetoed the bill. It is on record that subsequently he borrowed $100,000 from Cowperwood to stay himself from ruin.

CHAPTER LVI

The Ordeal of Berenice

At the news that Swanson had refused to sign the bill and that the legislature lacked sufficient courage to pass it over his veto, both Schryhart and Hand literally rubbed their hands in comfortable satisfaction.

"Well, Hosmer," said Schryhart the next day, when they met at their favorite club—the Union League—"it looks as though we were making some little progress, after all, doesn't it? Our friend didn't succeed in turning that little trick, did he?"

He beamed almost ecstatically upon his solid companion.

"Not this time. I wonder what move he will decide to make next."

"I don't see very well what it can be. He knows now that he can't get his franchises without a compromise that will eat into his profits, and if that happens he can't sell his Union Traction stock. This legislative scheme of his must have cost him all of three hundred thousand dollars, and what has he to show for it? The new legislature, unless I'm greatly mistaken, will be afraid to touch anything in connection with him. It's hardly likely that any of the Springfield politicians will want to draw the fire of the newspapers again."

Schryhart felt very powerful, imposing—sleek, indeed—now that his theory of newspaper publicity as a cure was apparently beginning to work. Hand, more saturnine, more responsive to the uncertainty of things mundane—the shifty undercurrents that are perpetually sapping and mining below—was agreeable, but not sure. Perhaps so.

In regard to his eastern life during this interlude, Cowperwood had been becoming more and more keenly alive to the futility of the attempt to effect a social rescue for Aileen. What was the use, he often asked himself, as he contemplated her movements, thoughts, plans, as contrasted with the natural efficiency, taste, grace, and subtlety of a woman like Berenice. He felt that the latter could, if she would, smooth over in an adroit way all the silly social antagonisms which were now afflicting him. It was a woman's game, he frequently told himself, and would never be adjusted till he had the woman.

Simultaneously Aileen, looking at the situation from her own point of view and nonplussed by the ineffectiveness of mere wealth when not combined with a certain social something which she did not appear to have, was, nevertheless, unwilling to surrender her dream. What was it, she asked herself over and over, that made this great difference between women and women? The question contained its own answer, but she did not know that. She was still good-looking—very—and an adept in self-ornamentation, after her manner and taste. So great had been the newspaper palaver regarding the arrival of a new multimillionaire from the West and the palace he was erecting that even tradesmen, clerks, and hallboys knew of her. Almost invariably, when called upon to state her name in such quarters, she was greeted by a slight start of recognition, a swift glance of examination, whispers, even open comment. That was something. Yet how much more, and how different, were those rarefied reaches of social supremacy to which popular repute bears scarcely any relationship at all. How different, indeed? From what Cowperwood had said in Chicago she had fancied that when they took up their formal abode in New York he would make an attempt to straighten out his life somewhat, to modify the number of his indifferent amours and to present an illusion of solidarity and unity. Yet, now that they actually arrived, she noticed that he was more concerned with his heightened political and financial complications in Illinois and with his art collection than he was with what might happen to be going on in the new home or what could be made to happen there. As in the days of old, she was constantly puzzled by his persistent evenings out and his sudden appearances and disappearances. Yet, determine as she might, rage secretly or openly as she would, she could not cure herself of the infection of Cowperwood, the lure that surrounded and substantiated a mind and spirit far greater than any other she had ever known. Neither honor, virtue, consistent charity, nor sympathy was there, but only a gay, foamy, unterrified sufficiency and a creative, constructive sense of beauty that, like sunlit spray, glowing with all the irradiative glories of the morning, danced and fled, spun driftwise over a heavy sea of circumstance. Life, however dark and somber, could never apparently cloud his soul. Brooding and idling in the wonder palace of his construction, Aileen could see what he was like. The silver fountain in the court of orchids, the peacelike glow of the pink marble chamber, with its birds and flowers, the serried brilliance of his amazing art collection were all like him, were really the color of his soul. To think that after all she was not the one to bind him to subjection, to hold him by golden yet steely threads of fancy to the hem of her garment! To think that he should no longer walk, a slave of his desire, behind the chariot of her spiritual and physical superiority. Yet she could not give up.

By this time Cowperwood had managed through infinite tact and a stoic disregard of his own aches and pains to reestablish at least a temporary working arrangement with the Carter household. To Mrs. Carter he was still a heavensent son of light. Actually in a mournful way she pleaded for Cowperwood, vouching for his disinterestedness and long-standing generosity. Berenice, on the other hand, was swept between her craving for a great state for herself—luxury, power—and her desire to conform to the current ethics and morals of life. Cowperwood was married, and

because of his attitude of affection for her his money was
tainted. She had long speculated on his relation to Aileen,
the basis of their differences, had often wondered why
neither she nor her mother had ever been introduced.
What type of woman was the second Mrs. Cowperwood?
Beyond generalities, Cowperwood had never mentioned her.
Berenice actually thought to seek her out in some inconspicuous way, but as it chanced, one night her curiosity was
rewarded without effort. She was at the opera with friends,
and her escort nudged her arm.

"Have you noticed Box 9—the lady in white satin with
the green lace shawl?"

"Yes." Berenice raised her glasses.

"Mrs. Frank Algernon Cowperwood, the wife of the Chicago millionaire. They have just built that house at 68th
Street. He has part lease of Number 9, I believe."

Berenice almost started, but retained her composure, giving merely an indifferent glance. A little while after, she
adjusted her glasses carefully and studied Mrs. Cowperwood.
She noted curiously that Aileen's hair was somewhat the
color of her own—a more carroty red. She studied her eyes,
which were slightly ringed, her smooth cheeks and full
mouth, thickened somewhat by drinking and dissipation.
Aileen was good-looking, she thought—handsome in a material way, though so much older than herself. Was it merely
age that was alienating Cowperwood, or was it some deep-
seated intellectual difference? Obviously Mrs. Cowperwood
was well over forty—a fact which did not give Berenice any
sense of satisfaction or of advantage. She really did not care
enough. It did occur to her, however, that this woman whom
she was observing had probably given the best years of her life
to Cowperwood—the brilliant years of her girlhood. And now
he was tired of her! There were small, carefully powdered
lines at the tails of Aileen's eyes and at the corners of her
mouth. At the same time she seemed preternaturally gay, kit-
tenish, spoiled. With her were two men—one a well-known
actor, sinisterly handsome, a man with a brutal, unclean reputation, the other a young social pretender—both unknown to
Berenice. Her knowledge was to come from her escort, a lo-
quacious youth, more or less versed, as it happened, in the
gay life of the city.

"I hear that she is creating quite a stir in Bohemia," he

observed. "If she expects to enter society it's a poor way to begin, don't you think?"

"Do you know that she expects to?"

"All the usual signs are out—a box here, a house on Fifth Avenue."

This study of Aileen puzzled and disturbed Berenice a little. Nevertheless, she felt immensely superior. Her soul seemed to soar over the plain Aileen inhabited. The type of the latter's escorts suggested error—a lack of social discrimination. Because of the high position he had succeeded in achieving Cowperwood was entitled, no doubt, to be dissatisfied. His wife had not kept pace with him, or, rather, had not eluded him in his onward flight—had not run swiftly before, like a winged victory. Berenice reflected that if she were dealing with such a man he should never know her truly—he should be made to wonder and to doubt. Lines of care and disappointment should never mar her face. She would scheme and dream and conceal and evade. He should dance attendance, whoever he was.

Nevertheless, here she herself was, at twenty-two, unmarried, her background insecure, the very ground on which she walked treacherous. Braxmar knew, and Beales Chadsey, and Cowperwood. At least three or four of her acquaintants must have been at the Waldorf on that fatal night. How long would it be before others became aware? She tried eluding her mother, Cowperwood, and the situation generally by freely accepting more extended invitations and by trying to see whether there was not some opening for her in the field of art. She thought of painting, and essayed several canvases which she took to dealers. The work was subtle, remote, fanciful—a snow scene with purple edges; a thinking satyr, ironlike in his heaviness, brooding over a cloudy valley; a lurking devil peering at a praying Marguerite; a Dutch interior inspired by Mrs. Batjer, and various dancing figures. Phlegmatic dealers of somber mien admitted some promise, but pointed out the difficulty of sales. Beginners were numerous. Art was long. If she went on, of course. . . . Let them see other things. She turned her thoughts to dancing.

This art in its interpretative sense was just being introduced into America, a certain Althea Baker having created a good deal of stir in society by this means. With the idea of duplicating or surpassing the success of this woman

Berenice conceived a dance series of her own. One was to be "The Terror"—a nymph dancing in the spring woods, but eventually pursued and terrorized by a faun; another, "The Peacock," a fantasy illustrative of proud self-adulation; another, "The Vestal," a study from Roman choric worship. After spending considerable time at Pocono evolving costumes, poses, and the like, Berenice finally hinted at the plan to Mrs. Batjer, declaring that she would enjoy the artistic outlet it would afford, and indicating at the same time that it might provide the necessary solution of a problem of ways and means.

"Why, Bevy, how you talk!" commented Mrs. Batjer. "And with your possibilities. Why don't you marry first, and do your dancing afterward? You might compel a certain amount of attention that way."

"Because of hubby? How droll! Whom would you suggest that I marry at once?"

"Oh, when it comes to that—" replied Mrs. Batjer, with a slight, reproachful lift in her voice, and thinking of Kilmer Duelma. "But surely your need isn't so pressing. If you were to take up professional dancing I might have to cut you afterward—particularly if anyone else did."

She smiled the sweetest, most sensible smile. Mrs. Batjer accompanied her suggestions nearly always with a slight sniff and cough. Berenice could see that the mere fact of this conversation made a slight difference. In Mrs. Batjer's world poverty was a dangerous topic. The mere odor of it suggested a kind of horror—perhaps the equivalent of error or sin. Others, Berenice now suspected, would take affright even more swiftly.

Subsequent to this, however, she made one slight investigation of those realms that govern professional theatrical engagements. It was a most disturbing experience. The mere color and odor of the stuffy offices, the gauche, material attendants, the impossible aspirants and participants in this make-believe world! The crudeness! The effrontery! The materiality! The sensuality! It came to her as a sickening breath and for the moment frightened her. What would become of refinement there? What of delicacy? How could one rise and sustain an individual dignity and control in such a world as this?

Cowperwood was now suggesting as a binding link that he should buy a home for them on Park Avenue, where such social functions as would be of advantage to Berenice and in some measure to himself as an occasional guest might be indulged in. Mrs. Carter, a fool of comfort, was pleased to welcome this idea. It promised to give her absolute financial security for the future.

"I know how it is with you, Frank," she declared. "I know you need some place that you can call a home. The whole difficulty will be with Bevy. Ever since that miserable puppy made those charges against me I haven't been able to talk to her at all. She doesn't seem to want to do anything I suggest. You have much more influence with her than I have. If you explain, it may be all right."

Instantly Cowperwood saw an opportunity. Intensely pleased with this confession of weakness on the part of the mother, he went to Berenice, but by his usual method of indirect direction.

"You know, Bevy," he said one afternoon when he found her alone, "I have been wondering if it wouldn't be better if I bought a large house for you and your mother here in New York, where you and she could do entertaining on a large scale. Since I can't spend my money on myself, I might as well spend it on someone who would make an interesting use of it. You might include me as an uncle or father's cousin or something of that sort," he added lightly.

Berenice, who saw quite clearly the trap he was setting for her, was nonplussed. At the same time she could not help seeing that a house, if it was beautifully furnished, would be an interesting asset. People in society loved fixed, notable dwellings; she had observed that. What functions could not be held if only her mother's past were not charged against her! That was the great difficulty. It was almost an Arabian situation, heightened by the glitter of gold. And Cowperwood was always so diplomatic. He came forward with such a bland, engaging smile. His hands were so shapely and seeking.

"A house such as you speak of would enlarge the debt beyond payment, I presume," she remarked, sardonically and with a sad, almost contemptuous gesture. Cowperwood realized how her piercing intellect was following his shifty trail, and winced. She must see that her fate was in his hands, but oh! if she would only surrender, how swiftly every dollar of his vast fortune should be piled humbly at her feet. She should have her heart's desire, if money would buy it. She could say to him go, and he would go; come, and he would come.

"Berenice," he said, getting up, "I know what you think. You fancy I am trying to further my own interests in this way, but I'm not. I wouldn't compromise you ultimately for all the wealth of India. I have told you where I stand. Every dollar that I have is yours to do with as you choose on any basis that you may care to name. I have no future outside of you, none except art. I do not expect you to marry me. Take all that I have. Wipe society under your feet. Don't think that I will ever charge it up as a debt. I won't. I want you to hold your own. Just answer me one question; I won't ever ask another."

"Yes?"

"If I were single now, and you were not in love or married, would you consider me at all?"

His eyes pleaded as never had they pleaded before.

She started, looked concerned, severe, then relaxed as suddenly.

"Let me see," she said, with a slight brightening of the eyes and a toss of her head. "That is a second cousin to a proposal, isn't it? You have no right to make it. You aren't single, and aren't likely to be. Why should I try to read the future?"

She walked indifferently out of the room, and Cowperwood stayed a moment to think. Obviously he had triumphed in a way. She had not taken great offense. She must like him and would marry him if only . . .

Only Aileen.

And now he wished more definitely and forcefully than ever that he were really and truly free. He felt that if ever he wished to attain Berenice he must persuade Aileen to divorce him.

CHAPTER LVII

Aileen's Last Card

It was not until some little time after they were established in the new house that Aileen first came upon any evidence of the existence of Berenice Fleming. In a general way she assumed that there were women—possibly some of whom she had known—Stephanie, Mrs. Hand, Florence Cochrane, or later arrivals—yet so long as they were not obtruded on her she permitted herself the semicomforting thought that things were not as bad as they might be. So long, indeed, as Cowperwood was genuinely promiscuous, so long as he trotted here and there, not snared by any particular siren, she could not despair, for, after all, she *had* ensnared him and held him deliciously—without variation, she believed, for all of ten years—a feat which no other woman had achieved before or after. Rita Sohlberg might have succeeded —the beast! How she hated the thought of Rita! By this time, however, Cowperwood was getting on in years. The day must come when he would be less keen for variability, or, at least, would think it no longer worthwhile to change. If only he did not find some one woman, some Circe, who would bind and enslave him in these later years as she had herself done in his earlier ones, all might yet be well. At the same time she lived in daily terror of a discovery which was soon to follow.

She had gone out one day to pay a call on someone to whom Rhees Grier, the Chicago sculptor, had given her an introduction. Crossing Central Park in one of the new French machines which Cowperwood had purchased for her indulgence, her glance wandered down a branch road to where another automobile similar to her own was stalled. It was early in the afternoon, at which time Cowperwood was presumably engaged in Wall Street. Yet there he was, and with him two women, neither of whom, in the speed of passing, could Aileen quite make out. She had her car halted and driven to within seeing distance behind a clump of bushes. A chauffeur whom she did not know was tinkering at a handsome machine, while on the grass nearby stood Cowperwood and a tall, slender girl with red hair somewhat like Aileen's own. Her expression was aloof, poetic, rhapsodical. Aileen could not analyze it, but it fixed her attention completely. In the tonneau sat an elderly lady, whom Aileen at once assumed to be the girl's mother. Who were they? What was Cowperwood doing here in the park at this hour? Where were they going? With a horrible retch of envy she noted upon Cowperwood's face a smile the like and import of which she well knew. How often she had seen it years and years before! Having escaped detection, she ordered her chauffeur to follow the car, which soon started, at a safe distance. She saw Cowperwood and the two ladies put down at one of the great hotels, and followed them into the dining room, where from behind a screen, after the most careful maneuvering, she had an opportunity of studying them at her leisure. She drank in every detail of Berenice's face—the delicately pointed chin, the clear, fixed blue eyes, the straight, sensitive nose and tawny hair. Calling the headwaiter, she inquired the names of the two women, and in return for a liberal tip was informed at once. "Mrs. Ira Carter, I believe, and her daughter, Miss Fleming, Miss Berenice Fleming. Mrs. Carter was Mrs. Fleming once." Aileen followed them out eventually, and in her own car pursued them to their door, into which Cowperwood also disappeared. The next day, by telephoning the apartment to make inquiry, she learned that they actually lived there. After a few days of brooding she employed a detective, and learned that Cowperwood was a constant visitor at the Carters', that the machine in which they rode was his, maintained at a separate garage, and that they were of society truly. Aileen would never have followed the clue so vigorously had it not been for the look she had seen Cowperwood fix on the girl in the park and in the restaurant—an air of soul hunger which could not be gainsaid.

Let no one ridicule the terrors of unrequited love. Its tentacles are cancerous, its grip is of icy death. Sitting in her boudoir immediately after these events, driving, walking, shopping, calling on the few with whom she had managed to scrape an acquaintance, Aileen thought morning, noon, and night of this new woman. The pale, delicate face haunted her. What were those eyes, so remote in their gaze, surveying? Love? Cowperwood? Yes! Yes! Gone in a flash, and permanently, as it seemed to Aileen, was the value of this house, her dreams of a new social entrance. And she had already suffered so much; endured so much. Cowperwood being absent for a fortnight, she moped in her room, sighed, raged, and then began to drink. Finally she sent for an actor who had once paid attention to her in Chicago, and whom she had later met here in the circle of the theaters. She was not so much burning with lust as determined in her drunken gloom that she would have revenge. For days there followed an orgy, in which wine, bestiality, mutual recrimination, hatred, and despair were involved. Sobering eventually, she wondered what Cowperwood would think of her now if he knew this. Could he ever love her anymore? Could he even tolerate her? But what did he care? It served him right, the dog! She would show him, she would wreck his dream, she would make her own life a scandal, and his, too! She would shame him before all the world. He should never have a divorce! He should never be able to marry a girl like that and leave her alone—never, never, never! When Cowperwood returned, she snarled at him without vouchsafing an explanation.

He suspected at once that she had been spying upon his maneuvers. Moreover, he did not fail to notice her heavy eyes, superheated cheeks, and sickly breath. Obviously she had abandoned her dream of a social victory of some kind, and was entering on a career of what—debauchery? Since coming to New York she had failed utterly, he thought, to make any single intelligent move toward her social rehabilitation. The banal realms of art and the stage, with which in his absence or neglect she had trifled with here, as she had done in Chicago, were worse than useless; they were destructive. He must have a long talk with her one of these days, must confess frankly to his passion for Berenice, and appeal to her sympathy and good sense. What scenes would follow! Yet she might succumb, at that. Despair, pride, disgust might move her. Besides, he could now bestow upon her a very large fortune. She could go to Europe or remain here and live in luxury. He would always remain friendly with her— helpful, advisory—if she would permit it.

The conversation which eventually followed on this topic was of such stuff as dreams are made of. It sounded hollow and unnatural within the walls where it took place. Consider the great house on upper Fifth Avenue, its magnificent chambers aglow, of a stormy Sunday night. Cowperwood was lingering in the city at this time, busy with a group of eastern financiers who were influencing his contest in the state legislature of Illinois. Aileen was momentarily consoled by the thought that for him, perhaps, love might, after all, be a thing apart—a thing no longer vital and soul-controlling. Tonight he was sitting in the court of orchids, reading a book—the diary of Cellini, which someone had recommended to him—stopping to think now and then of things in Chicago or Springfield, or to make a note. Outside the rain was splashing in torrents on the electric-lighted asphalt of Fifth Avenue —the park opposite a Corot-like shadow. Aileen was in the music room, strumming indifferently. She was thinking of times past—Lynde, from whom she had not heard in half a year; Watson Skeet, the sculptor, who was also out of her ken at present. When Cowperwood was in the city and in the house she was accustomed from habit to remain indoors or near. So great is the influence of past customs of devotion that they linger long past the hour when the act ceases to become valid.

"What an awful night!" she observed once, strolling to a window to peer out from behind a brocaded valance.

"It is bad, isn't it?" replied Cowperwood as she returned. "Hadn't you thought of going anywhere this evening?"

"No—oh no," replied Aileen indifferently. She rose restlessly from the piano, and strolled on into the great picture gallery. Stopping before one of Raphael Sanzio's Holy Families, only recently hung, she paused to contemplate the serene face—medieval, Madonnaesque, Italian. The lady seemed fragile, colorless, spineless—without life. Were there such women? Why did artists paint them? Yet the little Christ was sweet. Art bored Aileen unless others were enthusiastic. She craved only the fanfare of the living—not painted resemblances. She returned to the music room, to the court of orchids, and was just about to go upstairs to prepare herself a drink and read a novel when Cowperwood observed:

"You're bored, aren't you?"

"Oh no; I'm used to lonely evenings," she replied, quietly and without any attempt at sarcasm.

Relentless as he was in hewing life to his theory—hammering substance to the form of his thought—yet he was tender, too, in the manner of a rainbow dancing over an abyss. For the moment he wanted to say, "Poor girlie, you do have a hard time, don't you, with me?" but he reflected instantly how such a remark would be received. He meditated, holding his book in his hand above his knee, looking at the purling water that flowed and flowed in sprinkling showers over the sportive marble figures of mermaids, a Triton, and nymphs astride of fishes.

"You're really not happy in this state any more, are you?" he inquired. "Would you feel any more comfortable if I stayed away entirely?"

His mind had turned of a sudden to the one problem that was fretting him, and to the opportunities of this hour.

"*You* would," she replied, for her boredom merely concealed her unhappiness in no longer being able to command in the least his interest or his sentiment.

"Why do you say that in just that way?" he asked.

"Because I know you would. I know why you ask. You know well enough that it isn't anything I want to do that is concerned. It's what you want to do. You'd like to turn me off like an old horse now that you are tired of me, and so you ask whether I would feel any more comfortable. What a liar you are, Frank! How really shifty you are! I don't wonder you're a multimillionaire. If you could live long enough you would eat up the whole world. Don't you think for one moment that I don't know of Berenice Fleming here in New York, and how you're dancing attendance on her—because I do. I know how you have been hanging about her for months and months—ever since we have been here, and for long before. You think she's wonderful now because she's young and in society. I've seen you in the Waldorf and in the park hanging on her every word, looking at her with adoring eyes. What a fool you are, to be so big a man! Every little snip, if she has pink cheeks and a doll's face, can wind you right around her finger. Rita Sohlberg did it; Stephanie Platow did it; Florence Cochrane did it; Cecily Haguenin —and heaven knows how many more that I never heard of. I suppose Mrs. Hand still lives with you in Chicago—the cheap strumpet! Now it's Berenice Fleming and her frump of a mother. From all I can learn you haven't been able to get her yet—because her mother's too shrewd, perhaps—

but you probably will in the end. It isn't you so much as your money that they're after. Pah! Well, I'm unhappy enough, but it isn't anything you can remedy any more. Whatever you could do to make me unhappy you have done, and now you talk of my being happier away from you. Clever boy, you! I know you the way I know my ten fingers. You don't deceive me at any time in any way any more. I can't do anything about it. I can't stop you from making a fool of yourself with every woman you meet, and having people talk from one end of the country to the other. Why, for a woman to be seen with you is enough to fix her reputation forever. Right now all Broadway knows you're running after Berenice Fleming. Her name will soon be as sweet as those of the others you've had. She might as well give herself to you. If she ever had a decent reputation it's gone by now, you can depend upon that."

These remarks irritated Cowperwood greatly—enraged him—particularly her reference to Berenice. What were you to do with such a woman? he thought. Her tongue was becoming unbearable; her speech in its persistence and force was that of a termagant. Surely, surely, he had made a great mistake in marrying her. At the same time the control of her was largely in his own hands even yet.

"Aileen," he said coolly, at the end of her speech, "you talk too much. You rave. You're growing vulgar, I believe. Now let me tell you something." And he fixed her with a hard, quieting eye. "I have no apologies to make. Think what you please. I know why you say what you do. But here is the point. I want you to get it straight and clear. It may make some difference eventually if you're any kind of a woman at all. I don't care for you any more. If you want to put it another way—I'm tired of you. I have been for a long while. That's why I've run with other women. If I hadn't been tired of you I wouldn't have done it. What's more, I'm in love with somebody else—Berenice Fleming, and I expect to stay in love. I wish I were free so I could rearrange my life on a different basis and find a little comfort before I die. You don't really care for me any more. You can't. I'll admit I have treated you badly; but if I had really loved you I wouldn't have done it, would I? It isn't my fault that love died in me, is it? It isn't your fault. I'm not blaming you. Love isn't a bunch of coals that can be blown by an artificial bellows into a flame at any time. It's out, and that's an end of it. Since I don't love you and can't, why should you want me to stay near you? Why shouldn't you let me go and give me a divorce? You'll be just as happy or unhappy away from me as with me. Why not? I want to be free again. I'm miserable here, and have been for a long time. I'll make any arrangement that seems fair and right to you. I'll give you this house—these pictures, though I really don't see what you'd want with them." (Cowperwood had no intention of giving up the gallery if he could help it.) "I'll settle on you for life any income you desire, or I'll give you a fixed sum outright. I want to be free, and I want you to let me be. Now, why won't you be sensible and let me do this?"

During this harangue Cowperwood had first sat and then stood. At the statement that his love was really dead—the first time he had ever baldly and squarely announced it— Aileen had paled a little and put her hand to her forehead over her eyes. It was then he had arisen. He was cold, determined, a little revengeful for the moment. She realized now that he meant this—that in his heart was no least feeling for all that had gone before—no sweet memories, no binding thoughts of happy hours, days, weeks, years, that were so glittering and wonderful to her in retrospect. Great heavens, it was really true! His love was dead; he had said it! But for the nonce she could not believe it; she would not. It really couldn't be true.

"Frank," she began, coming toward him, the while he moved away to evade her. Her eyes were wide, her hands trembling, her lips moving in an emotional, wavy, rhythmic way. "You really don't mean that, do you? Love isn't wholly dead, is it? All the love you used to feel for me? Oh, Frank, I have raged, I have hated, I have said terrible, ugly things, but it has been because I have been in love with you! All the time I have. You know that. I have felt so bad—O God, how bad I have felt! Frank, you don't know it—but my pillow has been wet many and many a night. I have cried and cried. I have got up and walked the floor. I have drunk whiskey— plain, raw whiskey—because something hurt me and I wanted to kill the pain. I have gone with other men, one after another —you know that—but oh! Frank, Frank, you know that I didn't want to, that I didn't mean to! I have always despised the thought of them afterward. It was only because I was lonely and because you wouldn't pay any attention to me or be nice to me. Oh, how I have longed and longed for just one loving hour with you—one night, one day! There are women who could suffer in silence, but I can't. My mind won't let me alone, Frank—my thoughts won't. I can't help thinking how I used to run to you in Philadelphia, when you would meet me on your way home, or when I used to come to you in Ninth Street or on Eleventh. Oh, Frank, I probably did wrong to your first wife. I see it now—how she must have suffered! But I was just a silly girl then, and I didn't know. Don't you remember how I used to come to you in Ninth Street and how I saw you day after day in the penitentiary in Philadelphia? You said then you would love me always and that you would never forget. Can't you love me anymore— just a little? Is it really true that your love is dead? Am I so old, so changed? Oh, Frank, please don't say that—please don't—please, please, please! I beg of you!"

She tried to reach him and put a hand on his arm, but he stepped aside. To him, as he looked at her now, she was the antithesis of anything he could brook, let alone desire artistically or physically. The charm was gone, the spell broken. It was another type, another point of view he required, but, above all and principally, youth, youth—the spirit, for instance, that was in Berenice Fleming. He was sorry—in his way. He felt sympathy, but it was like the tinkling of a far-off sheep bell—the moaning of a whistling buoy heard over the thrash of night-black waves on a stormy sea.

"You don't understand how it is, Aileen," he said. "I can't help myself. My love is dead. It is gone. I can't recall it. I can't feel it. I wish I could, but I can't; you must understand that. Some things are possible and some are not."

He looked at her, but with no relenting. Aileen, for her part, saw in his eyes nothing, as she believed, save cold philosophic logic—the man of business, the thinker, the bargainer, the plotter. At the thought of the adamantine character of his soul, which could thus definitely close its gates on her forever and ever, she became wild, angry, feverish—not quite sane.

"Oh, don't say that!" she pleaded foolishly. "Please don't. Please don't say that. It might come back a little if—if—you would only believe in it. Don't you see how I feel? Don't you see how it is?"

She dropped to her knees and clasped him about the waist. "Oh, Frank! Oh, Frank! Oh, Frank!" she began to call, crying. "I can't stand it! I can't! I can't! I can't! I shall die."

"Don't give way like that, Aileen," he pleaded. "It doesn't do any good. I can't lie to myself. I don't want to lie to you. Life is too short. Facts are facts. If I could say and believe that I loved you I would say so now, but I can't. I don't love you. Why should I say that I do?"

In the content of Aileen's nature was a portion that was purely histrionic, a portion that was childish—petted and spoiled—a portion that was sheer unreason, and a portion that was splendid emotion—deep, dark, involved. At this statement of Cowperwood's, which seemed to throw her back on herself forever and ever to be alone, she first pleaded willingness to compromise—to share. She had not fought Stephanie Platow, she had not fought Florence Cochrane, or Cecily Haguenin, or Mrs. Hand, or, indeed, anybody after Rita, and she would fight no more. She had not spied on him in connection with Berenice—she had accidentally met them. True, she had gone with other men, but? . . . Berenice was beautiful, she admitted it, but so was she in her way still—a little, still. Couldn't he find a place for her yet in his life? Wasn't there room for both?

At this expression of humiliation and defeat Cowperwood was sad, sick, almost nauseated. How could one argue? How make her understand?

"I wish it were possible, Aileen," he concluded finally and heavily, "but it isn't."

All at once she arose, her eyes red but dry.

"You don't love me, then, at all, do you? Not a bit?"

"No, Aileen, I don't. I don't mean by that that I dislike you. I don't mean to say that you aren't interesting in your way as a woman and that I don't sympathize with you. I do. But I don't love you anymore. I can't. The thing I used to feel I can't feel anymore."

She paused for a moment, uncertain how to take this, the while she whitened, grew more tense, more spiritual than she had been in many a day. Now she felt desperate, angry, sick, but like the scorpion that ringed by fire can turn only on itself. What a hell life was, she told herself. How it slipped away and left one aging, horribly alone! Love was nothing, faith nothing—nothing, nothing!

A fine light of conviction, intensity, intention lit her eye for the moment. "Very well, then," she said coolly, tensely. "I know what I'll do. I'll not live this way. I'll not live beyond tonight. I want to die, anyhow, and I will."

It was by no means a cry, this last, but a calm statement. It should prove her love. To Cowperwood it seemed unreal, bravado, a momentary rage intended to frighten him. She turned and walked up the grand staircase, which was near— a splendid piece of marble and bronze fifteen feet wide, with marble Nereids for newel-posts, and dancing figures worked into the stone. She went into her room quite calmly and took up a steel paper cutter of dagger design—a knife with a handle of bronze and a point of great sharpness. Coming out and going along the balcony over the court of orchids, where Cowperwood still was seated, she entered the sunrise room with its pool of water, its birds, its benches, its vines. Locking the door, she sat down, and then, suddenly baring an arm, jabbed a vein—ripped it for inches—and sat there to bleed. Now she would see whether she could die, whether he would let her.

Uncertain, astonished, not able to believe that she could be so rash, not believing that her feeling could be so great, Cowperwood still remained where she had left him, wondering. He had not been so greatly moved—the tantrums of women were common—and yet— Could she really be contemplating death? How could she? How ridiculous! Life was so strange, so mad. But this was Aileen who had just made this threat, and she had gone up the stairs to carry it out, perhaps. Impossible! How could it be? Yet back of all his doubts there was a kind of sickening feeling, a dread. He recalled how she had assaulted Rita Sohlberg.

He hurried up the steps now and into her room. She was not there. He went quickly along the balcony, looking here and there, until he came to the sunrise room. She must be there, for the door was shut. He tried it—it was locked.

"Aileen," he called. "Aileen! Are you in there?" No answer. He listened. Still no answer. "Aileen!" he repeated, "Are you in there? What dammed nonsense is this, anyhow?"

"George!" he thought to himself, stepping back; "she might do it, too—perhaps she has." He could not hear anything save the odd chattering of a toucan aroused by the light she had switched on. Perspiration stood out on his brow. He shook the knob, pushed a bell for a servant, called for keys which had been made for every door, called for a chisel and hammer.

"Aileen," he said, "if you don't open the door this instant I will see that it is opened. It can be opened quick enough."

Still no sound.

"Damn it!" he exclaimed, becoming wretched, horrified. A servant brought the keys. The right one would not enter. A second was on the other side. "There is a bigger hammer somewhere," Cowperwood said. "Get it! Get me a chair!" Meantime, with terrific energy, using a large chisel, he forced the door.

There on one of the stone benches of the lovely room sat Aileen, the level pool of water before her, the sunrise glow over everything, tropic birds in their branches, and she, her hair disheveled, her face pale, one arm—her left—hanging down, ripped and bleeding, trickling a thick stream of rich red blood. On the floor was a pool of blood, fierce, scarlet, like some rich cloth, already turning darker in places.

Cowperwood paused—amazed. He hurried forward, seized her arm, made a bandage of a torn handerchief above the wound, sent for a surgeon, saying the while: "How could you, Aileen? How impossible! To try to take your life! This isn't love. It isn't even madness. It's foolish acting."

"Don't you really care?" she asked.

"How can you ask? How could you really do this?"

He was angry, hurt, glad that she was alive, shamed— many things.

"Aileen, this is nonsense. I will not talk to you about it now. Have you cut yourself anywhere else?" he asked, feeling about her bosom and sides.

"Then why not let me die?" she replied in the same manner. "I will someday. I want to."

"Well, you may, someday," he replied, "but not tonight. I scarcely think you want to now. This is too much, Aileen— really impossible."

He drew himself up and looked at her—cool, unbelieving, the light of control, even of victory, in his eyes. As he had suspected, it was not truly real. She would not have killed herself. She had expected him to come—to make the old effort. Very good. He would see her safely in bed and in a nurse's hands, and would then avoid her as much as possible in the future. If her intention were genuine she would carry it out in his absence, but he did not believe she would.

CHAPTER LVIII

A Marauder upon the Commonwealth

The spring and summer months of 1897 and the late fall of 1898 witnessed the final closing battle between Frank Algernon Cowperwood and the forces inimical to him insofar as the city of Chicago, the state of Illinois, and, indeed, the United States of America, were concerned. When in 1896 a new governor and a new group of state representatives were installed Cowperwood decided that it would be advisable to continue the struggle at once. By the time this new legislature should convene for its labors a year would have passed since Governor Swanson had vetoed the original public-service-commission bill. By that time public sentiment as aroused by the newspapers would have had time to cool. Already through various favorable financial interests —particularly Haeckelheimer, Gotloeb & Co. and all the sub-surface forces they represented—he had attempted to influence the incoming governor, and had in part succeeded.

The new governor in this instance—one Corporal A. E. Archer—or ex-Congressman Archer, as he was sometimes called—was, unlike Swanson, a curious mixture of the commonplace and the ideal—one of those shiftily loyal and loyally shifty who make their upward way by devious, if not too reprehensible, methods. He was a little man, stocky, brown-haired, brown-eyed, vigorous, witty, with the ordinary politician's estimate of public morality—namely, that there is no such thing. A drummer boy at fourteen in the War of the Rebellion, a private at sixteen and eighteen, he had subsequently been breveted for conspicuous military service. At this later time he was head of the Grand Army of the Republic, and conspicuous in various stirring eleemosynary efforts on behalf of the old soldiers, their widows and orphans. A fine American, flag-waving, tobacco-chewing, foulswearing little man was this—and one with noteworthy political ambitions. Other Grand Army men had been conspicuous in the lists for Presidential nominations. Why not he? An excellent orator in a high falsetto way, and popular because of good-fellowship, presence, force, he was by nature materially and commercially minded—therefore without basic appeal to the higher ranks of intelligence. In seeking the nomination for governorship he had made the usual overtures and had in turn been sounded by Haeckelheimer, Gotloeb, and various other corporate interests who were in league with Cowperwood as to his attitude in regard to a proposed public-service commission. At first he had refused to commit himself. Later, finding that the C. W. & I. and the Chicago & Pacific (very powerful railroads both) were interested, and that other candidates were running him a tight chase in the gubernatorial contest, he succumbed in a measure, declaring privately that in case the legislature proved to be strongly in favor of the idea and the newspapers not too crushingly opposed he might be willing to stand as its advocate. Other candidates expressed similar views, but Corporal Archer proved to have the greater following, and was eventually nominated and comfortably elected.

Shortly after the new legislature had convened, it so chanced that a certain A. S. Rotherhite, publisher of the South Chicago *Journal*, was one day accidentally sitting as a visitor in the seat of a state representative by the name of Clarence Mulligan. While so occupied Rotherhite was familiarly slapped on the back by a certain Senator Ladrigo of Menard, and was invited to come out into the rotunda, where, posing as Representative Mulligan, he was introduced by Senator Ladrigo to a stranger by the name of Gerard. The latter, with but few preliminary remarks, began as follows:

"Mr. Mulligan, I want to fix it with you in regard to this Southack bill which is soon to come up in the house. We have seventy votes, but we want ninety. The fact that the bill has gone to a second reading in the senate shows our strength. I am authorized to come to terms with you this morning if you would like. Your vote is worth two thousand dollars to you the moment the bill is signed."

Mr. Rotherhite, who happened to be a newly recruited member of the opposition press, proved very canny in this situation.

"Excuse me," he stammered, "I did not understand your name?"

"Gerard. G-er-ard. Henry A. Gerard," replied this other.

"Thank you. I will think it over," was the response of the presumed Representative Mulligan.

Strange to state, at this very instant the authentic Mulligan actually appeared—heralded aloud by several of his colleagues who happened to be lingering nearby in the lobby. Whereupon the anomalous Mr. Gerard and the crafty Senator Ladrigo discreetly withdrew. Needless to say that Mr. Rotherhite hurried at once to the forces of righteousness. The press should spread this little story broadcast. It was a very meaty incident; and it brought the whole matter once more into the fatal, poisonous field of press discussion.

At once the Chicago papers flew to arms. The cry was raised that the same old sinister Cowperwoodian forces were at work. The members of the senate and the house were solemnly warned. The sterling attitude of ex-Governor Swanson was held up as an example to the present Governor Archer. "The whole idea," observed an editorial in Truman Leslie MacDonald's *Inquirer*, "smacks of chicane, political subtlety, and political jugglery. Well do the citizens of Chicago and the people of Illinois know who and what particular organization would prove the true beneficiaries. We do not want a public-service commission at the behest of a private street-railway corporation. Are the tentacles of Frank A. Cowperwood to envelop this legislature as they did the last?"

This broadside, coming in conjunction with various hostile rumblings in other papers, aroused Cowperwood to emphatic language.

"They can all go to the devil," he said to Addison, one day at lunch. "I have a right to an extension of my franchises for fifty years, and I am going to get it. Look at New York and Philadelphia. Why, the eastern houses laugh. They don't understand such a situation. It's all the inside work of this Hand-Schryhart crowd. I know what they're doing and who's pulling the strings. The newspapers yap-yap every time they give an order. Hyssop waltzes every time Arneel moves. Little MacDonald is a stool pigeon for Hand. It's got down so low now that it's anything to beat Cowperwood. Well, they won't beat me. I'll find a way out. The legislature will pass a bill allowing for a fifty-year franchise, and the governor will sign it. I'll see to that personally. I have at least eighteen thousand stockholders who want a decent run for their money, and I propose to give it to them. Aren't other men getting rich? Aren't other corporations earning ten and twelve percent? Why shouldn't I? Is Chicago any the worse? Don't I employ twenty thousand men and pay them well? All this palaver about the rights of the people and the duty to the public—rats! Does Mr. Hand acknowledge any duty to the public where his special interests are concerned? Or Mr. Schryhart? Or Mr. Arneel? The newspapers be damned! I know my rights. An honest legislature will give me a decent franchise to save me from the local political sharks."

By this time, however, the newspapers had become as subtle and powerful as the politicians themselves. Under the great dome of the capitol at Springfield, in the halls and conference chambers of the senate and house, in the hotels, and in the rural districts wherever any least information was to be gathered, were their representatives—to see, to listen, to pry. Out of this contest they were gaining prestige and cash. By them were the reform aldermen persuaded to call mass meetings in their respective districts. Property owners were urged to organize; a committee of one hundred prominent citizens led by Hand and Schryhart was formed. It was not long before the halls, chambers, and committee rooms of the capitol at Springfield and the corridors of the one principal hotel were being tramped over almost daily by rampant delegations of ministers, reform aldermen, and civil committeemen, who arrived speechifying, threatening, and haranguing, and departed, only to make room for another relay.

"Say, what do you think of these delegations, Senator?" inquired a certain Representative Greenough of Senator George Christian of Grundy one morning, the while a group of Chicago clergymen accompanied by the mayor and several distinguished private citizens passed through the rotunda on their way to the committee on railroads, where the house bill was privily being discussed. "Don't you think they speak well for our civic pride and moral upbringing?" He raised his eyes and crossed his fingers over his waistcoat in the most sanctimonious and reverential attitude.

"Yes, dear Pastor," replied the irreverent Christian, without the shadow of a smile. He was a little sallow, wiry man with eyes like a ferret, a small moustache and goatee ornamenting his face. "But do not forget that the Lord has called us also to this work."

"Even so," acquiesced Greenough. "We must not weary in well doing. The harvest is truly plenteous and the laborers are few."

"Tut, tut, Pastor. Don't overdo it. You might make me larf," replied Christian; and the twain parted with knowing and yet weary smiles.

Yet how little did the accommodating attitude of these gentlemen avail in silencing the newspapers. The damnable newspapers! They were here, there, and everywhere, reporting each least fragment of rumor, conversation, or imaginary program. Never did the citizens of Chicago receive so keen a drilling in statecraft—its subtleties and ramifications. The president of the senate and the speaker of the house were singled out and warned separately as to their duty. A page a day devoted to legislative proceeding in this quarter was practically the custom of the situation. Cowperwood was here personally on the scene, brazen, defiant, logical, the courage of his convictions in his eyes, the power of his magnetism fairly enslaving men. Throwing off the mask of disinterestedness—if any might be said to have covered him—he now frankly came out in the open, and journeying to Springfield, took quarters at the principal hotel. Like a general in time of battle, he marshaled his forces about him. In the warm, moonlit atmosphere of June nights, when the streets of Springfield were quiet, the great plain of Illinois bathed for hundreds of miles from north to south in a sweet effulgence, and the rurals slumbering in their simple homes, he sat conferring with his lawyers and legislative agents.

Pity in such a crisis the poor country-jake legislator torn between his desire for a justifiable and expedient gain and his fear lest he should be assailed as a betrayer of the people's interests. To some of these small-town legislators, who had never seen as much as two thousand dollars in cash in all their days, the problem was soul-racking. Men gathered in private rooms and hotel parlors to discuss it. They stood in their rooms at night and thought about it alone. The sight of big business compelling its desires the while the people went begging was destructive. Many a romantic, illusioned, idealistic young country editor, lawyer, or statesman was here made over into a minor cynic or bribe-taker. Men were robbed of every vestige of faith or even of charity;

they came to feel, perforce, that there was nothing outside the capacity for taking and keeping. The surface might appear commonplace—ordinary men of the state of Illinois going here and there—simple farmers and small-town senators and representatives conferring and meditating and wondering what they could do—yet a junglelike complexity was present, a dark, rank growth of horrific but avid life—life at the full, life knife in hand, life blazing with courage and dripping at the jaws with hunger.

However, because of the terrific uproar the more cautious legislators were by degrees becoming fearful. Friends in their home towns, at the instigation of the papers, were beginning to write them. Political enemies were taking heart. It meant too much of a sacrifice on the part of everybody. In spite of the fact that the bait was apparently within easy reach, many became evasive and disturbed. When a certain Representative Sparks, cocked and primed, with the bill in his pocket, arose upon the floor of the house, asking leave to have it spread upon the minutes, there was an instant explosion. The privilege of the floor was requested by a hundred. Another representative, Disback, being in charge of the opposition to Cowperwood, had made a count of noses and was satisfied in spite of all subtlety on the part of the enemy that he had at least one hundred and two votes, the necessary two-thirds wherewith to crush any measure which might originate on the floor. Nevertheless, his followers, because of caution, voted it to a second and a third reading. All sorts of amendments were made—one for a three-cent fare during the rush hours, another for a 20 percent tax on gross receipts. In amended form the measure was sent to the senate, where the changes were stricken out and the bill once more returned to the house. Here, to Cowperwood's chagrin, signs were made manifest that it could not be passed. "It can't be done, Frank," said Judge Dickensheets. "It's too grilling a game. Their home papers are after them. They can't live."

Consequently a second measure was devised—more soothing and lulling to the newspapers, but far less satisfactory to Cowperwood. It conferred upon the Chicago City Council, by a trick of revising the old Horse and Dummy Act of 1865, the right to grant a franchise for fifty instead of for twenty years. This meant that Cowperwood would have to return to Chicago and fight out his battle there. It was a

severe blow, yet better than nothing. Providing that he could
win one more franchise battle within the walls of the city
council in Chicago, it would give him all that he desired.
But could he? Had he not come here to the legislature especially to evade such a risk? His motives were enduring such a
blistering exposure. Yet perhaps, after all, if the price were
large enough the Chicago councilmen would have more real
courage than these country legislators—would dare more.
They would have to.

So, after heaven knows what desperate whisperings, conferences, arguments, and heartening of members, there was
originated a second measure, which—after the defeat of the
first bill, 104 to 49—was introduced, by way of a very complicated path, through the judiciary committee. It was passed;
and Governor Archer, after heavy hours of contemplation
and self-examination, signed it. A little man mentally, he
failed to estimate an aroused popular fury at its true import
to him. At his elbow was Cowperwood in the clear light of
day, snapping his fingers in the face of his enemies, showing
by the hard, cheerful glint in his eye that he was still
master of the situation, giving all assurance that he would
yet live to whip the Chicago papers into submission. Besides, in the event of the passage of the bill, Cowperwood
had promised to make Archer independently rich—a cash
reward of $500,000.

CHAPTER LIX

Capital and Public Rights

Between the passage on June 5, 1897, of the Mears
bill—so christened after the doughty representative who had
received a small fortune for introducing it—and its presentation to the Chicago City Council in December of the same
year, what broodings, plottings, politickings, and editorial-
izings on the part of all and sundry! In spite of the intense

feeling of opposition to Cowerwpood there was at the same time in local public life one stratum of commercial and phlegmatic substance that could not view him in an altogether unfavorable light. They were in business themselves. His lines passed their doors and served them. They could not see wherein his street-railway service differed so much from that which others might give. Here was the type of materialist who in Cowperwood's defiance saw a justification of his own material point of view and was not afraid to say so. But as against these there were the preachers—poor windblown sticks of unreason who saw only what the current palaver seemed to indicate. Again there were the anarchists, socialists, single-taxers, and public-ownership advocates. There were the very poor who saw in Cowperwood's wealth and in the fabulous stories of his New York home and of his art collection a heartless exploitation of their needs. At this time the feeling was spreading broadcast in America that great political and economic changes were at hand—that the tyranny of iron masters at the top was to give way to a richer, freer, happier life for the rank and file. A national eight-hour-day law was being advocated, and the public ownership of public franchises. And here now was a great street-railway corporation, serving a population of a million and a half, occupying streets which the people themselves created by their presence, taking toll from all these humble citizens to the amount of sixteen or eighteen millions of dollars in the year and giving in return, so the papers said, poor service, shabby cars, no seats at rush hours, no universal transfers (as a matter of fact, there were in operation 362 separate transfer points) and no adequate tax on the immense sums earned. The workingman who read this by gas or lamp light in the kitchen or parlor of his shabby flat or cottage, and who read also in other sections of his paper of the free, reckless, glorious lives of the rich, felt himself to be defrauded of a portion of his rightful inheritance. It was all a question of compelling Frank A. Cowperwood to do his duty by Chicago. He must not again be allowed to bribe the aldermen; he must not be allowed to have a fifty-year franchise, the privilege of granting which he had already bought from the state legislature by the degradation of honest men. He must be made to succumb, to yield to the forces of law and order. It was claimed—and with a justice of which those who made the charge were by no means fully aware—that

the Mears bill had been put through the house and senate
by the use of cold cash, proffered even to the governor himself. No legal proof of this was obtainable, but Cowperwood
was assumed to be a briber on a giant scale. By the newspaper cartoons he was represented as a pirate commander
ordering his men to scuttle another vessel—the ship of Public
Rights. He was pictured as a thief, a black mask over his
eyes, and as a seducer, throttling Chicago, the fair maiden,
while he stole her purse. The fame of this battle was by
now becoming worldwide. In Montreal, in Cape Town, in
Buenos Aires and Melbourne, in London and Paris, men
were reading of this singular struggle. At last, and truly, he
was a national and international figure. His original dream,
however modified by circumstances, had literally been fulfilled.

Meanwhile be it admitted that the local elements in finance which had brought about this terrific onslaught on
Cowperwood were not a little disturbed as to the eventual
character of the child of their own creation. Here at last
was a public opinion definitely inimical to Cowperwood; but
here also were they themselves, tremendous profit-holders,
with a desire for just such favors as Cowperwood himself
had exacted, deliberately setting out to kill the goose that
could lay the golden egg. Men such as Haeckelheimer, Gotloeb, Fishel, tremendous capitalists in the East and foremost
in the directorates of huge transcontinental lines, international banking houses, and the like, were amazed that the
newspapers and the anti-Cowperwood element should have
gone so far in Chicago. Had they no respect for capital?
Did they not know that long-time franchises were practically
the basis of all modern capitalistic prosperity? Such theories
as were now being advocated here would spread to other
cities unless checked. America might readily become anti-
capitalistic—socialistic. Public ownership might appear as a
workable theory—and then what?

"Those men out there are very foolish," observed Mr.
Haeckelheimer at one time to Mr. Fishel, of Fishel, Stone
& Symons. "I can't see that Mr. Cowperwood is different from
any other organizer of his day. He seems to me perfectly
sound and able. All his companies pay. There are no better
investments than the North and West Chicago railways. It
would be advisable, in my judgment, that all the lines out
there should be consolidated and be put in his charge. He

would make money for the stockholders. He seems to know how to run street-railways."

"You know," replied Mr. Fishel, as smug and white as Mr. Haeckelheimer, and in thorough sympathy with his point of view, "I have been thinking of something like that myself. All this quarreling should be hushed up. It's very bad for business—very. Once they get that public-ownership nonsense started, it will be hard to stop. There has been too much of it already."

Mr. Fishel was stout and round like Mr. Haeckelheimer, but much smaller. He was little more than a walking mathematical formula. In his cranium were financial theorems and syllogisms of the second, third, and fourth power only.

And now behold a new trend of affairs. Mr. Timothy Arneel, attacked by pneumonia, dies and leaves his holdings in Chicago City to his eldest son, Edward Arneel. Mr. Fishel and Mr. Haeckelheimer, through agents and then directly, approach Mr. Merrill in behalf of Cowperwood. There is much talk of profits—how much more profitable has been the Cowperwood regime over street-railway lines than that of Mr. Schryhart. Mr. Fishel is interested in allaying socialistic excitement. So, by this time, is Mr. Merrill. Directly hereafter Mr. Haeckelheimer approaches Mr. Edward Arneel, who is not nearly so forceful as his father, though he would like to be so. He, strange to relate, has come rather to admire Cowperwood and sees no advantage in a policy that can only tend to municipalize local lines. Mr. Merrill, for Mr. Fishel, approaches Mr. Hand. "Never! never! never!" says Hand. Mr. Haeckelheimer approaches Mr. Hand. "Never! never! never! To the devil with Mr. Cowperwood!" But as a final emissary for Mr. Haeckelheimer and Mr. Fishel there now appears Mr. Morgan Frankhauser, the partner of Mr. Hand in a seven-million-dollar traction scheme in Minneapolis and St. Paul. Why will Mr. Hand be so persistent? Why pursue a scheme of revenge which only stirs up the masses and makes municipal ownership a valid political idea, thus disturbing capital elsewhere? Why not trade his Chicago holdings to him, Frankhauser, for Pittsburgh traction stock— share and share alike—and then fight Cowperwood all he pleases on the outside?

Mr. Hand, puzzled, astounded, scratching his round head, slaps a heavy hand on his desk. "Never!" he exlaims. "Never, by God—as long as I am alive and in Chicago!" And then he yields. Life does shifty things, he is forced to reflect in a most puzzled way. Never would he have believed it! "Schryhart," he declared to Frankhauser, "will never come in. He will die first. Poor old Timothy—if he were alive—he wouldn't either."

"Leave Mr. Schryhart out of it, for heaven's sake," pleaded Mr. Frankhauser, a genial German-American. "Haven't I troubles enough?"

Mr. Schryhart is enraged. Never! never! never! He will sell out first—but he is in a minority, and Mr. Frankhauser, or Mr. Fishel or Mr. Haeckelheimer, will gladly take his holdings.

Now behold in the autumn of 1897 all rival Chicago street-railway lines brought to Mr. Cowperwood on a platter, as it were—a golden platter.

"Ve haff it fixed," confidentially declared Mr. Gotloeb to Mr. Cowperwood, over an excellent dinner in the sacred precincts of the Metropolitan Club in New York. Time, 8:30 P.M. Wine—sparkling Burgundy. "A telegram come shusst today from Frankhauser. A nice man dot. You shouldt meet him sometime. Hant—he sells out his stock to Frankhauser. Merrill unt Edward Arneel vork vit us. Ve hantle efferyt'ing for dem. Mr. Fishel vill haff his friends pick up all de local shares he can, unt mit dees tree ve control de board. Schryhart iss out. He sess he vill resign. Very goot. I don't subbose dot vill make you veep any. It all hintges now on vether you can get dot fifty-year-franchise ordinance troo de city council or not. Haeckelheimer sess he prefers you to all utters to run t'ings. He vill leef everytink positifely in your hands. Frankhauser sess de same. Vot Haeckelheimer sess he doess. Now dere you are. It's up to you. I vish you much choy. It is no small chop you haff, beating de newspapers, unt you still haff Hant unt Schryhart against you. Mr. Haeckelheimer askt me to pay his complimends to you unt to say vill you dine vit him next veek, or may he dine vit you—vicheffer iss most conveniend. So."

In the mayor's chair of Chicago at this time sat a man named Walden H. Lucas. Aged thirty-eight, he was politically ambitious. He had the elements of popularity—the knack or luck of fixing public attention. A fine, upstanding, healthy young buck he was, subtle, vigorous, a cool, direct, practical thinker and speaker, an eager, enigmatic dreamer of great political honors to come, anxious to play his cards just right, to make friends, to be the pride of the righteous, and yet the not too-uncompromising foe of the wicked. In short, a youthful, hopeful western Machiavelli, and one who could, if he chose, serve the cause of the anti-Cowperwood struggle exceedingly well indeed.

Cowperwood, disturbed, visits the mayor in his office.

"Mr. Lucas, what is it you personally want? What can I do for you? Is it future political preferment you are after?"

"Mr. Cowperwood, there isn't anything you can do for me. You do not understand me, and I do not understand you. You cannot understand me because I am an honest man."

"Ye gods!" replied Cowperwood. "This is certainly a case of self-esteem and great knowledge. Good afternoon."

Shortly thereafter the mayor was approached by one Mr. Carker, who was the shrewd, cold, and yet magnetic leader of Democracy in the state of New York. Said Carker:

"You see, Mr. Lucas, the great money houses of the East are interested in this local contest here in Chicago. For example, Haeckelheimer, Gotloeb & Co. would like to see a consolidation of all the lines on a basis that will make them an attractive investment for buyers generally and will at the same time be fair and right to the city. A twenty-year contract is much too short a term in their eyes. Fifty is the least they could comfortably contemplate, and they would prefer a hundred. It is little enough for so great an outlay. The policy now being pursued here can lead only to the public ownership of public utilities, and that is something which the national Democratic party at large can certainly not afford to advocate at present. It would antagonize the money element from coast to coast. Any man whose political record was definitely identified with such a movement would have no possible chance at even a state nomination, let alone a national one. He could never be elected. I make myself clear, do I not?"

"You do."

"A man can just as easily be taken from the mayor's office in Chicago as from the governor's office at Springfield," pursued Mr. Carker. "Mr. Haeckelheimer and Mr. Fishel have personally asked me to call on you. If you want to be mayor of Chicago again for two years or governor next year, until the time for picking a candidate for the Presidency arrives, suit yourself. In the meantime you will be unwise, in my judgment, to saddle yourself with this public-ownership idea. The newspapers in fighting Mr. Cowperwood have raised an issue which never should have been raised."

After Mr. Carker's departure arrived Mr. Edward Arneel of local renown, and then Mr. Jacob Bethal, the Democratic leader in San Francisco, both offering suggestions which if followed might result in mutual support. There were in addition delegations of powerful Republicans from Minneapolis and from Philadelphia. Even the president of the Lake City Bank and the president of the Prairie National—once anti-Cowperwood—arrived to say what had already been said. So it went. Mr. Lucas was greatly nonplussed. A political career was surely a difficult thing to effect. Would it pay to harry Mr. Cowperwood as he had set out to do? Would a steadfast policy advocating the cause of the people get him anywhere? Would they be grateful? Would they remember? Suppose the current policy of the newspapers should be modified, as Mr. Carker had suggested that it might be. What a mess and tangle politics really were!

"Well, Bessie," he inquired of his handsome, healthy, semi-blonde wife one evening, "what would you do if you were I?"

She was gray-eyed, gay, practical, vain, substantially connected insofar as family went, and proud of her husband's position and future. He had formed the habit of talking over his various difficulties with her.

"Well, I'll tell you, Wally," she replied. "You've got to stick to something. It looks to me as though the winning side was with the people this time. I don't see how the newspapers can change now after all they've done. You don't have to advocate public ownership or anything unfair to the money element, but just the same I'd stick to my point that the fifty-year franchise is too much. You ought to make them pay the city something and get their franchise without bribery. They can't do less than that. I'd stick to the course you've begun on. You can't get along without the people, Wally. You just might have them. If you lose their good will the politicians can't help you much, nor anybody else."

Plainly there were times when the people had to be considered. They just *had* to be!

CHAPTER LX

The Net

The storm which burst in connection with Cowperwood's machinations at Springfield early in 1897, and continued without abating until the following fall, attracted such general attention that it was largely reported in the eastern papers. F. A. Cowperwood versus the state of Illinois—thus one New York daily phrased the situation. The magnetizing power of fame is great. Who can resist utterly the luster that surrounds the individualities of some men, causing them to glow with a separate and special effulgence? Even in the case of Berenice this was not without its value. In a Chicago paper which she found lying one day on a desk which Cowperwood had occupied was an extended editorial which interested her greatly. After reciting his various misdeeds, particularly in connection with the present state legislature, it went on to say:

He has an innate, chronic, unconquerable contempt for the rank and file. Men are but slaves and thralls to draw for him the chariot of his greatness. Never in all his history has he seen fit to go to the people direct for anything. In Philadelphia, when he wanted public-franchise control, he sought privily and by chicane to arrange his affairs with a venal city treasurer. In Chicago he has uniformly sought to buy and convert to his own use the splendid privileges of the city, which should really redound to the benefit of all. Frank Algernon Cowperwood does not believe in the people; he does not trust them. To him they constitute no more than a field upon which corn is to be sown, and from which it is to be reaped. They present but a mass of bent backs, their knees and faces in the mire, over which as over a floor he strides to

477

superiority. His private and inmost faith is in himself alone. Upon the majority he shuts the gates of his glory in order that the sight of their misery and their needs may not disturb nor alloy his selfish bliss. Frank Algernon Cowperwood does not believe in the people.

This editorial battle cry, flung aloft during the latter days of the contest at Springfield and taken up by the Chicago papers generally and by those elsewhere, interested Berenice greatly. As she thought of him—waging his terrific contests, hurrying to and fro between New York and Chicago, building his splendid mansion, collecting his pictures, quarreling with Aileen—he came by degrees to take on the outlines of a superman, a half-god or demi-Gorgon. How could the ordinary rules of life or the accustomed paths of men be expected to control him? They could not and did not. And here he was pursuing her, seeking her out with his eyes, grateful for a smile, waiting as much as he dared on her every wish and whim.

Say what one will, the wish buried deep in every woman's heart is that her lover should be a hero. Some, out of the veriest stick or stone, fashion the idol before which they kneel, others demand the hard reality of greatness; but in either case the illusion of paragon-worship is maintained.

Berenice, by no means ready to look upon Cowperwood as an accepted lover, was nevertheless gratified that his erring devotion was the tribute of one able apparently to command thought from the whole world. Moreover, because the New York papers had taken fire from his great struggle in the Middle West and were charging him with bribery, perjury, and intent to thwart the will of the people, Cowperwood now came forward with an attempt to explain his exact position to Berenice and to justify himself in her eyes. During visits to the Carter house or in entr'actes at the opera or the theater, he recounted to her bit by bit his entire history. He described the characters of Hand, Schryhart, Arneel, and the motives of jealousy and revenge which had led to their attack upon him in Chicago. "No human being could get anything through the Chicago City Council without paying for it," he declared. "It's simply a question of who's putting up the money." He told how Truman Leslie MacDonald had once tried to shake him down for fifty thousand dollars, and how the newspapers had since found it possible to make money, to increase their circulation, by attacking him. He frankly admitted the fact of his social ostracism, attributing it partially to Aileen's deficiencies and partially to his own attitude of Promethean defiance, which had never yet brooked defeat.

"And I will defeat them now," he said solemnly to Berenice one day over a luncheon table at the Plaza, when the room was nearly empty. His gray eyes were a study in colossal enigmatic spirit. "The governor hasn't signed my fifty-year-franchise bill" (this was before the closing events at Springfield), "but he will sign it. Then I have one more fight ahead of me. I'm going to combine all the traffic lines out there under one general system. I am the logical person to provide it. Later on, if public ownership ever arrives, the city can buy it."

"And then?" asked Berenice sweetly, flattered by his confidences.

"Oh, I don't know. I suppose I'll live abroad. You don't seem to be very much interested in me. I'll finish my picture collection—"

"But supposing you should lose?"

"I don't contemplate losing," he remarked coolly. "Whatever happens, I'll have enough to live on. I'm a little tired of contest."

He smiled, but Berenice saw that the thought of defeat was a gray one. With victory was his heart, and only there.

Owing to the national publicity being given to Cowperwood's affairs at this time, the effect upon Berenice of these conversations with him was considerable. At the same time another and somewhat sinister influence was working in his favor. By slow degrees she and her mother were coming to learn that the ultraconservatives of society were no longer willing to accept them. Berenice had become at last too individual a figure to be overlooked. At an important luncheon given by the Harris Haggertys, some five months after the Beales Chadsey affair, she had been pointed out to Mrs. Haggerty by a visiting guest from Cincinnati as someone with whom rumor was concerning itself. Mrs. Haggerty wrote to friends in Louisville for information, and received it. Shortly after, at the coming-out party of a certain Geraldine Borga, Berenice, who had been her sister's schoolmate, was curiously omitted. She took sharp note of that. Subsequently the Haggertys failed to include her, as they had always done before, in their generous summer invitations. This was true also of the Lanman Zeiglers and the Lucas Demmigs. No direct affront was offered; she was simply no longer invited. Also, one morning she read in the *Tribune* that Mrs. Corscaden Batjer had sailed for Italy. No word of this had been sent to Berenice. Yet Mrs. Batjer was supposedly one of her best friends. A hint to some is of more avail than an open statement to others. Berenice knew quite well in which direction the tide was setting.

True, there were a number—the ultrasmart of the smart world—who protested. Mrs. Patrick Gilhennin, for instance: "No! You don't tell me? What a shame! Well, I like Bevy and shall always like her. She's clever, and she can come here just as long as she chooses. It isn't her fault. She's a lady at heart and always will be. Life is so cruel." Mrs. Augustus Tabreez: "Is that really true? I can't believe it. Just the same, she's too charming to be dropped. I for one propose to ignore these rumors just as long as I dare. She can come here if she can't go anywhere else." Mrs. Pennington Drury: "That of Bevy Fleming! Who says so? I don't believe it. I like her anyhow. The idea of the Haggertys cutting her —dull fools! Well, she can be my guest, the dear thing, as long as she pleases. As though her mother's career really affected her!"

Nevertheless, in the world of the dull rich—those who hold their own by might of possession, conformity, owl-eyed sobriety, and ignorance—Bevy Fleming had become *persona non grata*. How did she take all this? With that air of superior consciousness which knows that no shift of outer material ill-fortune can detract one jot from an inward mental superiority. The truly individual know themselves from the beginning, and rarely, if ever, doubt. Life may play fast and loose about them, running like a racing, destructive tide in and out, but they themselves are like a rock, still, serene, unmoved. Bevy Fleming felt herself to be so immensely superior to anything of which she was a part that she could afford to hold her head high even now.

Just the same, in order to remedy the situation she now looked about her with an eye single to a possible satisfactory marriage. Braxmar had gone for good. He was somewhere in the East—in China, she heard—his infatuation for her apparently dead. Kilmer Duelma was gone also—snapped up—an acquisition on the part of one of those families who did not now receive her. However, in the drawing rooms where she still appeared—and what were they but marriage markets?—one or two affairs did spring up—tentative approachments on the part of scions of wealth. They were destined to prove abortive. One of these youths, Pedro Ricer Marcado, a Brazilian, educated at Oxford, promised much for sincerity and feeling until he learned that Berenice was poor in her own right—and what else? Someone had whispered something in his ear. Again, there was a certain William Drake Bowdoin, the son of a famous old family, who lived on the north side of Washington Square. After a ball, a morning musicale, and one other affair at which they met, Bowdoin took Berenice to see his mother and sister, who were charmed. "Oh, you serene divinity!" he said to her ecstatically one day. "Won't you marry me?" Bevy looked at him and wondered. "Let us wait just a little longer, my dear," she counseled. "I want you to be sure that you really love me." Shortly thereafter, meeting an old classmate at a club, Bowdoin was greeted as follows:

"Look here, Bowdoin. You're a friend of mine. I see you with that Miss Fleming. Now, I don't know how far things have gone, and I don't want to intrude, but are you sure you are aware of all the aspects of the case?"

"What do you mean?" demanded Bowdoin. "I want you to speak out."

"Oh, pardon, old man. No offense, really. You know me. I couldn't. College—and all that. Just this, though, before you go any further. Inquire about. You may hear things. If they're true you ought to know. If not, the talking ought to stop. If I'm wrong call on me for amends. I hear talk, I tell you. Best intentions in the world, old man. I do assure you."

More inquiries. The tongues of jealousy and envy. Mr. Bowdoin was sure to inherit three million dollars. Then a very necessary trip to somewhere, and Berenice stared at herself in the glass. What was it? What were people saying, if anything? This was strange. Well, she was young and beautiful. There were others. Still, she might have come to love Bowdoin. He was so airy, artistic in an unconscious way. Really, she had thought better of him.

The effect of all this was not wholly depressing. Enigmatic, disdainful, with a touch of melancholy and a world of gaiety and courage, Berenice heard at times behind joy the hollow echo of unreality. Here was a ticklish business, this living. For want of light and air the finest flowers might die. Her mother's error was not so inexplicable now. By it had she not, after all, preserved herself and her family to a certain phase of social superiority? Beauty was of such substance as dreams are made of, and as fleeting. Not oneself alone—one's inmost worth, the splendor of one's dreams—but other things—name, wealth, the presence or absence of rumor and of accident—were important. Berenice's lip curled. But life could be lived. One could lie to the world. Youth is optimistic, and Berenice, in spite of her splendid mind, was so young. She saw life as a game, a good chance, that could be played in many ways. Cowperwood's theory of things began to appeal to her. One must create one's own career, carve it out, or remain horribly dull or bored, dragged along at the chariot wheels of others. If society was so finicky, if men were so dull—well, there was one thing she could do. She must have life, life—and money would help some to that end.

Besides, Cowperwood by degrees was becoming attractive to her; he really was. He was so much better than most of the others, so very powerful. She was preternaturally gay, as one who says, "Victory shall be mine anyhow."

CHAPTER LXI

The Cataclysm

And now at last Chicago is really facing the thing which it has most feared. A giant monopoly is really reaching out to enfold it with an octopuslike grip. And Cowperwood is its eyes, its tentacles, its force! Embedded in the giant strength and good will of Haeckelheimer, Gotloeb & Co., he is like a monument based on a rock of great strength. A fifty-year franchise, to be delivered to him by a majority of forty-eight out of a total of sixty-eight aldermen (in case the ordinance has to be passed over the mayor's veto), is all that now stands between him and the realization of his dreams. What a triumph for his iron policy of courage in the face of all obstacles! What a tribute to his ability not to flinch in the face of storm and stress! Other men might have abandoned the game long before, but not he. What a splendid windfall of chance that the money element should of its own accord take fright at the Chicago idea of the municipalization of public privilege and should hand him this giant South Side system as a reward for his stern opposition to folderol theories.

Through the influence of these powerful advocates he was invited to speak before various local commercial bodies —the Board of Real Estate Dealers, the Property Owners' Association, the Merchants' League, the Bankers' Union, and so forth, where he had an opportunity to present his case and justify his cause. But the effect of his suave speechifyings in these quarters was largely neutralized by newspaper denunciation. "Can any good come out of Nazareth?" was the regular inquiry. That section of the press formerly beholden to Hand and Schryhart stood out as bitterly as ever; and most of the other newspapers, being under no obligation to eastern capital, felt it the part of wisdom to support the rank and file. The most searching and elaborate mathematical examinations were conducted, with a view to showing the fabulous profits of the streetcar trust in future years. The fine hand of eastern banking houses was detected, and their sinister motives noised abroad. "Millions for everybody in the trust, but not one cent for Chicago," was the *Inquirer's* way of putting it. Certain altruists of the community were by now so aroused that in the destruction of Cowperwood they saw their duty to God, to humanity, and to democracy straight and clear. The heavens had once more opened, and they saw a great light. On the other hand the politicians—those in office outside the mayor—constituted a petty band of guerrillas or freebooters who, like hungry swine shut in a pen, were ready to fall upon any and all propositions brought to their attention with but one end in view: that they might eat, and eat heartily. In times of great opportunity and contest for privilege life always sinks to its lowest depths of materialism and rises at the same time to its highest reaches of the ideal. When the waves of the sea are most towering its hollows are most awesome.

Finally the summer passed, the council assembled, and with the first breath of autumn chill the very air of the city was touched by a premonition of contest. Cowperwood, disappointed by the outcome of his various ingratiatory efforts, decided to fall back on his old, reliable method of bribery. He fixed on his price—twenty thousand dollars for each favorable vote, to begin with. Later, if necessary, he would raise it to twenty-five thousand, or even thirty thousand, making the total cost in the neighborhood of a million and a half. Yet it was a small price indeed when the ultimate return was considered. He planned to have his ordinance introduced by an alderman named Ballenberg, a trusted lieutenant, and handed thereafter to the clerk, who would read it, whereupon another henchman would rise to move that it be referred to the joint committee on streets and alleys, consisting of thirty-four members drawn from all the standing committees. By this committee it would be considered for one week in the general council chamber, where public hearings would be held. By keeping up a bold front Cowperwood thought the necessary iron could be put into his followers to enable them to go through with the scorching ordeal which was sure to follow. Already aldermen were being besieged at their homes and in the precincts of the ward clubs and meeting places. Their mail was being packed with importuning or threatening letters. Their very children were being derided, their neighbors urged to chastise them. Ministers wrote them in appealing or denunciatory vein. They were spied upon and abused daily in the public prints. The mayor, shrewd son of battle that he was, realizing that he had a whip of terror in his hands, excited by the long contest waged, and by the smell of battle, was not backward in urging the most drastic remedies.

"Wait till the thing comes up," he said to his friends, in a great central music-hall conference in which thousands participated, and when the matter of ways and means to defeat the venal aldermen was being discussed. "We have Mr. Cowperwood in a corner, I think. He cannot do anything for two weeks, once his ordinance is in, and by that time we shall be able to organize a vigilance committee, ward meetings, marching clubs, and the like. We ought to organize a great central mass meeting for the Sunday night before the Monday when the bill comes up for final hearing. We want overflow meetings in every ward at the same time. I tell you, gentlemen, that while I believe there are enough honest voters in the city council to prevent the Cowperwood crowd from passing this bill over my veto, yet I don't think the matter ought to be allowed to go that far. You never can tell what these rascals will do once they see an actual cash bid of twenty or thirty thousand dollars before them. Most of them, even if they were lucky, would never make the half of that in a lifetime. They don't expect to be returned to the Chicago City Council. Once is enough. There are too many others behind them waiting to get their noses in the trough. Go into your respective wards and districts and organize meetings. Call your particular alderman before you. Don't let him evade you or quibble or stand on his rights as a private citizen or a public officer. Threaten—don't cajole. Soft or kind words won't go with that type of man. Threaten, and when you have managed to extract a promise, be on hand with ropes to see that he keeps his word. I don't like to advise arbitrary methods, but what else is to be done? The enemy is armed and ready for action right now. They're just waiting for a peaceful moment. Don't let them find it. Be ready. Fight. I'm your mayor, and ready to do all I can, but I stand alone with a mere pitiful veto right. You help me and I'll help you. You fight for me and I'll fight for you."

Witness hereafter the discomfiting situation of Mr. Simon Pinski at 9 P.M. on the second evening following the introduction of the ordinance, in the ward house of the Fourteenth Ward Democratic Club. Rotund, flaccid, red-faced, his costume a long black frock coat and silk hat, Mr. Pinski was being heckled by his neighbors and business associates. He had been called here by threats to answer for his prospective high crimes and misdemeanors. By now it was pretty well understood that nearly all the present aldermen were criminal and venal, and in consequence party enmities were practically wiped out. There were no longer for the time being Democrats and Republicans, but only pro- or anti-Cowperwoods—principally anti. Mr. Pinski, unfortunately, had been singled out by the *Transcript,* the *Inquirer,* and the *Chronicle* as one of those open to advance questioning by his constituents. Of mixed Jewish and American extraction, he had been born and raised in the fourteenth, and spoke with a decidedly American accent. He was neither small nor large—sandy-haired, shifty-eyed, cunning, and on most occasions amiable. Just now he was decidedly nervous, wrathy, and perplexed, for he had been brought here against his will. His slightly oleaginous eye—not unlike that of a small pig—had been fixed definitely and finally on the munificent sum of thirty thousand dollars, no less, and this local agitation threatened to deprive him of his almost unalienable right to the same. His ordeal took place in a large, low-ceilinged room illuminated by five very plain, thin, two-armed gas jets suspended from the ceiling and adorned by posters of prizefights, raffles, games, and the "Simon Pinski Pleasure Association" plastered here and there freely against dirty, long-unwhitewashed walls. He stood on the low raised platform at the back of the room, surrounded by a score or more of his ward henchmen, all more or less reliable, all black-frocked, or at least in their Sunday clothes; all scowling, nervous, defensive, red-faced, and fearing trouble. Mr. Pinski has come armed. This talk of the mayor's concerning guns, ropes, drums, marching clubs, and the like has been given very wide publicity, and the public seems rather eager for a Chicago holiday in which the slaughter of an alderman or so might furnish the leading and most acceptable feature.

"Hey, Pinski!" yells someone out of a small sea of new and decidedly unfriendly faces. (This is no meeting of Pinski followers, but a conglomerate outpouring of all those elements of a distrait populace bent on enforcing for once the principles of aldermanic decency. There are even women here—local church members, and one or two advanced civic reformers and W. C. T. U. barroom smashers. Mr. Pinski has been summoned to their presence by the threat that if he didn't come the noble company would seek him out later at his own house.)

"Hey, Pinski! You old boodler! How much do you expect to get out of this traction business?" (This from a voice somewhere in the rear.)

Mr. Pinski (turning to one side as if pinched in the neck). "The man that says I am a boodler is a liar! I never took a dishonest dollar in my life, and everybody in the fourteenth ward knows it."

The Five Hundred People Assembled. "Ha! ha! ha! Pinski never took a dollar! Ho! ho! ho! Whoop-ee!"

Mr. Pinski (very red-faced, rising). "It is so. Why should I talk to a lot of loafers that come here because the papers tell them to call me names? I have been an alderman for six years now. Everybody knows me."

A Voice. "You call us loafers. You crook!"

Another Voice (referring to his statement of being known). "You bet they do!"

Another Voice (this from a small, bony plumber in work clothes). "Hey, you old grafter! Which way do you expect to vote? For or against this franchise? Which way?"

Still Another Voice (an insurance clerk). "Yes, which way?"

Mr. Pinski (rising once more, for in his nervousness he is constantly rising or starting to rise, and then sitting down again). "I have a right to my own mind, ain't I? I got a right to think. What for am I an alderman, then? The constitution . . ."

An Anti-Pinski Republican (a young law clerk). "To hell with the constitution! No fine words now, Pinski. Which way do you expect to vote? For or against? Yes or no?"

A Voice (that of a bricklayer, anti-Pinski). "He daresn't say. He's got some of that bastard's money in his jeans now, I'll bet."

A Voice from Behind (one of Pinski's henchmen—a heavy, pugilistic Irishman). "Don't let them frighten you, Sim. Stand your ground. They can't hurt you. We're here."

Pinski (getting up once more). "This is an outrage, I say. Ain't I goin' to be allowed to say what I think? There are two sides to every question. Now, I think, whatever the newspapers say, that Cowperwood—"

A Journeyman Carpenter (a reader of the *Inquirer*). "You're bribed, you thief! You're beating about the bush. You want to sell out."

The Bony Plumber. "Yes, you crook! You want to get away with thirty thousand dollars, that's what you want, you boodler!"

Mr. Pinski (defiantly, egged on by voices from behind). "I want to be fair—that's what. I want to keep my own mind. The constitution gives everybody the right of free speech—even me. I insist that the streetcar companies have some rights; at the same time the people have rights, too."

A Voice. "Where are those rights?"

Another Voice. "He don't know. He wouldn't know the people's rights from a sawmill."

Another Voice. "Or a load of hay."

Pinski (continuing very defiantly now, since he has not yet been slain). "I say the people have their rights. The companies ought to be made to pay a fair tax. But this twenty-year-franchise idea is too little, I think. The Mears bill now gives them fifty years, and I think all told—"

The Five Hundred (in chorus). "Ho, you robber! You thief! You boodler! Hang him! Ho! ho! ho! Get a rope!"

Pinski (retreating within a defensive circle as various citizens approach him, their eyes blazing, their teeth showing, their fists clenched). "My friends, wait! Ain't I goin' to be allowed to finish?"

A Voice. "We'll finish you, you stiff!"

A Citizen (advancing; a bearded Pole). How will you vote, hey! Tell us that! How? Hey?"

A Second Citizen (a Jew). "You're a no-good, you robber. I know you for ten years now already. You cheated me when you were in the grocery business."

A Third Citizen (a Swede; in a singsong voice). "Answer me this, Mr. Pinski. If a majority of the citizens of the fourteenth ward don't want you to vote for it, will you still vote for it?"

Pinski (hesitating).

The Five Hundred. "Ho! look at the scoundrel! He's afraid to say. He don't know whether he'll do what the people of this ward want him to do. Kill him! Brain him!"

A Voice from Behind. "Aw, stand up, Pinski. Don't be afraid."

Pinski (terrorized as the five hundred make a rush for the stage). "If the people don't want me to do it, of course I won't do it. Why should I? Ain't I their representative?"

A Voice. "Yes, when you think you're going to get the wadding kicked out of you."

Another Voice. "You wouldn't be honest with your mother, you bastard. You couldn't be!"

Pinski. "If one-half the voters should ask me not to do it I wouldn't do it."

A Voice. "Well, we'll get the voters to ask you, all right. We'll get nine-tenths of them to sign before tomorrow night."

An Irish-American (aged twenty-six; a gas collector; coming close to Pinski). "If you don't vote right we'll hang you, and I'll be there to help pull the rope myself."

One of Pinski's Lieutenants. "Say, who is that freshie?

We want to lay for him. One good kick in the right place will just about finish him."

The Gas Collector. "Not from you, you carrot-faced terrier. Come outside and see." (Business of friends interfering.)

The meeting becomes disorderly. Pinski is escorted out by friends—completely surrounded—amid shrieks and hisses, cat-calls, cries of "Boodler!" "Thief!" "Robber!"

There were many such little dramatic incidents after the ordinance had been introduced.

Henceforth on the streets, in the wards and outlying sections, and even, on occasion, in the business heart, behold the marching clubs—those sinister, ephemeral organizations which on demand of the mayor had cropped out into existence—great companies of the unheralded, the dull, the undistinguished—clerks, workingmen, small businessmen, and minor scions of religion or morality; all tramping to and fro of an evening after working hours, assembling in cheap halls and party clubhouses, and drilling themselves to what end? That they might march to the City Hall on the fateful Monday night when the street-railway ordinances should be up for passage and demand of unregenerate lawmakers that they do their duty. Cowperwood, coming down to his office one morning on his own elevated lines, was the observer of a button or badge worn upon the coat lapel of stolid, inconsequential citizens who sat reading their papers, unconscious of that presence which epitomized the terror and the power they all feared. One of these badges had for its device a gallows with a free noose suspended; another was blazoned with the query: "Are we going to be robbed?" On signboards, fences, and dead walls, huge posters, 4 by 6 feet in dimension, were displayed.

In the papers were flaring headlines; in the clubs, halls, and churches fiery speeches could nightly be heard. Men were drunk now with a kind of fury of contest. They would not succumb to this Titan who was bent on undoing them. They would not be devoured by this Gorgon of the East. He should be made to pay an honest return to the city or get out. No fifty-year franchise should be granted him. The Mears Law must be repealed, and he must come into the city council humble and with clean hands. No alderman who received as much as a dollar for his vote should in this instance be safe with his life.

WALDEN H. LUCAS

against the

BOODLERS

**Every citizen of Chicago should
come down to the City Hall**

TONIGHT

MONDAY, DEC. 12

**and every Monday night
thereafter while the Streetcar
Franchises are under consideration, and see that the interests
of the city are protected against**

BOODLEISM

*Citizens, Arouse, and Defeat
the Boodlers!*

Needless to say that in the face of such a campaign of intimidation only great courage could win. The aldermen were only human. In the council committee chamber Cowperwood went freely among them, explaining as he best could the justice of his course and making it plain that, although willing to buy his rights, he looked on them as no more than his due. The rule of the council was barter, and he accepted it. His unshaken and unconquerable defiance heartened his followers greatly, and the thought of thirty thousand dollars was a buttress against many terrors. At the same time many an alderman speculated solemnly as to what he would do afterward and where he would go once he had sold out.

At last the Monday night arrived which was to bring the final test of strength. Picture the large, ponderous structure of black granite—erected at the expense of millions and suggesting somewhat the somnolent architecture of ancient Egypt—which served as the City Hall and county courthouse combined. On this evening the four streets surrounding it were packed with thousands of people. To this throng Cowperwood has become an astounding figure: his wealth fabulous, his heart iron, his intentions sinister—the acme of cruel, plotting deviltry. Only this day the *Chronicle,* calculating well the hour and the occasion, has completely covered one of its pages with an intimate, though exaggerated, description of Cowperwood's house in New York: his court of orchids, his sunrise room, the baths of pink and blue alabaster, the finishings of marble and intaglio. Here Cowperwood was represented as seated in a swinging divan, his various books, art treasures, and comforts piled about him. The idea was vaguely suggested that in his sybaritic hours odalisques danced before him and unnamable indulgences and excesses were perpetrated.

At this same hour in the council chamber itself were assembling as hungry and bold a company of gray wolves as was ever gathered under one roof. The room was large, ornamented to the south by tall windows, its ceiling supporting a heavy, intricate chandelier, its sixty-six aldermanic desks arranged in half-circles, one behind the other; its woodwork of black oak carved and highly polished; its walls a dark blue-gray decorated with arabesques in gold—thus giving to all proceedings an air of dignity and stateliness. Above the speaker's head was an immense portrait in oil of a former mayor—poorly done, dusty, and yet impressive. The size and character of the place gave on ordinary occasions a sort of resonance to the voices of the speakers. Tonight through the closed windows could be heard the sound of distant drums and marching feet. In the hall outside the council door were packed at least a thousand men with ropes, sticks, a fife-and-drum corps which occasionally struck up "Hail, Columbia," "My Country, 'Tis of Thee," and "Dixie." Alderman Schlumbohm, heckled to within an inch of his life, followed to the council door by three hundred of his fellow citizens, was there left with the admonition that they would be waiting for him when he should make his exit. He was, at last, seriously impressed.

"What is this?" he asked of his neighbor and nearest associate, Alderman Gavegan, when he gained the safety of his seat. "A free country?"

"Search me!" replied his compatriot wearily. "I never seen such a band as I have to deal with out in the twentieth. Why, my God! a man can't call his name his own anymore out here. It's got so now the newspapers tell everybody what to do."

Alderman Pinski and Alderman Hoberkorn, conferring together in one corner, were both very dour. "I'll tell you what, Joe," said Pinski to his confrere; "it's this fellow Lucas that has got the people so stirred up. I didn't go home last night because I didn't want those fellows to follow me down there. Me and my wife stayed downtown. But one of the boys was over here at Jake's a little while ago, and he says there musta been five hundred people around my house at six o'clock, already. Whad ye think o' that?"

"Same here. I don't take much stock in this lynching idea. Still, you can't tell. I don't know whether the police could help us much or not. It's a damned outrage. Cowperwood has a fair proposition. What's the matter with them, anyhow?"

Renewed sounds of "Marching Through Georgia" from without.

Enter at this time Aldermen Ziner, Knudson, Revere, Rogers, Tiernan, and Kerrigan. Of all the aldermen perhaps Messrs. Tiernan and Kerrigan were as cool as any. Still, the spectacle of streets blocked with people who carried torches and wore badges showing slip nooses attached to a gallows was rather serious.

"I'll tell you, Pat," said Smiling Mike, as they eventually made the door through throngs of jeering citizens; "it does look a little rough. Whad ye think?"

"To hell with them!" replied Kerrigan, angry, waspish, determined. "They don't run me or my ward. I'll vote as I damn please."

"Same here," replied Tiernan with a great show of courage. "That goes for me. But it's purty warm, anyhow, eh?"

"Yes, it's warm, all right," replied Kerrigan, suspicious lest his companion in arms might be weakening, "but that'll never make a quitter out of me."

"Nor me, either," replied the Smiling One.

Enter now the mayor, accompanied by a fife-and-drum corps rendering "Hail to the Chief." He ascends the rostrum. Outside in the halls the huzzas of the populace. In the gallery overhead a picked audience. As the various aldermen look up they contemplate a sea of unfriendly faces. "Get on to the mayor's guests," commented one alderman to another cynically.

A little sparring for time while minor matters are considered, and the gallery is given opportunity for comment on the various communal lights, identifying for itself first one local celebrity and then another. "There's Johnnie Dowling, that big blond fellow with the round head; there's Pinski—look at the little rat; there's Kerrigan. Get on to the emerald. Eh, Pat, how's the jewelry? You won't get any chance to do any grafting tonight, Pat. You won't pass no ordinance tonight."

Alderman Winkler (pro-Cowperwood). "If the chair pleases, I think something ought to be done to restore order in the gallery and keep these proceedings from being disturbed. It seems to me an outrage that on an occasion of this kind, when the interests of the people require the most careful attention—"

A Voice. "The interests of the people!"

Another Voice. "Sit down. You're bought!"

Alderman Winkler. "If the chair pleases—"

The Mayor. "I shall have to ask the audience in the gallery to keep quiet in order that the business in hand may be considered." (Applause, and the gallery lapses into silence.)

Alderman Guigler (to Alderman Sumulsky). "Well-trained, eh?"

Alderman Ballenberg (pro-Cowperwood, getting up—large, brown, florid, smooth-faced). "Before calling up an ordinance which bears my name I should like to ask permission of the council to make a statement. When I introduced this ordinance last week I said—"

A Voice. "We know what you said."

Alderman Ballenberg. "I said that I did so by request. I want to explain that it was at the request of a number of gentlemen who have since appeared before the committee of this council that now has this ordinance—"

A Voice. "That's all right, Ballenberg. We know by whose request you introduced it. You've said your little say."

Alderman Ballenberg. "If the chair pleases—"

A Voice. "Sit down, Ballenberg. Give some other boodler a chance."

The Mayor. "Will the gallery please stop interrupting."

Alderman Hvranek (jumping to his feet). "This is an outrage. The gallery is packed with people come here to intimidate us. Here is a great public corporation that has served this city for years, and served it well, and when it comes to this body with a sensible proposition we ain't even allowed to consider it. The mayor packs the gallery with his friends, and the papers stir up people to come down here by thousands and try to frighten us. I for one—"

A Voice. "What's the matter, Billy? Haven't you got your money yet?"

Alderman Hvranek (Polish-American, intelligent, even artistic-looking, shaking his fist at the gallery). "You dare not come down here and say that, you coward!"

A Chorus of Fifty Voices. "Rats!" (also) "Billy, you ought to have wings."

Alderman Tiernan (rising). "I say now, Mr. Mayor, don't you think we've had enough of this?"

A Voice. "Well, look who's here. If it ain't Smiling Mike."

Another Voice. "How much do you expect to get, Mike?"

Alderman Tiernan (turning to gallery). "I want to say I can lick any man that wants to come down here and talk to me to my face. I'm not afraid of no ropes and no guns. These corporations have done everything for the city—"

A Voice. "Aw!"

Alderman Tiernan. "If it wasn't for the streetcar companies we wouldn't have any city."

Ten Voices. "Aw!"

Alderman Tiernan (bravely). "My mind ain't the mind of some people."

A Voice. "I should say not."

Alderman Tiernan. "I'm talking for compensation for the privileges we expect to give."

A Voice. "You're talking for your pocketbook."

Alderman Tiernan. "I don't give a damn for these cheap-skates and cowards in the gallery. I say treat these corporations right. They have helped make the city."

A Chorus of Fifty Voices. "Aw! You want to treat yourself right, that's what you want. You vote right tonight or you'll be sorry."

By now the various aldermen, outside of the most hardened characters, were more or less terrified by the grilling contest. It could do no good to battle with this gallery or the crowd outside. Above them sat the mayor, before them reporters, ticking in shorthand every phrase and word. "I don't see what we can do," said Alderman Pinski to Alderman Hvranek, his neighbor. "It looks to me as if we might just as well not try."

At this point arose Alderman Gilleran, small, pale, intelligent, anti-Cowperwood. By prearrangement he had been scheduled to bring the second, and, as it proved, the final test of strength to the issue. "If the chair pleases," he said, "I move that the vote by which the Ballenberg fifty-year ordinance was referred to the joint committee of streets and alleys be reconsidered, and that instead it be referred to the committee on city hall."

This was a committee that hitherto had always been considered by members of the council as of the least importance. Its principal duties consisted in devising new names for streets and regulating the hours of city-hall servants. There were no perquisites, no graft. In a spirit of ribald defiance at the organization of the present session all the mayor's friends—the reformers—those who could not be trusted—had been relegated to this committee. Now it was proposed to take this ordinance out of the hands of friends and send it here, whence unquestionably it would never reappear. The great test had come.

Alderman Hoberkorn (mouthpiece for his gang because the most skillful in a parliamentary sense). "The vote cannot be reconsidered." He begins a long explanation amid hisses.

A Voice. "How much have you got?"

A Second Voice. "You've been a boodler all your life."

Alderman Hoberkorn (turning to the gallery, a light of defiance in his eye). "You come here to intimidate us, but you can't do it. You're too contemptible to notice."

A Voice. "You hear the drums, don't you?"

A Second Voice. "Vote wrong, Hoberkorn, and see. We know you."

Alderman Tiernan (to himself). "Say, that's pretty rough, ain't it?"

The Mayor. "Motion overruled. The point is not well taken."

Alderman Guigler (rising, a little puzzled). "Do we vote now on the Gilleran resolution?"

A Voice. "You bet you do, and you vote right."

The Mayor. "Yes. The clerk will call the roll."

The Clerk (reading the names, beginning with the A's). "Altvast?" (Pro-Cowperwood.)

Alderman Altvast. "Yea." Fear had conquered him.

Alderman Tiernan (to Alderman Kerrigan). "Well, there's one baby down."

Alderman Kerrigan. "Yep."

"Ballenberg?" (Pro-Cowperwood; the man who had introduced the ordinance.)

"Yea."

Alderman Tiernan. "Say, has Ballenberg weakened?"

Alderman Kerrigan. "It looks that way."

"Canna?"

"Yea."

"Fogarty?"

"Yea."

Alderman Tiernan (nervously). "There goes Fogarty."

"Hvranek?"

"Yea."

Alderman Tiernan. "And Hvranek!"

Alderman Kerrigan (referring to the courage of his colleagues). "It's coming out of their hair."

In exactly eighty seconds the roll call was in and Cowperwood had lost—41 to 25. It was plain that the ordinance could never be revived.

CHAPTER LXII

The Recompense

You have seen, perhaps, a man whose heart was weighted by a great woe. You have seen the eye darken, the soul fag, and the spirit congeal under the breath of an icy disaster. At ten-thirty of this particular evening Cowperwood, sitting alone in the library of his Michigan Avenue house, was brought face to face with the fact that he had lost. He had built so much on the cast of this single die. It was useless to say to himself that he could go into the council a week later with a modified ordinance or could wait until the storm had died out. He refused himself these consolations. Already he had battled so long and so vigorously, by every resource and subtlety which his mind had been able to devise. All week long on divers occasions he had stood in the council chamber where the committee had been conducting its hearings. Small comfort to know that by suits, injunctions, appeals, and writs to intervene he could tie up this transit situation and leave it for years and years the prey of lawyers, the despair of the city, a hopeless muddle which would not be unraveled until he and his enemies should long be dead. This contest had been so long in the brewing, he had gone about it with such care years before. And now the enemy had been heartened by a great victory. His aldermen, powerful, hungry, fighting men all—like those picked soldiers of the ancient Roman emperors—ruthless, conscienceless, as desperate as himself, had in their last redoubt of personal privilege fallen, weakened, yielded. How could he hearten them to another struggle—how face the blazing wrath of a mighty populace that had once learned how to win? Others might enter here—Haeckelheimer, Fishel, any one of a half-dozen eastern giants—and smooth out the ruffled surface of the angry sea that he had blown to fury. But as for him, he was tired, sick of Chicago, sick of this interminable contest. Only recently he had promised himself that if he were to turn this great trick he would never again attempt anything so desperate or requiring so much effort. He would not need to. The size of his fortune made it of little worth. Besides, in spite of his tremendous vigor, he was getting on.

Since he had alienated Aileen he was quite alone, out of touch with anyone identified with the earlier years of his life. His all-desired Berenice still evaded him. True, she had shown lately a kind of warming sympathy; but what was it? Gracious tolerance, perhaps—a sense of obligation? Certainly little more, he felt. He looked into the future, deciding heavily that he must fight on, whatever happened, and then—

While he sat thus drearily pondering, answering a telephone call now and then, the doorbell rang and the servant brought a card which he said had been presented by a young woman who declared that it would bring immediate recognition. Glancing at it, Cowperwood jumped to his feet and hurried downstairs into the one presence he most craved.

There are compromises of the spirit too elusive and subtle to be traced in all their involute windings. From that earliest day when Berenice Fleming had first set eyes on Cowperwood she had been moved by a sense of power, an amazing and fascinating individuality. Since then by degrees he had familiarized her with a thought of individual freedom of action and a disregard of current social standards which were destructive to an earlier conventional view of things. Following him through this Chicago fight, she had been caught by the wonder of his dreams; he was on the way toward being one of the world's greatest money giants. During his recent trips East she had sometimes felt that she was able to read in the cast of his face the intensity of this great ambition, which had for its ultimate aim—herself. So he had once assured her. Always with her he had been so handsome, so pleading, so patient.

So here she was in Chicago tonight, the guest of friends at the Richelieu, and standing in Cowperwood's presence.

"Why, Berenice!" he said, extending a cordial hand. "When did you arrive in town? Whatever brings you here?" He had once tried to make her promise that if ever her feeling

toward him changed she would let him know of it in some
way. And here she was tonight—on what errand? He noted
her costume of brown silk and velvet—how well it seemed to
suggest her catlike grace!

"*You* bring me here," she replied, with an indefinable
something in her voice which was at once a challenge and
a confession. "I thought from what I had just been reading that you might really need me now."

"You mean—?" he inquired, looking at her with vivid
eyes. There he paused.

"That I have made up my mind. Besides, I ought to pay
sometime."

"Berenice!" he exclaimed reproachfully.

"No, I don't mean that, either," she replied. "I am sorry
now. I think I understand you better. Besides," she added,
with a sudden gaiety that had a touch of self-consolation
in it, "I want to."

"Berenice! Truly?"

"Can't you tell?" she queried.

"Well, then," he smiled, holding out his hands; and to
his amazement, she came forward.

"I can't explain myself to myself quite," she added, in a
hurried, low, eager tone, "but I couldn't stay away any
longer. I had the feeling that you might be going to lose
here for the present. But I want you to go somewhere else
if you have to—London or Paris. The world won't understand us quite—but I do."

"Berenice!" He smothered her cheek and hair.

"Not so close, please. And there aren't to be any other
ladies, unless you want me to change my mind."

"Not another one, as I hope to keep you. You will share
everything I have. . . ."

For answer—

How strange are realities as opposed to illusion!

IN RETROSPECT

The world is dosed with too much religion. Life is to be
learned from life, and the professional moralist is at best
but a manufacturer of shoddy wares. At the ultimate remove,
God or the life-force, if anything, is an equation, and at its
nearest expression for man—the contract social—it is that
also. Its method of expression appears to be that of gen-

erating the individual, in all his glittering variety and scope, and through him progressing to the mass with its problems. In the end a balance is invariably struck wherein the mass subdues the individual or the individual the mass—for the time being. For, behold, the sea is ever dancing or raging.

In the meantime there have sprung up social words and phrases expressing a need of balance—of equation. These are right, justice, truth, morality, an honest mind, a pure heart—all words meaning: a balance must be struck. The strong must not be too strong; the weak not too weak. But without variation how could the balance be maintained? Nirvana! Nirvana! The ultimate, still equation.

Rushing like a great comet to the zenith, his path a blazing trail, Cowperwood did for the hour illuminate the terrors and wonders of individuality. But for him also the eternal equation—the pathos of the discovery that even giants are but pygmies, and that an ultimate balance must be struck. On the strange, tortured, terrified reflection of those who, caught in his wake, were swept from the normal and the commonplace, what shall we say? Legislators by the hundred, who were hounded from politics into their graves; a half-hundred aldermen of various councils who were driven grumbling or whining into the limbo of the dull, the useless, the commonplace. A splendid governor dreaming of an ideal on the one hand, succumbing to material necessity on the other, traducing the spirit that aided him the while he tortured himself with his own doubts. A second governor, more amenable, was to be greeted by the hisses of the populace, to retire brooding and discomfited, and finally to take his own life. Schryhart and Hand, venomous men both, unable to discover whether they had really triumphed, were to die eventually, puzzled. A mayor whose greatest hour was in thwarting one who contemned him lived to say: "It is a great mystery. He was a strange man." A great city struggled for a score of years to untangle that which was all but beyond the power of solution —a true Gordian knot.

And this giant himself, rushing on to new struggles and new difficulties in an older land, forever suffering the goad of a restless heart—for him was no ultimate peace, no real understanding, but only hunger and thirst and wonder. Wealth, wealth, wealth! A new grasp of a new great problem and its eventual solution. Anew the old urgent thirst for life, and only its partial quenchment. In Dresden a palace for one woman, in Rome a second for another. In London a third for his beloved Berenice, the lure of beauty ever in his eye. The lives of two women wrecked, a score of victims despoiled; Berenice herself weary, yet brilliant, turning to others for recompense for her lost youth. And he resigned, and yet not—loving, understanding, doubting, caught at last by the drug of a personality which he could not gainsay.

What shall we say of life in the last analysis—"Peace, be still"? Or shall we battle sternly for that equation which we know will be maintained whether we battle or no, in order that the strong become not too strong or the weak not too weak? Or perchance shall we say (sick of dullness): "Enough of this. I will have strong meat or die!" And die? Or live?

Each according to his temperament—that something which he had not made and cannot always subdue, and which may not always be subdued by others for him. Who plans the steps that lead lives on to splendid glories, or twist them into gnarled sacrifices, or make of them dark, disdainful, contentious tragedies? The soul within? And whence comes it? Of God?

What thought engendered the spirit of Circe, or gave to a Helen the lust of tragedy? What lit the walls of Troy? Or prepared the woes of an Andromache? By what demon counsel was the fate of Hamlet prepared? And why did the weird sisters plan ruin to the murderous Scot?

> Double, double toil and trouble;
> Fire burn and cauldron bubble.

In a mulch of darkness are bedded the roots of endless sorrows—and of endless joys. Canst thou fix thine eye on the morning? Be glad. And if in the ultimate it blind thee, be glad also! Thou hast lived.

AFTERWORD

The charming remembered novelist William Dean Howells knew something of the business world, and Sinclair Lewis knew more. It might seem that, of the very small number of successful novels by Americans devoted to America's principal activity to date, *The Rise of Silas Lapham* and *Babbitt* are those to which Dreiser's Cowperwood series —in particular *The Titan*—ought to be compared. But it won't do, though to say why is not easy.

The three authors are obviously dissimilar (American "realists"); what I am thinking of is certain differences among the books. If more local points in novels were noticed in novels—the novels that matter—criticism might improve. Rereading *Babbitt* some years ago, for no special reason, I found myself indifferent to the apparent satire that brought it general fame but much impressed by its *poetic* quality. The products of the American business world glow and shine for George F. Babbitt and his creator. We come on something similar at a vivid point in *Lapham,* when the rough, rich paint-manufacturer declares, "deeply moved," to a young man of superior position he is thinking of taking on, "It's the best paint in God's universe"; the young man is impressed, and so was I. Now for all its energy and seeming dedication, *The Titan* lacks this glamour of faith in business, and comparison fails.

Perhaps now we can make the reasons clear. Though not wholly free of idealistic elements, Cowperwood can make no show of decency alongside Howells' and Lewis' heroes because he is not dealing with the real world as they are. Our position here is paradoxical but helpful. Paint and real estate are real things, real business. Finance is not; it is abstract. When Cowperwood hurls himself, in his "genial" way, on the growing city Chicago, it seems next door to accident that he fastens first on the gas companies and then on the street-railways as means to his ends. *Means.* So strongly is the insignificance of the facts of the means conveyed that it is with a tiny surge of definite surprise that one learns casually, late in the book, that one of his enormous New York backers, surveying the Chicago scene from Wall Street, feels that Cowperwood "knows a lot about running street-railways" and, elsewhere, that Cowperwood himself had personally gone so far, years before, on his visits to New York, as to inspect the new elevated line *physically*—just in case he should ever want to build one of his own. One never thinks of him as running a business— providing gas or transportation—but only as operating out of businesses. But as means to what end? Money? But he came from Philadelphia with money, and though it is true that he finally leaves Chicago enriched to the tune of twenty million there are ways to make money outside the dangerous and speculative world of high finance. Besides, I get a definite impression that he does not value money itself, and so we are still left with the matter of end. Sex? Love? Well, money is an element in his successes here, but one feels that like most of Dreiser's other heroes he could have had plenty of women without money. Political power? Not in itself. Social position? But in Chicago, with his Philadelphia reputation following him, he cannot have it, recognizes this without a tremor (though: *he wanted it*) and operates harder than ever.

What Cowperwood aims at is control—control of the fastest-growing, most involved services of a great crude city, control of his bankers and associates, control of his enemies financial and political, control of his passive and helpless wife (men of his sort in Dreiser never seem to have children; Cowperwood's two are rarely mentioned), control of big physical establishments, control of certain women (especially those theoretically least available), control of works of art. This is not a businessman, but a predator, comparable to nobody in *Lapham* or *Babbitt*—although we may think of the novels as comparable in artistic merit, all being second-class in my view, following on *A Hazard of New Fortunes* (along with parts of *The Landlord at Lion's Head*), *Arrowsmith* and *Main Street*, and—more clearly still—*An American Tragedy* and *Sister Carrie*. Thank the Lord for second-class novels, or what would we read after the age of twenty-one, and how insufferable would be a criticism that devoted itself solely to first-class novels (the fifty-two or eighty-six there are). It is an advantage, moreover, when not dealing with masterpieces, that it is easier to be candid. Nobody, perhaps, has ever thought Vronsky a successfully realized character; but who wishes to admit this fact?

Treacherous, brutal, corrupting, insolent, ego-sane as Dreiser presents his hero, we might reasonably inquire what means he has taken to recommend him, and how far they succeed, and here we come on tangles. I think his inventor has taken very few means indeed—I will mention some presently—to recommend Cowperwood to the reader. His point of view seems to be both lordly and helpless: lordly ("Take him or leave him") and helpless ("Can I help it if human nature—one human nature—is like this?"). These two qualities go far to describe Cowperwood himself, the man of imperious will who yet continually *wonders* why he *has* to do what he does. Several of Dreiser's favorite terms are already in play—"wondered," "Life was very strange," "necessary" ("As in the past they had made it necessary for him to work against them by bribery and perjury"—and he is also fond of "inconsequential" and "nebulous," and all these words come to us with a bearing practically programmatic, as if some vague "mood" philosophy of human life were being laid out or imposed.

I am prepared even to wonder whether Dreiser's failure to understand his hero, which so far we have considered as deliberate, may not be merely inadvertent. On one page we are notified, as if we needed to be, that "His greatest weakness, if he had one, was that he could but ill brook opposition of any kind." And twenty pages later: "Cowperwood, individual, reliant, utterly indifferent to opposition of any kind," etc. I believe this is called eating your cake and having it too, and it reminds me of the most important American novel yet written about a businessman—a real businessman—by that most improbable adept in the subject, Henry James: I mean *The American,* where an honest critic will have to confess that too much is *put into* Christopher Newman, for credibility, especially during the first half of the novel. But there we are dealing with a masterpiece: how shall we exonerate Dreiser?

A standard plea would be Whitman's "Do I contradict myself?" and so on. Remaining, to some extent, within the American scene, I prefer—and I think Theodore Dreiser would—a remark by a great master of pity, one of the areas human in which Dreiser perhaps was feeblest. There was until lately an English lyric poet named Ralph Hodgson, much admired in the early 1920's, hero of a delicious tribute by T. S. Eliot, who felt more for animal's mal-treatment by man in his left little finger than all the rest of even his own race felt put together; and wrote about nothing else for sixty years—"The Bells of Heaven" being one of the little masterworks of the age. At around eighty, in "retirement" on an Ohio hillside, thought long dead, he published a splendid new collection and was interviewed. "I don't try to reconcile anything," he said. "This is a damned strange world."

Cowperwood is not a villain, in his master's view. Let's begin with that. Nor is there anything tragic about his de-feats. One does not even suffer them. His second marriage is a horror. The wife claws his current mistress (a very good scene) in his own house and there is a problem of propriety, since the mistress may die. His bought men in politics do not stay bought—Kerrigan and Tiernan, I would say in passing, are the most effective ward leaders in Amer-ican literature, handled with something rare in Dreiser, humor, as well as complete understanding. He is finally wrinkled out even of the street-railways scene, and heads for New York and Europe, refreshed. With a larger fortune.

When Silas Lapham's paint is to be replaced by one equally good that costs less, one's heart hurts. Not in *The Titan*.

And yet Dreiser looms a far more formidable novelist than Howells. The general rage that went up when Lewis won the Nobel Prize—that overrated literary encomium—instead of Dreiser, I am happy to echo. (I am also glad that Dreiser cuffed Lewis physically—although any reader of Mark Schorer's biography of Lewis must feel intermittent sympathy with him—on a famous and absurd occasion in New York.) Dreiser remains one of the commanding writers we have had, for the readers who can bear him.

Mr. Alfred Kazin, a critic of bulky temperament, who understands the fantastic Dreiser as well as anyone, once committed himself to the following proposition: "Dreiser's success in handling social fact is due not merely to his doggedness and repetition but to the fact that his main characters are never shown in the round, are never complex." (*Major Writers of America,* edited by Perry Miller, 1962, Vol. II, p. 470.) This stricture, masquerading as an encomium, I would say is false. It is easy to agree that Dreiser is often dogged and repetitious but I would no more think of praising him for these weaknesses than I would praise the author of *Love's Labour's Lost* if that flashing play could be thought to possess them. Surely the truth is that Dreiser's power is felt in his strokes, like any other author's: for instance, the few sentences in which we learn that it was Cowperwood's habit, often, when returning home alone late at night, to go and sit in his gallery in front of one or the other of his art objects, and wonder. Dogged? Repetitious? In the fact of the immense assemblage of the primary materials of this ambitious novel—Money, Society, Sex, Politics, cunningly interacting—that is but a touch, only a strong one.

As for "never shown in the round," I have to be skeptical. Strength and geniality are Cowperwood's chief notes; need for control; need for women; amazement at art; blunt male egotism ("he could not forgive her for not loving him perfectly, as had so many others"); ruthless cunning—how complex does Mr. Kazin desire a character to be? But I would say more.

To put differently a matter adumbrated earlier, it is an oddity that an artist with Dreiser's views, or un-views, about life should have chosen for his most extensive character presentment a man of commanding activity and almost blind faith in his own destiny. (It is true that Cowperwood's career takes its origin in the actual Philadelphia-Chicago-London career of the tycoon C. T. Yerkes, but I think no critic has pretended that Cowperwood is a portrait of Yerkes, and in any case the question is irrelevant to our present concern, since Cowperwood is plainly Dreiser in temperament and thought, just as plainly as the artist-hero of *The Genius,* Eugene Witla.) When *The Bookman* once asked Dreiser for a credo, he wound up with a comprehensiveness unusual even for him and struck us out: "I can make no comment on my work or my life that holds either interest or import for me. Nor can I imagine any explanation or interpretation of any life, my own included, that would be either true—or important, if true. Life is to me too much a welter and play of inscrutable forces to permit, in my case at least, any significant comment. One may paint for one's own entertainment, and that of others—perhaps." Follows a genuinely Whitmanian, anti-Whitman, peroration that seems to me one of the most moving moments of this wonderfully candid and mysterious man: "As I see him the utterly infinitesimal individual weaves among the mysteries a floss-like and wholly meaningless course—if course it be. In short I catch no meaning from all I have seen, and pass quite as I came, confused and dismayed." (This in 1928, quoted in Robert H. Elias' reprehensible biography of 1949.) An antithetical reciprocity, or the modulation in the superman Cowperwood to this antiphilosophy, now and then seems to me to account for much of his attractiveness. Who fails to sympathize with a leader in despair?

At the same time, a composure hard to parallel, in Cowperwood, is pleasing. Without parallel, I mean, face to face. I have sometimes thought that our highest admiration ought to be reserved for those authors who find things for their characters to say when (manifestly) not only is there nothing to say, but even if there were, no human being could find out what it might be. Parolles in *All's Well that Ends Well*, Shakespeare's worst mature play, when taken "prisoner" by his own superior officers at night, blindfolded and questioned about the "enemy," spills his guts as fast as Dolon; his captors disclose themselves, taunt him and go off. Here would seem to be a case for suicide, and he says indeed:

> . . . If my heart were great,
> 'Twould burst at this.

But it is not great, and he also says earlier,

> Who cannot be crushed with a plot?

and finally

> . . . Simply the thing I am
> Shall make me live.

Now nowhere in Dreiser will we discover anything approaching the depth of this last line, but for similar composure under intolerable circumstances, consider an interview of Cowperwood's with Mr. Haguenin, editor of the *Press,* whose daughter he has seduced—to public knowledge. Mr. Haguenin bitterly reproaches him for his conduct, in a long tirade, and severs all business relationships with him:

> Cowperwood, who had listened very patiently and very fixedly, without a tremor of an eyelash, merely said:
> "There seems to be no common intellectual ground, Mr. Haguenin, upon which you and I can meet in this matter. You cannot understand my point of view. I could not possibly adopt yours. . . ."
> He turned and walked unconcernedly out, thinking that it was too bad to lose the support of so respectable a man, but also that he could do without it.

For years I've thought this one of the high points of the novel. It is certain that Cowperwood attracts us, if he does, by the same "appetite for the wonders of life" and "that instinct for the essential and vital which invariably possessed him," a certain sprightliness, that must have attracted Dreiser, in conception, to him. But I have never been quite clear as to what Dreiser really thinks about this hero to whom he devoted three long novels. His admiration is obvious, his irony far less so—if it were not for one episode one might deny him irony entirely. This is the masterly account—in two parts, very brief—of Cowperwood's entrapment and blackmailing of the mayor, Sluss (a blonde-chaser). For somebody—author, Cowperwood himself, the reader—it ought to exhibit his magnanimity, for he does not ruin Sluss publicly, as he could with impunity do (he only destroys poor high-minded Sluss's principles and peace of soul). But the truth is that Sluss exposed would be of no use to him.

It is time to say something of Dreiser as a poetic writer, as a chronicler of American urban life (many consider him, with whatever misgivings, the most impressive we have), and as a philosopher. The first two matters may be taken together, and some quotations prefaced with the observation that it is when Dreiser girds up his poetic loins that he becomes intolerable. "To whom may the laurels as laureate of this Florence of the West yet fall?" he wildly inquires (I am quoting exactly). "This singing flame of a city, this all America, this poet in chaps and buckskin, this rude, raw Titan, this Burns of a city!" How flatulent it seems beside the invocation of Saul Bellow at the beginning of a novel about Chicago that better evokes it: "Chicago, that somber city." (Chicagoans are so touchy that perhaps the present writer should explain that he has four or five reasons for being grateful to Chicago and nothing much in particular against it.) Intent as he is on it, Dreiser's evocation of the Chicago of the 1880's and later is not one of *The Titan's* most luminous features; Philadelphia, in the first volume of the trilogy, *The Financier,* is handled more freshly.

As for his ideas, perhaps Dreiser took them too seriously, confused as they were and remain. He never decided between Chance and Determinism—and why should he?—but he continually redecided and never knew quite on which side to place his magic "chemic" formula by which he hoped to explain to himself the mysteries of human life. Man sees woman: chemistry. Small wonder that he wound up half-Communist, half-Christian; dogmas, both, quite irreconcilable with the body of his published work. I am not objecting to his inconsistency but to his lifelong misconception of the role of ideas in imaginative work. It is true that he was uneducated, but even this, in my opinion, did not save him.

Something, but as little as possible, needs to be said about Dreiser's women. Women! At all points they strike one as emerging from his heroes' ears until one sits merely awaiting, with exasperation, the emergence of the next one, and as for the real women, it took him a very large work indeed (*A Gallery of Women*) to memorialize merely a few. He sweats over them, too—his anxiety that we should be hypnotized by Berenice is patent, and indeed she is one of his best portraits. But the whole topic does not represent Dreiser at his happiest. His interest in them, I think or rather feel, peaks with his hero's and flags with his hero's, and there is a want of objectivity which is fatal. A good instance is Aileen in *The Titan,* whose deterioration to smoking—smoking!—and liquor and adultery is grotesquely unconvincing. (Her lover Polk Lynde comes over poorly too—a caricature—Dreiser is numb with young men above a certain station in life.)

Here then are two reasons for the comparative failure: the pattern, destroying drama, and subjectivity. The major reason I feel to be a little different, and since at this moment in time it may seem strange to accuse an author of want of delicacy I want to take a counter-illustration from *The Rise of Silas Lapham.* The stupid beautiful sister and a well-bred young man are left alone briefly while a party is inspecting the half-finished house her father is building. For four pages, while a Jane Austen-ish conversation is taking place, Irene, to dissimulate her intensity (young Corey has no interest in her whatever—he is polite), follows shavings on the floor with her parasol. Finally he helps her get one, and Howells writes: "To a girl everything a young man does is of significance; and if he holds a shaving down with his foot while she pokes through it with her parasol, she must ask herself what he means by it." Returned home with her sister she bursts into storms of tears and smiles. It must be clear, even from this barren outline, that Dreiser would never have attempted such a scene and could not if he had tried. His women are mere objects. Perhaps, for all his experience, he really knew very little of women.

In summing up Dreiser's contribution to American letters, difficult though it may be to evaluate accurately, perhaps we should turn to Sinclair Lewis. I do not recall a more generous, more noble paean of praise to a fellow-worker than Lewis' statement to the Swedish Academy in 1930, when he accepted the Nobel Prize, which Dreiser had so begrudged him: "Suppose you had taken Theodore Dreiser," said Lewis nervously. "Now to me, as to many other American writers, Dreiser, more than any other man, is marching alone. Usually unappreciated, often hounded, he had cleared the trail from Victorian Howellsian timidity and gentility in American fiction to honesty, boldness and passion of life. Without his pioneering I doubt if any of us could, unless we liked to be sent to jail, seek to express life, beauty, and terror."

— John Berryman

Other SIGNET Classics
by American Authors